Penthouse
Uncensored III

The Editors of *Penthouse* Magazine Present...

Penthouse
Uncensored III

GC

GRAND CENTRAL
PUBLISHING

NEW YORK   BOSTON

Grand Central Publishing
Hachette Book Group
1290 Avenue of the Americas
New York, NY 10104

Visit our Web site at www.HachetteBookGroup.com.

First Compilation Printing: November 2002

Grand Central Publishing is a division of Hachette Book Group, Inc.
The Grand Central Publishing name and logo is a trademark of Hachette Book Group, Inc.

ISBN 978-0-446-67974-9
LCCN: 2002107734

Cover design by Susan Newman

CONTENTS

PART ONE

PART TWO

We've been keeping a finger on the sexual pulse of America, and you wouldn't believe what we're doing! Once again you'll find your niche or discover those you never knew you had, once you get started on this hot, erotic compilation of intimate adventures.

Leave your inhibitions at the door and set aside the world just for a little while; we promise you won't regret it. Bring your lover, bring your friend, bring your lover and a friend, or just keep all the enjoyment for yourself. Whatever your pleasure, you're bound to be swept away by the infinite combinations and endless possibilities. Enjoy!

Part One

From *Letters to*
Penthouse VII

Crowd Scenes

WANTON WIFE TAKES ON CREW OF FIFTEEN
DURING PLEASURE CRUISE

Like a lot of couples, my wife Dahlia and I spent the first seven years of our thirteen-year marriage getting over the sexual repressions instilled in us by our parents and the church.

Dahlia is thirty-one years old, five feet tall and a shapely one hundred twenty-five pounds. We both enjoy outdoor activities like swimming, biking and skiing, and this helps keep us trim. She maintains an allover tan, as do I. Although initially we both were a little uncomfortable with nudity, this inhibition was one of the first to disappear.

Like most couples, after about five years we were in a sexual rut. It took a while for us to open up to each other and talk about our fantasies. Predictably they ran the gamut of multiple-partner sex. Through various personal ads we answered in swingers' mags we were able to realize most of our fantasies. My two favorite fantasies are girl-girl sex and gang bangs. Luckily for me these are fantasies that my wife enjoys as well. I'd like to relate a memorable encounter that my wife and I had recently.

I planned to take a four-day boating trip with a group of about fifteen guys. Dahlia was going to make alternate plans, but when she heard that some of the guys' wives wanted to come along she decided she'd join us.

In the past we had swung with some of these people, but most were just friends or friends of friends. There was a lot of coordinating with so many people involved, but we managed to finally work out all the details.

We arrived about noon the day before we were to set out and joined the growing group. By late afternoon we learned that all the women except Dahlia had chickened out and two of the guys couldn't make it. Dahlia insisted that even though she was going to be the only woman she was still game for the trip. She had a certain gleam in her eye when she said that she had no problem going boating with thirteen guys, and I had a feeling we were in for an interesting trip. It turned out to be a weekend we will never forget.

The sun was already starting to heat things up the next morning when we started out just after sunrise. To keep cool, Dahlia decided to wear a pair of tight gym shorts and a halter top over a very skimpy thong bikini. By ten she had stripped down to her bikini and was lying on the deck sunning herself. Most of us guys had taken off our shirts and were just wearing shorts or swimsuits by then.

About that time we spotted a nice secluded little cove and decided to drop anchor and take a break during the heat of the day. Most of us gathered around the cockpit to have a few beers and shoot the breeze. As we talked I pulled Dahlia up to me with her back to my chest and proceeded to nibble on her ears and the back of her neck, which makes her really horny and causes her nipples to stiffen. I simultaneously stroked her belly and her legs, which is another way to get her horny, while I whispered in her ear that I wanted to fuck her.

When she started opening and closing her legs, a couple of guys sitting across from us said it was no fair for us to make out unless there were enough women to go around. Well, I didn't quit and neither did Dahlia. When I cupped her tits she didn't protest, so I went on to unhook her bikini top. I told the guys we were used to sunbathing nude and asked them if they wanted us to show them. To a resounding "Hell, yes!" I exposed her 34C tits and gave each nipple a tweak, then looked around to see just what the guys' reaction was. Dahlia's nipples were really swollen and when she spread her legs you could clearly see her slit outlined through the material of her bikini.

I tugged the crotch of her suit up into her slit, which exposed her shaved pussy lips and a small patch of pubic hair above them. By this time the head of my cock was poking out of the leg of my shorts. Dahlia felt it pressing into her, so she reached back and started stroking it. She told me later that at this point she was ready for things to go as far as I wanted them to. As I looked around at all the bulges surrounding me, I realized that I was going to have to share her with all of them if I was going to get any kind of relief myself.

When I stood her up and pulled her bikini bottom down, every eye was focused directly on her crotch. When I pulled my shorts off, I immediately guided her to my cock. My cock is thin and a little over seven inches long, but she had no problem deepthroating it. I know she's had bigger ones, but she can handle what I have quite well. I reached around to play with her tits and to probe her pussy. As I ran a finger up and down her slit, I realized it was dripping with juice! Not wanting to pass up a golden opportunity, I simply turned her around and backed her pussy onto my cock.

As my cock slid in to the hilt I looked around at all the staring faces and reminded the guys that her mouth was still available. The first one to respond just walked up to her and dropped his pants. In just a few minutes there were three very fine cocks lined up in front of her face awaiting their turn. One guy sat next to her and began sucking on her tits. The other seven just sat where they were, completely naked and stroking their cocks for all they were worth as they waited for an opening.

With all this activity going on around me I soon lost it and shot what seemed like a quart of come into her pussy. The spasming of my cock brought on her first climax. As soon as I pulled out of her the guys guided her down to some sleeping bags they had spread out on the deck. After they positioned her on her back, one of the guys immediately climbed into the saddle. She had come leaking down her thighs and she had to divide her attention between four cocks—one in her pussy, one in her mouth and one in each hand. One of the cocks in her hands and the one in her mouth exploded at the same time. She gulped down one load of sperm while the other flew into the air, raining down on the deck in pearly drops. I kept moving around, checking out the action from every angle. I was already sporting another hard-on, which I planned to soak in Dahlia's come-filled pussy after everyone else had come in it at least once. She was just getting ready to take another cock into her mouth when the guy in her pussy pulled out and shot his load on her pubic hair. With her eyes glazed over, her hair all in disarray and a nine-inch cock about to sink into her mouth, I could see she was drifting into a suck-and-fuck trance.

About an hour later I was finally ready to park my cock in her mouth. As I fucked her face I looked at her red lips caked with dried come. She also had several hickeys on her neck and tits. It made me so proud and excited all at the same time to know that my sexy wife was satisfying all these guys. When the guy in her pussy came, I told the next guy on line that I wanted to switch places with him so I could fuck her again.

By about one in the afternoon we had all come at least twice each—in most cases, once in Dahlia's pussy and once in her mouth. Dahlia was exhausted, so I decided it was time to take a break. I suggested we clean up, eat some lunch and head down the river a little way. We set up a cot on deck so Dahlia could get some rest, and no one was surprised when she fell right to sleep. She was stretched out on the cot, completely naked, but that didn't bother me in the least. After all, I wanted her to be ready for anything.

After we went a ways downstream, we came upon a swimming hole complete with several ropes for swinging tied to tree branches above it. The sun was still shining when we pulled to the side and dropped anchor. As we settled in for the night some guys went swimming while others set up camp. Dahlia and I opted to go swimming and she had quite a group of admirers around her. Since we wouldn't let her put on a swimsuit, she insisted that all the guys skinny-dip as well. They were happy to oblige.

When we walked into camp a little while later it was clear by the way things were set up that the guys were expecting a repeat of the afternoon's activities. The tents were all set up in a circle, but the sleeping bags were spread out in the center of camp. As we took in the sight I slid my finger into her pussy to check her response. She was already wet and her nipples were swelling. Dahlia whispered that it seemed like the more cock she got the more she wanted, and she was certainly up for one more round. I figured that this would be a good time to give her a thorough pussy-licking to lubricate her for what was to come. Fifteen minutes later her juices were flooding into my mouth as she came wildly.

Two nights later we were on a sandbar about two miles from our final destination. Dahlia had had two days and nights of fabulous gang-bang sex and was having a great time. The most clothing she had worn the whole time was that skimpy thong bikini. We had taken lots of photographs to help us remember our trip, but I have a feeling that even without any mementos we would be able to remember this vacation. I don't think I'll ever get tired of seeing her take someone else's cock into her mouth or watch someone else's come leak out of her pussy. Her pussy seemed to gape open continuously, and what I thought was a suntan on her neck and chest was just a permanent sex flush.

On our last night out we all agreed we should repeat the trip next year with the same people if Dahlia was up to it. She assured us she'd be more than ready and even suggested that next time we make it a week-long trip.—*Name and address withheld*

ADVENTUROUS COUPLE BRIGHTENS
THEIR SEX LIFE IN THE SUNSHINE STATE

My wife Lucy is five feet six inches tall and weighs around one hundred eight pounds. She has medium-size breasts and long blondish-brown hair. She has always expressed an interest in having sex with several partners at the same time.

This past winter Lucy and I planned a two-week vacation to Florida. During the few months leading up to our vacation she brought up the topic of group sex several times, asking what my thoughts were on her fulfilling her fantasy. I told her I would go along with just about anything as long as I was included in the fun, because one of my fantasies has always been to share my wife with other men. I'm not the type of guy who wants to sit back and watch my wife get screwed—I want a piece of the action!

We had been at the hotel for a couple of days, just lying around the pool relaxing. One afternoon on our way back from the beach we saw a notice posted informing guests about a poolside party that the hotel was throwing that evening. Lucy and I talked about it and decided to go. Lucy also decided that she was going to go out and buy a new bathing suit to wear at the party.

She went down to a boutique in the lobby to look for a new suit. She had not been gone that long when she returned with her new purchase: a two-piece swimsuit that covered very little of her body. I told her that she would definitely attract some attention with that on and she said that was exactly what she was hoping for.

We arrived at the party a little early to ensure that we got a table close to the dance floor. We had been sitting there talking and drinking for an hour or so when three somewhat older gentlemen came over to our table and asked if they could join us. We asked them to sit down and struck up a conversation. Vincent was tall and looked like he was in pretty good shape. He later admitted that he worked out a lot. Herman was much shorter and somewhat overweight. The last guy, Wayne, was black. He was tall and also looked physically fit.

I told them that we were here on vacation. They said they were in town for a golf tournament sponsored by one of the local hotels. They were not staying at our hotel but had heard about the party and decided to check it out.

I excused myself to go to the rest room, and upon returning to the table I noticed that Lucy had removed her coverup. I was not at all surprised to see that she was attracting considerable attention—not just from the guys at our table but from a few tables around us. We had been drinking pretty heavily, and even Lucy, who is not usually a big drinker, was pounding them back.

Wayne asked if it was okay if he danced with Lucy. I told him to go right ahead if Lucy was agreeable. As I sat there watching them dance I noticed how nicely her tan body contrasted with his ebony skin. I began to get somewhat horny as I watched her press her body into his as his hands caressed her bare skin. After a few dances they returned to the table, and Lucy asked if Vincent or Herman wanted to dance. Vincent led her onto the dance floor, his hands rubbing her ass-cheeks.

When Vincent and Lucy returned to the table, Herman suggested that we go over to their hotel where he had a suite complete with a bar and finish the party over there. I agreed and Lucy said it sounded great to her as she was getting a little bored with the party.

The guys told us that they had come over in a taxi, but I told them that we had a car and would be glad to give them a ride back. I went up to the room to get the car keys and Lucy took them out to the car. I got into the front seat with Vincent. Lucy, who was pretty drunk, climbed into the backseat with Wayne and Herman. As Vincent gave me directions I glanced in the rearview mirror and saw that Wayne's hand was creeping between Lucy's thighs from the left and Herman's was starting to do the same from the right.

A few minutes later we arrived at their hotel and headed up to Herman's suite. We all had another beer, and Vincent suggested that Lucy make herself comfortable by taking off her robe. Lucy stood up and said that she'd feel most comfortable if she just removed all of her clothes, and proceeded to do just that. First she unhooked her bikini top, exposing her firm round tits and dark brown nipples. But before she even had a chance to pull down her bikini bottoms, Herman was tugging them down over her hips. When they were down around her ankles she simply stepped out of them.

Wayne took her by the hand and led her over to the love seat. He sat her down, stood in front of her and began to take off his shorts. As his shorts dropped to the floor I noticed he was not wearing any underwear. When he turned around to motion for the rest of us to join in, I could see that he had a very large dick. Lucy had already begun to fondle it as Vincent and Herman walked over. Vincent began to cheer Wayne on, saying, "Give her that big black cock. Let her suck it. Give her a taste of your love."

With that Lucy took his cock into her mouth and began licking and sucking on the head. I almost couldn't believe that here was my wife, giving a blow job to an almost total stranger—and a black man with a big dick at that. Wayne cradled her head in his hands and began to fuck her face in earnest, gradually sliding his dick into her mouth deeper and faster.

By now both Vincent and Herman had removed their clothes and were getting ready to join in. Herman's dick matched his body size—short but very round and fat. Vincent's was about average size. Vincent and Herman watched for some time while Lucy continued to suck on Wayne. They finally interrupted, saying that they wanted to join in.

Wayne instructed Lucy to get on her hands and knees on the floor so he could fuck her from behind while she sucked off Herman and Vincent. As Wayne entered her with very fast, hard strokes, Lucy began to moan loudly. At the same time Herman slid his dick, which was becoming fatter and longer, into her mouth. She began to take turns on Herman and Vincent, sucking one dick at a time into her mouth. This lasted for several minutes until Herman warned her that he was about to come. Wayne sat Lucy on the couch with her head hanging over the back and Herman positioned himself so that she could continue to suck him off. Within minutes he was shooting a huge load into her mouth.

As she lay there with come leaking out the corners of her mouth, Wayne crouched down in front of the love seat, spread Lucy's legs as far apart as they would go and stuck his long black cock back into her wet and waiting pussy. He was fucking her very fast and hard, pushing his cock all the way in on each stroke. Lucy was going nuts. After several minutes he stood up, told her to lean forward and open her mouth wide, and began jacking off, aiming his cock at her mouth. I could tell by the way he was moaning that he was about to explode at any moment. He told Lucy he was going to shoot his come down her throat, and he proceeded to do just that.

Vincent, who had been standing on the sidelines the whole time, quietly watching and stroking his cock, reached down and picked up an empty glass. At first I had no idea what he had planned to do with it, but when I saw him hold it down next to his cock I knew exactly what he had in mind. He jerked off into the glass, filling it at least a quarter of the way with come. Then he wiped his dick around the rim, handed it to Lucy and said, "While I am fucking you I want to see you drink every last drop of my come."

At that he positioned himself between her thighs and rammed his cock into her pussy. After the first few strokes he told her to go ahead and drink down his come but to take her time and savor each drop. She raised the glass to her lips, licked the rim a few times and began to sip the come from the glass. This not only excited me, but I could see that the other two were riveted to the performance in front of them. Once the glass was empty, Lucy made a show of sticking out her tongue to lap up the last few remaining drops.

I watched for a few more hours as they each took a turn fucking her again. I finally wanted to have a little action, so I took a turn fucking my wife. When we left they gave us their phone numbers and said to give them a call if we ever were in their part of the country.

We enjoyed ourselves so much that weekend that we have since joined a swingers' club. Now we frequently swap partners or invite men over to the house so that we can continue to fulfill our fantasies.—V.D., Knoxville, Tennessee

MARRIED COUPLE SWAPS WITH FRIENDS
FOR TOTAL SATISFACTION

*M*y wife Beth has curly, raven-black hair, flawless olive skin, classic features and a beautiful body. In my opinion she rivals any Greek goddess. We've been married for three years and have always been faithful to one another. Beth and I have had an exciting sex life since the day we met. For some reason I've always had a fantasy of watching her fuck another man, especially someone with a bigger dick than mine. Beth has told me tales of her experiences with bigger-sized lovers, one who had a nine-incher and another who had a ten-inch cock. The thought of them fucking Beth has always excited me.

Last weekend Tracy, one of Beth's college friends, and Seth, her new husband, came in from out of town to visit. Tracy is a tall blonde with an absolutely stunning ass and mile-long legs. Seth has an athletic look, svelte and muscular. When this couple had first started dating, Tracy confided to my wife that Seth had the biggest tool she'd ever seen. Beth told me that since Tracy always tried to date men with big dicks, Seth's must be a whopper.

Our house has squeaky wood floors throughout so it's easy to hear everything that happens around the house. That night Beth and I became quite aroused listening to our guests fuck in the bedroom down the hall. I asked Beth if she ever missed being overstuffed by cock and she just smiled in a funny way. Although my cock is very fat, it is just under seven inches in length, and I've often wished I could give her more.

The next evening we were relaxing after dinner when the topic of sex came up. Seth was wearing a pair of jeans that clearly outlined just what he was packing. Beth is a bit mischievous at times, and that night was no exception. After eyeing Seth's crotch for a few minutes she blurted out, "So, Seth, Tracy tells me you're very well endowed. Is that true?"

Seth tried to ignore the question, but Tracy egged him on. "Come on, Seth, show them what you give me." With that Seth stood up, unbuttoned his jeans and pulled out a flaccid cock that hung to his mid-thigh. Beth just stared in awe, then her hand slipped down and started massaging between her thighs. Tracy went over and started sucking and stroking Seth's cock, and it started hardening and lengthening.

Even flaccid, he was several inches bigger than me when I'm hard, but as it thickened it was unbelievable. I had to ask how big it was, and as I did Beth was already searching for a measuring tape. His cock was over eleven inches long. Unlike my cock, which stands upright when erect, Seth's stuck straight out with a slightly downward curve and pulsed with each heartbeat. It was just too heavy to go any higher. Beth gave me a questioning look, indicating she wanted to join in, and I nodded my assent.

She and Tracy kept sucking his cock and playing with him until he told them they'd have to stop or he'd come. Tracy asked Beth if she wanted to feel him inside her. I gave her a nod and she lifted her miniskirt and peeled off her panties, tossing the soaked lingerie to me. She had a wild look in her eyes as she walked over to Seth and kissed him hard. She said, "Give me that big cock! Fuck me hard!"

Seth excitedly asked if he could fuck her from behind. Fortunately Beth loves it that way. Tracy came over to me and started sucking my cock, which I had been stroking. There in front of me was my beautiful wife with the first of eleven inches of meat sliding into her. With each thrust Seth slid in deeper. After a couple of minutes he was all the way in. His big balls were slapping against Beth's thighs. He turned to Tracy and moaned that he had all of his cock inside Beth. Apparently Tracy had never been able to fit his entire cock inside her.

While Seth fucked Beth, she reached back and fondled his big balls, which drove him nuts. Tracy released my cock and straddled me with her back to me so she could watch the show in front of us. Her pussy was pretty tight considering it was fucked regularly by Seth's big dick. As she rode me I watched Seth slam into my wife. He would pull back until we could see eight or nine inches slick with my wife's juices and then slam into her again. She was moaning, "Oh, Seth, fuck me with that pole. Give it to me." She was practically delirious. He finally came, pulling out and spewing his come in the air. He rested his huge cock on Beth's back and I could see just how far he had been in her. That was all I could take. I exploded inside Tracy. I watched as Seth pushed his softening tool back into my wife's pussy. Beth collapsed on the floor, exhausted but satisfied.

The sex continued on the rest of the weekend and the girls even put on a lesbian show for us. Tracy licked Beth's clit while Beth was riding Seth. Since then we've arranged to get together once a month. Beth says she really needs to be that full once in a while and Seth loves sinking all the way into a woman's pussy. That's okay with me, because Tracy and I get along pretty well too.—*T.R., Chicago, Illinois*

NOW WE KNOW THAT HE WEARS
THE PANTIES IN THIS FAMILY

Some time ago my husband Russell and I placed an ad in the local paper in search of a compatible couple to fool around with. We found a couple who changed our sex lives forever. Russ and I have always been interested in the new and unusual, and Russell never ceases to amaze me with his easy acceptance of some of the most outrageous things.

Andy and Elizabeth took us far beyond our wildest dreams. Our first sessions, rather tame, just involved swapping partners. We soon moved on to all four of us groping and fucking each other silly. I had no idea how wonderful it could be to have three other people licking, sucking and fucking me while I simply lay there and enjoyed it. I discovered during these sessions that I am a voyeur. I just love to watch my husband getting screwed. It was terribly exciting to watch Elizabeth riding up and down his prick, but I nearly lost all control the evening Elizabeth and Andy both took him on.

I had taken a breather after being sucked by Elizabeth as the menfolk watched. Russell was on his back on the floor of the living room when Elizabeth simply walked over and sat down on his face, offering him her dripping snatch, Russell really got into it, licking and sucking while Elizabeth purred in contentment. I was surprised when Andy joined in and began to suck on Russell's cock, but soon I was incredibly turned on. I'm not sure Russell realized who was licking his balls, but he was sure enjoying it. Before long his cock was standing tall and proud and Andy was milking it with his mouth, sliding up and down that steely shaft with his cheeks sucked in. I was getting very hot just watching the action and began to rub my clit and finger myself furiously. It wasn't long before my husband's tongue brought Elizabeth to climax, and she sank to the floor in exhausted satisfaction. I quickly sat on Russell's face to allow his hot tongue to penetrate my cunt. I watched Russell's eyes grow wide in surprise when it dawned on him who was sucking his cock, but my husband is, as I've already mentioned, the adventurous type. He didn't miss a beat as he buried his face deep into my crotch. I could feel him begin to move his ass as his own climax neared. Andy was a real expert at sucking dick. He slowed down his sucking and began to play with Russell's balls in order to slow him down. As I began to feel my own orgasm coming on I started to cry out. Andy took this as a signal to resume sucking my husband's engorged cock. As I came Andy redoubled his efforts and drank great gobs of Russell's sperm while I tried to keep from falling over from the excitement of the sight of seeing Andy relishing the sperm he seemed so ravenous for.

After a few months we were comfortable in any combination. I learned to love the taste of Elizabeth's cunt and Russell soon became an expert at cocksucking. I thought we had done it all but was in for another surprise. We were invited to Andy and Elizabeth's place for a special weekend, and both Russell and I could hardly wait. We arrived at their modest suburban home Friday evening and were greeted by Elizabeth and another woman. It was not until the other woman hugged Russell and spoke that we realized it was Andy. Russell simply hugged him back, then placed his tongue deep in Andy's mouth and kissed back. By this time their tongues were no strangers and had met many times, so it didn't really matter what clothes Andy was wearing.

It was odd to sit down and talk with Elizabeth and Andy/Becky at first, but soon our friendship overcame the strain. I found myself watching Becky closely. The illusion of a woman was not perfect, but fairly convincing nonetheless. I found myself wondering how he did it, so over dinner I got up the nerve to ask and Becky offered to show us. As we cleared the dishes Becky put on some music and began a slow striptease for us. First the skirt was removed and dropped to the floor, revealing a lovely pink slip. Button by button the blouse was undone and soon lay on the floor by the skirt. I found myself strangely excited by this cross-gender strip show. Next came the slip. With a flip of her hand Becky sent it sailing toward Russell, revealing a gorgeous black corset with red trim and real, old-fashioned stockings with garters. (I would have killed for the matching bra and panty set!) A pair of very convincing breast forms filled the bra and a very inviting lump filled the panties.

There was nothing else I could do. I went over to Becky, pulled down that silky black lace panty and took his/her cock in my mouth. It was still soft, hardly filling my dripping mouth at all, but I soon cured that problem. I ran my tongue up and down the flaccid shaft in my mouth, slowly applying more suction. I was rewarded with the feel of a rapidly growing prick and was soon sliding up and down, deep-throating that marvelous dong while I massaged Andy's balls through his panties. I couldn't believe how smooth his swollen nuts felt through the sheer fabric. By now his prick was fully erect. I grasped the tip of it between my lips and rapidly flicked my tongue down that slit with a wiggle. I began to slide my fingers up and down the shaft as I sucked. I could feel his cock twitching and returned to deep-throating him again. With a groan he began to fuck my mouth. I pulled back the black panties to grasp his balls as he filled my mouth with jet after jet of creamy white come. I swallowed furiously, barely keeping up with the flow until he had exhausted himself in my come-drenched mouth. As I looked up I saw Russell and Elizabeth in a 69 on the living room floor. They had not even bothered to take off their clothes. Russell's prick stuck up from his unzipped pants and was quickly swallowed by Elizabeth. They were moving furiously, and soon Elizabeth was squealing around Russell's massive meat as she started to come. She slowed her sucking for a few seconds as the contractions flew through her body, pulling up even more strongly on her lover's pecker with each wave of pleasure, then swiftly engulfing his dong to begin again. It wasn't long before Russell blew his load in Elizabeth's mouth. She tried her best to drink his entire load, but strings of white cream began to descend from her lips as he pumped faster and faster. At last she crawled off my husband and placed her head on his chest, smiling in pure pleasure. I gradually became aware of fingers probing my own pussy, and realized Becky had pulled down my panties and was finger-fucking me while I watched the show. I was so turned on by the action that I had barely noticed. With one hand caressing my tit and another probing my vagina, I closed my eyes and enjoyed the attention.

Before long I felt my legs being raised and I was filled by Andy's revived rod. I opened my eyes and was greeted by the sight of that lace-framed pecker plunging into my cunt. I felt unbelievably turned on by the sexy, feminine clothing Andy was wearing while he pounded his meat into me. Across the room my husband was watching spellbound at the sight of me being screwed by a man in women's clothing. I was turned on even further by knowing he was watching as Andy pounded my pussy. His prick once again exploded and filled me with globs of sticky white come. Elizabeth had been watching the action after her own orgasm and noticed that I still had not come, so she gently kissed Becky, moved her out of the way and proceeded to lap her husband's come from my snatch. Her tongue felt so good as it slid over my sperm-soaked slash, toying with my clit and probing my vagina. She sucked at the lips of my cunt and tried to draw out as much sperm as she could, then returned to my swollen clitoris to send waves of pleasure through my body. She began to suck on my clit faster and harder and I abandoned myself to the sheer joy of orgasm.

When I was able to open my eyes again I smiled up at Russell and thanked Becky and Elizabeth for one of the most wonderful screwings I had ever had.—*Name and address withheld*

CLOSE YOUR EYES, MAKE A WISH AND GET YOUR CANDLE BLOWN

*D*uring the week prior to my birthday, Angela, my wife of twenty years, was strangely silent. Normally she teases me with hints about my birthday present. Little did I know that this year's birthday experience would be the most memorable of my life.

Angela is gorgeous. She has long brown hair and brown eyes, but her best characteristic is her 38-26-36 figure. Many a time

I've smiled when other men turned and gave Angela a long, yearning look as we walked by.

Angela and I enjoy a spirited sex life. We often arouse each other during foreplay by describing our secret desires. My favorite fantasy involves having sex with two women. Angela has often told me that she would like to experience the sensation of satisfying several men at once. In all our years of marriage, however, our fantasies had still remained unfulfilled.

On the evening of my birthday I arrived home from work late and found the house empty. I walked through the darkened hallway and called out Angela's name, but there was no answer. I decided to go upstairs and sleep until she came home. When I entered the bedroom, I noticed a sheet of paper on the bed with my name at the top and a list of instructions. I recognized my wife's handwriting and read that I would receive my birthday present only if I followed her directions precisely. I felt the first stirrings of an erection as I tried to guess what surprise was in store for me.

Her first instruction told me to take a shower, dry off and cover my body with baby oil. Her letter then instructed me to relax on the bed and turn on the VCR. I followed her directions, and when I turned on the VCR an incredibly arousing X-rated movie started playing. I began gently stroking my penis as I watched the actors and actresses perform every sexual act imaginable. Just as I was getting really excited, the movie stopped abruptly and a message appeared on the screen ordering me to reach under my pillow for a blindfold, put it on and remain motionless.

I willingly complied and waited in the darkness for several minutes until I sensed that someone had entered the room and was standing next to me. I heard my wife say, "Trust me, Bill, and lie still. Your birthday surprise has arrived." Angela removed my blindfold and I saw that she had two female companions with her. Both were gorgeous and dressed in sexy lingerie that left nothing to the imagination. I recognized them as two of my wife's coworkers who I had met at last year's Christmas party. Their sexual exploits were legendary around her office. One of the women was named Pat. She was about twenty-five years old and had long auburn hair, green eyes and a shapely figure. The other woman was named Julie. She was much older than Pat (in her mid-fifties) and had long blonde hair, blue eyes and the most magnificent breasts I have ever seen.

As I stared dumbfounded, my wife said: "I've decided to give you the birthday present you've wanted for a long time. Pat and Julie are yours for the night. I know your fantasy has always been to have sex with two women at once." With that my wife winked at me and left, leaving me alone with these two sex goddesses. I smiled, knowing I was in for the night of my life.

Julie put on some soft music and sat next to me on the bed while Pat began slowly stripping in front of us. As she slowly undressed herself Pat caressed her breasts and massaged her clitoris. Julie leaned over and took my hard cock into her mouth and began sucking and licking the head. When Pat's pussy was dripping wet she climbed onto the bed and straddled me. Julie guided my swollen member into Pat's pussy.

We fucked in every possible position. Right before I was about to come, Pat abruptly climbed off. My pleasure was only briefly interrupted, however, because Julie immediately mounted my cock and began to rock back and forth. Meanwhile Pat leaned over me so I could suck on her nipples. I lost track of time as both women took turns pleasuring me, each one trying to outdo the other.

For a finale they both moved down below my waist and gave me the best blow job a man could imagine. As they took turns licking my balls and asshole and taking my shaft deep into their throats, I felt the biggest orgasm of my life building up within me. Suddenly I exploded with a tremendous load, shooting sperm all over. Laughing, we all collapsed on the bed, completely exhausted. I fell asleep thinking that this was the end of my birthday surprise. Boy, was I mistaken!

When I awoke, Julie and Pat informed me that my surprise had in fact just begun. They helped me to my feet, blindfolded me again and asked me to follow their directions.

They led me to our downstairs bedroom and sat me in a chair. I heard soft moaning coming from the other side of the room, but I could not determine who was making the noise. When Pat removed my blindfold I saw a woman in bed with two men, but the room was too dark for me to see their faces. The two men were both black and had athletic builds. As I watched, the taller of the two men knelt in front of the woman and she swallowed his cock to the hilt.

My member regained its hardness watching the men's coal-dark bodies pressing against the woman's milky-white flesh. My two female companions were also enjoying the show and becoming quite aroused. Julie sat on my lap and slowly inserted my cock into her pussy, moving up and down as Pat rubbed her breasts in my face. Within minutes Julie had a tremendous orgasm that almost knocked me off the chair. They traded positions and Pat's mature flesh engulfed my flaming rod. We began moving in unison. After a few minutes we came at the same time. Pat's orgasm was so overwhelming I was afraid her screams of delight would wake the entire neighborhood.

While recovering I noticed that the threesome on the bed were still locked in the heat of passion. Suddenly one of my companions reached out and turned on a lamp. Finally there was enough light for me to see who the trio was. Imagine my surprise when I realized that the woman was my beautiful wife Angela. Removing a large black penis from her mouth, she turned to me and said: "I hope you've enjoyed your evening so far. When I asked Julie and Pat to help me make your dream come true they agreed immediately, with the stipulation that I let them arrange to have mine come true also. I told them my wildest erotic fantasy was to have two ebony cocks in me at once. That's when they introduced me to John and Daryl. Why don't you relax and watch while I complete my fantasy."

With that Angela began furiously stroking both John and Daryl's cocks, one in each hand. The two men quickly hardened again and sucked on Angela's breasts while caressing her pussy. The taller of the two (I later learned he was John) positioned Angela on her knees and inserted his cock into her pussy doggie-style. Daryl kneeled in front of her so she could swallow every inch of his penis. They remained that way until I saw Angela's body begin to tremble. I knew from long experience that she was on the verge of coming. She cried out in ecstasy as her body shuddered with violent waves of orgasm.

Still in the throes of ecstasy, Angela turned over, grabbed the guys' huge pricks with her pretty white hands and jerked them off. Within seconds they had simultaneous orgasms. Julie and Pat then moved forward and hungrily licked a few stray drops of pearly white jism from her body.

At this point I could not restrain myself any longer and I climbed into the bed and mounted my sweaty wife. We made love in every position imaginable while our audience cheered us on. We both climaxed at the same time. I could tell I had pleased Angela when she cried out in pleasure, stiffened her body and then went limp with exhaustion.

As we calmed down, our fuckmates dressed and began to file out the door. After we recovered I thanked my wife for the best birthday present ever. We made wild and passionate love for the rest of the night. The next day we promised each other that all our birthday celebrations would be just like this one.—*B.S., Lynchburg, Virginia*

NEWFOUND FRIENDS GET BETTER ACQUAINTED DURING GROUP GROPE

My friend Tom and I were walking around downtown one night when we met two women named Sandra and Milena. Sandra was a ditzy blonde with big tits and a big, juicy ass. Milena had long black hair and a slim shapely figure. She was fun to talk to and she seemed to feel the same way about me. Tom and Sandra hit it off too, so we all decided to go to Sandra and Milena's place.

When we got there we paired off quickly. Milena and I sat on the floor, leaning against one couch while Tom and Sandra sat down on the couch right across from us. We talked for a while but soon I started to kiss Milena. Immediately her tongue was down my throat. Sandra turned out the light, and I could see that Tom was making a move on her. I unbuttoned Milena's shirt and was pleased to find that she was wearing a black bra—my favorite color. I asked Milena if her panties matched her bra and to my delight she replied that she wasn't wearing any!

I stuck my tongue in her ear and whispered how much I wanted to lick her pussy. She moaned and smiled a little. I looked over and saw that Sandra was sucking on Tom's cock. It was weird seeing her suck off my friend. She had one hand wrapped around the base and was bobbing her head up and down on his cockhead.

I took Milena's shirt off and flicked my tongue over her nipples a couple of times. I worked my way down her firm, flat stomach and stopped at her navel for a while. Next I unzipped her jeans and she wriggled out of them. Her pubic hair was black and nicely trimmed. I moaned and nuzzled her thighs. She moved around so that I was between her legs. I reached up for a pillow and slid it under her ass, telling her that I wanted to do a good job on her. She moaned and said that I was off to a good start.

She was wet and ready. I nibbled a little around the edges, then dove right in, making long, upward strokes with my tongue. She gasped loudly and put both hands on my head, spreading her legs as wide as they could go. I tongued her as deeply as I could, probing between her pussy lips. I found her clit and treated it to short, light, rhythmic licks. Milena started moving her hips in time with me and moaning, "Oh, yes. Oh, yes."

Finally I knew she was going to come. She clamped her legs around my head and pushed her crotch hard against my face. I grabbed her legs and tried to keep licking her, but it was difficult with her thrashing around. Finally she collapsed, sighed with pleasure and ran her fingers through my hair. I moved up beside her and she turned to kiss me. Then she started licking her juices off my face.

I had my clothes on throughout all of this. I now asked her if I could take them off. She said yes but warned me that she couldn't go all the way with me because she didn't know me well. I took off my shirt and slid off my jeans. I asked her if I could rub up against her ass and she said yes. We lay on our sides with me behind her and I kind of slid my cock between the cheeks of her ass and rubbed back and forth while we watched Tom and Sandra.

I don't know what they were doing while I was going down on Milena, but while we watched they were both on the floor with Sandra on top. Her back was to us so I had a great view of her tight little asshole as she rode Tom's cock. Sandra was making these little mewling noises every time she came down on Tom, and her back arched so that her hair fell down almost to her ass. I have to admit, even though she was kind of dumb, she sure did look hot.

Milena's ass felt great, but I needed something more. I asked her if she would go down on me. She said she didn't feel comfortable enough so instead she reached around, grabbed my stiff prick and started giving me a hand job. She worked my cock up and down while looking up at me and asking if it felt good. I said it felt great and told her she was beautiful. She thanked me and looked down at my cock. Then she surprised me by putting it in her mouth. I sighed and told her how good it felt to have my cock in her mouth.

With one hand she grabbed the base of my cock and with the other she grabbed my balls. She really knew how to give head. I looked up briefly and saw that Tom and Sandra were finished and were watching us intently. Sandra was sitting on the couch with her legs spread. When she caught me looking at her she reached down, fingered her pussy and smiled.

I looked down at Milena and she looked great. I whispered that I was about to come, but she didn't pull away. Finally I thrust my cock all the way into her mouth and exploded. I held it there as she kept sucking. After a while she looked up at me and I saw the come oozing out of her mouth as she sucked on my softening cock.

Tom and Sandra didn't stay together because Tom thought Sandra was too dumb, but Milena and I are still going at it whenever we can. She lets me fuck her now and I plan to talk to her about maybe getting Sandra into the act too. But I'll leave that for another letter.—*Name and address withheld*

IT WASN'T THE MOVIE THAT HAD THEM ROLLING IN THE AISLES

I was working at a small movie theater near my house one day when a hot babe with long legs and a great ass sauntered through the door. I noticed that she was alone and that all of my male coworkers were ogling her as she bought a ticket. She was the only patron in the theater.

My fellow usher Calvin and I walked into the theater after her and closed the doors. As she ambled down the aisle her perfectly shaped ass swayed and jiggled under skintight black jeans. We also noticed her huge tits. Her nipples were totally erect and clearly visible through her white tank top. At first Calvin and I decided to sit a few rows back and just watch, but after fifteen minutes we were both harder than the rock of Gibraltar. This made Calvin bold and he strode down to where she was sitting and said, "Hi. My friend and I were wondering if you would like to fuck us?"

After a few minutes I figured I might as well find out what was going on between them. When I got there Calvin was kissing her neck passionately. I wanted to get in on the action so I complimented her sexy-as-hell ass and told her I wanted to try her pussy on for size. She told us her name was Mariah and that she was ready to give us the fuck of our lives!

Calvin whipped out his cock and I revealed my own purple-headed warrior. Mariah knelt and took turns sucking our cocks.

In no time Calvin and I shot our wads. I didn't know about Calvin but I was still hungry for twat. I stripped off Mariah's clothes and uncovered a body that was even more ravishing than I had imagined. Her pubic hair was shaved and her pussy was covered with silky peach fuzz.

I thought I was going to explode. Instead I went to work licking her dripping snatch. While I was working on Mariah's honey-pot, Calvin was getting the best hand job of his life. After that Calvin dove for her bush and fucked her fast and furiously. After Calvin had pumped and humped to his satisfaction, I took his place.

I slid easily into her well-lubricated hole. She wanted it bad, and Calvin and I had every intention of giving it to her. As I slowly worked my throbbing member into her pussy, Calvin came around and entered her ass from behind. Soon she was moaning so loudly I thought the manager was going to burst in and catch us. She was screaming louder than the movie soundtrack and her moans let me know she was approaching the big one. Her orgasm was so violent it felt like an earthquake. I withdrew and shot my load on her creamy white thighs and seconds later Calvin took care of her other end and shot a huge load of come all over her ass-cheeks.

We gathered our clothes and got dressed. Calvin and I asked for the rest of the night off. Since it was so close to closing time and there weren't any customers, our boss granted our request. After a bite to eat, the three of us rushed to my house and screwed until the early hours of the morning. All I have to say is that this truly was the best fuck of my life!.—*J.C., Emerson, New Jersey*

CELEBRATE THE FOURTH OF JULY WITH A BANG—
A GANG BANG

My wife Judy and I had been having problems. Our sex life just wasn't the same after the birth of our first child. We hoped that a night on the town with another couple would help remind us of our days as passionate young lovers in college. So we left our child with his grandparents and drove to the park to watch the Independence Day fireworks. Little did we know what sort of fireworks the night had in store for us.

We had just parked the car when our friends showed up. Kevin is six feet four inches tall and very muscular. Jessica is only five feet two inches tall, but her full breasts and perky little ass make her stand out regardless of her height. She is a cute brunette but I still prefer my wife's shapely breasts, long legs and light blonde hair.

"Hey, Hank, ready for the fireworks?" Kevin called.

"Yeah, I can't wait," I answered enthusiastically. The four of us found a relatively deserted section of the park and spread out our blankets. Kevin and I sat down and the girls settled in front of us, leaning back to cuddle. We took out a thermos of lemonade heavily fortified with Jack Daniel's and soon everyone was enjoying a pretty good buzz.

After the sun set, the fireworks display began. Judy reclined against me and I gave her a hug and inconspicuously let my hands slip underneath her blouse to lightly touch her breasts. Her nipples soon stiffened under my tender caresses and she uttered a soft moan of pleasure. My cock grew in response and I shifted slightly to give it room to grow. I looked over to see if Kevin was enjoying the fireworks and was momentarily puzzled. He was looking up at the sky with a blissful smile on his face but his eyes were closed. I wondered what was up. Then I noticed that Jessica was cupping Kevin's balls and doing lots of other interesting things to him. I was glad that everything was turning out so nicely.

When Judy turned her head and slipped her tongue into my mouth, I lost interest in everything but her. We kissed until we noticed that the park had grown silent. When we looked around we saw the place was deserted. I glanced at Kevin and we realized that none of us had paid any attention to the fireworks. Laughing, we gathered our stuff and headed back to the car.

We weren't ready to call it a night so we decided to stop by a convenience store. While I chose the beer, Kevin perused the store's collection of X-rated videos. He said it might be fun to spring a dirty movie on the girls, so we grabbed one on our way out. We quickly drove back to our house where the four of us soon curled up on the couch to drink beer and watch the video.

Jessica gasped when she saw that the first scene in the movie involved two women locked in a 69, but neither of the girls suggested we turn it off. We kept getting drunker and drunker and hornier and hornier. Kevin could no longer sit still and watch so he began to knead Jessica's breasts as she reclined against him. She moaned and spread her legs wide, causing her short skirt to rise up and reveal that she wasn't wearing any panties. The alcohol, the sex on the screen and the sight of Jessica all combined to drive me to my knees. I began to lick Jessica's inner thighs and the delicious folds of her cunt.

As I ate her out, Jessica's moans became louder and her head thrashed from side to side. She shuddered and with a sharp cry she came, pulling my face between her legs tightly as she rode waves of pleasure. Then she pushed me away.

"We don't want Judy to feel left out, do we, boys?" Jessica asked with concern. Judy was lounging against the end of the couch. Her eyes were glazed over with lust. Jessica crawled across the couch and brought her face close to Judy's but Judy turned away, avoiding the embrace. She had never even thought of having sex with a woman and she wasn't sure what to do. Undeterred, Jessica slowly began to massage Judy's breasts through her flimsy blouse, causing Judy's nipples to strain against the confining fabric. Judy's breathing became labored. Jessica slid one finger up the leg of Judy's shorts and rubbed her pussy through her panties. Judy's hips started to rotate and heave, and when Jessica offered her lips once more Judy didn't turn away. Instead Judy pulled Jessica close and gave her a fiery embrace.

Jessica rose off the couch and motioned Judy to follow. The two girls stood in front of the TV and put the sex on the screen to shame as they devoured each other's mouth and rubbed their bodies together. Kevin stepped behind Judy and I got into position behind Jessica. As the women felt each other up, we removed their clothing. When they were nude we pulled them apart and I started tongue-wrestling with Jessica. Kevin wasted no time either. He laid Judy on the ground, spread her long legs, placed her ankles on his shoulders and impaled her with his thick cock until she was yelling with delight.

Next Jessica decided to take the lead. She pulled me over to the couch, laid me down on my back and lowered herself onto my stiff dick. She slowly rocked back and forth, leaning forward until her breasts were within reach of my mouth. I licked and nibbled on her tits while she rode my dick and wantonly rubbed her clit. In no time she had a screaming orgasm that lasted for a long time. After resting for a while with a contented look on her face, she climbed off my lap. She knelt on the floor before me and began licking my dick from the balls to the head, swirling her agile tongue around the most sensitive places. I closed my eyes and spread my legs to give her more room and she swallowed my entire dick.

Just when I thought things couldn't get any better, I felt another tongue on my balls. I looked down and saw that Judy was licking my balls while Jessica continued to slide my dick in and out of her throat. The image and sensation were too much and I exploded into Jessica's throat. She swallowed what she could and Judy licked up what was left on her face.

Judy kissed me and Jessica went over to Kevin, who had some fun of his own watching the three of us go at it. He pulled Jessica gently to the floor and began to fuck her slowly and sensually. Meanwhile Judy looked at my limp dick and pouted, "Too bad you don't have anything left to satisfy me with."

"I think I can come up with something to satisfy your hunger," I replied. Then I coaxed her to the floor and began licking her from stem to stern. She turned her head and watched Kevin and Jessica making love as I ate her sopping cunt. I moved up and concentrated on her clit until she screamed in ecstasy. Then I continued kissing my way up her sweaty body until I kissed her mouth one last time.

In the future I don't think we're going to wait till the Fourth of July to enjoy these kinds of fireworks.—*H.F., St. Louis, Missouri*

HIS DREAMS COME TRUE WHEN
THE SITTERS SIT ON HIS FACE

I never thought I would write to *Penthouse Letters*, but keeping this sexual experience to myself would surely be a crime.

I'm a working single parent and I have a steady baby-sitter named Caroline who comes over every weekday after school and on many Friday and Saturday nights. One Saturday evening a few weeks ago she called an hour before she was supposed to arrive and told me that something unexpected had come up and she wouldn't be able to sit for me that night. She didn't want to leave me in a bind, so she'd arranged for a friend of hers to take her place.

Precisely at seven the doorbell rang. When I opened the door, there stood Amy. Amy is a five-foot-three-inch, well-endowed eighteen-year-old who any man in his right mind would die for a chance to fuck. She was wearing a tight pair of cut-offs and a T-shirt that was cropped just below her gorgeous breasts. I almost forgot I was supposed to be going out that night!

I showed her around the house, introduced her to my son and went to my room to dress for the evening. Suddenly, as I was standing there in my birthday suit looking for something to wear, Amy walked into the room without bothering to knock. Her face turned bright red and, after staring at my semierect cock like a rabbit caught in the headlights, she hurried away, pulling the door closed behind her. When I'd finished dressing I went to the living room to say good-bye. Amy apologized for walking in on me. I told her not to worry about it and left.

When I arrived home, Amy was sitting on the couch with another girl who looked to be slightly older. Amy jumped up and told me that my parents had come over right after I'd left and invited my child to spend the weekend with them. Rather than waiting by herself to tell me the news, she'd invited her friend over to keep her company. I didn't say anything, but I wondered what they were really up to.

Amy took me by the hand, led me to the couch and introduced me to her best friend Betty. I told them to get ready so I could drive them home, but instead of putting on their coats, Amy and Betty stood up and took off all their clothes! What happened next was the equivalent of forty years of my favorite fantasies all coming true simultaneously.

Amy said she wanted to see my long, beautiful cock again because her friend hadn't believed her when she'd told her how big it was. It was a dream come true: Before me stood two unbelievably sexy eighteen-year-olds who wanted me to have my way with them. What was a healthy male to do?

As soon as I approached the couch, Betty started tugging at my pants. As she removed them, Amy took off my shirt and started kissing and licking my nipples, which drives me out of my mind. Next thing I knew, Betty had released my throbbing cock from my bikini briefs and was looking at it with awe and lust. She said she had never before seen such a huge cock. She reached out and touched it softly. As Betty held my cock with one hand, she began stroking her wet pussy with the other. Then she asked Amy to show her how to suck cock because she had never tried it before.

Without a word Amy fell to her knees and swallowed my cock. She licked, nibbled and sucked like an expert for about five minutes. Then she told Betty to join her. For the next ten minutes the two of them took turns sucking my cock for all they were worth. When Amy felt me starting to come, she told Betty to put my cock down her throat and enjoy it. It seemed as though I came forever while Betty sucked and swallowed till I was dry.

Once in a while I get a hard-on that lasts all night—this was one of those nights! After pulling my cock from Betty's mouth, Amy pulled me down to the floor and placed her moist young pussy lips right above my mouth. The fragrance was so sweet I reached my tongue up and started licking her cunt until she moaned loudly. All of a sudden Betty lowered herself onto my waiting cock and began rubbing it against her smooth, damp pussy lips. She held my cock with one hand and rubbed her friend's breasts with the other. I thought I was in heaven.

Then Amy turned around with her open pussy still pressing down on my hungry mouth. She told Betty to slide my cock into her dripping pussy and Betty obeyed with one swift push. Betty and Amy were both nearing climax, so I put everything I had into helping them along. They were playing with one another's perfect breasts when both of them reached climax together—flooding my mouth and my cock with their sweet love juices.

Betty got on all fours and begged me to fuck her doggie-style. I quickly obliged. Holding onto her waist, I shoved my rock-hard cock deep into her impatient love-hole. Amy left the room while I fucked Betty hard and fast. She squealed and whimpered with ecstasy until she achieved another shattering orgasm. When Amy returned, she said she had made a phone call and that I was in for a real surprise. What, I wondered, could be better than what I had already experienced?

Without further explanation, Amy motioned to Betty and both friends went to work licking me clean. They did this so well that I shot a load into the air.

Next Amy lay down on the coffee table and asked me to put her legs over my shoulders and slip my cock into her very slowly. Who was I to argue? I did as she requested. When I was only halfway in, Betty said she needed someone to eat her sopping cunt. I told her she would have to wait till I was through with Amy, but to my amazement she walked to the end of the table and placed her little love-box right on Amy's face. What a trip it was to see two lovely friends sucking and fucking their way to an orgasm! This time the excitement was too much for me to handle: I started coming harder than I ever had before.

I was still inside Amy, and Betty was still sitting on Amy's face, when all of a sudden I felt another set of hands rubbing my balls from behind. I turned around and there stood Caroline, my regular baby-sitter, wearing nothing but an ear-to-ear grin. She said she had always fantasized about fucking me but didn't know how to approach me. Caroline then told Betty and Amy that she wanted me all to herself for a few moments but added that they could watch if they wanted to.

Caroline led me to the shower and gently washed my dick. She admitted that a few times when she was baby-sitting for me she had peeked at me while I was dressing. She said she had been amazed by how long and thick my cock was. With that she got down on her knees and sucked me for a few minutes. Then suddenly she looked up and announced that she couldn't wait to get my dick in her pussy. I picked her up and carried her to my bedroom. She asked me to penetrate her slowly so she could feel every inch slide in. I did as she asked and she dug her fingers into my back and yelled, "Fuck me! Fuck me! Fuck me!"

When Betty and Amy heard her cries they came running into the bedroom. They lay down next to us and within seconds were locked in a 69. Watching the two of them while Caroline rocked on my cock was more than I could stand. I blew my load deep into her sweet love-canal as an orgasm flooded her body.

Caroline now started watching the girls eat each other out. She positioned herself on the floor so she could suck on my cock and still keep them in sight. I could see her left hand down between her legs rubbing her clit while she held me with the other. The girls started to orgasm, sending Caroline and me into climaxes of our own.

I could hardly believe what was happening! Here, on my bed, were four totally uninhibited bodies experiencing the finest fucking possible. The four of us spent the rest of the weekend sucking and fucking in every conceivable position. I watched the young women eat each other out while they took turns shoving my ever-ready tool into their greedy mouths or hungry pussies.

I thought that this could only be a once-in-a-lifetime weekend, but since then the four of us have gotten together at least once every two weeks. The funniest part is that all three girls come over separately sometimes and ask me not to tell the others. Of course, I always agree not to tell and we fuck away for hours. I'll go along with whatever they want in exchange for the fulfillment of fantasies they grant me every time I ask.—R.G., *Philadelphia, Pennsylvania*

REUNION WITH AN OLD FRIEND LEADS TO FUN WITH SOME NEW FRIENDS

*S*ince I moved to San Diego last year I hadn't had an opportunity to visit my best friend and ex-roommate Jean. Jean and I had gone to college together. After we'd graduated we'd shared an apartment in Manhattan for over a year. When I learned I'd be attending a week-long seminar in New York City, I phoned Jean to arrange a long-overdue reunion.

While we chatted, Jean told me that her latest boyfriend was incredibly good-looking and rather well-hung. She suggested we get together for dinner my first night in town and said she'd invite one of her boyfriend's friends to join us. When I asked about the friend, Jean responded that he was a total stud but might not be my type.

When I arrived in New York I checked into my hotel. Then I headed straight for Jean's apartment. Jean greeted me at the door. She's a very pretty blonde with a great figure. I am also blonde but my breasts are larger than Jean's. We were both quite popular in college. We were cheerleaders and we slept around a lot.

When Jean introduced me to her boyfriend James, I tried to hide my shock. He was a tall, handsome, well-dressed black man. Since Jean and I come from a small, conservative midwestern town with almost no black population, I was surprised.

As I regained my composure, Jean and I sat down on the couch and James went to fix us all a drink. Jean quietly asked me if I thought James was handsome, and of course I said he was. She went on to say that not only was he really nice but he was also incredibly talented in bed.

James soon returned with a tray of drinks. He was quite charming, handsome and debonair. I could easily see why Jean was so captivated by him. As we chatted, Jean mentioned that James was a very successful investment banker, as was his friend Alfred who would join us for dinner. As James began telling me a little about Alfred, I wondered if he was also black. I had never been on a date with a black man before, but if Alfred was anything like James I was beginning to look forward to it.

When we arrived at the restaurant Alfred was waiting for us. He, too, was a handsome, well-dressed black man. We thoroughly enjoyed our dinner, and Alfred and James were both perfect gentlemen. Afterward they suggested we go out dancing, and Jean and I agreed.

We all had another drink at the nightclub, and I danced with James as well as Alfred. After dancing to several fast songs with each man, a slow song came on and James escorted me to the dance floor. As we danced he held me tight enough for me to feel his penis pressed against my belly. He told me I was beautiful. I could also feel a dampness between my legs as I wondered what it would be like to be with a black lover. When the song ended, Jean suggested we leave since it was getting late.

Back at Jean's apartment, we reminisced about our wild and crazy college days. Jean was exhausted, and while we talked she fell asleep on the couch. James carried her to the bedroom and returned in a few minutes, saying that he had tucked her into bed.

I was getting ready to leave when James and Alfred convinced me to stay for a cup of coffee.

As we sat on the couch and sipped our coffee, the conversation got around to sex. James mentioned that Jean had told him we were both rather promiscuous in college. He also said that Jean had told them I gave great head. I was a little stunned and didn't respond when James added that Jean also loved sucking cock. My body language must have been very suggestive, because when I looked down I realized that my legs were spread and my panties were showing. I was feeling very horny but also a little nervous. When Alfred put his hand on my thigh I softly moaned. James kissed me softly on the neck. I'd never been with two men at once, never mind two black men, but I was too hot to stop and they knew it.

Alfred put his hand on my pussy and began rubbing my clit through my panties. James removed my blouse and bra and started caressing my ample tits. He complimented me on their firmness. Alfred lifted my skirt up around my waist and slid off my panties.

Having a few doubts as to whether or not I should let these two black studs have me, I told Alfred I wasn't sure if I wanted to go through with this. He stood up and dropped his pants, revealing a large, beautifully shaped penis. The sight of his cock dispelled any doubts I had. I decided I definitely wanted to go through with this. When he brought his cock to my mouth, I sucked on it. I was lying back on the couch, licking Alfred's huge cock, when James started licking my pussy. His tongue sent shock waves through my entire body. Just as I was on the verge of orgasm, he pulled away. When I moaned in protest around Alfred's cock, James told me not to worry, that my beautiful blonde pussy was going to be thoroughly satisfied. I'm not sure how long I sucked Alfred's cock, but when he came his load was so huge I couldn't swallow it all. I still hadn't orgasmed and I was ready for anything they had in mind.

Alfred then moved away. James positioned himself between

my legs and rubbed the head of his huge cock along my slit. He asked me if I wanted to be fucked. I replied yes. He told me to ask him to fuck me. I had never talked dirty during sex, but I asked him to fuck my hot pussy with his big cock. As he started to penetrate my cunt, I urged him to fuck me hard. Once he'd slid his cock all the way in, he quickly withdrew it and then slowly slid it in again. It was very exciting to watch his huge cock disappear into my cunt. My pussy had never been this full before. It felt as if it were being stretched to the limit with each thrust. After a few strokes I felt an orgasm building and I urged him to keep fucking me. He must have been hitting my G-spot, because I had a really intense orgasm. I was still spasming when I heard James comment to Alfred that I clearly loved to fuck. Alfred responded that it was going to be a long night.

After I'd recovered from my orgasm, I realized that James hadn't come yet. I was still lying on the couch with my pussy spread wide open when I asked James if he wanted to fuck me again. He moved up to my mouth and slid his cock in. At the same time Alfred rubbed the head of his cock against my clit and then slid it into my pussy. James asked me how I liked being fucked by two black cocks at once, adding that Jean always loved it. I told him I wanted him to come in my mouth. In just a few minutes James exploded in orgasm as I came a second time. After James withdrew, Alfred continued to fuck me, giving me multiple orgasms. Alfred also spewed his come into me, and I could feel it hit the walls of my pussy. Satiated for the moment, I just lay back and relaxed. James asked me how I'd enjoyed it. I replied that it was the best orgasm I'd ever had. Alfred told me that there was a lot more to come but it was Jean's turn next.

They went in and woke up Jean. She was not at all surprised to see me sprawled on the couch, naked and sweaty. James stripped off Jean's underwear, exposing a clean-shaven pussy. He told me to lay back and watch as they laid Jean on the floor and began to rub their huge cocks all over her body. Then James plunged his cock into her. While he fucked Jean, James told me that he and Alfred often took turns fucking her all night long. Jean was now in a frenzy as she begged them to fuck her. After what seemed like an eternity, James came in her pussy. Alfred, who hadn't come yet, pulled his cock out of her mouth, came over to me and asked me to mount him. I straddled Alfred, facing him, and bounced up and down on his cock. Fucking had never felt so good. James asked me to turn around so that he and Jean could see the expression on my face while Alfred fucked me. It was a real turn-on to have an audience watch me make love. We fucked until I had another serious orgasm and Alfred's come filled my pussy. Exhausted, I fell asleep completely satisfied.

When I awoke an hour or so later, I was alone. I went to take a shower. As I was dressing, James returned. Telling me they had more plans for me that night, he quickly stripped off my clothes, laid me down and spread my legs apart. He began to lick my pussy, telling me that he knew I loved to have my pussy eaten. He was right on target, and I couldn't resist humping his face.

After I came I began to give James a blow job. I was doing my best, but there was no way I could get his whole cock into my mouth. Finally he grunted and filled my mouth with his salty jism. This time I swallowed it all. After he came he had me get on my hands and knees. Then he fucked me doggie-style. His cock felt huge as it penetrated me.

I spent most of my visit with James's or Alfred's cock in my pussy. I had never enjoyed sex so much in my life, and I understood why Jean was addicted to their cocks. I even got to watch as they shaved Jean's pussy and then fucked her.

Soon after I arrived back home in San Diego, I received a round-trip plane ticket to New York from Alfred and James along with a note thanking me for a wonderful time and inviting me to visit them soon. I can't wait to see them!—*T.P.*, *San Diego, California*

BRIDE-TO-BE'S FINAL FLING TURNS INTO
A GANG BANG TO REMEMBER

I will be the maid of honor next weekend when Wendy, my very best friend, gets married. Wendy and I are both thirty-four. Wendy is five feet eight and weighs about one hundred forty pounds. She has short blonde hair, firm 38C breasts and a perfectly sculptured ass that everyone drools over! I am five feet six, with shoulder-length brunette hair. I have 34B breasts with large nipples.

Last Saturday the bridesmaids and I held a bachelorette party for Wendy. It was a very conservative luncheon, as both her mother and her future mother-in-law attended. Her fiancé comes from a rather conservative, straitlaced family. He's definitely a traditionalist, and he's insisted that Wendy quit her job since they plan on having children. Although Wendy is very much in love with him, I knew she was feeling apprehensive at the thought that her freedom would suddenly be curtailed.

After the luncheon we went back to my apartment to hang out. I whipped up a pitcher of frozen daiquiris and suggested we sit out by the pool. Wendy said she'd rather drive to the beach and find a motel so she could have one last bachelorette fling. She wanted to dance the night away and howl at the moon until the sun came up.

I agreed that sounded like a great idea, so I packed a few things for the two of us and changed into a sundress. Wendy had only the clothes she was wearing. We drove to the beach and found a motel on the ocean so we could watch the sunset before partying the night away.

We were sitting out in front of our room by the pool when we noticed several college-age guys going into the room next to ours. They eyed Wendy and me as we sunned ourselves. As the sun was on the descent, I suggested we go over to town, check out the shops and find a nice place to have a seafood dinner.

As we window-shopped, we came upon a window display featuring a mannequin wearing a skimpy thong bikini under a sheer white coverup. I followed Wendy into the shop, where she shocked me by telling the clerk that we each wanted an outfit like the one on the mannequin in the window. Wendy told me they were for the next day so we could work on our tans properly before leaving.

Wendy wanted to go back to the room, but I suggested we have dinner first. We found a raw bar that had a view of the sunset and ordered a platter of raw oysters, clams and steamed shrimp. Two very mellow guys joined us, and we were having a good time doing shooters and talking. I wanted to stay with them and party the night away, but Wendy wanted to go back to our room and lie down for a while. I told the guys we'd be back later when the band started.

As we walked back to our room, Wendy told me she really wanted this last fling to be memorable. But when she stopped at the pool to talk to a group of five or six college-age guys, I didn't think she knew what she was getting into. The guys invited Wendy and me to party with them, and we told them we'd be heading back to the bar later and they were welcome to join us then.

Wendy and I went into our room. We could hear the guys laughing and joking outside. I was looking longingly out the window, wishing that we'd taken them up on their offer, when Wendy came up behind me and suggested that we put on our new thongs and join them by the pool. Just then Wendy reached around and tweaked my nipple. I turned around to face her and she started to undress me. We'd never gotten it on together, so we very tentatively stripped one another.

When we were naked she began to suck my nipples. I pulled her face up to mine so we could tongue-kiss. After a few impassioned kisses she turned her attention back to my nipples, licking, kissing and sucking them. While she did that she asked me to tell her about the gang bang I had enjoyed last year. I'd gone to a black-tie social function that my company had sponsored. It was held in the ballroom of a luxury hotel, but it was such a stuffy bore that I wandered off to the lounge. I met five guys and I ended up going back to their suite with them. I let them gang-bang me and it was great!

Talking about my experience turned me on immensely. I was further aroused when Wendy told me that she wanted several guys to fuck her simultaneously. She said she knew that after her wedding she'd have to settle down to be a housewife and mother.

We put on our thongs and see-through coverups. Wendy twirled around in front of me to model hers. Her ass-cheeks were accentuated by the thong. She took off her top and suggested that I do the same, saying that she wanted these guys to know exactly what we wanted. Her tits were clearly visible, with dark red areolae topped by two very hard nipples sticking straight out.

When we stepped outside we were disappointed to see that the pool was deserted. We could hear music coming from an open door a few rooms down, so Wendy immediately headed toward it. I warned her there was no backing out once we got started. She told me not to worry.

Without further adieu we strode into the room. One guy was lying on the bed, thumbing through a copy of *Penthouse Letters*. His jaw dropped in surprise when he saw us. His gym shorts were bulging as he called to his buddy, who was in the bathroom showering. His buddy walked into the room with a towel wrapped around his waist. When he caught sight of us, he dropped his towel. I stood there in awe as his cock went from a limp noodle to a solid erection right before my eyes.

The guy on the bed said that they weren't over at the bar with the rest of their fraternity brothers because they'd forgotten their ID cards. He asked me if their frat brothers had sent us over as some kind of joke.

I locked the door as Wendy lay on her back on the other bed with her legs spread wide apart. The guy who had just come out of the shower climbed up between her legs. Wendy took hold of his stiff cock and guided it into her pussy. They began fucking each other wildly. I walked over to the foot of the bed where the first guy still sat stock-still. As I stripped, I asked him if he still thought I was a joke. He was too shocked to answer. I crawled up onto the bed with him and pulled off his shorts. I shifted to his right so I could see what Wendy was up to. My guy had a nice solid handful of stiff cock. I played with it as I watched Wendy.

The action on the other bed was a little more intense. The guy lifted Wendy's legs over his shoulders. She was fingering her clit. I could hear slurping sounds as his cock slid in and out of her pussy. As I started deep-throating the cock in my mouth, Wendy watched me intently. I sucked harder, massaging his scrotum. Suddenly I felt his balls start to twitch. I knew his orgasm was close. As he thrust into my mouth again, he stiffened, then erupted with an unbelievably powerful blast of come. The first blast was followed immediately by a second blast and then a third. When Wendy saw that I had swallowed his entire load of come without releasing his cock, she came with a groan. Wendy's orgasm triggered her partner's, and he tensed and shot his wad deep into her pussy.

I watched as Wendy climbed on the other side of the guy. She took his cock into her mouth as she stared at me intently. As I sucked my guy to another erection, Wendy matched me stroke for stroke, licking, sucking and deep-throating her guy's cock. As the cock in my mouth stiffened, I shifted my position, straddling his cock. Then I lowered myself down on it. As the stiff cock slid up into me, I could feel the familiar orgasmic twitches building up inside me. When he raised his head up to suck on my left nipple, I immediately started to climax. I rode him to orgasmic ecstasy. As he fucked my convulsing pussy, I felt him release a load of come. When I looked over at Wendy, she was sucking come from her guy's shaft. I climbed off my guy and sat at the edge of the bed so I could get a better view.

When Wendy caught sight of me, she crawled over her guy and off the bed. Kneeling next to me, she hugged and kissed me as the guys watched. The guys introduced themselves as Eric and Matt and asked us what our names were and where we were from. I told them that we wanted this to be an anonymous fling, so we'd prefer not to tell them anything about us. Then Wendy turned to face them and asked them if they would help turn her fantasy into reality. She went on to tell them she wanted the two of them to fuck her at the same time—one in her pussy and one in her ass.

Wendy looked at me with a lustful glint in her eyes, smiling like the Cheshire cat. I asked the guys if they had any lubricant. As Eric got out of the bed to look for some, I told Matt to climb on the bed with me. Wendy positioned him on his back next to me and straddled him, taking his cock into her pussy in one smooth movement. Eric was greasing up his cock with tanning butter. He positioned himself behind Wendy. As I held her ass-cheeks apart for him, he guided the tip of his cock to Wendy's anus, which winked at him like a bull's-eye. I told Wendy to relax and get ready for her double fuck. With one quick stroke Eric was buried balls-deep in her ass. Wendy began to chant, "Fuck me, fuck me, fuck me!"

At first the two guys had trouble establishing a rhythm between them. I kept telling Wendy to settle down on Matt's cock, and Eric to go slow and easy. Mere inches from the action, I watched in amazement as Matt and Eric started rhythmically fucking Wendy deep and slow.

Just then I realized that Eric was starting to shudder. I wanted him to pull out so I could watch him orgasm, but it was too late. As he buried his stiff cock deep in Wendy's ass one more time, he started coming. As he withdrew, I heard Wendy ask Matt to fuck her ass.

Matt rolled Wendy onto her back, then flipped her over like a rag doll, laying her on top of me. She began tongue-kissing me as he drove his cock into her ass. With a steady, stroking rhythm he reamed her ass. As my tongue probed her mouth, I wrapped my arms around her, hugging her tightly to me. She moaned in ecstasy as Matt exploded in her ass. His orgasm triggered hers, and her body shook so violently that she dislodged him. All I could do was hold her until she calmed down and started tongue-kissing me again.

I could hear the shower running and realized that Eric was nowhere to be seen, so I surmised he must be showering. Wendy and I continued kissing until Eric emerged from the bathroom, dripping wet. Matt asked Wendy if she wanted to take a shower with him, and the two of them walked into the bathroom hand in hand. I lay in bed, watching Eric towel himself off.

Suddenly there was a knock on the door and I heard someone call to Matt and Eric. Then the knocking turned to pounding. I looked over at Eric and, in a whisper, asked him to keep quiet. Wendy and Matt emerged from the bathroom to see what the commotion was. Eric put his finger to his lips to indicate that they should remain silent. Wendy sat down on the bed next to me, and we both breathed a sigh of relief when the noise outside stopped.

I was sitting up against the headboard with my legs spread when Wendy slid down between my legs. Both Eric's and Matt's eyes were glued to us. They stared at my matted pubic hair, my swollen red labia and my come-stained thighs. As Wendy ran her hand up my thigh, preparing to take a tongue-dive into my pussy, there was suddenly a quiet tapping on the door. I told Wendy to see who it was. As she cracked open the door, she put a finger to her lips. One guy walked into the room with his eyes wide and his jaw practically on his chest.

As he stood there staring at the sight before him, I asked him if he saw anything he'd like to fuck. All he had on was a pair of sweatpants, which he immediately pulled off. I was quite pleased to see that he had a big, stiff cock. I knew I was going to enjoy being fucked by him while the others watched.

I grabbed a pillow down and slid it under my hips to elevate my pussy. I told him I needed a nice, hard, deep fuck, and he said he'd be glad to oblige. I ran my hand over my nipples, which were rock hard. I asked Eric and Matt to suck on them while their friend fucked me. The three of them immediately went to work.

I looked over at Wendy and told her it felt heavenly. Then I told Eric and Matt that I wanted them to fuck me next. They immediately increased the intensity of their ministrations. I closed my eyes and let the sensations wash over me. I can come just from having my nipples sucked, and the added sensation of a stiff cock fucking me triggered multiple orgasms. I thought I was dreaming as I looked past the guy fucking me and saw four naked guys standing behind him, stroking their stiff cocks as they watched me fuck! I held onto Matt's and Eric's heads while I stared into the eyes of the guy fucking me. As he started fucking me with long, deep, rhythmic strokes, my body was wracked with one continuous orgasm. When I came back down to earth, I realized that my ass was propped up on a come-drenched pillow and a bunch of strange guys were standing around the bed watching me. Suddenly embarrassed at putting on such a wanton show of exhibitionism, I got up and went into the bathroom, closing the door behind me.

I was sitting on the edge of the tub trying to regain my composure when Wendy came in. She sat on the floor next to me and told me how awesome I looked fucking those guys. Wendy told me to calm down and take a shower, adding that she would be right outside with the guys.

I stood in the shower, leaning against the wall for support as I let a lukewarm spray of water cool my body down. The water rained down on my body, washing the come away. As crazy as it sounds, I became embarrassed when I heard a male voice talking to me through the frosted shower door. He told me he was leaving a pair of shorts and a T-shirt on the counter for me to wear. When I got out of the shower, I put on the clothes. I went back into the room, noting that Wendy had on a football jersey that hung below her knees and the five newcomers were all dressed. Matt and Eric were passed out on the bed. Evidently Wendy and I had worn them out.

Wendy told me the key to our room was under the doormat and suggested that I go back to the room and get some rest. She said she was going to party with these five guys in the room next to ours. She told me not to worry, saying that she'd be all right and would be back soon. As Wendy and the guys followed me out, I told Wendy I'd rather stay with her.

The guys were already in the room stripping when Wendy and I entered the dimly lit room. Loud music was playing in the background. The guys all sat on the edge of the bed and I sat in the chair next to the bed. Wendy stood in front of them and began to sway to the music. In one quick motion she pulled the jersey over her head. She rubbed her hands over her nipples, then slid them down to her pussy, spreading apart her labia. The guys were all stroking hard cocks as they watched, mesmerized. When she turned her back to them, one guy ran his hand between her legs while two others caressed her ass. When one guy stood up to get closer to her, she told them all to stay in their seats. She stepped back, leaned against the desk, and lifted each of her nipples to her mouth in turn so she could suck on them.

She asked the guys if they had any Vaseline, and one of the guys said he did, adding that he wanted to tit-fuck her. She said they could tit-fuck her, face-fuck her or butt-fuck her, as long as they gang-banged her first. She told them she wanted all five of them to fuck her at the same time.

I stripped and sat back down to watch. Wendy began orchestrating her gang bang. She asked the guy with the biggest dick to lie down in the center of the bed. The guy holding the Vaseline jar was awarded the honor of being the first to butt-fuck her. She told the other three she would suck on one cock while giving the other two hand jobs until it was their turn to fuck her. She said she wanted five guys filling her full of come!

I sat frozen in disbelief as conservative, soft-spoken, shy Wendy prepared to take on five hard cocks. Before she started, she kissed me and thanked me for helping her live out her ultimate fantasy. Then she climbed up onto the bed and straddled the guy who was lying there. She told him she wanted this to last, and if he could hold off his orgasm he'd be the fifth guy to fuck her ass!

As Wendy lowered herself onto his stiff cock, the others all watched. When her pussy made contact with his cock-head, she stopped for a moment, then dropped down onto his stiff cock, causing him to groan in ecstasy. She settled down, meshing their pubic hair together. She told the guy at her back door to ream her ass good. While buttman was stroking in and out, she reached out for the two cocks at her sides, saying she wanted them to fill her with come when it was their turn. She then deep-throated the fifth cock. Leaning in for a closer look, I stared in disbelief at my best friend in action with five hard cocks. The guy fucking her ass moaned and groaned as Wendy flexed her ass-cheeks. I could see Wendy rhythmically tighten her ass muscles, causing him to drive deeply into her ass on each stroke. Wendy let each guy fuck her ass for a few minutes, then she would start flexing her muscles and milking him to orgasm.

After the four guys had come in her ass, she continued to ride the guy beneath her for a few minutes. Everyone else settled down to watch. Finally Wendy raised her leg and the guy slid out from under her. She rolled onto her stomach and told the fifth guy to ream her ass full of come. As he entered her with one deep stroke, she winked at me. He started fucking her with long, deep thrusts, telling her he was going to fuck her silly. While looking me straight in the eye, Wendy tightened her ass muscles around his cock. The big-cocked guy slowed down his thrusts but the milking action of Wendy's ass was too much for him. Grunting, groaning and moaning, he came explosively in her ass. As I watched, he jerked backward and fell onto the bed. I looked at his totally limp dick, then at Wendy's smiling face. As she slid off the bed, she told the guys to sit in a row at the foot of the bed. She carefully walked over to the desk and bent over it, leaning on her elbows. As the guys all stared at her ass, she told them look at what they'd done to her. Then she parted her legs, allowing a torrent of come to run down her inner thighs to her ankles in a dozen streams.

Wendy told all the guys to go out to the pool and relax for a while. She said she was taking me into the shower with her, adding that they were all welcome back later when we were through. Then she took my hand and led me into the bathroom.

When Wendy and I reemerged some time later, the guys were still standing around the empty bed, looking in awe at the puddles of love juices that stained the sheets. When they caught sight of us, one guy said they wanted to watch us get it on together. Without a word Wendy walked over to the bed and lay down in the center of it. She looked at me, winked and licked her lips. With the guys cheering us on, I climbed onto the bed and straddled her head, facing her feet. As I lowered my face, we tongued each other's pussy. As I held onto her ass-cheeks I realized how well-muscled they were. They felt as if they'd been sculptured from a solid block of granite. I licked her from ass to clit, reveling in the firmness of her ass-cheeks.

Suddenly I felt the guys trying to push my knees up so one of them could fuck me. I told them that my pussy was too sore and that they should fuck me up the ass instead. Two guys spread apart my ass-cheeks as a third drove his cock in to his balls. I was moaning and groaning. After he came, two more guys fucked me in turn.

When I looked up, the big-dicked guy was asking Wendy if he and his buddy could double-fuck me. She looked down at me, and I told her I'd had enough. Wendy told the guy that he and his friend could double-fuck her, adding that this would be our last fuck of the night.

After they were through, Wendy and I dressed and returned to our room. After locking the door, we fell asleep in each other's arms.

When I awoke, Wendy told me to get my things together so we could head home. During the drive back to my apartment, Wendy asked me to write down the details of our gang bang so she'd have a memento of her final fling. I was relieved when she assured me that she still planned to go through with her upcoming nuptials and settle down to be the perfect little housewife. But with a devilish look in her eyes, she added that she was going to stay on the Pill, just in case married life got boring!—*Name and address withheld*

Serendipity

AN ORDINARY EVENING TURNS INTO AN
EXTRAORDINARY NIGHT

Yesterday started out as an ordinary evening. When I got home from work I had dinner with my wife and children. Afterward Tess and I put the kids to bed. I spent a few minutes longer than Tess tucking them in and saying good night. When I went back downstairs Tess was nowhere to be seen, but I heard some noise coming from the family room in the basement.

Figuring that Tess was just doing her exercise routine, I straightened up the kitchen before heading down to the family room. What I saw as I went down the stairs stopped me dead in my tracks. Tess had stripped down to her underwear and was sitting on the couch watching an X-rated movie. One hand delved into her panties while the other squeezed a pink nipple. Since my wife rarely masturbates, I watched from the stairs for a few minutes. When it appeared that she was close to orgasm I walked over to her. I slipped off her panties, revealing her wet pussy, and replaced her hand with my tongue. Her juices were flowing abundantly. Just before she reached the point of no return I slid a finger into her pussy. That sent her over the edge. She was moaning and groaning so loudly I had to remind her that the kids might not be asleep yet!

We sat and watched the movie for a few minutes to give Tess a chance to catch her breath. Her hand was resting on the bulge in my pants. Once she had recovered she unzipped my pants and worked my cock out into the open. She stroked it slowly before sliding her mouth over my shaft. I have always enjoyed watching her suck my cock. This time she took me deeper than usual and seemed to be sucking more vigorously.

I warned her I was going to explode if she didn't stop. She'd only let me come in her mouth once before, and I didn't want to push my luck. Instead of stopping like she usually does, she picked up the pace and told me she wanted to taste my come! I didn't argue with her. Instead I announced that I was coming and shot my load into her mouth. She let my come drip out of her mouth onto my cock and then licked it up again. She did this a few times before she finally swallowed it all.

I was so turned on that I couldn't wait to fuck her. I turned her around and thrust my cock into her doggie-style. I squeezed her firm ass-cheeks while my shaft slid in and out of her wet pussy. She began rubbing her clit (something else she rarely does) and screamed that she was coming again. That was enough to bring me off again too.

She had one last surprise for me. When I pulled my tool out of her pussy, she immediately turned around and began licking our juices off it, giving me a slow, languid blow job. This kept me hard as a rock. It took me a lot longer to come this time but Tess didn't seem to mind. Once again she let me explode in her mouth. I was in seventh heaven!

When I caught my breath, I asked her what had gotten her so horny. She told me she'd bet a friend that she could keep me hard and make me come three times in one night. I told her I'd be happy to help her win any future bets.—P.Y., *Dayton, Ohio*

IT'S DOUBLE TROUBLE WHEN
LOOK-ALIKE SISTERS DRIVE HIM WILD

Recently my wife went back to school to pursue her master's degree. This meant we had to hire a baby-sitter for our three kids. As luck would have it we found a great one in Gwen.

Gwen is a slim but well-built college freshman. She has beautiful shoulder-length blonde hair, blue eyes and a great body. When I first met her my wife had to take me aside and tell me to pull my tongue back into my mouth.

One afternoon I unexpectedly came home from the office for lunch. I found Gwen sunning herself in a small bikini in the backyard while my youngest child took a nap and the older two played at a friend's house. We chatted for a while as I ogled her chest. I was disappointed when she rolled onto her stomach, but my spirits picked up when she asked me to rub suntan oil on her back. I thought this might be my chance to seduce Gwen, but after a few minutes she thanked me and told me that was enough.

I went into the house, made myself a sandwich and ate it, then went into the bathroom to jerk off and relieve the tension in my balls while dreaming of being between Gwen's creamy thighs. I went back to work, but all I could think about was fucking Gwen.

About three weeks later I went out for a beer after work with a couple of guys from the office. There was a young woman sitting at the bar who bore an uncanny resemblance to Gwen. I couldn't keep my eyes off her. She was dressed in a conservative navy-blue business suit and a sheer white blouse. Her hair was piled on top of her head and she wore glasses, but I was certain it must be Gwen.

After staring at her for at least fifteen minutes she caught me eyeing her and smiled. She got up and began walking toward me. As she got closer I suddenly realized it wasn't Gwen after all. Nevertheless the resemblance left me hot and horny, as she was equally attractive. She introduced herself and I discovered she was Gwen's twenty-three-year-old sister Lori. I apologized for staring and she graciously accepted my apology. My friends left me alone with Lori and we ordered another round and began chatting.

When we left the bar I walked Lori to her car. It was parked near my brand-new bright-red Miata, which I had picked up from the dealer that very morning. Lori admired my car and said that she was planning to get one when the new model came out. "Have you driven one yet?" I asked.

"No, but I'd love a test drive," she answered. I tossed her the keys and told her to jump in. I was thrilled at the prospect of spending more time with Lori. I got in the passenger's side and told her we'd come back to get her car.

As we drove along I noticed that Lori's jacket was unbuttoned and her skirt had ridden up her thighs. I realized that Gwen's well-endowed chest and great legs were family traits. Lori's blouse was quite sheer, and I could see her bra underneath it as well as the outline of two hard nipples. I couldn't take my eyes off her as she drove.

Before I realized it we were in the country driving on a two-lane road. "Where are we going?" I asked curiously. Lori just smiled and told me to relax and enjoy the view.

Soon we turned onto a gravel road and drove down a winding, narrow lane before pulling up in front of a cabin alongside a lake. She turned off the engine and turned to me, a big smile on her face.

"Where are we?" I asked.

"This is where I come to get away from it all," she told me. "The cabin belongs to my folks. Get out. I'll show you around."

She left the radio on as she climbed out of the car. I watched that sweet ass sway back and forth, then I followed her around to the front of the car. Without warning Lori put her arms around my neck and gave me a long, deep French kiss that curled my toes. She backed me up against the hood of the car until I was sitting on it. She continued kissing me as she removed my jacket and loosened my tie. Then she began rubbing my crotch.

While I sat there stunned, Lori backed up a step or two and began a sensual striptease. She started by removing her glasses and tossing them into the car. Then she turned her back to me, let her hair down and began undulating her hips in time to the music. "Driving your car really got me hot," she announced. She continued to dance as I pulled off my tie and unbuttoned my collar. Soon she shed her jacket and turned back toward me. Her tits strained the buttons of her blouse and her nipples looked like they might pop right through the material. Lori turned around and backed up against me so that her ass was rubbing against my cock through my trousers. Over her shoulder she asked me to unzip her skirt. I dutifully obeyed.

Lori continued to dance, moving away from me again. She shimmied her skirt over her hips and down to her ankles, then danced back to me. "Now unbutton me," she instructed. Again I did as I was told, undoing the buttons of Lori's blouse while she stared right into my eyes. When I was done she held her blouse open so I could get a quick glimpse of her tits. Then she turned her back to me and let it slide off her arms to the ground.

By now I was ready to pop. My cock was straining at my zipper and I couldn't stop from rubbing my tin soldier through my pants. Lori smiled at my actions but made no move to assist me. She just continued to shimmy and shake. When the song neared its end Lori reached back and unhooked her bra, letting her tits spring free. She ran her hands over her tits while arching her back and moaning. I almost came right then!

Fortunately Lori had other plans. She dropped her panties as the song ended and tossed them over my shoulder. Then she undid my belt and zipper and tugged down my trousers and undershorts, allowing my cock to bob free. She lightly licked my cockhead before working the shaft into her mouth. In less than thirty seconds I shot a huge load down Lori's throat.

Lori stood up and kissed me. I could taste my love juice in my mouth. Then Lori lay back on the hood of the car and said, "Now it's my turn, baby. I want you to lick my cunt and make me come."

I ripped off my shirt and stood between Lori's legs. I bent over to kiss her lips, then began working my way down her luscious bod. My first stop was her magnificent tits, then I continued down her stomach to her pussy. I gently licked her labia until she began to encourage me to give her more. I love a woman to be vocal during sex, and Lori did not disappoint me. "You're a tease," she scolded. "Give it to me now. Don't make me wait any longer." With that I dove into her cunt, running the tip of my tongue across her clit every few seconds. I focused more attention on her clit until she clamped her thighs around my head and came. Her juices were so sweet. I couldn't get enough. She finally had to push me away.

I lay next to her on the hood of the car with my cock at half-mast. Lori saw that I was coming back to life and rolled on top of me. She stroked my cock back to full hardness, then slid it up her pussy. We fucked there on the hood of the car for ten minutes. Several times we were on the brink of a mutual orgasm, but each time Lori slowed the pace to prevent it. Suddenly we heard a car approaching. Lori slid off me and told me to follow her. We ran inside the cabin until the car passed. Laughing, Lori and I proceeded to the bedroom, where we enjoyed a leisurely fuck.

On the drive back to her car Lori was very quiet. A few blocks from the bar I asked her if everything was okay. When we reached the parking lot Lori confessed that the sex had been great but she felt a little guilty about fucking another woman's husband and hoped I wouldn't tell Gwen. I assured her it would be our little secret. Before Lori got out she leaned over to kiss me. It began as a soft goodbye kiss, but I couldn't bring myself to break it off and it gradually developed into a very hot French kiss. As soon as I touched her breasts Lori grabbed for my cock and it was off to the races again.

Soon we were sitting in my little convertible in a dark corner of the parking lot. Lori turned her back to me and said, "I want you to fuck me from behind." She knelt on the passenger seat and held onto the headrest as I positioned myself between the dashboard and her tantalizing ass. I slid her skirt up and massaged her ass-cheeks as I worked my cock between her thighs.

She reached between her legs and guided my rod into her cunt. "Oh, baby, your cock feels so good in me. Make it last, lover," she exhorted me. By then I had wrapped my hands around her breasts. My cock was buried in her cunt. As I began humping her from behind, Lori lost control. She became quite vocal and I was afraid we might attract too much attention but, despite the danger that someone I knew might see me fucking this girl, I couldn't stop.

"C'mon, baby, fuck me," she spurred me on. "Fuck my pussy. Make me come, baby. I want to feel you come with me. Fuck me, baby. Fuck me!" I held her swaying tits in my hands while pounding my cock into her from behind. "Oh, God, baby. Your cock feels so good. Keep fucking me, baby. I want you to come in me!" In less than a minute we came together.

As soon as our orgasms subsided Lori and I started to laugh as we got dressed again. I walked her to her car, kissed her good-bye and watched her drive away. I hurried back to my car and checked my appearance in the rearview mirror. I was worried that my wife would be able to tell what I had been up to from my guilty expression and the stupid grin on my face. I hoped she'd just attribute it to my new sports car.

As it turned out I needn't have worried. When I got home I learned that my wife had left town on an unexpected business trip. Gwen was there to watch the kids until I arrived. I called my wife at her hotel and we chatted for a few minutes. Gwen had put the kids to bed and was standing at the door waiting for a ride home. My brother showed up just then to watch the football game with me, and he said he'd watch the kids while I drove Gwen home and got a bite to eat.

As we walked out to the garage Gwen asked me what had kept me so late at the office. "An unexpected opportunity came up," I responded. I noticed that Gwen's ass resembled Lori's but filled out her jeans a little better. The sight of her firm young body caused my cock to stiffen.

"Wow, I love your new car!" Gwen exclaimed as we entered the garage. "Could I drive it home? I know how to drive a stick shift and I promise I won't go too fast."

In response I just tossed her the keys. I watched as she slid into the driver's seat. She turned to me as she fired up the engine and said, "I know just where I want to go. There's a two-lane road that goes to my parents' place by the lake. It's a beautiful drive on a clear night. Maybe we could grab some food on the way out of town and have a little party. How does that sound?"

Well, what could I say? I'll tell you one thing though—I'm never selling this car!—*Name and address withheld*

FOOTLOOSE FARM BOY SOWS
A FEW WILD OATS ON THE SIDE

I had just turned eighteen and was working as a farmhand on a large farm for the summer. Mike, the farmer's son, was four years older than me. One Friday night he invited me to accompany him and his friend Billy to a nearby city for a dance at the civic center.

I was surprised when Mike asked me if I wanted to drive his car, and I gladly accepted. Of course when they directed me to stop in town to pick up two girls, Nancy and Maria, I realized I was being used as a chauffeur. It soon became apparent that other duties were also expected of me.

The girls had been promised they'd be taken to the dance, but neither Mike nor Billy could dance. That task was left to me. Mike and Billy split shortly after we arrived and were gone for over two hours. I had the time of my life dancing with Nancy and Maria.

Both Nancy and Maria had beautiful bodies. Their firm, bra-less tits swayed nicely in their clingy sweaters. They had my cock as hard as steel in no time and kept me that way all evening. It looked like I had a horseshoe in my pants. Fortunately my sports jacket and the dim light hid my erection, but of course the girls noticed it and teased me unmercifully.

As we danced, Maria slid her legs between mine and nibbled on my neck and ear.

When it was Nancy's turn, she whispered, "Maria says you're

getting nice and hard. I love the feel of a hard cock." Her hips moved suggestively against mine as we danced.

After the next dance Maria suggested we walk up to the balcony that encircles the arena. It was fairly dark, but the music sounded great. I stood between them with an arm around each of them as we looked down at the dance floor below. Their hands caressed my back and buttocks as they removed my tie and unbuttoned most of my shirt. I kissed each of them in turn.

We decided to dance again. It was Maria's turn. This time her hand traced the outline of my cock as I played with her breasts. Then her hand slid down inside my pants and positioned my cock pointing upward. My cockhead peeked over the waistband of my pants. "I think you'll like him even better now," she said to Nancy as they switched.

Nancy's hand crept down the front of my pants as we danced to a slow song. She looked at me, smiled and said, "I'm going to make you come." The combined effect of her hands, breasts and legs soon made her prediction come true. I erupted into her hand as she pumped my cock. The sight of her licking the come off her fingers brought me to another erection. Then Maria stepped in, made sure my cock was still peeking over my waistband and danced me away.

Her fingers were on my crotch, my sports jacket was unbuttoned and my arms were wrapped around her as we slowly moved to the music. She played with my cock with both hands and never stopped talking about how she loved cocks in general and mine in particular. "I'd love to taste your come," she said.

When the music stopped her fingers never left my cock. When it started again I told her I was going to make a mess right there on the dance floor if she didn't stop. She smiled and said, "No you're not. I have everything in hand." My knees buckled when I came. She caught every drop in her hands.

Shortly after that Mike and Billy returned. We left to go to a drive-in restaurant. After we parked at the rear of the parking lot (at Nancy's suggestion), Mike and Billy went in to get some food.

Maria, who was sitting beside me, started getting friendly before the guys even reached the door to the restaurant. "I want to thank you for dancing with us," she cooed as she unzipped my pants. Her nimble fingers had me hard in no time and then her head dropped down into my lap. I got the blow job of my life. She sucked and licked my cock while her hand slid up and down the shaft. Nancy leaned over the seat, massaging my neck and chest while nibbling on my ear. Her whispered comments about the magnificent job that Maria was doing brought me to a thunderous climax. Maria swallowed every last drop.

Before we dropped off the girls that night, Nancy slipped me something and whispered, "Here's something to help you remember this night." It was a pair of slightly moist silk panties.—*T.D.*, *Topeka, Kansas*

VIVACIOUS VIXEN TURNS IRON WORKER
INTO A MAN OF STEEL

On certain bright, crisp autumn days I can't resist letting the top down on my little MG. I know I probably look silly—freezing and hair askew—but even making bank deposits and picking up groceries become celebrations! This particular perfect day was no exception, and it was a payday to boot.

I still had one last errand to run. I'd had an iron gate built that week and it had turned out beautifully. The man who'd done the job had simply left a handwritten bill. His eyes told me he took his commitment seriously, so when payday rolled around I didn't blow it all on Ma Bell and the power company. Looking at my watch, I saw that it was nearly six o'clock. Hoping that he hadn't closed up shop yet, I stepped on the gas.

I pulled up in front of his place a few minutes later. It was a small shop covered with ornamental wrought iron. I was relieved to see that lights were still on inside. As I got closer I could see through the window. Sparks were flying through the air like a comet's tail.

I entered a small, unkempt office and stuck my head in the shop door, holding up my check to indicate my intentions. The man who had built my gate motioned for me to sit down and wait, then he flipped down his protective face plate and continued working. The bright blue light from the blowtorch was too intense for me to look at and I had to turn away, but not before I noticed his beautiful physique. On our previous encounters he had been dressed in baggy jeans and work shirts, but here in the shop, with the heat from the forge to contend with, he was dressed only in a ragged T-shirt and cutoffs. When he turned his blowtorch off I continued checking out his body. He removed his mask and gloves, revealing wild eyes and reddish-gray hair as disheveled as mine. My heart quickened at the sight of his demonic look against the fiery backdrop. Red hair covered his arms and chest. I was mesmerized. He stood still for what seemed hours, just meeting my stare, until I stammered something about the check. He walked into the office with a catlike grace and I handed the check to him, our eyes still locked. He put the check on a desk without even looking at it.

When he invited me in to see the shop, I eagerly accepted and followed him in, feasting my eyes on his butt. Usually doctors and lawyers were my mainstay, but here I was, incredibly turned on by a manual laborer. A jolting surge of lust almost made me reach out and touch him, but he was heating a piece of metal in the forge while he explained the process. Placing the glowing red end on the anvil, he twisted and banged it with a huge hammer into something entirely new. Every movement he made excited me even more. I longed to feel his callused, scarred hands all over my body.

At last he laid down the tools. I tried to feign interest in his work, but I was really only interested in him. We stared into each other's eyes until I reached out, took hold of his battered hand and kissed it. That was all it took. The man of steel collapsed and an avalanche of the most perfect kisses and hugs poured over me. As I reveled in his smell and his taste, I heard him whisper something about not wanting to get me dirty. My response was to let my silk jacket fall in the shavings of steel behind me and pull him closer.

He quickly stripped and yanked off my lacy underwear. Like an excited child unwrapping birthday presents, he gasped and cooed with delight at each body part that was unveiled. I felt like an unfinished sculpture in the hands of an artist as he kneaded, kissed and buried himself in my flesh. His soft red body hair teased my skin with its feathery touch, contrasting markedly with his rough, scarred fingers. My juices were flowing with excitement and I started looking around for a place to lie down. He was so tall that I didn't think we could make love standing up. He was evidently in no hurry as we stood naked except for the boxer shorts around his ankles. Usually slow to arouse, I longed for him to just plunge into my being. Even without any foreplay I knew I would climax instantly. I had never seen a cock with such a beautiful upward curve, and I longed to ride it. But he just stared longingly at me, not making a move. Finally I couldn't take it any longer. I grabbed his prick and tried to embrace him. He lifted me without effort and sat me on the workbench. I begged him to fuck me, but he spread my legs and, with the tenderest touch, explored the warm wetness there. Staring intently into my eyes, he ever so softly stroked and probed. I told him I had to have him in me. He whispered for me to let go, so I allowed myself to explode in a series of orgasms and melt into his arms.

He tenderly stroked my thighs before kissing down my abdomen. When he reached my pussy he lapped up my sweet come. Never before had I come so hard. I could feel my orgasm from my head to my toes. Before I could catch my breath he stood up and slid his penis into my still-quivering cunt. He didn't move at first, delighting in the pulsating aftershocks. Deep within me he touched places that had never been touched before. It was as though I hadn't just come a few minutes before. A deep new chord was struck as that beautifully curved cock stroked me like a glowing rod of metal. It was so primal, yet so natural and powerful. Every other sexual encounter I'd ever had paled in comparison. Animal noises escaped my lips as I began to meet his thrusts. Each seemed harder and deeper than the last. I was transported to another state of being, transfigured into a wholly sexual creature. Gyrating his hips, he moaned, "Come with me, baby," and together we crested the wave, sliding down into the trough of orgasm. Quivering and moaning, he held me tightly in his arms. I wanted to stay there forever, safe and warm. Words of endearment poured from my lips as I tenderly kissed his earlobe. I would have never believed one could fall in love so instantly and intensely had it not happened to me.—R.E., *Amherst, Massachusetts*

MIKE LOOK-ALIKE SCORES BIG WITH FOXY FEMALE GUARD

I would like to share a wonderful sexual experience with the horny readers of *Penthouse Letters*. I am an incarcerated twenty-eight-year-old African-American, five feet seven and one hundred and eighty pounds of muscularity. About six months ago a female guard named Joan began making sexual advances toward me, probably because I'm so pretty. You see, I look for all the world like Michael Jordan. I had not been sexually active for quite a while and it really turned me on to hear her talking about licking me from head to toe. Our steamy conversations always led to me jerking off afterward.

Now let me tell you about this female guard. Joan is a forty-eight-year-old white woman, five feet tall, with amazing 40-27-38 measurements. She had just recently started working the night shift. One night around one o'clock, just as I was beginning to jerk off, Joan was making her rounds and caught me in the act of furiously stroking my dick. She just stood there in front of the bars with her eyes glued on my dick. I poked it out through the bars and, without a word, Joan dropped to her knees and took my cock into her mouth. She cupped my hairy nuts tenderly in her hand and started licking and sucking my dick like I had never experienced. After about five minutes Joan slipped a rubber band down around the base of my dick as a makeshift cock-ring to prolong our pleasure. Then she continued working on me with her mouth for at least another twenty minutes. Finally she slipped the rubber band off. After just a few more sucks I started squirting warm come into her mouth and throat. She managed to swallow every drop, and I figured we were done for the night. But it was only the beginning.

Joan continued making her rounds, and nearly an hour later she returned and quietly unlocked my cell door. My sweet love guard came in and lay on the bed. She was wearing a skirt uniform and I had her spread her legs. I pulled up the skirt and was surprised to see she had no panties on. Joan mentioned that she had removed her panties and bra just for me. Then she unbuttoned her shirt and two gorgeous mounds of white flesh appeared. I grasped a tit in each hand and, while kneading them, started licking her neatly trimmed blonde-haired pussy. The sensation of my tongue darting in and out of Joan's tight hole, slipping up between the fleshy folds over her erect clit, had her squirming and biting her lip to keep from moaning out loud. She began to push my head farther down, rocking furiously and enjoying the sensation of her pussy rubbing on my bald head. I lifted up, inserted two fingers into her tight pussy and, with the aid of my tongue, made Joan have four orgasms in about fifteen minutes.

Joan had had enough oral sex and wanted to feel my dick in her. I started rubbing my throbbing cockhead up and down between her wet, warm, soft, pink pussy lips. This caused moans of pleasure to rumble deep in her throat. I slowly pushed forward. The lips parted and my dickhead slipped in. Joan's hole was really tight. I slowly inched in until I felt the head of my dick touching the back of her pussy. Then I started pistoning slowly in and out, withdrawing until just the head was inside and then shoving it all the way in again. It took a few minutes for her pussy muscles to relax around my dick.

Joan wrapped her legs around me and we started gyrating our pelvises in rhythmic fury as our tongues played a game of hide-and-seek in each other's mouth. Within five minutes her body started spasming uncontrollably as orgasmic bliss took her to heaven. This triggered my climax and I flooded her pussy with warm come. I slipped my softening dick out of her with a slurp; Joan licked it clean of our love-juice mixture, wiped her oozing pussy with one of my washcloths, locked my cell and walked away with a satisfied smile.—R.J., Memphis, Tennessee

WHAT WILL THE JONESES SAY TO
A NAKED NEIGHBOR? COME ON IN!

I had just stepped out on the porch of my apartment building, trying not to spill any more coffee, when I heard the voice: "Hello!"

I looked around. "Hello!" I heard again. I stepped to the edge of the concrete.

"This is Patsy, your upstairs neighbor." I looked up, but I still couldn't see her. "Don't look," she said, sounding alarmed. "I've locked myself out." Our apartments have self-locking doors, which can be tricky if you're not used to them.

"I have some bad news for you," I said. "The office doesn't open until noon on Sunday. Sorry." I took a sip of coffee. It was cooling down.

"Well, I can't stay here until noon. I'm not wearing anything." She had moved in earlier that week, and I had seen her a few times. She was a cute, small woman with long, dark hair. I stepped out onto the sidewalk and looked up. She was standing by her window, trying to cover her tits and her bush. "Don't look!" she screamed.

"Sorry, I couldn't resist," I admitted. "I have something you could wear. Come on." I stepped back into the apartment and grabbed a towel. When I turned around I saw her standing in my living room, still covering as much of herself as possible. I was very aroused by then. I handed her the towel.

"Is that it? This is what you have for me to wear?" Patsy asked, incredulous. She took the towel with the arm that was covering her tits. They were full and stood very firm, with light-colored nipples. I caught just a glimpse of them, but it was enough. She stood there, the towel covering her body from her nipples to just below the junction of her thighs. "I can't sit down," Patsy said, less embarrassed than she had been.

I had an amusing idea. "Here," I said, unbuttoning my shorts and dropping them, showing her my hard, firm cock. "Now we're even." She was very surprised by my actions, but I could see the smile on her lips as she checked me out.

"Would you like something to drink?" I asked.

"Men are never shy about their bodies," Patsy said, laughing. I laughed with her. "I've known you for five minutes and here you are, already standing in front of me practically naked."

"You must have that effect on men, although I do tend to walk around in my apartment naked most of the time," I said. I sat down in a blue armchair, my erection still hard. "Sit down, get comfortable. We have four hours before the office opens," I reminded her.

"Do you mind if I take a shower?" Patsy asked.

She walked over to me, tempting me with her body. She stopped when she had straddled my right leg. I leaned forward and slid my hands up her legs, cupping her ass. Her towel dropped. Her pussy was wet, with just a fringe of hair. I pulled her to me, letting my tongue trace the delicate folds of her cunt. She was hot and tasted sweet. She moaned. "Whatever shall we do for four hours?" she joked. I felt the hair of her bush. I moved my hands back and forth between her ass and her pussy. My finger circled her heat and I slowly probed her opening, careful to take my time. I licked her clit, enjoying the sounds she made. She humped my mouth and hand. When she came, I felt her body shudder.

She curled up on top of me. I kept one hand on her ass-cheeks, delighting in the curves and firmness of her flesh. My other hand played with her nipples, stimulating them. We kissed, our tongues dueling. I kissed her face, nibbled on her earlobes and took playful bites of her neck. She played with my nipples. Her small hand stroked me. I had gone soft, but her actions made me strong again. She moved down my body, placing lingering kisses on my most sensitive places. Her hands cupped my balls as she poised her mouth over the tip of my cock. I leaned back as I felt the wetness of her tongue mingle with the pre-come. I felt her nipples grazing my legs. She was very good, and soon I felt the familiar rising of my body. She stopped and kissed me, saying, "I don't want to waste this." She mounted me, guiding me into her with her hand. She was tight, and I felt her muscles grip me. I rested my hands on her hips as I moved into her. She undulated her hips, bringing me in still farther. I gripped her ass, fingering her asshole. She arched her back, delivering her nipples to me. My mouth was dry as I tried to cover them with saliva, then sucked them into my mouth. Her hands were in my hair. We kissed, sharing the hot breath of sex. I came, my fingers on her nipples. She moaned as I grunted. She rested her head on my shoulder. "Is there more?" she asked.

"Yes."

"Good, we have so much time to waste."

"And all I wanted was some morning coffee on my porch."

"This was a better idea," she pointed out.

"I can't argue with that." We kissed some more, leisurely touching each other. "You know, I do have a bed," I offered.

"You do?" She smiled as she kissed me. "What about that shower?"

"I always shower after I get out of bed."

"That's a wise policy."

"Thank you."

"Let's try something different. Let's shower and then go to bed."

"That will only confuse me." My tongue was tracing lazy circles on her neck.

"A little confusion is good in life." She stood up slowly, holding out her hands. "Come on. I feel sweaty." I gave her my hands and she pulled me out of the chair. We hugged standing up, although she barely came up to my neck. I bent my head down to kiss her. She fondled my balls. "You like sex, don't you?"

"Actually I hate it. I'm just doing this to be polite to company," I wisecracked.

"Your company is impressed." She turned and I followed her cute ass into my bathroom. We took a shower and spent the day fucking and sucking.—F.S., *Dayton, Ohio*

HE OFFERS A HELPING HAND TO
A WOMAN WHO WAS HELPING HERSELF

I was staying with Jim, an old Army buddy, and his wife Lynn, while attending a training course for the company I was working for. Jim was unexpectedly called away on business, leaving me alone with Lynn.

My wife and I had known Jim and Lynn for years, so none of us really thought twice about the two of us being alone together.

Late one night after turning off the TV and heading for bed, I passed Lynn's room. The door was open a crack and I heard moaning. I peeked inside. She had a night-light on and I could see clearly inside the room.

Lynn was lying on the bed with nothing on. She had a vibrator in one hand and was thrusting it in and out of her cunt, digging her fingertips into her breasts and pulling on her nipples with the other hand. Her motions were a blur as she stroked her tits and fucked her box.

Compelled by a feeling of boldness I'd never felt before, I walked into the room and immediately got on the bed. I ran my hands along her body and took the vibrator from her hand. I grasped her legs and opened them, leaving her thighs and cunt exposed to my gaze.

Lynn's hips arched toward my hand as I parted her legs, and I made contact with the juicy flesh of her cunt. Parting her puffy, wet lips, I inserted my fingers between the folds.

Until then Lynn had been in a little bit of a daze, but her eyes flew open when she realized that someone was finger-fucking her and in a shaky voice she whispered, "Oh my God, what are we doing?"

I removed my fingers from her cunt and moved up alongside her, gently kissing her, trying to reassure her. She was as turned on as I was, and moaned into my mouth as we continued to kiss, our lips and tongues sucking and licking.

Satisfied that she was as into this as I was, I slid back down the bed to her cunt. She writhed in ecstasy as I once again crammed my fingers into her and began to rove around the fleshy folds.

I shifted my attention to her clit, pulling and rubbing faster and faster until she climaxed. I pulled my fingers out of her, and she gave a short mew of protest. I slid my knees beneath her buttocks and placed my shaft at her open pussy lips.

She lurched with excitement as I approached her cunt. Wanting to take some time, I thrust just the head of my cock inside her, until I could feel the walls of her cunt gripping at my hot flesh, her muscles tightening and holding fast.

I knew she wanted it all, but I withdrew a little, teasing her with just the tip of my cock. Lynn was jerking her ass up and down, trying to take the whole thing in. I grabbed her legs and pushed them to her chest. She responded with a surge of powerful thrusts that sent my cock so deep into her soft opening that I repeatedly touched her cervix.

We pumped against one another. I released her legs and she clamped them around my waist, gripping tightly as my balls banged against her bottom. The sound of her wet, sucking cunt filled the room.

With a mutual groan we came, my come washing her cunt and leaking out the side of her pussy. Lynn just held on with her legs until she had drained me of my last drops with her cunt muscles. I rolled off her, totally exhausted, and quickly went to sleep.

I woke the next morning with Lynn's mouth on my cock. I groaned and reached to touch her brown, curly hair. I moved her face closer to my body so that my cock could go a little farther down her throat.

She raised her head, causing my dick to slip out, smiled and then ever so lightly she licked it, giving feather-light little tongue sweeps across the tip, causing me to jump and twitch as the flicks of her tongue darted over the most sensitive spots.

Her moistened lips closed around the head, and she sank her mouth down my throbbing shaft a little at a time, stopping every time I was all the way inside her, then sucking hard and pulling back to the tip before plunging down the length again.

My balls were cupped lightly in the palm of her hands and she squeezed them softly, tickling my sac.

Her mouth filled with warm spit as she began to work up and down frantically. Her head was a blur as she ate my cock. It was too much to bear and I pumped my hips up hard, lifting my buttocks off the bed and ramming my cock into her throat.

I knew I was going to come and tried to warn her, but she wrapped her lips around the head of my cock and sucked on it like a vacuum cleaner, then grabbed the shaft in her hand and started to jack me off.

She pumped at what I thought was the speed of light and within seconds I could feel the juice coming up the shaft. It exploded out of the tip of my dick and blasted down her throat. She used her lips to milk me dry. Keeping her mouth wrapped around it until it had softened, Lynn licked off the last remaining drops of sperm.

Suddenly her mouth was all over mine, her tongue darting passionately around mine. I kneaded her breasts and twiddled her nipples between my fingers as she broke our kiss to let out a moan that shook her whole body.

She pulled away from me, though without letting go of my dick. As she stroked my cock a flood of obscene words and suggestions poured out of her mouth.

I could hardly believe what I was hearing, considering how quiet and ladylike Lynn had always been, but it was incredibly exciting.

She rolled on her back, spread her thighs wide and guided the head of my dick against her pussy. She was screaming for me to fuck her, to make her feel full, relieve her passion.

Since I've always believed in helping out a friend, I lifted her legs over my shoulders and rammed my dick straight into her cunt without any further thought. Her ass rose off the bed to meet my thrusts. The harder I fucked her the more she begged for it. I pounded my dick into her again and again, yet she was begging for more. Her head was tossing from side to side as I continued to fuck her. She shrieked as she came. I pulled out of her and rolled her onto her knees, doggie-style, and gave it to her hard from the back, gripping her tits in my hands. I fucked her ruthlessly until I shot gobs of come into her, and she surprised me by coming again.

My erection peacefully wilted away. Lynn had a huge smile on her face, giving me the strong impression that she was every bit as happy as I was.—A.N., *Baltimore, Maryland*

LOVE ASIAN-AMERICAN STYLE:
WITH ONE YOU GET ANOTHER

*T*hanks to your publication my wife and I enjoy a much better life. I have been reading *Penthouse Letters* for years, as has my wife. Reading the letters from all kinds of people of all ages has really opened up our relationship and has allowed both of us the freedom to enjoy each other more.

Recently my wife went off to visit her parents, so I was a bachelor for two weeks. We had just relocated to this area. Our house has a beautiful screened-in porch that offers us a great deal of privacy. Because of this we often opt to go naked around the house, and since we live in the South we are able to spend a great deal of the year outside on the porch in the nude.

My wife had been gone for three days. I was sitting on the porch reading the paper and drinking coffee as usual when I was surprised by my neighbor from across the street. Singh is a wealthy Korean, around thirty-five or forty years old, and has a twenty-year-old maid named Lucy. Singh is tall for an Asian woman, about five feet ten inches I'd say, and Lucy is around five foot seven. Singh is small-breasted, but her maid has tits that need to be carried around in a wagon. Anyway, there they came, Singh and Lucy, up to the porch, where I was sitting around nude. They were both giggling. Singh explained that they'd been watching Joy and me wander around naked every day for about two months, and when they realized Joy had gone away they decided to come over. Singh had on shorts and a loose blouse. Lucy was wearing a one-piece, micro-mini sundress with spaghetti straps. Without any more ado they both proceeded to strip, which seized my attention in a serious way. Singh has a small, barely noticeable patch of pubic hair. It looked like you could lick it off. Lucy's mound was shaved bald. Lucy's tits were even bigger than I had imagined, 40D's, with areolae the size of a pocket watch. Both had dark, fleshy nipples whose color contrasted with their much lighter skin coloring.

We all tried to make small talk for a while. Finally Singh made the kind of move I'd been praying she would, coming over to me and rubbing her tits against my neck. My dick did the thinking from that point on. I was hard in microseconds. Singh kept rubbing, and I was ready to burst even before Lucy came over and started stroking my dick with her velvety soft hands. My moans were pouring out like music from the moment that she touched me.

Singh and Lucy each took a hand and led me into the house and onto my bed. Lucy started by sucking my dick into her mouth until her lips were nuzzling my pubes. Singh straddled my face and lowered her treasure onto my waiting mouth.

Now, I am not a superhung stallion, nor do I possess a monster dick with supernatural powers to fuck and fuck forever and then start over again without any time to reload. I was therefore grateful when Lucy, sensing I was close to erupting, took a breather, came around to face her employer and began tonguing her tits. Singh exploded into an orgasm over my face that almost drowned me. After settling down a little bit she backed away so that Lucy could take a turn riding my face. The little maid sat straight up so that Singh could bury her tongue alongside mine in this hairless slit. I was tonguing from the back, and Singh licking from the front. Lucy was responding with energetic humping.

Soon I felt Singh mount my dick, and I sensed that she wasn't going to release me until I came. The wild sexiness of this adventure went straight to my cock, and although she rose and fell as slowly as she could on my pole, I wasn't going to last long. Before many exquisite strokes had passed I could feel the buildup and then the spew. I was sweating, gasping for air and crying out like a dying man.

I finally recovered long enough to make the room stop spinning, in time to watch Lucy suck my sperm out of Singh like it was going to be the last meal she would ever get. Next I felt Singh sucking my shaft back to hardness, which was a total surprise to me, as I had thought that after that much ecstasy I'd have to spend a month in a splint before I could raise another hard-on. When she saw that I was up and at 'em, Lucy pushed Singh aside, rolled over on her back, threw open her legs and pulled me on top of her. As I started moving in and out I felt a tongue on my balls. Next they were sucked into Singh's mouth, and gently rolled around by her tongue and lips. I don't know how long they kept this up, but it can't have been too long before I was again gasping for air and pounding against Lucy's cunt with every ounce of strength I could muster. The head of my dick expanded like a hot air balloon, then poured forth its contents. Riding the wave of pleasure, I drifted asleep.

Maybe an hour later I awoke to find Lucy lying next to me, also lightly napping. When I started moving around she reached over and kissed me. She whispered that while the two of them had been watching Joy and myself, they had seen us in animated conversation with another couple. When we all disappeared inside, holding hands, they realized that we were swingers. Lucy said that she wanted to be mine for as long as Joy was away, but that when my wife came back she would like to party with us as a couple. She stated that Singh couldn't always join us because her husband was very old-fashioned. She had told him that she was going to a friend's house for a few days. That was how she got out.

Joy came home two days earlier than expected and came into the bedroom to find Lucy there. Because of the openness of our relationship, instead of being upset she just stripped and joined us.—*Name and address withheld*

Head & Tail

TO THE MOON, LORI! DARING WIFE EXPOSES HER BUTT AND MORE TO POKER PALS

My wife Lori and I are both thirty-three and have been happily married for nine years. My wife is a very sexy and passionate woman and has a body made to love. She is tall—nearly six feet—with very long legs leading up to a very hairy, thick brown bush (to match her auburn hair) and possesses lovely thick, protruding snatch lips and a luscious ass, which she always loves to have licked and fingered. She is very cute and turns heads wherever we go.

When we met, Lori was very free-spirited and sexually active. Even during the time I was courting her I knew she dated many guys and was having sex frequently. After we were married it took some prodding, but during our lovemaking Lori would tell me some of the more memorable fucks she had during her single days. It really turned me on. She got laid at drive-ins, at picnics, and once even had two guys after a toga party!

Lori described how she enjoyed the foreplay of sucking a guy's cock and tonguing his balls, how she asked her dates to stick their tongues and fingers into her asshole; the many positions they fucked her in; and how much she enjoyed feeling the hot come squirt in and fill up her cunt. Hearing this really turned me on. I could easily picture my wife in these scenarios.

One night I had a bunch of guys over for poker. Lori always joined us. Into the night we went on drinking, joking and telling stories from our high school days. When the subject of mooning came up, Lori chimed in and stated that she too used to moon, the guys kidded her and said that girls didn't have the guts to moon. At that Lori stood, turned her back to the group, hiked her skirt up to her waist to reveal her pink satin panties, hooked her thumbs in the waistband and slowly lowered them to her ankles, completely exposing her creamy white ass. No one said a word as she spread her legs, bent over and looked back up at us. Through her long legs she said, "No guts to moon, huh?" All eyes were glued to her spread ass-cheeks that revealed her puckered asshole and her hairy beaver with the cunt lips hanging down.

Lori remained in this pose for a few seconds, then straightened up and pulled up her panties. The guys said they believed her when she said that she used to moon and conversation continued, but there was a definite aura of excitement and sex in the air. A half hour or so later the gathering started to break up and Lori and I retreated to our bedroom. I told her it excited the hell out of me when she showed her ass to the guys. I reached into her panties and slipped a finger easily into her. She was hot and excited too. My wife whispered into my ear that she found it exciting also and asked if I would object to her having sex with the two guys in the room next to ours.

I told Lori to go for it and kissed her, whereupon she went into the adjoining room occupied by our friends Sean and Ron. She left the door slightly ajar so I had an unobstructed view of the entire room. My wife told them that I had too much to drink and had passed out but that she still wanted to party. The guys made Lori a drink and idle chat continued. Sean said that my wife still looked too prim and proper to moon. She replied, "Sean, kiss my ass!" Sean jokingly got down on his knees at Lori's feet, but she turned her back to him, knelt on the bed and once again pulled down her cute, lacy panties to fully expose her butt. Sean saw the opportunity with my sweet wife's ass only inches from his face and started to plant kisses on her soft cheeks.

"Make sure you hit the bull's-eye," Lori whispered as she reached back with both hands and spread her cheeks apart to reveal her asshole. Sean stiffened his tongue and sank it all the way in her butt. Lori moaned in ecstasy, which caused Ron to remove his trousers and kneel by my wife's face. She hungrily gobbled up his hot cock and began slowly sucking it. Sean, who had been alternately licking Lori's butthole and pussy from behind, stood up and unzipped his pants to reveal a huge, hard, throbbing piece of meat. He placed it at the entrance to my wife's vagina and slowly started to push and inch its entire length into Lori. She growled deeply when it was all the way in and continued to deep-throat Ron's entire length. Sean wet his finger and pushed it all the way into my wife's asshole as he continued to fuck her.

I had to free my own hard dick and slowly started to stroke it as I watched excitedly as Lori was getting it from both ends. They changed positions. Sean lay on his back and Lori straddled him, reaching back and placing his large swollen head at the entrance to her wet hole. I watched in fascination as her large, hairy cunt lips enveloped the head and I could hear the liquid sound of her wet snatch as it slowly swallowed the entire shaft right up to his balls as she slowly started to ride it. It was such a turn-on to watch his whole dick appear then disappear into my wife's pussy.

Ron, his cock still wet from my wife's saliva, stepped behind and placed his cockhead against her butthole. He slowly started to push his dick into her hungry rectum. They got into rhythm and moans and sounds of lovemaking filled the room. They fucked like this for fifteen or so minutes until first Lori bucked into a deep orgasmic moan, whereupon both Sean and Ron let go, filling her butt and cunt with a load of come. Sperm dripped from her asshole and also out of her cunt as the shrinking cocks popped out of her holes. Lori kissed each guy good night and then said she was spent. She came back into our room where I lay on the bed waiting.

I knew Lori was still hot and horny, and one look at my hard-on told her I had witnessed the whole scene and enjoyed it. Lori straddled my head and lowered her well-used pussy onto my mouth as she engulfed my organ. I could taste both guys' loads mingled with hers as I dug my tongue deep into her sloppy pussy and asshole. It soon became too overwhelming and I shot my load deep into Lori's sucking throat as I tongued her clit to a shattering orgasm. We then collapsed and fell asleep.—*Name and address withheld*

CITY BOY GOES DOWN ON THE FARM AND PLANTS HIS SEED—IN HIS BOSS'S WIFE

*M*y name is Jake and I am eighteen years old. I graduated from high school last spring and am now attending college. Because I was unable to obtain a scholarship, I was extremely short on cash, so last summer I went job hunting. Jobs are scarce in this part of the country, and after a couple of weeks of searching, things were looking grim. I picked up a copy of the local newspaper, hoping someone was looking for help. After finding all the usual ads for experienced workers, I came across an ad looking for help on a farm. Now, I am the first to admit I'm a city boy and didn't know a thing about farming, but I needed money, so I thought I'd give it a try. I called the phone number and had a nice talk with the farmer, Sam. Sam told me to be at the farm first thing in the morning and we would see if he could find work for me.

It was a long drive out to Sam's farm and I got there around nine in the morning. Sam was already working on some machinery when I drove up. "Come on up to the house," he told me. As Sam and I sat down at the table Sam's wife Trisha entered the room. Trisha was in her late thirties, but it was very evident she was in great physical shape. She was dressed in a pair of very short cutoffs that showed her well-rounded ass, and a skimpy T-shirt. She was braless and her nipples showed through the flimsy material. It was hard not to stare at Trisha as she moved around the kitchen, but I was able to concentrate on Sam's questions well enough so that he hired me.

I spent the next few days doing farm work, which lasts from sunup till after dark. When I hit the bed each night I was asleep in minutes. I loved working for Sam and Trisha. I thought they were the typical conservative farm couple. All that changed one night.

I had stayed up late, beating my meat, dreaming of dicking Trisha's well-muscled country ass, when I heard voices downstairs. I had to investigate, so I peeked around the door into Sam and Trisha's bedroom. I got the show of my life. Trisha, on her knees in front of him, opened her sweet mouth and Sam drove his dick into it. Sam fucked her hot mouth a few minutes, then had Trisha bend over a chair. He greased up his dick and slipped it up his pretty wife's ass. Sam butt-fucked Trisha a long time. The sight of all this had me rapidly beating my cock. I let a load of my come fly onto the wall as Sam let loose into his sexy wife's ass. I stuffed my dick back into my shorts and hurried back to my room. I was so horny at what I'd just witnessed that I jacked off three more times before falling asleep.

The next day Sam told me he was going to be gone for a couple of days and gave me a list of chores. It was a hot July day and after ten hours in the sun I was ready for a nice shower and one of Trisha's home-cooked meals. I got into the shower and cleaned up good. As I stood drying myself the door opened. There stood Trisha in the skimpiest bikini I had ever seen. I tried to hide my growing boner with the towel. Trisha looked at me and smiled. "Did you like what you saw last night?" she asked. I tried to act dumb, but Trisha pulled the towel away. "Ah, what a beautiful teenage cock," she cooed as she began to fondle my dick. "I want to make love to you," she said. "You can live out your every fantasy with me." I led Trisha to the table in the kitchen and laid her down on it. I sucked her hard nipples awhile and then put my mouth to her fresh pussy. I ate Trisha's cunt like a wild man, causing her to come several times before I fucked her brains out. After

I filled her with my sperm I told her to stay on the table. I went to the refrigerator and took out a nice fat ear of corn and a carrot. I placed the ear of corn at Trisha's slit and slowly began to inch it deeper into her. When I had it halfway into her cunt I took the carrot, buttered it up and slipped it into her red-hot ass. She was going bonkers as I fucked her in both ends with the vegetables. Trisha came violently, coating the ear of corn with her own sweet butter. I removed the veggies and had Trisha get off the table and onto the floor on her hands and knees. "Now, baby," I told her, "I'm gonna fuck your farm-fresh butt." I shoved my dick into her buttered buns and fucked her anus hard, filling her ass with my hot cream. We both collapsed on the floor, my dick going limp in her ass. Trisha and I fucked in all kinds of places and ways that summer, but all good things come to an end. Hopefully I can get a job with Sam and his sweet wife again this summer.—*R.W., Lincoln, Nebraska*

AMATEUR STRIPPER TAKES ON ALL COMERS
AND GOES ALL THE WAY

I knew when I married Kim five years ago that I had married a woman who thoroughly enjoyed sex. She quite frankly told me about her past exploits, knowing how much her detailed descriptions turned me on. Likewise she knew that I had dated a lot of girls and also enjoyed my extracurricular fucking and sucking. Occasionally we would really let our hair down and tell each other about our ultimate sex fantasies. In the case of Kim it involved her getting fucked while I sat by and watched. My favorite fantasy was getting involved with two females and, while I was eating out one of them, having the other stick her finger or an anal stimulator up my ass. We certainly knew what each other wanted and about two months ago my charming, sweet, beautiful and oversexed wife got what she wanted.

I had taken Kim along with me on a business trip to the West Coast. As usual we were very horny when we took trips together, and the first couple of nights we really went after each other in our hotel room. When Kim gets a heavy load of fucking it really seems to get her engine turned on, and I could tell by the look in her eyes that she really wanted to do something nasty on this trip. I had heard about an after-hours club that held amateur strip contests for women who wanted to pick up some extra cash and show themselves off. I suggested to Kim that we check out this place, have a few drinks and see what it was all about. Kim eagerly agreed to my suggestion, and after a few inquiries I found out where the place was located.

That night we found ourselves in a roadhouse type of tavern. The food was good and the drinks were very good. We noticed that the majority of clients were unescorted men, but there were also a few women who were surveying the field. As the evening wore on the music from the stereo system got louder and very much into a hot Latin beat. Finally the owner and host of the tavern got up on the small stage in the corner of the dance floor and announced that there was going to be a strip contest for any woman interested. He added that the first prize, based on applause, would be one hundred dollars. Kim and I noticed a few of the women go up to the owner and enter into a discussion, then disappear through a door that evidently was a dressing, or undressing room. Kim, who had had more than her usual quota of drinks, whispered to me that she wanted to enter the contest. I looked at her and the look in her eyes and told her to go for it. As she walked away from our table I could see almost all the eyes of the males in the room follow her. At this point may I say that Kim is a fabulously sexy-looking woman. She has long auburn hair, a lovely face, and tits and ass that defy description. I knew that this would be a night to remember.

As it turned out Kim was to appear last among five other entrants. The other girls put on some very good and very erotic performances. One girl even stripped down to nothing and feigned an orgasm as she fingered her clit. The crowd went wild and wanted more, much more, as she left the stage.

When Kim came out on the stage there was a pronounced silence. First of all, she looked so very sedate and proper in her conservative blouse and skirt. She even had left her glasses on, which gave her an almost professional look. Despite all that, her figure and facial beauty were readily apparent.

When the music began, so did Kim. Her initial moves were slow but very sensuous. It didn't take too long before she had seductively removed her blouse. When her magnificent tits came into view through her bra the cheering started. Kim moved her body in time to the music. Her hands explored every inch of her body. The crowd was really getting into her performance. Kim began to teasingly unzip her skirt and finally let it fall. She was dancing in only panties and her bra plus high-heeled shoes. The crowd was clapping and screaming, "Take it all off!"

Kim looked in my direction and smiled at me. I knew that she was about to live out her favorite fantasy. Her bra was next to disappear and her very erect, delectable nipples sprang into view. She tweaked them and massaged her breasts as she continued to dance to the Latin beat. Her panties were next and as she slowly, very slowly slid them down past her hips there was an audible gasp from the audience. Even the women present seemed to be entranced by what they were watching. As I looked around the room I could see lustful looks from almost every man present.

Once Kim was completely nude she really went to work. She danced, twirled and moved like a pro on the stage. She even got down on the floor, on her hands and knees and, with her ass facing the audience, she spread her legs wide apart and began playing with her cunt and asshole. The crowd went wild.

Suddenly I noticed the owner get up from his table and walk over to the entrance to the club. He locked the door and then went up on the stage. He was a good-looking, very muscular young guy. He said something in Kim's ear and she smiled at him.

He turned to the spectators and announced, "Any of you who don't like sex better leave now. The show is just beginning."

With that announcement he began to take his clothes off. Kim helped him and it wasn't long before he was naked. His giant cock stuck out like a telephone pole and my wife took it eagerly in her mouth. The two of them put on quite a show. Kim got fucked in a variety of positions: on her back, doggie-style and riding on top of him. After the owner came, Kim stared out into the audience and asked if there were a few good men out there who wanted a good fuck. Well, that started an evening of wanton sex. Kim must have fucked at least a dozen men. They took her every which way. Some of the women who were there joined in. It was an on-stage orgy I'll never forget.

Just when I thought that Kim had had enough, she stood up and announced that she wanted someone to give her a good ass-fucking. With that she looked me straight in the eye, pointed at me and said, "How about you, guy? Would you like to fuck my ass?" All eyes were on me, so I decided to take advantage of the situation. I approached the stage and removed my clothes. My cock was like a rock. All the men and women around Kim backed off as I approached. One of the women had thoughtfully found a tube of hand cream. "Take this," she said. "It will help her." As she handed me the cream Kim said something to her in her ear. I coated my cock with the lube and positioned Kim on her hands and knees. The next thing I knew I was ass-fucking my wife in front of about forty men and women. They applauded as I drove my stiff prick into Kim. My wife went wild as I did her. Suddenly I felt someone playing with my asshole. It was the gal with the cream. The next thing I knew she was probing my asshole with her finger and then slipping it in. I blew my load in short order.

When we were finally done we were the center of attention. Drinks were on the house, and guys and their dates were slapping us on the back and telling us how great we were.

After our trip was finally over and we were back home reminiscing, I asked Kim what her next-best fantasy was. All she would say was that it involved leather and chains. Needless to say, my imagination has been running overtime ever since.— B.L., *New York, New York*

LOVER MAN, OH WHERE CAN YOU BE? OH, YOU'RE BACK THERE!

*I*t's okay, he will call, I think to myself, losing all hope. Well, there's always tomorrow. My mind, however, rebels at the thought. In my head the images of us together clamor for recognition.

"Call me," I whisper, my fingertips lightly caressing the phone, hopefully, sending out a mental signal. My mind is silent now. And only my eyes staring at the phone hint at my need.

How long the phone has been ringing I can't imagine as the noise finally registers. Praying, I close my eyes and, crossing my fingers, I answer.

"Hello," I barely manage to say.

"Hey," he replies, "what's up?"

Thank you, I mouth up to heaven as his voice excites me. I smile in anticipation. Now that I know how the night will end I can relax and enjoy.

"I need to see you," he says. "I have a surprise for you."

I giggle, remembering the last surprise he had for me.

"What?" I manage to gasp out, along with a not-too-convincing yawn.

"Little brat, I'm closer than you think. Get ready, I am on my way."

I ponder our unusual relationship. We have been friends for ten or more years, lovers for just a few, keeping our trysts to just a few times a year, which for us is perfect. Every time we meet we have open, uninhibited, passionate, great, nasty sex! Of course, we do tend to go a little fuck-crazy, winding up in the strangest places. Just imagine being over forty years old and fucking your heart out at the drive-in or in your driveway at home. God, if anybody catches us, I hope it's not at the Kmart parking lot!

I think about how much I enjoy driving around the backroads of our small town, my skirt up to my waist, panties on the dashboard, legs spread wide, my blouse open, my body turned toward him as he finger-fucks me, his hand wet with juices from my pussy. Or watching him trying to watch me. Occasionally I will slowly fuck myself with a large vibrator. It generally doesn't take too long for the car to stop and us to start.

Hearing his car in the driveway, I race to answer the door. Just seeing him at the door is enough to make my pussy throb. Taking him by the hand, I lead him right into my bedroom. Turning toward him, I gasp with delight as he takes this huge dildo from his coat. Smiling, I take it, placing it close to the bed. Reaching out, he pulls me into his arms. As he kisses me his hands, as if of their own will, rove all over my body. Stopping at the waistband of my skirt, he rips off both it and my panties in one swift motion. He pulls me tight against his cock, holding me close while his hands grip my bare ass-cheeks. Moaning, I twist to the side, giving him better access to my well-rounded buns. He cannot resist turning me the rest of the way around. Holding on to my wrists, he pushes my hands high upon the wall, telling me not to move from this position.

"I told you to be ready," he whispers into my ear. He begins massaging my ass, first one side and then the other. I whimper just a little, keeping my ass well within his reach. He continues, rubbing me until my cheeks are the color he desires. My butt feels like it's aglow. Placing his palms on my rosy cheeks, he whispers, "Miss me, love?"

I can't think straight. I nod my head in agreement. My knees are shaking. My pussy is hot and wet. Turning toward him, I wiggle my butt around so his hand can slide right into the crack of my ass.

"Baby, sometimes you just wait too damn long between phone calls," I reply as I pull him down on my bed.

Ripping my shirt open, he reveals my breasts to his hungry gaze. Trailing kisses down my throat, he nibbles and licks at my breasts until I'm begging him to take one deep into his mouth. Finally, as I push my breasts up to his mouth, he takes one nipple, deep, sucking hard on it. Gasping, I feel the sparks of lust rampaging throughout my body. The heat between my thighs causes my legs to spread.

Slowly he slides his mouth down to my neatly shaved pussy. My fingers hold open my pussy lips for his kiss. His tongue goes straight for my hard, throbbing knob of desire. Licking and nipping, he sucks in all my juices.

With his hands on my legs he easily turns me onto my stomach, moving me around like a puppet. I wind up on my hands and knees. From behind me he likes to bury his face into my waiting pussy. However, with my ass in the air he can't resist licking up between my cheeks. I hold my breath as he licks closer to my butt. I love it when he pushes his tongue into my asshole. The sensation jumps through me, jerking me forward. I almost come off the bed. I look around to see that his face is covered with my juices. From my pussy up to the crack of my ass, my juices are flowing freely.

I turn over, pushing him back up against the dresser. I run my hands up and down his chest. Undoing his pants, I let them fall down around his ankles. I start kissing his chest, licking and nipping at his nipples. He holds my face on his nipples. I can feel his body trembling as he lowers my head down past his chest to his cock. My mouth starts watering as I get closer to his hard shaft. Getting on my knees, I open my mouth. I lick the head of his erection. I run my tongue up his cock, getting to the head. I'm ready as it slips into my mouth. Slowly he begins to fuck my face, controlling the rhythm and depth of his thrusts. With each thrust he makes I try to take him deeper. My lips stretch as he slides past them into the warmth of my mouth. I know he wants to go deep into my throat. His thrusts get faster. When I feel his cock swelling, I lift my chin and feel him slide down into my neck muscles. Groaning, he holds on to my head. Pulling my face fully onto his cock, he bends his knees, fucking my face with deep, powerful strokes.

Pulling out of my mouth, he picks me up and carries me to the bed. Jerking my legs apart, he shoves his hard cock into my waiting pussy. He kisses me, sweeping his tongue into my mouth. My pussy lips grip his swollen shaft, keeping him inside me. Putting my legs up on his shoulders, he proceeds to fuck me with slow, powerful strokes. Kissing me, he tells me how he loves to be in me. He jerks his cock quickly out of me, then slams it home deep inside of me. Feeling his cock swelling inside me, my climax starts. Suddenly he stops moving. Breathing heavily, he puts his forehead to mine.

"Don't stop," I cry, clutching at his waist.

"Wait, baby," he whispers. "We have plenty of time. I don't want to come yet, baby. Lie still."

His smooth caress and soft whispers prove to be calming for both of us. Nodding my head in agreement, I try to breathe slowly.

"How about a smoke," he says, planting a light kiss on my lips.

"Okay, let me up so I can find them." Slapping his shoulder, I try to get him off me. Grinning, he lays his head on my shoulder as he shakes his head no. Pushing him off, I'm amazed that I feel so empty as his cock slips out of my pussy. Finally he rolls over onto his back, pulling me with him for a quick kiss.

Eventually I spot the cigarettes on the dresser. Stepping over him, I lean over the dresser to pick them up. That's when I feel his hands on my ass-cheeks. He pulls them wide apart, plunging his tongue deep into my asshole. I can hear myself moaning while he tongues my butt. It feels so good that I bend over farther, giving him better access, so he is able to shove his tongue deeper into my ass. My legs give out as lust overtakes me. Slowly I sink down to my knees and then even lower as I crouch down so that my shoulders are lower than my butt. Following me down he licks my cheeks as he kneels behind me. Again he pulls my cheeks wide apart. Excitement rushes through me as he tongue-fucks my asshole. I find myself pushing back toward him, wanting more. I moan, begging him not to stop. I feel his finger, still wet from my pussy, slip easily into my ass. The slight discomfort I feel is quickly forgotten as pleasure radiates from my backside. I start pushing back, begging for more, much to his delight. Much to my delight, he keeps alternating between his tongue and his fingers. My ass is throbbing. I get to the point where I can't tell if it's his fingers or tongue in my ass.

I try to reach around, wanting to give him some head. Before I even try he grabs at me, urging me back down. His large hand is between my shoulder blades, holding me down before him.

"This is what I want," he growls, fingering my asshole. "This is what I'm here for."

I shiver in my fear. I shiver in my need.

"Tell me, love, tell me to fuck your ass. Tell me to shove my cock deep into your ass. Tell me to fuck you, baby," he says, growling fiercely, his fingers keeping a steady rhythm, plunging into my ass.

"I'm going to fuck you the way I want to, baby. I'm going to shove my cock up your willing ass." Moving his hand to my shoulder, he starts pulling me back toward him. "You want it too, don't you?" he asks.

"Yes," I weakly whisper while nodding my head. "Please," I cry. "Please fuck me. I need you to come inside me. Oh, God, I want your cock in my ass. I want you to fill me up. Fuck me. Do it. Fuck my asshole!" Eagerly I crouch lower on my knees, putting my ass higher in the air. Pulling his fingers out of me, I feel him coming closer. I feel the head of his cock brush against my thighs. I know how this is going to feel. I want this. Still my mind runs rampant and the size of his cock magnifies in my mind. I'm not ready, I think, as fear washes over me.

When I feel him place the head of his cock against my twitching asshole I panic and try to jump away. Holding me down, he gently leans over me. Wrapping his arm around my waist, he gently brings me back against him. Quickly he slips his fingers back in my ass.

"Relax," he says, his voice soft in my ear. "Your ass is ready for me. You know I won't hurt you. I want you so much. Feel my fingers slipping inside your wonderful ass. I can feel how much you want me. I love fucking your asshole. Let me in, love. Man, this is going to be good."

While he talks to me he removes his fingers. Moving closer, he pushes his cock just inside of my well-lubricated, tight hole. I come back to reality as the shock jolts me. Breathing hard, I force myself to relax, accepting him inside me. Sighing, I feel him push farther in. Crouching under him, I start panting, letting him push his cock deeper into my anus.

He catches his breath. "Hold on, baby, it's almost there." Grabbing a hold of my shoulders, he pulls me back against him, surging forward at the same moment. The full length of his cock is now buried deep inside my behind.

Breathing hard, he reaches under me to play with my nipples, kissing the back of my neck. Lying still, he waits for me to adjust to his cock. I know he won't move until I let him know that I'm ready for more. As I relax I start to move my ass in tiny little backward thrusts. I feel him get up on his knees behind me. Pulling back on my hips, he raises my butt high. He slowly starts to move, gently matching my small strokes. When I want to feel more of his cock I begin to drive myself back into each thrust, harder each time. He lies down on top of my crouching form, which enables him to shove his cock deeper into my willing hole. Spreading my legs just far enough to get my hand between my thighs, I plunge my two fingers into my pussy. Grabbing a hold of my clit, I masturbate furiously. My whole body is throbbing, needing release. Steadily he plunges his cock in and out of my asshole with strong, even strokes.

"God, I knew this would be good. Baby, how I love to fuck you. Your ass is mine. It's so tight. So fucking good," he gasps between strokes.

His words ignite me. I clench my ass-cheeks together. I push back hard toward him.

"I know what you want." Chuckling, he gets up on his knees. Grabbing hold of my waist, he pulls me up onto my hands and knees. He begins to fuck me with strong, deep strokes. My hand is swirling around in my pussy. My ass clenches his cock as I start to climax, pulsing as wave after wave of pleasure overwhelms me.

"Fuck me," I scream. "Fuck me hard, shove your prick deep in my ass, baby. God, I love your prick in my ass. Harder, baby, fill me up." I can feel my lover's cock swelling in my ass. His pumping becomes faster, gradually becoming almost frantic.

With a shout he starts to climax. Jerking his cock back to the edge of my hole, thrusting toward me, he presses his hard cock back into my asshole. Again and again he thrusts his cock deep into me. I climax again as he yells his pleasure. I feel his cock spurting its come deep into my butt. Collapsing on top of me, he gently turns my head so he can kiss me.

Reaching behind me, I stroke his head as he kisses my neck. I can still feel his cock pumping seed into my well-fucked ass. I sigh with contentment as he slides out of me. Turning over, I cup his face in my hands and gently kiss his lips.

"You know that we forgot about your gift?" he asks.

Reaching over him, I grab the new toy, giving him the dildo. I look into his face. Smiling, I whisper, "Relax, baby, we have all night."—*R.T., Atlanta, Georgia*

MARRIED COUPLE FINALLY DECIDES TO OPEN UP THE BACK DOOR

This letter will prove to your readers that not all fantastic sex involves liaisons with other people, singly or in groups. My greatest experience involves my wife, imagination and romance.

It all started during one night of "normal" sex: deep kissing, intense fondling, mutual oral pleasures and then penetration of the tightest, wettest love-box known to man. After several minutes of rolling in her love-canal we would achieve mutual orgasm. Not the stuff of *Penthouse Letters*, but not a bad way to spend an evening. However, in grabbing my wife's firm and skinny cheeks while she rode me I brushed against her tight little puckered asshole and an audible gasp slipped out of her. Later, in bed, snuggled in each other's arms, I asked if she enjoyed my little brush with her tight hole. She acknowledged not only that it felt good but that she sometimes fantasized about anal sex.

I decided to embark on a seduction that would end with my firm cock embedded in her tight little ass. I asked her out on a date and bought her a new outfit: short denim shirt, snug spandex top and tiny G-string panties. She did not know of my ultimate intentions but figured I was obviously kissing up for sex. After dinner at a trendy restaurant where my wife received several admiring and well-deserved looks, we went out dancing and stayed until closing time. On the way home she nestled up to me and mentioned impure thoughts about what she was going to do to me once we got home. Exciting, but my plans were even better.

Once home I suggested a shower together, where we engaged in mutual fondling. She wanted to suck me off in the shower, and I almost consented but remembered greater treasures in store. After showering I presented her with an all-white silk camisole and bikini panties. She looked radiant with her lean body, pert breasts with pointed nipples and neatly trimmed bush. She lunged at me, hungry for sex, but I held her off and explained further.

I told her I too had thought about anal sex and was presenting her this all-white ensemble for a reason. Together we were going to be initiated into the pleasures of anal sex. The white symbolized her virginity, and my inexperience would find me to be an equal novice. She looked at me with beaming eyes that suggested we begin our adventure at once.

We kissed deeply before I placed her on her stomach. I massaged her backside and the sides of her breasts until I heard the sigh that preceded her willingness to give all of herself. She stood up, the moonlight through the window glowing all over her, and slowly took off her lingerie, looking me right in the eyes. She looked magnificent in the light, and her gentle swaying was another indication of her sexual need. Then, lying again on her stomach, she murmured the encouragement to proceed. I squeezed an amount of needed K-Y jelly and slowly lubricated the crack of her tiny little ass. She lifted her hips and spread her legs slightly. I continued to apply jelly down her crack and approached her pucker. Slowly and with quickening breath she further raised her ass to encourage my advance. Gently I glided over her little hole and worked the jelly around. My wife became more aroused and rose to her knees, offering herself for even more. My cock was rock hard as I appraised the sight before me. I kneeled behind her and slowly inserted my middle finger up the tight hole. She gasped as I circled my finger and applied more jelly. Her anus became looser. I knew this would be the night my cock would slip in and fulfill our desires. I then slid a second finger up to my knuckles and my wife was in ecstasy. I positioned myself directly behind her and in full view of the mirror along the side of our bed. I had to drape one leg up and over hers for more leverage and slowly greased my thick cock as she approvingly watched in the mirror.

Our time was now at hand. I placed the tip of my cock against her asshole. Her breathing quickened. I pushed against her sphincter and stretched her hole with my finger. She pushed back against me and started moaning. I encouraged her to relax as her ass was tight with anticipation. Then, with an audible gasp, she felt my thick member push past her sphincter and enter her anal orifice. It felt like heaven; she was so tight! My wife had meanwhile released her inhibitions and began slowly rotating her ass for a better feel. It was obvious she had wanted this for some time. As she moved her ass seductively I felt myself coming and released my load in a way that aroused her further. As my spent cock came out of her ass dripping with sperm, she rolled over and I began showering her with kisses. I gently reached down and found her clitoral hood between her splayed legs. I lovingly stroked her lightly. This woman had unleashed her newfound desires and soon came with a shattering orgasm that she felt to the depths of her being. She collapsed in my arms and, thoroughly spent, we lay together and basked in our new experience.

My wife often initiates anal play now; and we only wish we had embarked on these adventures sooner.—*Name and address withheld*

SHE GRADUATES SUMMA CUM LOUDLY
FROM ANAL UNIVERSITY

*A*fter forty years of waiting I finally met the girl of my dreams, and I haven't been the same since. Missy was introduced to me on a blind date. When I saw her, it was love at first sight. Our date went so well that she invited me into her bed that same night. The rapport between our bodies was remarkable. Man, was she hot!

Missy is a stunning redhead. She just turned forty, but she has a figure that any twenty-five-year-old would kill for. Her body is soft and feminine, but well defined and nicely toned. Her breasts aren't very big, but she has the sweetest ass and pussy I've ever seen! She makes her pussy even sexier by shaving it completely bald. This compels me to spend many hours licking it and driving her to mind-bending orgasms. Her tight ass is always beautifully accentuated by thong panties. This has kept me in an almost constant state of horniness since the day we met.

After that incredible first night, over the next few weeks we fucked in every way and every place we could think of. Missy had not yet experienced some of the finer pleasures of sexual diversity, so I decided to be her teacher. In no time at all she'd mastered the art of sucking cock, and every time she'd get me off she'd eagerly swallow my thick load. Since I have a sizable cock, her jaw often got tired of being stretched open for long periods of time. In order to avoid this oral fatigue I often told her to just suck around the head of my penis until I was ready to explode. Then I'd have her open up her mouth and extend her tongue so I could watch my cream shoot into her mouth. When I finished coming, she would close her mouth and gulp down my hot load. Then she'd smile sweetly and tell me how much she liked doing it. God, what a sexy lady!

After many cocksucking sessions she eventually conditioned her jaw to accommodate me. I'd often wake up to find her sucking my big, pink tool and I'd always reward her with a nice liquid breakfast. On several occasions while I was driving around town she slid her hot, wet mouth down onto my tool. I often saw people in nearby cars watching my short-haired, redheaded angel bobbing up and down on my thick-veined cock. When the bobbing stopped, my cock was drained.

We eventually started experimenting with anal sex. Missy was receptive to it because she knew I was a gentle, patient teacher. I knew that in order to give her the same multiorgasmic pleasure that I'd given her in her pussy, everything had to be just right. Her anal debut occurred while we were visiting her mother in Alabama. It marked the beginning of many future sexual triathlons, as all three of her holes were used that day.

We woke up on Saturday morning and had a hot, wet session of intense fucking. Then we went jogging. Later that afternoon, in her old bedroom, Missy treated me to a sensuous blow job as we got ready to go out partying with some people she had gone to school with.

After an enjoyable evening of drinking and dancing, Missy was real mellow. I felt the time had come for the real fun to begin, so I suggested we call it a night. When we got back to her mother's place, I took her to her bedroom and gently undressed her. She was relaxed from the alcohol, so she was quite compliant.

When she was naked, I picked her up and placed her on the bed. After a lot of kissing and caressing, I rolled her onto her stomach, exposing the sweet, curvy mounds of her cute little ass. I moved my head down between her shapely legs and spread apart her ass-cheeks with my hands, revealing her tiny, pink butthole. I licked it lovingly and speared it with my tongue several times, causing her to shiver and moan quietly. After letting her suck my cock to steely hardness, I smeared myself with Vaseline and applied a generous amount to her anal opening as well. I whispered to her to relax and very slowly began to penetrate her tight hole.

She stayed relaxed and I eventually slid all of my meat into her slick rear channel. I took my time so that she could get used to accommodating each inch that was impaling her. As I started to pull back she gasped. She started panting as I plunged forward again. I asked her if she was okay, and she reassured me, "Yes. Don't stop!" We got into a nice steady rhythm and she had one orgasm after another. She had to keep a pillow near her face to muffle her cries of ecstasy so she wouldn't wake her mother. Finally I couldn't last any longer and I shot my hot wad up her ass. What a sensational fuck that was!

Missy is very noisy when she comes, and if I pleasure her correctly she often has multiple orgasms. Fucking her tight ass accentuates this condition and we continue to derive wonderful satisfaction from the experience. Of all the dozens of women I've made love to, Missy is the most incredibly exciting, sexy and sensual woman I've ever known! She's open to just about any erotic suggestion and is always willing to learn more about pleasuring herself and her man.—*Name and address withheld*

SHE BUYS SOFTWARE FOR HER HARD DRIVE AND
GETS HIS HARD DICK FREE!

*A*fter my second divorce I had more debts than good memories, so I got a second job on weekends in a computer store. I had been working several months and had not seen many women, much less any good-looking women. Then, when I least expected, I met a woman who surpassed my wildest fantasies.

She walked into the store on a quiet Sunday afternoon, wearing a tight white blouse that showed off perky dark tits. She was so sexy I was about to point her out to another salesman, when I was called to the front to help her. I almost ran.

She wanted software to help her make a newsletter for her church. As she talked, I noticed how sweet and soft her voice was. Her skin was a warm chocolate brown and her eyes looked vaguely Oriental. I didn't want her to just buy and run, so I took my time telling her about different options. Finally I recommended a program and demonstrated it for her on the store computer. All the while I took advantage of any opportunity to touch her hand or arm.

As we chatted, I could feel the electricity building between us. My hand lightly caressed her spine and I felt her shiver. "I'd be happy to come by after work and load the software onto your computer," I offered.

"It would make my life much easier," she replied. "Of course, I'll pay you for your time," she added, and ran her hand over my arm.

"I won't be there long enough," I said. "It should only take ten minutes."

"Great." She smiled. "How about letting me buy you a beer, then?"

"That would be perfect." I grinned. We arranged to meet at a nearby bar after the store closed.

When I got to the bar she was already there, still dressed in the white blouse and black skirt. After a beer each we decided to get on with our project. As we ambled out of the bar, I casually took her arm. She looked up at me and I wanted to kiss her, but didn't. I noticed that several men were checking her out as we left. She had the kind of legs men just couldn't help paying attention to.

We got into our cars and I followed her through the winding maze of her neighborhood until she pulled into the driveway of a large white house. She led me to the library, where her computer was set up, and offered me a drink. Then she told me to get started while she changed into something a little more comfortable.

I was installing the second diskette onto her hard drive when she returned wearing a cutoff T-shirt and sweatpants. Her tits were free under the T-shirt, and as we talked I watched her nipples rise and harden.

While I sat at the keyboard, she played with my hair and I felt her fingertips brush my neck. "If you want to give me a massage, go right ahead," I said, and she began lightly rubbing my shoulders.

"You seem tense," she commented. "Are you always this tense?"

"I'm as relaxed as I can be when a woman is turning me on," I answered.

"Am I turning you on?" she cooed in her sultry, sexy voice.

"Just a little," I replied coyly. "Not so that you'd notice."

"But I am noticing," she said. I felt her tongue circle my ear and probe it gently. "Would you like to take a shower?" she asked, but before I could answer she pulled me to my feet and led me to the bathroom. As I undressed, she pulled off her T-shirt. Her tits were much larger than I had expected and her nipples were hard, dark points. "You might need someone to wash your back," she purred, and pulled off her sweatpants and panties. Her sweet pussy was smoothly shaven.

"It's not my back I need washed," I said, and as I unzipped my pants I saw her stare at my hard cock.

We quickly hopped into the shower and began kissing and stroking each other all over. She playfully took my cock in her mouth. I squeezed her tits and thumbed her nipples. She took great care in washing my balls and cock, inspecting every inch with her agile tongue. I turned her around and cupped her ass, delighting in its firmness. She kissed me and rubbed her cunt against my genitals. "I want you," she moaned, and without another word she faced the wall and spread her legs wide. I guided my cock into her with one hand on her hip to steady myself. "That feels so good. Give it to me. Give it all to me," she panted.

I started slowly pumping into her, watching my white cock slide between her dark folds and pink lips. She bent over, gripped the sides of the tub and lifted her ass up to me. She was pushing back against me with every stroke. I held on to her hips and enjoyed the ride.

"I love to fuck. Fuck me some more. Fuck me harder. Oh God, you're so big. Fuck me!" she kept moaning as I increased my speed. "Yes, yes!" she gasped, and lost herself in an orgasm that left her shaking and whimpering. The water pounded on our backs as I neared my climax.

"I'm coming," I said, and shot what felt like gallons of come deep inside her. She arched her back and came again, and as I slipped out of her she surprised me by coming a third time.

Finally I helped her up, held her against me, cupped her tits and thumbed her nipples. We kissed. "My legs are getting tired," I said, "do you have a place to lay down around here?"

"I think there's a bed somewhere," she giggled. "What do you think?" she asked wickedly, wiggling her butt as she stepped out of the tub. I just stared at her bare cunt and grinned, then I followed her into the bedroom with my hands cupping her sassy, bouncy ass.

With an I'm-getting-fucked smile on her face, she proudly led me to an enormous bed. She lay back shamelessly with her legs spread wide and fingered her slit. "Is it true that white men love to eat pussy?" she teased.

"Actions speak louder than words," I replied, and lowered my mouth to her clit. She tasted sweeter than honey. As I ate her I pushed two fingers up her swollen cunt and played with her asshole with my little finger. She was very vocal, urging me on and begging for more.

After she had come twice, she pushed my face away. "I want your cock!" she insisted, and slowly worked her tongue down my body till she reached my tired tool. She started by licking the tip and fingering my balls, then she swallowed a little at a time until my hard dick was all the way down her throat. I had never been deep-throated before. The feeling was incredible!

When she sensed I was about to come she stopped, straddled me and guided my throbbing cock into her hot, wet slit. I held her hips and she rode me faster and faster while I tweaked her erect nipples and squeezed her ass-cheeks. My left hand stroked her clit, urging her on. She came over and over again but kept right on fucking. We switched to the missionary position and I thrust into her harder and harder, but she still wasn't satisfied. She lifted her ass off the bed and I put two pillows under her hips so I could penetrate her greedy little cunt even deeper. She came several more times before I rolled her over and took her from behind, doggie-style.

"Take my ass! I want my ass fucked!" she demanded, so I pulled out of her, lubricated her little pink asshole with her cunt juice and popped the head of my dick inside.

Savoring the tightness of her tiny orifice, I buried my cock into her again and again. "More, more, more," she kept saying. I sank my full length into her and she pushed against me greedily. "Harder. Come in my ass. Come in my ass," she gasped, her voice ragged. I only lasted a few more minutes before shooting a torrent of hot jism into her ass. We collapsed on the bed, unable to move. Even breathing seemed to be a considerable accomplishment.

I think we must have set a world record for the greatest number of orgasms two people shared in one night. The next morning I woke her up by eating her pussy. Then we both called in sick. You wouldn't believe how many different ways I fucked her and how many orgasms we enjoyed. We still get together once in a while to fuck a weekend away, but I will always cherish that first special night.—*L.R., Chicago, Illinois*

A HOT TIP AT THE RACES LEADS TO
THE RIDE OF HIS LIFE

I'm a thirty-five-year-old married man and I'm in excellent shape, if I do say so myself. Until the age of thirty-two I enjoyed being a bachelor, but getting married was the best thing that ever happened to me. Not only do my wife and I both share similar interests and goals, but my wife Carol has the body and looks of a college coed. Her thirty-two-inch chest perfectly complements her small waist, perfect hips and firm little ass.

One night while lying in bed beside Carol, thumbing through one of our many issues of *Penthouse Letters*, I came across a series of photographs that made me do a double take. The model in the photos was the spitting image of Carol! I scrutinized the pictures for several minutes before sharing them with Carol. She marveled at the resemblance as well. Seeing my wife's look-alike in an erotic magazine really turned me on. It also inspired a plan.

The next day I dug my photography equipment out of a closet and set it up in the rec room. Then I went out and bought Carol a sexy set of white silk lingerie. That evening I took her out to a fancy restaurant for dinner and presented her with my gift. She loved it and said she couldn't wait to get home and try it on. Five minutes later the check was paid and we were on our way.

Once home, I ushered Carol into the rec room. The camera and spotlights were ready to go.

When she saw the setup, she smiled mischievously and said, "I guess I'd better go change into my new lingerie, don't you think?"

When she stepped back into the room she looked absolutely stunning. The lingerie fit her beautifully, flowing gracefully over her body and emphasizing every curve of her gorgeous feminine physique. She had applied fresh makeup and she looked like a sultry tramp. She leaned against the pool table and gave me a pose. I felt like forgetting about the camera and taking her right there on the pool table, but I managed to compose myself and start snapping pictures.

Carol really got into it. She knew how to make love to the camera. Each pose she struck was sexier and more revealing than the last. Soon she was on the couch with her legs spread, fingering herself as I took shot after sexy shot. After a few minutes of this I couldn't take it anymore. I put the camera aside and stripped faster than I ever had before. The camera wasn't the only tool that did a lot of shooting that night!

Several months later things were getting a little dull, so we decided to spend a day at the horse races to add some excitement to our lives. Carol added a bit more excitement to the event by wearing a low-cut top and tight denim shorts that exposed her ass-cheeks. Like all females, Carol really enjoys attracting male attention.

We bet on the first three races and lost each time. When I went to place our bets on the fourth race, I noticed a handsome, young, blond-haired man collecting his winnings. I struck up a conversation with him. It seemed that lady luck had favored him that day. He had won his first three picks.

We walked outside and talked for several minutes. After advising me on how to bet the next race, he nudged me with his elbow, pointed and said: "Now, there's a real winner."

He was pointing at Carol, or rather at Carol's ass. Her tight denim shorts were quite an eye-catcher and left little to the imagination.

"She's a winner, all right," I agreed. "And I should know— she's my wife."

At first John (that was his name) seemed embarrassed, but I quickly put him at ease and introduced him to Carol. Then I hurried to place our bets according to John's suggestion.

When I got back to the grandstand I immediately noticed that my wife was very interested in John. They were flirting outrageously. She kept leaning up against him, and more than once I noticed his hand graze her plump ass.

Soon my attention was diverted by the race. John's tip paid off and we won a bundle on a long shot. Carol thanked John with a big hug that he obviously enjoyed. I went to cash in on our winnings, leaving Carol and John alone together. This time I made a point to discreetly observe Carol and John before returning. I saw John slip his hand into Carol's back pocket. Carol giggled and pulled out some of the erotic photographs that I had taken of her and showed them to him.

When I returned, John seemed unfazed by the fact that he was browsing through naked photos of my wife. He just told me what a lucky guy I was and kept right on looking, obviously enjoying himself immensely.

After the last race we all headed out the gate together. I wanted to thank him for his tip but didn't know how. Then, just as we were about to go our separate ways, Carol invited him over to our place for a barbecue. I thought I knew what she had in mind and I liked the idea, so I quickly seconded the invitation. He accepted readily.

Once home Carol strolled off to the master bedroom and slipped into a thong bikini. John's eyes nearly popped out of his skull when she returned. Carol's bikini was two sizes too small and her pussy hairs were peeking out the sides. Carol noticed John's reaction and seemed quite pleased with herself. She stepped up beside John, placed a hand on his shoulder and said, "Let's all go relax in the Jacuzzi."

John immediately went to the cabana to get undressed, while I headed to the kitchen for some wine. When I returned I found John in the hot tub, buck naked. He couldn't take his eyes off Carol. I stripped off my clothes and joined them. Carol immediately stood up, water cascading over her firm, scantily-clad breasts. She must have felt our eyes devouring her as she poured us each a glass of wine.

After a few minutes of awkward silence Carol boldly made the first move. Laughing mischievously, she sat down between John's legs and began rubbing her ass against his erect penis. I could see why Carol was so attracted to him. He had a well-developed chest and a dark complexion that contrasted nicely with his sandy blond hair.

When Carol turned around, their lips met. As they kissed passionately, John's hands began roaming over Carol's body. He unfastened her bikini top and her beautiful breasts bounced free. Carol moaned with delight as he sucked and licked her swollen nipples. At the same time she reached back and gently stroked my throbbing hard-on.

After getting us both hotter than hell, she calmly slid out of the tub to refill our glasses. She handed us our wine, smiled at John and reached for a sex toy she had hidden beneath a towel. It was a short, fat vibrator. Carol, it seemed, was about to give us a show. She sat on the edge of the Jacuzzi, spread her legs wide, switched on the vibrator and started rubbing it across her swollen pussy lips. Then she penetrated herself with it. We watched in awe as her pussy engulfed the plastic cock with a soft, squelching sound. Over and over again she plunged that vibrator deep inside her pussy until she was shrieking with intense pleasure.

But the show had only just begun. After catching her breath Carol turned around, reached behind her and slowly began inserting the dildo into her asshole. Slowly her tight chocolate tunnel took in inch after inch of hard, vibrating plastic. When half the vibrator had entered her butt, she began to have trouble reaching it. "Help me, John," she said. "Shove it in really deep."

Like a shot John was at her side, helping her work the vibrator into her ass. I was a little disappointed that she hadn't asked me to help her, but I was enjoying the show so much that I didn't let it trouble me long.

Soon the vibrator was buried deep in her ass. Only the last inch of it was peeking out between her ass-cheeks. The pulsations of the sex toy were driving Carol crazy. "Fu— Fu— Fuck me, John," she panted. "Fuck me deep and hard!"

John stood eager to comply, and Carol wrapped her legs around him and drew him to her.

His big dick slipped effortlessly into her wet and swollen pussy. John grunted with pleasure. Carol moaned with delight.

At first John pounded his penis into her fast and furiously. Soon, however, he discovered the titillating pleasure caused by the vibrator still pulsing in Carol's ass. He buried his shaft in her to the hilt and let the tickling sensation wash over his cock. He was on the verge of coming when Carol pushed him away. She pulled the vibrator out of her ass and demanded that I take its place.

Now it was John's turn to watch and my turn to play. Carol's ass was tight and firm and I could feel her powerful ass muscles repeatedly tightening and loosening their grip on my shaft.

Watching Carol get butt-fucked really seemed to turn John on. At Carol's direction he rolled Carol and me onto our sides and buried his penis in her cunt. Soon both John and I were slamming away. Carol was screaming in ecstasy as my balls bounced into John's. After a few minutes of this I exploded inside her ass.

I pulled my penis out of Carol and sat back to catch my breath. Meanwhile Carol had again pushed John away in order to stop him from coming too soon. She had something else in mind.

She quickly maneuvered John into the 69 position. Her hands rubbed John's balls as she began working her bright red lips down to the root of his shaft. Finally, with apparent effort, she managed to work his cock into her throat. She began bobbing her head up and down, making his long dick fuck her tight throat.

This drove John crazy. Impulsively he wrapped his hands around her head and started fucking her face. Carol took it in stride and seconds later John's balls tensed up and he shot his load deep inside her gullet. As his cries of pleasure subsided, a trickle of stray come dripped down the corner of her mouth.

But Carol was by no means finished with her newfound stud. She never even allowed him time to recuperate. Still craving more sex, Carol began expertly massaging and kneading John's rapidly shrinking cock until it was a rapidly growing cock once again.

Then John fucked her pussy again and after a little while I joined the action and worked my dick back into her ass. We must have ridden her for over an hour before calling it a night. I lost track of how many orgasms Carol had.

John showered and left us with a warm good-bye. We never saw him again. I guess that sure was his lucky day!

That night my wife and I once again curled up with a copy of *Penthouse Letters* . . . but that's another story.—*Name and address withheld*

THEY ENJOY A SEXUAL SUNDAY
WITH AN ANAL CHERRY ON TOP

*W*ords simply cannot describe the excitement, intensity and ultimate joy of the experience I want to share with you. I am not especially kinky or perverted, but I recently had an experience that was truly remarkable and filled with the kind of passion that only two open-minded people can share.

Last September I met a very special lady. She isn't a perfect beauty like Cindy Crawford, but she certainly is one of the most striking women I have ever seen. Talia has an incredible body. She's five feet tall and weighs only one hundred pounds. She has a firm gymnast's body with a perfectly flat tummy, beautiful long legs and an absolutely amazing ass.

Talia is a businesswoman who can dress elegantly and erotically at the same time. Our sexual relationship was great right from the start but not nearly as fantastic as it became once we had learned all the subtle ways to tantalize each other's body.

Our bedroom takes up the entire top floor of an old house. Basically it is a six-hundred-square-foot space completely covered with deep, white shag carpeting—an ideal playpen and love-nest. We often disappear up the stairs early each evening to indulge in hours of pleasure. Both of us are equally turned on by giving or receiving. I delight in giving her orgasm after breathless orgasm. I am incredibly turned on by the way her tiny, lithe body convulses during her orgasms. She is better than any fantasy I have ever had.

For many years I was very promiscuous, and all that practice made me very good in bed. One of the first things I learned about women was that if I took pleasure in giving them pleasure I would rarely be rejected. Since then I have had the pleasure of helping many women achieve powerful orgasms. I have also learned that (unfortunately) only a handful of women are willing to try anal sex.

When Talia and I were first getting to know each other better, she asked me if I had ever experienced anal sex. I thought she was only asking to find out more about my past, but one evening as we were playing with each other's body, I discovered that her asshole was very sensitive.

I had just finished giving her a total body massage and she was lying on her stomach feeling very relaxed. I leaned over and ran my tongue slowly up her spine. Her body curled up the way cats do when you scratch them in the right place. I did this a couple more times and Talia's moans and sighs were delightful. As I licked between her legs she spread them wide and I was transfixed by the glorious sight before me.

The mounds of her plump ass and the pink lips of her pussy glistened with the oils I had used during the massage. Then, ever so slowly, I saw the lips of her pussy open. I ran my tongue up the soft, sweet skin of her inner thighs and lightly and tenderly probed the folds of her precious flower. Her hips undulated with the rhythm of my tongue. She spread her legs even wider and my tongue started dancing on her clit. As she got increasingly aroused, her hips moved faster and faster. I wanted to make the pleasure last longer, so I stiffened my tongue and ran it over her asshole and the crack of her ass up her spine to the base of her neck. I did this again and noticed that she really enjoyed it when my tongue lingered on the little bud of her asshole.

Gently I stuck my tongue inside it and Talia squirmed with delight. Moments later I pushed my cock through the folds of her pussy deep into her love-canal. A few strokes later we exploded in intense simultaneous orgasms. Exhausted, I collapsed on top of her. She sighed and moaned with satisfaction.

A couple of days later, after we had just made love, Talia was soaking wet. I playfully wriggled two fingers into her hot, wet box. She responded by grabbing my still-stiff rod and planting herself on top of it, pushing it into her as far as possible. Moments later, as she neared orgasm, I reached around and slipped my pussy-drenched middle finger into her tight little asshole. I pushed deeper and deeper until she came, shuddering uncontrollably.

Even after this experience I only fantasized about anal penetration. She was so small and tight that I was afraid it would hurt my precious little baby. Little did I know that she was having fantasies about giving me what she had never given any other man—her perfect, tight ass.

It was a Sunday morning, and as usual we started the day by making love. She really likes me to take my time in the morning and slowly awaken her passion. The rewards are always well worth the trouble. She was sleeping with her legs gently spread, one leg lying over my leg. I started running my fingers through her closely cropped bush, tenderly tugging on her pubic hair. Her bush was always trimmed and the hair on her pussy lips was just long enough to avoid the prickles. Slowly, in her sleep, her hips started moving with the rhythm of my hand. I gently lifted her leg and pressed my cock tenderly against her pussy lips as she started to wake up.

Drowsily, she pushed against my cock until it filled her completely. I put a finger on her clit and stroked it in time with the thrusts of my cock. Her gasps got shorter and shorter until she came. It was a long, drawn-out orgasm.

After she recovered from the high of her orgasm, she flipped me onto my back and lay on her back on top of me—snuggling her cute little ass into my crotch. As soon as my cock was hard again, she reached down and guided it back into her sopping pussy. Then she ground against me, rolling her hips in ways that drove me crazy. She creates tremendous pressure on the underside of my cock and usually makes me come very quickly. She delights in exerting this sort of control over me.

She continued working my cock in and out of her pussy until I succumbed to a breathtaking orgasm. While we paused to rest, I played with Talia, spreading her pussy lips wide with one hand and massaging her clit with the other. We watched ourselves in the full-length mirror conveniently placed on the wall near the bed and saw my come oozing out of her pussy.

Usually this sight gets Talia so excited that she immediately impales herself on my dick and begs me to fuck her again. But this time was different. Talia rolled over and slowly stroked me back to hardness with her expert hands and luscious mouth. As I approached orgasm she swallowed as much of my dick as she could and pushed the tip of one of her fingers into my ass. I exploded almost instantaneously. Gasping for breath, I watched as my cream trickled out of the corner of her mouth. Wow, talk about the rockets' red glare!

When I came back down to earth I really needed time to recuperate. Talia rolled over on her side and I snuggled up behind her. I hadn't yet had enough time to go soft, and she wiggled until my stiff cock was right up against the crack of her incredible ass. I wondered what it would be like to slip it into her asshole, but I worried about hurting her.

While this was going through my mind, Talia reached behind her, wrapped her fingers around my cock and pressed the head against her little rosebud asshole. I could hardly breathe in anticipation. With her hand still firmly wrapped around my cock, she slowly, ever so slowly, began feeding my cock into her virgin asshole.

A fantasy beyond my fondest dreams was suddenly unfolding. I didn't dare move for fear of disturbing the moment. Slowly Talia worked the crown of my big cock into her ass. When she paused for a moment to relax, we noticed that we were both sweating and trembling like virgins.

Talia was really getting into the groove. Gently and tenderly she worked my thick member in and out of her, taking a little more of my meat every time. With a little effort her fine ass finally swallowed my whole cock.

I increased the speed of my thrusts and Talia rocked her hips against me, straining to take in every inch. The pleasure was beyond description. After a couple more strokes I came harder than I ever had before. My cock popped out of her ass, shooting come everywhere, then plunged back in, lining her tight canal with jism.

Totally spent, we remained in the spoon position with me still buried deep inside of her for what seemed like hours. Talia had given me something that I had never before experienced—an anal cherry. The experience surpassed any that had come before. Since then we enjoy anal sex at least five or six times a month.—S.T., *Tucson, Arizona*

GAL'S AN ASS-TONISHING WOMAN
WITH ASS-TOUNDING ASSETS

I'm a six-foot-four-inch black male with an average-size cock. I'm an avid reader of *Penthouse Letters*, so I thought I should make a contribution of my own. My story begins three years ago with a business trip to a large East Coast city. At one of the meetings I attended I met a very thin black woman named Beryl. She has tiny tits, a pretty face and a delicious ass. We went out for dinner the first night of my trip and she showed me some of the sights. Afterward we returned to her home and had a few drinks.

Soon I began kissing her on the lips. My kisses were tentative at first, but then I threw caution to the wind and pushed my tongue deep into her mouth, practically down her throat. She opened her mouth wide and sucked on my tongue. I wasted no time unbuttoning her dress and unsnapping her bra. While her tits were very small, her nipples were quite large and had already hardened from excitement.

I started pulling on her big nipples and she moaned loudly. Then I bent my head down and sucked each nipple enthusiastically. I couldn't believe how large her nipples became. They stuck out at least an inch and she moaned loudly every time they were tweaked or sucked. Suddenly she broke the kiss and suggested we retire to the bedroom.

She told me to get comfortable and disappeared into the bathroom. I undressed completely and when she came back she was clad only in panties. She joined me on the bed and, as we kissed, I rolled her extra-large nipples between my thumb and fingers. She moaned loudly. She grabbed my cock and squeezed it tightly and I pulled off her panties and rolled her onto her back. I sucked on her nipples and then slowly worked my tongue down to her pussy.

She had a very hairy pussy, but I parted the hair and licked her pussy lips. Her clit was as big as her nipples. I licked and sucked it, and within a few minutes she came, screaming with pleasure. By now I was desperate to fuck her, so I quickly positioned myself between her legs and slid my dick into her pussy. It was the tightest pussy I had ever felt, but it was so wet that my cock slid in easily. I pushed it all the way in and then pulled it all the way out. At first I fucked her with long, slow strokes so I could feel her tight, wet pussy caressing my cock like a glove. She came again in less than five minutes, but I was able to hold my orgasm back.

I positioned her on her hands and knees and took her doggie-style. I knew I wouldn't last long, because in this position her pussy felt even tighter and she was moaning loudly with every stroke. I came hard and filled her pussy with sperm. Thus sated, we both fell into a deep sleep.

The next morning I ate her pussy until she had an orgasm and then we decided to shower together. When she asked me to wash her back, I couldn't take my eyes off her beautiful ass. The soap was running down her back and into her ass-crack. I bent her over and fucked her doggie-style once again. After she came, I pulled my cock out of her pussy and started eating her out from behind. This time I let my tongue pass over her asshole and she moaned and asked me to tongue her asshole more. I reamed her with gusto as water cascaded over us. She gasped that she was about to come, so I took my tongue out of her ass and replaced it with my middle finger. I slid my finger into her tiny asshole to the second knuckle and she shook all over and came.

The next day I called her but got no answer. I thought I was going to be stuck with nothing better than TV and room service. I was looking at the room service menu when I heard a knock on the door. To my delight it was Beryl. I invited her in and she told me that she had thought about me all day and just had to see me again. I told her the feeling was mutual. We rapidly got undressed and climbed into bed. This time she was much more aggressive and grabbed my cock and sucked it hard. Her mouth was so small it made my cock feel incredibly large. It also made it very hard. It grew so large and hard she could no longer get much of it into her mouth, so she mounted me and slid her tight little pussy onto my rock-hard cock. She was so aroused she fucked me very hard and fast. She came quickly, but again I was able to hold back.

She fell back onto the bed and I sucked her nipples until she was hot once again. Then I positioned her on all fours and entered her pussy from behind. As I was fucking her, I looked down at her beautiful ass. I could clearly see her asshole wink every time my cock pulled out of her pussy. Suddenly I had an idea. I reached over to the nightstand, coated my finger with lotion and inserted it into her tight asshole. She went wild, screamed and came. Her pussy squeezed my cock so hard, all I could do was come.

Later she confessed that her asshole was very sensitive and she often fingered it when masturbating. That's all I needed to hear. After thirty minutes of talking about what we liked sexually, I went to my suitcase, got a tube of K-Y jelly and coated my cock with it. Beryl stroked my jelly-covered cock until it grew larger and harder than ever. Then she got on her hands and knees and looked at me imploringly. I knew she wanted it in the ass, so I obliged. She moaned loudly and begged me to fuck her ass extra hard. To my surprise, I fucked her ass for over ten minutes and Beryl came without me even touching her pussy. When I felt myself coming I pushed my cock into her asshole as deeply as I could and let my come erupt deep inside her bowels. For the next two years I fucked Beryl every time I visited the East Coast—most of the time in her sweet little asshole.—C.G., *Baton Rouge, Louisiana*

THAT'S A SWITCH!
THE BOSS IS KISSING HER BUTT!

As far back as I can recall, I have been a true "ass man." The finest feature of a pretty girl is her bottom. Nothing in the world is sweeter than a round, shapely behind that jiggles and wiggles. The beach is a great place to see a variety of butts covered only by tiny pieces of cloth. Sometimes you can see the entire outline and the white, untanned cheek bottoms and you can easily picture the deep cleft of a butt crack splitting those soft orbs—so luscious and hot!

My name is Philip and I have been married to Joanie for eleven years. She is thirty-three and has a fantastic body. Shoulder-length blonde hair frames her cute face and she is tall with good-sized, big-nippled boobs. Her mile-high legs join at what I consider to be the greatest ass on the planet. Her body is tanned, but her butt is milky white and slightly plump with a deep ass-crack. What really makes Joanie's ass unique is an abundance of soft, brown, kinky hair that surrounds her asshole and protrudes prominently from her behind. Such a pretty, feminine woman with such a luscious growth of hair is sexy as hell.

Joanie loves all kinds of sex, but she's especially turned on by anal sex. Since the start of our relationship, we have been very open with each other. One of the many things that gets both of us hot is when Joanie describes some of the lovers she had before we met and how she always asked them to make love to her ass. The thought of my wife on all fours with some guy pushing the head of his hard dick into her sweet, hairy back door and shooting his load into her is enough to get my blood boiling.

My wife works as a receptionist for a small consulting firm two days a week. Her boss is a thirty-six-year-old guy named Skip who she finds very attractive. A few months ago, she confessed that he had made several advances toward her and that she had playfully turned him down. After consulting with me and obtaining my blessing, Joanie decided to grant Skip access to her succulent body—especially her ass. She immediately made this clear to him, and she didn't have to wait long for his gratitude.

According to Joanie, a typical day at the office now begins when Skip summons her to his office. Skip then invites her to kneel on all fours on his desk with her backside facing him. He scoots up his chair until his face reaches her plump rear end and lifts the hem of her skirt over her back to expose a pair of pink or white see-through satin panties. Next, Skip nuzzles her butt. I get incredibly excited just thinking about this guy sniffing her sweet ass through her panties. From personal experience, I know exactly how turned on he must be.

Skip then pulls her sexy panties off her round bottom and licks and kisses her pale white moons. He tugs gently on her hairs with his lips and makes her purr with delight. After that, he tells Joanie to reach back and part her cheeks. She happily complies and spreads her ass-cheeks wide so that Skip can push his tongue deep into her ass and swirl it around—a sensation that causes my wife to become so excited her pussy begins to juice. Skip gives her butt-hole a thorough reaming before pressing against her well-lubed entrance with his finger and slowly inching it into her.

My dick gets hard as a rock as Joanie recounts how, after all this foreplay, Skip removes his pants and frees his huge hard-on. She says his cock reminds her of a long English cucumber with a large head. He eases it first into her wet pussy to lubricate it and then into her asshole. He pumps her hard until he comes. All the while my wife is frigging her clit until she reaches a shattering orgasm. These days, Joanie's workday always begins with this ritual and it is often repeated just before quitting time.

I usually arrive home from work early, and when Joanie returns from one of Skip's afternoon workouts, she is still pumped up and raring to go. She grabs my hand and leads me into the bedroom where she kneels on the bed and lifts the hem of her dress to show me her come-soaked panties. I kneel behind her (as Skip has done) and slowly peel down her undies, whereupon she reaches back and spreads her cheeks wide.

Joanie's pussy lips are usually still swollen with excitement. Skip's come flows freely from her sweet, stretched asshole and droplets of jism cling to her kinky hairs and drip from her snatch. I savor the hot sight in front of me before I lick up all the goo from her well-used ass and pussy. For the next fifteen minutes or so, I administer a thorough tongue-job. By then my cock is throbbing with excitement and I roll her onto her back and sink my meat into her until we both come in a powerful, shaking climax.

We have repeated this scenario many times and it always turns us both on. We also love to flash whenever possible, and I love the looks we get when her whole white ass is exposed and opened wide! Joanie is beautiful and I love her dearly. These little episodes certainly heighten our sexual appetites.—*P.I., Charleston, South Carolina*

DOUBLE YOUR PLEASURE DOUBLE YOUR ENJOYMENT WITH DOUBLE PENETRATION

*M*y wife Jean and I recently enjoyed a great evening that I'd like to share with your readers. My wife is about five feet seven inches tall and has a great body. Her long and shapely legs accentuate the sex appeal of her lovely ass. I love to hold Jean's hips while fucking her from behind, and Jean seems to like this position too. We've also experimented with anal sex a few times. When properly relaxed Jean really enjoys it, and I love it as an outlet for my lust.

Yesterday morning I informed Jean that I had something special planned for the evening. I instructed her to spend the day fantasizing about being fucked in her pussy and her ass at the same time. I explained that I intended to give her a very memorable experience with my own cock and a dildo designed for anal use. I described the dildo and assured Jean it would fill her perfectly and without pain; it was larger than my finger but smaller than my cock, so I knew it would fit quite well. I told her to close her eyes from time to time during the day and think about my lust for her and how she'd enjoy having two cocks inside of her at the same time!

Jean later confirmed that she had found the mental image very exciting when it unexpectedly popped into her mind several times during the course of the day. She said she had found it particularly exciting when standing in line at the supermarket; thinking about my planned double penetration while surrounded by strangers in a public place got her soaking wet. She said it also made her realize how lucky she was and how unlikely it was that any of the other housewives around her had ever received as much lustful attention.

We started our evening with a great dinner accompanied by plenty of wine. Jean wore an incredibly tight short skirt that accentuated her ass. Her hips looked fantastic and her body language was a clear invitation to fuck her from behind. I couldn't keep my hands off her ass when we began necking after dinner.

When I felt we were both sufficiently aroused, we moved to the bedroom. I then instructed Jean to remain standing and bend over. This position exposed her ass fully and made it easily accessible. Jean followed my directions and bent over a sewing machine cabinet for support. From past experience we both knew that the cabinet was the perfect platform for her to comfortably rest her upper body upon while being plugged from the rear. It exposed her hips and ass fully to my sight and grasp, and aligned her pussy and my cock perfectly.

I removed my clothes and stripped off Jean's skirt and panties. Jean soon felt my hands exploring her entire body. I spent the most time feeling her sexy ass, hips and thighs, but my hands strayed all over her sexy body from her firm calves to her hardened nipples.

I then moved in very close behind her and pushed my hard cock between her buttocks. As I pressed my hardness against her ass, I reached around and grasped Jean's hanging breasts. My hands squeezed her breasts, enjoying their sensuality in a raw rather than gentle way, and she reveled in the sensation.

After a while I backed away so that Jean's ass could give and receive other pleasures. I began by kneading her buttocks very firmly. Then I applied some oil to her ass so that my hands could slide over her more sensuously. I now squeezed and grabbed her ass as tightly as possible. Next I channeled some oil between her buttocks and worked it over and into her anus. The sensation was incredibly tantalizing to both of us. It felt so good that I slipped my finger all the way into her ass. Jean gasped with my first penetration and pushed back against my hand.

I decided it was time for the dildo. Initially I pushed the dildo in slowly and carefully, but I soon realized that Jean's ass was eagerly accepting it with no hesitation or discomfort. This was yet another turn-on for me, so it was with feverish excitement that I thrust the dildo the rest of the way into my wife's eager asshole.

I then began to fuck her ass with the latex cock. It slid back and forth with ease, and I could tell Jean loved it. With each stroke she pushed her hips back against her inanimate lover in order to force it deeper within her. After a few minutes of this, Jean was super hot and my cock was aching to get in on the action. Keeping Jean's ass full with the dildo, I quickly moved into position and buried my anxious cock inside her. I slid into her dripping wet pussy with ease. She was incredibly wet! Once I'd gotten in as far as I could, I began a slow fucking motion that she responded to by thrusting back against me.

Each time I thrust my cock into Jean's pussy, I also drove the latex cock into her ass with my stomach muscles. When I pulled back, the lover in her ass would start to slip out, only to be reintroduced to her nether regions by my next thrust. Jean moaned loudly the first time she felt both cocks moving inside of her. I loved hearing and sensing her excitement. It was exactly as I had fantasized it would be: my wife was enjoying being taken by two hard cocks.

Our position allowed me to reach around Jean's hips and actually feel the shaft of my cock where it disappeared into the stretched folds of her pussy. My other hand moved up and down her body, alternately grasping her hip and fondling her breasts. Both cocks continued to move together, filling her totally! In a very few minutes the raw sexuality of being together this way overpowered us both. Our hips moved faster and with much less control. An intense orgasm swept over both of us. We then moved over to the bed and collapsed in a satisfied heap.—V.C., *Denver, Colorado*

OLD DOG LIKES TO STICK IT TO NEW TRICKS AND TEACH THEM A THING OR TWO

I am a fifty-two-year-old man and I get most of my sex from call girls. Once or twice a month I call an escort agency and tell the person who answers that I would like some companionship.

If I speak to someone who is not yet familiar with my tastes, I make it plain that the escort should be young (under twenty-four) and slender. Unless you have been using the same agency for years, you can't get too explicit about what you want. Otherwise you shouldn't expect to get your heart's desire. Recently, however, I got exactly that.

About a month ago I called a service I have used for years and asked for Rachel, who is prized for her deep-throat technique. The girl who answered the phone said Rachel was no longer with the service but there was a young Puerto Rican girl she could call for me. I told her to go ahead, hung up the phone and waited. Soon the phone rang and a girl introduced herself as Alba from the agency. I gave her directions to my house and she arrived soon after.

Alba is about five feet two inches tall and weighs one hundred pounds. She has flashing black eyes and black hair, and she claims to have just turned twenty.

After calling the escort service to let them know she had arrived, we went into my bedroom. Alba saw the one-hundred-fifty-dollar fee lying on the bed and she quickly picked it up, counted it and put it into her purse. She undressed on one side of the bed and I undressed on the other. I noticed that she had a very dense bush of curly black pubic hair that started just above her pussy and disappeared between her legs. When she turned around I saw that the hair went clear up the split of her buttocks to her anus. I simply love hairy women!

I slid on a one-inch cock ring, which is the diameter of my dick when it is flaccid. When my dick is fully erect it is one-and-a-half inches wide and five inches long. We got on the bed and she started sucking my dick. Alba managed to deep-throat me with no problem. I felt nothing but tongue and throat.

We swung around into the 69 position with me on my back and Alba above me. As she continued to bury my dick in her throat, I started to gently lick her pussy lips. She was as hairy a woman as I have ever seen! I really enjoyed parting her thick pubes with my tongue as I searched out her clit. She got more and more excited as my tongue moved faster and faster. Lubrication started to flow from her pussy. She foamed for a good ten minutes and I drank down every drop of it.

While I was licking her clit I stuck my index and middle finger into her pussy. These digits got so wet and slick that I was then able to insert my middle finger into her anus with ease. Alba started moaning, and after I finger-fucked her pussy and ass at the same time for about five minutes she came. As she orgasmed, I moved my tongue down and buried it in her ass. Alba must have kept coming for almost a minute.

As we repositioned ourselves for fucking, I asked Alba, "How much for up your butt?" She didn't understand, so I restated it. "How much to fuck you in the ass?" She thought for a few moments and then replied, "Fifty dollars."

I got off the bed, got fifty dollars out of my billfold and handed it to her. She then dropped it into her purse.

When I got back on the bed, she pointed to the K-Y jelly on the nightstand and said, "We'll need a lot of that, because I've never done this before."

She started to get on her hands and knees. "No," I said. "I'll fuck your ass after I fuck your pussy." I lay down on my back and she straddled my tool and fucked me for five or six minutes. I then got out from under her and flipped her over for some missionary-style action. With her legs over my shoulders I fucked her furiously for about ten minutes.

Alba then asked, "How about my ass?" Always ready to comply with a lady's wishes, I reached over to the nightstand and got the K-Y jelly. I lubricated her asshole with the K-Y. Then I slid my middle finger into her ass. My index finger soon went in alongside it. I then must have pumped those two fingers in and out of her ass a hundred times until her anal sphincter was nice and relaxed. Finally her ass was ready.

I applied some of the lubricant to my dick and proceeded to slowly embed the head of my pole in her tight puckered asshole. I stopped moving for a couple of minutes to allow Alba to get used to it.

I then slowly resumed pushing in a fraction of an inch at a time, until about half my dick was in her ass. I stopped and asked her if she was all right. She moaned with pleasure and begged me to shove my dick in all the way. Again I readily complied with her wishes.

Once I had my dick fully buried in her rectum I started to thrust rhythmically in and out. I used very short, slow strokes at first, but then I picked up the tempo until I was fucking her at a frenzied pace. Alba began to finger her clit furiously and she soon started having multiple orgasms. Finally I had the best orgasm I have ever had. It must have lasted a full minute. I pulled out and collapsed next to Alba.

After resting for a few minutes I started questioning Alba about her life. She said she was a nurse in a nursing home and that she worked for the escort service only part-time. Before she left I got her personal phone number. I can't wait to call her again!—*J.L., Ann Arbor, Michigan*

WORKING GIRL TAKES ON THREE BUSINESSMEN
DURING MARATHON SESSION

My colleagues Newt and Ollie and I were on a business trip. We were driving from the airport to the hotel when something caught our attention: a buxom hooker in a short, tight black skirt was standing at a nearby street corner.

Realizing that she had caught our eyes, she approached our car. To excite us, she turned around, slipped up the black skirt and exposed her firm buttocks and her meaty snatch. We knew what to do next. At our eager invitation, the hooker jumped in the backseat between Newt and Ollie. I then took off for the nearest hotel. I had difficulty keeping my eyes on the road, since the rearview mirror afforded me a clear view of the action taking place in the backseat. Samantha (that was her name) had a dick in each hand that she was working like an expert.

While we were climbing the hotel stairs we ogled Samantha's

full, voluptuous body. By the time we got in the room we were all panting with excitement. Appraising the king-size bed, we all stripped and, without so much as a word exchanged, we all decided to share Samantha and the bed at the same time!

Samantha told us that she was really horny and that she intended to get fully satisfied that night. We didn't argue. Samantha was about thirty years old and had long legs, wide hips and big succulent breasts. I sat on the bed first and beckoned for Samantha to join me. She didn't hesitate. In a moment she had straddled my legs and parked her fragrant pussy within easy reach of my tongue. She then engulfed my engorged member. While she oiled my dick with her lips, I grabbed her ass-cheeks and dove my mouth into her juicy snatch.

After coming in my mouth she turned herself around and began riding my dick. Watching this action got Newt and Ollie very excited. Newt climbed on the bed next. He approached Samantha from behind, spat on his hand and lubricated her asshole with his saliva. Then he inserted his long, banana-shaped dick into her tight, rosy opening. He pushed it slowly inside of her, right up to the hilt.

Ollie then joined in from the other side. Kneeling above my head, he slid his engorged dick into Samantha's hungry mouth. Even though she was a hooker and was doing this for a living, I believe she truly enjoyed it. She had three dicks inside her body.

By now all three of us were close to coming. I lost control first and exploded in her pussy. Next Newt emptied his load in her asshole. Right after that Ollie arched his back and filled Samantha's mouth with milky liquid. One by one we pulled our softening tools from her body. Semen dripped from her pussy and it trickled from her puckered anus. Watching Samantha lying on the bed oozing come, moaning and fingering herself soon had all three of us hard again.

This time we changed positions: Ollie lay down on his back and let her straddle his pole. Newt began fucking her mouth and I got behind her and inspected her recently invaded asshole.

After applying lubricant I impaled her on my love-tool, stuffing inch after inch of my meat into her puckered anal opening. Ollie and I were pumping back and forth with the same rhythm, while Newt was installing his stick deeper and deeper inside her throat. Samantha now began moaning with ecstasy. This pushed us over the edge again and all three of us exploded within her almost simultaneously.

After that, we paused a while to gather our strength. Then we all moved onto the floor so we could have more room to maneuver in. Ollie lay on the floor and Samantha sat on him. He then spread her sweaty buttocks and inserted his dick into her ass. From the front, Newt spread her legs wide and slammed his prick in and out of her pussy. With every thrust Newt's balls and Ollie's balls would collide. Meanwhile, I was letting her suck and lick my balls. Then I pushed my cock down her tight throat.

Samantha began shaking like she was possessed. Soon her ass and her twat were again filled with Ollie and Newt's sticky juice. Only I had yet to come again. I took my dick out of Samantha's mouth and prepared for a special treat: shooting my load between her tits.

Samantha kneeled and I stood up and directed my shaft between her hot breasts. My tool was already well-oiled, so I could easily slide it back and forth. It felt great! Soon I felt an eruption building up from deep in my balls. Then I unloaded the biggest load of semen I've ever produced!—*R.V.*, *Toronto, Ontario*

ONE GOOD TURN DESERVES ANOTHER TILL THEY DON'T KNOW WHICH END IS UP

I am a twenty-six-year-old professional woman and I work in the insurance industry. My blonde hair and five-foot-six-inch athletic frame perfectly complement my husband Bob's dark hair and five-foot-eight-inch muscular build.

A recent promotion I received prompted Bob to reward me by fulfilling one of my sexual fantasies. Bob works with several really cute guys. Stan is the cutest of these guys, and he always seems to have several females chasing after him.

Last Friday I got home from work and found that Bob had left a message on our answering machine instructing me to meet him and Stan at our favorite bar. I was anxious to eat, drink and party, so I quickly changed from my business clothes into a sexy outfit and headed for the bar. When I arrived both Bob and Stan greeted me with kisses. Although Stan had never kissed me before, I wasn't really surprised, because he had always been friendly toward me and I knew he'd been drinking. What did surprise me was the length of the kiss and the fact that he smiled and winked at me when he finished. I didn't read too much into it at the time, but it soon became obvious that Bob and Stan had something up their sleeves.

The joint was soon jumping and I was having a great time taking turns dancing with the guys. At one point we all decided to go on the dance floor together for a group dance. The floor was packed and I was happily sandwiched between Bob and Stan. I was glad that I had worn my shortest, sheerest and sexiest black dress. Bob rubbed against my front while Stan pressed against me from behind. I felt Stan's hard bulge dry-humping the crack of my ass.

The three of us became very hot (and bothered), so Bob suggested we go outside to get some fresh air. Once outside, Stan pointed out that the bar was really overcrowded, so, instead of going back inside, we decided to invite Stan to our house to listen to some CDs and have a few more drinks.

When we arrived at our house I put on some music while Bob got us some beers. Stan headed to the bathroom while Bob and I started slow-dancing and kissing in the living room. Bob caressed my butt-cheeks, then my breasts. I moaned and became weak in the knees when he rubbed my nipples through my dress. I had not realized that Stan had returned, so I was pleasantly surprised when I felt his hands rubbing my butt. At first I was worried that Bob might object, but my doubts vanished when he lifted up my skirt in order to give Stan better access to my ass.

Within seconds the guys stripped me naked and began rubbing, kissing and licking every inch of my body. It was great having four hands and two tongues all over me. Bob sucked on my tits while Stan knelt between my parted legs and tongued my pussy. I pulled Bob's face up to mine so that I could kiss him deeply as I felt Stan's tongue probing my clit. Stan then treated me to one of my favorite pleasures: he pulled my ass-cheeks apart with his hands and worked my butthole with his tongue. Between Stan licking my ass and Bob fingering my pussy, I had my first of many orgasms of the night. Not wanting to remain the only one who was naked, I began to help both guys out of their clothes. I then had them stand next to each other so I could marvel at the view of their great bodies. I dropped to my knees, grabbed a cock in each hand and took turns sucking them. Bob then suggested that we move to our king-size bed, and we all agreed.

The three of us jumped on the bed with me in the middle. We began licking and sucking every part of each other's body. As Stan was licking me and I was sucking Bob, I had my second orgasm. I then told Bob that I needed a cock inside me and he quickly obliged. As Bob and I fucked, Stan continued to lick my clit and pussy lips. As Bob slowly worked his shaft in and out of my pussy, he whispered to me that he could feel Stan's tongue grazing his cock and balls. This greatly excited me. I became even more excited when I realized that Stan had begun licking Bob's balls exclusively. I came again quickly, and Bob's orgasm was not far behind.

After Bob pulled out of me I turned Stan onto his back and knelt between his legs. I began pumping the base of his cock with my right hand while using my left to play with his balls. I then wet my lips and lowered my mouth onto the head of his beautiful cock. Bob had left the room, but he now returned to find me on my knees sucking off Stan.

Bob quickly rejoined us on the bed and positioned himself behind me. Then he slid completely under my body on his stomach. At first I couldn't figure out what he was up to; I then saw that he had a tube of K-Y jelly and that he intended to use it on Stan. I continued sucking on Stan's cock as Bob rubbed K-Y on Stan's balls and ass. Stan moaned his approval and excitement. I turned around and assumed a 69 position with Stan so that I could get a better view of what Bob was doing to him. I was pretty sure that neither Bob nor Stan had ever had any sexual contact with another guy before, so I found this moment especially exciting. Knowing how much he likes having it done to himself, Bob slid a lubricated finger deep into Stan's butt. Stan's muscles soon tightened around Bob's finger and his cock erupted into my mouth. I kept my mouth on Stan's cock and savored every last drop.

After a short rest Stan and I started kissing and he became hard again. As we lay on our sides facing each other, he grabbed my butt-cheeks and slid his cock into my pussy. I was savoring the sensation of Stan's cock in my pussy when I heard the click of the K-Y tube cap opening. I opened my eyes and saw Stan squeezing some K-Y onto his open palm. I heard Bob let out a moan and I realized that Stan was greasing up his rigid member. Stan then rubbed K-Y onto my butthole and pulled apart my ass-cheeks. Bob put his cock against my asshole and began penetrating my rectum.

I had always imagined that it would be too much to have a cock in my ass and my pussy at the same time, but how wrong I was. It was actually incredibly satisfying and exciting. When the guys told me they could feel their cocks rubbing against each other through my inside walls, I began to have multiple orgasms. Stan and Bob soon came too. As I caught my breath I told Bob how much I had loved having his cock in my ass.

After a very enjoyable three-person shower we all fell asleep for a few hours. I was awakened by Stan's tongue on my clit, and I opened my eyes to the sight of his engorged cock swaying in front of my face. I eagerly began sucking his cock and licking his balls as his tongue worked its magic on my clit.

After we had both orgasmed again, Stan asked me why Bob's balls are hairless. I told him that I let Bob keep the hair above his cock, but insist that he shave the hair from his balls to his ass. This intrigued Stan, so while Bob slept we went into the bathroom and started shaving away. Stan's cock looked delicious without any hair, but then he turned the tables on me. Since Stan had lost his pubes he said mine were fair game. He soon had my pussy shaved bald.

We slipped back into bed as Bob slept. I told Stan that I had a special request and that if he performed it I would do anything he wanted at a later date. He agreed to my terms. I told him that my fantasy was to watch a guy suck off another guy. He seemed nervous about this idea at first, but I think the excitement of the night (not to mention my hand on his cock) helped me coax him into it.

Stan slid his head under the covers and began sucking on Bob's limp and sleeping dick. Bob's dick awoke before he did, and Stan soon had a raging hard-on in his mouth. Then Bob woke up and discovered that it was Stan sucking him off. I thought he might object, so I kissed him deeply to keep him from saying anything. He moaned as I forced my tongue into his mouth and Stan continued sucking his dick. That told me it would be okay.

With Stan's cock up by our faces I got an even better idea. I grabbed Stan's ass and pulled him closer so that his hard cock was between my face and Bob's face. I sucked on Stan's cock, then told Bob to lick his balls. At first Bob was reluctant, but after I promised to fulfill any fantasy that he chose, he went for it. He started by tentatively licking Stan's balls, but soon he was sucking off Stan as hard as Stan was sucking him off. I just sat back and watched those two gorgeous guys in a 69.

Bob pulled Stan's cock out of his mouth and began jerking him off furiously as he fondled his balls. The scene in front of me was so exciting, I had to play with my clit. Stan began bucking wildly as he came all over Bob's hand. When Stan had finished shooting his load, Bob brought his hand up to my mouth so I could taste Stan's come. I slurped it up and then kissed Bob, giving him a taste of semen too. I then told him he had to lick the remaining come off of Stan's cock if he wanted me to fulfill his fantasy. He quickly (and I think happily) complied.

Stan then flipped Bob onto his back and knelt between his legs. I pulled up a seat and watched intently as I began to finger myself again. As Bob began to get closer to orgasm, I told Stan to swallow his come. When Bob came, Stan raised his mouth just over Bob's cock so that I could see the come spurt into Stan's mouth. The scene was more than I could stand, and I came instantly.

Now I owe both of these guys a fantasy of their choice. I don't know all the details yet, but I know one of them involves me licking at least one other girl's pussy and possibly being filmed in the act. To tell you the truth, I can't wait to hear what they've dreamed up for me!—*P.Y., San Antonio, Texas*

TRIO SERVES UP A FUCK SANDWICH WITH RELISH

Joyce and I have been married for over twenty years. I'm forty-five and she is forty, but she has the body and looks of a twenty-five-year-old. Joyce is five feet two inches tall, one hundred fifteen pounds and measures 34-28-35. She has brown hair and the sexiest blue eyes you've ever seen. The way they sparkle and dance leaves no doubt that she is one hot and impish little lady.

Joyce likes to make her own clothes to ensure that her best assets are always prominently displayed. These include shapely legs, pert breasts and a sweet, tight little ass. Yes, my wife has it all—beauty, body and brains.

We have always had a good sex life, but Joyce always seems to get a little hornier than usual after watching adult videos showing two guys fucking and sucking one woman. One day I decided to treat her to a little threesome of her own. One night, after watching a three-way video and doing our share of fucking and sucking, I told Joyce about my plans for a threesome. At first she was reluctant and declined, but that sweet wet pussy of hers was contradicting her. I kept bringing up the subject until she agreed to give it a try.

Joyce and I made a list of all possible participants and finally selected a friend named Ed. We didn't think Ed would turn us down, because he had been separated from his wife for over five months and we knew he hadn't had any female companionship in a long time. In addition, he had often told me what a lucky prick I was for having such a good-looking woman and he had even complimented Joyce about her fantastic legs and sultry body.

The following weekend Joyce dressed to the nines in an outfit she had created especially for the occasion. She wore a black satin miniskirt and a black scoop-necked blouse that exposed her beautiful creamy white tits each time she leaned forward. Underneath she wore a red bustier with a shelf-style bra cup that let her nipples stick out freely, matching G-string panties, black silk seamed nylons and four-inch heels. She was clearly hot to trot.

We went out to our usual hangout hoping that Ed would show up, and we weren't disappointed. Ed was sitting at the bar hoisting a beer. Joyce and I found a table and I went to the bar to order drinks. I greeted Ed and asked if he cared to join us. He looked over and saw Joyce sitting on a stool with her legs crossed and her skirt hiked up above the tops of her stockings, exposing creamy thighs and red garters.

Without hesitation, Ed came over and sat down in the chair that afforded the best view of Joyce's legs. Joyce rewarded his stares by crossing and uncrossing her beautiful legs. Sometimes she crossed them with deliberate slowness, teasing Ed with quick peeks of her barely covered snatch. We soon saw that Ed was getting pretty excited watching this show, and frankly so were we.

Joyce kept bending forward to sip her drink so that Ed would be able to see her tits and steadily hardening nipples.

Ed didn't miss a thing. His eyes darted back and forth trying to take in all these lovely sights at one time. I thought he was going to get whiplash from turning his head so quickly and so often. I found it all perversely humorous, to say the least.

When Ed finally excused himself to use the men's room, Joyce and I figured that it was time for me to make him our offer, so I followed him into the john.

In the john, I asked Ed what he thought of Joyce's latest outfit. He said, "It's just too fucking hot for words," adding that he wished he could also see beneath the outfit.

"You'll see all you want to see if you come home with us." I said bluntly. He pretended to be angry and said that teasing a horny bastard like him was not funny. I told him that I was not joking and repeated the offer. This time he readily assented. As we made our way back to the table, Joyce saw us coming and flashed a slow, leg-crossing snatch shot, which left Ed with no doubt that we were serious.

When the bar closed, I told Joyce that Ed was going to stop over at our house for a few more cold ones. She said that would be great. I told Ed to come over in half an hour—time enough for me to get home and load the VCR with Joyce's favorite three-some video.

When Ed arrived, the three of us headed for the couch to drink more beer and watch the video. I told Ed to sit next to Joyce so that he would have the best view of the TV. About twenty minutes into the tape, Joyce and I started rubbing each other's thighs. Her hand worked its way toward my stiffening cock as my hands reached up her skirt toward her wet, waiting pussy.

Ed was fidgeting, and we could tell he was getting very excited watching the movie and even more excited watching Joyce and me play with one another. Joyce looked at me lovingly and passionately, her blue eyes sparkling, and gave me a deep soul kiss. My hand went right to her wet snatch and began rubbing her panty-covered clit and cunt. Meanwhile Joyce's left hand found Ed's hard, throbbing cock. I guess she liked what she felt, because she made a noise of surprise and her other hand grabbed my cock.

Ed and I removed Joyce's blouse while she clung to our cocks, which were still trapped in our pants. Ed's mouth found Joyce's left nipple, which was now rock-hard and desperate to be sucked. While nibbling on her other nipple I moved her panties to one side and worked a finger into her juicy, dripping pussy. Joyce leaned against the couch, moaned softly and arched her body upward, forcing my finger deeper into her love-tunnel. She grabbed the backs of our heads and pressed our faces into her heaving tits.

The three of us were definitely ready for action. Ed and I stripped off Joyce's skirt and panties and exposed her glistening pussy lips and pale thighs while she helped both of us out of our pants to get at our cocks. Joyce had a big smile on her face. She knew she was in for some terrific cunt-cramming experiences.

By now I had two fingers up her snatch and Ed was rubbing her hard little clit. My fingers shoved in and out of Joyce in time with Ed's rubbing, and soon Joyce had her first orgasm of the night. She bit her lower lip and moaned and groaned louder than I had ever heard her moan before.

I worked yet another finger into Joyce's eager cunt and replaced Ed's finger on her clit with my tongue. While I was busy working over Joyce's cunt, she leaned over and took Ed's cock into her mouth. The sight of Joyce playing with another man's balls while her head bobbed up and down on his cock was almost too much for me to take. I had to fuck her now. I needed to shove my dick into her up to the balls and coat her inner walls with my jism.

She lay on her stomach on the couch, and soon I was thrusting my meat into Joyce's wet snatch in time with the bobbing motions she was making over Ed's cock. After a few minutes of serious pussy pounding, I shot a load of come into her that I thought would never end. When I pulled out, she focused all her attention on Ed's cock, sucking, rubbing and licking as though possessed by the cocksucking God himself!

I was in the kitchen getting another beer when I heard Joyce cry out, "Oh yes! Oh fuck me, Ed! Fill my cunt with your meat!"

I hurried back to the living room, and the sight that greeted me produced an instant hard-on. Ed had Joyce splayed on the couch with one leg on the floor and the other draped across the back of the couch. Her long legs were spread as wide as possible, giving Ed the room he needed to stuff her box full of his fat, long cock. I could tell he was stretching her cunt like it had never been stretched before.

Ed had pushed his tool into Joyce's snatch inch by inch until he was as far inside her as he could be. I was envious because he was thrusting deeper into Joyce's cunt than I ever could. But I was glad for her sake, and that's what really mattered.

Ed was thrusting into Joyce hard and fast, and she was loving every stroke. He had worked that pussy into a fucking frenzy! Joyce's head rolled from side to side and her hands gripped Ed's ass, pulling him into her as she strained to meet his every stroke.

I laid my cock against Joyce's lips and she sucked it into her mouth. Ed's pussy stimulation was making Joyce suck on my cock like it was the last one she would ever get. Suddenly she released my cock and hollered, "I have to come! Fuck me! Fuck me! Fuck me!"

Ed complied and started pounding that pussy for all he was worth. My mouth and hands found Joyce's tits and I sucked and tweaked her nipples. After three minutes of unbelievable pounding, Joyce screamed, "Oh God, Oh my God!" and had her second intense orgasm. Ed made one last deep thrust into her frothing tunnel and sent his jism deep into Joyce's womb. He ground his pelvis into her clit and sent her over the edge one more time. I put my cock back into Joyce's mouth and she sucked me off again. When I couldn't hold back any longer, I shot a load of come down her throat.

After Joyce had licked my dick clean, I bent over and kissed her passionately. Joyce looked into my eyes and said softly,

"Thank you and don't forget how much I love you." I told her I loved her very much too.

The three of us rested for a while and decided to move to the bedroom. In no time Joyce was hungry for more of Ed's cock and she began to work on sucking him back to hardness. Ed slid underneath her and started to tongue-fuck her love-box. I needed to be involved, so I rolled Joyce onto her side so that I could fuck her from behind while she sucked on Ed's cock.

Ed turned around to face Joyce and they kissed. He played with her nipples with one hand and slowly ground his dick into Joyce's clit with his other hand. I pulled out of Joyce's hot box and she immediately grabbed Ed's hard meat and placed its head on her cunt. As Ed eased into Joyce's well-lubed cunt, I started rubbing my cock up and down her juice-drenched ass-crack.

Joyce lay on her side with one leg up over Ed's body to accommodate Ed's dong. This left her little rosebud of an anus fully exposed and available. Joyce reached behind her and guided my cock to her butthole. She rubbed it up and down her asshole, using the come and pussy juice seeping from her cunt to lube my cock. Finally I was able to ease my cockhead into her back door. She moaned and pulled back to lube it some more. Then she eased it in again. Joyce and I rarely engaged in anal sex, so this was a real treat.

While all this was going on, Ed had pulled his dong out of Joyce's box in order to give us room to maneuver. Joyce was slowly rocking back and forth, working my cock into her tight asshole. The feeling of being balls-deep in such a hot, tight opening was fantastic.

Ed went back to eating Joyce's cunt, and she began thrusting her burning cunt against Ed's probing tongue and then down just as hard onto my rigid dick. In no time Joyce had another orgasm, but I had stopped counting how many she had had.

With my cock still deep in her asshole, I slowly rolled onto my back so that Joyce was lying faceup with her tits and cunt fully available to Ed. I reached around with my right hand and started working on her nipples, and she rolled her head to the side to kiss me passionately once again. Her tongue jabbed in and out of my mouth like a piston as Ed rubbed his cock up and down Joyce's greedy clit.

Desperate to have her cunt full of cock and to come again, Joyce grabbed Ed's meat and guided the head into her sopping snatch. Ed worked slowly, pushing in an inch at a time until he had his whole member inside her hot tunnel up to his balls. I could feel his nuts hitting mine. Joyce was now completely filled in both of her sexholes.

Ed's cock was stretching her snatch even further than before and I could feel his thrusts through the thin membrane that separates box from butt. With Ed's weight on top of us and his cock packing Joyce's box, it was impossible for me to work my cock in and out. But that didn't stop Ed. As he pounded in and out of Joyce's cunt, I could feel every inch of meat sliding across my cock. I guess you could say he was fucking both of us at the same time.

Finally Joyce couldn't take Ed's slow fucking anymore and she strained to shove up and down onto our cocks. Ed took the hint and started pistoning his meat in and out of Joyce with determination. Using hard, full-length strokes, he had himself, Joyce and me ready to come in a matter of minutes. While all three of us grunted and groaned, he gave Joyce three super-hard thrusts against her clit and into her box and sent us all over the edge at the same time. Ed's come oozed out of Joyce's pussy and my jism oozed out of her ass.

Ed and I eventually pulled out of Joyce's limp, sated body. Ed kissed her softly and thanked us both for a wonderful evening.— A.C., *San Francisco, California*

WIFE TRANSFORMED INTO SEXUAL DYNAMO
BY THE GIFT THAT KEEPS ON GIVING

*E*ven though my wife Eva and I have always had an excellent sex life, I recently gave her a book entitled *How to Drive Your Man Wild* as a gift. I had no idea that I was about to create a sexual monster.

A couple of weeks after I gave Eva the book, we were scheduled to attend a formal affair being held in the ballroom of a luxury hotel for some of my business associates. I was facing a full day of meetings, so we decided that Eva would meet me at the party. Late that afternoon, as I was getting ready to leave the office, a courier arrived with an express package.

My curiosity got the better of me and I decided to take a moment to open it. Inside I found an unlabeled video cassette along with a typewritten note. The note said that I should view the enclosed confidential videotape immediately.

I closed and locked my office door before popping the cassette into my VCR. I was stunned to see my wife suddenly appear on-screen, dressed only in white, thigh-high stockings and a translucent white G-string. She smiled mysteriously at the camera and said: "Honey, I love you very much. This is just the beginning of what is going to be one of the wildest nights of your life. Tonight I intend to make as many of your dreams and fantasies come true as I possibly can."

My brain began spinning, trying to imagine what this could mean. We had always been sexually active, but, as in most marriages, there were a few things that seemed destined to remain fantasies forever.

As I pondered this, the scene on the screen abruptly changed from our bedroom to our bathroom. Eva looked lustfully at the camera and said: "You have often asked me to shave my pussy for you so that you can lick and stroke me without pubic hair getting in the way. I am about to grant you that wish."

With that, she slowly pulled down her G-string and sensually massaged shaving gel all over her mound. I could see that she was already beginning to enjoy her performance, because her nipples rose to hard points and she began to emit soft purrs and sighs as she massaged the foam between her open legs.

Finally Eva picked up a razor and began to stroke it over her mound. Using her free hand to hold the skin taut, she carefully shaved each side of her vagina. By this time my hand was rubbing my prick through my pants, which felt like they were going to burst open any minute.

Once Eva completed shaving, she moistened a washcloth and wiped away the foamy residue between her thighs. Before ending the scene she spread her legs for the camera with a smile, allowing me to admire her handiwork. Then she stood and said, "Now for your second wish."

The scene switched back to our bedroom. Eva was lying on her back on our bed wearing only white stockings. Her voice had become huskier. She said: "Thinking of all the things we are going to do later this evening has turned me on so much that I can't wait for tonight's dinner to be over." Then she picked up a bottle of oil and began to lubricate her pussy, holding the lips open so I could see right into her. "I'm ready for you right now," she continued, "but since you can't be here, I'm going to give myself a little orgasm so that I can wait until later."

To my knowledge, Eva had never masturbated in her life and certainly had never done so in front of me, even though I had encouraged her to on many occasions. Sweat was running down my temples and my balls were beginning to ache. I watched helplessly as Eva picked up a large vibrator and began to tease her lower lips with its tip. It wasn't long before she raised her knees and slowly, inch by inch, sank the vibrator into her oiled cunt.

She made a soft humming sound and said, "This is my favorite love-toy because it feels so much like your hard cock. I am imagining that this is you burying yourself in me. It feels best when the base is buzzing right up against my clit, like this." At this point the vibrator nearly disappeared into her cunt.

She continued plunging the vibrator in and out of her pussy. After a few minutes I could see her juices were creating a noticeable wet spot on our bedspread. By this time I had undone my pants and was matching her stroke for stroke. All of a sudden she stopped and said, "I know you've got that big cock of yours in your hand by now, but you've got to put it away this instant. First, because you are going to be late for the party, and second because you have to save all that come for me later tonight."

Her reasoning seemed sound, so I stopped stroking myself immediately and put my penis away. Meanwhile Eva had rolled onto her side and pulled one knee up to her tits, giving me a full view of her ass and of the vibrator still buried in her clean-shaven cunt.

She reached back, began to apply lubricant to her asshole and said: "I want you to save your biggest orgasm for something else you have desired for a long time. Tonight I want your cock up my ass and I want you to come as hard as you have ever come in your life." It took some considerable restraint on my part to keep from creaming my shorts right there and then.

Eva was merciless. Knowing full well the effect she was having on me, she grabbed another vibrator and gently worked it into her ass as I watched. In between grunts and moans she managed to say, "I'm getting my asshole all stretched out so you can fuck it later."

Those were the last intelligible words on the video. As I watched, my beautiful wife worked the vibrators in front and back until she began to shake uncontrollably in the grips of a massive orgasm. My eyes were riveted to the screen. I sat open-mouthed as she finally pulled the vibrators out of her ass and pussy. Still teasing, she licked the vibrators clean. Just before the screen went blank she looked up at the camera and said, "I need to see you very soon. I'm sure you know why."

I must have broken a dozen traffic laws on the way to the hotel to meet Eva. In spite of my speeding, Eva was already in the reception area having a glass of wine with two of my associates and their wives when I arrived. She was wearing a cream-colored cocktail dress with the same white stockings that she'd worn in the video. I knew that the dress was probably the only thing between me and that freshly shaved pussy of hers. I was soon forced to keep my hands in my pockets to hide my condition.

Eva gave me an innocent smile as I kissed her hello and greeted our friends. The next two and a half hours were an exercise in teasing. My wife made it a point to quietly inform me that she had forgotten to put the G-string back on after making the video, so she was completely naked under her dress. She also took every opportunity to grab my crotch or ass to ensure that I didn't forget what was in store for me later. As if I could forget!

Eva told me she had reserved a room at the hotel so that we would be free to get right at it as soon as dessert was over. "This seems to be one of those nights we should skip dessert," I replied.

It seemed as if the affair would never end. During the sit-down dinner I couldn't keep my mind off what was to happen later. Afterward, as everyone was preparing to leave, Eva came up to me with a lascivious grin on her face and said: "Tonight I will grant you three wishes. Shouldn't we go upstairs so we can begin?" We said some very brief good-byes and quickly made our way to the elevators. As luck would have it, we managed to be alone in one on the way up to our room.

Eva coyly lifted her dress, showing me her moistness. She slipped a finger into her crease, raised it to my lips and said, "You can have a little sample now and you can look at me all you want, but don't touch me until I say so. That is the only rule for the next couple of hours. Can you live with that?" I'm not sure what I mumbled, but I must have agreed to abide by her rules.

When we arrived in our room, it was obvious that Eva had found time to make preparations for the evening. The bedcover and blanket had been removed from the large, four-poster bed and a long red ribbon had been tied to each bedpost. Eva quickly took control of the situation and instructed me to strip off all my clothes and lie completely still on the bed. By this point my rod was poking me in the navel.

Eva slowly removed her dress and shoes, leaving only the white stockings, and approached the bed. I soon found out that she had brought along our entire love kit, including all our favorite love-toys and lotions. Eva slowly oiled her thighs and pussy, then gently sat astride my immobile body, kissing me and lightly stroking my sides. She rubbed oil on herself and then used her body to transfer the oil to mine. Soon we were both covered with lotion. Eva continued to massage my legs and chest with her cunt.

Finally Eva seemed satisfied with her work. She turned around and started licking my cock and balls, keeping her ass and pussy just far enough away that I couldn't reach them with my tongue. She took my prick in her mouth and ran her tongue around the head while her hand rubbed the vein underneath. As my breathing became faster and heavier, Eva slipped her other hand around my leg and began to poke gently at my asshole. A few seconds later I gasped, "Please make me come."

Eva just smiled and said, "Not just yet. Remember what I said in the video? I've got some very special plans for the evening. I need you to be as hard as you can be so that I can feel that cock of yours all the way up my ass. Okay?" Then she added, "I think I should slow things down a bit so that I can have some time to get even hornier."

Eva climbed off the bed and stepped into the bathroom. She was only gone a couple of minutes, but it seemed like an eternity. When she returned she said: "Now that your hard-on has gone down a little, I think I'd better do something to help you control the urge to come whenever I get near your cock." She came over, kissed me fiercely and grabbed my semi-rigid pole. Before I knew what was happening, she rolled a black cock ring down to the base of my rod.

Eva used her mouth and hands to tease my cock back to its rock-hard state and said: "This ring will keep you as hard as nails.

It won't stop you from coming if you absolutely have to, but it will restrict your ability to come until you are just about ready to explode. It should help you last until I am ready for you. While I am bringing myself up to your level, would you like to see a re-play of the video I made for you this afternoon?"

I didn't know how to answer her question, so I just lay there mutely. What I really wanted to say was that she should finish me off before something important burst. But it was obvious that Eva had choreographed every movement in her scenario. As I tried to think of something to say to convince her to give me some relief, she slipped a cassette into the VCR and turned on the television.

As the same video I had seen that afternoon in my office began to play, Eva pulled a chair up beside the bed facing me. When her shaving scene began she asked, "Does my bare cunt meet your expectations?"

"You have always had the best-looking pussy I've ever seen," I answered. "I wanted you to shave it so I could lick and caress it even more."

With a mischievous grin Eva climbed onto the bed and strad-dled my face. "You can have a little sample right now," she said, and lowered her wet crotch to my hungry mouth.

Hoping to regain some control over the situation, I very lightly licked the crease between her thigh and labia. Then, moving very slowly, I ran the tip of my tongue up the entire length of her pussy.

"You just don't understand," she moaned. "The faster you help me get as hot as you are, the sooner it will be time for you to come."

I immediately thrust my tongue into her as far as I could. She lowered her body even more to give me better access to the depths of her love-nest. As my tongue began to spread her juices around, I moved up to work on her clit, knowing that it was the best button to push if I wanted to speed things up and get relief. After a few minutes of this, Eva's breathing quickened. Suddenly she lifted herself up and moved back to the chair. The scene on the video was just changing from her shaving to her vibrator play. Once again I thought about how Eva had planned every second of this, and how she seemed to enjoy being in control.

Glancing at the television screen, Eva said, "That gets me very excited. Should I just let you focus on the video or should I give you a choice between it and some live action?" Then she picked up a cock-shaped vibrator and began running it up and down her sopping gash.

I don't know if it was the cock ring or the video or the live show on the chair next to me, but my dick was at full attention—veins bulging as if they were going to burst any second. It was truly amazing. It had been at least fifteen minutes since I had been touched, yet I was still as hard as ever. Eva was staring at my pole and working the vibrator between the folds of her pussy. From the look on her face, it was obvious that her self-control was slipping away. Her sounds of pleasure, both live and taped, filled the room. "I'm just about ready to fuck you now," she informed me as she reached into her bag. I had never seen my wife so immersed in giving herself pleasure. When her hand emerged from the bag, she held a tube of K-Y jelly. With one hand on the vibrator in her pussy, she took a glob of the ointment and began to dab it around her asshole. With her legs over the arms of the chair and her buns at the very edge of the seat, I had a full view of Eva's enticing preparations.

"Is this where you want to be?" she asked as she darted the tip of her finger into her ass.

A hoarse "Uh-huh" was all I could manage. After a couple more applications of K-Y jelly, Eva wormed a second finger into her asshole. I watched transfixed, longing to replace those fingers with my dick.

Eva pulled the vibrator from her pussy and said, "We'll have to see if I am open wide enough to fuck you." Then she rubbed some of the lubricant on the vibrator and placed the tip of the cock-shaped dong at her anal opening. I saw her muscles relax as she slowly worked the head in. She sighed loudly as the vibrator slid in another inch. As I watched, the skin around the intruding tool got taut. With a bit of twisting, she slid the thing in another inch before pulling it out entirely.

Without a word, Eva stood and mounted me again. After a lingering kiss, she reached back, grasped my cock and said, "Are you ready for your third wish to be granted?"

I was so filled with desire and lust that I couldn't manage a response. Kissing me again, she positioned her pussy over my engorged cock and guided it into her. As she slowly rocked up and down I could feel my balls tightening with every stroke. The smile on her face was diabolical. She knew that I was ready to beg for any kind of release. She also knew that I had fantasized for twelve years about this sex act, which neither of us had ever experienced. I wanted to bury my cock inside Eva's virgin ass.

She lifted herself off my throbbing prick, leaving her juices dripping all over me. I could tell from her state of arousal that she was nearly as close to climax as I was. Reaching behind her and holding my cock like a handle, she repeated the rotating motion she had used to insert the vibrator up her ass. I felt her sphincter open to engulf the head of my cock, and she released her grip and began to push her body backward.

I think it took at least ten minutes as she rocked and moved my dick deeper into her anal canal millimeter by millimeter. I could feel the tightness of her ass gripping me with each stroke. Once I was in her most of the way, she sat up and totally impaled herself on my cock. Then she slowly began moving her hips, fucking me. Actually it was more like milking me with her ass. The tightness around my cock was incredible, and not just at her opening. My entire shaft felt like it was being massaged by hundreds of internal muscles.

Instinctively she knew that I couldn't hold back long enough for her to reach her climax without some help, so she continued rocking, put her hand on her clit and started rubbing hard and fast. Eva was nearly incoherent. She pushed against my cock with wild abandon as she neared her peak. When the contractions that signal the onset of orgasm began, it seemed like every muscle in my body was vibrating. As she convulsed, I could feel my body tensing, building up the pressure necessary to shoot my come up the tight canal gripping my cock. When I exploded inside her, it felt like my lower abdomen and groin had been turned inside out.

For quite a while afterward, neither of us could move at all. As our breathing slowly returned to normal, we held each other, kissed and stroked each other gently. Eventually Eva let my cock slip out of her backside and I felt some of the fluid I had shot into her drip back onto my flaccid cock.

As I lay under my lover with a contented smile on my face, I realized that she had given me a part of herself and an experience that would never be forgotten. After resting, we got up and showered together. Then we celebrated our lovemaking with a bottle of fine wine. It wasn't long before we were kissing and stroking each other with renewed energy. Finally I was able to fully savor her newly shaved pussy and enjoy the memory of having all of my fantasy wishes come true in a single night.—B.D., St. Paul, Minnesota

Girls & Girls

AN OVERNIGHT CONVENTION, A SEXY ROOMMATE, A FIRST GIRL-GIRL ENCOUNTER

I recently attended an out-of-town convention. My assigned roommate turned out to be a very pretty and shapely twenty-two-year-old brunette from another city. I am an eighteen-year-old blonde female. This was my first convention.

I didn't get to talk to my roommate, whose name is Terry, until after the dinner and the party. I couldn't help noticing the way she kept staring at me all night at the party. I was wearing a white miniskirt, a tight, low-cut blouse and high heels. Terry wore a skintight black miniskirt, black stockings and high heels.

When I returned to the room, Terry was removing her heels and rubbing her feet. Her dress was hiked way up her thighs. She looked really hot.

She greeted me with a big smile and said that I really looked great in my new dress. I watched as she pulled her black skirt up and slowly peeled her black stockings off. She wore no panties, so I had a great view of her pussy. It looked like she had shaved most of her pubic hair away.

She caught me looking at her and smiled. Then she stood up and pulled her dress off. She was now completely naked. Her tits were nice and round, and they stood out boldly from her body with no hint of sag. Her nipples were hard and brown. She sat down on the bed, ready to watch me undress.

I had never been with another woman before, so I was somewhat amazed at how wet my pussy was from the sight of her lovely nakedness. Part of me wanted to go into the bathroom to undress, but the alcohol I had consumed at the party and the wetness between my legs made me feel randy. I turned away from her and slipped out of my dress. I then turned around to face her, wearing only a white bra, panties and high heels. I then reached behind, unsnapped my bra and peeled it off my erect nipples. My breasts are small, but firm and pointed. Terry was staring right at them.

She drew her knees up to her breasts and smiled, completely exposing her glistening slit. I slipped my thumbs under the elastic band of my panties and pulled them down, showing her my pussy with its blonde hair and protruding pink lips. After drinking in my beauty, she looked into my eyes, smiled and licked her lips.

"Wanna take a shower with me, baby?" she asked, standing up from the bed. She took my hand without waiting for a reply and led me into the bathroom. We stepped into the stall and she turned on the water, adjusting it so that it was nice and hot. She grabbed the bar of soap and told me to turn around so that my back was facing her. I closed my eyes and enjoyed the feeling of her soaped hands gliding up and down my back, paying extra attention to my small, tight ass. Then she knelt down and ran her hands up and down my legs and thighs, teasing me by lightly brushing against my pussy lips.

She told me to turn around so that I was facing her. She started to lather my breasts and nipples. I was getting dizzy and horny. Her hands were on my belly now. Soon she was working on my pussy, soaping my pubic hair. She looked me right in the eye and ran two fingers up and down my slit, casually rubbing my clit. I closed my eyes while feeling her arms reaching around me. She pried my lips open with her pointed tongue, and we started French-kissing. Then she inserted two fingers inside my pussy and stroked my clit with the ball of her thumb. I gasped and came, holding tightly on to her to keep my balance.

She smiled and handed me the soap. "Your turn, baby," she said with a smile. I soaped up her tits and her nipples in the same manner in which she had done mine. I reached down below her belly and rubbed her pussy. Hers was the first pussy I had ever touched.

"Let's go lay on the bed," she said.

She toweled me dry, then dried herself. "Have you ever licked a girl's pussy before?" she asked. I told her I never had. "You'll like it, baby. Come lay down with me," she said.

We went into the bedroom. I lay down beside her on the bed. She pressed her lips firmly against mine, sliding her tongue into my mouth. Then she broke the kiss and held my head with both of her hands. "Make me come with your mouth," she said, guiding my lips down to her pussy. She spread her legs wide and used two fingers from each hand to hold her pussy lips open, exposing herself completely to me. "Just lick up and down, from my hole to my clit. Then stick your tongue inside and twist it around and fuck me with it. When I'm ready to come, I'll guide you up to my clit. I want you to suck it into your mouth and lick it until I scream."

I closed my eyes and had my very first taste of pussy. It tasted slightly salty and smelled soapy and clean. I licked her up and down and all over. "Fuck me with your tongue," she moaned. I stuck it inside her and pushed it in and out, swirling it all around. I did this over and over, until she guided me to her clit. I did just what she had said, sucking and flicking her clit until she moaned louder and louder and finally creamed in my mouth.

She pulled me up and kissed me, licking my lips and neck. Then she sucked my tits. I was gasping with pleasure as she spread my legs open and looked right at my pussy. "Can I shave you?" she asked.

Drunk with passion, I whispered a throaty "Yeah."

She quickly returned with some shaving cream and a razor. She handed me the cream, telling me to rub it onto my pussy and show her how I make myself come. She watched me masturbate with the cream for a minute or so, and then she carefully shaved my pussy so that it was completely bald. After she finished, she pressed a hot, wet towel against my pussy.

"Make yourself come," she whispered. I slowly moved my hand between my legs and massaged my clit, fingering my pussy as she stared into my eyes. I arched my back and thrust my nipples up into the air. She gently slid her finger inside me. I couldn't believe what she was doing could possibly feel so good, and I was completely out of control.

She started fucking me with her finger. Then she bent down and licked my cunt as I screamed and went into multiple orgasms. I couldn't stop coming. I broke into tears as she continued sliding her finger in and out of me. I almost passed out. When I finally regained my senses, she was kissing my face and saying that I was a wonderful lover.

When I woke up the next morning, she had already packed and left. I couldn't find my panties. I guess she took them for a souvenir.—J.K., New York, New York

LOOKING FOR SOME ACTION, LAST CALL WAS JUST THE CALL SHE NEEDED

I am a twenty-seven-year-old brunette with a 38C-24-34 figure. I work for a computer company, and my work takes me on the road much of the time. I have no time for a serious relationship. I find myself alone most nights, and I get very horny sometimes. Masturbation is okay, but sometimes you need more than that.

I was at a computer show. It was my last night in town, and I decided that I was going to get laid. I have a short leather skirt that I've only worn twice. It makes me look like a walking fuck-machine. That night I wanted to be one. Along with the miniskirt I wore fishnet hose, high heels and a halter top that lifted my tits up and made them look huge.

I went to a club, confident that my outfit would help serve my purpose. Before I even reached the bar, two guys asked me to dance. Neither was attractive to me, so I turned both of them down.

I danced all night with a lot of different men. It was really a turn-on to have so many men coming on to me. I finally found the man I was looking for. He was tall and well-built, with a gorgeous face. I caught him undressing me with his eyes. I turned slowly on my stool and spread my legs. His eyes moved down to my trimmed pussy. I wasn't wearing underwear, and he nearly dropped his drink when he found this out. He worked his way over to me.

The ensuing conversation seemed to be based solely on how much of a bitch his wife was, and how he would love to leave her if only he had the chance. I could not think of a bigger turn-off.

So there it was: last call and no man worth my time. On my way out of the place I ran into a friend. She wanted to get one more drink before the bar closed. I told her I had some champagne back in my room if she was interested.

We ended up getting drunk. We were sitting on the bed, discussing the pressures of our jobs.

"Let's get comfortable and I'll show you what I do to relax after a long day," she said.

I pulled out a silk nightshirt for her and she started to change. As she got undressed, I couldn't help but be a little jealous of her body. She had big, firm tits with dark nipples. Her long blonde hair ran down almost to her firm, tan ass. She had a G-string tan line.

"I have never been able to wear a G-string in public," I said.

"You should!" she told me. "I love to tease men on the beach."

She turned and lowered her shirt. I stole a glimpse of her blonde pussy. It was nicely trimmed. She got on the bed and took my foot in her hand. "Nothing is better than a good foot rub at the end of the day," she said.

She's right. It felt great. I lay back and closed my eyes. After a minute she lowered my foot down between her legs. It caught me totally off guard. I never thought she was going to do anything like that. I stayed quiet and still, not sure how to handle what was happening. Then I felt the heat of her pussy on my foot. God! I've never gotten turned on so fast in my life. She moved my foot slowly against the soft hair around her pussy. Her juices were running down her leg.

I knew what she was going to do next. There was no way I would stop what was going to happen. As her tongue touched my clit, chills ran through my whole body. My hot juices flowed. She put her finger inside my pussy and sucked my clit. Men have licked my clit before, but I never got off from someone just sucking it. I came so fast and so hard.

I sat up, pulled off my shirt and then pulled off hers. Before I could do anything, she began licking my nipples. I pushed her back onto the bed and kissed her on the mouth and down her neck. I sucked her firm tits, and I could feel her nipples get hard under my tongue. I moved down to her pussy. Her hair was much softer than mine. Until then, I had never tasted the sweet juice of a pussy. It was fantastic. It was so easy to bring her to orgasm. She came fast and got much wetter than I usually do.

We played all night and tried everything I had never fantasized about doing with another woman. She made me feel so comfortable about it all.

My friend and I met at a show two weeks ago. What do you think we did? I'm at home now, but let's just say I can't wait until next month's show.—A.T., *Fort Worth, Texas*

WHEN LESBIAN LOVERS GET IT ON, THEY FLOOD EACH OTHER'S SENSES

My lady is twenty-one, a gorgeous, hazel-eyed brunette. I am twenty-three, a Dutch, blue-eyed blonde. Our night of pleasure began when she said she had a surprise for me and that I should take a shower and wait for her in bed. I did as she asked without hesitation, but not before opening a bottle of wine and smoking a joint. Then I took a quick shower and eagerly awaited her in bed. I was feeling very love-crazed by this time.

My heart skipped a beat when she appeared in the doorway wearing a short, black lacy negligee. I must add that negligees are a super turn-on for me. She lay down on top of me. Our tongues touched and we melted into each other's mouth. I explored every inch of lace with my hands, occasionally stopping to feel her hard nipples and firm breasts straining through the fabric. We were both moaning with pleasure.

Her delightful tongue danced down my neck and stopped at my tits to languish on my nipples for a while. I moved my hand from her ass to the crotch of her panties, which by this time were soaked with honey. I exclaimed my delight and rolled her over onto her back.

We kissed for what seemed an eternity, slowly entwining our tongues. I lay on top of her between her luscious legs. My tongue drifted across her neck and caressed her ears. I moved down to her breasts and sucked them through the lace, pulling at her engorged nipples with my lips. Our hips were moving in rhythm as we rubbed our soaking mounds together. I supported myself on my toes and elbows, moving back and forth, matching her thrusts as we engaged in a whirlpool kiss. It was her night, so I concentrated on her total pleasure.

In a short time she was writhing in delight. We were moaning and whispering breathlessly in each other's ear. Her body tensed as she arched her back and thrust her hips upward. I kept moving over her love-button as she climaxed. Once was not enough, however, because she was soon holding my hips and guiding me back and forth. We were drenched in sweat and love juice when she came again, more powerfully than the first time. I clung to her as if I were riding a bucking bronco. We collapsed into each other's arms. We rested and had some more wine.

Once we had rested enough, I said I wanted to get a closer look at her new panties. I moved down to her triangle and found it to be entirely drenched. I loved it! I began to eat her through the sheer fabric, pushing my tongue as far as I could into her steaming hole, my nose rubbing her clitoris. I hummed happily as she told me how good it felt. No longer wanting the restriction, I pulled her panties off with my teeth. After running my tongue along her thigh, I was soon nibbling on her box. After teasing her, I drove my tongue in as far as I could. At the same time my upper lip massaged her clit. She reached down, grabbed my hand and brought it to her lips. As she sucked on my finger, I did the same to her swollen knob. I knew she was near another orgasm by the way her body jerked and from the words she gasped. She felt and tasted so damn good. I didn't want it to end, so I withdrew.

I gently blew my hot breath over her box. I slowly moved up her body until my tits were over her mouth. She raised her head and eagerly devoured one of my breasts. She massaged the other. While keeping a mouthful, she reached down to my dripping box. I wasted no time in straddling her face. Her hot tongue darted in and out of my hole and dashed up to my clit. I was in heaven. It felt so good. I moved my hips over her face so her tongue could go deeper, and soon I was having one hell of a climax. We held each other tightly while we regained our senses and landed back on Earth.

I'm not one to leave a project incomplete. I told her I wanted to finish what I had started. She agreed one hundred percent. Since she had surprised me with her negligee, I thought it only right to do what turned her on.

I started to kiss her all over, sucking here and there, until she could take it no more and begged for relief. Wanting some relief myself, I got out one of our toys, a double-headed dildo. I was well-lubricated, so I was able to easily slip one end inside me. Then I proceeded to enter my moaning lover with the other end. She gasped as the first couple of inches slowly penetrated her, and then she relaxed and took the rest with ease. We moved nice and slow at first, letting our senses run wild. Then our pace quickened, and I could hear the sounds of her orgasm as the toy moved in and out of our tunnels of love. With both of us on the verge of climaxing, we thrust deeper and ground our pelvises together. I held on to her ass as she sucked my tongue deep into her mouth, and we exploded together in ecstasy. I lay on top of her as we caught our breath. We held one another, shaking, and within a short while fell asleep in each other's arms.—*Name and address withheld*

THIS SERGEANT REALLY GETS INTO HER PRIVATES

I'm a twenty-six-year-old female and a military instructor in Utah. I'm considered attractive by my peers, and I work out at the gym every day to stay in shape. One of my most memorable experiences was with one of my female trainees. I don't consider myself a lesbian, but I do enjoy a sweet pussy time and again.

One day when I was sitting in my office, one of the trainees came to me with a problem. She had been crying, and told me she had gotten a letter from her boyfriend telling her they were through. We talked for about an hour, and while we were talking, I couldn't help noticing that she had a very lovely figure. Although she was no beauty queen, she was very cute. I consoled her and told her to let me know if she needed anything.

As the days went by, she seemed to become attached to me and was always offering to help me or ask a question. I myself was starting to get hot for this little lady. I would find any excuse to go into the dorm while they were in the showers just to get a look at her lovely body.

One night, on about the twentieth day of training, I was in the office rather late doing some paperwork, and decided to stay for the night. I have a bed in my office, so it was no problem.

I locked the doors and started to get ready for bed. I always sleep nude. When I got into bed, I started stroking my pussy, thinking of my trainee. I closed my eyes and started to stroke my skin and rub the insides of my thighs with my fingers, imagining they were her soft lips. As I worked on my painfully hard nipples,

I worked my other hand feverishly over my cunt lips and clit. I keep a large rubber dildo by my bed at home, and was wishing I had it then. Suddenly there was a knock at the door. At first it startled me. I was so deep into what I was doing, I must have made more noise than I thought.

I asked who it was, and it turned out to be my trainee. She was pulling dorm guard and asked if I was all right. I got up, put my pants on, and opened the door. She obviously must have known I was terribly aroused, as my nipples were still very stiff. She asked if she could come in, and I opened the door.

Without a word she started to kiss my nipples, undoing my pants at the same time. Her hot little mouth felt so good on my aching nipples. She sat me down on the bunk, put my legs over her shoulders and immediately dove into my pussy, sucking like crazy, nibbling and rubbing her face all over my soaking-wet pussy lips. I thrust my hips at her face as she made me come.

She kissed me very deeply, our tongues battling. Then she got up and quietly left.

The next day she didn't say a word about what had happened between us. I just got a cute smile from her when no one was watching.

I couldn't stand it. I had to have her. The trainees were due for a town pass the last Saturday they were there. I discreetly told her to plan on coming to my house. I got soaking wet just thinking about it.

The day finally came. I had a friend of mine pick her up and bring her to my house. We sat around the pool for a while and did some swimming and sunbathing. I couldn't keep my eyes off of her. We went in for lunch, and after we ate I just couldn't control my lust any longer. I pulled her to me and gave her a deep, hot kiss. She readily embraced me and returned my passionate kiss.

In no time we were totally nude and on my king-size water bed. I laid her down and told her to just lie back and enjoy. I kissed every inch of her body from head to toe. She hadn't had any sex for a long time, except masturbating, as I found out later;

she was so hot she couldn't keep still. I sucked her nipples into my mouth. God, they were so large. This drove her wild. While still sucking her nipples, I used my right hand to work on her pussy lips. I would lightly rub her clit with the tip of my finger, then plunge my finger deep into her steaming hole. Then I'd use two fingers, working them in and out and twisting them while I used the knuckle of my index finger to put pressure on her clit. Her hips were swaying out of control as I sucked her nipples one at a time.

I turned her over and got my dildo out of my nightstand. It's twelve inches long and plenty fat. I slowly filled her pussy with it. She raised her hips up off the bed and begged me to fuck her harder. I started slowly and gradually building up speed, shoving the rubber cock in and out of her swollen pussy. She was bucking wildly. I wanted to taste her come, so I withdrew the dildo and sucked feverishly on her swollen clit. Her juice tasted sweeter than I had imagined. I couldn't get enough.

Then it was my turn to feel the dildo. She had me get on my knees and proceeded to fuck me doggie-style. The pleasure was incredible. My breath came in digging pants, and my stomach muscles grew hot and started trembling as she tirelessly thrusted the dildo in and out of my hot, clutching hole. I was quickly overcome by a strong orgasm that left me completely breathless.

We spent the rest of the afternoon in bed, sucking and fucking like there was no tomorrow. It was one of the best sessions I've ever had.

She calls me from her new base from time to time. I told my boyfriend about the experience. He got so worked up, we ended up in bed, enjoying one hell of a terrific fuck session. We're going to call her to see if we can get together for a threesome. We can hardly wait.—*Name and address withheld*

FROM THE BIBLE BELT TO BLOW JOBS:
A YOUNG COED LEARNS THE TRICKS

Over the past ten years I've come a long way. I went from being a sweet, innocent, extremely naive eighteen-year-old from the Bible Belt to, with the possible exception of Paula, the best cocksucker and blow job artist to be found.

I left home when I was eighteen to attend college in southern California. My parents were very strict. My father is a Baptist minister and my mother teaches Sunday school and leads the church choir. They only agreed to my going to school there if I stayed with Paula, who was an old friend of theirs and who lived within a few blocks of the college. Paula is only ten years older than I, but had a master's degree in library science, with a minor in economics. Mom and Dad approved of her highly and felt that she would be a fit guardian for their sweet little virgin daughter.

I arrived at Paula's house in June, two and a half months before my freshman classes were to begin. She was very sweet and nice to me. She didn't look at all like the photographs we had of her back home. Paula was a foxy woman. After she taught me how to fix myself up a bit, we looked so much alike that men often thought we were sisters.

Paula lived in a nice house in a quiet suburban neighborhood and drove a fire-engine-red Corvette. When I asked her how she could afford all of these nice things living by herself, she just smiled and didn't say much. All she would say was that she was in the entertainment industry. She didn't bother to elaborate. She was somewhat mysterious about her work and the odd hours she kept.

It all started about three weeks after I moved in. Paula had gone out dressed to kill, carrying her purple gym bag, as she always did. Alone in the house, I was in her bedroom looking through her drawers for a pair of panty hose when I found a ten-inch vibrator underneath some of her black lace panties. I couldn't believe what I found. I'd heard about dildos and vibrators from some of the girls back home, but I'd never actually seen one before, let alone used one. As I switched it on, its vibrations sent a shiver through me and gave me a knot in my stomach. Not expecting Paula to come home for a few hours, I let curiosity and temptation get the best of me. I was soon almost hypnotized by the rhythmic vibrations of my new find.

Holding the vibrator to my breasts, I could feel my nipples getting harder and my crotch and panties getting wetter and wetter. This was all so new to me. It felt so good that I just couldn't help exploring my entire body with it.

Well, I can tell you it didn't take long for me to strip naked and fall back on Paula's big brass bed with my new toy. I even tilted her big mirror in such a way that I could watch myself.

After teasing myself with it, I placed the tip of the vibrator into my moist, steaming crack and pushed it gently in. As I watched it slowly slide into me, I could feel my vaginal muscles tighten around it. I had been masturbating with my finger for years already, but I'd never felt anything like this before. With both hands working that vibrator in and out of my hot little cunt, I was soon beside myself in ecstasy. That afternoon I had one loud, thundering orgasm after the other.

It was great! I felt so deliciously wicked and nasty watching myself masturbate in that big mirror. I was like an addict who couldn't stop.

I must have been at it for quite some time. I was so absorbed with ramming that vibrator in and out of my tunnel of love and moaning like an animal that I didn't hear Paula come into the house. You can just imagine my embarrassment when I looked up and saw her leaning in the doorway, staring at me with a rather wry grin on her face. (She later told me that she had been standing there enjoying my "performance" for about ten minutes.) Before I could open my mouth to say anything to her, I was seized by another mind-blowing orgasm.

I thought I was going to just die, but all Paula said to me was, "When you're finished, come downstairs and we'll have dinner. I brought home Chinese food." She didn't say anything about what she had caught me doing, but carried on as usual—except that every time she looked at me she had that same smile on her face. We made an early night of it, and all she said to me before turning in was, "Sweet dreams, baby." I went to bed that night red with embarrassment, but drifted off to sleep rubbing and fingering my cunt, thinking about the next time I could get that vibrator up my yearning snatch.

I was out of the house for much of the next afternoon, still feeling quite embarrassed. When I returned home around six that night, I saw Paula's car in the driveway and went straight to my room. As I entered the doorway I was surprised to find a brightly wrapped package on my bed. Attached to the package was a note that read: "Since you seemed to enjoy mine so much, I thought it was time you had one of your own, baby. With love, Paula." I ripped the package open to find a beautiful ten-inch vibrating dildo.

I rushed downstairs to find Paula waiting for me in the living room. She was standing there, feet apart, hands on hips, wearing a short purple silk robe that barely covered her shapely ass and proud, jutting thirty-eight-inch breasts. She had that familiar coy, seductive smile on her face. She stood before me—wanton, raw sex personified. Rushing up to her, we embraced. I knew this was going to be quite a night, one that I'd never forget and that would change me forever.

After our touching embrace, Paula went to the kitchen and returned with a silver tray of shucked and iced oysters on the half-shell, two chilled glasses and a bottle of wine. Next, she dimmed the lights, lit some candles and put a tape on the stereo. I was surprised to hear the erotic sounds of heavy fucking and sucking rather than music.

For the next half hour I sat on the sofa opposite Paula as she made an erotic show of eating those oysters. Occasionally, between slurping oysters and sipping wine, she would slip her hand down to finger her twat, then slowly suck the pussy juice from her fingers. After some more of this, she stood up and said, "It's time we expanded your horizons, sweet baby."

She took me by the hand and led me downstairs into her finished basement. The lights were dimmed real low. There was a lamp directly over the pool table, which bathed it in a warm, pinkish glow. The pool table was covered with an orchid-color satin quilt, and Paula had about a dozen of her favorite vibrators and dildos lined up along the edge of it, within easy reach. She placed me in a big leather easy chair. She put on a tape of rock music with a slow, heavy beat and a lot of sax. She lit some incense and said, "You wanted to know what I do in the entertainment industry. Well, Paula's gonna entertain you."

I was so excited. Paula walked around behind the pool table and stood with her back to me. She shot me a sultry "fuck me" smile over her shoulder as she deftly slipped off her robe, letting it fall to the floor around her ankles. She mounted the table in one swift, catlike motion. There she was, kneeling in front of me, resting on her knees, legs bent under and thighs spread wide. Her thatch of brown pubic hair was neatly trimmed into the shape of a heart. Paula reached back, without looking, and selected a fourteen-inch vibrator that not only moved in and out like a piston, but also made small, circular motions while it hummed and vibrated.

She moaned softly as she worked the vibrator over her gorgeous, tan body, paying special attention to her jutting boobs. Her ruby-red areolae were as big as half-dollars, and her nipples stuck out hard as rocks. She held each breast to her mouth, licking and sucking her nipples, leaving them shiny with saliva.

Turning her attention to her steaming-hot crack, she ran that pulsating dildo up and down her cunt lips and clit, moaning louder all the time. Then she brought the dildo, now gleaming with her cunt juice, up to her hungry mouth and licked and sucked it from its bulbous head down to the base. Still kneeling in front of me, her twat and thighs glistening from the flow of her pussy juice, she set the vibrator on full speed and slowly guided its massive cockhead into her cunt, taking all fourteen inches of it.

Then she slowly pulled it almost all the way out. Using both hands, she rammed that big fucker in and out.

Paula left that massive vibrator pulsating and churning deep inside her cunt, using her well-conditioned vaginal muscles to hold it in. Next she spun around quickly onto her knees and elbows, thrusting her beautiful ass toward the ceiling. She began playing with her clit while the dildo was humming away inside her. Within seconds, Paula's entire body was shuddering in a violent orgasm that brought tears to her eyes. It was incredible watching her wailing out loud like a wild animal, hips and ass undulating in rhythm to the music as she fucked herself.

Paula had all the practiced movements of a real pro. I couldn't believe it. Without missing a beat she spun around again, kneeling, thighs spread wide. She then leaned way back and, again without looking, put a hand over the far edge of the pool table. When she pulled it back up, she was holding a beautiful, twelve-inch, lifelike rubber cock that was covered in syrup.

Paula shook her head, her beautiful mane of brown hair slapping at her face. There was a look of pure, unadulterated lust in her eyes as she dangled that glistening monster cock over her face. Slowly she lowered it and tickled its head and underside with her darting tongue. Resting on one elbow for support, she raised up slightly, arching her back and neck. She then brought the sticky, dripping dildo to her hot, waiting mouth. Clear syrup, oozing from her glossy wet lips, ran down her chin and cheeks as she slurped and sucked the dildo into her mouth, devouring it deeper and deeper until she had finally deep-throated it all the way to the very base of its rigid shaft, moaning loudly with pure pleasure and delight the whole time.

Completely oblivious to everything else, Paula, thighs splayed wide, slowly pulled the rubber cock from her mouth while stroking the steaming slit of her cunt with her other hand. She withdrew the cock from her pursed lips, leaving only a slender thread of syrup and saliva between the two. Her tongue darted out to lick up the excess around her smiling, wet lips.

The vibrator in Paula's cunt was still driving her wild with lust and, caught up in another approaching orgasm, she began to writhe and squirm. Her hips and ass were rising in response to that incredible onslaught. Now using her hands to pull at her rock-hard nipples, Paula went over the brink. Her cries rising to a near wail, she went off like crazy. Her entire body bucked and jerked wildly as if an electric shock had been applied to her. She was the whole time moaning and crying out. No doubt Paula was savoring every minute of it.

I was really enjoying it too. This was the most fantastic thing I had ever seen. I didn't know it was possible for a woman to give herself so much pleasure and satisfaction. I couldn't take my eyes off her.

The show wasn't over yet. After that last orgasm, Paula didn't miss a beat. Repositioning herself on the pool table, she immediately launched into a routine of hot, nonstop action. Before it was over, Paula had used all seven vibrators and five dildos that she had laid out on the table. Even she lost track of how many orgasms she had had.

When she was through, I glanced at my watch and realized that she had been going at it hot and heavy for over an hour. Paula rolled over to face me, her head propped up on one hand, tousled hair across her face. One leg was bent at the knee, giving me a full view as she gently stroked her hot, juicy crack and massaged the insides of her aching thighs.

I was so excited just from watching her. My own nipples were hard and taut against the material of my blouse, and my crotch and panties were soaked through. When Paula smiled that smile of hers and asked me if I would like to join her "onstage," I didn't hesitate for a second.

Paula was sweet and gentle as she watched me treat myself to the pleasures I had just seen her enjoy. Using my new vibrator, as well as my own fingers, I learned how to bring myself to countless orgasms. It felt so good!

After we both took cool showers, Paula explained to me that

the masturbation show she had performed earlier for me was really a dress rehearsal. She would be doing the same act the following week at a stag party for about fifty guys. She told me that she had been working as an exotic dancer and performing live sex shows onstage at bachelor parties since college. She laughed and said, "In what other line of work can you get a roomful of guys to cream in their jeans over you all at once?"

The next week I lost my virginity to a real cock when Paula brought home one of her special lovers just for that purpose. I was a little scared, but Paula was careful in her selection and did everything she could to make that first time a special one.

He was a very handsome man. He had blond hair and reminded me somewhat of a young Robert Redford. Paula helped me undress and cradled my head in her arms while he went down on me, licking and sucking my clit. Paula kissed me, and I enjoyed having a tongue in my mouth, while, at the same time, another one was penetrating my pussy.

Then Paula had me lie flat on my back. She spread my legs and had him get on top of me. Paula grabbed his thick, meaty cock and started rubbing the fat tip up and down the length of my slit. She made sure my clit received plenty of attention. I closed my eyes and gasped with pleasure, and suddenly he rammed his cock all the way inside me. I saw stars. He started fucking me with long, deep strokes. All the while Paula was nibbling on my lips, gently tweaking my nipples and whispering sweetly into my ear. When he orgasmed, his hot seed trickling inside me brought me over the brink.

During the next four years that I lived with her, we often wound up sharing lovers. Paula taught me as much about sex as anyone ever could.

Mom and Dad were paying for my education at college, but I also worked weekends and summers to help. Little did they know that I was applying my newly learned talents working in nightclubs featuring "all-nude coeds" and doing some performances with Paula. I finally graduated with honors and a degree in physical education. You might say that I also graduated with a degree in general sex, with a concentration in cocksucking. Mom and Dad would just die if they knew the truth.—*Name and address withheld*

HER FIRST TIME WITH A WOMAN WAS
THE TIME OF HER LIFE

Most of us remember our first time, even when other memories become faded and jumbled. For me, my first time with a woman is still extremely vivid.

Her blouse was open and her bare breasts stood straight out, tipped with long, dark nipples. I reached out to touch them and she took a deep breath and closed her eyes. The smooth flesh and hard nipples felt strange to my inexperienced hands, but the excitement of touching her was like electricity.

She reached down and lifted my face to hers, kissing me full on the lips. Her tongue snaked into my mouth and I felt myself answering her probe. A rush of excitement coursed through my body. She urged my head downward until my mouth was even with her breasts. Then she lifted one to my mouth. I closed my lips around the tough, pink knob and began to suckle. I could feel my body beginning to ache, and dampness puddle in my panties.

She moved my mouth to the other breast, and I sucked the nipple into my eager mouth. She moved me gently away from her, unsnapped her shorts and let them slide down her long, long legs. Her thin, white underpants did little to hide her triangle of dark red hair, and she quickly slid them down and away as well.

I stared openmouthed at the dark lips of her vagina. My lover reached for my hand and pressed it against her opening. Her pubic hair felt strange against my palm. The tips of my fingers touched the wet folds of her vaginal lips. "Go on, baby, touch me. Feel me up and down and all around, honey," she cooed. I slid my hand further into the wetness and felt her lips part and close around my fingers.

"I want to show you how to love me," she whispered, and urged my head down until my face was against her vagina. Her scent rose in waves and soon became an aphrodisiac. "Use your tongue, darling," she purred. "Stick out your tongue and taste me deep inside." She guided me to the places she wanted touched. The salty taste of her excited me as much as the feel of her slippery lips.

She held me against her opening, then encouraged me to slide up until my tongue was pressing hard against her clitoris. "Yes! Yes! There! Yes! Lick me there! Suck my clit into your mouth. Oh! Yes, yessss!" she screamed.

Her body began to undulate beneath me, but she held my face to her body and the pressure continued to mount inside her. She kept moaning and writhing. Finally she pressed hard against my mouth one last time and then relaxed. "Oh, my sweet!" she said between labored breaths, "That was good, so good. Let me taste your lips."

My mouth was wet, covered with the smell and taste of her. She bent forward and kissed me. She reached down, tugged my T-shirt over my head and tossed it aside. Her soft hands began roaming over my skinny chest. She started kissing my body, down my neck and chest until she sucked one nipple into her mouth. I closed my eyes and tensed at the powerful and wonderful feelings rushing through me.

Her hand moved gently down my stomach, across my shorts, and to my inner thighs. She slid her long, elegant fingers beneath the elastic waistband and pulled my shorts and underpants down my legs. Her hand moved slowly up one leg, feeling each curve, each muscle and bone, until she reached my sex. She rolled over so her body could lie against mine. Her breasts pressed into me, her nipples rubbed against mine, her breath was on my neck and her fingers were teasing my most secret parts.

She slid between my legs and her tongue began playing with me, teasing me, tracing a line through my lips until she touched my engorged clitoris. She sucked my clit into her mouth, her tongue rubbing rapidly against the tip, until I fell apart in orgasm. An eighteen-year-old girl was introduced to wonderful sex by a thirty-six-year-old woman on an old park bench in a small-town park.

I'm twenty-seven now and married, but Lucia and I continue our woman-to-woman relationship.—A.O., *Salt Lake City, Utah*

SHE WAS WARM FOR ROOMIE'S FORM
IN THE COLLEGE DORM

I was a senior at an all-girl college. I have short hair, brown eyes and a generous figure that both men and women admire. I am—and was—bisexual, but not many people knew that, including my roommate Stephanie.

One evening I was in my room studying when Stephanie burst in, threw herself on the bed and started weeping. I went over to comfort her and she put her arms around me and started to sob into my chest. When I asked her what was wrong, she told me that her boyfriend had dumped her for another girl.

Stephanie continued to cry for several minutes, which made the front of my nightshirt wet and clingy. I was not wearing a bra, and the feeling of her tears and her breath was erotic. She hugged me even tighter, which sent shivers down my spine and beads of moisture into my panties.

I tilted her head upward and wiped the tears off her face. We looked directly into each other's eyes. I desperately wanted to kiss her, but I didn't want her to feel uncomfortable. Stephanie glanced at my breasts and saw the effect she had had on my nipples. Then she looked back into my eyes. She reached her hand out gingerly and began to rub my tits.

"Make love to me," she whispered.

She wrapped her arms around my shoulders and placed her lips on mine. Her tongue entered my mouth. As our breasts rubbed together, I felt her nipples harden under her sweater. While we kissed, she began to run her fingers up and down my back under my nightshirt.

I grabbed the bottom of her sweater and pulled it up and over her head. I had seen her naked several times in the shower and while she changed, but this was the first time I'd felt a sexual charge for her.

With her tits totally bare, I bent down and clasped a nipple between my lips. I gently tugged on it, then licked it with my tongue. Stephanie moaned and lay down on the bed as her hands continued exploring my tits. As I licked her cleavage, the faint smell of her perfume filled my nostrils.

My hand slowly traveled down her body, stopping between her legs. She was incredibly hot. I moved my hand back and forth across her crotch, causing her to whimper and her legs to stiffen. Still wearing her jeans, she ground her cunt against my hand and slowly moved her pelvis up and down. Her breathing became more rapid. Finally she let go of my tits to unbutton her jeans. I grabbed the waistband and tugged them off. After I pulled down her undies, I took off my nightshirt and peeled off my own moist panties.

We were both naked, and the feel of her hot skin and the cool air was sensational. Stephanie began to play with my nipples again, and I returned to sucking hers. My hot breath caused her nipples to get as hard as rocks in my mouth. Stephanie moaned and I continued licking and sucking her tits.

After a few minutes, Stephanie spread her legs and motioned shyly for me to go down toward her pussy. "Lick me there," she sighed. "I want to know how another woman's tongue feels on my cunt."

My tongue darted in and out of the folds of her pussy. I could taste her juices as her hips began bucking. She pushed my face into her crotch with her hands, and I got a mouthful of her come as she climaxed. Her groans of pleasure filled our room.

Once Stephanie caught her breath, she urged me to continue. But first she had another request: "Kiss me now. I want to taste my come on your lips."

I moved up and put my dewy lips on hers. Her tongue began to lick and explore my mouth. As she pressed her lips against mine, her muffled groans told me that she enjoyed what she was tasting.

As we continued to lock lips I put two fingers into her cunt. I rubbed my fingers inside her, moving them around so that she would get the full effect. Then she hit her second orgasm, this one even hotter and wetter than the first.

As she lay on the bed catching her breath I worked my hand back up her body. Then I whispered in her ear, "I'm hot for you. Please get me off with your fingers and tongue."

Stephanie and I switched places. Before she began to play with my sex, however, she reached into her drawer and pulled out a bottle of baby oil. She squirted the oil all over my tits and stomach and rubbed it in slowly. I began to groan and move my hips in response as she had done minutes before.

"I'll get you off like you've never felt it before," Stephanie said.

She put my legs over her shoulders so that my gap was wide and exposed for anything that she had in mind. She put three fingers into my cunt and began to play with me, saying, "Come all over my fingers. I want to taste you on my fingers. I want you to taste yourself when you come on my hand."

Her fingers danced over my clit and I quickly covered them with my cunt juice. She pulled her fingers out, put two of them in her mouth and licked them clean, then put the other two fingers she had used in my mouth.

"Don't you like the way this tastes?" she asked. "Don't you like the way your come tastes on my fingers?"

My skin was burning like never before. In fact, Stephanie and I remained hot all night and into the early hours of the morning, when we took a long, cool shower. She soaped me from head to toe and I returned the favor. We didn't overstay our time in the shower for fear that some of the other girls might walk in on us. Instead, we ran naked back to our room and jumped into her bed.

We continued dating guys, but if we were dumped, it didn't bother us.—*S.L., Lincoln, Nebraska*

SHE COULDN'T FIND A BRA THAT FIT—
SO SHE FOUND ANOTHER'S TITS

*I*t was a rainy day and I was bored, so I thought I'd go to the mall to pick up some new lingerie. I'm a full-figured woman who's a bit overweight, so I can't buy average-size clothing. But I like going to department stores anyway, to browse through the latest styles and designs.

I was in the bra section when one bra in particular caught my eye. As I picked it up a lady walked by me and knelt to look at some bras hanging at about knee height. As she reached past my knees to get the one she was looking at, her hand brushed my thigh and her face passed within six inches of my leg, causing my pussy to tingle.

"Excuse me," I said, moving a bit to the left.

She put back the bra she had and said, "You smell very nice."

"Thank you. It's lily of the valley soap," I answered.

"Mmmm, nice," was her response.

I experienced more tingling sensations and felt juices stirring in my love-hole. I've never been with anyone but my husband, so I didn't know what to make of this. I took a long look at her while she was busy browsing. I thought she was nice looking, almost beautiful, with beautiful, hip-length blonde hair.

"Do you like this one?" she asked. I just about jumped, I'd been so lost in my own thoughts.

"What?" I asked.

"I'm sorry. You were looking at me, so I thought I'd ask your opinion," she responded, smiling.

"I was admiring your hair," I answered, hoping she couldn't read the truth. My cheeks were turning pink.

"Don't be embarrassed. I enjoy being looked at. My name is Terry," she said.

"Mine is Wednesday," I answered, blushing madly.

"That's a beautiful name. You know I can never find anything in my size in the styles I like. How do you do it?" she asked.

"I don't usually get my stuff in the stores. I order most of it. But I do get lucky every once in a while, so I come in and look around."

"I thought so," she said, looking at my tits. "I'm a 38B and I have a hard time. And you are much better endowed than I." This really got me tingling, because while she was looking at me she was licking her lips. Then she stepped closer, reached across at tit level and grabbed a bra. God, I thought she was going to grab my tit! By this time I felt all wet and ready to be fucked. "Do you like this?" she asked, holding the bra tightly across her chest.

"It's okay, but this one is much prettier," I said, passing her the one I had been looking at.

"Yes, I agree. It's beautiful," she nodded. "But do they have my size?" We both began looking for the bra in her size. As I began searching the upper rack, she bent over and reached for one at knee level. When she stood up she said in a husky voice, "Yes, you do smell good. Your soap mixed with pussy juice smells quite edible."

"I'm sorry?" I gasped, jumping back nervously.

She reached up and laid her hand on the inside of my thigh, just above my knee. "Don't move," she whispered. "I enjoy smelling you. You smell very sexy."

"Please, don't," I said in a quavering voice. I hadn't been this turned on in a long time, and I had never been turned on by another girl.

As I was deep in thought, she said, "I think I'll buy the one you chose. It's very nice." Then she found a pair of panties to match, looked at me, smiled and said, "Thank you for the help and for such an interesting hour." Then she left. I was shaking so badly I don't know how I made it to my car, but I do know that once I was there the first thing I did was put my hand under my skirt.

I was so wet that my fingers emerged covered with juice. I lapped it off.

A truck pulled in and four guys got out and went into the mall. I spread my legs a bit and started playing with myself. Because of where I was parked and how I was sitting no one could see me fingering myself.

I was really getting into it, so I didn't see the men come back until I heard voices. I opened my eyes and one of them was smiling at me. Then, making sure the men were busy talking among themselves and that no one else was watching, I very slowly eased my index finger in and out of my pussy.

I knew they couldn't see me or what I was doing, so I wasn't worried when the guy who smiled at me kept looking over once in a while. I slowly continued what I had been doing. Every once in a while I would suck my fingers clean.

Now, if it wasn't for a slight change in my breathing, no one would ever know when I get off. So after about ten minutes I came, not the least bit worried that anyone knew. But God I felt so much better!

I removed my fingers, sucked my come off and started my car. Then the guy who had watched me walked over to my car, bent down and said, "I couldn't help noticing you getting yourself off. I just wish it was me eating your pussy juice," he said with a big grin.

I stared at him for what seemed forever and stammered, "I'm very quiet and no one usually knows. What gave me away?"

"Hon, with tits like yours, anyone who enjoyed sex would notice the change in your breathing. Anyway, thanks for letting me watch," he said, and walked away.

About a week later I went to the beach. I was lying on my stomach reading a book when someone started rubbing my shoulders. A female voice said, "Fancy meeting you here. Lie still and I'll grease you up so you won't burn."

After she rubbed lotion on my back and shoulders, her hands moved down to my thighs. I looked around and, Lord have mercy, it was Terry from the mall. Man, she was a knockout in her swimsuit! She tenderly stroked my thighs, occasionally slipping her fingers up to my crotch but not quite touching it.

As she rubbed a bit more, she said: "You're a very naughty girl.

You made me so horny last week I had to go to the ladies' room at the mall to get myself off. And I'm loud when I come!"

Then I related my story to her. "Such a pity," she sighed. "You should have gone to the ladies' room with me and I'd have eaten you out . . . Such a waste."

I smiled and asked, "What makes you think I'd let you eat me?"

"I'd like a chance to prove just how enjoyable it can be," she whispered.

I looked at her and said: "I've never been with a girl. I wouldn't know where to start."

"Hon," she replied, "I'd be pleased if you would let me be the first. Come with me." Well, by this time I was so turned on that I was weak in the knees. We got up and I followed her into a nearby beach house. I sighed as she put her arms around me and kissed me full on the lips. She tasted sweet. Her tongue forced my lips open and she French-kissed me. I just about melted. She broke the kiss, led me into the bedroom and took off her suit. I looked at her body, wishing mine was built more like hers.

"How do I look?" she asked.

With a voice made husky by lust I answered, "You're breathtaking." She walked close to me so that our boobs touched. Then she stood there swaying so that our tits rubbed back and forth. I closed my eyes, enjoying the sensation. Then I felt my suit leave my shoulders, and we were flesh against flesh.

I thought I was going to come right there and then. She gently pushed me backward until my legs touched the bed. Then she knelt and removed the rest of the suit. I felt the suit land around my ankles. "Lift your foot," she told me. As I did so, she planted a kiss on my pussy fur. Then she moved between my legs and slid her tongue in between my pussy lips, brushing my clit. My knees gave way and I landed on the bed. She was on top of me as fast as you could blink. She rubbed her titties against mine and I started coming.

"My God, I'm coming!" I screamed. She quickly slid down between my legs and lapped my come-juice until it stopped flowing.

"Well, that didn't take long." She smirked. "How about we start all over?"

"I've never done this before, and I don't know where to start," I said.

"Sure you do. Look, let's start with a 69. Whatever you want done to you, do to me and I'll copy you. It's great. You get an extra thrill because you actually feel like you're doing it to yourself." She turned herself around so her pussy was on my face and her face was in my pussy. Not sure what to do, I blew on her triangle. I felt her blow back on mine.

This might be okay, I thought, as I reached up and very lightly rubbed her cunt lips. She did the same. I eased apart her cunt lips and played with her clit with the end of my index finger. Again she did the same. The more I got into this, the more I felt like I was playing with myself. I decided to get braver. I lapped at her clit and the outer edges of her hole. As I in turn received these manipulations, I felt my juices drip down my ass-cheeks. I stuck my tongue into her hole and wiggled it in and out as if it was a small dick.

"I thought you said you'd never done this before," she gasped. Then she screamed, "Ohhh, I'm coming!" I kept working her with my tongue, every once in a while replacing my flicking tongue with small butterfly kisses. By this time I was in my own world, so I was completely unaware of the fact that the closet door had opened.

I was on the verge of coming all over Terry's pretty face when I felt a hand rub my titties. "I told you I'd help get you off," said a deep male voice.

I must have jumped ten feet. Then I turned to see a hunk of a man with the biggest dick I'd ever seen. He smiled and I recognized him from the mall parking lot. It was the man who had watched me masturbate.

"Now I know I just died and went to heaven," I said.

"Think you could handle ten inches in that pussy?" he asked as he mounted me.

He slid it in as smooth as silk. His penis was so enormous it felt as if it was reaching up to my chest. As he fucked me, Terry kissed and licked my belly and chest. Then she moved down and started lapping and kissing my ass and his balls. At that point I lost it. I came so hard I think I must have had five orgasms all at once. I felt like I was going to pass out. Moments later he pulled out, shooting his load all over my face and mouth. I tried to catch most of it with my mouth, and what I missed Terry was quick to lap up.

The man explained, "I came home that night and told my wife about this hot chick who got herself off in the parking lot. Then she told me about this girl with great tits she had met in the mall. Well, we put two and two together and discovered we had both met the same girl. By the way," he added, "thanks for allowing me to watch . . . again." *W.T., Los Angeles, California*

GO, GIRLS! SUPERCHARGED LOVERS CAN'T WAIT TO FONDLE IN THE FAST LANE

*T*his past summer my lover and I, while on a road trip to Florida, had an experience that I won't soon forget.

I am twenty-seven years old and stand five feet five inches tall. I have a dancer's body: lean, well-shaped, muscular. With blondish-brown hair and eyes that change color, many men find me attractive. My lover is twenty-six. Susie is five feet six, with short brown hair, beautiful light blue eyes and a fabulous body. A real knockout, she is always turning heads.

It was a very pretty afternoon. We had been driving quite a while and were becoming restless with the monotony of the highway. To relieve the boredom we decided to talk about the things that make us horny. Susie said she loved seeing me in skirts. Just to get her going I mentioned that I was wearing a lacy G-string underneath my skirt, which I casually pulled up a little higher so that she might catch a glimpse.

As the conversation continued we became more and more aroused. While I was driving Susie reached over and kissed me, her hands sliding underneath my blouse to feel my breasts. I have small tits, and they almost always have erect nipples. Susie began to roll the ends around in her fingers until they became rock hard. The next thing I knew she pulled a pillow from the back-seat and placed it between us, partially on my lap. She laid her head down on it. With one hand on the wheel I stroked her hair, caressing and touching her face, ears, nose and lips. Susie has full lips, soft to touch and wonderful to feel. She looked up at me with those beautiful eyes and said she wanted me right there. I could feel myself getting excited just by the thought of it.

I could hardly believe what happened next. Susie started nibbling, licking and kissing her way up my stomach until she found my breasts. She started sucking on my nipples, making me hot with anticipation of what was to happen next. Her hand slid up the insides of my thighs until she found my crotch, which by this point was wet with excitement.

Susie loves playing with my hair. Exploring, teasing and arousing me to greater heights, she soon lifted my skirt over my hips.

Being the athletic type, I am pretty flexible, a trait that comes in handy when you're having sex in a car. I found myself with my right leg stretched across Susie's body. Susie repositioned herself so that she was able to slide her tongue down from my belly button to my hot pussy, rolling it around until she found my clit. I reached over and felt the small of her back, my hand meandering lazily to her beautiful ass. How I wished I could lick and suck on this wonderful creature in my car. I could see her body contracting with pleasure, which made me want more. She told me to continue driving or else she would stop.

By this point my love juices were flowing. She slipped one finger inside my pulsating cunt, sliding it in and out, driving me crazy! In seconds her head was buried deep between my legs and I found myself driving faster. Her tongue found my clit and her lips surrounded it and sucked. I moaned with pleasure, at which point Susie stuck a second finger in my cunt and began pistoning them in and out of my soaking hole. I felt as if I would come all over us both. I really had to concentrate on not losing control of the car, as traffic seemed to be picking up. I think this excited Susie even more.

Susie loves to be inside my butt. She says it is so soft, tight and welcoming. So I was not at all surprised when I felt a finger probing my other hole. Lifting my hips and thrusting deep inside my ass as her tongue teased my clit, Susie sent me skyrocketing into the most exciting orgasm I have ever experienced. Realizing that I was speeding down the highway and that the truck drivers probably had a wonderful view made it even more exciting.

That was one road trip I'll never forget. I'm looking forward to our next trip so that I can return the favor to my sweet lover.—
Name and address withheld

True Romance

HE WAS BORED WITH HIS SAILBOARD
UNTIL SHE CAME ABOARD

*I*t was while I was working to increase my windsurfing skills to the competitive level that this unforgettable experience occurred.

I was training in the Caribbean because of the cold weather up north, and also because of the excellent competition to be found in the islands. As you can imagine, I didn't have a large budget. Hence I was living in a small inn on the water far from the fancy resorts. That's why I was totally taken by surprise when I entered the inn's tiny bar one evening and found a stunning blonde sitting by herself.

The proprietor quickly introduced me to her because she was also a sailboarder in training. I invited her to join me for dinner. As we ate we talked about windsurfing. Since I had been sailing alone I asked her to join me the next day. If nothing else, I said, it would add an extra measure of safety if we sailed together. She quickly agreed.

When I arrived for breakfast the next morning, she was already there eating a large bowl of fruit and wearing only an oversize T-shirt. Her long blonde hair was flowing freely halfway down her back. Her blue eyes were bright and smiling. Her well-formed, well-muscled legs got my attention, but the rest of her was concealed by her T-shirt.

We finished breakfast and went to get ready to sail. I was rigging up on the beach when she arrived carrying her board on her head. I almost whistled when I saw her. Even though she was small (five feet four inches), her shape and proportions were perfect. She was wearing bike pants that were as tight as a second skin and a very small top that barely covered her large, full breasts. It was going to be hard to concentrate on sailing with her near me!

We sailed all day, and I discovered that not only was she a very good sailor but she was also great fun to be with.

The next morning at breakfast she complained about the visible tan lines caused by her bike pants. We had both been sailing with seat harnesses the day before, which is much more comfortable with long shorts or bike pants.

"Why don't we skip the harnesses so we can get an allover tan?" she suggested.

"I'm game," I answered, "but let's leave the beach with suits on. I've got a little bag in my board we can put them in once we're farther out."

"Great," she said with a dazzling smile. "Let's go!"

She appeared on the beach wearing a truly tiny bikini that hid none of her terrific body. Those great legs I mentioned before ended at slim hips and a round, apple-like ass. Her stomach was hard and flat with a really cute belly button. Her breasts were so firm, it seemed as if they wouldn't budge if she dropped her top.

We sailed out of the bay toward a secluded beach I had discovered earlier. When we got there she jumped off her board and took off her suit, to my surprise leaving behind a tiny thong that just barely covered her triangle. The reason I was surprised was that I was wearing the same garment under my trunks.

"I guess you sail naked a lot too," I said as I stepped out of my trunks. She laughed and told me she'd figured I knew that trick. (You see, when you windsurf all day you can really get burned without feeling it; and who likes to burn that part of the body?) I took her suit, put it in my bag with mine and started to sail.

"Is that all the attention I get for being almost naked?" she yelled while walking her board up the beach. "From the way you were looking at me earlier, I thought you wanted me!"

I made an about-face and sailed, swam, ran, splashed and stumbled to her. There I was on my knees, my face inches from that tiny red triangle, trying to say something that made sense. She just grabbed my head and pulled it to her crotch.

"So you do appreciate me," she said. "Well, if this beach really is secluded, show me just how secluded right now."

In a second I was kissing her belly and running my hands up and down her body from her beautiful tits to her firm ass. I hooked my thumbs over the elastic band in her thong and pulled it down as she pushed her pussy into my face. Her soft blonde fuzz was trimmed in a mohawk and showed off her pink lips beautifully. As I squeezed her ass-cheeks I buried my nose in her folds. Her smell was a combination of the sea and womanhood. I had to taste her! As I tried to part her legs, she stopped me and said, "No. Let's find somewhere comfortable in the shade where we can really enjoy each other."

Ten yards away was a patch of grass under a palm tree that became our bed of lust. I licked her, sucked her and drank her juices. Her taste was like nectar and I couldn't get enough. I let my hands wander across her belly, her hips and finally to her soft, firm breasts. Her nipples were hard and she moaned as I tweaked them, but I never let my face move from that wonderful-tasting pussy. Suddenly she lifted her hips, spread her legs more and thrust her crotch against my face. I knew what she wanted, so I sucked more and more of her lips into my mouth. As she began to shiver I nibbled gently on her clit. Her orgasm gave her goose bumps all over and seemed to come in waves. I guess she really was a girl of the sea.

After she calmed down, she pulled me up beside her and held me tenderly. She kissed my whole face and licked her juices from my nose, lips, chin and cheeks. Her gentle touch made me feel warm and loving and took away the urgency of my desire. I enjoyed feeling her hands holding me and softly caressing me. The moment was tender and I knew I should not change that. I let her set the rhythm and mood of the moment and just lay back looking at her incredible body.

Bit by bit her caresses became more insistent, and she began to pay more attention to my stomach and thighs. She brushed off every grain of sand and then slid down my thing, exposing my salute to her beauty. I was becoming so inflamed I just about lost all control, but I was saved from embarrassment by the urgency of her desire to have me. In one fluid movement she straddled my hips and lowered herself onto my pole. Oh, it felt good! Her warm wetness enveloped my manhood as I gazed up at her lovely face. I was in bliss. Using her athletic legs, she bobbed up and down like a carousel horse. Her head was thrown back and her hands were on my knees as she lost herself in her own rhythm.

I knew I wouldn't last long. My desire was too strong to control. I grabbed her hips and thrust myself deep inside her as I felt myself go over the edge. I lost all restraint and bucked wildly while exploding into her. Suddenly, just as I was calming down, she reached back, grabbed my balls, thrust me in farther than I thought possible and came with a shriek. She lay on top of me, panting, and I held her as tightly as possible, not wanting the moment to ever end.

We rested, still joined together, until she slid off, took my hand and drew me toward the water. As we played and laughed in the sea I knew we had started something wonderful and exciting that would last much longer than this trip.—M.M., *San Francisco, California*

A SLOW START LEADS TO LOVE ON WHEELS
FOR COMMITTED COUPLE

I'm writing to tell you about the most sensuous, desirable woman I've ever known. Jessica was just eighteen when I first met her. She was reserved, uncomfortable with her sexuality and not at all responsive in bed.

We started slowly back then. I was both gentle and careful. Yet whenever I touched her secret places, instead of arousing her my touch would actually disturb her.

One night I suggested that we strip to just our underwear and gently caress each other. We touched very little. Then I removed her panties and started kissing my way down to her mound. I was sure that Jessica would enjoy the wetness of my tongue. Unfortunately this also made her uncomfortable. I began to worry about her psychological health. Here was a desirable girl who was unable to enjoy any aspect of sex.

Without going into details, let it be said that Jessica's introduction into womanhood had not been a pleasant one. Because of this I knew I would have to be patient. I had no idea how long it would be before she responded to me in a sensual way.

One evening when we smoked some marijuana, her inhibitions seemed to fade. I licked her hard nipples and she suddenly put her hands on my shoulders and pushed me down toward the wet warmth between her legs. I turned around on the bed so that I could gain better access and started licking her wildly. Jessica began to moan softly, letting me know that she actually was enjoying our encounter. Suddenly she tensed up and I realized she was experiencing an orgasm. I had no idea that this was her very first climax. Since I was turned around in the right position, I was hoping that she might also want to taste me. I gently coaxed her, but to no avail. She had rarely even touched my cock, much less had any desire to taste it.

Even though I continued to find ways to help her relax and enjoy her sexuality, I was afraid that Jessica and I were destined to no-frills sex with little passion. The breakthrough came one evening when she made a strange request: She wanted to begin our lovemaking by lying on her back immobile in a spread-eagle position. As she held still, I was to have my way with her. At this point I was willing to try anything, so I readily complied.

Once she had assumed the position I straddled one of her hands and rubbed myself over her outstretched fingers. Then I removed my underwear and began to rub my cock across her hand, up her arm and up to her shoulder. My pre-come was oozing from my cockhead as I positioned my dick over her breasts and began to rub the sticky substance over her nipples. Jessica started writhing on the bed, and at first I didn't know whether she was turned on or trying to avoid me. I kissed her deeply, pressing my tongue into her mouth. Sensing her hot response, I pushed on. I turned around so that my cock was bouncing above her nose and my balls were almost touching her mouth. Then I moved down and began licking her thighs. When I found her clit and began licking and sucking it, I felt her muscles begin to tighten. She dug her fingernails into the sheets and I fell forward onto her, losing my creamy load all over.

This seemed to free her. If Jessica could relinquish control, then she seemed able to enjoy herself and do things that she previously would not have done.

One summer night, when we were coming back from a party, I told Jessica that I would love to see her sitting in the car without her blouse. Much to my delight, she took it off. She had on a lacy black bra. I then asked her if she had on black panties as well. She responded by taking off her skirt. Here we were driving down the interstate with her in only her underwear. I slowed down since I was coming up on a truck. I didn't want to pass him and put on a show. She then moved over on the seat and began to unfasten the buttons on my shirt. Next she began stroking my chest. Then she unbuckled my belt, unzipped my pants and began to stroke my dick through my underwear. When I glanced in the rearview mirror I saw that a truck traveling at a good speed would soon overtake me. I could either speed up and pass the guy in front of me or let this guy pass me. Either way, one of the drivers would get himself a show.

Suddenly Jessica arched her back and took off her bra. The truck behind us slowed, honked its horn and then roared by. Now she was really turned on. She moved back over to her seat and began rubbing her tits and moving one hand between her legs. Another truck passed. I reached over, placed my hand on hers and helped rub her pussy. Jessica responded by pulling my dick out of my underwear and sliding her fingers up and down my shaft. When I exploded all over her hand she just smiled. I exited the highway and headed home so we could continue our adventures in privacy.

Since then, we've made love in the park, on our back deck, in the lake, in the ocean, in the hot tub, in front of mirrors and all over the house. I give her sensuous massages and she strokes me, makes love to me and sucks my cock. Besides being my best friend, she is the woman who knows my deepest needs and how to satisfy them. She is my soulmate. She is my wife.—C.A., *Rhinebeck, New York*

LOVING WIFE KEEPS THE DOCTOR IN THE HOUSE FOR ROUND-THE-CLOCK CARE

I have read Penthouse publications for many years. In the early seventies I read *Penthouse* every month. Later I added *Forum* because I particularly liked their letters. After I got married I continued to read these magazines but started sharing them with my wife. Many times we used your letters to add spice to our lovemaking. Now we mostly read *Penthouse Letters* because I think they have the best letters around.

All these years I have been waiting to have an experience worthy of your magazine. It never happened! It's not that I haven't tried. Rita (my wife) and I have gotten ourselves into some really interesting situations. We have been to swinging parties, met with couples and have even had a couple of threesomes. Now, don't get me wrong. These experiences were fun, but none reached what I considered to be *Penthouse Letters* quality. Finally, however, I suddenly realized that I have been living for years with a woman worthy of the *Penthouse Letters* Hall of Fame: my wife Rita.

I knew that Rita was something special when we went to bed together on our first date. Rita is forty now and she has gotten better each year of our marriage. The spontaneity of our early years have lessened, only to be replaced by less inhibitions and a better understanding of how to excite each other.

What I am going to tell you about happened two weeks ago. Because of our three young children, Rita and I do not get the opportunity to make love as often as we'd like. Maybe it's better this way, because when the time does come Rita can be a real fireball. I masturbate every day, usually while reading the latest issue of *Penthouse Letters*. When Rita is interested in having sex that day she will tell me in the morning to save myself for her. The reward is always worth the wait. On this particular day I was planning to take off early as I do every other Friday. I'm a physician, and this day I'd gotten through my rounds early. Usually I call on the way home, but on this day I decided to surprise Rita instead. She didn't hear me pull up, so when I came in the door she was pleasantly surprised.

Rita is five feet six inches tall and has reddish hair, blue eyes and a 36-27-38 body that I find every bit as desirable as on the day we met.

I have learned over the years that, if the timing is right, Rita prefers to be approached aggressively. So that is what I did. I met her in the hallway and, without a word, took her in my arms, held her tight and kissed her strongly, letting my tongue feel the roof of her mouth. I led her into our study and started to undress her. At the moment I was interested in giving her pleasure. Once her clothes were off I had her kneel upright. In this position I can easily play with her pussy, rub her ass and suck her nipples. More than anything else I love to masturbate Rita and bring her to orgasm. I get more excited doing this than anything else.

Rita can get unbelievably turned on. The first time we made love I discovered that she is multiorgasmic. The last time I counted, she had twenty-five orgasms during a single session. I'm sure she's broken that record since.

Once Rita was on her knees I began to play with her pussy by wetting my fingers and letting them part her shaved vulva. Her clit was sticking out, so I began to rub it rapidly with one finger. She came quickly and intensely. Next I put two fingers inside her. They slipped in easily because she was already wet. If I'm kneeling at her side I can slide two fingers deep in her pussy from the front while I squeeze her ass with my other hand from behind. In this way I can stimulate her from both ends. My thumb rubbed her clit while two fingers stroked her G-spot. She came violently, soaking my hand and her inner thighs with her delicious come.

Although I could play with her like this all day, she wanted something different. In our study we have a wooden rocking chair that is just the right height. With her ass at the edge of the chair, my hands on the arms, and her legs over my arms, I can fuck her the way she likes best.

After about thirty minutes of this I came and we relaxed together. We were just getting started.

While Rita went upstairs to dress, I went to the kitchen, opened a bottle of champagne and put it in an ice bucket. When I brought the ice bucket and two glasses upstairs, Rita greeted me dressed in black high heels, black thigh-high stockings and a black silk robe that stopped just below her black thong undies. Just looking at her gave me a hard-on. I really love sexy lingerie even though it usually doesn't stay on very long. We danced to some music and sipped on the champagne.

It didn't take long before she was lying on our recliner. Our recliner is also just the right height for sex. When she's in the recliner I can hold on to her hips and fuck her with fast, hard strokes or long, slow ones. Rita likes it when the kids are out so she can make as much noise as she wants. She began emitting a kind of rhythmic keening while orgasming continuously.

A couple of times I pulled my penis out of her, stood beside the recliner and fingered her so that I could feel her juices wash over my hand.

When I felt the time was right I lay back on the floor, hoping that Rita would join me in my favorite position: her on top facing my feet. This allows me to see her beautiful ass and to watch her pussy lips sliding up and down my cock. Rita joined me and I put a thumb in her ass and felt my penis in her vagina while her juices dripped over my balls. I came again, pulled out of her and collapsed onto my side, exhausted.

I must have done a good job warming her up on this particular day, because she still wasn't satisfied. She needed one or two more climaxes. We were lying on the floor opposite each other so that I could get a good view of her pussy. She started playing with herself a foot or so from my face. With her middle finger rigid, Rita vigorously rubbed her clitoris to give herself a few more orgasms. By this time my penis was once again fully erect. I started masturbating to add to her excitement. I came for the third time that morning while Rita had the last of her uncountable orgasms. Not including breaks, we had been at it for an hour and forty-five minutes.

This session was memorable only in that I had three orgasms. The intensity and excitement are always there. I could tell you about times on our boat that put this encounter to shame. Maybe someday I'll fulfill one of my fantasies that include me, Rita and someone else, but if it never happens it really won't matter, because I live with a fantasy every day.—*D.M., Seattle, Washington*

RUBBERS MAKE A GREAT CONDOMENT FOR
THEIR FEAST OF LOVE

I never would have believed it, but safe sex has improved my sex life tremendously. I have always been dead set against condoms. My wife Beverly and I don't swing, and I had a vasectomy years ago, so I always figured there was no need to worry. But Beverly is a woman of strong opinions and she felt I should get over my irrational attitude regarding condoms.

Beverly and I have always had a good sex life, even though I have always had problems with what is kindly referred to as premature ejaculation. After only a dozen strokes I usually shoot my load and that's that. Consequently I have become one of the best practitioners of cunnilingus on the planet. There's nothing Beverly loves more than to lie back on a pillow while I eat her out.

Anyway, the improvement in our sex life began a few nights ago. We started the evening with our favorite sex toy: the electric heater. (We always warm the room to semitropical conditions before we remove a stitch of clothing.) When all was ready we sat on the edge of the bed and I began to slowly unbutton her blouse while kissing her neck. Next I freed her 38D boobs from their restraints, fastened my hot and horny lips over the closest nipple and proceeded to suckle until it stood up tall and proud in my mouth. I then began to slide my tongue over her erect nipple while massaging her breasts with my hands. Before long each pass of my wet and willing tongue caused a spasm of pleasure to run through her body.

I knelt before her and worshiped her body as I began to intensify my sucking and licking. Without warning I switched tits and began to work on the other side. I then gently began tweaking one nipple while sucking the other until Beverly could stand it no longer and collapsed onto the bed.

Once she was on her back I reached for her skirt and deftly slid it down along with her panties. Still kneeling, I gently eased her legs apart to reveal the soft, curly hair of her bush. I stared at her lovely pussy and then slowly and sensuously parted her hair, revealing her large cunt lips and the inviting nub of her clit. As I parted her hair the scent of her pussy burst forth. I could hardly wait to taste her juices.

I placed her legs on my shoulders and stealthily worked a finger around her labia, darting into her love-tunnel for lubrication.

The smell of her arousal was overwhelming and soon I was finger-fucking her madly, spreading her slippery love juice all over her burning crotch. When she was ready, I lowered my eager lips over her waiting clit and began to suck greedily. My mouth flooded with the sharp taste of her womanhood. As I ran my tongue over her she began to moan, softly at first and then with increasing volume as I felt her clitoris stiffen in my mouth.

Sensing that her orgasm was imminent, I slowed down and began gently running the tip of my tongue down the slippery channel below her clit. Placing my lips around her hole, I sucked her juices greedily. This caused her to start bucking furiously, pleading for release. I inserted two fingers deep inside her to stimulate her cervix.

Having decided to grant her release, I returned to her clit. I worked it madly with my tongue and upper lip until, with a groan, she lifted off the bed in a shattering orgasm. My tongue began to slow as she descended from her peak. I kept my lips cupped over her sensitive clit as she began to relax, licking ever so gently once in a while to remind her I was still there.

At last she relaxed and stared into my eyes. Then, without warning, she grabbed my shirt and pulled it over my head. Next she reached for my belt. I stood up, more than happy to cooperate, and allowed my pants and shorts to slide down my legs. Before they reached the floor my cock was engulfed by her eager lips, and her tongue began to circle the flaccid head. I love the feel of my member growing and filling her mouth. Her strong lips squeezed the base of my prick, milking it as it continued to grow. Before long I was rigid and she was slowly bobbing up and down my pole as I tried to keep my balance.

When I could take it no longer I collapsed onto the bed. Once I was on my back, Beverly got on all fours and began a blow job of epic proportions. As she teased me by sliding the tip of her tongue up one side of my cock and down the other, I reached over and grabbed her tits. I timed my squeezes with her sucks, and we soon developed a rhythm. Just as I felt my sperm begin to rise, my cock

was suddenly left alone pointing into the air as Beverly reached
into the nightstand. Before I knew what was happening, she had
covered my penis with a rubber and impaled herself upon me.

Well, I'm no fool. I went along with her surprise and began to
move beneath her. Her strong legs lifted her up and down on my
latex-covered cock. I was amazed. It didn't feel like it does without the condom, but it wasn't all that bad. As she continued
bouncing up and down on my rod I grew more amazed. Even
though I could feel her hot, slippery vagina milking my rod, I was
not coming. I lay there and enjoyed pumping in and out of her
longer than I have ever done before. I stayed hard and felt her rise
and fall over my penis for ages. In fact, we even changed position
several times, ending up with me pumping into her from behind
(a position she enjoys only when she is especially excited).

I continued pumping into her from behind, feeling her love-
muscles squeezing my cock but not sending me over the edge. I
felt like a porn star ramming my boner into a beautiful woman for
all the world to see. As I kept pumping, Beverly began to grunt
with each thrust and soon she was pushing back hard against me.
I couldn't believe it! I was going to give her an orgasm by fucking her silly. She came and still I stayed hard, driving into her
cunt with joy. I fucked her harder and harder, and soon I felt my
cream rising. I rammed even harder and filled the condom with a
prodigious amount of creamy spunk.

It was an absolutely amazing experience. We now use rubbers
regularly to enhance the pleasure of sex for both of us.—A.H.,
Portland, Oregon

WHEN SHE HIKES UP HER SKIRT
SHE REACHES HER HIGHEST PEAKS

Kiki is a natural redhead who could easily pass for a Penthouse Pet. She is five feet eight inches tall and her measurements

are 38-23-35. Her D-cup tits are all natural—no silicone there. She has the beautiful long legs of a dancer—the kind that make men fantasize about having them wrapped around their heads. When she lets her pussy hair grow it is a beautiful shade of red, but most of the time she keeps her cunt shaved smooth as silk.

Before I started dating her, I knew Kiki was an exhibitionist but I never knew to what extent. I soon discovered that she never wears any clothes around the house and doesn't even own any underwear.

When we go out, Kiki often wears four-inch spike heels, a micro-miniskirt and a thin silk blouse with nothing underneath. When her nipples get hard they are very noticeable. Whenever we are in a crowded place, I like to drop something and make her bend over to pick it up. Her skirt rides up in back so that her ass and pussy are exposed to anyone who cares to look. Whenever we go to a bar, Kiki likes to sit on a bar stool and spread her legs wide enough to allow the other patrons to see up her skirt.

Showing off her body always makes her so horny that she usually sucks me off in the cab on the way home. She is an excellent cocksucker and can take my cock to the root. You can bet I take advantage of this every chance I get.

A few months ago I left Kiki at home in Colorado to go on a business trip to Chicago. While there, I visited an adult bookstore and theater. That week the theater had hired a well-known porn star as a dancer. After stripping on stage, she got out her toys and actually fucked a dildo on stage. I had seen this woman in adult movies fucking guys with huge dicks, and suddenly there she was two feet in front of me, pumping a dildo in and out of her famous pussy. I was so hot I pulled out my cock and began to stroke it. When she looked down at it and licked her lips I nearly came.

After her act, she put on a G-string and went through the audience, sitting on guys' laps and collecting tips. When she got to me, she stuck her tits in my face and moaned as I squeezed them and sucked her nipples. Then she put a rubber on my cock and turned around. When she sat back down, my cock slipped deep into her. She squeezed it with her pussy muscles and wiggled her ass. Within seconds I came deep inside the porn star's pussy. When I looked up I saw that dozens of people were watching us. I was not the only one arousing attention, though. A few tables away I noticed a pretty brunette with her blouse undone and her skirt pulled up to expose her pussy. Her companion was finger-fucking her while she jacked him off. Several guys sat around watching avidly and stroking their cocks.

When I related my experiences to Kiki, she made me promise to take her to Chicago on vacation the very next weekend. On our way, she was so excited she kept pulling out my cock to suck on like it was a pacifier. By the time we pulled into town Kiki had earned herself more than a few mouthfuls of hot come.

Before checking into our hotel we stopped at the adult book-store. Kiki got all sorts of looks—especially when she squatted down to look at the fuck books on the bottom shelf. Each time she shifted position everyone watching could see her pussy. Finally Kiki picked out an enormous dildo and I bought it for her.

We continued on to the hotel and checked in. We got a room on the top floor facing another hotel. As soon as we were settled in, I opened the drapes and turned all the lights on. I lay on the bed, switched on the radio and told Kiki to strip for me. Then I tossed her the dildo and told her to fuck herself with it. After she had come several times I got up, positioned her with her ass pressed up against the window and fucked her hard until we both came.

The next day we decided to try a peep show. We got a few rolls of quarters and headed for the booths in the back. Kiki entered one booth and I told her I was going to go into the next one, but instead I let a black guy enter in my place. I went into the booth on the opposite side of Kiki's. There were six-inch holes in the walls between the booths, so I could peek into Kiki's booth and see what was going on. Kiki fed some quarters into the machine and made her selection. As she watched the film, she opened her blouse and played with her tits until her nipples were hard as diamonds. Then she pulled up her skirt and started to finger-fuck herself. She spread her juice on her nipples and stuck one of her tits through the hole. The black guy sucked her nipple until she pulled back and reached through the hole for his cock. Until that moment she was under the impression that I was the one in the next booth. When she suddenly saw that she had a black cock in her hand she gasped and squealed. She started to lick and suck his cock ravenously, but no matter how she tried she couldn't get the whole thing in her mouth. Resourceful as ever, Kiki slipped a rubber onto his bulging cock and carefully backed up to the hole until her dripping pussy was impaled on his steely tool. I could hear them breathing hard and moaning. Kiki cried out, "Fuck me with that big black cock! I'm coming!"

He answered, "Fuck me, baby! You're so tight!" Soon after, I watched him leave with a shit-eating grin on his face. A little later Kiki came out and tied her blouse loosely below her tits so that they were exposed with every swaying step she took.

The next day we bought her some sexy lingerie and went to the adult theater that showed X-rated movies and had live entertainment. After watching a movie with a few topless dancers, Kiki said she wanted to get up onstage and perform. At first the manager refused, but after she pleaded and cajoled, he relented and told her to go ahead and do her thing. From the instant Kiki started dancing, every guy in the audience knew something special was going to happen.

It only took Kiki a few seconds to strip naked. Moments later she was playing with her tits and pussy like she had been doing this professionally for years. After a few minutes everyone could see that she was wet enough to fuck. She proved this by reaching for a bright red dildo and pushing it slowly into her steaming cunt. Soon she was pumping it in and out for all she was worth. I noticed that all the guys in the front row had their dicks out and ready. To oblige them, Kiki got on her hands and knees right at the edge of the stage and let a grinning fat guy pump the dildo in and out of her until she came. Each guy in the front row got a turn fucking Kiki with the dildo.

Finally Kiki got up and pulled on a tiny G-string. Instead of covering her, it rose further up into her pussy with every step she took. I helped her off the stage and gave her tits and ass a squeeze before I let her move through the audience to collect tips. I told her that if a guy had a rubber on she could fuck him but not to let anyone see whether his dick was really in her cunt or just being rubbed between her ass-cheeks.

As Kiki made her way around, guys played with her tits, grabbed her ass and fingered her cunt. Just about everyone slipped her a bill or two. If she saw a guy she liked, she sat on his lap and wiggled while he felt her up. Sometimes she sat facing a guy while he sucked on her nipples and caressed her tits. After collecting about seventy-five dollars in tips she came back to our seats and I told her it was almost time for the next movie to begin.

We went to the front counter so Kiki could exchange the smaller bills for larger ones. Kiki was still wearing only a G-string and high heels. While she was changing the bills, a young guy stood next to her and played with her nipples. When she was done she took off her G-string and gave it to him as a souvenir. She pulled on her miniskirt and slipped on her blouse, again tying the ends loosely underneath her breasts instead of using the buttons.

We got back to our seats just as the next movie was starting. Several guys sat near us to see if Kiki was going to put on another show. Little did they know what was in store.

Soon I had her blouse untied and pulled back over her shoulders. I played with her tits until her nipples were as hard as rocks and sticking out almost an inch. Then I pulled her skirt up to her waist and began probing her pussy with my fingers.

About this time another couple entered the theater and sat across the aisle from us. The woman had long blonde hair and was wearing a miniskirt and halter top. Her enormous tits looked like they were about to fall out of her top and the skirt barely covered her pussy. Obviously they were there for the same reason we were: to fuck in front of an audience.

At first the other couple didn't notice what Kiki and I were up to, but it soon became obvious. Kiki was leaning over the armrest and sucking my cock like a pro. I'd lifted her skirt up over her delicious ass and was playing with her ass and pussy.

By this time the other couple was watching us instead of the movie. I took our new dildo out of Kiki's purse and slowly started fucking her with it. The blonde got up and pulled her boyfriend over to sit next to us. The blonde took the dildo out of my hand and started playing with Kiki's ass. Soon she was licking Kiki's bald pussy from behind. The blonde's guy yanked off her halter top and we both played with her tits until her nipples were as hard as Kiki's.

About this time Kiki realized that it wasn't me who was sucking her pussy, so she turned around to see who it was. When she saw the blonde, she leaned over and kissed her full on the lips. They both caressed each other's tits and pussy. Then Kiki leaned back and put her legs up on the seat in front of her. I started sliding my fingers in and out of her hairless pussy while the blonde sucked Kiki's tits. The blonde's boyfriend slid between Kiki's legs and started licking her bald cunt and sucking on her clit. The blonde leaned across Kiki, rubbing her tits in Kiki's face, and started to suck my cock. After sucking me for a while, the blonde pulled out a rubber and put it on my cock. Then she turned around, sat on my cock and started riding me. I squeezed her tits and tweaked her nipples to encourage her to quicken the pace. The blonde's boyfriend put on a rubber and guided Kiki onto his cock. Not to be outdone, Kiki sucked off the guy in front of her, and jacked off two more. Soon we were all coming like crazy.

Finally the four of us sat back and relaxed for a while. As Kiki looked around and saw all the guys smiling at us, she realized that we must have put on quite a show. The other couple finally introduced themselves as Ray and Tina. We chatted awhile about how much fun it had been to make love in front of so many people. When I told them how Kiki had danced on stage and collected tips, they were fascinated. Ray and I asked the manager if Kiki and Tina could get up on stage and he agreed.

When the music started, Kiki and Tina stripped off their clothes before they climbed up onstage. Everybody in the theater began whistling and applauding. Once onstage, Kiki went to one side and Tina to the other, and they masturbated in front of everyone. Then they kissed and fondled each other's tits. Next Kiki spread Tina's legs so that everyone could see Tina's blonde pussy. Kiki used her fingers to pull Tina's pussy lips apart, then leaned over and started to lick her. Tina started coming right away, and it was all Kiki could do to keep her tongue on Tina's clit. Finally Tina couldn't take any more. She rolled Kiki over so that Kiki's pussy faced the audience and paid her back in kind. After they had both come, they got up and circulated through the audience wearing nothing but high heels. Each time they approached a guy, one of the girls would kneel down and play with his dick while the other stuck her pussy in his face. They each fucked or sucked several guys.

When the manager finally caught on to what was happening he threatened to call the cops, so Ray and I grabbed our girls' clothes and headed for the door. Kiki and Tina had no choice but to walk out wearing nothing but their high-heeled shoes. As Ray fumbled with his car keys, the girls waited under the parking lot lights and got a lot of catcalls and wolf whistles.

We cruised around in Ray and Tina's convertible with the top down for a while. The girls sat in the back and flashed every car that passed by. In between flashing they kept themselves busy by playing with each other. By the time we got to the hotel we were all aroused again so the four of us hurried to our room and fucked and sucked each other until the sun came up. Before Tina and Ray left they promised to come visit us in Colorado next summer for some high mountain fucking and sucking.—*R.P.*, *Aspen, Colorado*

IF THE CORSET FITS, WEAR IT—
OR THE BRA AND PANTIES

*I*t was a hot summer Sunday and Judy and I had been picnicking and enjoying the sun all day. We were walking in the park several blocks from her house when the sky started to darken and the clouds began to look ominous. Suddenly we were running through a downpour, encumbered by a picnic basket, blankets and other heavy items.

When we got to Judy's place we were thoroughly cold and soaked, so we quickly stripped off our soggy clothes. She was soon dressed in dry clothes, but I had nothing to change into. I was getting pretty cold until Judy offered me her pink flowered robe and I put it on. (At least I tried to put it on; it was several sizes too small and my arms barely fit the sleeves.) Thus attired, I sat beside Judy to watch the tube and finish our picnic as my clothes dried.

After a little while I noticed that Judy kept looking at me in a peculiar way. At last I realized her attention was on my prick, which had worked its way out of the robe. There was the head of my cock lying against the feminine floral pattern of her robe. I hadn't even noticed, but Judy sure had. At first we both laughed at the discovery, but then, before I knew what was happening, Judy began kissing my wayward prick.

She started slowly, barely nibbling the exposed tip of my member. Then she switched to long, slow, hot licks along the full length of my growing tool. My cock soon pulsed to life, parting the robe and standing tall and proud. As I lay back and felt her hot tongue slide up and down my cock I was very aware of the silky fabric of the robe clinging to my body.

With my eyes closed I felt her warm wet mouth slowly engulf my cock until it reached the very root. Then, slowly and sensually, her lips once again slid upward as she milked my throbbing prick. This was turning out to be the best blow job I'd ever had! Every time she reached the top of my cock she would pause a bit and wiggle her tongue into my slit or run it around the glans be-fore starting downward again.

Soon her fingers were tracing patterns on my balls while she held my cockhead in her mouth. This brought me to the edge. I arched my back and got ready to come, but she suddenly stopped her ministrations. I felt only the barest touch of her fingertips sliding over my cock and a sudden coolness when she removed her mouth and whispered, "I have a great idea for next weekend. If you agree to go along with it, I'll finish you off now!"

After I gave her my solemn promise that I would accede to her wishes next weekend, she began a frenzy of sucking that soon had me erupting into her mouth, filling it with hot come. As I lay there recovering she quickly peeled off her clothes and spread her legs provocatively in front of me.

I had never felt her so wet, and I don't mean from the rain! My lips had barely touched her curly black hair before she began to moan with pleasure. She began to writhe as I ran the tip of my tongue over her cunt lips. Without any hesitation I rammed two fingers deep into her love-tunnel and began to suck her clit. This was no time for subtlety. She was more turned on than I had ever seen her and she wanted it fast and hard! I pumped my fingers in and out of her dripping snatch and licked for all I was worth, try-ing to keep pace with her bucking hips. In moments she screamed and abandoned herself to an orgasm of staggering intensity.

My prick was soon hard again and I quickly drove it into her soaking snatch. There was virtually no friction as I fucked her fu-riously, driving my prick deep into her lovely cunt on each stroke before pulling it out again. I remember that as I was pounding into her I became aware of her robe around my body. With each thrust the silky fabric tightened around my body, adding a sensu-ous dimension to our lovemaking. At last I felt my come rising and, redoubling my efforts, I filled her drenched twat with yet more hot and sticky fluid.

After the most intense lovemaking we had yet experienced I hated to go home, but I had to go to work the next morning. As

I left she reminded me that she had some special plans for next weekend and I had promised to do anything she asked of me. I happily agreed I'd do anything she wanted.

When Friday finally came I rang her doorbell with intense anticipation. I'm not sure what I was expecting, but it sure wasn't what I got: an evening of looking through her family's photo albums! Though I was bitterly disappointed I soon began taking an interest in the photos in spite of myself. The women of Judy's family were all beautiful, and the gowns they were wearing in many of the portraits were exquisite.

After such a tame evening I was convinced Judy had forgotten about the promise she had exhorted from me the previous weekend. I was therefore quite surprised when I entered Judy's bedroom and discovered two matching sheer, lacy nightgowns. Judy picked the larger one up and handed it to me. "Time to make good on your promise," she said.

She explained that seeing me in her robe last week had really turned her on, and that she wanted to sleep with me while I wore the nightgown. I was a bit nervous, but since I had enjoyed the feel of the robe last week and since it seemed important to her I decided not to protest. I must admit it was convenient. All I had to do was hike my nightgown up and we were screwing away.

The next morning we ate breakfast in our nightgowns, and when I suggested we get dressed, Judy said we had to visit the attic first.

The attic? We had christened just about every room in the house with our lovemaking, but the attic? I started to ask questions, but she put her finger to my lips and shushed me. Taking my hand, she led me up the staircase. As we entered the attic she explained, "I hope you don't think it's too weird, but there are trunks full of my mother's and aunt's clothes up here that should fit you just fine."

Call me a pervert if you must, but after last night's session I was actually getting turned on at the thought of wearing a dress. There were several trunks of clothes. In one we discovered a collection of corsets and stockings and sexy lingerie that told me

Judy's mother and father must have had an active and imaginative sex life. Holding up a heavy, boned corset, Judy said, "It's you! Try it on! If anything will give you a woman's shape, this will."

With her enthusiastic help I put the corset on, padding the hips with soft fabric from the trunks, while Judy pulled the lacing in the back and tightened the garment around my belly. The trunk produced further treasures, including a classic brassiere with circular stitching on the cups, a silk slip and several petticoats. Judy's mother was a statuesque woman and her old clothes fit much better than last weekend's robe.

I must admit it felt rather good. After selecting a satin dress from the collection, Judy slipped it over my head and zipped up the back. The style may have been out of date, but it was soft and feminine and felt strangely comforting.

A bit more rummaging produced a vintage outfit of her aunt's that fit Judy very well. We went downstairs to her bedroom where Judy produced a pair of stockings and one of her wigs. Of course, they were both added to my ensemble. I drew the line when she tried to put makeup on me, though. Enough was enough.

When our outfits were complete we stood in front of the mirror and surveyed the results. I was surprised. While I was obviously a man in a dress, I didn't look too bad, and it sure felt good!

For the rest of the morning we could hardly keep our hands off each other. We took every opportunity to caress each other through the silky fabric of our gowns. I was getting really excited and could feel my cock growing beneath the pressure of my corset. Judy teased me continuously as we went about the domestic routines of housekeeping, telling me in great detail what she would do to me when the chores were done.

Every move in my corset and dress brought new and pleasurable sensations. The tightness of the corset made me all the more aware of my maleness. At last I could stand it no longer and I began to nibble on Judy's bare neck above her silky dress. She sighed and I began to inch her skirt upward. The fabric of our dresses slid between us and I was aware of the pressure of my bra as she leaned against me.

I could barely feel her nipples beneath the thick layers of old-fashioned fabric, but she began to sigh as I cupped her breasts and then slowly slid a finger under the bodice and stroked her tits. I worked my way in deeper until I reached her nipples, now hardening and pressing against the heavy stitching of her bra.

Gathering and lifting her skirts, I began to trace the outline of her panties. I could feel the wetness from her cunt seeping into them. I worked a finger under the fabric and began to gently stroke her clit. This caused her to collapse in my arms. I led her to a chair and sat her down.

Kneeling before her, I raised her skirts and removed her panties. I began to lightly caress her crotch, brushing the hair with my finger and blowing gently on her dripping snatch. I wanted this to last, so I began to kiss her thighs, just barely brushing her pubic hair as I moved from one leg to the other.

After teasing her for a good long time, I began to lightly tongue her snatch, barely touching the soft wet lips of her cunt, then flicking at her clit. Judy writhed in the chair, grinding her hips in pleasure and urging me to make her come. Her skirts and petticoats had fallen over my head, so I was in a soft, feminine cave of cloth and flesh as I ate her cunt with delight. I licked a finger and inserted it into her slit. It slid in with unbelievable ease. She was really turned on by this!

I began to probe the inside of her crack with my finger, tickling and wiggling. Now she was screaming at the top of her lungs: "Make me come! Fuck me!" I redoubled my efforts. My tongue flew over her erect clitoris, slurping up her juices as fast as they gushed forth. She suddenly began bucking up and down and with a wordless cry went over the edge of orgasm.

She recovered slowly, and as her breathing slowed I continued to lick her soaking cunt. I felt her body shiver with satisfaction.

Then it was my turn. I stood up, lifted my skirt and pulled down my panties, freeing my cock to swing in the air before her.

She quickly turned around in the chair and offered me her pussy doggie-style. Holding up my skirt, I drove my pecker into her with a single thrust and began to ram my rod in and out of her cunt. With each thrust I heard the rustle of my skirts and felt the tightness of the corset around my middle.

What a picture we must have made! There I was pounding my hot stiff pecker into a receptive woman while I wore her mother's clothes. I couldn't see what was happening beneath the layers of fabric, but I could feel my love-rod being sucked into her and my balls slapping against her with each stroke. I grunted in time to her sharp cries of ecstasy, feeling the shock waves of pleasure run through her ass as I continued to pound my pecker into her sweet cunt. Again I could feel my come rising from deep in my balls, and I savored the feeling as I prepared to fire jets of thick, creamy spunk deep into Judy's slippery tunnel. Grabbing her waist through the layers of vintage cloth, I pulled her onto my rigid pecker, pressing her ass against me as I blew my load. We collapsed into a pile of soft cloth and snuggled for some time, glowing with the pleasure of our fabulous lovemaking.

Since then we have moved much of the clothing from the attic to a spare bedroom and I have gotten deeper and deeper into cross-dressing. I keep my legs shaved and I've even been bold enough to venture out of the house dressed in more contemporary feminine clothing. However, Judy and I still love to dress up together in her mother's clothes and return to fantasies of an earlier age.—Y.E., *Omaha, Nebraska*

HARNESSING THE ENERGY OF AN INVENTIVE COUPLE LEADS TO SUPER SEX

My wife Cyndy and I recently had a great experience. After experimenting with anal sex, we talked about how we might be able to hold a dildo in Cyndy's ass while I fucked her pussy.

I showed Cyndy a picture of a strap-on dildo in a catalog. It also had an extra attachment to hold a second dildo that would penetrate the wearer, which was really the part of it that interested us.

I told Cyndy that what we needed was a harness that would keep her pussy area exposed so that I could fuck her while the dildo was up her ass. The device in the picture had a strap that covered the crotch, so it was no good for us. We'd either have to keep looking or make one ourselves.

To my total surprise, when I arrived home the next day Cyndy presented me with a harness she had designed and sewn by cutting up a black leather corset that didn't fit her properly. The harness had Velcro fasteners at the waist and was intended to hold anal dildos of various sizes. More importantly it was designed to leave the pussy easily accessible.

I couldn't get over Cyndy's resourcefulness. The idea clearly had intrigued her and she'd wasted no time designing this device. I was particularly turned on when she told me that repeatedly trying on the harness to ensure a proper fit had gotten her very aroused. She even showed me how her love juices had stained the leather in a few spots. This made my cock rock-hard.

Unfortunately we both had other things to do that night, so we put our new toy away until we had enough time to experiment more fully. I couldn't get over the fact that my wife had designed and created this device for our mutual enjoyment, and I couldn't wait to show my appreciation.

Luckily the next night found us free of other commitments. To get in the mood we necked on the couch like teenagers and got one another incredibly aroused. When I sensed that we were both more than ready, I suggested to Cyndy that we try the harness on her without a dildo so that she could get the feel of it and make any necessary adjustments.

We adjourned to our bedroom, where I stripped her from the waist down. My cock throbbed as I encircled my wife's waist for the first time with the leather strap and buckled it in place.

I told Cyndy how excited she had made me and asked her to bend over a nearby cabinet so I could really test her work. She readily moved into position and wiggled her ass back and forth, blatantly teasing me. I fumbled to insert a small dildo into the leather holder that connected to the Y-shaped strap at the crotch.

After applying some lubricant to the dildo, I attached it to the strap. I gradually pushed the dildo into her ass with my right hand as my left hand pulled the front harness strap back into place. Cyndy moaned as the dildo disappeared into her and again as the leather was pulled up tightly on either side of her pussy.

I could feel my cock throbbing as the dildo filled my wife's ass. The harness held it in place and prevented it from slipping out. I told Cyndy that the harness fit her perfectly and she had done a great job. When I added that I hadn't been this excited for a while, she said she could feel my excitement in my hands and hear it in my voice.

I told Cyndy to stand up, walk around the room a little and see if she could sit down comfortably with the dildo up her ass. Cyndy followed my instructions and reported that the dildo felt fine. I envisioned sitting in a fancy restaurant with Cyndy, or in a movie theater, while a dildo was up her butt. Only she and I would know that it was there. The thought that she could wear this device in public without anyone being the wiser made me so hard I thought my cock was going to explode.

Sitting down and standing up obviously moved the dildo and heightened the physical sensations. I particularly enjoyed hearing Cyndy's soft murmurs of pleasure as she rocked back and forth in her seat. Cyndy said the dildo made her more aware of her ass but not inherently arousing. She admitted that the sensation of the leather harness rubbing against her pussy as she walked turned her on the most.

I was so hot I couldn't wait any longer. I stripped off my clothes and positioned her near the cabinet. As I crouched down to adjust the divided front harness strap to better expose her pussy, I saw that her pussy glistened with her juices. This told me that she was more than ready for sex.

Positioning myself behind my wife, I spread her feet about eighteen inches apart and bent her forward so that she was leaning on the cabinet. I guided my cock past the leather straps to her dripping wet honey-pot.

She gasped as I entered her. I grabbed her hips and pulled her pelvis toward me, pressing our bodies together as tightly as possible. We both enjoyed the resulting deeper penetration in her pussy and her ass.

Keeping my hands on Cyndy's hips, I guided them back and forth to begin a controlled thrusting in and out of her pussy. It was incredible! Seeing my wife's handmade leather harness disappear between her ass-cheeks added an extra edge to my pleasure. I could imagine the dildo being forced in deeper each time I thrust forward. It felt as if I were fucking my wife with two cocks!

Within a few minutes both of us were nearing orgasm. I reached around to fondle Cyndy's clit. As soon as I made contact with her wetness, Cyndy's body began to spasm out of control. This of course pushed me over the brink as well. It was all I could do to hold us both upright so we wouldn't fall down. It was great!

I can't wait for another evening when we can prolong our foreplay with the harness and an even larger dildo. And on some future occasion I look forward to stripping the harness off and burying my cock in Cyndy's well-conditioned ass.—L.C., *Tenafly, New Jersey*

Different Strokes

A NIGHT OUT WITH THE GUYS
UNLEASHES WIFE'S DESIRES

I am a twenty-five-year-old fitness instructor at a local gym. My husband Rick is a tall, blond, handsome businessman. Although we spend most of our free time together, on Friday nights he always goes out with his coworkers and comes home very late. This never bothered me, but eventually I became curious to know what they did all night.

One day I told Rick that I wanted to go with him one night so I could see what an evening out with the guys is like. He was reluctant at first, but I let my fingers do the talking. I put my hands in his pants and cupped his balls, squeezing lightly until he gave in.

When Friday night came around I was very curious about what we would be doing. Knowing that we would be with a bunch of stuffy businessmen, I wore a high-neck blouse and slacks.

Rick and I drove to his friend's house to meet up with the others. When we got there I smiled and said that I hoped they didn't mind me accompanying them. Both men were very well built, and I couldn't help noticing their bulging muscles. Although I have very large breasts I had kept them well covered, but my excitement had made my nipples harden. It was obvious by the way their eyes bulged that they could tell. I told them not to pay any special attention to me, and to do whatever it was they normally did. One of my husband's friends, Brandon, said, "I thought your wife preferred cock?" I had no idea what he was talking about. Brandon always was strange, so I quickly forgot all about his comment.

It took us over an hour to drive to our destination. From the outside it seemed to be an ordinary bar, so I asked them why they drove all this way just to go to such a place. Rick said, "Just don't wiggle that great ass of yours too much. It may be the only one in here that they can touch." The rest of the men smiled.

Sure enough, when I walked into the bar I discovered that I was the only woman in a bar full of men. Some were in business suits, some in jeans, and all of them stared at me as I walked in. An enormous man wearing a leather vest and very tight pants was working the door, and he leered at me as we sat down. I slid self-consciously into a chair and looked at my husband. He was smiling, seemingly enjoying all the attention I was getting. "Why are there no other women in here?" I asked. He patted me on the arm and smiled again.

After we ordered drinks, the stage in front of our table lit up and a tall girl with long blonde hair, wearing a short skirt and blouse, came out onto the stage.

Music started playing, and she danced and shook her ass. I couldn't believe my eyes when she wiggled around on the stage and removed her clothes. I was so shocked that I couldn't take my eyes off her, and when she revealed her enormous breasts I saw that her nipples were as big as silver dollars and fully erect. I started to feel very warm. My eyes remained glued to her nipples as Rick and his friends watched me and chuckled. I told Rick that I felt funny being there, and that maybe I should leave. He said, "Just relax and watch. I'll get her to show you her pussy."

He took a dollar bill out of his wallet and put it on the stage right in front of me. We all stared as she danced over to us, her hands on her tits, and picked up the dollar bill. Then she bent over and put her pussy so close to my face that I thought I could smell it. I had never been so close to a woman's pussy before. She spread the lips of her cunt open so I could see everything. I turned red with embarrassment, but something inside me wanted to dart my tongue out and get a taste. My own pussy tingled and moistened at the sight of this beautiful, naked dancer.

The next girl to come to the stage had short hair and small, teacup-size tits that bounced up and down as she shook them. As I gazed at her clean-shaven cunt I could feel my own cunt getting hotter. I fidgeted in my seat, squeezing my legs together, hoping that no one would discover my furtive attempts at masturbation. I fantasized about licking her erect nipples. I guess my nipples were still erect, because the bouncer had his eyes glued to my breasts.

I made my way to the ladies' room, hoping to find a place where I could stick a finger deep inside myself. Once in the bathroom I stood before the mirror, yanked my pants down and stuck my finger into my cunt. My pussy was soaked.

One of the dancers came in to get changed, and I quickly removed my finger from my slit and pulled my pants back up. The girl smiled at me as I tucked in my shirt. There was no hiding what I had been doing. The dancer leaned against the mirror and continued to watch me fidget as she put down her clothes and began to rub the insides of her thighs. Her tits were swollen and beautiful, her pussy exposed to my gaze. I quickly left the bathroom and hurried back to my table. My pussy was now aching with desire.

After three more girls had made their way on and off the stage, we decided it was time to call it a night. On the way home I kept thinking about the naked woman in the bathroom and began to rub my husband's cock, which was more than a little stiff. The men in the front seat didn't seem to be paying much attention to us so I leaned over and said, "I want to suck it."

Rick whipped out his beautiful cock. I leaned down and sucked hard, going all the way down to his balls and back up to the huge head. Thinking of all the men leering at me in the bar made me so horny that my pussy throbbed. I had to have something, *anything* inside it. I knew that this was impossible while I was in the car, so I focused my attention on the cock in my mouth.

My husband had no problems coming and, although he tried to be very quiet, I knew it was hard for him not to scream. Since we had nothing with which to clean up the mess, I knew I would have to swallow all of the come that poured out. So, without releasing my lips from his pulsating meat, I gulped all of his juice without missing a drop. By now my cunt was drenched. I couldn't wait to get home and get fucked.

Rick could tell how horny I was and whispered, "I want to eat you." The words were music to my ears, but I motioned to the front seat, explaining that we were sure to be caught if we hadn't been already. Without hesitation he unzipped my pants to reveal my hot cunt. He touched my wetness and, knowing that it was too late to stop, I shimmied my pants down to my ankles.

As he licked me I tried to use my coat as a shield between the men in front and my husband's face buried between my legs, but I was so excited I forgot about everything except my pleasure. I dropped the coat and started bucking like a horny pony. I came in an explosion of pleasure, and Rick had to hold his hand over my mouth to muffle my moans of ecstasy. It was a futile attempt. The sweet smell of my cunt was already permeating the car.

Finally we arrived at Brandon's house, where our car was parked. As we said our good-byes, Brandon said, "I guess you enjoyed yourself after all." I smiled and said yes. I could see by the bulge in his pants that he had been watching my pussy being eaten the whole time.

When we got back into our own car I was so hot I couldn't stand it. Rick suggested that I take off my shirt and let my breasts hang loose on the drive home. It felt so good to massage them. Rick watched me tweak my nipples while he drove. Then, at my husband's request, I took off my pants. I couldn't stand it any longer. I said, "You have to fuck me now."

Instead of pulling over, Rick asked, "Did you like the sight of all those pussies tonight?"

I moaned, "Fuck me now, please, or I'll have to sit on the gearshift."

"You'll have to wait," he said, reaching over and tapping his fingers on my clit. I was so out of control that I gushed my juices all over his hand. I moaned louder than I ever had. The smell of my pussy filled the car and I began to finger-fuck myself. His cock grew to mammoth proportions as he watched me fingering myself next to him. "Fuck me," I moaned, my fingers buried in my pussy.

He took out his cock and pulled me onto his lap as he put the car on cruise control. One car on the highway slowed down in order to witness this unusual show. We moaned with ecstasy until we came. His come spurted through me as my pussy grabbed at his cock in the most powerful orgasm I have ever experienced. Luckily he was able to keep the car on the road.

When we got back home I thanked him for letting me go out with him and the guys, and told him that I had really enjoyed it. He said that everyone had enjoyed themselves. Last week we got a call from Brandon, inviting us both out on Friday night. This time, he said, his wife would join us too.—*P.F., New Brunswick, New Jersey*

HORNY MUD WRESTLER GIVES
NEW MEANING TO THE WORD "COCKPIT"

One night I was drinking with some of my old college friends. The bar we chose was near the airport, where I work as an airplane mechanic. I wasn't there more than ten minutes when a tall, blonde vision pranced through the door. She scanned the room and headed right for the video game machines, where my friend Doug and I were busy trying to save the universe. She watched us quietly.

When Doug needed to go to the bathroom, he told the girl to take his turn. He never came back. She and I played and drank for hours, betting shots of tequila on each game. We got smashed.

The girl's name was Elizabeth, and she was a mud wrestler at a bar down the street. She said she was tired of the geeks who hung around after the show to hit on her, so she had snuck out the back and come here. When I told her that I worked for the airlines, she squealed with delight. She said she had never been in an airplane, so I offered to show her one of the planes. She squealed again, grabbed my arm and ran for the door.

As we walked to the airport, I tried to think of a way to let her know that I wasn't a pilot. I figured she'd leave if she knew. Suddenly Elizabeth ran ahead of me and climbed into one of my company's Lear jets. I tried to stop her, but she was too fast.

Suddenly the flaps on the wings started moving up and down. I climbed into the cockpit to find Elizabeth playing with the controls and giggling. It looked as if she had bared her breasts, but it was so dark I couldn't tell for sure. I reached forward and flicked a switch. Elizabeth's beautiful, thirty-seven-inch chest was now drenched in the bright red light of the control panel. "Airplanes make me so fucking horny," she said, grabbing my head and pulling me to her tits.

I sucked on those creamy beauties for all I was worth. Her nipples became rock-hard. I pushed her jugs together so I could suck both nipples at the same time. Elizabeth mashed my head into her heaving chest, bucking wildly and screaming loudly.

When I finally came up for air, I realized that Elizabeth was removing my pants. As she did this I moved the seats back, preparing for the action that was about to begin.

Grasping my nine-inch cock in both hands, Elizabeth kissed my swollen cockhead. She looked up at me, than rammed my huge pole all the way down her wet throat. I watched in amazement as her lips locked around the base of my root. Her agile hands worked magic on my swollen balls. I threw my head back, opened my mouth and shouted with delight. Then I came—and came—and came. Elizabeth swallowed every thick, gooey drop.

After I had caught my breath, Elizabeth stood before me and thrust her hot, dripping pussy into my face. I thrust out my tongue, pushing it as far as it would go into her lovely, blonde hot-box. Elizabeth yelped and gyrated her hips. I nibbled her clit and she screamed again, smashing her slippery twat against my face. I held on to her hips as she bounced and wriggled in orgasm. I stopped for a second or two, then sucked on her button again. She shuddered and jumped again and again until she finally went limp.

By this time my giant tool was rigid and ready for more. I pulled Elizabeth onto my lap, where she positioned her sopping cunt above my throbbing pole, slowly pushed my blood-engorged head between her cunt lips and rubbed it along the length of her slit. Then I shoved my cock all the way into her vagina. I pulled out until only the head remained inside, and reached for her gorgeous jugs. Elizabeth started gasping and squealing, so I rotated my hips, sinking inch after inch of my joystick into her hot love-tunnel. Soon my pulsating prick was completely buried inside this blonde bombshell. I reached around to grab two sexy handfuls of her beautiful ass. Elizabeth shuddered and began bouncing up and down. When I fingered her clit, she yelled and bucked even faster.

I began to feel the rumblings of another orgasm deep inside my balls. Elizabeth leaned back as she thrashed around on top of me. This continued for about ten minutes. Our bodies were covered with sweat, bathed in the red light of the control panel. I was in ecstasy.

As my body began to shudder with pleasure, I heard a high-pitched whine coming from far away. All at once my muscles tightened and I pushed my cock deep into Elizabeth's twat. She shrieked and clamped her inner muscles around my prick. I grunted loudly and shot my load, pumping load after load of hot juice into her cunt.

As I came down from that incredible high I heard the high-pitched whine again. When I regained my senses I realized that Elizabeth had leaned back against the ignition switch, causing the engines to rev. I quickly shut everything off and dressed. I dragged Elizabeth out of the plane and over behind some parked cars. Just then the night watchman came running. He went into the jet, and came out holding a pair of pink, juice-soaked panties. He looked quite confused.

I never said a word to anyone about my adventure in the cockpit, even though Elizabeth's pink panties still hang from the bulletin board in our office.—K.C., *Riverside, California*

YOU KNOW A PARTY IS A SUCCESS WHEN EVERYBODY COMES!

*R*ecently I attended a party thrown by Mae, one of my coworkers. Mae lives with several other women in a beautiful old mansion set deep in the woods. When I got there the party was rocking. All of the guests were very attractive. I mingled, ate, drank and danced.

Shortly after midnight, Mae gathered all the men in the living room and explained that we were going to play a sex game, promising that it would be the hottest "safe sex" any of us had ever had. We were puzzled, but intrigued.

Earlier in the evening, each woman had chosen the man she wanted for her partner. Each man was led to a different room and instructed to stand facing a corner.

The room to which I was assigned was softly lit by candlelight. I stared at the wall for a few minutes before I heard someone enter. A woman's voice told me to step away from the wall so that we were standing back-to-back in the center of the room. I recognized the voice from earlier in the evening, but couldn't remember the woman's name. I did recall that she was very beautiful, with full, round, firm breasts. I had caught a glimpse of them when she bent over to retrieve a dropped napkin—the neckline of her loose blouse gapped, revealing her lovely treasures.

She then requested that I undress. We quickly shed our clothes as we stood back-to-back. She asked me to sit down and we slumped to the floor, our bare backs and asses pressed firmly against each other. By this time I was extremely excited. My eight-inch cock was as hard as a rock.

The woman then explained that we were going to masturbate and describe what we were doing to the other person. The goal was for us to come at the same time.

My cock got even harder as I envisioned this gorgeous stranger getting herself off right behind me. She asked me to describe my cock in detail, then gave me a verbal tour of her own body. When she described her excellent tits, I knew I had correctly guessed her identity. She moaned as she caressed them and pinched her nipples. I told her how I was tugging gently on my dick with my thumb and index finger, and that it was throbbing as if it were about to burst. She moaned softly as she touched her clit. I could feel her back arch a little when she told me she was slipping a finger into her dripping pussy, all the while tracing little circles around her magic button with her other hand. Then she told me that there was a bottle of baby oil within reach if I wanted it, and I enthusiastically greased my raging hard-on. She wanted to know exactly how I was stroking it, what it looked like as the head poked out of my fist on the downstroke, and how my balls felt cradled in my other hand. I described my movements in exquisite detail.

Whenever we were silent we could hear the slurpy sounds of the other's movements, which were steadily becoming faster and faster. This whole situation was really blowing my mind. I was afraid I was going to shoot my wad up to the ceiling before she was ready, but it wasn't long before she was near climax. The timing was a bit off, and she started quivering and shaking against me before I had reached the point of no return. Feeling her shudder violently and hearing her sharp grunts of ecstasy pushed me over the edge, though, and I blew a giant load while furiously jacking my swollen shaft. She had quieted down enough to hear my come splashing onto the hardwood floors, and it was enough to send her into another round of quakes and groans.

We were still so hot that we started all over again and repeated our self-pleasuring at a more leisurely pace. After we were both spent, she thanked me for playing along with the game and quickly left the room.—N.C., *Huntsville, Alabama*

NYLON: IT ISN'T JUST FOR LADIES ANYMORE

*M*y wife Lynn and I are both in our late twenties and have been married for seven years. Our sex life is never dull.

Lynn knows that I love when she wears panty hose, as I believe that nylon is sensual. One day she suggested that I put on a pair of panty hose the next time we made love. The idea sounded pretty harmless, so I did.

On that particular night, Lynn gave me a pair of sheer-to-waist panty hose to wear. At first they felt strange, but after a few minutes the nylon felt great against my balls and legs. Needless to say, my cock was rock-hard in seconds. Lynn had also put a pair of hose on, and as our bodies rubbed together we became even more excited. I nearly shot my load right then and there.

Lynn stroked my cock through the panty hose, and ripples of pleasure ran through me. We lay down on the bed, and I placed my leg between hers so she could hump my thigh. After a few minutes I felt her juices on my leg. I was glad she was enjoying this as much as I was.

We didn't want to take off our panty hose to fuck, so I cut the cotton panty shields out of both pairs. Lynn's pussy was fully exposed now, as was my cock. When I entered her, she wrapped her legs around my waist. The feel of nylon against our skin brought us to the point of no return.

Just as Lynn was about to come, she grabbed my ass and pulled me in deep. I shot an endless load of come at the same time she came.

After I was through, Lynn stroked my cock until I was ready

for round two. Wearing the panty hose kept me hard throughout the night.

Since that night, there has rarely been a time when we haven't worn panty hose when we screw. Each time is as great as the first!—*N.N., Albuquerque, New Mexico*

MIRROR, MIRROR ON THE WALL, WHO'S THE GREATEST LAY OF ALL?

*M*y husband Sean is my best friend, but he's a lousy lover. I can easily satisfy his sexual needs, but he does very little to sate my lusty sexual appetite. Luckily for me, he gets very turned-on when I make love to others. During our fifteen years of marriage I have had hundreds of lovers. Sometimes we set up situations where he can watch—other times I just tell him about my affairs.

He likes me to wear sexually revealing clothing, which, of course, helps me attract men. I have a good figure and beautiful face, so when I dress to show myself off, I get a lot of attention. I am five feet two inches tall and weigh one hundred pounds, with nice, plump tits and a delectable, round ass. When I wear a short skirt with fishnet stockings and a see-through blouse, I drive men wild.

In our bedroom is a large, walk-in closet. We installed a special mirror on the closet door so Sean can sit comfortably and watch when I bring one of my lovers home.

I usually go out three or four times a week to pick up men. I seldom go to bed with the same man twice because I like variety, and because I have no interest in having a long-term relationship with anyone but my husband.

One of my most sexually satisfying experiences was a foursome with two handsome black studs and a young white girl.

I met the three of them at a dance club. It was a rainy night, and the place was fairly empty. As soon as I walked in I noticed one of the black guys dancing with the girl. She was wearing a very short skirt and a tight tank top. He had his hands all over her ass as they mashed their bodies together. When the song was over, they sat at a table with the second black guy. Since I didn't notice anyone else with them, I went up and asked if I could join them. I mentioned that the sight of the two of them dancing had made my juices flow. They immediately asked me to sit down.

When I took off my raincoat, the man who had not been dancing immediately grew a tremendous boner. The bulge in his pants was quite impressive. I had worn a see-through blouse without a bra and a short, tight leather skirt. They ordered a drink for me and, before I knew it, began touching me. The one with the hard-on put his hand up my skirt and was thrilled to discover I wasn't wearing panties.

I invited them all over to my place. Before we left I called Sean so he would have time to get himself comfortable in the closet. I took my bulging black stud in my car, and the others followed. All the way there he told me how he was going to give me the best fucking of my life. He also mentioned that his friend was a great lay too, and that the girl loved to eat pussy. My juices were really gushing—particularly because he kept massaging my nipples and fingering my twat. It's a miracle I managed to drive home without getting us killed in the process.

Once in the house, I told them that I was dying to see their big, black pricks. They didn't hesitate and dropped their pants for me in the living room. I immediately went down on my big hunk as the other girl went down on hers. We had them rock-hard in seconds. Their pricks were huge! Each was at least ten inches long and as thick as a beer can. Suddenly I jumped up and ran to my bedroom, dropping my clothes along the way. My new friends followed suit.

By the time we reached the bedroom we were all naked. I jumped onto my king-size bed and invited them to join me. The guys each took a tit, and the young woman dove for my clit. The guys really liked my large nipples, which are extremely sensitive.

Just having them licked makes me come. My clit is also large, so my female friend was able to have a field day with it.

We spent six hours doing everything imaginable. I must have come a dozen times. The guys each came several times, and the girl came even more than I did. She kept screaming in ecstasy. Needless to say, Sean had seen everything from his vantage point in the closet.

After my guests had left, Sean and I enjoyed a quick fuck and fell into a deep sleep.—S.M., *Santa Monica, California*

FORGET COKE AND PEPSI—SPUNK'S THE CHOICE OF TODAY'S GENERATION

*H*aving had a strict religious upbringing, I never dreamed I'd actually be writing to *Penthouse Letters*. But with the help of both my loving husband John and such liberating publications as your magazine I've gradually learned to let go of my old sexual inhibitions. Now I feel free to enjoy all kinds of kinky lovemaking experiences.

I guess what really surprises me most, however, is that I've become uncontrollably obsessed with one aspect of sex that many women may not find exciting. Without any shame or regrets I can now finally admit to the world that I'm totally addicted to the smell, the feel and especially the taste of my man's hot sticky come.

Here's one girl who really has come a long way! I was once too ashamed to perform anything but the standard missionary position with the lights out. Now I love to suck and fuck in every way possible, and I crave jism like a come-hungry junkie.

Up until recently I always thought that most women didn't share my passionate interest in cock juice. But some of your magazine's recent letters have convinced me otherwise. Reading these hot stories about other sperm-slurping women makes me cream my panties as I picture performing these naughty acts with my sexy man.

I am now John's come-slut and every weekend we act out a hot new come-fantasy. We both have wild imaginations and we manage to come up with some pretty incredible scenarios. Of course, they all revolve around me consuming mass quantities of his hot pearly jism! I'd like to tell your readers about a few of our more memorable spunk sessions.

I remember one weekend when I knew I just couldn't get enough of my man's sperm—I was so damn hot and come-thirsty! We started off with one of our favorite fantasies, where John plays a bartender and I play a sexy woman looking to get picked up. After dressing for our parts we headed down to the bar we have in our basement and let the fun begin.

John looked real fine, but I was dressed to kill if I do say so myself. I had on my hottest skintight black dress, no bra or panties and my brightest crimson lipstick was smeared on my lips. I thought John would blow a gasket when I sat down on a stool, sensuously crossed my long legs and then lit a cigarette, all the while staring at him with my best fuck-me eyes.

I ordered a drink and began to flirt with him while my nipples strained against the flimsy fabric of my dress. After a few long drinks I could tell that he was on the verge of creaming in his tight pants, so I told him to fix me a very special drink. I licked my wet lips and said, "A shot of sperm straight up, please." I then grabbed a shot glass from the counter, brought it to my teasing lips, snaked out my tongue and probed erotically inside in search of fluid. My eyes never left his as I continued my little act.

Immediately a bulge appeared at his crotch. He pulled his pants and underwear down and started feverishly jerking off his fat thick cock before me, the tip of his meat oozing delicious precome. I lowered my mouth onto his rigid purple head and slurped up his sticky secretions while cooing and begging for more. "I want to drink your tasty come. Give it to me now," I demanded as I held out the shot glass to catch his sticky load. Seconds later he shot spurt after spurt of thick hot sperm into the glass, grunting and groaning for all he was worth. He must have been quite excited as he almost completely filled the shot glass with his salty white jism.

When John was through I licked the end of his sexy dick dry and told him to relax while I had my drink. I then brought the shot glass full of hot come to my lips and dipped my tongue into it for a small taste. His eyes were locked on me as I said, "Here's looking at you, honey," and chugged the whole glassful down in one sexy gulp. It was quite a mouthful, but I managed to swallow the whole gooey wad without any problem.

It was absolutely delicious! My tongue quickly licked up what I hadn't swallowed, then I slammed the shot glass down and told him how tasty it had been. "I think I'll have one more for the road, if you please," I said with a smile. Then I opened my mouth to show my man the fruits of his labor: my tongue and lips were coated with his pearly come just like my pussy is after a good fucking.

John's erection never faltered as he eagerly began frigging his stiff pole, frantically trying to get himself off again to quench my insatiable thirst. I really didn't expect him to be able to come so soon; nor did I expect him to produce so much spunk right after such an impressive series of big juicy squirts. Boy, was I mistaken! His cockhead soon turned beet-red and he shot thick wet streams of sperm from his wet slit. His mighty second load managed to fill the shot glass more than halfway! I licked my lips in anticipation as I contemplated my second shot of come.

My fingers were busy on my lusty crotch as I prepared to gulp down load number two. I eased the glass toward my wanton lips and, with agonizing slowness, tipped the glass and let his steamy seed slide into my eager mouth. I let it drip slowly down my throat, savoring the texture and flavor. I then surprised my hubby by suddenly embracing him and driving my tongue deep into his mouth.

"Do you like the taste of your come on my tongue?" I whispered with a grin. He nodded his head and we continued to kiss and share his tangy spunk between our taste buds.

I'm surprised but very pleased that John has acquired a taste for his own sperm. He had always been a super pussy-sucker, but I feel especially lucky to have a man who doesn't get turned off by his own masculinity. He now enjoys come almost as much as I do. He's even admitted that sometimes he sucks down his own goo after masturbating. I've also jerked him off to orgasm, caught his spunk in the palm of my hand and then fed it to him.

One experience I'll never forget took place one recent weekend. John announced that he had a very special treat prepared for me. My pussy instantly turned to jelly and my mind started to wander as I conjured up one sexy scene after another. I wondered what in the world he could have cooked up. Well, I didn't have to wait long as we settled in for some hot juicy sex. Soon we were all over each other whispering dirty phrases as we kissed and hugged and licked each other's genitals. Before we reached the point of no return, John got up and went into the kitchen.

When my man returned I saw he was carrying a large juice glass. It looked frosty and cold, as if he'd just pulled it from the freezer. He placed it down before me on the coffee table and my jaw fell open as I realized what it held. Our eyes met and, with the most devilish grin he'd ever given me, he said, "I hope you feel real thirsty tonight, honey. I've been working extra hard just for you. Every morning for the past two months I've jerked off into this glass. I had it hidden way back in the freezer so you wouldn't find it."

I almost had an orgasm just looking at the glass before me. "I would say there are over forty orgasms in that glass," he continued. "And I want you to give me the sexiest show ever and drink down every drop of this treat I've stored up for you." A wave of ecstasy washed over me and I shuddered to a fantastic orgasm. My whole body shook violently as I slammed two fingers up my dripping pussy.

"Suck your fingers clean for me, because the next thing I want in your mouth is my delicious cock cream," he told me. I obliged him and licked my fingers dry, all the while staring at the full glass before me.

As I relaxed after my orgasm, the realization of just how much come was in the glass suddenly hit me. I wondered if even I—obsessive come-drinking woman that I am—could actually drink down all that jism. But soon my doubts left me and I knew that I wanted nothing more than to savor this super-size glass of come.

At first we planned to wait while John's "come-sicle" melted gradually at room temperature. I was soon drooling and licking my lips as I yearned for the huge load of come. What would it taste like? Could I actually drink it all down? The anticipation got to be too much for me, so John suggested he use the microwave to heat it up.

Before John had a chance to take it into the kitchen to warm it up, I brought the glass of frozen cream to my mouth and stuck out my tongue. Then I licked it like a Popsicle for a couple of minutes. My man couldn't believe how horny I was for his come as he watched me slurping his frozen sperm. It was delicious! I could barely wait for the meltdown.

My mind raced with images of all that come going down my throat, or passing between our mouths as we shared a kiss afterward. When the microwave timer rang John returned with the now steamy glass, a plastic spoon, a straw and a small paintbrush. My goodness! What artistic endeavors did he have planned?

"Now, my little come-slut," he announced, "here's your glass full of my spunk all steamy hot for you. First it needs to get stirred so it's mixed thoroughly. Then show me how much you love to eat come!"

I stuck one finger into the glass, coating it up to the first knuckle and then using it like a swizzle stick to stir. His semen felt warmer than usual, but this made me even hotter and juicier. This was the ultimate in sexiness! I withdrew my sticky finger and sucked it dry right before him. It was delicious! It made me squirm to think I could drink down a load of come just like a glass of milk.

My man was frigging his huge dick rapidly as I continued to finger-feed myself with his sticky sperm and rub it all over my hungry lips. It was so hot and tasty that it took a lot of restraint not to just pick up the glass and chug it all down. Instead I decided to give him a show, so I grabbed the spoon from the coffee table. It looked as if his heart would pound out through his chest as I scooped up a spoonful of sloppy spunk and took it into my sultry mouth.

"Mmmm, it's so good and gooey," I cooed. "I feel just like a come-queen, and I won't be happy till I've swallowed every sticky drop. Oh, honey, I live to eat your hot sperm. I just can't get enough."

After indulging in a couple of more lovin' spoonfuls of John's yummy jism, I pulled him toward me, kissed him hard with my come-soaked lips and transferred some hot juice from my mouth into his. He swallowed and then screamed that he was about to come, so I gave him the good old squeeze technique to stop him in his tracks and then proceeded with my wild exhibition.

I tried the straw next and, to my delight, it worked marvelously. Here I was, actually slurping up stored-up wads of spunk through a straw as if it were a milk shake! This thought drove me to drink down quite a portion of the glass—probably a third of it. The come was not as hot as it first was, but it was still warm enough to suck down. I even let a few drops ooze out from the corners of my mouth and dribble down my chin, to give John the total effect.

My sweetie then joined in the fun. Dipping his paintbrush into the glass, he began to paint my stiff nipples with his come. I complimented his artistry, then softly said, "Now suck 'em clean, baby. You know you want to."

After lapping his come off my nipples, John painted my pouty pussy lips and clit. Then, naturally, he licked them clean. I came quickly as I sucked his white love goo through the straw while he gave me head.

"Why don't you make me up, honey. Spread your gooey gunk all over my pretty cheeks and lips," I cooed in a husky voice. With that I closed my eyes and enjoyed the feel of his warm sperm slowly covering my lips like a musky lip gloss. He told me that I looked like a goddess from heaven as he coated my cheeks with his come as if it were rouge. The semen dried quickly, making me feel like I had a mud pack on. Of course, I'd never had a facial quite like this one.

I asked my hubby if he would reheat my glass of come in the microwave. Needless to say, he was more than willing to oblige. When he brought back my drink I told him, "Honey, this is the best thing you've ever done for me. I feel so sexy, I could suck down come all night long."

With that I brought the warmed glass to my full dark lips and tipped it back, letting a river of cock juice surge into my hungry mouth. John watched in total amazement as I took one gulp after another and almost emptied the contents of the glass within seconds.

My man then let loose a huge load of sperm, covering my swollen tits and nipples with his latest love sauce. "Lick it off my tits! Lick it all off like a good come-sucking hubby!" I bellowed. He did, swirling his tongue and lips all over my juicy chest, sucking up every drop of his fresh wad.

I looked at my near-empty glass of come and felt a bit sad it was almost gone. Who would have thought anyone, particularly someone like myself, could be so erotically uninhibited as to drink all that semen. I had never realized until then just how feminine and satisfied drinking spunk could make me feel.

With one last tip of the glass I took the remaining pool of jism into my pungent-smelling mouth. I then grabbed my sexy guy by the back of the head and we lip-locked tightly. The flow of steamy sperm moved like a slow river between our mouths as I encouraged him to swallow the last swig from the glass.

With a sigh of total satisfaction, I sat back limply and reveled in the afterglow. Wow, what an incredibly kinky thing to have done!

Since then John and I have maintained our insatiable love life, but nothing yet has compared to that one juicy weekend. I think I'm going to have my man come inside me more often, especially in the morning before work. That way I can run to the bathroom and taste him with my fingers all day long.

I've also been thinking about our future weekends of lovemaking. Perhaps for the next few months I'll suck John off and let his come ooze out of my mouth and into a glass. That way, I can get a sexy taste and still store up another huge supply of spunk. Maybe this time I'll save up enough for a come shampoo. I'll be sure to keep your readers abreast of all the naughty deeds to come!—*T.C., Bangor, Maine*

Someone's Watching

HER SKILL WITH THE STICK GETS HER
THREE BALLS IN HER CORNER POCKET

*I*t all began late Friday night. I'd had to work overtime every day that week and I figured my wife Helen would be mad at me. We hadn't had a minute alone together in a long time. It was now the weekend, and all I wanted to do was spend some time with her.

I expected Helen to be waiting for me when I got home, but the house was empty. I checked the bedroom and found a note on the bed. Helen had written, "Your wildest fantasy will come true! Meet me at Larue's when you get home for the night of your life."

I didn't know what to expect, but I was so horny I couldn't wait to see her. I already had an erection from just thinking about the night to come!

When I got to the bar, I didn't see Helen at first. When I did, my eyes nearly popped out of my head! She was sitting on a stool at the bar wearing a short, black, low-cut Lycra minidress that I'd never seen before. She was surrounded by three guys who were obviously hitting on her and she was happily flirting right back.

The bar was kind of cold and Helen obviously wasn't wearing a bra, because her nipples were hard and perfectly outlined by her tight dress. She had her skirt hiked high up her thighs, exposing the tops of her black stockings. God, she looked sexy!

Instead of greeting her I walked quietly to the other side of the bar, ordered a beer and waited to see what would happen. I have always fantasized about watching Helen with another man, and even though I was jealous of all the guys around her I was excited by the knowledge that they all wanted to fuck my wife! After a few minutes, she got up and came over to me. She smiled seductively and asked if I liked her outfit. All I could do was nod. I asked her what was going on, but she would only say that we needed a change.

She had reserved a table in the corner of the bar. We started to play pool, but I found it hard to concentrate because Helen was teasing me the whole time.

We played for an hour or so and had several more drinks. Helen becomes an exhibitionist when she drinks. She was beginning to brush against my crotch and rub me with her ass every time she walked by. By this time I had a rock-hard erection and was dying to get her alone. I glanced around the bar and noticed that every guy there was taking long looks at her while she played. I knew exactly what they were thinking. I was thinking the same thing myself!

I couldn't stand her teasing any longer, so when she bent over the table to shoot her next shot I slipped my hand under her skirt. We were both surprised: Helen was surprised by feeling my finger inside her cunt, and I was surprised to find she wasn't wearing panties and was soaking wet!

As we continued to play, I noticed two guys at a nearby table watching Helen closely. Helen was still teasing me and I noticed that every so often, she would glance over to the two guys and smile. One guy was a typical cowboy type from his hat to his boots, and the other was a big jock and obviously a bodybuilder.

After watching for a while, they sauntered over to us and asked if we wanted to play pool with them. Before I could say anything, Helen consented. They introduced themselves as Ed (the cowboy) and Al (the jock) and then racked up the balls.

I was sure Helen would stop her little show with two strangers there, but I was wrong. She continued as if the two guys weren't even there. To make matters worse, she started teasing them too—giving them a good look at her cleavage by leaning seductively over the pool table, sitting with her skirt hiked high up over her thighs, even accidentally brushing against them when she bent over.

After a while I had to excuse myself and go to the bathroom to cool down. As I made my way back, I was struck dumb by what I saw. Helen was standing against the table taking a drink while Ed stood behind her, kissing her neck and rubbing her ass. She just stood there drinking wine as if nothing unusual was happening!

I stood there watching in amazement as Al walked up to my wife, took the glass out of her hand and gave her a deep French kiss. Helen returned it vigorously and Al reached up and began caressing her breasts through her dress. After they broke off and composed themselves, I walked back to the table. Helen winked at me and asked if I'd liked the show.

We kept playing, and before we knew it the bartender was announcing the last round. I excused myself again, explaining that I had to go to the bathroom. Instead I peeked around the corner to see what Helen would do. In no time, I saw Al kiss Helen, pick her up and sit her on the corner of the pool table. She lay back and he bent over her, kissing her and feeling her breasts. I heard him ask about me, and she told him that this was what I'd always wanted.

His fears allayed, Al continued kissing Helen and motioned for Ed to join in. Ed came over, slid his hands under Helen's dress and pushed it up over her waist.

Ed didn't waste a minute. He knelt down and started licking her clit and fingering her pussy. Helen loves to be eaten out, and soon she was moaning in ecstasy. Finally I lost all control and rushed over to the two men and my wife. Helen glanced at me and asked me to join them.

After a few minutes Ed stood up, unzipped his pants and took off his underwear. I looked on in amazement—his cock was almost nine inches long and twice as fat as mine. He moved up to Helen, lifted her legs up onto his shoulders and slowly sank his dick all the way into her cunt. Helen started moaning louder and humping for all she was worth. Ed grabbed her ass and pulled her even closer to him, slamming his dick all the way into her with a grunt.

Meanwhile, Al had peeled down the top of Helen's dress and was sucking her breasts. I walked up to Helen and quickly took off my pants. She pulled my cock into her mouth. Helen usually doesn't let me come in her mouth, but I was so excited at what was happening I came in seconds and she sucked it all up.

Ed began ramming his cock harder and faster into Helen. Just before he came, he pulled out and shot several huge loads of come onto Helen's belly and dress. After that he collapsed in a chair to watch.

Al took his place in front of Helen, picked up one of her legs and flipped her over onto her stomach. Then he shoved his dick into her from behind. Helen began yelling at him to fuck her harder, so Al grabbed her hips and started thrusting into her for all he was worth. Suddenly he let out a loud groan and came deep inside her. After he pulled out of her Helen got up, took her dress off and walked over to Ed, who was sitting in a chair. She slowly spread her legs, bent over, and started licking and sucking his cock. Watching this, I was hard again in record time.

I stepped behind Helen and shoved my dick into her. She was so wet with her own juices and the come from the other guys that I slipped into her cunt easily. Watching her give Ed a blow job was an incredible turn-on, and after a few minutes I came deep inside her. Ed was hard by this time, so Helen straddled him on the chair, grabbed his dick and stuck it inside her. She grasped his shoulders and started riding him like a bronco, throwing her head back and screaming.

After a few minutes Helen started shaking in the throes of a violent orgasm, while Ed shot another load into her. We rested for a few minutes, then Helen and I got dressed and said good-bye. The guys told Helen she could come back anytime and patted her crotch gently as they kissed her good-bye.

When we got home Helen asked me if the show had been worth it. I told her it was all I had fantasized about and more. I then asked her if she had enjoyed it. She said she'd be lying if she said she hadn't.

Helen says that next month I should expect a new surprise. I can hardly wait.—M.S., *Sandpoint, Idaho*

HE'S NICE ENOUGH TO SHARE HIS WIFE
WHO'S NAMED CLAIRE

*M*y wife works in the entertainment industry, so she gets the chance to meet a lot of hot young guys. Over the years we've come to an understanding: She can fuck anyone she wants as long as I get to hear about it or, even better, watch.

Recently we went out to a club to check out a band her firm was interested in signing. The band turned out to be a bust, but we decided to stick around for drinks and dancing. Claire was looking great, as always, in a short black dress with a low-cut front that showed plenty of cleavage. The short skirt showed off her long, lithe legs. Three-inch black pumps with leather straps running up her calves set everything off perfectly.

We'd already had quite a few drinks and were resting in a se-cluded corner booth when a man came up and greeted my wife with a big hug. He was about twenty-five, with long hair and a muscular body. My wife introduced him to me as Gary, a col-league recently recruited by the firm she worked for. We invited him to join us for a drink.

As we sat and talked, I noticed Claire's hand slip beneath the table. I excused myself to go to the men's room, so I could observe them from afar. As I walked away, I looked over my shoulder and discovered that Claire was actually kneading Gary's cock through his jeans. Suddenly she unzipped his pants and pulled out his big, erect cock. I could see Claire licking her lips in anticipation as she gently stroked its delicious length.

When I returned to the table Claire grinned mischievously. Then she turned back to Gary, licked his neck like a big cat and sank her head into his lap. I watched as she gently played her tongue up the pulsing vein of his hard rod, licking and sucking up the drops of pre-come glistening on its bulbous head. She took him into her mouth and started sucking on his steely length, one hand caressing the shaft. Her long, red nails drifted over his hairy sac and Gary moaned softly.

Claire engulfed him in her hot mouth, and he buried himself in her hot throat while her slippery serpent's tongue squirmed and slithered. She inched forward, sucking him deeper into her throat. She then began bobbing her head up and down, her tongue swirling over the swollen head on each stroke. Gary was quivering, his hips thrusting back, trying to fuck himself even deeper into her throat. My own cock was getting hard as I watched the scene, and I pulled it out and started rubbing its head against Claire's silken thigh. She moaned softly and reached back with one hand to jerk me off as she continued to deep-throat Gary.

Gary's movements became more urgent, and I knew he was about to come. He gave a sharp gasp as his cock exploded. As he came, Claire drew off him for an instant and a huge stream of come shot into the air. She aimed his throbbing cock at her mouth and hungrily caught huge gobs of hot juice. Finally, she engulfed his spurting rod and sucked every last drop out of him. A trickle of goo was running down her chin when she sat up. She kissed him deeply, swirling his seed around in his mouth with her tongue.

Apparently Gary wasn't through. Taking Claire's hand, he led her out of the club. I followed. I didn't have far to go. Gary took Claire into an alley behind the stage. The area was deserted, even though we were only a few feet from the main entrance and the crowd waiting to get inside. We could hear people on the street talking about the show, but we couldn't see them and they couldn't see us. Gary grabbed Claire roughly and kissed her hard. She melted into him while his hands played over her naked back. He unhooked her dress and it fell away. Her breasts jiggled in the dim light and Gary dropped his mouth to her rock-hard nipples.

As his tongue swirled each areola, Claire moaned, raised her right leg and humped her pussy against his crotch.

He backed her against the wall of the club and hurriedly unzipped his jeans. His big dick sprang into view, fully hard once again. He pushed the thin material of her panties away from her wet, aching cunt. Raising her leg up with a strong arm, he sank his hard meat into her humid depths in a single stroke. I could hear the warm, welcoming wetness of her hole suck him in as he began fucking her with long, hard strokes. Claire's head was thrown back and she was grinding her pussy into him, flexing her taut ass muscles. She clutched at him, trying to pull him deeper.

"Oh yes, yes, fuck me hard. Your cock feels so good! Oh please, fill me up with sweet, sweet come!"

With a wail, Claire came. Her long fingers ran over Gary's back and her hips shivered with the intensity of her orgasm. Her eyes were glazed and her full, red lips formed a perfect O. Her strong legs pulled his thrusting ass hard against her. Suddenly her eyes snapped shut and she moaned loudly as a second wave of pleasure coursed through her. Her hips thrust back and forth involuntarily, her feet were splayed out and her tongue licked her swollen lips. She pulled Gary to her and gave him a deep, wet kiss, fucking him with her tongue like he was fucking her with his dick.

I exploded in my hand and covered it with sticky seed. Gary was fucking Claire with furious thrusts of his huge cock and Claire had locked her legs around his strong ass. With a guttural cry he buried himself in her one last time and shot warm jets of come deep into her spasming pussy. As he continued to fuck her streams of come dripped out, running down her thighs and onto the silky material of her stockings. I watched as she kneaded his balls, milking every drop into her pussy with her long, supple fingers.

Since that night, Gary and Claire get together at least once a week. Sometimes I watch, but often I wait and ask my wife to describe it for me. This always gets her hot and ready for more action which is just how I like her.—B.E., *Detroit, Michigan*

HAPPY BIRTHDAY HONEY—NOW BLOW OUT THE
CANDLES ON THE BEEFCAKE

I'm writing to let readers know about the wonderful birthday present I gave my wife. She was about to turn forty. For several years, especially during lovemaking, Jody had mentioned how every woman dreams of having two men simultaneously. I don't think she believed she would ever have the chance to experience this, and I never said anything about making her dream come true.

As a regular reader of *Penthouse Letters*, I have always been fascinated by letters from men who liked to watch their wives making it with other men. The idea was a little frightening, but it always got me very excited.

I finally chose two friends I thought my wife would like. I also made sure I would be able to observe and join in. Ross and Ken were shocked at first, but it soon became clear they were also very interested. They both thought my wife was very attractive. I later learned that Ross and Jody had exchanged passionate kisses at a party a year ago, but Jody had stopped his advances when his hands had strayed too far.

Jody and I began her birthday celebration by going out for dinner. Arrangements had been made for Ross and Ken to accidentally meet us afterward at a local lounge. They sat at our table and the four of us spent the evening drinking and dancing. As the evening wore on I danced with Jody less, letting Ross and Ken keep her busy. During one long, slow song I noticed Ross's hands on Jody's shapely rear end. When the song ended, they kissed before coming back to the table.

As Ross and Jody danced to another slow song, Ken joined them on the dance floor and snuggled up against Jody from behind. His cock was obviously straining to escape from his trousers as he humped my wife's ass on the dance floor. As the three of them moved to the music, I could see Ken kissing her neck. I knew it was time to move on to our house for step two.

I announced that Jody and I had to head home while we were still able to drive. Jody protested, until I asked Ross and Ken to follow us home for a nightcap.

Earlier that day I had asked a friend to leave a message for me on our answering machine telling me I had to go to my office to take care of an urgent security problem. These kinds of emergencies have happened before, so Jody was not suspicious. The scene was set for Ross and Ken to fulfill my wife's fantasy while she felt safe to enjoy herself.

Instead of driving to the office I drove around the block and parked not far from our house. Then I went through the backyard, climbed up onto the deck and looked through a sliding glass door. I had left the drapes open, so I had a full view of the living room and its three horny occupants. Even Ross and Ken didn't know I'd planned to watch.

The first thing I saw through the glass door was Ken and Jody slow dancing. After a few moments, their lips locked together for what must have been a deep and probing kiss. Ross joined them and Jody kissed him with equal passion. While this was happening, I noticed that the two men's hands had begun exploring Jody's curves. At first she brushed them away, but soon she gave up and started enjoying the attention.

The three friends stood in the middle of the living room and Jody kissed one and then the other. As Ross kissed her, Ken began undressing my very horny wife. First he unfastened her skirt and let it fall to the floor. Then he unbuttoned her blouse, revealing a lace bra. His hands cupped each breast and massaged them. Jody, however, seemed lost in a passionate embrace with Ross.

Luckily for Ken, my wife's bra fastens in front. As her white, rose-tipped breasts tumbled free, he sucked one of her hard nipples into his mouth. Jody reacted by placing her hand on the back of his head, as if to make sure he stayed put. As Ken focused his attention on her top half, Ross slid his hand down Jody's stomach until he reached her bush.

He found her pussy and slid a finger inside. Jody broke off the embrace and spread her legs a bit more.

Ross removed the rest of Jody's clothing, and I could see her love-juices glistening and running down her long, slim legs. Ken was still sucking her tits, while Ross kneeled and began licking her slit. At that point Jody's legs finally gave out and the two men gently helped her to the floor. As she was lying back, she reached for Ken's trousers and released his long, hard cock. She immediately took it in her mouth. Then, as she hungrily sucked Ken's cock, she wantonly used her free hand to release Ross's tool.

Soon the two men were devouring my wife's body with their hands and mouths. Ken was getting the blow job of his life, while Ross was eating away at her snatch. It was only a matter of time before a cock found its way between my wife's legs.

Ross grabbed a pillow, placed it under Jody's ass and gently eased his throbbing, red cock inside her. Jody didn't miss a beat sucking Ken's cock. After a few easy strokes, Ross's thrusts took on more power.

As Ross entered Jody, Ken had his first explosive orgasm while I (still behind the glass door) shot my load into my hand. After that Jody lay back and enjoyed the fucking Ross was giving her. One thing I know about my wife is that she arches her back and toes when she is reaching orgasm. As Ross pumped into her, her back and feet arched for what seemed like more than ten minutes. My love was obviously in sexual heaven.

After giving Jody a wonderful fucking, Ross's muscles tensed up and he unloaded into her. He collapsed on top of her and remained there for several minutes before rolling off. The three of them sat there exhausted. It looked as though the evening was over, until Ken picked up my wife and carried her into the bedroom. It took me a few moments to get into position to see what happened next.

By the time I reached the bedroom window, Jody was on the bed on her back and Ken was holding her left leg straight up in the air. He was standing beside the bed and his huge cock was easily sliding in and out of her sopping wet hole. Ross was licking and sucking her nipples, and I knew it was only a matter of time before his cock would find its way between her lips. It was time for me to rejoin the party.

By now, Ross was receiving a blow job while Ken was thrusting deep into Jody. I slipped out of my clothes before any of them noticed I was there. I waited until Ken unloaded his second load into my flushed and panting wife, and then I immediately replaced him. Jody looked up, saw it was me inside her and said, "Welcome home. We missed you." We spent the next several hours in a variety of positions. I have yet to tell Jody I watched the whole event.—*R.W., Altoona, Pennsylvania*

GUY LEARNS HIS LADY HAS A JOB ON THE SIDE—ON HER BACK

*M*y girl's name is Sue. She was born and raised in a ritzy part of Philadelphia and she's a snob.

She's a sweet girl in many ways but she doesn't realize she's a snob, though she inarguably is. Anyway, Sue loves sex. She really, really loves sex. And she's never had any trouble getting her fill of it.

Sue is twenty-six years old and beautiful. She has gorgeous hair, a terrific body, a knockout face, a super-tight pussy, long legs and adorable feet. Her perfect, long fingernails and toenails are always expertly manicured and painted to match.

Next to sex, Sue loves money best. She expects anyone she dates to pay for everything, even though she says she's a feminist. Her logic tells her that, because men have most of the power and money in society, the least they can do for a woman is pay for everything.

Although Sue has always loved sex, during her college days she used to worry about her reputation. She was convinced that all her boyfriends bragged to their frat brothers about how the hottest-looking girl on campus was also the wildest lay around. Maybe that's why, when we first met, she pretended that she didn't like doing it doggie-style and that she never gave head. Over time, though, her powerful sex drive overcame her false modesty and she willingly engaged in both practices.

Sue often has more than ten orgasms when we make love. Sometimes she wants to switch positions every five minutes. She turns into a complete animal—squealing, squeaking, snorting and whining as I fuck her tiny brains out. (And tiny is what they are, believe me.) We've even tried anal sex. At first she said she was sure she would hate it, but now when my dick's up her ass she can come without either of us even touching her pussy.

Sue and I discuss our fantasies quite often. Her fantasies involve having several men at once—older men who are there solely to pleasure her. Her fantasies also involve men paying for the privilege of fucking her. She's also obsessed with huge cocks. Sue's the first girl I've ever met who absolutely insists that size matters. She claims all her friends agree with her too. She says they all laugh at guys with little dicks.

I always enjoyed hearing about Sue's fantasies, but I was sure they existed only in her head. I believed there was no way this princess would ever actually do the nasty things she loved to talk about. I don't mind admitting that I was wrong.

Last Thursday I left work early and decided to surprise Sue. I went to my place, changed and strolled over to Sue's. As I neared her building, I saw a man in his early fifties get out of a shiny new Lexus. He stopped, reached into his pocket and pulled out a piece of paper. He looked down at it and then up at the number on the apartment building before putting the slip back into his pocket. Then I saw him pull out a money clip and thumb through it before entering Sue's building.

I thought nothing of it and followed him in. As I walked through the main door, I was surprised to see the door to Sue's place closing. I ran up to the door and knocked, but there was no answer. I started to worry, so I quickly left the building and went around back to look in her windows. There was nothing to see in the living room, nothing in the dining room or kitchen, and nothing in her roommate's room. The sight from her bedroom window was a different story. My panic left me and so did all the feeling in my body. I was rooted to the spot in shock. Through half-open blinds I saw Sue. She looked fine. So did the man I'd seen outside her apartment building. So did the other two guys.

Sue was naked save for one of the Victoria's Secret push-up bras she always wears because she doesn't think her terrific tits are big enough. She was on the bed with her ass in the air and her head and shoulders down on her Ralph Lauren comforter. One of the men knelt behind her, holding her hips and slamming his dick into her greedy pussy. Her swollen cunt lips clung to the shaft of his dick as he pumped it in and out of her. Her eyes were closed and her lips were pursed in pleasure.

All three men had gray hair and looked like they were in their fifties. All three were exposing extra-large dicks. The other two were patiently waiting for the third to get his rocks off.

When he did he pulled his pants up, said a few words to Sue (who was still on the bed with her perfect white ass in the air), put three fifty-dollar bills on Sue's vanity table and left the room.

The second guy stepped over to Sue. She lifted her head up off the bed, crawled to face him, slurped his hard cock into her big mouth and started sucking. Sue bobbed her sweet head up and down on the old guy's prick. This time it was the lips on her face that clung to a thick cock as it moved in and out of her. She massaged his balls as she slurped on him. She sucked him there on her hands and knees for ten minutes before he said something and she hauled his log out of her mouth. She kissed his cockhead, rolled over onto her back, spread her legs and pulled her knees up to her chest. Her pretty feet were pointing toward the ceiling.

The guy got down between her thighs and began lapping her perfect pussy. Sue closed her eyes. Meanwhile, the man I'd seen earlier stroked his dick and watched them, just as I was doing. The guy between her legs reached up and held Sue's ankles in the air as he ate her out. Sue has the kind of pussy you can eat all day without getting tired. This guy savored it for quite a while before climbing up into her arms and positioning his dick at the entrance to her pussy. He teased her with his cockhead, and I saw her bucking her hips in an effort to get it into her. She said something (probably "fuck me") and grabbed his ass. He responded by plunging his dick in up to the hilt. Sue stuck her feet up in the air as the guy's ass started pumping up and down. He really fucked her hard.

I stared at her slender ankles and shapely feet. Sue was wiggling and spreading her little painted toes in pleasure. Then all of a sudden, after a few final hard thrusts, the man stopped. It was clear that he'd come.

Sue lowered her feet down to the bed and waited patiently for the guy to climb off her. When he did, she propped herself up on her elbows and watched him pull his pants on. He left four bills on her vanity, said good-bye and left. She gave him a smile as he closed the bedroom door behind him.

The man I'd followed in was now the only one left. He and Sue talked as he stroked his very large dong with one hand. Of the three men, he had the biggest dick by far. Sue was watching it, rather than the man, as he talked.

This guy talked with Sue longer than the others had. Then he reached into his pocket and showed her his money clip. The money clip distracted her from his big dick, but only for a second.

He put five bills down on her vanity and she flashed him a big, toothy smile. She was obviously very excited to see that much cash. Still smiling, she rolled over onto her stomach and slowly raised her spectacular ass into the air. Her head was down on the bed, her eyes were closed and that big smile still graced her lips.

The man walked up behind her and massaged her pussy for a moment. He spread the mix of her juices and the other fellows' come all over her with one hand while he stroked his big schlong with the other. Sue said something, in response to which he slammed his whole dick into her pussy with one thrust. After two more thrusts, Sue quite obviously came. Sue said something else and the guy slowly pulled his dick free of the grip of her pussy lips.

The man then put his fat dick up against my pretty girlfriend's tight little asshole and pushed. The smile left her face. Her hands clutched the comforter on her bed. Her face was contorted as the man slowly pushed inch after inch of his penis into her rectum. He slowly pulled it out and repeated the process, picking up speed this time. Sue held on to the sheets and kept her head down, but the look on her face slowly changed. Her mouth opened and she began to pant with pleasure as the man fucked her ass. He held her hips and pumped into her tiny asshole like a steam locomotive. I could see her swollen, gaping cunt lips very clearly as the man's balls slapped into them over and over again.

After a few minutes of steady ass-fucking, he leaned back and cried out so loudly that I could hear him outside. He'd clearly had a very powerful orgasm. Then he held still, his dick stuffed deep inside Sue's ass, while that big smile returned to her gorgeous face. She kept smiling as the man held on to her hips and tried to catch his breath. After a minute he slowly pulled his dick out of her ass. The man pulled his pants up and looked at his watch as his come started to ooze out of Sue's ass. He then reached into his pocket, pulled out another crisp bill and folded it. Sue was still on the bed with her ass in the air, smiling that great smile. The man reached down and slid the folded bill right between Sue's fleshy ass-cheeks. He then tickled her pretty foot, gave her a kiss and turned to leave.

Sue just stayed there with her head down on the bed and the bill in her ass-crack. "Thanks!" she called out as the satisfied customer left her bedroom.

I kept watching, dumbstruck and rock-hard, as Sue lay quietly on her bed for a while. I heard the Lexus drive off. When Sue finally moved, it was to reach back, remove the bill from between her cheeks and unfold it. She grinned when she saw he'd given her a one-hundred-dollar tip. She then got off the bed and walked to the vanity. I watched as she pulled a jewelry box out of her drawer, opened it and put the bills in with a bunch of others already there. She then took her bra off, grabbed her towel and went off to shower, I guess.

I snapped out of it at that point and decided to just go home. I still don't know what to think.—*K.M., Philadelphia, Pennsylvania*

HUBBY HIRES A STRIPPER TO
UNLOCK HIS BRIDE'S WILD SIDE

Your letters sometimes show that extraordinary things can happen to ordinary people. I'd like to relate an extraordinary occurrence that happened to me recently.

I play racquetball with a friend of mine named Dan. He's in great shape and has a terrific body. After our games we'd usually hit the sauna together. We talked about a lot of different things, but neither of us ever broached the subject of sex. So I was pretty surprised one day when Dan stated that, in his opinion, most married women were interested in having wild sexual experiences but that they would never confess this to their husbands.

I told him I agreed and that I believed my own wife, Phoebe, had always wanted to see a male strip show but had never admitted it to me. "What a coincidence!" he replied. "Before I was married I auditioned for a job as a stripper."

A week later I half-jokingly asked Dan if he wanted to audition again—this time for Phoebe. She and Dan had never met, so I thought he would be the perfect choice. He looked at me and smiled. We made a deal then and there.

It took a while to set things up, but I finally convinced Phoebe to spend a weekend with me at a posh hotel.

We checked into a nice suite. After sharing a bottle of champagne, we went downstairs to the restaurant for a light supper and a lot more wine. Once Phoebe was feeling very relaxed, I told her there was a special surprise visitor coming at exactly eleven. She thought I was joking, but I convinced her to return to the room with me as eleven approached.

When there was a knock on the door promptly at eleven, Phoebe seemed genuinely surprised. She threw her robe on as I went to answer the door. When I let Dan in, Phoebe didn't know what to think. During dinner I had mentioned the possibility of taking her to see a male strip show one day, and now here was a tall, well-built stranger wearing a silk shirt, skintight pants and dark Revo sunglasses.

Dan introduced himself as "your entertainment for the evening." Dan then opened up a gym bag, took out a tape player and started his routine. He was good—real good.

I sat on the bed behind my wife. "This is all for you," I whispered to her. She put her hand on my thigh and gave a little squeeze, but she never took her eyes off of Dan's body.

Dan was putting on a great show. He'd taken off his shirt and had started to slowly unzip his pants when he turned around to face Phoebe, who was sitting on the edge of the bed. She reached over and ran her hand over his well-muscled back and across his tight behind. She felt him flex his buttocks as he slowly moved his body back and forth. She wrapped both arms around him and helped him remove his pants. I could tell by the way they both flinched slightly that she must have checked out his equipment.

Dan, now wearing only black bikini briefs, started a pulsating rhythm that seemed to mesmerize Phoebe. When the song ended, I poured more of the champagne and we all had a glass. Dan then went into the next room to change his costume. Phoebe gave me the most passionate kiss ever. She was really flushed. She told me that this was the most exciting surprise I'd ever given her.

Phoebe was even more excited by Dan's second number. He came out wearing red silk shorts and a fishnet T-shirt. I knew by the look on Phoebe's face that she wanted to get those shorts off him fast. Dan took her by the hand, pulled her to her feet, put his arms around her waist and started slowly moving to the music. I saw her grind her crotch against his leg. Then she slid her thumb into the waistband of his shorts, knelt down and pulled the shorts to the ground. He was left wearing a black G-string that was even smaller than a jockstrap. Phoebe's face was less than a foot away from his bulge. The sexual tension in the room suddenly grew thicker. Nobody moved for what seemed like a minute. There was, however, something moving. Phoebe and I watched silently as Dan's cock unfurled and grew until it strained the flimsy material of his G-string.

I got up and helped my mesmerized wife back to the bed. She put her arms around my hips and pressed the side of her head against my cock while continuing to stare at Dan's body. At this point the song ended and Dan again left the room. Without a word, Phoebe turned her head, opened my robe and hungrily took my cock into her mouth. She looked up and met my eyes— something she'd never done before during oral sex. That simple act signaled a revolution in our sex life. I knew that, from that moment on, sex with Phoebe would be hotter, more exciting and less inhibited.

Phoebe was glowing with sexual energy. She was in control and she knew it. She stood up and gently pushed me down onto the bed. Then, with her back to me, she straddled me and guided my penis into her wet pussy. We had just started rocking back and forth when Dan came back into the room.

The atmosphere in the room crackled with sexual electricity. Dan was wearing a cape and little else. He began to dance slowly, rotating his hips in front of her face as we fucked. She began to hungrily explore his body with her hands. Phoebe reached behind her and pushed down on my chest until I was lying flat on the bed. Then she pulled the cape off him and draped it over my head so that it blocked my view.

I felt her weight shift a little, so I pulled the material down a bit so I could see. Have you ever imagined your wife with another man: the flush of her cheeks, the jiggling of her breasts, the hardness of her nipples? I have; but seeing it for real was still a shock.

There was my wife, breathing deeply through flared nostrils, her cheeks hollowed as she sucked with abandon on Dan's dick. Her head bobbed and her tongue swirled around his shaft. I felt my cock grow another inch inside her. I was sure she felt it too: She moaned low and long.

Phoebe had one hand on his butt, pulling him toward her. Her other hand was between his legs, toying with his balls. Half of Dan's eight-incher had disappeared between her pouting lips.

His hand was on her head, gently encouraging her to take more of his cock into her eager mouth. I could tell that Dan's cock was up against the back of her throat. Phoebe had never deep-throated a guy before, but I had a feeling this time might be different. I watched enthralled as, ever so slowly, they worked more of his cock into her. As with all her previous attempts, she couldn't do it and had to take his cock out of her mouth. He moaned in disappointment.

But Phoebe wasn't quitting. "Wait," she said. Then, taking him by the hips, she guided him back a step so that she would have to crane her neck forward to reach him. Now, with her neck stretched and her head tilted back, she was lined up for another attempt to take him down her throat.

I felt her grip me tightly with her pussy and grind her clit against the base of my cock. She was getting ready to come as she once more began fucking him with her mouth. Then she took a deep breath and, once again, pressed the swollen head of his cock against the back of her throat.

She steeled herself and took him down her throat with one quick thrust. For the first time in her life she was deep-throating. I had never seen her so aroused. As Dan's cock penetrated her virgin throat, she had an orgasm that shook her whole body.

Phoebe's trembling body had become a conductor of sexual energy. As I rapidly approached orgasm, Dan clutched her face tightly and, with a resounding groan, pumped his load deep inside her. She pulled his cock out of her mouth and milked the last drops out of him with her hand. Then she turned her attention to me. Glowing with passion, she pulled me out of her pussy, turned and took me into her mouth. She then worked my penis down her throat for the first time ever. The sensation was incredible, and I started to come almost immediately. My orgasm seemed to go on and on.

That night was the most erotic I have ever had. Phoebe and I never made it a habit to have an extra lover in bed with us, but we did make it a habit to have exciting and uninhibited sex.— *Name and address withheld*

CAROUSING COUPLE GETS A BLAST FROM THE PAST

*M*y wife Sylvia and I have been reading *Penthouse Letters* for about a year now, and we both love it. Sylvia is thirty-two years old and I am thirty-five. We have been married for eleven years.

Sylvia was born and raised in a small town in South Dakota. Last summer we went there to attend a family reunion. Long before this, Sylvia had told me she had lost her cherry to a guy named John who'd lived in her neighborhood. She'd had sex with him a number of times until he got married shortly after she turned nineteen. Sylvia hadn't seen John since we were married, but he was expected to attend the reunion.

Sylvia and I have done a little swinging in the past. We even swapped a couple of times with other couples. Sylvia once had a short affair with a fellow worker. One night I watched her in bed with a guy we met at a party. Ever since she'd told me about John, I'd been curious about him and had wanted to meet him.

As anticipated, I finally got my chance to meet John on the first day of the reunion. He turned out to be a very good-looking guy. He is about my age and had been divorced for several years. He and Sylvia spent most of the day together talking. At one point, I saw them heading toward the lake.

That night Sylvia told me that John had asked her if they

might get together one more time before she went back home. I asked her if she had given him an answer. She said she had told him she would talk to me and let him know later. I asked her if she wanted to do it. She said she did, but that it was up to me. Since I had watched Sylvia in bed with another guy in the past and had found it very exciting, I asked her if John would let me watch. She said she would talk to him about it the next day.

As it turned out John was a little hesitant at first, but when Sylvia told him we had an open marriage and that I had watched her have sex with another guy before, he agreed to let me watch.

John lived alone in a mobile home, and Sylvia and I paid him a visit there that night. We had a few drinks and sat around talking for about an hour before anything happened. John and Sylvia were sitting on the sofa together. At one point I got up to use the bathroom. When I came back they were kissing and John's hand was up Sylvia's dress. They kept right on kissing as I walked in and sat down in a chair facing them.

Things started heating up and I saw Sylvia reach for John's zipper. When she opened it and took his cock out, I got a big surprise. John was hung like a horse! His cock looked to be at least ten inches long. Sylvia is a small woman, and I wondered if she could accommodate a cock that large.

Before long they were both naked. Sylvia got on her knees in front of John, took his cock in her mouth and began to suck on it. After a few minutes of that, John lay down on her. He licked and sucked her pussy until she was moaning and rolling her head from side to side. Then she had an orgasm.

They decided to move to the bed. John started to ease his cock into her pussy. I was amazed at the way she took his large cock into her body.

He lasted only a short time before he shot his load inside her, but after a short rest he was soon hard again. John then put her on her hands and knees and got behind her. With a single thrust he rammed all ten inches into her up to the hilt. At first he fucked her with long, slow strokes. Then he started banging her really hard.

Sylvia loved it, and I watched her have several more orgasms.

When he threw back his head and bellowed, I knew John was shooting another load in her.

Sylvia let out a scream at the same time. After watching all this I was so turned on that I couldn't wait to get Sylvia back to our motel room so I could fuck her myself.

We invited John to visit us during his next vacation, and both of us hope he will come . . . and that we'll come too!—*S.B., Omaha, Nebraska*

SNEAKY WIFE FUCKS YOUNG STUD, BUT HUBBY'S ONTO IT—AND INTO IT

*L*ast weekend I saw something I hoped I would never see—my wife fucking another man. If that wasn't bad enough, she fucked a guy young enough to be her son. As far as I know, last weekend's encounter was the first time she ever cheated on me.

Brenda, my wife, is a statuesque woman, standing six feet tall with flowing curly brown hair, muscular thighs, a plump ass and two big tits—40DDs. We met years ago as college freshmen. I was a computer nerd, and she was a loner because of her big size and brains.

After she survived a serious car accident ten years ago, my wife started changing. She started jogging, eating low-fat foods and doing strenuous aerobic exercises every day. She also threw out all her old clothes and bought a stylish new wardrobe. I loved her, but I wasn't changing. I was still the same old computer nerd, working my way up the corporate ladder at a computer company.

I often wondered if my wife was unhappy sexually. My six-inch cock isn't all that big, and I'm shorter and smaller than my wife. With her voluptuous size, my wife has an extremely deep pussy, which my cock can't fill completely. A couple of years ago, when the kids were away for the weekend, we rented some X-rated videos. When I woke up in the middle of the night and realized my wife wasn't in bed, I suddenly was aware of the murmur of the television downstairs. I walked to the top of the stairs and watched something I had never seen before—my wife masturbating. She was slumped down in a chair, her thick, well-muscled legs draped over the wide chair arms, playing with her hairy pussy. On the screen men with bulging muscles and solid, tanned bodies slammed in and out of the women.

Last weekend we headed to a mountain resort for my company's annual retreat. We unpacked our suitcases on Friday afternoon and settled into our small, secluded cabin in the mountains of North Carolina. That night at dinner we sat with my coworker Tom, his wife Georgina and their son Jeff, a muscular football player at a local college. I initially dismissed Jeff as a dumb jock, but he held his own in conversation with the adults sitting at the table, revealing the brains he possessed along with the brawn.

As couples moved onto the dance floor, I endured a dance with my wife, stepping on her feet several times. After we sat down, Jeff walked over from the bar and asked my wife to dance. Giving him a big smile, she accepted. I felt like a fool as that young man expertly whisked my wife around the dance floor, leading her through some complicated steps.

"Thank you," my wife gushed, blushing, when Jeff escorted her back to the table. "You're a great dancer."

They danced two more times during the next hour, and one of those dances was a long, slow dance. As the night wore on, I noticed my wife looking around the cavernous room, but Jeff had obviously disappeared. I was jealous of that damn quarterback's ability on the dance floor, and I drank a few too many beers.

Back in our cabin, when my wife stripped off her dress and playfully pounced on me, I couldn't get an erection. She certainly didn't hide her irritation as she yanked on a nightgown and walked out into the living room. I fell asleep a few minutes later, but when the alarm clock woke me up the next morning my wife was curled up next to me.

After a quick shower, shave and breakfast, I hurried to my first meeting of the day, agreeing to meet my wife in the dining room at five-thirty that evening. During the first speech of the day I realized that I had forgotten my laptop computer in the cabin. Glancing at my watch, I decided to go back and get it during the midmorning break. When the speaker finished talking, I scurried out of the lecture hall and hurried up the steep steps leading to our cabin. I rushed into the cabin, grabbed the computer and started to dart back out the door when two things caught my attention: First, I heard my wife moan from the direction of the bedroom. Second, I saw her nightgown lying in a heap in the middle of the kitchen floor. Realizing that I might catch a glimpse of her masturbating again, I quietly set the computer down and tiptoed to the bedroom door. Luckily the old wooden doors had decorative doorknobs with huge keyholes. I squatted down in front of the door, and I had a perfect view of the bed.

My wife was naked, crouched on her hands and knees with her big butt stuck up in the air—a different position than the first time I'd seen her masturbate—and she was gasping and grunting, "Oh Lord! Ahhhh! Yeah!"

Then I realized something very strange. Both of my wife's hands were tightly gripping the bedspread. Something odd was going on here. How could she be masturbating if she was holding on to the bedspread? The mystery was solved when Jeff stood up on the other side of the bed. I almost screamed. I had not seen him kneeling on the other side of the bed with his face buried in my wife's pussy.

As he straightened up, my heart sank, but my cock hardened in my pants. Bulging, thick muscles rippled under his tanned, golden skin, but the thickest muscle of all was the huge cock sticking out from between his hard thighs. My God, he was hung. Blue veins throbbed along the length of his swollen rod of flesh. If my wife had fantasized about getting her ample pussy filled, her wish was certainly about to come true.

"Why did you stop?" my wife asked, looking back over her shoulder. "You do that so well."

"I enjoy eating pussy," Jeff said, staring at my wife's naked body. "But we'll have time for more of that later. Right now I want to fuck that pussy. Isn't that what you want?"

"Yes."

"Yes, what? I want you to tell me exactly what you want me to do."

"I want you to fill my pussy with that big cock," my wife responded.

Turning around, she grabbed Jeff's cock and guided it into her mouth. As she sucked and licked the head of his penis, she reached underneath his dick and cupped his bulging nuts.

While my wife serviced him with her mouth, Jeff closed his eyes as he fastened his fingers on my wife's sensitive nipples. He teased and twisted her dark brown nipples, cupping her tits in his callused hands.

My wife jerked her mouth away from his cock and flopped back on the bed with her ass hanging off the edge of the mattress. Grabbing her knees, she pulled her legs apart, presenting her pussy for that hunky young stud. She had never done anything like that with me.

"Oh please, please fuck me, Jeff," she implored him.

Jeff did just that. He grabbed his cock and guided it to my wife's dripping cunt.

"Uhhh," my wife groaned as Jeff's cockhead slipped past her pussy lips. Jeff slowly guided his dick into my wife until his balls were pressed against her white ass-cheeks. From where I was watching, I could see past Jeff's tight ass to the direct point of penetration. I quickly unzipped my pants and slipped out my penis.

Jeff stood there next to the bed with his cock completely buried in my wife's big pussy for several minutes, then he reached down, wrapped his arms around my wife's knees and started fucking her. My wife has always been a vocal lovemaker, but fortunately we were staying in an isolated cabin. Her screams and moans echoed inside the bedroom. As I watched, I realized I had never seen an X-rated video as raw as the solid fucking my wife was getting.

Using his upper-body strength, Jeff jerked my wife's legs up and down, yanking her ass back and forth off the mattress. He also started bending up and down, shoving his cock as deep as he could into my wife's pussy. My wife's ass bounced up and down on the mattress as Jeff hammered in and out of her. With her arms pressed flat on the mattress, and legs kicking and jerking in the air, my wife screamed and grunted as she got the fucking of her life. Her pussy stretched tight around his massive cock, filled completely for the first time in her life.

Jeff was also a vocal lover. He grunted and groaned as he talked dirty to my wife, which was something I had never done. To my shock, my wife talked back to him the same way.

"I wanted to fuck this pussy last night," Jeff said. "When I came up here this morning, I wasn't going to take no for an answer. But I didn't have a problem, did I? As soon as I slid my hand onto your leg out there in the kitchen, you parted those thighs and pulled my hand right onto your wet pussy."

"Oh God!" my wife cried. "Oh, oh yes! I knew you would be good. I wanted to sneak off and fuck you last night, but you disappeared."

"I didn't want to go to bed horny," Jeff said. "So I got a plump redhead to follow me down to my cabin."

I couldn't believe what he was saying. The only plump redhead I knew of was the vice-president of our company, and she was happily married with three kids. My God, didn't this stud have any sense of decency?

"Her big fat ass shook like a bowl of jelly when I fucked her from behind like I'm going to do to you in a minute," Jeff told her.

My wife reached down and started tugging on Jeff's nuts. "She might have been good, but I'll do anything you want. I'll be the best lover you ever had," she boasted.

As Jeff's movements sped up to a virtual frenzy, his ass started jerking erratically back and forth. Slipping his hands down, he cupped my wife's ass, then pried her ass-cheeks apart and shoved his index finger into her anus. Jeff fell across the bed, dropping his full weight onto my wife's thighs and driving his dick all the way inside her.

My wife moaned and groaned. Her legs wrapped around Jeff's ass as she wrapped her arms around him, pulled his face into her cleavage and let out a monstrous scream. She didn't move for several minutes, and neither did he. Finally he rolled off her with a loud grunt. Breathing shallowly, my wife sat up and stared at him.

"My God," she said, gasping for air, "that was the best goddamn sex I've ever had, or even dreamed of for that matter."

Raising up on one arm, Jeff ran his fingertips down my wife's sweaty stomach.

"Thank you," he said. "I was doing my best to please you."

When I saw the thick, white spunk dripping out of my wife's pussy, my cock exploded.

They started kissing and cuddling, and Jeff's cock suddenly hardened again. Rubbing her fingers down the thickness, my wife bent her head down and kissed the tip.

"Before we do anything else," she said, "I want to take a bath." When Jeff followed my wife into the large bathroom, I snuck into the bedroom and slipped quietly into the large walk-in closet. I could see the bed and the bathroom perfectly from where I stood inside the closet.

My wife and Jeff took a long, leisurely bath. Neither of them seemed the least bit awkward or regretful of their earlier sexual encounter. As I watched, they climbed out of the bathtub, dried each other off and ended up on the floor, fucking doggie-style. Jeff hung on to my wife's hips and yanked her back and forth on his dick, sending her big titties flopping every time he pounded into her. His hard stomach slapped against my wife's thick ass, and the sound of flesh hitting flesh filled the bathroom and the bedroom. I tugged on my aching penis and shot a wad of thick come as my wife arched her head back and let out a deep-throated groan as she orgasmed again.

I hid in the closet all day—watching my wife fall under the spell of that thick-bodied jock with a blond crew cut. I wanted to cry as he lathered K-Y jelly onto his cock and fucked my wife in the ass for the first time. She whooped and hollered as she orgasmed with a cock inside her ass.

He also tit-fucked her. Then she got on top and rode his thick cock, her ass bouncing up and down on his thighs. She also sat on his face as he licked her to a mind-blowing orgasm.

After lunch I got the shock of my life when someone knocked lightly at the cabin door. My wife jumped up and yanked on a bathrobe, telling Jeff to hide in the bathroom.

"I think I know who that is," he said. He stayed where he was on the bed, naked, his stiffening cock bobbing back and forth, as my wife went to see who it was.

"It's Carol," my wife hissed, sticking her head through the bedroom door. "She says that she knows you're in here."

"Bring her in," Jeff responded.

My wife looked at him with an odd expression, then opened the door all the way.

Carol burst through the doorway, ran to the bed and started licking his slick cock. "I don't care if you watch, and I could care less if he makes it with other women," Carol said to my wife as she yanked her dress over her head. "But I couldn't go another minute without fucking this sweet boy's hard dick."

I watched as the vice-president of my company unhooked her bra, releasing a pair of breasts bigger than my wife's. Then she slid her panties down. "You probably have the same problem I do," Carol said, climbing onto the bed and straddling Jeff's cock, "finding a cock big enough to fill up your big pussy."

Jerking her ass forward, Carol started bouncing up and down on Jeff. "Suck my titties, big guy," she said, shoving her thick, pink nipples into Jeff's open mouth.

"Come join us, Brenda," Carol said. "It'll be fun."

I watched as my wife dropped her bathrobe onto the bed and started licking Jeff's balls. Inhibitions soon crumbled, and when my wife slipped her pussy onto Jeff's face, she leaned forward and started sucking Carol's nipples. I proceeded to witness my wife's very first lesbian encounter. It was certainly a weekend of firsts, and I only hope that my wife and I can share such adventures in the future.—*R.K., St. Petersburg, Florida*

SATURDAY NIGHT'S ALL RIGHT
FOR FUCKING—AND FOR WATCHING

*M*y name is Russ and I'm married to my high school sweetheart Cindy. She was a cheerleader then and I played football. My dad has a successful chain of dry-cleaning stores and we both went to work for him right after graduation. We've been married for fourteen years and our sex life is great. We get it on three or four times a week, which is plenty for me, but every once in a while Cindy uses a vibrator to give herself a little something extra.

We love to read the letters in your magazine where the husband watches his wife getting it on with another man. We watch porn videos once in a while, and the men with especially big cocks really turn her on. She'll make comments like, "I wonder what a cock that big feels like. I don't even know if I could handle one like it."

We live in a large condo complex with a pool, and I've noticed Cindy eyeing some of the men as they walk around. There's one guy she pays particular attention to. Andy is about thirty years old and single. We both took a liking to him when he first moved in. We became good friends and have gone out many times together. We play cards and drink on Saturday nights and usually get a good buzz on. A few times at the pool I've said to Cindy,

"Look at how much meat he's packing into those trunks. How would you like to try that monster on for size?"

She'd just say, "You've got to be kidding. There's enough cock there for two women."

I knew that Andy had the hots for her, because he was always checking her out in her bikini. I wanted to see whether Cindy would fuck Andy if she didn't think I'd find out. A plan gradually formed in my mind. I worked out a deal with one of my friends to call me around eleven o'clock that Saturday night to say there was an emergency and that he needed my help. That would leave Cindy and Andy alone to play cards . . . or whatever. But of course I'd be nearby to find out what actually happened.

That Saturday night we were drinking and playing cards as usual. We were all a little drunk. The phone rang at eleven o'clock, right on schedule, and I told Cindy and Andy that I had to take care of an emergency but wouldn't be gone long.

Cindy was upset and pouted, "Oh shit, we were having such a good time. When will you be back?"

"In about an hour," I answered. "You can play cards until I get back."

I got in my car, drove to the next lot over and parked. Then I walked back to my condo, which is on the first floor and has a wooden fence around the patio. I let myself into the patio area. From there I could see into the kitchen where Cindy and Andy were talking and playing cards. Soon they stopped their game and moved into the living room. Andy pulled out a fat joint. Through the open window I could hear him ask Cindy if she wanted to smoke with him. "Just a few hits," she said. "That shit makes me horny." Andy laughed when she said that and didn't waste any time lighting up and offering her a toke.

Cindy had on shorts and a T-shirt with no bra. I could see her nipples getting hard from where I was standing. Andy had been staring at her boobs most of the night, and he took this opportunity to squeeze one through her shirt. She turned to say something, but Andy kissed her. Then he caught himself and backed away, mumbling an apology.

"No," she said, "you don't have to apologize. I'm just not sure this is a good idea. Besides, my husband will be back soon." He sat back and picked up his drink, but suddenly Cindy grabbed his free hand and put it on her thigh. He was soon working his way toward her cunt, toying with her zipper.

But then Cindy pushed his hand away and moaned, "I'm sorry. I just can't do this."

"That's okay," he responded. "You shouldn't do anything you don't want to do."

"I didn't say I didn't want to," Cindy muttered. "Oh, I don't know. Russ would probably even like it if we fucked. He's always dropping hints about how much I'd enjoy sucking your big cock." She leaned over and gave Andy a friendly kiss. It quickly grew passionate and I knew that she wasn't going to stop this time. Andy lifted her shirt and started sucking on her nipples. There was no turning back. I know my wife. She's unstoppable once you start playing with her tits.

After a couple of minutes Andy's hand was back on her thigh, and this time there was no resistance from my wife. His fingers were soon under her shorts and she was moaning, "Oh yes, yes, please touch me there." Whenever he took his hand away from her pussy she put it back, softly muttering, "I'm so wet. I can't believe I'm doing this with you."

Cindy lifted her ass and Andy pulled her shorts and panties down. He knelt on the floor, pulled her ass to the edge of the couch and started licking the insides of her thighs. She moaned, "Deeper, stick your tongue in all the way." Her pussy lips were swollen and gaping, and clear juice was pouring out of them. I would've loved to be lapping up that delicious fluid myself, but in a way it was even more of a turn-on watching Andy do it.

Cindy's head was rolling from side to side. She kept moaning, "Oh God, oh God," and playing with her clit.

"Do you want me to stop?" Andy teased.

Cindy groaned, "No! No way. I'm almost there. Don't stop!" He tongue-fucked her to an orgasm that left her legs flailing in the air and her body spasming. Her loud cries of "Jesus, I'm fucking coming!" filled the air.

After Cindy caught her breath Andy pulled his shorts down and asked, "What do you say? Are you ready for a great fuck?"

Cindy opened her eyes wide at the sight of his giant pole. She took him in her arms and said, "God yes. Fuck me. Fuck me with that big dick!" Kneeling between her knees, Andy tapped his cock against her cunt a few times to get it hard. It was eight or nine inches long and quite fat: the head was the size of a plum. He lifted her legs up and eased them apart. Her waiting cunt was shiny with her juices. Andy placed the head of his dick at her hole and started pressing against it, wetting just his dickhead but not trying to squeeze all of his cock into her cunt just yet.

Cindy sighed, "Oh God, you're big!" Once his tip was well lubricated Andy eased more and more of his shaft into her. It seemed to take him forever, but he finally got it all in. Once when he pulled the whole length out of her she sucked in her breath and begged, "Please, please put it back!" He obliged and Cindy let loose a long, low growl of pleasure. Andy started fucking her with strong thrusts, mashing his pubic hair against hers at the end of each push. Whenever he pulled out, his shaft was glistening with her juices. His cock looked so good even I wanted a piece of it. It was the first time I'd ever had the urge to suck a dick. For a few minutes I actually considered bursting into the room and having Andy fuck my mouth instead of my wife's cunt.

After a few minutes of thrusting Andy asked, "Do you want me to come inside you?"

"Yes!" she urged. He grunted loudly, his balls drawn up tightly against his body. After several especially deep plunges he shouted, "I'm coming . . . now!" Cindy wrapped her legs tightly around his ass as he pumped his load into her hole. They were both trembling all over with excitement, their bodies spasming as the waves of orgasm raced through them.

When Andy pulled out he rolled off to the side and kissed Cindy. Her cunt was tomato-red and wide open. I could see his sperm running out of her pussy and down her ass-cheeks. For some time I'd been jerking off, and as I watched the semen drip out of her cunt I shot my load.

Andy continued playing with her cunt as they talked about what they'd just done. It was getting late, so Cindy kissed him and said, "You'd better get going before Russ gets back."

He started getting dressed, so I left for my car. After I saw Andy leave I waited about fifteen minutes before walking in. Cindy was in a robe and I casually asked, "Where's Andy?"

"You just missed him. He was tired and went home." I asked her to make us a drink and waited for her in the living room. When Cindy handed me my drink I inquired, "So how was it?" Before she could think of what to say I told her, "I watched it all from the yard." Cindy started to cry, but I said, "Hey, honey, it's okay. You two got me so hot I had a fantastic orgasm."

We started kissing and soon we were in a 69 position. Some of Andy's spunk was still in her cunt, and when she came it oozed out mixed with her own juices. We fucked for a good hour and decided that the next time Andy was over we'd have a threesome with him.—R.P., Columbus, Ohio

"JOHNNY COME LATELY?"
"OH, ABOUT AN HOUR AGO," SHE REPLIED

I travel extensively in my line of work, which is what I was doing a couple of weeks ago. But after another night of sitting in yet another strange hotel in another unfamiliar city I found myself really missing my wife Ella. I canceled the rest of my business trip and booked a flight home so I could surprise her by returning a day early. All I wanted was to wrap my arms around my beautiful Ella, carry her to the bed and get a little of the hot pussy I'd been dreaming about all week.

Wouldn't you know it—when I got to the house I discovered that Ella wasn't home. With a cry of disappointment I threw myself on the sofa. I was too restless to sit still for long, though, and decided to take a quick shower and cool my heels at a local bar for a few hours.

I quickly shed my clothes and stepped into the shower. After standing under the hot water for about fifteen minutes I began to masturbate, thinking about how good Ella's soft pussy lips were going to feel in my mouth. Her cunt has a strong scent and flavor and gets incredibly wet when she climaxes. I brought myself to orgasm imagining that she too was coming, filling my mouth with her tasty nectar.

As I went into the bedroom to get dressed I noticed a plain brown envelope lying on the floor in front of the TV set. I casually picked it up and read the note on the outside: "I thought that you might enjoy this—Johnny."

The envelope was empty, but I noticed a tape in the VCR. It had been ejected but not removed. Obviously Ella had already watched the tape. Johnny is my boss, a thirty-year-old self-made millionaire who puts the moves on every woman he meets and is successful with most of them. My curiosity was piqued as I stood there naked. I wondered why he'd left a videotape for my wife. As far as I knew they'd only met a couple of times at company functions and Ella didn't seem to care much for his womanizing ways.

I tried to forget about the tape, but I couldn't. With my heart beating a mile a minute I turned the TV on, put the tape into the VCR and hit the Play button.

The screen was flooded with the image of a man on his hands and knees. He was kneeling behind a woman, thrusting his hips forward as he drove his hard meat into her. I recognized Johnny but couldn't see much of the woman, covered as she was by his tall frame. Her hands reached back over her head as she ran her fingers through his thick hair. His hands were kneading her large tits as he continued to drive his cock into her. The woman was obviously enjoying the fucking she was getting. Johnny has a lot of tapes of him screwing the many women in his life and he's always handing them out to people. He's a little disgusting, really, and I was sorry that Ella had been subjected to his grossness.

Just as I was about to stop the tape the woman leaned forward and rolled onto her back. My eyes just about popped out of their sockets. The lady getting fucked so powerfully by Johnny was my own wife! I was transfixed by the lustful look in Ella's eyes as she begged Johnny to stick his huge cock back into her pussy. I had no idea how they first got together, let alone how many times my wife had made it with my boss by the time this videotape was shot. All I knew was that they were very exciting to watch, their powerful, energetic bodies well-matched—one of those couples that looked as though they'd been born to fuck each other's brains out.

I watched Johnny lean over and lick the beads of sweat off Ella's neck and breasts. Even though I was shocked that my wife had given in to someone as crude and obvious as Johnny, I have to admit that the scene before me was getting me really turned on. I felt my cock hardening and unzipped my pants to give it room to grow fully erect. I found myself stroking my cock as I watched my boss kiss Ella's wet, open mouth, then work his way down to her snatch and plunge his tongue between her moist cunt lips.

"That's it, Johnny, suck on my pussy. Fuck me with your hot tongue. Oh baby, make me come. Oh yes! Yes! I'm coming, baby! I'm coming for you! Feel me come!" she screamed as I watched her hump his face with her cunt. It was more than I could stand. I masturbated heatedly until my prick erupted in my hand, spewing sticky sperm all over the place.

By the time I'd licked the last thin dribble of jism off the palm of my hand Johnny had managed to sink his large cock into Ella's cunt and was fucking her hard, clutching her hips and plowing into her with his man-machine. Ella's tits surged up toward her chin like an ocean wave in the aftershock of each powerful thrust of Johnny's hips. Fascinated once more by the pair on the screen, I watched as Johnny moved his hands to Ella's tits, kneading them powerfully as he continued to fuck her with long, hard strokes.

"That's it, Johnny, give me your cock. Harder, baby, fuck me harder. Come on, do it—fuck me!" she screamed. As she experienced another in a string of massive orgasms my cock, hard as stone again, let loose another torrent of come—this time without me even touching it!

I rewound the tape to where I'd started it, cleaned up my mess, dressed and headed to the bar for a much-needed drink. The look of ecstasy on Ella's face while Johnny's dick was inside her wouldn't leave my mind. So you can imagine my surprise when I stepped into the dark bar and saw my wife sitting in the nearly deserted room surrounded by four handsome young men. One of them was Johnny! I was also shocked to see the way Ella was dressed. Her big tits were barely covered by the sheer, skimpy blouse she wore. Her black lace bra clearly showed through for everyone to see and her skirt was so short it had crept up to the point where it looked more like a belt. With her legs slightly apart I could see the black lace panties that shielded her pussy lips from the eyes of all present.

My head felt hot and I was a little dizzy as a jolt of undeniable lust raced through my body. What was this new feeling I'd discovered, this enjoyment I was getting out of seeing Ella flirting with and fucking other men? Shouldn't I be upset that she was fooling around on me? Shouldn't I go over there and demand that she stop this nonsense and come home at once? I quickly ducked back into the shadows to safely watch them laugh and talk, the stares of all the men in the place fixed on my wife's nearly-exposed tits and crotch. No one but the waitress even noticed me.

Johnny leaned toward Ella, placing his hand on her thigh about halfway between her knee and her cunt. At that distance it was impossible to hear what they were saying, so after the waitress brought me a beer I moved closer, being careful not to be spotted. Ella's gorgeous breasts were a beautiful sight, rising and falling from her excited breathing. She turned to face Johnny and spread her legs a little wider apart for him. His hand slowly worked its way up her thigh, squeezing and caressing the flesh until her whole body jumped as his fingers slid past her panties and brushed against her cunt lips.

"Well, aren't we getting fresh!" I heard her giggle. Then she leaned forward and pressed her lips to his, pushing her tongue deep into his mouth. I had to shift positions because my dick was completely hard again. Two of Johnny's fingers disappeared into her snatch, which was no doubt dripping by now. His friends stood wide-eyed and drooling, shifting their weight as their pants became tight and uncomfortable around their swelling dicks.

"Save some for us, Johnny boy!" they said.

"Hey, I'm a married woman," Ella joked, and the men burst out laughing. I could feel pre-come leaking from my penis.

Johnny's fingers continued to work on Ella's cunt as she writhed on the stool. "Oh, Johnny, I want to be fucked now, before Robert gets home. I need it," she begged, and they all laughed. She drove her tongue hungrily into his mouth again as she reached out and stroked Johnny's prick through his jeans.

"Aren't you hot!" he commented as he withdrew his hand from her lap. "It's time we got going," he continued, holding his pussy-soaked hand to her mouth. Without hesitating she wrapped her lips around his fingers and sucked them like a cock, nibbling and moaning around their hardness. Johnny broke their embrace and turned to his friends, tossing his keys to one of the other guys. "Here, take my car and follow us," he instructed. "It's getting late."

Before they could move I was out the door. Looking over my shoulder, I saw my wife slide off her bar stool and, grinding her pelvis against Johnny, kiss him passionately.

I headed home, expecting them to go to our place. I wanted to make sure I was safely hidden away in the closet from where I could watch my wife fuck all these guys. But it wasn't meant to be. After half an hour I realized they must've gone somewhere else. Damn! It was six o'clock by then and I lay naked on the bed stroking my dick as I watched the tape of Johnny reaming my wife's cunt with his gargantuan cock. I couldn't help but wonder who was behind the camera as he slammed his meat into her.

I jerked off grumpily, wondering where they'd all gone. All I could think about was Johnny and his friends pumping huge loads of come into Ella's tight cunt, making her tits heave back and forth as they screwed her without letup. I pictured her on her hands and knees, those big boobs rocking wildly as she was pumped from behind, a second prick pistoning in and out of her mouth, a third and fourth spewing their goo into her hands as she masturbated them vigorously, urging them on with her filthy talk.

When I heard the front door open and Ella come in, I looked at my watch and was startled to realize that it was already ten o'clock. It was still sooner than I was supposed to be home, however, and Ella walked into the room not expecting to see me. She looked even hotter than she had earlier in the evening. Her black lace bra was gone and her huge tits and dark nipples were clearly visible through her sheer blouse. I couldn't take my eyes off her breasts as they swayed back and forth.

"Hi, baby, you're home early," she said seductively when she saw me on the bed. It was obvious she was still quite hot from the evening's activities, and I wanted to make sure I took advantage of the situation. She leaned over to kiss me and the front of her blouse opened slightly, allowing me an unobstructed view of her tits. It was as though she was flaunting her sluttishness, wanting me to know that she was letting other men sample the forbidden charms of her sensational body.

Without saying a word, I leaned forward and cupped her tits in my hands, feeling the hard nipples bore into my palms. As I buried my face between her firm mounds I inhaled deeply and smelled the sweat and come from her lovers' cocks lingering on her skin. I know she loves to have her big tits fucked—I've done it dozens of times myself. I could just picture Johnny's hard slab surfing between her breasts.

"You're a horny bastard tonight, aren't you!" she purred as she gently pushed one of her tits into my mouth. "Well, I'm horny too. Suck that tit, honey. Pull on my nipple." When I sucked her hard nipple I savored the faint taste of semen on her flesh. As she shoved her hot tongue deep into my waiting mouth I began to explore her body with my hands, once again detecting the taste of another man's sperm.

Ella pulled away from my embrace and climbed onto the bed. She rolled over on her back as I again went for her beautiful tits, but that was obviously not what she wanted. She pushed me down across her firm stomach until my face was opposite her cunt. She certainly knew I would quickly realize that I wasn't the first visitor there that night, but she didn't seem to care. Her disregard for my feelings made my cock pound like a drum.

I was overcome with lust as I looked at her swollen red cunt lips. She had obviously taken quite a pounding from those four young studs. As I looked closely I could see a small trail of white sperm leaking from her cunt. I went wild and began rubbing her freshly fucked bush all over my face. Then I pulled away a little and slowly ran my tongue up and down the full length of her slit, lapping the white liquid up with my tongue. She freely began to tell me about the four lovers she'd just enjoyed and how beautiful their cocks were. I placed my lips over her hot gash, snaking my tongue deep into her hole as she told me how they'd given her the best fucking of her life.

She was going crazy as I sucked on her cunt. The come of her four studs was streaming out of her pussy and onto my tongue. I swallowed hard, trying to consume each and every drop that my wife had squeezed out of them. As my tongue wiggled against her erect, rubbery clit she grabbed my head, shoving her hot pussy into my face. Her climax was intense and filled my mouth with a mixture of her juices and the rest of her lovers' spunk.

"Oh, baby, suck on my clit," she moaned. "That's it, honey, you get me so hot. Oh God, you don't know how good you make me feel. Eat me out, drink the come out of my pussy." I ate and ate until, after hearing her describe every detail of her night and bringing her to several gut-wrenching orgasms, it was time for me to come too. I wrapped my wife's tits around my hard shaft and fucked them until I pumped my load onto her stiff nipples. Naturally, after massaging my come into her soft mounds I lapped them clean with my tongue.

I learned a lot of things that night. One of them was that another man's semen can taste quite good if you're eating it out of your wife's pussy. I no longer hesitate to eat Ella out after I've shot my load into her. I also encourage her to have a good time with other men, and lately she's been enjoying a steady diet of big fat cocks. When she gets home she always feeds me a cuntfull of hot sperm while telling me about how great it was to get fucked by her latest hunk. Just yesterday as she was kneeling over my face frigging herself to another orgasm, Ella told me about the seven men who had fucked her for five hours straight in an adult-book store that afternoon while I was at work. It seems she went into the store looking for a dildo and found something a little more lively to play with.—R.M., *Madison, Wisconsin*

APARTMENT FOR RENT:
EAT-IN KITCHEN AND A ROOM WITH A VIEW

I am twenty-five years old, five feet four and one hundred twenty pounds, with short blonde hair. I am also an exhibitionist.

For the last three years I have been working as a realtor. When a great side-by-side duplex came on the market at a bargain price, I decided to buy it for myself. I moved in and began looking for a tenant.

While I was screening applicants, I thought of a way to indulge my exhibitionist desires. I bought a two-way mirror and installed it in such a way that my tenant would see me but I would not see them. Then I bought a hideously ugly painting and hung it over the tenant's side of the mirror. I figured that whoever moved in would have to get rid of the painting (it really was quite ghastly). Then they would see into my bedroom because of the mirror.

I interviewed five people and finally settled on Kurt, a good-looking man in his thirties. It didn't take long. One day I peeked in his window to see him taking down the painting to put up one of his own. His painting was never hung, though, after he discovered that he could see into my bedroom anytime he wanted.

It was perfect. Kurt didn't think I knew he was watching me. I could show off my naked body to my heart's content. I went through my daily routine as I always had. I would get up in the morning and exercise in the nude, knowing that Kurt was watching me.

One Saturday afternoon I summoned up all my courage and provided him with a show that turned us both on. First I went outside to make sure he was standing by the mirror. I ran back in and stripped for him, then lay down on the bed. He must have been thrilled when I reached under the bed and took out my vibrator. I then proceeded to masturbate, climaxing with the vibrator in my cunt and my left hand pinching my nipples.

From that day on, every Saturday afternoon was show time. One day I was wondering what it would be like to shave my cunt. Then I realized that it would be a golden opportunity for another exhibition.

The following Saturday I looked through the window and was shocked to see Kurt and four of his friends sitting by the mirror. My pussy really got wet when I saw that they had set up a video camera.

I went into the bathroom and brought out a razor, shaving cream, a towel and a bowl of water. I then lay down on my back, on the floor, with one foot on each side of the mirror.

I began shaving my cunt, doing my best to make sure the guys saw plenty of pink. When I was done, I stopped and got my vibrator. I went back to the mirror, turned away from it and bent over. I could almost feel their eyes on me as I reached between my legs and slid the small vibrator into my slit.

For thirty minutes I gave the guys the show of their lives. I came, bucking my hips and screaming.

The next day, as I was clipping my toenails in the nude, I wondered who had the videotape. The thought of one of the guys watching the video and jerking off propelled me to masturbate for Kurt yet again.

Kurt hardly ever leaves the house now. I can't wait until next Saturday. My friend Stephanie is coming over and we're going to put on a show that will knock Kurt's socks off.—L.R., *Newport News, Virginia*

WATCHING A SEXY RUBDOWN MAKES HIS ROD STAND UP

*M*y wife Teresa is gorgeous, with a great set of tits and a gorgeous ass. She was a virgin when we got married and didn't experience another cock until she started cheating on me a few years ago. I never caught her and she never told me, but I'd been keeping count of her contraceptive sponges. Every time she was working late, another sponge would disappear. I would always wait up for her—the fucking that followed would be great, as her cunt was well lubricated with her lover's come. I never said anything to her because I'd always wanted to watch her fuck another man—this was a step in the right direction.

After a while I was finally able to fulfill my fantasy. We took a vacation to St. Maarten. Our hotel was near a nude beach. After much coaxing from me, Teresa agreed to go.

When we got to the beach she removed her top, but refused to take off the bottom of her bikini. I really enjoyed the admiring looks she received as we played in the water.

The next day we went back to the beach. This time she went

totally nude. The fact that her beautiful tits and cunt were exposed for all to see gave me a raging hard-on. When she lay down on her back and spread her legs slightly, I wanted to fuck her right then and there. A number of guys walking the beach made it a point to walk by as closely and slowly as possible. One guy, about twenty years old, sat down about ten feet in front of us. His position gave him a clear view of Teresa's furry cunt. After a few minutes he had to roll over onto his stomach to hide his hard-on.

When we got back to the hotel I suggested we both get a massage. I called the front desk and made arrangements for the masseur to come to our room. John, the masseur, was about thirty years old and black. He wore a white T-shirt and a pair of thin white running shorts. The glow of his ebony skin through the white shorts made it obvious he wasn't wearing anything underneath them.

Teresa went first, lying facedown on a mat John had placed on the floor. John straddled her hips and, with professional ease, untied her bikini top. Teresa's eyes widened a bit, but she didn't say anything. With his nylon-covered cock resting against her bikini-covered ass, John proceeded to massage her back and shoulders. The feel of his fingers grazing the sides of her tits as he worked on her back began to get to her. She squirmed slightly as his hands moved down.

Pushing her legs slightly apart, he reached up and removed Teresa's bikini bottom, exposing the smooth white globes of her ass-cheeks. He didn't move for a moment, feasting his eyes on her exposed ass and cunt. His view was spectacular. I couldn't believe I was sitting on the bed, watching a black man enjoying the sight of my naked wife.

Starting with her calves he worked his way up, alternately kneading and caressing them. Using one hand, he squeezed and massaged her thighs, his other hand resting against her cunt. Teresa's eyes were squeezed shut as she squirmed against the pressure of his hand.

John then took one white ass-cheek in each black hand. Gently kneading them, he pulled them apart, exposing Teresa's slit.

His thumb moved toward her entrance and moved in circles around her dripping-wet hole. Teresa's eyes flew open, she moaned out loud, and she rotated her hips to meet the pressure of John's teasing thumb. Smiling broadly, John sat back. He poured some oil onto his hands and gently massaged her ass, then inserted two fingers into her gushing cunt. Teresa raised her hips to meet the thrusts of his fingers. Her eyes were glazed with lust and she was biting her lip to keep from crying out. She was on the brink of orgasm when he withdrew his fingers.

After telling her to roll over onto her back, John stood up and removed his clothes. Teresa stared at his glistening black body in awe. His cock was semi-erect, six inches long and much thicker than mine. Trailing his fingertips along her body, he positioned himself next to her head. Kneeling down, his cock just inches from her face, he began massaging her breasts.

Teresa couldn't stand his teasing any longer. She grabbed his cock, brought it to her lips and began sucking with abandon. The sight of her sucking that big, black cock went beyond my wildest fantasies. After what seemed like an eternity, John pulled his wet cock from my wife's lips and knelt between her legs. In one smooth stroke he buried his cock to the hilt. She screamed with the intensity of her orgasm.

I couldn't hold back any longer. I knelt by Teresa's head and she sucked my cock like a woman possessed. I watched John's cock slide in and out of my wife's beautiful cunt as she sucked me. John and I came at the same time. She gasped as she came again and swallowed the torrent of come filling her mouth.

The rest of our vacation was an endless stream of fucking and sucking. We've already made our reservations for next year.— T.D., Wichita, Kansas

NEXT ON NATIONAL GEOGRAPHIC:
THE SEXUAL HABITS OF AMERICANS

I would like to share an experience that happened nine years ago when I was living in the Midwest. I am an avid hunter and fisherman, and one day I witnessed something in the woods I'll never forget.

It was a Saturday afternoon, and I was trudging through the woods with my rifle by my side. The neck of woods in which I was hunting is filled with valleys, trees, bushes and cliffs. I crawled onto a cliff that hung about thirty feet above the valley below. I looked down and saw a man and a woman engaged in a hot and heavy petting session. They were completely unaware of my presence on the cliff above them, and I was in a perfect position to hear and see everything they said and did.

I quickly crouched down behind a boulder. The young woman was about twenty-five years old, and I judged the man to be about the same age. She had long black hair and a sexy body. She had a beautiful face, with high cheekbones and big, brown eyes. The man was short and stocky, with broad shoulders and a powerful build. They were lying in the grass, their rifles by their sides, kissing and petting up a storm. Her hand was on his crotch, rubbing it vigorously while his hands massaged her groin. They were shoving their tongues down each other's throat as if they were feeding each other. Suddenly the girl stopped kissing him and said, "Let's fuck."

The dark-haired man stood up and removed her pants and underwear, revealing her hairy black bush. He then pulled his own pants and underwear down to his ankles. I couldn't believe the size of his cock. Although it was only about six inches long, it was as thick as a beer can. I watched as he spit into his hands, then applied the saliva to his dick, taking special care to lubricate the entire shaft. He knelt down and she spread her luscious legs as wide as she could. He eased himself inside her, and petite though she was, she seemed to accommodate him easily.

After about ten gentle strokes, he grabbed her ass and began to pound her. He continued ramming her fiercely, and the expression on her face turned from love to lust. She eagerly arched her hips to meet every one of his thrusts.

After only five minutes of this heavy-duty screwing she grabbed his hairy ass-cheeks and began to gasp heavily as she neared climax. The man must have sensed this, as he quickened his pace and drove into her even harder. Her whole body shuddered and then she went limp.

Her boyfriend wasn't through yet. He continued to pound her, pulling her hips into his with each stroke. After another two or three minutes of this he announced through clenched teeth that he was coming. I watched his muscular ass-cheeks clench and unclench as he strained to drive his cock even further inside. "I'm going to fill your pussy full of come," I heard him growl. Then he grunted, and I knew he was shooting his load into this dark-haired doll.

He rested on top of her for a few minutes, then she tapped him on the shoulder and said that they had to get dressed before someone came along and saw them.

As he started to get up, he ground his crotch into hers and said, "I love your pussy." She simply smiled.

I never saw them again, but the memory of that day is as clear in my mind as the day it happened. I'll never forget it.—*N.T., Rochester, New York*

GETTING CAUGHT UNEXPECTEDLY
LEADS TO UNEXPECTED REWARDS

*L*ast week I met Christine, a real sweetheart of a girl, at a friend's party. Every guy there had his eyes glued to her cute ass, but I was the only one who worked up the nerve to talk to her.

Christine's eyes were big and cornflower-blue, and while we

made small talk I noticed her looking me up and down, not even trying to hide her interest in the region below my belt.

"Do you like what you see?" I asked her, hoping to catch her off guard.

"Yes," she answered. "Judging from what I can see from here, your cock is about eight inches long and very thick."

We left the party soon after that. I'm no slouch with women, but it's not often I find one who looks as fine as Christine, with a great personality and a sex drive to match.

While driving to her house she took off her top and pressed her soft, round tits against me as I drove. "My husband's at work. We'll have the place to ourselves for hours," she said.

I cupped her gorgeous ass with my free hand, then ran a curious finger into her pants and felt her hot snatch, which was as moist as my cock was hard.

When we got to her place she took me directly to the bedroom. In two seconds flat she had her clothes off, and did a couple of pirouettes around the room so I could get a good look at her.

She had a tiny waist, which made her full breasts look even bigger. Her nipples were hard little roses begging to be touched.

The bedroom had a floor-to-ceiling mirror that covered two walls, and I could tell she liked watching her luscious body as much as I did. Soon I had her incredible ass backed up against my big bulge as she watched me cup her tits and kiss the back of her neck in the mirror.

"Take it out, baby. I can feel how big it is through your jeans," she moaned as she squirmed against me.

By this time I had her cunt in my hand, and she was so wet it was as if my fingers were fish swimming in a slippery stream. I unzipped my pants and my cock sprang free. She thrust back against me impatiently, but instead of ramming my cock inside her hot pussy I made her wait. I pushed the head of my cock between her velvety thighs, which were slick with pussy juice. She closed her legs around my rod, rocking with me as I slid forward and backward, pressing the tip of my cock against her swollen clit. Her whimpers told me how much she was getting off on riding my cock.

In the mirror I could see the knob of my cock peeking out between her legs, and it looked as if she had a small cock of her own. "You're making me crazy," she moaned.

The sight of her tits swinging with the force of my strokes and her hand on my cock made me come so hard I nearly passed out.

I quickly turned her around and began kissing her hot cunt. Suddenly we heard a car door slam. "Oh shit!" she cried. "You're going to have to hide in the closet." Christine was so horny she was on the verge of tears, but I ran to the closet, leaving the door open a crack.

She barely had enough time to grab a magazine off the dresser and fling herself onto the bed before her husband walked into the room.

"Jack, what a surprise!" she exclaimed.

"Hello there," he said, running his eyes over his naked wife. He laughed when he saw that the magazine she was reading was *Penthouse Letters*. "Now I know why you're so horny when I get home."

Christine made a move to get up, but he gently pushed her back onto the bed. I could see the bulge in his pants from my vantage point in the closet.

"Actually, I was just getting ready to take a nap. That's why I took off my clothes," she said. I could see her glancing nervously at the closet door.

He knelt in front of her, gently running his hands over her hard nipples. Then he discovered the wetness between her legs. She threw another worried look my way, but when he traced her swollen lips with his finger she let out a long sigh. He began to lap at her cunt the way I had wanted to. It was clear that his tongue was driving all thoughts out of her mind except how good he was making her feel. The sounds of their lovemaking were getting to me. I stroked my cock, watching Jack go down on her.

Suddenly she came with a small scream, bucking her hips

against his face. He gently turned her over onto her stomach and, with a sigh of joy, sank his cock inside her pussy. Now they were both facing me, and I could see her nipples standing erect. I remembered how wonderful it felt to press against her round ass, and envied Jack more than I'd ever envied any man.

I imagined that she could see me watching her from the closet, jacking my throbbing cock while watching her getting fucked by her husband.

He fucked her with long, slow strokes that were so deep I could almost hear her pussy sucking his cock into her. She came first, and at the sound of her groans he went crazy, pumping hard and fast, making the same sounds she'd made, but a couple of octaves lower. I shot my load onto the bathrobe that was hanging on the inside of the closet door. Jack slid out of Christine and a pool of their juices puddled onto the bed. "I just stopped by to get a few papers," he said, kissing her. "I'll see you tonight. Save some for me." The second he left I came out of the closet. We had a good laugh together, although she was somewhat ashamed. I said, "Don't worry about it. I liked watching you." My cock began to rise again, remembering how sexy she had looked.

Christine took me into her mouth, licking me with her warm, wet tongue. I noticed that she was stroking her clit at the same time. We fucked like crazy until about an hour before her husband was due home.—G.S., Los Angeles, California

ROOMMATE FINDS THAT WHEN THE CAT'S AWAY, THE MICE DO PLAY

About twelve years ago I decided to share an apartment with a man. It was strictly platonic. My girlfriends told me they suspected Dave was bisexual, but it didn't bother me. We hardly interacted with each other until one fateful night.

I had told Dave that I was going to be out of town for the weekend, but my plans got screwed up and I didn't go. Late Friday night I was in bed when I heard Dave and his friend Harris come in. They went straight to Dave's room. They were making a lot of noise, since they didn't think I was home. I got up to ask them to be quiet, but when I opened my door I received the shock of my life.

The door to Dave's room was open. Standing before me were two completely naked men. I was stunned, but I didn't move for fear they would see me, causing even more embarrassment for all of us.

I watched in awe as Dave sat on the edge of his bed and Harris moved in front of him. It didn't take a genius to figure out what was going on. I remember thinking what a hunk Harris was, and wondering how Dave met such beautiful men.

After a few minutes Harris and Dave changed positions. I stared at Dave's hard-on, but when Harris climbed onto the bed my jaw dropped even lower. He had the biggest dick I had ever seen, and Dave wasted no time taking it into his mouth.

After seeing the way Dave licked and kissed Harris's huge penis, I knew how he was able to bring hunks like that home. I thought I would be repulsed by something like this, but I found it fascinating. Dave began sucking harder and faster, and soon Harris spurted semen all over my roommate's bed. There was a lot of it.

I quickly and silently got back into bed. Dave seemed worried the next morning when he saw that I was home, but I told him I had had a change of plans, had gotten home real late and was so tired I'd slept like a baby. He looked relieved. I couldn't get what I had seen out of my mind, so during the week I told Dave that I was definitely going away for the weekend. I couldn't wait to see what would happen when Friday night rolled around. I parked my car a couple of blocks away and walked back to our apartment, then hid in my bedroom.

When Dave finally came home late that night he had two friends with him, Harris and a guy named Jimmy. I waited for another performance in the bedroom, but I heard them getting started in the living room. This was even better, because I wouldn't be spotted in the dark hallway. This time I had *three* naked men parading around in front of me!

To my pleasant surprise, Jimmy was just as impressive as Harris. His cock must have been at least ten inches long, and it wasn't even hard.

Soon Dave was doing what he apparently does best, going down on these gorgeous men. Believe it or not, I actually became bored watching him suck for so long, but finally Harris said he was about to come. He came so forcefully that some of his sperm poured out of Dave's mouth. Jimmy used his penis to scoop up the cream from Dave's lips and had him lick it off, making sure he had swallowed every delicious drop.

While Harris and Jimmy got dressed, Dave sat on the sofa and masturbated. He ejaculated all over his chest and stomach. When he started walking to the bathroom to clean up, I ran back to my bedroom before he saw me.

I left early the next morning so he wouldn't know I was there, but I think he was suspicious. He moved out a few weeks later.— *B.F., San Francisco, California*

PRIM AND PROPER LADY BECOMES
A VIXEN WHEN THERE'S AN AUDIENCE

I recently went on a date with a very attractive woman named Alicia. When I picked her up that evening, I couldn't help but notice her voluptuous breasts, which threatened to burst out of the blouse she was wearing. She kept it open to the third button. Alicia normally acted very prim and proper, so this blatant display of sexuality took me by surprise. I'd originally thought we'd have a quiet little evening, but now my fantasy machine went into high gear.

As we sat in the restaurant I kept trying to find a way to tell her how hot she was making me, without being offensive. I never found the words, but I couldn't help feeling as though she'd gotten the message when she slid one foot up my leg and tickled the inside of my knee with her toes. This was not the Alicia I'd been expecting, but I had no complaints!

After dinner I drove Alicia home, and asked if I could come in to make a telephone call. She responded, "As long as it's not to another woman. I want you all to myself." Before we'd even gotten past the foyer, Alicia dropped to her knees and unleashed my tool. She let the tip of it rest on her tongue, which she swirled around the knob a few times, as if trying to get it good and wet. My cock was rock-hard in seconds. Smiling up at me, Alicia kissed the tip of my dick and asked, "Anyone ever done this for you before?" Then she let her mouth run down, down, down the length of my dick until we were practically playing tonsil hockey. As a matter of fact, no one had ever taken me that deep before. I let her know my response with a groan, which seemed to make her happy. When she slowly eased my shaft back out of her mouth again and ran her tongue once more around the tip, she made a kind of purring sound.

As her mouth moved back and forth on my hard prick, I grabbed on to her shoulders just to keep from passing out with pleasure. Watching my cock disappear inside her stroke after stroke was carrying me to a plateau of pleasure I'd never known. The sensation was intensifying so rapidly that it didn't take long for me to shoot jets of come into her mouth. She kept me deep inside her mouth the whole time I was coming, as though she understood how sensitive my dick gets when it reaches that point. When it seemed as though I'd stopped, she licked the vein up the center of my pecker with just the tip of her tongue, and it shuddered, squeezing out one last spray of sperm.

After Alicia had sucked up all of my load, she led me to her bedroom. I spent a long time patting and enjoying those gorgeous tits. Too long, apparently, because she finally screamed, "Don't tease me! Eat me!" I bent down and lapped at Alicia's wet vagina. I continued to eat her tasty pussy until she splattered my face with her juices.

Suddenly we noticed two men looking through the window. I thought this would scare my shy, proper friend, but it had the opposite effect—Alicia became even more aroused and climbed onto my totem pole to give them a show.

Alicia's wet cunt swallowed my prick to the hilt. She bounced up and down on my dick with delight. We shifted position, and I fucked her doggie-style until she had another orgasm. I kept pumping into her tight, hot cunt until I exploded, collapsing with exhaustion and delight.

My shy princess wasn't done with me, though. She bent down and darted her long tongue over my balls until I shot another mammoth load.

The next time I have a date with Alicia, I think I'll sell tickets!—B.D., *Hartford, Connecticut*

Domination & Discipline

TABLES ARE TURNED WHEN WIFE DECIDES THAT
TWO CAN PLAY THE DOMINATION GAME

*A*fter ten years of marriage I decided to spice up our sex life. After telling my beautiful wife Erica that she was bad for not cleaning the house that day, I tied her up and lightly spanked her ass. Erica really responded favorably to this.

I let a few weeks go by before I decided she was ready for a re-peat performance. When we went into the bedroom one night, I gave her ass a slap and told her she had been bad again and needed to be punished. But this time she surprised me. She spun around and said, "Bullshit, you were the one who came home shit-faced tonight after going out drinking with the boys."

With that she grabbed one of my bandannas and tied my hands to the headboard in a flash. She undid my pants and pulled them down to my ankles. Erica roughly rolled me over on my stomach and gave me the spanking of my life. While she spanked me she lectured me on how bad I had been and told me that she was going to spank my ass until it was beet red. When she was through, she even got a mirror and made me look at my red ass so I would bet-ter remember it.

Then she rolled me over onto my back. I was relieved, because my dick had been trying to drill a hole through the mattress and was real uncomfortable. She said that even though she was mad, she still loved me and would prove it. Erica ran her tongue over my balls and gently scraped them with her fingernails. I almost came in her face.

She sensed I was close to the edge, so she backed off. She continued her attentions but would not let me come.

She said that as soon as I was finished with my punishment and chores, she would let me come. I didn't know what she meant, but when I saw her pussy moving toward my face I got the idea. She was more turned on than I was, and I could see her delicious juices running down her thighs. I strained at my bonds to get my tongue on her, but she teased me by only allowing quick licks and then backing away and fingering herself. She knew this was driving me wild, so she played her game until she couldn't stand it anymore. Then she planted her pussy firmly on my mouth and I licked everywhere my tongue could reach. Erica climaxed violently, drenching my face with her juices.

I was willing to continue this for a while, but she got up and went to her dresser. She returned with her eight-inch vibrating dildo and straddled my chest. With one quick thrust, she shoved the dildo up her pussy. The plastic dick was fairly large in diameter and I was really getting turned on as I watched it slide in and out, stretching her drenched pussy. Soon Erica climaxed and flooded my chest with her juices.

After she'd rested, I said, "Okay, you've had your fun. Now get down and suck my dick till I come in your mouth." Oops, that was a mistake. She let me know it by flipping me over and slapping my ass hard for talking to her that way. I said I was sorry, but that right now I could use a good fucking. I guess I got a little carried away.

"Oh, you want a good fucking?" she asked. "Well, fine, I'll give you one." I felt her run the dildo up the crack of my ass and I nervously told her that wasn't exactly what I had in mind. Erica said she didn't care.

She got out the K-Y jelly and lubed up my asshole. I tried to relax, and she stuck the tip of the dildo in. Erica moved the vibrator in and out real slow. The more she did, the better it felt, and I was beginning to lose control. I couldn't help myself. Soon I was bucking backward to meet each thrust.

The next few minutes were a blur, because she turned the vibrator on. I was in heaven. I had never been so totally consumed by anything like that before. She reached around and started jerking me off. Within seconds I blasted my load onto the sheets.—R.P., *Detroit, Michigan*

SPENDTHRIFT WIFE GETS A SOUND SPANKING FOR HER NAUGHTY WAYS

*M*y name is Donna and I am a twenty-four-year-old housewife. I enjoy a great sex life with my husband Walter. We are like most young couples, except Walter is very dominant in our relationship. I enjoy playing the submissive role most of the time, because Walter takes good care of me. As long as I don't neglect my household duties and keep my spending down to reasonable limits, there is no problem. Unfortunately sometimes I let my housework slide or spend too much. Walter's response is always the same: he punishes me with a sound spanking.

After about three months of marriage Walter found out that I enjoy playing a submissive role and took full advantage of that knowledge. He said if I wanted him to continue handling everything, I would have to agree to do things his way. Of course, I agreed.

He told me I was to go to the mall and purchase a few implements for him to spank me with. I bought a wooden hairbrush and a Ping-Pong paddle and gave them to him that night. I was surprised to find how much it turned me on to think that Walter would actually spank me with these things.

After I gave him the brush and paddle, he put them on the bureau up in the spare room and told me that that's where I would be sent when I was going to get spanked. The subject was then dropped.

As strange as it may seem, by that time I wanted to get spanked, and I began doing little things to goad Walter into carrying out his threat. I wasn't successful though, until I didn't do a single load of laundry for fifteen straight days. On the sixteenth day he ran out of clean underwear. He was really pissed when he looked in the hamper and found a ton of dirty laundry. He told me to go to the spare room, strip down to my bra and panties and wait for him. He added that I better enjoy sitting while I still could.

When he finally came upstairs, first he scolded me soundly. He said that since this was my first offense, he would only use his hand, but I had better stay still. He sat down on a straight-backed chair and had me stand next to him. He pulled down my panties, which embarrassed me even though he's my husband. He positioned me over his knees and started to rub my bottom. I enjoyed that until he started to spank me really hard.

He kept this up until I was crying out loud. I kicked my legs and squirmed around, but this only seemed to make him spank me even harder. He stopped after I finally lay still. He kept me over his knees until my cries faded into sobs, and then he let me up. I stood there, frantically rubbing my poor little bottom. I was exhausted and figured I'd just go to bed. But Walter informed me that I'd better get the laundry done if I didn't want another spanking.

Walter gave me my most recent spanking just last night. Unlike the spanking I just described, this one was severe. But I must admit I really deserved it. I had charged a lot of new clothes that I had no way of paying for. While I was on my shopping spree, I foolishly thought I'd be able to pay it off in time, but by the end of the day I knew that I was in for a sound spanking if Walter found out. Of course, when the credit card bill came in, I was caught red-handed. Walter was not just annoyed—he was furious. He coldly informed me that I was really going to get it this time.

I was really nervous as I waited for him up in the spare room. After two and a half hours, he finally came upstairs. By that time, I was almost looking forward to getting it over with.

First he yelled at me for about a half hour for being such a spendthrift. Then he picked up the paddle and told me to touch my toes. He yanked down my panties, put his arm around my waist and warned me that I wasn't going to be able to sit for a week.

He cocked his arm back for a full swing, and the paddle made a loud crack when it made contact with my bottom. The pain was intense, and by the third stroke I was in tears. He told me that I was going to get one stroke for every dollar I had spent. This terrified me, because I had spent over five hundred dollars. The few strokes I had already received hurt so much that I could not even imagine five hundred strokes of the paddle.

The paddle was large enough to cover almost my entire bottom on each stroke, so Walter did not have to move it around to cover all the territory. He aimed for the same spot with each stinging blow. After what seemed like a very long while, he stopped, stood me up, sat down and pulled me across his lap. Then he continued the spanking with the back of his hand. I begged and pleaded with him to stop. My poor bottom felt as if it were on fire. I finally stopped begging, because I was crying so loud my pleas could not be heard.

When he finally stopped and released me, I went straight to bed and cried myself to sleep.

Walter gave me a copy of *Penthouse Letters* today and told me as part of my punishment I had to write a letter to you about this incident. He warned me that if I didn't write a good letter I'd get another spanking.

It may sound strange to some people, but I have to admit, even though it hurts to get a spanking, I know that my husband does it because he loves me.—*D.T., Buffalo, New York*

DELIVERANCE II: SUBMISSIVE HAS MOUNTAINS OF FUN WITH THREE RURAL ROUGHNECKS

*M*y name is Lena and I'm a true submissive who enjoys bondage and humiliation. I serve my husband Henry in any way he pleases. I have been Henry's slut-slave for over ten years. In a previous letter to your magazine, I related my experience as a sex slave to three of Henry's friends: Michael, Wayne and Steve. They share a hunting camp near ours in the Adirondack Mountains. My husband had set everything up and given the men permission to use me in any way they wished. When I left Michael, Wayne and Steve Sunday morning, I left behind a pair of my panties and a note telling them I would be back.

Henry and I talked about my experiences all the way home and I told him I would enjoy spending one more weekend with his three friends. Henry was pleased and gave me permission to do so.

A week later, Michael called to find out when I'd be coming back. I assured him that I would return as long as he promised that our second weekend together would be as good or better than the first. Michael assured me that it would be and promised to call me as soon as all the necessary arrangements had been made. Anticipation of a delicious weekend drove me wild with lust all week long.

On Wednesday night Michael called to say he had contacted Wayne and Steve and that all was ready. He instructed me to bring only three items of clothing: the tightest, shortest shorts I could find, a bikini top and a pair of extra-high heels. He also told me to bring my slave collar, wrist and ankle cuffs, and a leather belt.

They had all the rope we would need at the camp already. I was to arrive at four o'clock Friday afternoon, ready for the most humiliating weekend I had ever experienced. Michael also promised to capture everything on video for Henry.

On Friday afternoon I kissed Henry good-bye and drove to their camp. Along the way, I kept checking my face in the mirror. For a thirty-two-year-old broad I still looked pretty darn good.

I arrived right on time wearing my slutty shorts and sky-high heels. No underwear was allowed. Michael met me at the car and told me to strip and bring my things inside and then to serve the guys a beer on the porch. Things were starting well. I had only been there two minutes and I was already completely naked!

After putting my stuff away, I brought the guys their beers. "Get on your knees, slut, and start sucking," Michael ordered. As I sucked each of the guys, I knew that this was going to be a fantastic weekend. After they had all been satisfied orally, they put on my slave collar and wrist and ankle cuffs, and tied me to a nearby tree. Then all three took turns whipping my ass with willow switches as a preview of what I would get if I displeased them.

I cooked supper for everyone. After cleaning up I became the center of attention once again. First I had to dance for them. I fetched my overnight bag, took out my biggest dildo and put on a sexy show guaranteed to shock and arouse them. I was so hot myself that I got myself off with the dildo several times as I danced. After another round of blow jobs, I was tied to a bed and fucked by each of them in turn. After that, Michael said that the foreplay was now over and that the real humiliation was about to begin.

I was released from the bed and told to sit on a chair with my legs spread wide. Then I had to tell them what a worthless slut I was and all the nasty things I wanted them to do to me. During the entire interview, I also had to fuck myself with my dildo. Of course, it was all recorded on video.

After telling them how they were to fuck me any way, any time and any where they wanted, I described in detail how I wanted to be tied up, forced to march naked through the woods and have my ass whipped.

I was told to get on my knees. After hooking my hands behind my back, they took me outside for a walk down the road. It is a dead-end dirt road, but even so, anyone could have driven by and seen me. After returning to the camp, I was asked to slither across the lawn like a snake: not an easy task when your hands are tied behind your back.

The rest of the night, the guys fucked me in the pussy, the ass and the mouth. Then each of them wanted a tongue bath and each one wanted his ass licked clean.

The next morning after breakfast, I was taken out to a tree and hung spread-eagle. The guys took turns whipping my ass with switches. It really didn't hurt. In fact, it felt fucking great! Next I was suspended upside down. With me in this position, the guys were able to fuck my mouth while Wayne used my dildo to fuck my ass. Naturally the camcorder continued to roll.

In the afternoon, I was staked spread-eagle on the lawn and the guys all jacked off over me. I was then taken for a walk in the woods, tied over a fallen tree and fucked in the ass by each of the guys. These guys had amazing staying power! As for me, running through the woods on a leash while having my ass whipped had made me hotter than you can imagine.

When we got back to the camp, I was made to stack firewood while the men sat around drinking beer and commenting about how nice it was to have their wood stacked by a naked slut.

After dinner, we all got dressed up and went to a small country bar that Michael liked. I was wearing such skimpy cutoffs that there was only a thin piece of fabric hiding the crack of my ass. On top I wore my string bikini top. To complete my ensemble I put on a lot of makeup. Everything about me shouted "slut."

The bartender and the two other customers all knew Michael and his friends. We all sat together and had a couple rounds of drinks. I could see the locals staring at my slave collar.

When Michael noticed their stares, he explained that I was their slave for the weekend and that I would do anything they asked.

When the bartender put on some music, Michael told me to dance and then to strip. There I was, in a bar wearing nothing but my heels with six very horny men. Michael told me to put on a good show for his friends. At his instructions, I played with myself, slithered across the floor and finally allowed everyone to feel me up and run their hands all over my body.

As an encore, I jacked off the bartender and the two locals. As each was about to come, I knelt down and let them shoot their loads on my face. My pussy was really dripping by this time and I desperately needed to be fucked, but my masters would not hear of it. We stayed at the bar long enough for one more round of drinks. I was still completely naked with my hands tied behind my back as we walked to the parking lot.

The locals watched from the bar window as the guys laid me over the hood of the car and fucked my ass one after the other. Then I sucked each of them until they came in my mouth.

Finally we headed back to the camp. When we were about half a mile from the camp, Wayne told me to get out and walk in front of the car, illuminated by the headlights. The men rode behind, shouting lewd comments about my ass and various body parts.

When we arrived at the camp, they had me stand in the front yard and tell them what a slut I was. All I could do was beg them to fuck me and let me come. Michael lay down on the grass face first and told me to lick his ass while Steve and Wayne fucked me from behind. He insisted that he wanted to feel my tongue inside his ass or he would give me a whipping I would never forget. I spent the rest of the night crawling from one man to the next, servicing them in any way they desired.

On Sunday morning, my last official act as slave was to fuck and suck each of the guys and have my picture taken with each of the guys whipping my ass. Finally, each guy jerked off on my face while I lay exhausted on the grass. When they were all finished, I spoke into the camera, describing what a great weekend I had had and how Michael, Wayne and Steve had been among the toughest masters I had ever known.

That afternoon I drove home in my come-covered cutoffs and bikini top. After dinner, Henry and I spent the night watching the videotapes from my weekend at the camp. Although I will probably never do this sort of thing again, it was an experience I will always cherish.

Henry and I wish more submissive women would write letters about their experiences. We would love to read them.—*Name and address withheld*

WHIP-WIELDING CALIFORNIA BEACH BABE
GETS TO BE BOSS FOR ONE YEAR

I am married to a woman who causes traffic jams as she walks down the street. Sylvia weighs about one hundred five pounds; and her weight is beautifully distributed within a very sexy, five-foot-six-inch, 35-21-34 frame. She is the blonde and blue-eyed epitome of the Southern California beach babe. She is also my mistress.

My wife became my mistress on the eve of our first wedding anniversary. We started off the evening by sharing a great dinner at a plush restaurant. She looked so damn hot that husbands at nearby tables were being repeatedly chastised by their wives for sneaking peeks at her. Sylvia never wears any bras or panties, and her provocative dress had the place buzzing.

After dinner we went dancing and then to a movie. When we arrived home we, as usual, shed our clothing. (Nude is the norm in our household.) Then we fired up the fireplace, turned out the lights and opened a bottle of champagne, all in preparation for exchanging our anniversary gifts.

Sylvia had often mentioned that she wanted a tattoo of a sexy nude lady with a whip on her left tit. She had also always wanted one of her bald pussy lips to be pierced with a gold ring.

Sylvia's pussy and anal hair had all been electrically removed while she was in college; the ring would be the final decoration of her womanhood.

My presents to Sylvia were a gold ring for her pussy, an artist's rendition of her tattoo and gift certificates for the tattoo and the pussy piercing. She was ecstatic.

After a few sips of champagne, Sylvia left the room to get my gift. When she returned, my heart almost stopped beating. Before me stood my glorious wife with a strap-on cock attached to her loins and a whip in her hand! She strolled over to me, her fake cock bouncing in the air with each step. Tickling my nipples with the handle of the whip, she asked if I was up to being her complete slave until our next anniversary.

I was so excited that all I could do was nod in reply. She then announced that her tattoo would be modified to show the strap-on cock she now wore. At that statement, my cock gave a lurch and a drop of pre-come leaked from the tip.

Noticing my excitement, my new mistress ordered me to milk the pre-come from my cock, wipe it up with my finger and place it in my mouth. You know, it tasted rather nice! Next my mistress had me go to our nightstand and fetch a tube of anal lubricant she had placed there.

When I returned, my mistress had me apply the lubricant to her "cock" and then to my own asshole. Following her directions, I inserted one, then two fingers into myself to ensure good lubrication.

Mistress Sylvia then instructed me to get on all fours facing the fireplace. No sooner had I done this than she was on her knees behind me with her "cock" against my asshole. Mistress suggested that I relax, and told me that my virgin asshole was going to be fucked by her, relaxed or not. I tried to relax, but not successfully enough. Mistress grew impatient. With one giant thrust she filled my ass with her cock.

Shit, it hurt! Tears came to my eyes, but as Mistress Sylvia began to fuck me, my asshole relaxed and I began to enjoy the fullness of her in me. The whole time my mistress was banging my asshole, I had a hard-on as hard as steel. Mistress reached around and started to pump my cock with her hand in time with her fucking of my butt. I was instructed to catch my come with my hand and then to lick my hand clean. I shot my load and drank my come like it was my last meal. Once I had swallowed my come, Mistress Sylvia pulled out of my sore asshole and went to the bathroom for a wet towel. As I cleaned her cock with the towel, my mistress laid down the new rules for the house. She told me that the upcoming year was going to be real fun for both of us. She would be bringing home any man who turned her on and having sex with him as I watched. As soon as her pussy was full of his come, I would have to suck it all out. I would also have to orally clean off her new sex-mate's cock. If my mistress's new lover became aroused while I was licking his cock clean, I was to offer him his choice of a blow job or my ass for fucking. If Mistress Sylvia was pleased by my performance, I would be allowed to masturbate to orgasm and then to eat my own come.

Well, it has been a year since I became a sex slave. Mistress Sylvia has had at least one new sex partner per week. I have had the pleasure of sucking all of their come from her glorious, bald pussy, and of using either my asshole or mouth to drain a second load of come from their balls. Nude was still the norm in our home; but whenever Mistress Sylvia went out to find a man, I wore a butt-plug up my ass. This kept my asshole in constant readiness for whomever my lovely mistress brought home.

Tomorrow is our second anniversary. I intend to have seven couples over for an orgy on the mats in our basement exercise room. Sylvia will be tied down. Sex acts will be going on all around her, and she will be sucking all the come from whatever fuck-hole it is leaking from on each woman. Once a woman has had her cunt or asshole orally cleaned by Sylvia, she will then strap on a dildo and fuck Sylvia up the ass. The woman's lover will fuck Sylvia up the ass as well.

By the end of the evening, Sylvia's asshole should be as accustomed to cock as mine is.

And for my anniversary present to her? Why, she will be my sex slave for a year, of course! I can hardly wait to begin bringing home women and making Sylvia guide my prick into their fuck-holes. Sylvia will watch as we fuck like maniacs, then I will command her to lick up all my juices from the woman's cunt. And of course, if the woman wants, there is always the fake cock on the nightstand that she can use on Sylvia's asshole!—S.B., *Eugene, Oregon*

Three-For-All

GREEK SISTERS PLEDGE ALLEGIANCE TO
FRAT BOY'S FLAGPOLE

Once in every guy's life there comes a chance to be big man on campus. Mine came during senior year in college when, after three years in a fraternity, I was elected pledge master. This is a great position because not only do I get to be in charge of the male pledges, but also the pledges for our "little sister" auxiliary organization. Of course, this is all handled on a very professional level. There is no fraternizing allowed between the brothers and the pledges.

One day a little-sister pledge named Terry came to my room to see me. She was someone I definitely wanted to get to know better when pledging ended. She had a long flowing mane of red hair and full pouty lips. She was also very slim and had full breasts and a nice round ass. Terry explained to me that her close friend and fellow pledge Sara was considering dropping out of our fraternity. She added that she was even thinking about dropping out herself. I didn't want to lose either of them as pledges, so I asked Terry if the three of us could get together and talk about it.

When Terry and I arrived at Sara's room she was sitting on her bed. Sara was also very attractive, but in a much darker way than Terry. Her hair was long and black and her body was tan and hard. She was a dance major and she had the body to prove it.

"What's wrong, Sara?" I asked, getting right to the point. "You've come too far to quit now."

"We don't really want to quit," she replied as I stared at her dark nipples peeking through her flimsy white tank top, "but we really don't know how else to solve our dilemma." Her sultry brown eyes followed my stare. She touched a nipple gently with her fingertips. "You see, we both want you, and we don't know any other way around the rules."

"Well, you know that I make the rules for all the pledges," I reminded them. "And I'm deciding to temporarily suspend the non-fraternization clause for, let's say, the next two hours."

I turned as I heard the door close behind me. Terry stood there, smiling sexily. "Is it okay if I take off my pledge pin?" she asked.

"Absolutely," I said. I felt my cock harden as I watched her pull her pink sweater up over her head. She then popped off her bra, revealing two perfectly round pink-nippled breasts. She giggled as she wriggled out of her black leggings. From behind me, Sara reached around my chest and began rubbing my nipples.

"We just wanted to thank you for being so nice to us during pledging," Sara purred as she began nibbling my earlobe. She ran her hands over my chest and down to my jeans. She gently rubbed my crotch as she licked my neck. Terry then kissed me, her mouth open, her tongue flickering in and out. Sara unbuttoned my shirt with one hand and stroked my crotch with the other. Terry was kissing me deeply, her mouth pressed hard against mine. I felt my zipper go down. Then a hand reached in, grabbed my throbbing cock and pulled it out.

When Terry finally came up for air, she and Sara took me by either arm and pulled me to the bed. Terry sat me down as Sara pulled my jeans off. I sat there naked, my cock standing straight up like a flagpole. Sara tore off her clothes with abandon, exposing her amazing body. She was tanned all over and had small firm breasts and a tiny patch of fine black hair just above her pussy.

Terry's face came closer to mine and her hand started pumping my dick. Sara leaned in and brought her lips to Terry's glistening mouth. Their tongues met. Then Sara grabbed Terry's head, pulled her close and drove her tongue deep into Terry's eager mouth.

The girls pulled me toward them. My tongue entwined with theirs and I kissed them both. Terry rubbed my cock the whole time. Sara gently pushed me onto my back, her mouth over mine. She then straddled my chest with one leg on either side of my head, her pussy inches from my face.

"I'm gonna make you come now," Terry announced, jamming my cock inside her. "Yeah, baby, fuck me! Fuck my pussy!" She moaned as she rode my throbbing cock. I thrust myself up into her, simultaneously sticking my tongue deep into Sara's pussy. Sara responded by grinding her snatch into my face. My chin and cheeks were soon smeared with her wetness. I tensed up and was about to come when they both leaped off me.

"Hey, come on. What are you doing?" I cried out in desperation.

"Not yet, baby," Sara said as she sat beside me and rubbed my leg softly. She touched my rock-hard cock and I lurched toward her hand.

Terry ran her tongue along my shaft and then lifted my balls with her fingers. She pumped my cock once, then released it. "Please let me come," I gasped. "I was so close!"

"Right after you make me come," Sara said, lying on her back and spreading her legs. Her dark pussy glistened wetly. I rolled onto her and shoved my aching prick deep inside her. She kept up a lively patter as I fucked her. "Yeah, baby, yeah. Do it. You're gonna make me come." She wrapped her legs around my ass. "I love it! I love it! Make me come, baby!"

Terry crept behind me and began pushing me deeper into Sara's pussy with every stroke. "Yes! Yes! I'm coming! I'm coming!" Sara screamed.

Next it was Terry's turn. Before Sara had even stopped twitching, Terry pulled me back, spun me around and positioned me on top of her. I shoved my cock into her with a deep, hard stroke. Terry moaned with pleasure and tugged her swollen pink nipples.

"Fuck me! Fuck me, baby!" Terry grunted as I pounded into her. I brought my mouth to hers and she kissed me hungrily as I continued to fuck her hard. "Oh, oh oh!" she panted. "I'm gonna come! Oh, make me come! I love your cock! I love it!"

Her body began to spasm wildly as she reached orgasm. I gave her one last hard thrust and shot my load deep inside her. Then I collapsed on her chest. I lay there for a little while before Terry pushed me off.

"Okay, pledge master. This is our little secret, right?" Sara asked.

"Yeah. You know the rules. No fraternizing with pledges," Terry said with a smile.

"Well, you won't be pledges much longer," I said. "And after that, who knows?" I was hopeful, anyway.—*J.S., Boston, Massachusetts*

WHEN IT COMES TO MASSEURS
HE LEARNS HE PREFERS A MONSIEUR

*M*y wife of five years recently surprised me with a holiday weekend trip for my birthday. It's been a while since we've been able to get away together, so I was immensely pleased at the prospect of four days with Christine.

After checking into a very pleasant hotel, we spent the afternoon shopping and taking in some of the local sights. Later that evening we went out for dinner and an adult movie. Watching the movie triggered a session of fondling and petting in the cab back to our hotel.

As soon as we were in the hotel elevator, Christine unzipped my slacks, pulled out my fully erect cock, dropped to her knees and took my penis deep into her mouth. At that point I don't think I would have cared if the elevator had stopped for another passenger. Fortunately it didn't. When the elevator reached our floor, she reluctantly tucked my dick back into my pants and stood up for the long walk to our room.

We fucked twice that night (which is unusual for us) and once when we woke up the next morning. Our bold exhibition of the previous night was out of character for either of us, but it had definitely inspired some great sex.

As I showered and shaved, I heard Christine making phone calls. She came into the bathroom to let me know that she had made an appointment for herself to get a manicure, a pedicure and a facial. She said that she would be back in time for us to grab a late lunch. I must have looked a little disappointed at the prospect of being left alone, because she then told me she had also made arrangements for a massage for me, and that the masseur would be at our hotel room in about a half hour. I tried to tell her that I would be just as happy watching a ball game on television, but she insisted that this was my birthday weekend and that I deserved to be pampered.

After she left I slipped on a pair of shorts, not knowing quite how to dress for my first-ever professional massage. When I heard a knock on the door, I answered it. The masseur introduced himself as Donald. He told me that Christine had told him I was stressed out and sorely in need of relief. We both laughed, and I soon found that Donald was a pleasant conversationalist with a disarming manner that was undoubtedly an asset in his business. He was dressed in white tennis shorts and a matching knit shirt, and he looked to be in his late twenties or very early thirties.

Donald explained that he would be using a combination of Swedish and Oriental techniques that included the use of a lightly scented oil which would have a warm, relaxing effect on the skin. Not knowing what to expect, I walked ahead of him into the bedroom and lay facedown on the bed. He then suggested that I lie on the padded sheet he had brought and that I remove my shorts in order to prevent them from getting stained by the massage oil.

I followed his advice even though I felt a little self-conscious about being completely nude in front of a man I hardly knew.

He laid out his various containers on the nightstand and then began kneading and manipulating the muscles of my neck and shoulders. As he worked down my spine his touch varied from extremely relaxing to almost painful, and I soon found myself thinking that this was something I could easily grow accustomed to.

Donald continued working his way down my ribs and lower back. Then he switched over to my feet and began working his way back up. I spread my legs slightly as he worked the muscles of my legs and knees. Suddenly, and to my great surprise, I felt my cock begin to stiffen as he worked the backs of my thighs just below the cheeks of my ass. I tried to think of other matters in order to avoid the embarrassment of sporting an erection when I rolled over.

When it was time to roll over, in spite of my efforts I was obviously semierect. I had no idea how Donald would react. Would he be offended? Would he make fun of me? But Donald didn't say a word about it. He just asked me if I was enjoying myself and resumed manipulating my feet and leg muscles. Try as I might, I could not deny the effect his hands were having on my near fully erect penis. I was almost disappointed when his fingers stopped within inches of my swollen balls. My breathing was heavy as he traced oil across my chest and began working downward from my neck.

Embarrassed, I thought this was his way of allowing me to regain my composure until I felt him caressing my nipples between his oily fingers. I looked up and our eyes locked. Turning, he took my throbbing erection firmly in his hand and asked, "Would you like me to take care of this?"

I was surprised by the huskiness of my voice as I responded, "Yes, please."

I expected him to use his oil-slicked hands to relieve my discomfort. Instead he took my cock deep into his mouth. I moaned as my surprise was overwhelmed by the waves of pleasure I felt as his tongue swirled over the head of my cock. He sucked my shaft deeply into his mouth, burying his nose in my pubic hair while gently fondling my balls. It was incredible! I found myself comparing this to blow jobs from my wife. Christine is a fantastic cocksucker, but at this point, feeling the warmth of his mouth and tongue on my engorged member, I could not say that her technique was any better. He knew just what to do without asking.

I felt his finger tenderly probe my anus. I spread my legs to allow unencumbered access and he gently slid it into my asshole. I was quickly approaching what I knew would be an outrageous orgasm. With my last remnants of self-control, I told him that I was about to come. His sucking intensified and I pumped what must have been my biggest load ever into his mouth. He swallowed every drop, pulling his finger from my anus only as my orgasm began to subside. Withdrawing my still-stiff organ from his mouth, he licked the last few drops from the head.

Only then did I see Christine sitting in the corner. Her face was redder than I had ever seen it. I was speechless with shock. I realized there was no excuse that could explain what she had just witnessed. A moment of silence passed before Christine said, "Okay, Roger, now it's your turn to suck cock!"

Donald unzipped his tennis shorts and let them fall, exposing a thick, smooth member much larger than my own. I sat up, still not fully comprehending what was transpiring as Donald stroked his shaft and brought it close to my face. I looked over at Christine to find her completely undressed except for her bra and panties.

As Donald's bulbous head temptingly slid across my lips, I began to realize that this whole scenario had been planned and orchestrated by my loving wife. Reaching up to grasp the huge dick being fed to me, I now saw that the flush on Christine's face was unmistakably sexual excitement. This made me feel better as I turned my attentions to the fleshy firmness of Donald's prick. I laid him down and positioned myself between his legs. The musky sweetness of his groin was incredible, much different from a pussy but exciting nonetheless. I stroked his shaft with my hand and sucked as much of it as possible into my bulging mouth.

Feeling a clumsy poke at my anus, I turned to see that Christine had strapped on a rubber dick and was attempting to fuck my ass. Momentarily suspending my oral manipulations of Donald's cock, I spread my legs in order to assist Christine's penetration of my anus. Expecting some discomfort, I was pleasantly surprised as the long dildo slid slowly in and out of my rectum. I then resumed my attentions to Donald's prick, concentrating on doing to him what I like being done to me. My inexperience was soon overcome by my enthusiasm, and Donald began to moan appreciatively as I sloppily sucked his big dick.

He soon reached orgasm, and the feel of Christine's rubber cock sliding in and out of my asshole had my cock stiff and swaying as I felt his jism spurt deep into my mouth. Hesitating only momentarily, I began swallowing as he pumped spurt after spurt of thick hot come down my throat. As his orgasm began to subside I came again, shamelessly spraying the padded sheet as Christine buried her dick deep in my ass.

I let Donald's cockhead slip from my mouth and turned to share the remnants of his come with Christine as I kissed her deeply. Donald and I then turned our attentions to pleasing Christine, who was a more than willing recipient of our combined efforts.—R.W., Helena, Montana

SHE MAKES NEW EMPLOYEE FEEL AT HOME BY
FEELING HIM AT WORK

I had been laid off after twenty years with the same company and I was nervous about starting over. I had sold everything I owned and had a new job in a new town. On Monday I showed up at the plant for the night shift. My supervisor, a guy named Harvey, showed me the ropes and got me started. I'd been hired as the plant repairman, but that day nothing broke down so I had no work to do. Instead Harvey and I talked for several hours, comparing notes on everything from cars to computers to sex.

At about four in the morning I began to nod off. Harvey shook me awake and said, "Come on, kid, let's take a walk and maybe I can find something that will keep you awake." As we strolled around the place, Harvey showed me the various machines and described the problems I should expect from each one. There were a lot of women working the lines, and because of the warm weather there was a lot more to look at than machinery.

Finally at the shipping dock we ran into Martha. One look was enough to make me drool. Martha was almost six feet tall and she had huge boobs that stretched the fabric of her thin sleeveless shirt to the limit. Her nipples were clearly visible. As she bent over to pick up a heavy box, I noticed wisps of cunt hair protruding from her short shorts. Suddenly I was wide awake.

Harvey introduced us and asked Martha if she had time to welcome a new worker. Her eyes practically sizzled as she inspected me. Finally she licked her lips and said, "I think I just might have enough time to welcome you both." Without another word she came over to me and kissed me full on the lips, driving her tongue deep into my mouth. Then she unbuttoned my shirt and tickled my nipples.

When the kiss broke I noticed Harvey had opened the door to the stockroom and was removing his clothing. I followed Martha into the stockroom. She bolted the door and led us to the back, where we found several pallets of fluffy shipping material. I slid up behind Martha and cupped her heavy breasts. Sliding my hands under her shirt, I pulled it over her head and unclasped her bra, freeing her quivering hooters. Eagerly I placed my lips around a large nipple and felt it grow and harden in my mouth as I slowly circled my tongue around it. I felt her move slightly and saw Harvey slide her shorts and panties down her legs. Soon he was stroking her pussy and kissing her ass-cheeks.

After a few minutes Martha lay down and spread her legs. I

skinned off the rest of my clothing and dove in. Harvey began feasting on her oversize boobs as I worked my tongue through her matted cunt hair. I took my time and kept her guessing as to where my tongue would land next. She squirmed beneath me and made soft purring noises. When I finally reached the inside of her sweet pussy lips, she lifted her ass and ground her steamy cunt into my face. I circled her outer lips with my tongue to lubricate her twat for the fucking to come.

Soon I had my tongue deep in her fuck-hole, darting in and out as my upper lip brushed her clit. I worked my tongue up toward her mound. Then I licked a finger and inserted it into her vagina so it wouldn't miss my tongue. As soon as my tongue touched her clitoris she cried out and bucked wildly. I nibbled her sweet flesh, and in seconds she came. I didn't stop probing her pussy, though. Instead I drove my finger deeper into her twat and sucked her clit deep into my mouth.

Up above I could hear Harvey's lips smacking Martha's breasts, and in no time she was moaning loudly. I ran my slippery tongue up and down her hot gash, periodically flicking her clitoris. Her moans grew louder and she came again, raising her ass off the soft padding and screaming: "Fuck me!"

Wasting no time, I buried my cock in her wet cunt and drove it in and out of her. Harvey straddled her, pressed her massive tits together and tit-fucked her as I rammed my rod into her cunt. Though she was so wet I barely felt her around my pecker, each time I drove deeper into her cunt I felt an incredible warmth around my rigid tool. In all too short a time I felt an ache in my balls and I shot my load deep into Martha's snatch.

I had barely pulled out when Harvey climbed off Martha and positioned her on all fours. Soon he was fucking her from behind. I could see drops of Martha's sweet cunt juice and my own come dripping from her twat. Martha motioned me over and had me lie down where she could get at my spent stick. She blew new life into my tool as Harvey banged away. In an amazingly short time I was hard again and her blazing red lips were riding up and down my pole. I closed my eyes and enjoyed the feeling. I could hear Harvey grunt each time he slammed into Martha. Moments later I filled Martha's mouth with a load of cream, but Harvey was still going strong. I watched in amazement as he drove his dong in and out of Martha's sopping cunt. She was totally absorbed in being fucked. Harvey thrust harder until spasms racked his body and he filled Martha with come.

We sat there a few minutes recovering and then slowly got dressed. Oddly enough, Martha put on my underwear and handed me hers. She told me that I had to wear her panties for the rest of the night and that I could return them the next day. I think this may be the job I've been looking for all my life.—*P.L.*, *Pittsburgh*, *Pennsylvania*

THEIR PERSONAL TRAINER GETS
MORE PERSONAL THAN THEY EXPECTED

*M*y wife and I are both from small towns in the Midwest. We met in college and went on to law school in New York together. Now we both practice law there for different firms. We were both raised with very old-fashioned values: We'd had almost no sexual experience when we met and we held off having sex until we married.

Elizabeth is on the petite side. She has beautiful blue eyes that nicely contrast her dark brown hair. I am not much taller than she is. I am also slender and somewhat under-endowed.

After eleven years of practicing law, Elizabeth and I were both getting out of shape because our long hours at work prevented us from taking advantage of our health club membership. Then one day someone at the club suggested that we install some equipment at home and hire a personal trainer. We both liked the idea, and soon we had converted a spare bedroom into a gym and put out the word at the club that we were looking for a trainer.

We have no idea who referred him to us, but nearly two years ago the person who was to become such a major part of our lives appeared at our door. His name was Andre. He has a last name neither of us can pronounce, but it sounds Polish. He is fit, with a flashing smile and rugged good looks. The most striking thing about him is his commanding presence—he seems to take charge as soon as he enters a room.

The first night Andre had us perform sit-ups and other physical tests while he took notes. Then we arranged for him to come over three nights a week. Though things started out normally enough, soon we noticed that as he guided us through our exercises he touched us in all sorts of places. The strangest thing about this was that he seemed completely unaware of the fact that the places he touched us were in any way intimate. In fact, when he would help Elizabeth do her last few push-ups, his hands were usually on her breasts. She blushed at first but didn't object, because he seemed so oblivious to what he was doing.

Within a couple of months we were getting back into shape. We knew we were going to stick with it, so we decided to enlarge the room into a real gym, installing a sauna, a Jacuzzi and a high-tech shower big enough for both Elizabeth and me. The first time Andre saw the new setup he seemed impressed. He especially liked the shower and asked us if he could use it before he left each night. This was okay with us, because we liked using the sauna first anyway.

We agreed and to our great surprise he proceeded to remove his clothes right in front of us. Our eyes bulged when we saw his huge cock. I never knew a cock could be that big. Elizabeth blushed, but she also stared intently. Andre calmly entered the shower, adjusted some of the many nozzles and, when he had them right, started singing some strange song. From then on, nudity became quite common with all three of us, even Elizabeth.

One night Andre walked into the sauna while I was rubbing Elizabeth's sore shoulders. He stood there watching us, his cock red and semierect. He had probably turned the massaging jets onto it, discovered that it felt good and had just kept the water going. That's the way he is. Completely unembarrassed by his semiaroused state, Andre watched us for a few minutes and then calmly suggested that we purchase a massage table so that he could take the kinks out of us before our sauna.

I was the first to get a massage the next week. As he worked my legs, his fingers brushed my balls but he didn't seem to notice. When he stroked my front his oily hands went right over my cock, making me hard. This was embarrassing to me but not to him. Without saying a word he took my cock in his hand and, with a few strokes, got me off. There was no change in his expression as he wiped the mixed oil and come off my belly.

Elizabeth was next, and his hands wandered everywhere on her. Every time his fingers touched her clit she moaned. I don't know if he made her come that first time or not, but she did make an interesting discovery. She found out that the only thing to get him going sexually was actual contact with his cock. In the course of massaging Elizabeth, his penis brushed against her hand. When she closed her hand around it, he grunted and immediately started thrusting his pelvis. It was the first time he got fully erect in our presence. His cock grew to at least ten inches long and got as thick as a cucumber. Entranced, Elizabeth kept stroking him while staring at his dong. With a moan he came, squirting jism clear across the table. Then he went right on with the massage!

Elizabeth and I both got experimental with Andre. The next time he helped her with her bench presses his crotch was right over her face and the head of his cock was hanging out of his shorts looking as huge as a plum. She reached up and pulled his cock into her mouth. He almost went into spasms trying to hold his position with bent knees. When he came he filled her mouth and semen leaked out the corners.

We have tried several things with our hunky trainer. Elizabeth's favorite is to have him straddle her rear when he massages her back. She squeezes her oiled buns together until his cock gets hard. Then she raises her butt so his cock slides down between her pussy lips and the head rubs her clit. That feels so good to him he stops the massage and starts thrusting his pelvis. He has never come that way, but she bounces and moans until she has a great orgasm.

The last time she did this was different. She raised her rear as she usually does, then moved her hand under her crotch until I heard her sigh. She had obviously maneuvered until his cock was starting to enter her cunt. Her face was something to see! Her expression was torn between ecstasy and uncertainty due to his huge size. Once he was all the way in her, however, they started fucking violently. After a while Elizabeth came, screaming into the towel. He kept right on pumping into her until he came, which brought her off again!—T.V., *New York, New York*

IT PAYS TO ADVERTISE! COUPLE FINDS
DICK OF THEIR DREAMS IN THE CLASSIFIEDS

I have to tell someone about the first night my wife and I spent with another guy. My wife Caroline and I wanted to find out what it would be like to have another guy in bed with us. So we went to an adult bookstore to get a swingers magazine. We responded to a personal ad that sounded good to us, and a few weeks later we received a response from this guy named Tim.

Tim's letter included his picture and his phone number. Liking what we saw in the picture, we called him up and invited him to visit us the following Saturday.

We couldn't wait for Saturday to come. Tim arrived at our house at five in the afternoon. At first we just sat around and talked for a while. Then we had supper and polished off a few beers. It wasn't until about ten that we decided to get things started. We put an X-rated movie into the VCR. It started off with a girl getting fucked by two guys—one fucked her ass while the other fucked her pussy. We all looked at each other and then quickly undressed.

Tim and I joined Caroline on the couch, sitting on either side of her. I started sucking on one of her tits and Tim started sucking on the other while she stroked both our cocks. Caroline soon made clear her desire to suck Tim's dick. I can't say that I blamed her. Tim had the biggest, fattest dick I had ever seen. Watching my wife trying to take that huge hunk of meat into her mouth was a sight to remember. We were all really getting into it when Caroline suggested we move to the bedroom.

Once on the bed Caroline immediately started to suck me off while Tim got busy eating her out. I came in no time. Then I told Tim that it was his turn and we switched places. I gave Caroline a really good tongue-lashing. When she said that she was about to come I backed off and told her that she would have to wait.

Tim then suggested that Caroline sit on his face. He lay down on his back and she eagerly lowered her dripping snatch onto his waiting tongue. As Caroline was moaning and squealing in ecstasy, my eyes strayed to Tim's big hard cock. I decided this was an opportunity to do something that I had always wanted to do: suck cock. I positioned myself between his muscular legs and started gently licking the head of his engorged tool. Then I slowly worked it into my mouth.

I was really getting into the sensation of sucking cock when Caroline's groans reached a fevered pitch and she screamed, "I need to be fucked!" To my disappointment but to Caroline's delight, Tim pulled his big dick out of my mouth, laid Caroline down on her back and started to fuck her hard. I slid my cock into Caroline's mouth so she could suck me off one more time. Watching her get fucked by Tim's big cock got me so turned on that I came in her mouth after just a few seconds. As I shot my load into her hungry mouth, Tim's ramming piston sent her over the edge and she exploded in orgasm.

After a brief rest Caroline declared that she wanted to get fucked by both of us at the same time. I lay down on the bed first.

Then Caroline got on top of me and slowly eased her pussy down on my cock. Tim positioned himself above us so that his dick was lined up with her asshole. Unfortunately Tim had trouble getting his cock in her ass and after a few futile attempts he went soft.

Caroline, clearly disappointed, excused herself to go to the bathroom. On the way out of the room she turned back and said to me, "Why don't you see if you can get Tim ready to double-fuck me?"

I was delighted by the suggestion. I started by taking his balls in my mouth and then slowly licking my way up to his cock. I worked my way up to the head of his dick and started to nibble on it. I could tell that I was doing a good job, because his cock quickly sprang to attention. I sucked on the head of his cock until he started moaning. Then I worked his big tool all the way down my throat, which was not an easy feat.

When Caroline walked into the room she gasped, "Wow! What a sight!" I'm sure Caroline never imagined she'd see her husband deep-throating a well-hung man. Watching us made her flush with excitement. She quickly jumped on the bed and begged to be the meat in a fuck sandwich. Needless to say, neither of us hesitated to comply.

Tim stayed where he was and Caroline mounted his cock, letting it sink deep into her pussy. I got behind Caroline and slowly fed my cock into her tight asshole. To describe the feeling this produced would be difficult. Let me just say that I could feel Tim's dick in her pussy through the thin membrane. Caroline groaned with pleasure and kept repeating that she never wanted us to stop and that it was the greatest feeling she'd ever had. Well, with all that stimulation I didn't last long. I shot my load into her ass in no time.

Now, Tim did not come during all this, so he was pretty hot and wanted to come badly. Caroline obliged him by getting on her hands and knees and letting him fuck her pussy from behind. Meanwhile I got under Caroline so I could lick her clit while Tim fucked her. It was great! As Tim pounded into her I licked her pussy and also helped myself to some cock and balls. This really got them going. Tim soon said that he was about to come. He asked Caroline if she wanted him to come in her mouth. She said yes, so he pulled out of her pussy and shoved his dick in her mouth. He came moments later, showering her tonsils with sticky white semen.

After we were all satisfied we sat there and talked some more. Tim said that he was pretty worn out and should be getting home. But he also said that he had enjoyed himself and wanted to do it again sometime.—*Name and address withheld*

WHEN AN OLD FLAME TURNS UP THEY BURN THE CANDLE FROM BOTH ENDS

When I was eighteen and a senior in high school, I went out with a guy named Brad. He dated a lot of girls and was quite popular. We had typical teenage sex—quick and not very satisfying.

We hadn't seen each other in five years when we ran into each other at a friend's wedding. When he saw me his eyes just about popped out of his head. I was never really obese, but I weighed about one hundred forty pounds in high school. I am five feet four and now weigh one hundred ten pounds. I have long blonde hair and brown eyes, and I work out three times a week.

The first thing he said was, "What happened to your big ass?" We laughed, had a few drinks, danced and talked about old times. Now let me tell you, Brad is not hard on the eyes. He has black hair that he keeps in a ponytail, crystal blue eyes and a six-foot-two-inch body that doesn't quit. At the end of the reception he invited me back to his place. I suggested that we go to my place, but he insisted that we go back to his town house instead. Little did I know why he was so persistent.

When we arrived at his house he told me to make myself comfortable while he made a quick telephone call. When Brad returned we couldn't keep our hands off each other. He cradled my head and kissed me deep and hard. Then he unzipped my dress and exposed my breasts. He cupped his hands around them and sucked them till my nipples were hard. I reached for the bulge in his pants, but he pushed my hand away. He slipped off my dress and pulled down my panties. When he took off his shirt I admired his well-defined chest. He slowly kissed my stomach and licked my navel. I was so hot. I desperately wanted his cock, but again he stopped my attempts to free it.

He began flicking my clit with his tongue while he fingered my hole. Brad pulled off his pants and let his member spring from its prison. I tried one more time to reach for his tool, but to no avail. He leaned close to me and asked me if I remembered what he had once offered me. I had no recollection at all until I looked up and saw Jeremy, another gorgeous high-school chum, walking into the living room with a huge smile on his face. I suddenly remembered that Brad and Jeremy had once offered to "double-team" me back in high school. I'd never taken them up on their offer, but now I was going to go for it.

Brad positioned me on my hands and knees so he could fuck me doggie-style. Jeremy undressed and stood in front of me. He slid his dick into my mouth and asked me to suck on it, which I did without hesitation. Brad got behind me and drove his cock into my love-box. I could feel my wetness dribbling down my thighs. I think this was the wettest I'd ever been in my life. All of a sudden I felt an intense orgasm rising up inside me. I exploded, and by the way Brad and Jeremy were moaning and groaning I figured they were about to come as well.

Much to my surprise they both pulled out. I was yearning for more as I sank to the floor. Brad slid two fingers into my pussy and used my juices to lubricate his cock. Jeremy lay on his back and pulled me on top of him, impaling me on his cock. Brad got behind me and stuck his dick into my tight ass. It felt weird at first, but then it was pure pleasure. Brad came first and shot his load all over my ass. Jeremy continued to pound me hard. When he finally came, we all went into Brad's bedroom and fell into a deep sleep.—*L.W., Knoxville, Tennessee*

LUCKY MAN SCORES TWICE WITH OPEN BALL TRICK

My wife Pearl and I recently rented out the room in our basement to a student going to the local university. Her name is Tanya and she is a knockout—nineteen, with perky tits, tight ass, and a beautiful face framed by long blonde hair. She's a cheerleader for the university football team, and that helps keep her in terrific shape. Once I got a look at her, my objections to renting out my former study seemed trivial. Not only was the extra rent money good, but sex with Pearl has never been better.

Not that it was ever bad. You see, Pearl has black hair, big firm tits with enormous nipples that stand out about an inch when fully erect, and long, tanned legs that go on forever. As good a time as we have together, thoughts of a threesome occupied my mind from the day that Tanya moved in. One day it happened.

We had just driven home from the football game, where the sight of Tanya in her short skirt, white panties and tight wool sweater, prancing on the sidelines, had turned my attention from the game and onto my rigid goalpost. Tanya asked if she could use the shower in the bathroom attached to our bedroom. I said yes, sensing my opportunity. I cornered Pearl in the kitchen and began nuzzling her neck and squeezing her tits and hard nipples. She didn't need much encouragement to follow me up to the bedroom.

I threw her on the bed, stripped off my clothes, and covered Pearl's body with my own, our tongues intertwining as we kissed and licked each other. I tore off Pearl's blouse, revealing her heavy breasts. I squeezed them in my hands and began sucking on them hard. Then I licked all over her tits, trying to swallow them whole, as Pearl moaned and undulated beneath me.

As I had hoped, I caught sight of Tanya out of the corner of my eye. She had just finished her shower and, clad in nothing but a towel, had opened the bathroom door to leave. Her eyes widened in astonishment at what she saw. I was between Pearl's legs, tearing at her panties with my teeth, still fondling her tits. She wrapped her legs tightly around my neck as my tongue shot into her wet pussy. I quickly located her clitoris and began sucking and tonguing it, my face already bathed in cunt juice. She pushed my head into her cunt, thrashing her body on the bed in a frenzy, completely oblivious to Tanya.

But not me. As I came up for air I noticed that Tanya had let the towel drop away, revealing her young, moist body. She was cupping her tits with her hands, her fingers pinching and tugging at her pink, rock-hard nipples. She was really turned on, and the musky smell of sex filling the room added to her abandon. I stood up, pulled Pearl to the edge of the bed and shoved my cock into her pussy. I motioned Tanya over.

Tanya, eyes glazed, unsteadily made her way over to the bed. "I was hoping you would join in our games," Pearl breathed, much to my relief. Tanya lay on the bed next to my wife.

"I . . . I . . . don't know much about sex," Tanya stammered. She was cut short by Pearl, who pulled her close and kissed her on the mouth. She filled Tanya's mouth with her tongue, then began kissing her neck, sticking her tongue in Tanya's ear. Tanya's body shook with sexual awakening, as she felt another woman's passionate kiss and hot body for the first time.

"Your hair is so soft," Pearl moaned, as she buried her face in Tanya's blonde tresses, all the while rubbing her tits against the youngster's breasts. Pearl then pushed Tanya on her back, pulled my cock out of her red-hot cunt and crawled on top of Tanya. The sight of my wife, with her jet-black hair, lying on top of that blonde, innocent, their bodies rubbing together, all the time sucking each other's tongue, almost sent me over the edge. "Shove that big dick in Tanya's tight cunt," my wife groaned, snapping me back to beautiful reality. I spread Tanya's legs, holding them by the soles of her feet, and inserted my throbbing cock into her blonde bush. It was tight, and Tanya's moans filled Pearl's mouth as they French-kissed. I slammed in and out of Tanya, sucking on her toes at the same time.

I then pulled my cock out of Tanya and shoved it into Pearl from behind. Her ass-cheeks bounced against my body as I buried my cock into her over and over. We were all drenched in sweat by this time, and the air was filled with Pearl's moaning and Tanya's cries as my wife fingered her to multiple orgasms. Tanya flailed away on the bed, her body tensing and untensing as the orgasms rolled over her. Pearl was like a woman possessed, finger-fucking Tanya while slamming her ass onto my cock. As my come reached the boiling point, Pearl suddenly crawled across the bed, leaving my dick hanging erect in the air. She took some ice out of the mini-fridge next to our bed.

"You're overheating," she purred. She repositioned herself on the bed, her cunt now directly over Tanya's face. She began rubbing my cock up and down with the ice. Tanya tentatively licked my wife's cunt, until Pearl shoved her pussy hard down into Tanya's face. Tanya got the message and began licking and lapping it like a cat licking a bowl of milk. My knees buckled and my cock got even heavier as Pearl continued to massage my hard member with the ice. She then popped one of the cubes into her mouth. After sucking on it, she pulled it out and began sucking on my cock. The coolness of her mouth made my legs quake, and I had to clutch her head to keep from passing out. She licked up and down my shaft, icing my balls with a cube to keep me from shooting jism down her throat.

As Pearl deep-throated me, I felt Tanya's mouth on my nipples, sucking hard, sending shivers down to my cock. I grabbed my wife's head with one hand and began fucking her mouth, while I played with Tanya's tits with the other hand. The ice on my balls was melting fast and Pearl knew it.

Tanya knelt down next to my wife, who pulled my big, soaking-wet dick out of her mouth and put it in Tanya's. Tanya was learning fast, and her teeth lightly scraping my manhood sent tingles throughout my body. They took turns sucking me off, stopping only to kiss each other, until I could take it no longer. Pearl pulled my cock out of Tanya's mouth and ordered her to keep her mouth wide open. Tanya willingly obliged, reaching out with her tongue for my come, her head tilted back in anticipation. Pearl stroked me until the jism burst out of my cock in torrential spurts. My whole body shook as the come covered Tanya's beautiful face and hair. Pearl licked Tanya's lips and face, drinking in the come as Tanya swallowed the load that was in her mouth. I slipped to the floor, exhausted.—*H.L., Ogden, Utah*

LONELY GUY DISCOVERS THAT
HIS SEXUAL FUTURE IS ALL BEHIND HIM

I'm a thirty-year-old male, recently divorced. I've always liked to have my ass played with. Sometimes I used to slip one finger in my ass when I jerked off, wanting to enhance the sensation. I recently purchased a vibrator to use on my ass. I was only able to get about six or seven inches up my ass, until one recent occasion.

It started when I asked a friend a weird question. I was hanging out one night with a good friend of mine named Floyd. We were drinking, and in a moment of serene inebriation I asked him if he would let his girl use a strap-on dildo on him. He laughed and asked me would I. I said yes.

He said, "I'll fuck your ass." I answered that I wasn't gay, but the bulge in my pants told a slightly different story.

I was real nervous, and asked if he would use a vibrator on me. He said, "Sure, but I may want to fuck you afterward."

The next time we hung out I brought my vibrator along just in case. We were in our favorite bar and he started making time with a girl. She had a real kinky look.

To my shock, when he introduced me she said in my ear, "Want me to use a strap-on to fuck you?"

My mouth dropped and I looked at Floyd. Then I realized that a chance like this doesn't come along every day. I looked back at her and said, "Come on, let's go do it!"

The three of us jumped into my car and headed to Floyd's place. When we got inside his apartment Angela wanted to shower. She went into the bathroom and we followed. Before long we were all naked in the shower.

Floyd seemed to take a long time washing his cock. I'd never realized how big it was. We went into the bedroom and Angela asked, "So, where's the strapper?" I told her I only had a vibrator, which I pulled out. I got up on my knees. Angela put some lubricant on my ass and worked it into my anus with her fingers. My buddy was behind her working her clit. My cock was hard from the feeling of Angela's fingers on my greased asshole. Before I knew it she was thrusting two fingers in and out of my ass. When she stopped I knew what was coming. The rubber cock slipped in easily, but even though Angela pushed pretty hard she couldn't get more than seven inches in.

Then I heard Floyd say, "Relax, and breathe out as she pushes." He got in front of me and was coaching. Looking at his big cock put me in a trance. My mouth must have dropped open, because his cock slipped between my lips. I just started sucking. While sucking his cock I must have really relaxed my ass muscles, because I felt the vibrator slide all the way in.

Angela said, "I can't believe this whole huge thing is buried in his little ass." At that Floyd thrust his cock all the way down my throat. What a rush! Angela got under me and, while holding the vibrator in my ass, began to suck my cock. I couldn't hold out, and started to come. Just as I came I felt Floyd tense up. He grabbed my head so I wouldn't pull away as he started coming. I nodded to let him know I understood. His cockhead felt enormous in my throat as his salty come began to pour. It was great!

We all collapsed, and Angela said, "You guys are great. Now I

want to get fucked!" We were both hard in an instant. She straddled my buddy's cock and came quick. She kept riding him, and
I positioned myself so she could suck me.

After about twenty minutes she got off him and said she
wanted a 69 with me. I got on my back and she got on top. Her
pussy lips were pink and swollen. The taste was a mix of cunt
juice and come. As she was sucking my cock she spread my ass
cheeks. I felt something warm bump my anus, and before I could
say anything I felt Floyd's cock begin to slide up my ass. It was a
tight fit, so I said, "Push my legs back." As he did, his monster
cock slid in to the hilt. I felt his balls and pelvis against my bottom.

Angela stopped sucking my cock and started to lick the area
under my balls. I started jerking off and told Floyd to come in my
ass. As I got close to coming my anus tightened around his cock.
I felt him getting harder, and we came at the same time. As I
started to come, Angela sucked the head of my cock. I let out a
loud yell. Floyd just grunted as he busted a load up my ass. I told
him, "Don't pull out fast." He just left his cock in my ass and
flexed it, until eventually it got soft and slipped out.

After Angela left I asked Floyd if he thought I was gay. He said
no, just bisexual. Then he confessed that he also likes anal pleasure, and said maybe he'd let me use the vibrator on him one day.
Can't wait.—R.J., *Asheville, North Carolina*

ATTRACTIVE COUPLE SEEKS WELL-ENDOWED MAN
FOR INTIMATE FUN . . . SEEK AND YE SHALL FIND!

I recently answered a personal ad in a local newspaper placed
by a couple seeking a threesome with a single, well-endowed
male. I left a phone message with the paper's answering service
and in no time I got a call back from Sal. We chatted briefly
about our interests and we hit it off right away. It turns out that

Sal's wife, Becky, was very sexual and above average in terms of orgasms per intercourse. Plainly, she was looking for even more attention than she was getting at home.

I invited Sal and Becky to my apartment that very evening. They are a very physically attractive couple in their early forties. Becky has shoulder-length brown hair, firm breasts and a very tight ass. Sal has gray hair but is tanned and in great shape. I'm in my early thirties and I work out regularly too. Needless to say, I am also very well endowed.

All three of us were nervous at first because we had never done anything like this before. I suggested I give Becky a massage to break the ice. I had some scented lotion which I generously applied across her shoulder, down her back, over the cheeks of her ass and down her thighs.

It didn't take long for me to get over my nervousness. My hardening cock rubbed against Becky's well-oiled ass, and I could tell she wasn't feeling shy anymore either.

I rolled her over and dove face first into her moist muff. Oral sex is one of my favorite pastimes and Becky responded with two quick orgasms, her tan, firm thighs wrapped snug across my cheeks.

All our shyness by now had flown out the window. I lay back on the bed and Becky climbed on top of my swollen cock. She faced away from me toward her husband to give him a better view of her riding my manhood. Becky came again just seconds after easing down on my massive length, and was soon building toward another even stronger orgasm. Sensing this, Sal moved in and started licking and sucking her clit while I continued to thrust deep inside her. She collapsed backward onto my chest and I grabbed her breasts and held on as I shot my load into the deepest regions of her body.

Sal didn't miss a beat. He entered Becky the instant I pulled out. I watched as their bodies ground against each other. Watching them was very arousing, and my member quickly sprang back to life. Sal had been very aroused from watching Becky and me, and he came quickly. I turned Becky so that she was lying on her back on top of Sal, and penetrated her from above, making a delicious pussy sandwich.

Sal and Becky enjoyed themselves as much as I did that night. They called me again two weeks later and we got together for a much different evening. It started out the same—a nice back rub to get things rolling—but Becky had different plans. She asked me to use even more oil and to fuck her in the ass this time.

I was hard immediately. Precome oozed from the tip of my cock when I applied lotion to Becky's puckered rim. "Oh that feels so nice, would you lick me there?" she asked.

I played dumb. "You want my tongue in your ass?"

"Please!"

"OK," I said, graciously plying her cheeks wide so I could French-kiss her sexy round rectum. Becky's finely wrinkled asshole tasted like Juicy Fruit and made me wildly hot.

Within moments I was hip deep inside her most intimate cavity. Her asshole was so tight and strong against my cock that I lasted only a minute. I came with an explosive blast just as Becky murmured that she was coming too.

Sal had known this was the plan for the evening, and he lost no time plunging his tool down the same tight pathway. Becky squirmed as Sal slid in and out of her, his deep penetration aided no doubt by the puddle of come I had just deposited in excess inside her bowels. I stood in front of her, and Becky eagerly took my limp cock into her mouth and sucked it back to its manly state. Sal exploded in her asshole with a satisfied groan. To my surprise, however, Becky was not satisfied. She can't get enough. She is a veritable fuck machine incapable of being sated when it comes to cock. Sal and I are bringing one of those foot-long dildos with the width of a dictionary into play on our next get-together. Obviously there will be plenty more to come.—J.P., *Philadelphia, Pennsylvania*

JUST WHAT HE ALWAYS WANTED—LUCKY STIFF
GETS A BIRTHDAY THREESOME

For as long as I can remember I've fantasized about making love with two women at the same time. I guess it's a pretty typical male fantasy, but I was lucky enough to have it become a reality on my last birthday!

Let me tell you how my wish came true. My lover Cory is a slender, attractive brunette with a wicked sex drive. One afternoon we were lying in bed in a blissful, post-orgasmic haze, when the conversation turned to our sexual fantasies. I hesitated to mention my favorite, but when I did I was surprised at how curious she was about it. Cory asked me to describe my fantasy threeway, and it seemed to excite her when I poured out the details.

She asked if I really wanted to live out my fantasy. "Definitely," I said, hoping someday to find myself in bed with her and another woman but never really expecting it. But Cory stunned me by asking if I would like her to bring another woman to bed with us as my birthday present. I couldn't believe it!

Of course, I agreed. Cory volunteered to make the arrangements. She told me a friend of hers thought I was handsome and might agree to sleep with us. I asked who the woman was, but Cory refused to disclose her identity until she consented.

I went crazy with anticipation for the next few days. Finally Cory called to say that her friend was very interested in joining us. Again I asked for a description. "Well, she's twenty-two and quite pretty," Cory replied. "She's also black." I developed an instant hard-on. Making love with an attractive black woman was another of my favorite fantasies. I could see I was in for an incredible treat. I suggested the three of us meet for a drink to see if we liked each other enough to go through with it.

We met at an outdoor café on a warm summer night. The three of us drank, chatted and got to know one another. The air was soon filled with sexual tension. Cory was right. Linda was beautiful. She had short hair, pretty eyes, a good figure and a sexy laugh. I liked her immediately and couldn't take my eyes off her. My mind raced as we talked, trying to imagine Linda in bed with us. Linda and I soon agreed that we wanted each other. Cory was still game, so we lingered over our drinks, flirting and laughing, and let the tension build. Finally we couldn't wait any longer. We paid the tab and left for my apartment. I felt as if I were in a dream as I walked down the street arm-in-arm with two attractive women.

At my apartment, I poured Cory and Linda some wine, then excused myself to take a quick shower. It somehow turned into a long, hot shower. Suddenly I heard the bathroom door open and in came the girls. My two partners quickly stripped and joined me under the pulsing spray. Linda stepped into the shower first and kissed me deeply, her tongue swirling around in my mouth. I put my arms around her and pulled her close, pressing her breasts against my chest. A minute later I felt Cory's familiar breasts against my back. She held me by the shoulders and rubbed her hard nipples in circles on my skin.

As Cory kissed and licked the back of my neck, Linda slid her body down over mine until she was kneeling in front of me. She cupped her hand around my balls and began making sweet love to my cock with her mouth. I still couldn't believe this was real. There I was in the shower with my lover and a beautiful black woman sucking my cock. What an incredible birthday this was turning out to be!

It was getting so hot and steamy in the bathroom, we decided to towel off and head for the bedroom. Cory made a beeline for the bed. Linda and I only made it as far as the hallway. We were all over each other. We started kissing furiously. I couldn't get enough of her full, tender lips. She kissed hard, sliding her sweet tongue deep into my mouth to let me suck on it.

We sank to the thick carpet without breaking our kiss. Our arms were wrapped around each other and our legs were inter-twined. I wanted to explore the rest of Linda's firm, sexy figure more than anything in the universe. After covering her face with kisses, I began moving slowly down her body. I kissed her beautiful neck and shoulders, her firm breasts, her hard nipples and her sensitive ribs and hips. We were both breathing hard and sweating with lust. I continued working my way down the outside of her thigh and calf. Then I worked my way back up the inside of her other leg.

I could smell the sweet, musky scent of her pussy as I neared its pink folds. Her inner lips were swollen, slightly parted and very wet. Linda gasped when I slid my tongue between them. I groaned in pleasure and felt the pre-come leaking from my cock. She was so delicious I never wanted to stop eating her. Soon it was clear from Linda's writhing and moaning that she was close to orgasm. I sent her over the edge by sliding two fingers deep into her pussy and flicking my tongue over her clitoris.

After Linda had regained her senses, I moved up to let her taste her juices on my mouth. As we kissed, she reached down, dipped her fingers into her pussy and spread her wetness over my cock. I held her legs up while she guided my stiff cock into her. With one long, slow thrust I was deep inside her cunt. She felt incredibly good. I started pumping with everything I had. In no time at all I had a powerful orgasm. Linda came right after me.

We lay on the floor for a while before joining Cory in bed. The two women took turns making love to me for the next few hours. Finally, after my sixth orgasm, I was worn out. My final image of the night is the most vivid. I can still see Linda and me watching ourselves in the full-length mirror as I fucked her from behind. That was one birthday party I will never forget.—H.D., *Hartford, Connecticut*

Part Two

From Letters to Penthouse VIII

Clusterfucks

WIFE TAKES THE BAIT ON FISHING TRIP

*L*ike many men who have been married for a while, my marriage had become sexually stale. My wife, Cindy, wasn't the problem. She has kept herself in great shape. Her five-foot frame is one hundred five pounds, and her 34C-22-36 figure complements a pretty face and natural red hair. Several times I have mentioned swinging with another couple, but Cindy always got angry. I just dropped the subject and kept my fantasies to myself.

A few weeks before the end of the summer, Cindy and I went to a national forest near our home to enjoy a few days of camping and swimming. My job allows me to get away during the middle of the week, but I'm still on call via a pager. In the middle of the week we had our choice of prime camp sites and we selected a shaded one by the lakeshore. It was like having the park all to ourselves. Later that day we were disappointed when a large R.V. drove by just as Cindy was coming back from a swim. I saw the man driving checking her out. He then pulled into the site next to ours.

Cindy was ready to move camp to another site, but I talked her out of it by reminding her of the hassle of breaking camp and setting up again. While we were talking we noticed four men get out of the R.V. One was a young black man, who was about twenty years younger than the rest of the group.

Later that afternoon the men came over and introduced themselves. They were on a fishing trip and all worked for the same firm. Jim, the young black guy, was a college student working as an intern. Chris and Joe were both engineers, slightly overweight and middle-aged. Kevin was tall, thickly built, with a coarse, aggressive personality. He was a production manager.

It was obvious their main reason for coming over was to get a closer look at my wife. Cindy surprised me by enjoying the attention of these men, flirting and returning their jokes. After a few beers the guys left to try to get some fishing in before nightfall. Chris came back over later and invited us to dinner.

The R.V. was a big one with all the comforts of home. While the steaks were grilled we drank red wine and let Kevin give us a tour of the motor home. I noticed a VCR in a large entertainment center and jokingly asked Kevin if he had any porno movies. He opened a cabinet door and pulled out a couple of tapes. "Like this?" he asked.

Everyone had been drinking so it didn't take much convincing to get Cindy to agree to watch at least a little of a movie. We all settled in with another drink as Jim turned down the lights. Cindy and I sat down on a low-backed couch. Chris sat down next to my wife and Kevin started the movie. It was clear to me that there was a lot of sexual tension in the room as the movie started.

The movie was a hot one: a blonde giving head to some guy built like a small horse. As the movie continued Cindy cuddled up to me and started to nibble on my ear and neck. This show of affection before these men surprised me, but also made me proud. I noticed that when the guys weren't watching the film, they were eyeing my wife's shapely, tanned legs and round, firm breasts.

About this time the blonde in the movie was taking on two men at once. She was on her hands and knees, fucking one guy and blowing another, all the while imploring the men like a wanton slut to fill her up. I sensed Cindy was thrilled by the action because she was squirming and fidgeting in her seat.

Kevin noticed this, too, and wasn't shy about cutting to the chase and breaking the ice. He looked over and asked Cindy if what she was watching looked good.

"Oh shut up Kevin," she said, but she never took her eyes off the screen. I knew then that it was now or never. I reached back and cycled my pager so it would go off.

"Well shit," I said, as the movie was shut off and the lights came back on. "I have to go in to work," I told them. "Go ahead and watch the rest of the movie. I should be back in a couple of hours, max."

"Oh, all right. As long as the guys promise to behave themselves," Cindy said with a smile. Of course they were quick with their assurances that she had nothing to worry about. As I left I pushed the curtain on the door window back so there was a gap big enough to scope the action from outside. I gave Cindy a kiss and drove down the access road to an unused site about a quarter mile away. On the short walk back, my hard-on was pushing against my pants.

When I got to the R.V. I was happy to see that there was enough light on inside to see easily. The opening allowed me to see most of the living area. The movie was still on, but Joe had taken my place on the couch beside Cindy. The mood, I noticed, appeared a little cheerier, owing to the consumption of drinks while I was gone. The real clincher, however, was the location of Chris's hand. It was on Cindy's leg, stroking the top of her tan thigh with soft but deliberate caresses. When Joe scooted closer to her, Cindy sat up and downed Chris's glass of scotch in one gulp. I knew then that the dam of sexual frustration was about to break.

Everyone was watching her as she leaned back on the couch and put both arms out. Chris moved his hand inside the leg opening of her shorts. Slowly moving his hand under the loose-fitting cloth, he began to rub my wife's pussy through her panties.

"You're very juicy tonight," I heard him mutter into Cindy's ear. Joe turned and kissed Cindy's long, smooth neck as he moved his hand up and under her sweatshirt to knead her full round tits. Cindy sat up a little so Joe could pull her shirt up and over her head. He gave her other tit a nice squeeze as he placed the shirt next to her on the couch.

I was going nuts, breathing in shallow gasps and massaging my cock as this tense action unfolded. Nobody was saying anything, which gave it kind of a dramatic intensity. Cindy was doing most of the expressing, and it was all in her body language. Her eyes were almost closed to tiny slits as she pressed their heads against her heaving chest, allowing them access to her ripe melons. Their hands were in her panties. They were finger-fucking her tight twat at the same time they kissed her tits. Her eyes closed as she blanked out in sexual euphoria, giving in to the temptation of servicing a whole group of men. I loved what I was seeing.

Both Kevin and Jim had been raptly watching the show on the couch, and now Kevin got up to move the coffee table out of the way. He got down on the floor and spread my lovely wife's knees apart, exposing her panty-clad muff to the whole room. Kissing and nibbling the inside of her thighs, he reached up and pulled her shorts and panties down with the help of the other two men. As he eased the panties off her feet, Kevin took her foot and sucked on her toes.

This was too much for me, watching my beautiful naked wife about to fuck four strange men. I pulled out my cock and shot the night's first load of come into the bushes. When I looked back Kevin had his head between Cindy's legs, where he was licking and sucking away on her sweet, red-trimmed pussy.

Chris and Joe continued to suck her tits. Jim now got into the act and moved around behind the couch. Looking down at my wife's face, he pulled down his zipper and pulled out his hard, seven-inch cock and pointed it right at her pouting lips.

Cindy gazed at his black pole as it oozed pre-come. Jim caught it with his finger and spread it over the helmet of his cock, as if she were dipping an ice cream cone in a rich topping. Cindy stared into Jim's face and, with a wicked smile, opened her mouth to accept the phallic treat.

Jim slipped his cock past her red lips and shoved it deep into her mouth. Moving his hot ebony meat in and out over my wife's pink, wet tongue was an extremely erotic sight. It really got to me and it must have done it for him, too. Jim grabbed the back of her head and thrust his dick deep into her throat until her chin was pressed against his balls. She was gagging slightly, but still sucking on him hard enough that I could plainly see the bulge of his cockhead against her cheek, sawing in and out.

Chris and Joe sat on the coffee table watching and toying with their meaty packages. Cindy sucked hard on Jim's pole, while Kevin licked her inflamed cunt. It was totally depraved, I thought, when Cindy grabbed her hot tits and squeezed and pinched her taut nipples.

Kevin got up and turned her around so she was leaning against the back of the couch. Her knees were spread on the edge of the seat. Kevin pulled down his pants and shorts, exposing his thick, hard cock. He eased it up and down Cindy's slit and between her titillating ass-cheeks.

Cindy moaned, still gurgling with a mouthful of Jim's dick. She wiggled her hot cunt back toward Kevin's probing cock. He got the head in the opening of Cindy's pussy, and held back until she was positioned as far back as she could while still keeping Jim's cock in her mouth. Kevin roughly jammed his cock to the hilt. He let it rest there for several seconds before he began to quickly stroke her. Kevin was banging Cindy so hard that Jim had to pull out of her mouth. He stood back, joining Chris and Joe in watching the free sex show.

By now, Cindy was concentrating on Kevin's dick, which was hammering her hungry cunt. Kevin grabbed her hips and stroked so hard and deep that all she could do was grunt and moan on each thrust. Finally, he came, filling her love-hole with his come and leaving Cindy wanting more. Kevin let his cock shrink out of Cindy's red-hot pussy. When he pulled out I could see their combined juices flowing down her thighs.

The other three men had been busy talking among themselves

while removing their clothes. They moved the coffee table against the wall and had Cindy move to the center of the room. Chris stood behind her and reached around to cup her tits in the palms of his hands. Jim lay down on the floor and Chris guided her over to him. She leaned over Jim and placed her knees on either side of his body.

Her alabaster skin and red muff made his skin seem even darker as she reached back and placed the head of his throbbing cock against her pussy lips. The other men didn't want to miss this sight and gathered around to watch as she slowly lowered her well-lubed twat onto his pole. She sat there for a few seconds and slowly started to bob up and down.

Jim's black cock was slick and shining with my wife's love-juice as she repeatedly impaled herself on him. Chris came up and gently pushed her down so her tits jiggled over Jim's chest. Jim reached up and pinched and rubbed one while lifting his head up and taking the nipple of the other into his mouth.

Chris spread Cindy's ass-cheeks apart and slowly worked his finger deep into her ass. Cindy has never let me fuck her there, so I watched with another hard-on as Chris sawed two fingers in and out of her hole. Chris moved closer and put the head of his dick on Cindy's ass, then pushed past her sphincter and plunged into her ass.

Cindy was now in a state of passion I had never dreamed she was capable of. She tossed her head from side to side as she was being sandwiched between the salt-and-pepper team. Joe moved around and put his cock before her face. Jim and Cindy came at the same time, but Cindy continued to work on the other two men, humping back against Chris's rod and bobbing her lips on Joe's.

Joe pulled back and shot his come all over Cindy's tits, laughing and telling the others he had always wanted to do that. Cindy reached up and licked the wet cock like a lollipop until it was clean. Chris was hammering into Cindy's ass, which caused her to collapse against Jim. A few minutes later Joe filled her ass with his come, and Jim fucked her cunt.

I left then and went back to the car. Later that night when I got back to camp Cindy was already in the tent. She was almost asleep and I asked her if she had been bored without me. She laughed lightly and said she had a good time playing cards. The guys had entertained her. It's been a few months now and we are going to Jamaica for the holidays. Hopefully I'll have another reason to write later. —R.K., *Sausalito, California*

SOME PARTIES YOU NEVER FORGET

*L*et me tell you about a party that my husband, Gary, and I went to about five years ago. On the day of the party, Gary and I had a leisurely Saturday morning together. I woke him up by sucking his beautiful cock to life. He reciprocated by licking my nipples and clit until I screamed with joy. Most of the morning was spent making love. In spite of all of the hot action with Gary, I was still very horny.

The party was at the home of Brenda, one of my close friends from work. Most of those invited were coworkers, so I anticipated a relatively sedate party. I made it a point not to seduce or be seduced by anyone from work, feeling that I should keep my wild side separate from these people.

Because we were both horny, Gary was able to convince me to wear a backless summer dress. I was braless, wearing only bikini panties, thigh hose and garter belt. The fabric was sheer enough that my nipples and areolae were visible. The thought of showing off my big breasts excited me. I figured that Gary and I would park on the way home for some heavy necking and a little oral sex. The outfit was too sexy for my work image. They only saw me in conservative suits and dresses.

When we arrived, I could tell that several of the men appreciated this new look. After two or three drinks, I relaxed and enjoyed all of the attention I was getting. Most of those at the party were married couples, but there were a few who didn't bring their spouses. One who came alone was Dave, Brenda's new boss. She had told me how hot he made her just working together. I knew that she would love to have him make a move on her.

He was in his forties, at least fifteen years older than Brenda and me. Dave was tall, athletic and had great blue eyes. In spite of his quiet, mature manner, I found myself getting turned on when he talked to me at the office. I loved the way he looked at me.

Brenda had a very revealing dress on, cut low between her breasts, barely concealing her nipples. It also was slit on the side showing her leg to mid-thigh. The green dress was a dramatic contrast to her white skin and beautiful red hair. Looking at this outfit, I wondered if she had known that Dave's wife wouldn't be there. They stood in a corner talking, very close to one another. Dave's eyes roamed over her exposed cleavage. It made me hot to watch them, but I was concerned that Brenda's husband, Jerry, might become upset. I decided to find him and keep him away from Brenda and Dave.

As I looked for Jerry in the crowd, I saw Gary dancing with Tina, one of my friends who was there alone. She didn't get enough attention from her husband and always wanted to hear about my sex life. I knew that Gary turned her on. Maybe I should let him seduce her tonight, I thought. As horny as she was, I knew that he would drive her crazy. He would love to put his tongue in her sweet little pussy.

She held his face in her hands as they danced, staring into his blue eyes. One of Gary's hands was slowly caressing her ass, cupping her cheeks. I knew that he would go much further if Tina let him. Either way, Gary would be extra hot for my pussy when we got home. Thinking about this, I smiled.

Looking around the room again, I spotted Jerry. He was a

handsome man, with blond hair, full beard and moustache. He was talking to Doug, a sexy black man who had worked with me for the past year and lived next door to Brenda and Jerry. Doug also played on the company's coed softball team with me and loved to flirt and tease when his wife was not around. She was out of town on business, so I knew Doug would be in good form tonight.

They both smiled at me as I approached. "That's a very sexy dress, Pam. I've never seen you in anything more becoming," Jerry said. Doug didn't say a word, but his eyes were glued to my breasts. His stare caused my nipples to grow hot and hard.

"Thank you. It's nice of you to notice," I responded. "Since you're so sweet, would you like to dance? It looks like I've lost Gary."

Jerry didn't answer, but took my hand and led me to a corner of the room. He pulled me against him as we began to dance. His hands explored the bare flesh of my back as we moved with the music. The feel of him against me made me hot. I knew I would have to be careful and control my emotions.

Luckily the next song was a fast rock number. Doug appeared and led me back to dance with him. As I moved to the music, my breasts moved wildly against the fabric of my dress. Doug smiled as he watched my breasts, a wicked grin covering his face.

I found myself getting horny. It was exciting to display my sexy side to my coworkers. Shaking my tits even more, I began to move my ass under the short skirt, turning to make sure that Doug had a good view of both. My feelings were getting out of hand, but I really didn't want to misbehave in front of these people from work. The impact of my behavior on the other men was predictable. I was a popular dance partner for the next three hours. I did not miss a fast or slow dance. Many different hands caressed my back and ass as I danced with the men. But I liked dancing with Jerry and Doug the best. It was their flirting and touching that turned me on.

At about one-thirty the crowd began to thin out. As a slow

number began, Doug appeared and pulled me to him, pressing my breasts against his muscular body. While we danced, he talked softly in my ear, telling me how beautiful my breasts looked in the soft dress.

"Honey, you always look great, but your breasts are fantastic without a bra. I can tell that you love showing them off. You need to let me see them. I'll bet you have never had them licked by a black man. I know how hot I would make you if my beautiful black skin touched those sexy white titties. I'll bet you love to have your titties fucked. You need to have my big, black cock rubbing on your nipples and squirting all over you. I'll bet your pussy is wet just thinking about it."

He was right. My panties were soaked.

As he talked his hands caressed my ass. He reached under the hem of my dress and his long fingers stroked the crack of my ass. His fingertips traced the lips of my pussy through the soft lace. His talk and touch made me even wetter. Before he could do more, a rock number began, saving me from my sexy thoughts. My body shook to the music. Dave and Brenda were dancing near me. As she danced, the slit in her dress would open to reveal glimpses of her panties and stocking tops. Dave's eyes were glued to her body as she moved.

I decided to distract him before Jerry noticed the sexual tension between them. I danced very close to them, then turned quickly to rub my braless breasts against Dave's arm. As he turned and reached for me to apologize, I moved again so that his hand ran across both of my breasts, touching my erect nipples. This produced a reaction in me that I had not anticipated. My pussy was on fire, needing a mouth or cock to make love to it.

Dave laughed, saying he was sorry, but his face was flushed and he watched me until the song ended. Brenda headed toward the bathroom, as a slow dance began. Dave came toward me and took my hand, leading me back to dance. He pulled me tightly against his body, with his hands on my hips as we moved to the music.

"I really wasn't sorry that happened," he said, grinning. "Judging from how your breasts felt, you weren't either. I've always loved looking at your beautiful face, but I never knew what a fantastic body you were hiding under your suits at work. Or how much you liked to play and show off. I noticed that nobody could keep their hands off of your cute fanny, and I am jealous. But I think they were missing the two best parts. Your husband shouldn't let you go out like this. I won't be able to concentrate anymore at work when you are around."

As he spoke, he moved his hands to my back, running them over the bare flesh. His arms were so long that they easily wrapped around me. He ran his fingers under the fabric of my dress, stroking the sides of my breasts, almost reaching the nipples. My body responded to his touch. I wanted more. I needed for him to play with my nipples. Closing my eyes, I imagined the feel of his face against my thighs, his mouth kissing my pussy.

Almost involuntarily, I brushed my leg between his, feeling his hard cock on my thigh. He took my hand and put it between us, on his cock. It was hot and very big. As he held my hand there, I traced my fingers over the head. Moving my fingers over his bulge, I could feel the wetness of his pre-come through his slacks. I raised my wet fingertips to my lips and licked them, looking into his eyes.

"Something on my fingers sure tastes good," I said, smiling at him. Before we could go further, Brenda came back to take Dave away. I hadn't seen Gary for over an hour when he appeared to dance a slow number with me.

"It looks like you're having a good time," he said.

"I saw the big boss trying to get into your panties." As he talked, he leaned forward to kiss me, frenching me with passion. Watching me with Dave had made him hot too.

I asked, "Do you want to watch him suck my nipples? Or would you like to see him eat my pussy?" I could tell that this talk was turning Gary on. And me too. Until now, Gary had only had me tell him about my experiences with other men. Maybe it was time to let him watch. I knew that it would turn me on to perform for him, and I was sure it would make him hot too.

Heated up from these thoughts, I headed for the rest room with Gary when the music stopped. Looking in the mirror, my nipples were still hard and clearly visible through the fabric of my dress. Standing behind me, Gary squeezed them with his fingers, causing me to shudder. Turning me around, he kneeled and slid my panties down my thighs. Leaning forward, he put his mouth on my cunt, licking the swollen lips.

"You're sure wet. Did someone already play with this sweet pussy?" he asked.

"Not yet. Eat my pussy now. Make me come," I begged. It only took a minute for Gary to send me over the edge. As my body relaxed, I had to taste Gary's cock. Pushing him against the sink, I undid his belt and zipper to reveal his meat.

"Do you want to watch me with Dave later tonight? He has me so turned on that I have to fuck him." I said, licking the head of Gary's cock. Undoing my dress to expose my breasts, I asked, "Do you think he will like these?"

"You will drive him crazy with that body. You know I want to see you with him. How can you fix it so that I can watch?" he asked.

"Don't worry. I'll find a way," I responded. "You play with Tina to stay horny. Drive her home. I know that she wants to suck you off. And you'll love to touch her little titties. Just be home before two-thirty. I'll find a way to get Dave away from Brenda long enough for him to take me home. Once we're in the house, he won't be able to resist my goodies."

With that, I worked on Gary's cock until he filled my mouth with his come. Standing, we kissed tenderly and Gary went back to the party as I fixed my dress. Opening the bathroom door, I looked into Jerry's smiling face.

"I brought you a tequila shooter. I think you will like it," he said. He took my hand and led me into a room away from the party. He then took the glass and raised it to his lips, taking a large swig. Lowering the glass, he put his hand behind my head and pulled my mouth to his.

Surprised, I felt his tongue go between my teeth, then tasted the tequila. Swallowing, I said, "That was nice, but you are very naughty. We are both married and we can't do this."

Ignoring me, he raised the glass again, taking another mouthful. Again he pulled my face to his in a kiss. This time my lips opened and I ran my tongue into his mouth, drinking in the booze. I wanted Dave, but Jerry was making my pussy hot now. My panties were drenched again.

I knew that I was losing the battle to control my emotions. I also knew what to say to make Jerry try harder. "We have to stop now, Jerry. I'm only human and you're turning me on. Brenda is my good friend. We can't do this."

With that, he pulled me to him as his beard rubbed my face. Automatically, my arms wrapped around his neck, pulling him to me as my mouth opened to accept his tongue. I loved the feel of his hands as they caressed my naked back.

"Don't worry about Brenda. She told me earlier what she had planned. It was no accident that her boss showed up without his wife." As Jerry kissed me again, I felt hands cup and caress my ass. Turning, I saw Doug. He put his hands on my face and kissed me, running his thick tongue into my mouth. My battle to maintain my work image was quickly being lost.

"Relax and enjoy, Pam. You obviously need more loving than Gary can give you. You need to try two men at once and let yourself go. See how hot we can make you," Doug said, reaching under my dress to run his long fingers over my pussy again. My panties were getting wetter as he rubbed my clit. I pulled his face to my mouth, opening my lips to suck in his tongue. Gently, he slid his fingers under the leg of my panties to touch my pussy lips.

"I knew you were wet," he said as his fingers stroked my pussy.

"Come with us for a minute and we'll show you something that will really make you hot," Jerry said. With that, they led me out a back door and around the side of the house. Jerry motioned for me to be quiet as we neared his bedroom window. A soft light came through the louvers and I could hear Brenda's voice. "Oh yes, Dave, tell me, please."

"You've made me hot since my first day in the office. When I saw you leaning over a file cabinet, showing those beautiful legs, I wanted them wrapped around my neck so I could lick your sweet pussy. I wanted you to take my cock and suck it until my come shot all over you."

As Dave talked, I saw him unzip Brenda's dress, easing the fabric down her arms to expose her bra. Brenda then took a step back, pushing her dress over her hips. As it fell to the floor, I noticed that her panties were around her knees, leaving the beautiful red hair on her pussy exposed to view. Dave had been busy even before we got to the window. Brenda reached to put her panties and dress on a chair, followed by her bra. She then stood to proudly display her body, clad only in hose and garter belt. Dave quickly leaned down to lick her nipples.

"Please let me see your cock. I've wanted it for two months. I'll take it in my mouth and suck it until you come. I'm so glad you came to my party," Brenda said.

Dave pulled his shirt over his head. He then reached to undo his belt, stepping out of his pants and shoes. Standing in briefs, he said, "You come take these off, Brenda. Then we will 69 until we both come."

Kneeling, she pulled his briefs off. His cock stood out, about seven inches long and incredibly thick. While Brenda licked Dave's cock, I felt Doug and Jerry's hands undo my dress, letting it fall to expose my naked breasts. Their hands worked on the hot flesh of my breasts as I watched Brenda and Dave fall to the bed in a hot 69. Dave was working his tongue in and out of her pussy as she bucked on the bed.

I was definitely hot. I was somewhat surprised that Jerry seemed to be turned on by his wife fucking other men, but also glad. As we watched, Brenda got on her knees while Dave fucked her from behind. Watching him pull her nipples while they fucked made me need a cock. It had been a long time since I had made love to two men at once. But I wanted Jerry and Doug now. Turning, I kissed Doug and then Jerry. Then I pulled a mouth to each of my breasts. They licked and sucked them until I could not stand it. Taking my hands, they led me to Doug's house, not bothering to cover my naked tits. Fortunately, no one saw me in my partially clothed state as we left the party.

We went into the master bedroom and Jerry removed my dress. He sat me on the king-size bed and began to lick my cunt through my panties. I could not believe how good his hairy face felt against my thighs. He pulled my panties off and ran his tongue over my clit, back and forth until I was bouncing on the bed in anticipation. I reached to take off my garter belt, but Doug stopped me.

"You look fantastic like that," he said. Doug had taken his clothes off and climbed on the bed to lick my breasts while Jerry ate my cunt. His body was gorgeous, with large muscular shoulders and chest. His small hips set off a long, very thick cock. I laid back on the bed to touch his tool while Jerry's mouth devoured me. The black cock looked beautiful in contrast with my white skin. My body shook in a climax as soon as I put Doug's cock in my mouth. I continued to lick and suck, needing to taste his come.

Just as Doug was about to climax, Jerry pulled me to my feet and kissed me. The taste of my juices on his beard was great. I needed a cock in me now. "Suck my cock, Pam. I need that," Jerry said. "Show me what a hot woman you are."

I sat back on the bed and pulled his belt and pants off to see his bikini underwear. Pulling them down, I looked at his beautiful cock, devouring it with my wet lips. I wanted to suck him more, but I wanted Doug's thick muscle in me too. While I continued my blowjob on Jerry, I got on my knees with my ass high in the air, toward Doug. He quickly went to work on my pussy with his tongue. With one hand, I reached back for Doug's cock, pulling it toward my hot cunt. He pushed the fat head into me, stretching me. Finally, he pushed it all into me, taking my breath away with its size.

I was on fire, working my pussy on Doug while I ate Jerry's cock. Jerry was also driving me crazy, playing with my breasts and nipples. I had almost forgotten how fantastic it could be with more than one man.

Watching Brenda must have turned Jerry on too much, because he quickly squirted his come into my mouth. I licked the head clean, smiling up at him. Then I concentrated all my energy on Doug, working my hips and ass against his cock. He did not last long, filling my pussy with his come. I was not done. I wanted more fucking and more cock in my mouth. "Please fuck me now, Jerry. I need to feel you inside me."

He sat on a chair and pulled me on his lap, my back against him as he put his cock into me. Doug stood in front of me, offering me his thick tool while he pinched my swollen nipples. I was crazy with lust. For over forty-five minutes, the three of us made love in every possible position. Both men were worn out, but I was getting even hotter from this activity, unable to get enough. Kissing Jerry and Doug, I dressed and headed back to the party.

I saw Dave as I entered the house. He and another man were talking with Brenda. Her hair was combed, but her dress was wrinkled and her face was still flushed. Her neckline gaped, exposing most of her breasts, including her areolae. She had obviously not bothered to put her bra back on. Both men seemed to like the view, and Brenda did not try to conceal her nipples.

Doug and Jerry had not returned. Only one couple besides Brenda's group remained. Trying to sport an innocent look, I walked over to Brenda and asked if she knew where Gary was. She told me that Tina had asked for a ride home and that Gary had looked for me to go with him to drive her home. "He asked me to have Jerry take you," she said.

"I don't see Jerry now," I responded. "Dave, would you drop me off on your way home?"

"I'll be glad to. Let me get my things in the kitchen," he said, walking with Brenda to the other room. Not wanting him to have too much time alone with Brenda, I waited only five minutes before I went to the kitchen. To let them know I was coming, I made plenty of noise as I entered. Hearing me, they broke a passionate kiss. As Dave pulled back, both of Brenda's breasts were totally exposed. I smiled to myself as Brenda turned her back to fix her dress. Dave would still be very horny, I thought.

Sitting in Dave's big Lincoln, I decided that he would have to initiate any sexual activity. I made sure that my dress did not even reveal too much of my legs. In a couple of minutes, we were parked in front of my neighbor's house.

"It looks like your husband is not home," he said. "Let me check the house for you."

"I'll be okay, but I would appreciate it if you would come in until I'm sure that the house is safe."

Dave came in with me and I asked him to sit in the living room while I went upstairs. He asked if he could fix us a drink, and I told him that would be nice. I told him to open some champagne for us. Gary was hiding in a bedroom adjoining the master bath. He kissed me passionately, telling me what a sexy woman I was. He then whispered to me to play the answering machine when I went downstairs.

Dave was waiting for me with my champagne when I returned. He handed it to me and we raised our glasses in a gesture, as if to toast each other. "I love this stuff but it makes me silly," I said as I drank the glass dry. He was quick to refill it.

I went to the answering machine and pressed playback. Gary had left a message saying that he had had too much to drink and was resting on Tina's couch until he sobered up. Dave seemed very happy to hear this. "I'm glad that I have some time to talk to you. You don't need to be afraid of me," he said. "I don't bite. Not too hard anyway," he said grinning. "Come sit by me, please."

"I don't think that would be too smart," I answered. "After all, we're both married. You had me so turned on earlier that I don't think I can trust either one of us. Besides, I noticed that you and Brenda were heavily involved tonight. You were playing with her breasts in the kitchen. Watching that just made me hornier. Judging from tonight, you know too much about making young women like Brenda and me hot."

Dave seemed to love what I said. He walked over and refilled my glass. Setting his glass on the table, he put his arms around me, pulling my body against him. Then he raised my glass to my lips until I drank all of it. Hoping to work on his ego, I said, "You have to go now. We can't do this. I love my husband and I don't need to get involved. Also, I don't want to interfere with you and Brenda. Please leave now."

Dave ignored what I said and pressed his lips to mine. I kept my lips closed so he could not get his tongue in my mouth. I knew this would make him try harder. Two more times he kissed me, but I kept his tongue out. This was not easy because I was getting hot. But I wanted to make him work to get into my panties. Pushing away, I turned my back to him. He then wrapped his arms around my waist from behind me, kissing my neck and licking my shoulders. Then his hands began to work on my breasts, pinching my nipples through the fabric of my dress. I moaned as he worked his hands under my top to touch my naked flesh.

"Please stop, Dave. You need to leave now. You're making me too hot and Gary isn't even home to take care of me. It isn't fair to do this to me. I can't take any more."

This was what Dave had wanted to hear. As he kissed me again, I opened my mouth to let him know I was at the edge. His tongue worked against mine as he undid the top of my dress to reveal my breasts. He took each nipple into my mouth, expertly using his tongue and lips to arouse them further. I held his head as he worked on my breasts. I had to admit that he was very talented.

His hands pulled my zipper down and he removed my dress. I stood back to let him look at me, clad only in bikini, garter belt, hose and shoes. "You bastard! You don't play fair," I said. "Don't stop now. You can't leave me this hot. I need you." Taking his hand, I led him to the couch, which was in full view for Gary.

He pulled off my panties and began to lick my thighs, above the tops of my hose. He then started talking to me, telling me how beautiful my blonde pussy looked, what incredible breasts and nipples I had. He told me he couldn't believe how wet my pussy was as he slid his tongue into me. He didn't know that I was full of come from two other men. He knew things to say that drove me wild as he ate me. I had an incredible orgasm.

Even I was surprised that he brought me off before I saw or touched his cock. I could wait no longer. I had him stand as I took off his pants and underwear. I was excited. His cock was even longer and thicker than it had looked while he was with Brenda. Maybe I turned him on even more. I got on my knees so he could fuck me from behind. As wet and turned-on as I was, his cock seemed to stretch my cunt even further. I started to talk to him, telling him what a fantastic lover he was and how I loved his fat cock. Listening to me, he worked on my clit and nipples while we fucked, again taking me over the edge.

Knowing that Gary was watching and listening to all of this was almost too much to stand. Dave's sexual imagination was unbelievable. We did things that I had never done before. He told me sexy things constantly, keeping the intensity very high. I liked sexy talk, but he took it to new levels. Several times he had me suck him to orgasm, but each time he squirted his come over my breasts, having me rub the jism into my skin. Never believe that people over forty have lost their sexual prowess.

It was after four in the morning when he left. He made me promise that I would let him fuck me whenever we could get away. That was a promise that I would be happy to keep over and over again. Gary was so hot from watching that we made love and talked until nine that morning. Gary fell asleep, exhausted. But I was so turned on from fucking four men that I couldn't sleep. All I could think about was more sex. After hiding my sexy body and my horniness from all of my coworkers for over a year, I had totally blown my quiet, proper image in one night. I had flaunted my body in front of all of the men at the party. But you know what, it really didn't matter. Neither work nor softball would ever be the same. So much for a quiet party with my coworkers. — P.D., *Savannah, Georgia*

True Romance

A SOLDIER'S RETURN PROVES WELL WORTH WAITING FOR

*M*y lover's overseas military duty is almost over. It has been a long six months. The slightest thought of him brings a smile from deep within. I can hear his soft voice whispering in my ear and it fills me with excitement. I imagine his touch, so gentle, and it warms my entire body. Knowing today is the day our eyes will meet again, I dress myself in something comfortable, yet soft and sexy, just for him.

At work, anxiously waiting for him to arrive, I turn around just in time to see him walk in. I lose my train of thought as we embrace. I can feel myself getting excited as he holds me in his arms. After he greets everyone, we leave.

Arriving at his place, he makes himself comfortable as I freshen up. I slowly enter the bedroom. The lights are low, the music soft. Standing at the foot of his bed, I slowly remove my dress, dropping it to the floor. I drop to my knees and crawl toward him. Kneeling between his legs, my hands begin to caress him.

Passionately massaging his strong legs and thighs, feeling the warmth of his body, my hands roam freely. Gently rubbing his crotch, I feel the hardness of his cock through his shorts. Feeling his excitement build, I slowly remove his pants, exposing his big, hard cock. Using my tongue, lips and hands on him, I begin to lick and suck his big cock, taking it into my mouth. He spreads his legs to give me more room.

My juices start flowing, as again and again he fills my mouth and throat with his hard, hot cock. My body tingles from the sensation of his hands, so soft and warm, caressing my breasts, my body. My legs spread as I feel his fingers slip inside my hot pussy, making me squirm with every thrust.

My excitement increasing even more, the anticipation of feeling his hard cock deep inside me is overwhelming. I lie back on the bed next to him, my back against his chest. I feel the hardness of his cock against my ass and his warm hands touching me. I get on all fours and stick my ass in the air. At last his cock penetrates my wet pussy.

His hands on my hips, he starts pumping me as fast as he can. My pussy juices flow, my muscles grip him, and before we even settle into a steady rhythm, I come. My juices gush all over his balls, while his fingers play with my ass, heightening my excitement even further. After I come he continues to fuck me, deeper and deeper. As I grow juicier, he pumps harder, deeper, our bodies moving together in perfect rhythm. I start playing with my clit, my body shaking with each stroke as he pushes his cock deeper into my hole, until my body is seized with one orgasm after another. Finally, his cock pulsing, I feel him shoot his load of come deep inside me.

He continues pumping until his cock softens, and, as he pulls out, a flood of juices run over my pussy and down my legs. Lying there in complete exhaustion, our bodies tingling from head to toe, we drift off to sleep together in each other's arms. —M.S., Rochester, New York

HE GETS OFF ON HER RANDY BEDTIME STORIES

One night a couple of weeks ago, lying in bed while my husband tenderly played with my clit and sucked on my tits, he asked me if anyone had ever made a pass at me when I was out dancing with my friend Theresa. You see, when we first got married, my husband was still in graduate school, working toward his doctorate, and he spent every spare minute studying and cramming for exams. Rather than sit home bored, I would go out dancing with my best friend.

Well, to answer my husband's question, I told him about a man I had met who was in town on business. I told him how we had danced together a couple of times, how we had rubbed up against each other, and how he tried to feel me up.

On hearing this, my husband became extremely aroused—his dick seemed to grow another two inches. He quickly mounted me and we had one of the best fucks we'd had in a long time. Since then, he's often asked me to tell him the story again. Whenever I do, we fuck with wild abandon. However, I've never told him the whole story and I think he suspects as much. Our tenth anniversary is approaching and I asked him what he wanted. He said he wanted to hear the whole story of what happened that long-ago night. Well, honey, happy anniversary. Here it is.

I danced with Tim a couple of times that night and I enjoyed teasing him by pressing up against the bulge in his pants. I knew he was getting turned on by that and by the sensation of my rather large tits pressing into his chest. After one slow song ended, the band went into a hot, fast number and we stayed on the dance floor bumping and grinding away.

By the time the number ended, we were both soaked with sweat and out of breath. The alcohol we had consumed didn't help either. Tim suggested that we take a walk outside to cool off.

We went out the side door of the club, which opened onto a darkened quadrangle of shops. It was after midnight and we found ourselves completely alone. To tell the truth, I kind of suspected what would happen next.

Tim encircled me with his arms from behind, pressing the bulge in his trousers into the crack of my ass. He kissed my neck, then slowly ran his tongue up and down the side of my neck, sending shivers through me. I closed my eyes and moaned softly as his obviously talented mouth continued on its path up and down the side of my throat.

My eyes still closed, I felt his hands move from my waist to the front of my blouse, which he slowly began to unbutton, kissing and licking my neck all the while.

I knew I should stop him, but it felt so good! Almost of its own volition, my hand found its way to the lump in his trousers. Even through the fabric, I could feel the heat being generated by what felt like a massive prick.

After Tim had unbuttoned my blouse, he cupped both of my bra-clad tits and gently squeezed them, sending yet another shiver through me. He then slid his hand around to my back, deftly unhooked my bra and lifted it up, baring my tits to the cool evening air. Tim then took both my naked tits in his large, warm hands, and slowly squeezed and massaged them, lightly rubbing and tugging on my tender, swollen, fully erect nipples.

Still holding me from behind, he let go of one of my tits and, with his free hand, lifted the hem of my skirt. He slid his questing fingers between my thighs and directly to my pussy. I parted my legs to give him better access. The feelings that rippled through me as he massaged my hot, wet cunt were indescribable.

While Tim manipulated my drenched pussy with one hand, playing with my tits with the other, all the while kissing me up and down my neck, I kept right on rubbing his cock through his pants. It wasn't long before I decided that this just wasn't enough. I turned in his arms and kissed him deeply.

There I was, married just about a year, standing in the dark outside of a nightclub, my blouse open, my bra hanging loose, my breasts exposed, kissing the hell out of a stranger while he played with my pussy and tits and I stroked his cock! At this point though, I was too far gone to care. Still kissing him, I reached down and unzipped his pants, sticking my hand in to touch his cock.

I pulled his underwear aside and, with my thumb and two fingers, started to caress and stroke his dick, causing him to shudder. He again lifted my dress and, this time, reached into the top of my panties and slid his hand straight down to my hot, throbbing cunt.

As we kissed again, he slipped a finger inside my pussy, causing me to moan loudly. Breaking the kiss, Tim leaned down and started sucking on my tits, first taking one nipple into his warm, moist mouth, circling it with his tongue, then gently sucking on it, before turning his attention to my other tit.

Tim kept right on finger-fucking me as his thumb played with my clit. I could feel my resolve weakening by the moment, and I knew that if I didn't do something to defuse him soon, his cock was going to wind up buried in me to the hilt, marriage or no marriage. I decided the only way to stop him from coming in my cunt was for him to come in my mouth.

My decision made, I freed his cock from his pants and continued to stroke it, feeling it throb in my hand. Dislodging his fingers from my pussy, I quickly glanced around and, seeing no one, crouched and slid Tim's thick penis in my mouth. I didn't know what was more erotic—sucking a cock outside a busy nightclub, with the possibility of being seen by anybody walking nearby, or sucking a cock that didn't belong to my husband!

Anyway, I eagerly took Tim in my mouth, feeling his cock slide all the way to the back of my throat, before I pulled it out and began to lick and suck it like it was a big lollipop.

Taking him in my mouth again, I deep-throated him, sliding my lips down the length of his shaft to his pubic hair, my nose bumping against his zipper. Tim held my head in his hands as his hips started to buck, and I knew it wouldn't be long before he came. Tim thrust in and out, furiously fucking my mouth.

With one last thrust, Tim erupted, spurting his warm and slightly salty come in my mouth. I swallowed it and proceeded to lick his dick clean, then stood up to kiss him, letting him sample the taste of his come still lingering in my mouth. As he stood there swaying, overcome by the force of his orgasm, I hurriedly fastened my bra and buttoned my blouse.

Just as I finished, he asked me to go back to his hotel room with him so he could repay the blowjob by fucking me. I regretfully told him that I couldn't, and that we shouldn't have even done what we did. He pulled me close, reached under my dress again and, placing the palm of his hand between my legs and pressing my aching mound, told me that he knew I was hot and that he knew a good way to cool me off.

I was wavering, torn between a desire not to cheat on my husband and a desire to feel a strange cock in my cunt, when my girlfriend, who had been looking for me, found us. With that, I told him I had to leave.

I dropped my friend off at her apartment and, from there home, I kept one hand on the wheel and the other between my legs, frantically rubbing my inflamed pussy. My husband was sound asleep but awoke rather abruptly when I grabbed his cock and started sucking it like there was no tomorrow. When he was both fully awake and fully erect, I climbed on top of him and buried his cock in my oozing snatch. With my hands on his shoulders, I bounced up and down on his shaft. He sucked my tits as we fucked, which I love him to do when he's inside me.

Finally I couldn't stand any more and I erupted in a long, violent orgasm just as he, too, came, mingling his come with my cunt juice, soaking the sheets.

After I collapsed on top of him, he asked me what, or who, had gotten me so worked up. I told him that it was just a cute guy I had seen at the club!

If giving him only some of the details led to such wild fucking, I wonder what this letter will do! Maybe I ought to tell him about the time the neighbor downstairs made a pass at me! —*Name and address withheld*

JUST PLAIN FOLKS ENJOYING OUTSTANDING FUCKS

*T*his is not one of those letters where everybody looks like a model, but it did happen and we both enjoyed our time together.

I was just coming in the front door from the worst day in my life. Everything that could go wrong had, and the phone was ringing off its hook.

"Barry, I want you to come down here and fuck me!" she said when I picked up the phone. An obscene phone call, I thought, just the ending I needed to an already perfectly lousy day.

"Barry, I'm horny and need to be serviced," she continued. "Since we used to talk all the time, I thought of you as a possibility."

Over the next fifteen minutes, I gradually realized that the woman at the other end of the phone line was Jo. We had worked for the same company for years. I was a branch manager and Jo worked in the head office. We had spent lots of company time talking on the phone about our lives, our problems and, when we thought of it, company business.

We made a date for dinner and a movie the next night, even though I'd never actually met her and had no idea what she looked like. Jo hung up, saying, "It will be nice to finally meet you. But you're staying all night so remember to bring some protection."

Dinner and the new Stallone movie were great! My date was not a Penthouse Pet. She was a mature woman with a great personality and great boobs. But, then, I'm not Fabio, so we suited each other.

When we got back to Jo's place, we sat and talked for a while before heading off to bed. When we did, we didn't tear off each other's clothes. Instead, we were more like a long-married couple. After quietly undressing ourselves, she helped me put on a condom. We got into bed and snuggled with each other. We knew that the first time was important, and we wanted it to go right.

I started kissing Jo while my free hand explored her breasts and her hardening nipples. With our bodies pressed together, one of her hands wandered over my back while the other moved up my leg until she held my hardening cock.

My mouth moved from hers to kiss her eyes, then to her ears and gradually down her neck to her breasts. My tongue circled first one breast and then the other, working my way to her large nipples. Jo's breasts were too large to be just a mouthful, but none of the excess went to waste. I played with her other breast while one hand moved down to her pubic hair. I gently stroked it and then slid farther down so my hand could run up and down the inside of her legs. I almost touched her slit but didn't. Jo's fingers were driving me crazy, playing with my nuts while squeezing my cock.

I started nibbling gently on her erect nipples and rubbing them between my finger and thumb. Jo raised her knees and spread them apart. My hand moved higher on her legs until I felt the heat and moisture of her cunt on my thumb. I ran my fingers up and down her slit several times and she squeezed my cock hard in response. "Play with me. Make me come," Jo whispered. I spread her cunt lips, slipped a finger into the wet hole and then moved my moistened finger to diddle her clit. Jo came for the first time that night.

"I want your cock in me now. I need to feel you shoving your prick in my cunt. I need to be fucked!" Jo almost shouted, as she tried to pull my cock to her hole, I let her lead the way. She wasn't the only one who needed to fuck. Jo was so wet I slid the first inch or so in easily. After I backed out a little to ensure that I didn't hurt her and that all of me was wet, I slid back in a little farther. I kept going farther and farther into her tight hole.

"Oh, you feel so good. I feel like a virgin on her first night. I don't care if I can't walk tomorrow, I want all of you now," Jo said as her hands pulled at my ass to get more of me.

"I'm trying to go slow, so you'll only walk bowlegged tomorrow."

"I don't care, I want all of your cock. Go faster, faster! Fuck me harder! I want to feel all of you inside me!"

When my whole cock was in her and I could rub against her clit, I began to move faster. Then I stopped moving and let Jo do all the work. I wanted her to come without me orgasming, so I could last the night.

"It feels so good. Don't stop! Keep fucking me. I need you to fuck me." Jo said, moving wildly up and down. I barely held on while Jo's hips bucked as she came. Her contractions squeezed my cock so much I almost came too.

Jo laughed as she squeezed her pussy around my prick. I slowly began to slide my cock in and out, and I felt Jo start lifting her hips to match me stroke for stroke.

Within minutes we were going full tilt as we tried to get my cock as deep into Jo as possible. My pubic bone rubbed her clit whenever I drove my cock deep into her pussy. We carried on until I thought one of us would have a heart attack, but what a way to go!

"I'm going to come! Come with me, baby," she cried, as I felt her cunt start contracting. "We'll need a rest after this, so don't hold back, come with me!"

"I'm coming too!" I yelled as I felt my balls tighten, and I shot spurt after spurt of come.

We held each other until we cooled down and could think straight again. Jo got a wet cloth and wiped off our sweat-covered bodies and our come-soaked genitals.

After carefully taking off my rubber, she cleaned my cock last. She kept running her hands along it and playing with my balls. Her manual resuscitation became oral when my cock showed some signs of life. "I like to suck cock," Jo announced before taking my shaft into her mouth. She sucked like a woman just off a desert island.

It became mutual when I slipped my head between her legs for a 69. You'd have thought I hadn't eaten for a month the way my tongue dove into her cunt. I stopped every few strokes to suck up her juices, and then ran my tongue up and down her slit. I paused at her clit, which I gently stimulated and sucked. Her asshole received an occasional lick and visits from my fingers. Jo seemed to like that, as it made her suck extra hard and moan. When I finally shoved two fingers into her pussy while licking her clit, Jo came again and again until she collapsed.

Next, after another rest, Jo insisted I had to lie perfectly still while she did whatever she wanted. Leaning over my head, she started by rubbing her breasts and nipples all over my body. It took willpower to remain still as Jo rubbed them over my face, eyes and lips. Jo gradually worked her tits down to my cock, rubbing all of me with them as she moved. When all I could see and smell was pussy, Jo began rubbing her nipples all over my prick and balls.

Jo then showed me an oral way to put on a rubber. Within moments my cock was at full attention. She continued to play with it, alternately rubbing my cock between her breasts and sucking on it, until she felt I was ready to come. Jo sat up, turned around and carefully lowered herself onto my cock.

As she raised and lowered herself, I slid my fingers between our bodies and gently played with her clit. Jo came almost immediately and collapsed on top of me.

I got up and positioned Jo facedown on the bed with her pussy at the edge, fully exposed between her widely spread legs. I asked, "Which hole do you want me to fuck? Your cunt or your asshole?"

"I want your cock in my pussy until I can't come anymore, then you can use my asshole if you have any cock left."

I couldn't let that dare go by, so I started driving my cock into her pussy as fast and hard as I could. I slid two fingers around front to collect her juices and then rubbed the fingers into her asshole, first one finger, then both. I slid my other hand back to her clit and gently squeezed it, and continued pumping until she came, gripping the sheets and screaming.

We crawled into bed and fell asleep with my cock locked between her thighs and a breast in each of my hands.

I later awoke from a sexy dream of fucking a Penthouse Pet to find I really *was* fucking. I was madly fucking in my dreams and fucking Jo in reality. "Didn't you get enough?" Jo asked sleepily as I came. She soon followed.

The next morning came all too soon and we both had to drag our tails to work, but with that just-fucked look on our happy faces. I never hang up on an obscene phone call now, and gladly invite Jo over for many weekends. —B.O., *Milwaukee, Wisconsin*

THE LOVE MACHINE UPSTAIRS GOT THEIR MOTORS RUNNING

I enjoy camping with my wife and kids, but after a week in a tent at Yellowstone all four of us wanted to sleep in a real bed. We drove into a nearby town in the early afternoon and found a motel with a pool. We all were a little edgy after having shared close quarters for so long, so we decided to get the kids a room that adjoined ours. That way they could each have their own bed, and my wife and I could have some much-needed privacy.

After we had settled in, the kids headed straight for the pool, which could be seen from our first-floor window. The water looked inviting but Trudy and I desperately wanted to shower first. Trudy must have seen me watching appreciatively as she removed her blouse, because she slowed down her actions and made a dramatic show of it. Then she untied her ponytail and threw her head back, running her fingers through her hair.

I stepped behind her, unhooked her bra and slid it off her lightly freckled shoulders. I cupped and lifted a full breast with one hand while I pulled back her long brown hair with the other so I could kiss her behind the ear where it arouses her the most. She leaned her head back, closed her eyes and smiled contentedly, a sure sign that she's enjoying my sexual attention. I gently released her breast and slid my hand down her soft, flat belly and into her panties. She turned, kissed me on the mouth and said she wanted to shower so she'd smell nice and clean for me. She then ran her tongue around her lips and gave me a playful wink as she disappeared into the bathroom.

We normally have an active sex life, but spending seven days in a tent with our kids had put a damper on our libidos. When Trudy emerged, I greeted her in the nude with a kiss and proceeded to nibble her ears and neck. She caressed my cock for about five seconds. Then she told me I needed a shower worse than she did and pushed me into the bathroom. When I finished my shower and stepped out of the bathroom, I saw that she and her bathing suit were gone.

Knowing how much she likes to tease me, I put on my own suit and joined the family at the pool. The kids were swimming in the shallow end with others their own age. I jumped in next to Trudy and stayed in the water until my cock returned to its dormant state and everybody started getting hungry.

After we came back from dinner, the kids stretched out in front of the TV in their room and I went out for some wine coolers. When I returned, Trudy was propped up in bed watching TV, wearing my favorite short silky nightie and looking flushed and excited. I could smell one of my favorite perfumes, one that I hadn't even known she had packed for the trip. She hopped out of bed, turned down the TV and told me to listen. I heard a familiar steady squeaking sound coming from the room above us. Suddenly I knew why she was in such a state! Whoever had the room upstairs was really going at it!

I knew the kids wouldn't be going to bed for almost an hour, and since they might barge in at any time we had to keep ourselves under control until they were asleep. Believe me, after what had transpired earlier in the afternoon, I knew it was going to be tough! But I also knew that the delayed gratification might take our sex to that deeper, almost spiritual, level we sometimes reach after a romantic evening alone.

I changed into some comfortable shorts, put two of the wine

coolers on ice and joined her on the bed with two open bottles. We cuddled with my arm around her shoulders while her fingernails traced designs on my inner thigh. After a while we made some romantic small talk about how lucky we were to have each other. Trudy sighed softly and moved her hand up my leg to tease my balls through my shorts. We kissed deeply, and then I put my own hand to work pleasing her. I love the feel of her full breasts through the silk of her nightie. As I tweaked her hardened nipples, she moaned and squirmed in pleasure.

Thankfully it was soon time to kiss the kids good night and put them to bed. Since the bulge in my shorts would have raised embarrassing questions, Trudy did the honors while I pulled down the spread, dimmed the lights and turned off the TV. To my surprise, I could hear that they were still going at it upstairs! When Trudy returned I told her to listen. Her eyes widened and her jaw dropped when she realized the couple upstairs had been going at it for over an hour. That did it! Nothing could keep us apart any longer.

Trudy pulled her nightie over her head as I took off my shorts. Her arms went around my neck and her tongue went crazy in my mouth as my hands traveled down her back and squeezed her buttocks. My cock pressed against the warm softness of her heaving belly, leaving hot sticky trails on her smooth skin. Still standing up, she locked her hands behind my neck and brought first one leg and then the other up and around my back. She gyrated her pelvis as we endeavored to get her dripping pussy positioned above my thrusting rod. I soon felt the familiar wet softness surround the tip of my cock, and Trudy cried out in pleasure as I lowered her the rest of the way. I turned us so her back was to the bed and then fell forward, never leaving that wonderful pussy. We tried to take it slow but I was too far gone. I came mere seconds later, shooting semen into the farthest recesses of her body.

I lay on top of her for a minute, still panting. Then I gently withdrew and lay down next to her. She hadn't had an orgasm yet, but we both knew I would be hard again in a few minutes.

Kneeling on the bed, she began to administer a lip massage to my flaccid penis. I told her I wanted to reciprocate, so she stretched out next to me on her side and resumed work on my now-stiffening cock. I lifted her legs at the knees, spread her labia with my fingers and licked her protruding love-button, making her moan with delight.

My cock was now fully recuperated, and she let go of it to concentrate on her own pleasure. She placed her hand firmly behind my head and began arching her hips toward my face. I put two fingers deep into her pussy and began massaging her G-spot. She lay back on the bed and cried out as she experienced the first of many orgasms.

Finally she pulled me up, got on her knees and rested her head upon a pillow. I got on my knees behind her, taking hold of her hips as she reached between her legs to guide my organ to its favorite place once again. I began pumping into her, slowly at first, then harder and faster as we found our rhythm. After we both came, I collapsed on top of her.

As we lay together catching our breath, I couldn't believe my ears. I could still hear the squeaking sound coming through the ceiling!

In the morning, as we loaded the car, I kept an eye on the room above us to see if I could catch a glimpse of the love machine that had been operating up there. I didn't see any activity, so I decided to investigate more closely. Trying to look casual, I strolled across the second-floor landing. The curtains to the room were closed tight, but when I stopped I could hear the squeaking again—only I suddenly realized it wasn't coming from the room after all! Standing there was an old ice machine whose compressor was apparently about to give out. Trudy and I had a good laugh over that one! —E.H., San Diego, California

Three-For-All

EVERYTHING I NEED TO KNOW I LEARNED IN
PENTHOUSE LETTERS

*M*y wife and I are avid readers of *Penthouse Letters*. We started reading a couple of years after we were married, to add some extra spice to our lovemaking. We would slip into bed wearing something silky and with a bottle of wine in hand. As we read the stories we soon discovered we were both turned on by a certain scenario. Whenever we read about a threesome involving a woman and two men we both got hornier than hell. Soon we were fantasizing about two big cocks slipping one after the other into my wife's sweet slit. As we fucked I would whisper to her "I want you to be filled up with two big rods." She would pump my cock like crazy.

We happened to be very close at this time to a buddy of mine named Thorpe, and of course the fantasies started to center around him. Whenever he came over to watch TV or play cards, we got really horny. I would recommend a slutty top for Angela to wear and tell her she should go without her bra. Like the sexy wife she is, she always went along. When the opportunity arose for us to be alone, I would quickly pull out my cock for her to have a suck. We'd put it back in before Thorpe returned to the room, but we knew he suspected us of fooling around behind his back. Angela always made sure she had lots of tit showing, knowing it was turning us both on.

After a while we became more daring. Thorpe began to enjoy our teasing, and I'm sure he went home and had a great jack-off.

We always had great sex afterward. Soon Angela was modeling lingerie and wearing only a see-through silk jumpsuit with no bra or panties.

Then a day came when we all decided to go to the cabin up at the lake. When we set up our sleeping bags I made sure Angela was in the middle. We decided to have a hand of cards and go to bed, so we could have an early start. Angela told us to turn around while she undressed. She slipped into a cute lace teddy. Thorpe and I started a game of cards, and Angela joined in. Our cocks began to swell instantly.

After playing a couple of hands and enjoying a few beers, I could see that Angela was getting really horny. I leaned over and kissed her neck, while sliding my hand up her leg toward her wet crack. I pinched open the clasps with no resistance from her. My fingers found her pussy. Her snatch was soaked. By this time Thorpe had pulled off her shirt and begun to fondle her breasts. Soon she was naked, squirming on the floor, as her fantasy unfolded at last.

Thorpe and I both released our hungry monsters. She begged to kiss the shafts. She sucked each of our tools, and we stroked ourselves while the other was having his turn. I buried two fingers deep in her hole and Thorpe played with her tits. Angela was totally out of control. She began to shake, and screamed "Give me cock! I want to be filled up right now!" Thorpe lay down, with his pole pointing straight up. Angela aimed her asshole at his shaft, then eased slowly down, gasping at first as he penetrated her tight butt.

I laid her on her back on top of Thorpe, and she directed my meat into her cunt. Once it was fully inserted she began to buck. She had two cocks inside her, and she was totally wild. As she squirmed, I felt a mind-numbing sensation spread upward from my balls to my dickhead.

"I'm going to come," I shouted.

"Me too," Thorpe immediately added. I could feel the warmth of our jism spread around our cocks and jet into Angela's horny pussy and ass. With a few final thrusts we emptied our balls into her. I got off this wild ride and let Angela stand up. Her cunt and ass were soaked with wetness and come. Long white strings oozed out of her cunt.

She lay down on the floor, legs spread open and said, "Come finish me, baby." I knelt down and pushed my cock into her. Thorpe sat a couple of feet away and stroked his cock. I started slowly, pushing hard at the end of every stroke. Her tits jiggled with every pump. Her hand went down to her clit. I increased my speed, and she came in tremors. Her ass came off the floor and she screamed, "Fuck that's good!" Just as she said that, Thorpe began shooting cream all over, obviously turned on by watching us fucking.

I was ready to blow again too. I pulled out of Angela and knelt over her face. I beat my cock, and she encouraged me. "Come on, baby, squirt it between my lips." I shot my load into her waiting mouth, and she licked both our dicks dry. We all relaxed for a while before taking showers and cleaning up.

Over the years since, we've had several sexual encounters with Thorpe, and I hope we will again. —R.L., *Helena, Montana*

IF YOU MARRY THE PERFECT WOMAN, IT'S ONLY FAIR TO SHARE

Six years ago, after a long and very dull marriage, I found myself single. I hadn't dated much before marriage and, believe it or not, was a virgin on my wedding night. Consequently, I didn't have a clue about being single. Fortunately for me, my dream woman found me.

Let me tell you about Tiana. She's Hawaiian, Filipino and Spanish. She is a delicious shade of golden brown, with dark, luminous eyes. Unlike most of the local ladies here, she is really built. Exquisite 34D breasts, a small waist and full hips, topped off with long, glossy black hair. She calls herself a "full-bodied" woman. We dated for over a year before we married.

I thought that women like Tiana only existed in horny men's imaginations. She really enjoys sex. It really blew me away to discover that she has multiple orgasms, sometimes from just my kissing her neck or sucking her nipples.

On our third or fourth date, the subject got around to sex. I mentioned that I really love pleasing a woman with my tongue. A few dates later, after lots of necking, I bent her facedown over the dining room table, pushed up her miniskirt, pulled her panties aside and stuck my tongue in her pussy. I just had to taste her. It was just for a few seconds. That was all she needed. From then on she was stuck to me like glue. I just can't get enough of tasting her sweet cunt, listening to her scream and having her talk dirty to me, while I flick my tongue over her clit, then thrust it deep into her succulent cunt. The neighbors are always flicking their porch lights on and off to quiet us down. Tiana says I must have been in a closet saving my horniness all this time just for her.

About three years ago, while on a trip to San Francisco, I talked Tiana into having her beautiful brown nipples pierced with gold rings. Some people may think we're kinky, but to me there's nothing quite so erotic as feeling those rings dragging over my balls, across my cock or up my chest.

I noticed that during our lovemaking she would often suck her fingers, or reach back and spread her cheeks as if inviting an extra lover to join us. When I finally worked up the courage to ask her about it she admitted that she likes to imagine having sex with two guys. That was what I'd been hoping for, because my favorite fantasy is of watching and listening to my wife having sex with another guy. I'd never told anyone. With my heart beating like a trip-hammer I told her about my fantasy, and added quietly that I would love for her to have sex with another man if she wanted to.

She was silent for a while, and later told me she was a little hurt at first, wondering if I was trying to get rid of her. I assured her that was the furthest thing from my mind. She then confessed that, during her single days, after a few too many at a party, she had once experienced two guys at the same time and it had really turned her on. She added that she might like to try it again if the right guy came along.

Over the next few months we enjoyed some of our best sex ever, fueled by Tiana's memories of that one wild incident. I was anxious for Tiana to find someone to help us live out our fantasy. She's very particular, and would obviously have to do the choosing herself. Many guys were eager to have an affair with a beautiful and sexy married lady behind her husband's back, but when she told them that she doesn't hide anything from her husband they got cold feet.

I had about given up, until about a month ago. Tiana came home from a business meeting and said she'd met a single guy named Tim. He seemed nice, and was certainly handsome. I asked if she thought he might be the one. "We'll see," was her only reply. Tim called the next day, while I was home, and during the conversation he asked if she was married or single. My playful wife replied, "Both." That got his attention. They made a date for lunch the following day, and hit it off well. Tiana explained that her husband was not jealous and allowed her to have male friends. He didn't seem fazed at all, and asked if there was a possibility of a threesome. He had never had one, and was intrigued by the idea. I was a little nervous, now that it seemed like it might really happen.

After a few more phone conversations, Tim asked her out for dinner and drinks. They had a few drinks, then went to his apartment to relax and talk. No sooner had the door closed than Tim was kissing her hands, then all over her neck and face, maneuvering her onto the couch. My horny wife got busy with her hands, checking out the big bulge in his pants. Tim slid his hand inside her blouse (she wasn't wearing a bra), and discovered her nipple jewelry. He stopped for a moment, then asked if he could see. Tiana helped him take off her blouse. He sat there for a moment with his mouth open, just staring at my wife's erect brown nipples with the little gold initials glittering and swaying back and forth. He quickly recovered and was soon stroking and kissing her breasts all over.

He tried to get his hands into her tight jeans, but she said no, she never sleeps with a man on the first date. She did, however, offer to give him an oil massage. Later she told me she'd never seen a guy get out of his clothes so fast. He had a nice, long cock with a large head. Straddling him, she massaged his back, legs and ass with baby oil. She then had him turn over, and noticed a lot of pre-come leaking from his cock. She smeared some on her lips and nipples with her finger. "Would you like to lick them for me?" she asked him. He was only too happy to lick her lips clean.

During the massage, Tiana told me, Tim was about to burst, shivering and moaning each time she lightly tickled her way up the insides of his thighs, over his throbbing cock and balls and up his chest. When she slipped her fingers down into her panties and got them wet, then offered them to him to suck, he almost lost it. She offered to give him some relief with her hands, but he wanted the real thing.

"Not tonight. Besides, I have to go soon," was her reply. Tim couldn't believe it when she left him standing at the front door, naked, with a huge, throbbing hard-on, wondering when he would see her again.

A few days later they went out for dinner. I had chosen her outfit. It started with a pair of black pants, but it was the top that really set it off. After dinner she slipped the jacket off her shoulders and her twin beauties, with their erect nipples and their special jewelry, were plainly visible through her sheer top. "How about some dessert?" she asked. Tim was speechless.

During the ride home, Tim made full use of his hands and lips, but that was as far as he got. He must have had a case of blue balls that wouldn't quit. I felt sorry for him when she told me. Tiana called him later that night, after she'd gotten into bed. When he found out where she was and what she was wearing (nothing), the topic quickly turned to sex. Tiana gets aroused very easily, and in no time she was rubbing her fingers rapidly over her clit, and moaning in orgasm, with Tim's encouragement. He told her that he was stroking himself at the same time and, when she came for the third time, the line was very quiet. She knew that he had come all over himself while listening.

Tim's birthday was coming up soon, and he kept asking if she would be his birthday present, and stay overnight with him at a hotel in Waikiki. She was noncommittal for a while, but finally agreed. They planned to spend one night together, and then I would join them the next.

The evening I dropped her off, we had a few glasses of wine and made small talk. He thanked me sincerely for letting her stay with him. I had her promise that when they got back from dinner she would call and let me listen on the phone. He was happy to agree to anything. I went home and waited nervously.

Tiana finally called, and said that Tim already had her stripped down to her panties. She lay down on the bed to talk with me while he slid her panties down and off. He began kissing her passionately, working his way down her neck to her breasts, where he lingered for quite a while. She was already starting to come, and I had an incredible erection from listening. Trailing kisses down her belly, Tim headed for her juicy cunt. After a few minutes of this she was more than ready for Tim's hard cock.

Now it was his turn to tease. Tim licked and sucked her swollen cunt lips and clit while she had one huge orgasm after another. My lovely wife was screaming, bucking and begging him to fuck her. I was loving every moment of it. My cock was leaking drops of come, and hard as steel. When Tim finally slid his throbbing cock into her sopping wet cunt, I heard her give a long, low sigh as she felt his big cockhead stretch her open and go all the way in. After a short pause, he began to slowly stroke in and out, while she shook her head from side to side and screamed in one orgasm after another. She shouted, "Give me your cock. Oh my God!" and "Fuck me harder and deeper," while coming nearly nonstop.

After half an hour of this she needed a break. We chatted on the phone while Tim continued to suck on her nipples and run his fingers over her pussy. He hadn't come yet, so I knew she wouldn't get much sleep that night. Neither would I. After promising to call me later, she dropped off to sleep.

Sure enough, about three A.M., she awoke to find him under the covers with his tongue between her legs. I've awakened her that way myself, so I knew she would soon be begging to have her cunt filled with his hard cock again. Tiana was arching her back and sliding all over the bed, begging him to fuck her again. She got what she asked for, and it wasn't long before she could feel his hot come shooting into her depths. She really gets off on feeling a big, throbbing cock swell and then explode inside her. She had one last earth-shattering orgasm before they fell asleep.

About eight in the morning she called to let me know that Tim had awakened with a huge hard-on and wanted to do her doggie-style. This is her favorite position, and I lay back to enjoy her pleasure. She didn't need any foreplay. She just got up on her knees with her beautiful ass in the air, head down on the pillow and said, "Take me. Take me now. I want your hard cock. Fuck me." She screamed into the phone as Tim shoved his cock into her sopping cunt all at once. He grabbed her hips and started really pounding into her hot pussy. She moaned "Harder. Oh yes! Fuck me! Deeper, harder. I love your cock!" She reached back between her legs for Tim's balls and began squeezing them and pulling him in deeper. It wasn't long before she had another hot load of come filling her and running down her thighs.

How I wished I could be there. While Tiana was resting, and talking to both of us, she was absentmindedly fondling and stroking his soft, wet cock. It wasn't long before she had another handful of hard cock and wanted some more fucking. Tiana was still quite wet, so she pulled her legs up over her head, spread them as wide as possible and invited him to enjoy her warm pussy again. I couldn't believe it when she said he filled her with yet another big load of come.

I met them for lunch about mid-afternoon, with plans for just the two of us to go back to the hotel. Tim had some business to take care of before he could join us for dining, dancing and what we all were waiting for after that. When Tiana and I returned to the room I lost no time in getting her naked and sprawled on the bed. I wanted my tongue inside her. I spread her legs wide and used my fingers to open her lips so I could shove my tongue deep inside. In a few seconds I was savoring a long string of her lover's come. Up to that point I didn't know how I would react to having someone else's come in my mouth, but was willing to see. I was pleasantly surprised at how good it tasted, and delved deeper for more.

I had to get my aching cock into her. I fucked her powerfully while she described her morning with her lover. In very short order I added a huge load of come to what was left of his. It felt like the top of my head was going to come off.

Unfortunately, Tim called later with bad news. He had a family emergency and wouldn't be joining us. We were disappointed, but also somewhat relieved. Tiana was pretty well fucked out, and I was groggy from lack of sleep.

Tim seemed anxious to try a threesome, since it would be a first for him also. He had taken care of the family problem and was ready for some fun. We invited him to our house the following afternoon. I felt a little strange having another man come to our house to make love to my wife, but was very excited also.

After some small talk, we went into the bedroom to lie on our king-size water bed. At that time I was glad that we had decided to get the one with mirrors on the ceiling. Tim and I quickly stripped to our shorts, while watching my beautiful wife slowly remove her sheer white teddy and matching panties. She lay between us, enjoying the feeling of four hands massaging her all over with oil. I didn't wait long to get the ball rolling. I slid down between her spread legs and slid my tongue into her cunt. Meanwhile, Tim was sucking on one nipple while squeezing the other. Not one to be selfish, I soon moved up to her gorgeous breasts, so Tim could enjoy the taste of her sweet cunt.

After a seemingly endless series of orgasms, Tiana was begging for a hard cock, she didn't care whose. I told Tim to go ahead and give her what she wanted. We straightened her around on the bed (she was all over the place while we were eating her). Tim got on top and placed the head of his cock at her entrance. He started to enter her slowly, but she would have none of that. She grabbed his ass with both hands and shoved his hard cock all the way in, while letting out a long "Oh-h-h-h!" She held him still for a few moments, savoring his throbbing hardness, before allowing him to begin stroking in and out in earnest. I watched in the overhead mirror as she spread her legs wide and urged him to fuck her faster and harder. I could see the muscles in his ass flex as he thrust into my wife's hot pussy over and over. I loved every moment of it. Tiana screamed and arched her back, meeting his thrusts. She wanted to have every inch of his beautiful cock buried in her hungry cunt.

Tim could hold out no longer, and came deep inside her. Tiana screamed out one final, huge orgasm and collapsed. Tim withdrew his softening organ, and I watched his come overflow and run down the crack of her ass. I wanted to lick her clean, then spray my own hot load deep in her swollen cunt, but I knew she needed a breather. Tim had to go. After thanking us again for an unforgettable afternoon, he let himself out. My beautiful wife had a very contented smile on her face as she lay there with her long hair splayed out on the pillow, her big breasts slowly rising and falling and her wet and swollen pussy glistening in the late afternoon sun.

I was never more proud or more in love with her than at that moment. She had made my fantasy come true, and it was even better than I had hoped. We spent the rest of the afternoon suck-ing and fucking till we just weren't able to go anymore.

Since then we've had more threesomes with Tim, and she's also visited him alone. I encourage her to have sex with him as often as she likes, because I love the contented, just-fucked look on her beautiful face when she comes home. I don't know how long this will last. Tiana says she doesn't need another man be-sides me, but she's clearly enjoying herself. Who am I to deny her pleasure? Especially when I enjoy it myself. —F.B., *Honolulu, Hawaii*

IT TAKES TWO TO RESCUE A FRIEND IN
DEEP SEXUAL NEED

In my last letter, I related how my wife Gail got picked up by two strangers in a bar—a black man and the bar bouncer, and made it with all three of us in the back of our van. Later, Gail said she felt guilty that she was getting all the new cock and I wasn't getting any new pussy. I told Gail about another of my fantasies, watching her make it with another woman. Gail replied that she liked cock too much to be interested in another woman, but I saw the horny glint in her eye as she thought about it, and decided to drop the subject and bide my time.

One day Gail asked if I'd like to make it with Allison, a friend of hers who worked in her office. Allison is about thirty, but looks barely twenty. She's under five feet tall and weighs about ninety pounds, is drop-dead gorgeous and has long blonde hair she usu-ally wears in a ponytail. Her tits are small and her waist is about twenty inches.

Allison was getting divorced from an abusive and insanely jealous husband, and kept telling Gail how lucky she was to have a good husband and marriage. She also complained that she hadn't had sex for months, and wished that she had a good man.

Gail decided she would give Allison to me, as a present to us both. I told Gail that I would get it on with her and Allison if that was what she really wanted me to do. I tried to sound reluctant, but I was getting hard just thinking about plunging my cock into Allison's pussy, or hanging onto her ponytail as she sucked me off, not to mention the thought of watching Gail and Allison lapping each other's clits.

Gail and I invited Allison to our house for dinner and drinks. We figured that after getting Allison toasted we would all play cards, turning the game into an excuse for us all to get naked. We know a game in which each player starts with four chips and loses a chip to the pot with each hand lost. If a player loses all his chips he's out of the game. A marked deck of cards and prearranged signals allowed Gail and me to control who won each hand. I quickly lost all my chips. Gail said I could stay in the game if I sold her a piece of my clothing for one of her chips. I agreed, and she bought my workout pants, leaving me in white bikini underwear and a tank top. Gail insisted, of course, that the purchaser got to remove the clothing from the seller. As she pulled down my pants, Gail scraped the underside of my cock with her lips, causing the head of my cock to nearly poke up above the top of my briefs. I tried to act embarrassed in front of Allison, but it was obvious that she was getting excited.

We continued to play, Gail secretly controlling the game. Gail lost, and I bought her blouse, leaving her in her shorts and black lace bra. We made Allison lose her chips, but spared her by just taking her shoes. In the next two games I removed Gail's shorts and then her bra, leaving her sitting in her pink lace panties, her tits bare. Then it was her turn, taking my top and then my shorts, leaving me completely naked. As Gail was starting to remove my briefs I began to protest, telling Gail that Allison probably didn't want to see my naked ass. When Allison said no, it was her lucky night, getting to keep her clothes and see me lose mine, I knew we had her.

Surprisingly, Allison's luck changed, and she lost the next several hands. Soon I was buying her bodysuit, which she was wearing under gym shorts. She protested. "No fair! I'm not wearing anything under the bodysuit. You can't take off the bodysuit without taking the shorts first." She relented when I stood up and walked around the table toward her, bare-ass naked, my half-erect cock waving back and forth as I walked. I stood by her seat, my prick becoming stiffer as I held it an inch from her face. I raised her to her feet, grabbed the straps to the bodysuit and slowly pulled it and her shorts to the floor.

As I stripped Allison I held my face next to her body, staring up into her eyes and rubbing my hands down her flanks as I knelt down. I could see that she was very excited. I was also surprised to find that she had shaved her pussy clean. As she stepped out of her clothes, I said, "You're right, Gail, she has a fantastic body. I don't think I can bring myself to put her shorts back on."

Gail replied, "I don't think you have to. I think she wants to stay naked. I think what she really wants is for you to fuck her. Isn't that right, Allison? You want to fuck my husband, don't you?"

"You mean you'd let me?" replied Allison.

"Sure I will," said Gail. "You're my friend, and I know you need it. Rick's a great lover. He'll have you coming all night. Rick's watched me get fucked by other men, watched me suck their cocks and swallow their hot come. Now it's my turn to watch him show off his big cock. If you want him, just take him."

Without another word, Allison reached out and took my rapidly stiffening prick in one hand, cupping my balls in the other. She began by gently rubbing my balls. The sensation was incredible, and I returned the favor by stroking her pussy lips, which I found were already wet, hot and ready. I slid a finger into her canal, while my thumb began to massage her clit. She tilted her head back and began to moan. We were both getting a little weak in the knees, so I picked her up and laid her on the sofa. She spread her legs and began to hunch her pussy up and down. Gail had said that Allison hadn't fucked in months, and it showed, so I knew that I could get her off quickly.

I looked over at Gail, who had shed her panties and was fingering her pussy. I said, "Come here, Gail. I want you to watch while I make another woman come. I want you to get real close so you can see my tongue lapping another woman's pussy, like I've watched other men's tongues lapping at yours." She got down on her knees beside me as I began to suck on Al's red, engorged clit and lick and suck her pussy.

As I stuck my tongue up into Allison's tight, shaved pussy, I began to work a fingertip into her tight butthole. She began to come—screaming, crying and hunching her crotch furiously. As she came, the pussy juice literally ran out of her cunt. I eagerly lapped up some of it, then put my hand behind Gail's head and gently guided her toward Allison's pussy. "Go ahead, baby," I encouraged, "Give Al's sexy, shaved pussy a little kiss." To my pleasure and surprise, Gail put her head down and flicked the end of her tongue across Allison's clit. Al, who was still ready for more pleasure, moaned and trembled. This apparently pleased Gail, and she began to lap at Allison's cunt lips like she'd been doing it all her life.

After a minute, Allison was getting ready to come again. Gail pulled back and said, "I think what she needs now is your big cock, and a load of hot come!" I was more than ready to prong Al's hot, bare pussy, so I lifted her off the sofa, laying her on the big shag throw rug. I climbed on top of her sexy little body. I held her hands as I licked and sucked on her hard nipples. My cockhead found her pussy, and I pushed into her about an inch. She struggled to get the rest of my cock inside her.

"Do you like my cock, Allison?" I asked.

"Oh God, yes!" she moaned. "Stop teasing and give it to me!"

"Did you like it when I licked your pussy?" I continued, as I slowly fucked her with only the first inch of my cock.

"Oh yes, you made me come hard, but now I want your cock inside me!" she cried.

"And did you like it when Gail licked your pussy?" I persisted, sliding my cock in another inch.

"Gail licking my pussy?" Allison exclaimed. "It felt great! Gail can lick my pussy whenever she wants, as long as she makes you fuck me now!" While I'd been teasing Al, Gail had reached for the jar of Albolene and now she jammed her well-lubed index finger right into my asshole. I pushed into Allison's cunt so hard my balls slapped against her ass. As I slammed in and out of Al, Gail kept working her finger in my ass. Gail knows from experience that this not only drives me crazy, but makes me come fast and hard. Al held her legs straight up and out, spreading her pussy open, so my stiff pubic hairs rubbed against her clit as I thrust into her. Soon she tensed, began hunching her pussy hard against my cock, and screamed as she had her second orgasm. Again her hot pussy juice flowed all over our genitals.

As Allison came, Gail rubbed the tip of her finger against my prostate, and my cock erupted with a huge load of hot spunk, which shot deep into Al's canal. This was followed by a second and third spurt, and I began to think I would never stop coming.

The spasms finally subsided as Gail pulled her finger out of my ass, but my cock stayed hard, and I continued to slowly slide in and out of Allison's wet pussy. As Allison began to get into the rhythm of the slow fucking she was getting, Gail surprised me by moving around and straddling Allison, facing me, her pussy only about an inch from Allison's face.

"Come on, Allison," Gail said. "It's your turn to lick pussy. I tasted yours and let you fuck my husband. I need to get off, too."

Allison looked at me and smiled. "This is your idea, isn't it? You want us to lezzie each other, don't you?"

I just smiled back. Allison raised her head slightly and wiped her tongue across Gail's slit. Gail moaned and lowered herself onto Allison's face. Allison began to lap at Gail's pussy and suck on her clit. I watched Gail as her nipples hardened and extended, and she got that expression on her face that she gets when she's really turned on.

"Is this what you wanted to see me do?" she asked. "I hope you like it as much as I do. She's got my pussy on fire! You're going to see me come in a minute if she doesn't stop!" Allison didn't stop. Instead she began sticking her tongue into Gail's snatch and rubbing her clit with her thumb. Gail was grinding her crotch on Al's face and gently twisting her own nipples.

I pulled my cock out of Allison's pussy and began rubbing the head of my prick up and back through Allison's pussy lips, across her clit. This caused Allison to go wild. She began bucking her pussy against my cock and went completely crazy on Gail's clit. As hot as Gail was, that caused her to come. She hunched so hard that Allison's tongue was lapping her ass as well as her cunt, and Gail's pussy juices flowed down all over Allison's face.

Feeling Gail come on her tongue, and my cockhead rubbing on her clit, pushed Al over the edge into another orgasm. Once again my cock and balls were flooded with Allison's juices. I was near coming myself, and kept thrusting my cock between Allison's pussy lips.

"Go ahead and shoot a load, baby!" yelled Gail, who was getting turned on by the thought of watching me come on Allison's pussy, where she could see me spurt. Gail moved back, so Allison could look down and see, as well as feel, what was happening. I was about to lose control, and the thought of two naked, sexy women watching me humping, eager to see me spew my jism, was more than I could stand. I felt myself tense, my cock pulsing, and I let go, shooting a huge stream of spunk into the air. I spewed gob after gob of jism onto Allison's pubes, and finally the last one dribbled down the side of my prick.

Gail was highly excited by my explosion. She called me a sexy bastard, and then she leaned over and sucked on Allison's right nipple. She continued down her belly, licking up all of my come, including that on my cock. As she licked my cock clean she gave Allison's snatch a few good laps as well.

After a short rest I made us all another drink, then suggested we get into the hot tub, which is on the deck outside. The deck is surrounded by a fence, rather than a railing, for privacy, and there is a large platform for sunbathing attached to the hot tub frame. We all got in, and I turned on the jets.

After we'd relaxed for a few minutes I turned on the air pump, which forced air bubbles through hundreds of holes in the seats. The bubbles tickled the girls' pussies, my cock and balls and our asses. Gail commented that the hot tub jets were a girl's best friend. Allison replied that she didn't understand. "My God, girl!" exclaimed Gail, "Haven't you ever masturbated on a hot tub jet?"

"No," said Allison, "Wouldn't it hurt?"

Gail replied, "No, it only gets you off faster and harder than any dildo or vibrator that I've ever used."

"Yeah, and it works on cocks too!" I added. Gail had become turned on by the air bubbles washing over her crotch and the thought of the water jet on her clit. She swung her legs over the side of the tub, lay back and aimed the jet of water at her pussy.

"Damn, it feels so good I can barely stand it!" cried Gail. "Help Allison get her pussy on that jet, Rick." I put my arm under Allison's legs and swung them over the side of the tub. I put my hand under Allison's pussy and when I felt the water jet hit my hand, I slid it under her butt, allowing the invisible stream to hit her pussy lips. Within three seconds, Allison gasped and spread her legs wide. Immediately she was thrashing in the water, moaning with pleasure and moving her crotch up and down, directing the water jet across her clit, aiming at her pussy, then her asshole, and back again.

Within seconds both women were having continuous, multiple orgasms. This was making me hot, of course, so I knelt on a seat, allowing the water jet to strike the head and glans of my cock. In seconds I was as hard as a stone column.

As I was masturbating, I happened to glance up, and noticed that our neighbors, an attractive young couple that we hadn't met yet, were standing in their darkened kitchen window, trying to see what we were doing in the faint moonlight. They couldn't see anything over the fence, but obviously could hear the moaning of the women, and didn't realize that I could see their outlines. I decided to give them a little better view, so I got out of the hot tub, walked over to the fence gate, and swung it open, standing naked in the opening. Our house was dark, and the moonlight was faint, but I'm sure that my outline, including the erect cock I was slowly stroking, was visible as I turned to get back in the hot tub. Even with the gate open, they would see very little of us, but they would see enough to have an idea what was going on. I figured if they disapproved, fuck 'em, they shouldn't be spying on us. If we were turning them on, then maybe they would introduce themselves. I thought that maybe I would like to fuck the wife and let the husband fuck Gail, if they were interested.

As I returned to the hot tub, I found the girls still fucking the jets, but now they were teasing each other's nipples. I gently pulled Gail off the jet and laid her on the platform. She was still humping from the sensations of the jet, and began to finger her pussy. I turned to Allison and lifted her off the tub and placed her on the platform, so that her pussy was in Gail's face. Both Gail and Allison were by now completely abandoned to the sexual hunger that they were feeling. Gail didn't hesitate a second before starting to tongue Allison's pussy. She licked at Allison's clit, tongue-fucking her pussy, then began to push her tongue into Allison's pink, puckered little asshole.

Allison began to come again, flooding Gail with pussy juice, which made Gail suck Al's pussy all the harder, while she continued furiously finger-fucking herself. I climbed onto the platform and began to rub my cock against Allison's face. She got the hint, popped my cock into her mouth and began to suck it. Soon she was swallowing my entire shaft, then pulling it out to suck and lick around the head. I couldn't take much of that. Soon I felt that familiar pulsing of my cock and balls and I began to spew, pumping a load of hot jism into Al's throat.

As soon as she had sucked me completely dry, she turned

around to Gail and kissed her, pushing her tongue into Gail's throat, and said, "I just sucked your husband's cock and swallowed his spunk. Now I'm going to eat out your pussy and tongue your ass, like you did to me. Rick can watch and jack off if he wants, but it's time to show what us girls can do!"

The girls got into the 69 position and began to lick and suck each other's pussy, clit and asshole. I was content to watch the show from the hot tub, holding my semierect cock in the water jet. I glanced back toward the open fence gate and saw that our neighbors had moved to a bedroom window, where they had a better view of the hot tub and platform. There was a small nightlight of some type that they had left on, either accidentally or intentionally. It was plain to see that he had bent her over and was fucking her from behind as they watched us through the gate. Watching my wife and her friend shamelessly making love on the platform right in front of me and knowing that our neighbors were watching us and fucking in their house, combined with the powerful sensations of the water jet, caused me to come once again, shooting my load of spunk into the hot tub.

Hours later we finally tumbled into bed. Lying on my back, with two sexy, naked ladies lying across me, their breasts and nipples rubbing on my chest, was wonderful. Before we went to sleep, Gail told Allison that she would never have to get that horny again. She could come over and use our hot tub jets, or use us, whenever she wanted. —R.V., San Luis Obispo, California

A BROKER BLESSED WITH TEN-INCH MEAT MAKES A PERFECT BIRTHDAY TREAT

My husband Scot and I have a wonderful marriage. We are very open with one another, and we tell each other everything. We have participated in threesomes, foursomes and moresomes. We also go to a nude beach on a regular basis, and we are very comfortable with our bodies. We both have powerful sex drives and we fuck at least once a day. One Sunday I got Scot off five times in six hours. I lost track of how many times I came that day.

One day at the beach we met a nice young black man whom I will call Bill. Bill is a stockbroker whose cock is at least ten inches long when limp. The very first time we saw him and his bulge, I said to Scot: "Boy, would I like to see that cock hard."

As time went by, we often ran into Bill at the beach and we got rather friendly with him. Scot knew I used Bill as a fantasy lover when I masturbated. My birthday was coming up and Scot told me he was giving me a special present. He had invited Bill to come over for the sole purpose of fucking me silly. The mere thought of it got me soaking wet.

We were helping the kids with their homework when Bill arrived. We got him a beer, finished up with the kids and sent them to bed. Then we invited him upstairs.

As soon as we had closed and locked the door, Bill said: "So, if this is your birthday present you should be wearing your birthday suit." I immediately stripped and lay down on the bed.

Scot came over, spread my legs wide and said: "This is the cunt I want you to fuck. She gives the best deep-throat I've ever had and she can take it up the ass. I want you to take her and fuck her like she's never been fucked before."

Scot played with my tits as Bill got on top of me. Scot said: "Suck that big, black cock. Go on and make it hard." I finally took the cock I had been fantasizing about for months into my hungry mouth. I got Bill hard in no time. All the while Bill kept commenting that it was the best head he'd ever had and that most girls got scared when they saw the size of his dick. Bill was in heaven, he said, because it was his first deep-throat. I was in heaven because I was able to give it to him.

Bill got up and repositioned himself to fuck my pussy. Chills were running up and down my spine as he stuck his huge hard-on into me. He filled me like I'd never been filled before. Scot asked me if it felt good. "God, yes," I gasped. "I feel so full." Scot has a nice seven-inch cock but it just couldn't compare to Bill's tool. I hoped Scot wasn't jealous of the pleasure Bill's prick was giving me.

After fucking me for a while and giving me several orgasms, Bill announced that he had never fucked a girl in the ass before and really wanted to try it. I got a little scared. He was so big! I knew I could handle Scot's cock but I wasn't sure any woman could handle Bill's.

Scot opened up my nightstand drawer and took out the K-Y jelly. Bill slathered it on his huge cock. Then, ever so gently, he inserted it into my rectum. It took a long time, but finally he had it buried up to the hilt. Soon he was fucking my white ass with his big black dick. By the third or fourth stroke I was coming in one long nonstop orgasm. As he fucked my ass, Bill spotted my dildo in the open nightstand drawer. He took it out and proceeded to poke my pussy with it while pounding my butthole. Both he and Scot watched as I writhed and moaned in ecstasy. Scot played with my tits the whole time. I'd never had such a good fuck.

Finally Bill pulled out and proceeded to cover my asscheeks with his sweet cream. Scot suggested I give Bill another blowjob, and went to the bathroom to get a washcloth to clean us off. Scot cleaned me off while I was deep-throating Bill. It didn't take long to get him hard again. I relished playing with that big cock. I kissed it, poked my tongue into the slit, and gently sucked his testicles. All Bill could do was moan in delight.

Soon Bill said he wanted to fuck me in the ass again. This time I wasn't nervous and he entered me with ease. Scot kept spurring him on, saying, "Go for it! Give it to her! Fuck her hard! She loves it!" Bill came in yet another massive orgasm. I did love it. He was so gentle, yet so masculine. Afterward he told me he felt like it was *his* birthday because this was the first time he had ever made love with a white woman. It was also the first time he had ever fucked a woman up the ass and the first time he was deep-throated.

Scot and I are closer now than ever before. He did not feel at all threatened by my encounter with Bill. As a matter of fact, he said he had been proud to show off my talents. He wants us to have a threeway again, this time with another woman. I'm working on setting it up right now. —*E.U.*, *Austin*, *Texas*

Someone's Watching

GOLFING BUDDIES BALL CLUB SECRETARY IN
HEAD PRO'S INNER SANCTUM

During the first six years of our marriage, I tried talking to my wife about things like swapping, or possibly engaging in a three-way, but Amanda never had the nerve to do anything. However, shortly after I got her a job, as the director's secretary at the country club where I'm the physical training instructor, she had an adventure I'd like to share.

It all started one morning when Amanda was in my office, which is next to the men's locker room. Right in the middle of our conversation, I noticed her staring out the door with her mouth hanging open, her eyes bulging. Out in the hallway, two of the members, who are always playing stupid macho games, were standing stark naked, arguing over which one of them had the biggest dick. Amanda couldn't take her eyes off them, and I couldn't blame her; even hanging limp, it was obvious that both these guys had huge cocks. I waited a minute, but when they didn't go back into the locker room I yelled, "Gentlemen please, there's a lady present." They stopped horsing around but made no effort to cover themselves. Instead, when they saw Amanda's expression, they just stood there letting her have a good, long look. It had such an effect on her, I wondered if Amanda could be tempted to experiment with someone who was really hung.

The director goes home at two o'clock, leaving Amanda alone on the second floor until five. If I'm not busy, I go up and visit with her when no one's around. A little after three o'clock, I was approaching her office when I heard voices. Not wanting to disturb her, if whatever she was doing was important, I crept forward and peeked around the corner. As soon as I saw Butch and David, the same two men from that morning, I knew what they were up to. My only problem with it was, when I'd talked to Amanda about a threesome, I'd assumed I'd be one of the three.

The two men had come to Amanda on the pretext of checking their memberships. While she was going through their files, David said, "We're sorry about what happened earlier. Did we embarrass you?"

Amanda gave them a sheepish smile and replied, "A little."

Butch then asked, "Since you had the opportunity to check us out, which one of us do you think has the biggest cock?" I was shocked by my conservative wife's boldness; without looking up from the file she was holding, she meekly answered, "Before I can make a definite statement, I'd have to see them again, up close and hard."

In an instant, the two men were out of their clothes and around the desk, with both their dicks being stroked to erection by my sexy wife. They were so similar, it took Amanda a while to choose, but when she picked Butch, he yelled, "Yes, and to the victor go the spoils. I get to go first."

He quickly spun Amanda around, bent her over the desk, pulled her slacks and panties down and moved in to fuck her from behind.

Right then I nearly panicked. Even though I had encouraged this, and even though I was standing there watching it happen, I suddenly wasn't sure if I wanted another man screwing my wife. Well, it was too late. Amanda had a look of pure ecstasy on her face as Butch pushed his thick, ten-inch pleasure stick inside her, stretching and filling her vagina like I'll never be able to. His equipment was so much larger than she was accustomed to, he had to go slow. But he eventually got it all the way in.

*   *   *

It must have felt wonderful, because Amanda climaxed after just a few full strokes. She bit her lower lip and pumped her ass backward to make sure she was getting everything Butch could offer. Feeling Amanda's pussy contracting must have been too much for Butch because, unfortunately, Butch quickly blew his load. Amanda's disappointment (and Butch's embarrassment) caused him to leave without saying another word.

Meanwhile, David went to Amanda and repositioned her so that she was lying longways atop the desk, on her back. I watched with fascination as my wife spread her legs and guided the second stranger's erection to her love-hole. With one slow but steady push, he sank his big shaft all the way inside, once again filling Amanda's pussy to the brim. Then, as he began pumping into her, she sighed with joy, wrapped her legs around his hips, and humped her pelvis to meet his every thrust.

He had her hold the edge of the desk, to prevent her from sliding. This freed his hands to unbutton her blouse and open the front hook of her 34C bra. He then squeezed her titties and pinched her nipples while he plunged in and out of her love-nest. David turned out to be a much better lover than Butch, giving Amanda three good orgasms before he climaxed. Then, as his cock exploded inside her, she had one more superstrong orgasm. They were really slamming into each other, all squishy and hot.

When they were finished, they went to the director's private bathroom. Amanda stopped at the door, saying, "I have to use the toilet." What she wanted was for David to wait while she went, because she's very shy about anyone seeing her going.

When Amanda returned, she licked David's dick and balls, and when he started getting hard again, she took his cock into her mouth and sucked him back to full erection. This really knocked me for a loop, since Amanda always insisted that oral sex is dirty and didn't want anything to do with it. Yet there she was, lovingly slurping away on David's big, fat boner, giving him her first blowjob.

I think she would have continued until he came down her

throat, but a phone call interrupted them. While Amanda sat on the director's chair talking on the phone, David crawled under the desk and buried his face between her thighs. It was kind of funny watching my wife trying to carry on a conversation while her new friend was licking her slit and nibbling her clit. By the time the call ended, Amanda's legs were spread wide open, hanging over the chair's armrests, and her free hand was pushing on the back of David's head. Shortly after she hung up, she began jerking and letting out a series of short, raspy sighs as David brought her to another tremendous climax.

After her orgasm subsided, Amanda sat David down and mounted him right there behind the director's desk. Unfortunately, their location greatly limited my view. I could see Amanda from the chest up, as she rocked back and forth, humping David's big dick. And I saw her placing his hands on her breasts, but the real action, down below, eluded me.

Then, when David stood up and laid my wife back on the floor, I had to be content with the sounds of my wife's moans and that unique sloshing noise that only a well-fucked pussy makes. I think David gave Amanda four more strong orgasms, as once again he proved to be a very apt lover. He lasted a good twenty minutes before shooting his second load deep inside her.

After that, Amanda was really cute when she took hold of David's spent cock and led him back to the bathroom, where this time she insisted that they bathe each other. The two of them then jumped into the shower together where, incredibly, David got another erection and fucked Amanda again, filling her full of his seed for the third time.

After that day, Amanda was very receptive to the idea of a repeat liaison with the two men. But unfortunately we haven't seen either of them since they found out she's my wife.—*T.O., Gainesville, Florida*

HOW ARE YOU GOING TO KNOW WHAT YOUR WIFE
WANTS IF YOU DON'T ASK HER?

I never thought I'd be writing our experiences to *Penthouse Letters*. I have enjoyed reading *Penthouse Letters* for years, but that's precisely why I've never written in, because I've never experienced anything like what I read in your magazine.

It happened like this: The air-conditioning system at work broke down. It was hot, humid and claustrophobic, so I decided to go home early. I told my secretary to forward any important phone calls to me at home.

Well, the phone was ringing as I entered the house. I thought, Not already. I put my briefcase down and answered the phone—just seconds after my wife had evidently answered it upstairs.

Before I could say hello, I realized a conversation was already beginning. I heard a man's voice identifying himself as Stan. This Stan, who was a stranger to me, was evidently very intimate with my wife. He was telling Cheryl, my wife, that he wanted to bring a friend of his over on Wednesday. He said he'd bragged to his friend about how sexy, talented and enthusiastic Cheryl was. He interrupted his train of thought to ask if Cheryl was playing with her clit.

"Of course I am, you silly man. Didn't I tell you that I finger myself every time we talk on the phone? I get turned on just by the sound of your voice."

It sounded like bad phone sex.

Stan went on, saying that he'd told George that when Cheryl gave him a blowjob, she'd not only blow his cock, she'd blow his mind! "So when I bring him over, I want you to really gobble his dick like he's never had it before."

I was astounded, to say the least.

Cheryl then asked what he looked like. Stan said he had sandy-colored hair and a good build—they knew each other from the gym. He also said that he knew Cheryl liked her lovers to be well hung, and he didn't think she'd be disappointed with George.

Stan wanted to know if one o'clock Wednesday afternoon would be okay. Cheryl said it would. Stan then said he'd still be by for their regular fun and games on Friday. He said that yet another guy, Nick, would also be along on Friday, but that he was really pissed that he couldn't get off work on Wednesday. Stan said, "We could have really given you a good workout if all three of us could have made it. Maybe some other time. How would that suit you?"

"You know I'm always open to new experiences, Stan-the-Man."

I hung up confused, angry, intrigued and uncertain. But one thing was sure—I had an aching hard-on.

Now, Cheryl and I have shared a lot of fantasies and viewed a lot of erotic videotapes. We especially dig threesomes, and I've always told Cheryl that I'd like to see her take on two guys like in the movies. She was always turned on by the fantasies, but she would never commit to actually trying one.

From the sound of this phone call, however, she had suddenly taken on a second personality. The prim and proper housewife had given way to a new personality—a liberated, free-loving, open-to-anything (or anyone) sexpot.

When Cheryl came downstairs, I decided not to say anything. I decided to let circumstances follow their own path, but I took my lunch hour Wednesday a little late so that I'd be able to observe my wife's "friends" arrive at the appointed hour. I recognized Stan. He was a fellow who worked at the garage where we get our cars fixed. He had dark, wavy hair, a perpetual five-o'clock shadow, a dark complexion and a great build. The other guy I'd never seen before, as far as I could tell. I watched them enter the house, and I wanted desperately to observe whatever was going to happen, but I had to get back to work. Visions kept forming in my mind of Cheryl servicing these two hot studs. I realized I wasn't angry or even jealous, really. I was excited, and I couldn't get rid of my rock-hard cock.

I made a point on Thursday of stopping for gas at the garage on the way home from work. When I saw that Stan was working, I decided to get a quick oil change as well.

Stan was seated in the office. His broad shoulders and muscled chest tapered to a narrow waist. His hefty thighs were spread wide—I imagined how he would look naked, seated like that with my wife kneeling between his thighs, sucking his cock—which I was sure she had done. More than once.

I stuck my head in his door. "How you doing, Stan?"

He was cool as a cucumber. "I'm great, Joe. How's that sexy wife of yours. Haven't seen her in here in a while."

"She's fine, Stan. She's fine."

The next day, Friday, I went by our house to see if Stan would show with Nick. As it happened, Stan's car was already there, as was another. I wasn't pissed that the three of them were having a wild time. I wanted to be there with them.

I suddenly remembered that there had been a recent change in our sex life. I recalled that Cheryl was much more randy lately, and that she seemed to enjoy sucking my cock more and longer than she used to. So I related this increased interest in sex to what she was learning from these guys, her lovers.

I decided I would quietly enter the house, just to see how things were transpiring, and leave undetected, if possible, without having interrupted things.

I successfully entered and heard Stan yelling, "Fuck her, Nick, fuck her hard. Oh shit, I think she's going to suck my nuts right through my cock. Go, Cheryl. Yeah, baby, suck my cock, sweet thing. Oh, God, I'm coming, I'm coming."

Then there was a silence. Finally Stan said, "Eat it all! Oh God, yes. You are the one."

I walked up to our bedroom and peeked in through the crack in the door. There was my loving wife, lying back on the bed naked, a white man's dick in her mouth and a black man's dick between her spread legs.

Just as I looked in, Stan was pulling his spent dick out of Cheryl's mouth and Nick was speeding up his humping motion.

Cheryl lifted up her legs so that the backs of them were flush against Nick's dark chest. Nick started reaming my wife like I've seen nowhere else before, not on videotape, not in real life. I started sweating just watching.

When Cheryl started yelling that she was going to come. Stan started nibbling on her engorged nipples. This really set her off, and as her pussy started contracting around Nick's dick, Nick started shooting into Cheryl's cunt. Their natural rhythm was incredible and they came simultaneously for close to five minutes.

I decided to hightail it out of there before I was discovered. I was glad I finally knew what the deal was.

That night I told my wife that I'd seen her that afternoon. I told her that I'd forgotten some papers and had to come home to get them at lunchtime. Cheryl looked like a doe caught by a pair of headlights, but I assured her that I wasn't angry. I just wanted her to be honest with me and keep me informed of her activities. I said, "You know we used to fantasize with that black rubber dildo. I'd fuck you with that rubber dick and you'd suck my cock and we'd pretend to be having a threesome." I felt responsible for pushing the idea, and I wanted to let Cheryl know that it was all right with me.

I asked her how she had gotten it started. She explained that it began when her car had needed work. She took it to the garage, and Stan offered to drive her home, saying he'd bring her car to her when it was repaired.

When he drove her home, Cheryl invited him in for a cup of coffee. Stan started putting the make on her, but nothing actually happened. When he brought her car back, however, Cheryl had just gotten out of the shower and was wearing only a dressing gown. When she tried to write out the check, her left breast popped free. She apologized.

Stan said "Don't apologize. It's beautiful, and I bet you have another just like it." He got behind her, kissed her on the back of the neck and reached his right hand around her and into her gown to grab hold of a tit. From then on, she became putty in his hands, and before he left she sucked him off and got him hard again so he could fuck her.

They started seeing each other regularly. Stan used to quiz her a lot about what she and I did in bed. She'd even gotten out the black dildo and had Stan use it on her as I did. He told her he had something better. He said, "Why pretend we're having a three-some when we can have the real thing?" and that's how he introduced Nick to the equation.

The next date she had with Stan was at his place. He got her all naked and hot and ready to be fucked, and then he asked if she would like a big black dick to fuck her while she sucked his cock. She agreed and he called Nick in. He was already stripped, and he came in sporting the biggest, blackest, thickest cock she'd ever seen. She let Stan's cock drop out of her mouth in amazement as Nick got on the bed between her legs and rubbed his big purple head all over her cunt lips. Then he gently eased into her and stuffed her cunt with more cock than she had ever imagined. She said she thought she'd go out of her mind with ecstasy as Stan fucked her mouth and Nick reamed her deeper and wider than she'd ever been reamed.—*Name and address withheld*

BASS PLAYER STOPS PLAYING SECOND FIDDLE AND SCREWS LEAD SINGER'S WIFE

*M*y wife hadn't been on a lot of dates before I met her—she's too damn shy. She hasn't really turned into a party animal since we've been married, either. 'Bout the only socializing she does is when she helps me out with the band I play in—on the few gigs we get.

She's known the bass player for years, and she really loves talking to him. Sometimes Kelly cooks dinner for the band, and on those occasions she and Paul will talk for hours. After dinner, Paul would sit on the couch across from Kelly and completely monopolize her time.

One night I noticed him playing with his crotch, and I wondered why. I looked over at my wife, and there was Kelly, sitting with her legs just slightly open. Kelly's white lace panties were showing, and you could see just a few light brown hairs curling around from behind her panties. I'd never known my wife to be an exhibitionist, and I wondered if she knew what she was doing.

Every time Paul came over, he would sit across from Kelly and look her over. If she crossed her legs, or got up, or sat down, he would quickly look over.

Another night Kelly became a little drunk and Paul got bold and just stared at her pantied crotch all night long. Later that night, after everyone had gone, I talked to Kelly and asked if she knew what she was doing. Having had too much to drink, she admitted that she was fond of Paul and she didn't care if he was sneaking a peek. She said that it was kind of exciting, the idea that Paul would want to see her. I suggested she should go the whole nine yards and wear a nightie next time he's around. She looked at me with those chestnut eyes and said she could never do such a thing. She didn't mind flirting, but that was as far as she could go.

After that night, however, she became more adventurous, leaving her shirt halfway unbuttoned, wearing see-through panties. I must admit, I was starting to feel sorry for poor Paul. He would leave horny, and I would get the best sex of my life.

One night we were watching Mary Poppins on TV. Kelly was wearing a dark blue negligee. We had been drinking wine, and right when Kelly went to get another bottle from the kitchen, I heard the doorbell ring and went to answer the door. There I found a very sad-looking Paul. He had just broken up with his girlfriend and needed a shoulder to cry on.

Kelly came back with more wine, poured Paul a glass and we

all settled down to watch the rest of the movie. I'll be damned if Paul wasn't constantly looking at Kelly throughout the whole goddamned movie. Kelly was getting tipsy (it doesn't take much) and with every commercial seemed to slide closer to Paul. Before long, she had her head in his lap and he was playing with her hair. She would giggle and purr each time he tickled her ear, and Paul started looking down the length of her body. When he got to her toes, he looked up and saw me looking at him. He knew he was caught, and he stammered something about how pretty Kelly's lacy nightie was.

I sarcastically told him he should see her underwear. Kelly got up at that moment to get another glass of wine, and Paul remarked that he could see plenty. When Kelly sat back down, she said, "If you show me yours, I'll show you mine."

"How far do you want to go?" Paul asked.

"Well, let's just start with the undies. Are you game, honey?" she asked me.

"You guys are on your own," I said. "You don't need my approval."

"All right, Paul," Kelly said. "You first."

"You come uncover whatever you want to see," Paul intoned.

Kelly slowly undid Paul's shirt and pulled it open. Giggling, she pinched his nipples and then rubbed her hands over his hairy chest. Then she licked her finger and attacked his belly button. Paul jumped at having a wet finger stuck in his belly button, but Kelly was not deterred. She reached down and started unbuttoning his fly.

When she got them all the way open, there was this huge bulge of dick and balls encased in tightie-whitie Calvins.

"Holy shit," my wife said in genuine surprise. When she realized that she'd said it out loud, she covered her blushing face and ran into the kitchen.

"C'mon, honey," I yelled into the kitchen, "a deal's a deal."

She came sheepishly back into the TV room but soon broke into a shit-eating grin.

"All right, Paul, what do you want to see?"

"Whatever you want to show me, Kelly."

She stood in front of my band mate, and I watched as Kelly's eyes grew bigger and bigger. Paul took each of Kelly's hands and pulled her toward him. I could not believe the look of lust in this man's eyes. He untied the bow at the front of my wife's nightie and gasped as the thing fell open. Kelly was wearing panties, but she wasn't wearing a bra, and Paul looked like he was trying to stare at everything all at once.

"Man, Kelly," Paul gasped, "you're tits aren't particularly big, but they're the most perfectly shaped tits I've ever laid eyes on."

Turning to me with a salacious smile on his face, he said, "Damn, Ned, now I know why you're always late for our jam sessions. You been bonin' this fine piece of meat all day long."

"Watch it, Paul, " I solemnly said. "That's my wife standing naked in front of you."

We all laughed, and in his mirth Paul took the opportunity to slide his hand up the back of Kelly's leg and grab ahold of her ass. "Jesus, Kelly, I never realized you were so sexy," Paul said. Kelly, who had suddenly become very nervous, stammered a thank you and quickly grabbed her wine glass.

As she drank, the room became very quiet. We went back to watching the movie, and Paul continued to look Kelly over. After a while, Kelly's wine glass was empty again, and she got up and walked over to Paul, where the wine bottle was. When she started to go back to her chair, Paul asked her to put her head back in his lap.

"Oh, what the fuck," Kelly said. Once her head was in his lap, it was my turn to feel that lovely butt. From my end of the couch, I slid my hand up Kelly's taut legs and firmly grabbed a cheek. Paul's right, I have to admit it: she's a fine piece of meat.

Toward the end of the movie, when I knew that Paul was catching a buzz himself, I slid Kelly's panties away from her crotch and stared down at her twat. I could clearly see her pussy lips—they had started to glisten with her juices. Paul started to play with her hair again, and Kelly started to purr just like before. Then Paul bent over and kissed her ear, whispering how great she looked. Kelly smiled and stated that she was really very plain.

Paul started to laugh and asked if she could feel anything getting hard in his pants. I had failed to notice her hand under her head. She very quietly said yes, and she did not remove her hand.

Paul started to get very interested in Kelly's back. He started to rub her neck and lower back and Kelly mentioned how great it felt. He asked if she would like a back rub.

"Only if you stay right where you are," was her answer.

"You mean my hand?" Paul asked.

"That's right."

Paul started rubbing Kelly's back through her nightie, and with each stroke, more and more of her back became visible. Paul was acting like he was watching the movie, but most of the time his eyes were glued to Kelly's great ass.

I said to myself, Oh, what the hell, and proceeded to pull Kelly's panties off. Kelly's pussy lips were bright pink, and juices were starting to run into the couch.

Paul kissed Kelly's neck and asked her if she would like to undo his pants. All Kelly could say was yes. Paul stopped rubbing her back, and she sat up and threw her nightie to the floor. Paul quickly started unbuttoning his pants, and Kelly said, "Wait a minute, that's my job."

When Kelly saw Paul's underwear-clad package again, all she could say was, "Oh, Paul." She slowly started to play with Paul's dick and Paul started to rub Kelly's ass, then lightly scratching her back all the way up the back of her neck.

He kissed her again and asked if she wanted to see his cock. Kelly said nothing and Paul said, "I'll take that as a yes."

Kelly still did not say anything, and so Paul decided to wait, turning his attention instead to Kelly's hot torso. Paul looked over my wife's body, touching her very softly and telling her how soft her skin was. I got on the floor behind Kelly and started to tickle her ass, running my fingers over her pussy lips.

Judging from the wetness of it, I could tell that Kelly's pussy was ready to be fucked, and my cock just ached to do that. I had been playing with Kelly's pussy for so long that I did not notice Paul starting to moan. I looked at Paul's crotch, and there was my wife's little hand, slowly rubbing his cock up and down. I hadn't even seen her pull his underwear down!

Paul quickly pulled his pants off, and Kelly's full attention was on his cock. She started to cup his balls and then kissed each one. Then she licked them and rolled her face into his crotch. I couldn't believe my eyes when I saw my wife sit all the way up and then slowly lower her head to Paul's pole, sucking him all the way into her mouth. Paul started to moan, begging Kelly not to stop before he came.

All of a sudden we had gone from light petting to serious love-making. Kelly pulled her mouth away and blew on Paul's wet cock before engulfing the thing again. My wife is kind of small, and it was so sexy watching her dainty little head being skull-dragged by Paul's huge dick. She was huffing and puffing but she was not giving up.

After about twenty minutes of this, I watched as Paul's toes started to go straight, then limp, then straight again. Then a look of absolute pleasure crossed Paul's face as he started to pump his hips. I guess my wife figured she didn't have anywhere else to put his come, so she decided to put it in her stomach. Kelly started to giggle as Paul continued to pump come into her mouth. As he started to relax, he looked down and could only see her back and butt. He slowly rubbed her and told her how great she was. He was trying to see her pussy as I fingered and licked her pink hole.

Even after he was soft, Kelly continued to play with Paul's cock. She told him how beautiful it was, and with that Paul started to get hard again.

All this time I continued to finger my wife, and I could tell it would only be a matter of minutes before she came. Presently, Kelly started to moan, and I continued to work on her pussy. Her butt started to go up and down on my hand. All of a sudden Kelly turned around and said she didn't want Paul to see her come.

"Honey, he just shot his wad down your throat. I think you guys are beyond the coy stage."

With that she let go, vigorously humping up and down on my hand. I was working my two big fingers all the way in to her cervix, and when my entire hand was wet I slipped my thumb up her tight asshole. She really started going crazy, crying out the high-pitched scream she emits every time she comes.

"See, goddamn it, I don't want Paul to hear how silly I sound when I come." To muffle her cries, she stuck Paul's cock back in her mouth. I had two fingers up her dripping twat and my thumb up her ass: I felt like we were connected.

Then, about five minutes later, I watched her legs straighten and, popping Paul's cock out of her mouth, she slammed her ass down on my hand and started coming, screaming out loud like a madwoman.

When she was done, she hid her face in Paul's lap and said how embarrassed she was. Paul was lightly playing with her hair and said how sexy it was to see her come. Kelly asked for a glass of wine, and Paul refilled her glass, handing it to her.

After one sip, Kelly announced that she had to pee. She jumped up and ran for the bathroom. Paul followed her pussy lips all the way. After Kelly left, Paul apologized, but I would hear none of it.

Suddenly realizing that I was the only one who was dressed, I stripped, and when I saw my cock and how hard it was, I brought it to Paul's attention and said, "Judging from the size of this thing, do you think I mind?"

"Man, I've been wanting to see your wife in the buff ever since I met her. She's incredible, Ned."

"Don't I know it, Paul."

Kelly came back in time to hear the last of our conversation. Seeing her bush for the first time, Paul had to catch his breath.

"I wish I could have some of that," Paul said, and Kelly just walked right up to Paul and straddled his lap.

Paul's cock was so hard, the head was purple. It was just grazing her pubic hair, and he grabbed hold of her ass and started to pull her closer to him. All she could say was, "Paul, I can't stop you," and with that she closed her eyes and he kissed her. I watched as she took hold of his cock, lifted herself up and put it into her. She opened her eyes and whispered into his ear, "Fuck me, please."

Paul slowly started to push his cock in, and with each push, Kelly would gasp. Kelly started to move up and down, and Paul started to push it deeper. They both started to moan, and soon Paul was seriously banging his cock into her. He slowly turned her so that she was lying down and he was on top. Kelly wrapped her legs around him and begged him to go faster. She started to cry and laugh at the same time, saying how great it felt. I could tell she was coming when she spread her legs and hands, then pushed her groin into him and grabbed his ass. Then he started to come into her. With each spurt, he moaned aloud. They were truly bumping uglies, slapping into each other's sweaty body.

Finally, he let out a shriek and collapsed onto Kelly's chest.

Kelly looked at my pole sticking up and said, "You poor dear, you need some help." With that she pushed Paul onto the floor, got on all fours and put that beautiful butt in the air. I could see Paul's come on her pussy, and it felt really weird as I slid my cock into her. I started to fuck her and Paul just watched her breasts swinging.

"I didn't think anything would be hotter than fucking you," Paul said, "but watching Ned fuck you like that is so incredibly hot . . ."

As soon as he said that, she seemed to change and started to come one more time. I could hardly contain myself. I could feel the pressure in my balls and Kelly knew I was ready to come. As she reached under to play with my balls, Paul stood up and positioned himself before my wife's face. She opened her mouth to take Paul's cock one more time. When I started to come, Kelly was so taken with Paul's cock that she leaned forward and my dick popped out. I grabbed my cock and jerked off all over Kelly's ass.

Right about the same time, Paul started coming again, and when Kelly could take no more in her mouth, she pulled her mouth away and took a couple of last squirts in her face before collapsing onto the couch.

Paul looked at me and said, "I guess we burned her out." Kelly could not move. She had her finger on her clit and all she could do was moan. Paul looked at me, and asked if he could look at her pussy, as he'd really never gotten a good look at it. I turned Kelly over and Paul sat at my end of the sofa. He very gently opened Kelly's legs and pulled her pubic hair back. He separated her lips, bent over and softly kissed her pink hole.

Then Paul said he'd better be going, he had to be at work at six in the morning. Just before he walked out the door, he went back to Kelly, and I heard him say, "I've always loved you, and I will always be jealous of Ned."

He touched her right breast, kissed her lightly on the head and said good night.—N.H., Barnwell, South Carolina

HUBBY HIRES AN ITALIAN STALLION TO GIVE WIFEY THE RIDE OF HER LIFE

Michelle and I have been married for ten years. We have a good marriage because we are always very understanding of each other. Michelle was a virgin before our honeymoon and, up until recently, I was the only man she had ever known sexually.

For quite some time I fantasized about Michelle in the hands of other men. Her conservative style always made me reluctant to ask her what she thought of this fantasy. One morning, I told her that I had dreamt she was having an affair with her favorite soap star—a tall, dark Italian stud. She didn't say much, but I could tell by the look on her face that she wished it were true.

Michelle has a good body for a thirty-year-old. She stands five feet two inches tall, has medium-sized tits, shapely legs and a nice, round ass. Her curly reddish-brown hair and deep blue eyes are eye-catching, and so is her soft smile and graceful body. She has creamy skin and powder-pink nipples atop firm, perky tits. Working out daily has kept her in top form.

I am a very wealthy, thirty-two-year-old businessman. I am five feet eleven inches tall and of average build. I travel quite a bit and my schedule changes constantly, often on very short notice. Unfortunately, my business causes me to neglect Michelle. It also causes some erection problems when we make love. Even when erect, my penis is only five inches long. I've always thought Michelle needed more than I can give. Several times I have hinted at this—telling her how I've heard women love big, thick cocks. She always blushes and compliments the things I can do with my own apparatus. I wonder if my hints have made her think I'm insecure.

Anyway, I thought of a way to find out if she could use something more. I had to create a situation behind her back because she is much too shy to help in the planning. I remembered the son of one of my clients who lives a hundred miles away. Tom is unemployed, twenty-one years old and looks a great deal like my wife's television idol. I knew he would catch Michelle's eye with his six-foot frame, dark complexion, thick black hair and self-assured style. I hired Tom for a few days to do yard work on the back acres of our country estate. Since Tom lives so far away, I invited him to stay with us until completing the job.

The first morning, Michelle cooked breakfast for us. As we ate, I noticed Michelle furtively inspecting Tom from head to toe. He was wearing a T-shirt, shorts, and old sneakers. She was pretty slick about her inspection, but I could tell she had noticed the magnificent bulge in the young stud's shorts.

After we were through eating, I helped Tom get started on the landscaping project. That evening Tom and I showered while

Michelle started dinner. I went to the master bathroom and Tom went to the shower in the guest room. I hurried, hopping in and out of the shower. As I dried off I noticed, through the partially open door, that Michelle was standing in the doorway of Tom's room. She could see him, but he couldn't see her. She stood watching him dry himself for a few minutes before she walked back into the kitchen.

When Tom and I came to dinner, he was wearing nothing but a blue pair of loose-fitting satin shorts that magnified the heft and length of his large penis. I could tell that he was having an effect on Michelle, even though she was trying hard not to look at him. She had a worried look on her face, as though she were having troubled thoughts.

As we ate, music became the topic of conversation and it became apparent that Michelle and Tom had quite a few tastes in common. As they were reminiscing about some old favorites, Michelle started loosening up. She got up to refill Tom's glass, brought it back and sat down in the chair beside him. I caught her looking Tom over more openly. There was a look in her eye that I had never seen before. As they got deeper into a discussion of early punk bands, I excused myself.

I left the room, but instead of going into my office, I crept around to the backyard and hunched down next to the glass patio door. I could barely see them but, as I had hoped, Michelle soon led Tom into the den and put some music on the stereo. I had a completely unobstructed view.

They started to dance very innocently, holding hands only. Then, about halfway through the song, Tom put his hands around Michelle's waist and she put hers around his neck. Michelle had the look of a woman who needed attention. She stared up into Tom's eyes as they swayed slowly across the floor, and his hands began to rub and caress her ass. She let him pull her against his hard body. Suddenly, the song ended and Michelle seemed to snap out of a trance. She rushed to the kitchen to clean up. I passed the kitchen on my way upstairs and told Michelle I would be leaving town in the morning and that I'd be gone on business for three to four days.

I left the next morning, driving to a path just down the road that led to the back of our property. I parked my car and walked back to the edge of the woods surrounding our backyard. Once there, I made myself comfortable, took out my high-powered binoculars and waited.

Tom had already started working in the yard. Towards noon, Michelle left in her car and returned about an hour later carrying a shopping bag. A little while later she came out wearing the tightest shorts I have ever seen. The shorts were shiny black vinyl and cut shorter than any she'd ever worn. She also had on a loose black blouse made entirely of lace that glided over her beautiful figure. She had come out to bring Tom a glass of water.

She handed Tom the water and bent over to inspect some of the new shrubs. Tom stared at her sassy-looking little body, and I noticed his shorts change shape as his dick rose within. It was so big, the head almost came out the top of his shorts. When Michelle turned around, she was staring right at Tom's dick.

Without a word, Tom reached out his hand and lifted her to him. Immediately they started kissing. Michelle started running her hands all over his back while he kissed her and pressed his hands against her cute little ass. She kissed his neck, sucked on his nipples and then ran her tongue all over his chest. Then she made her way down his dark body, raking her lips and tongue over his rippled abdomen and his waist as she slipped her hands into the back of his shorts to feel his butt.

She stood up and quickly unbuttoned her shorts and Tom pulled them down. He kneaded her beautiful ass while she felt up his dick and pulled his shorts completely off. They headed for the patio where Tom sat in a lounge chair. I was sure they would start fucking immediately. Instead, Michelle knelt down and started kissing Tom's enormous erection. This shocked me. Michelle has never given me head.

There she was, French-kissing the big swollen head of Tom's

huge dick, causing his pre-come to glisten. She noticed it, touched the tip of her tongue to it and swirled it around, spreading pre-come all over the head of his dark red cock. Then she placed little wet, warm, sticky kisses all the way down the underside of his long, thick shaft.

I was so caught up in the action, it took me a while to notice that my own dick was harder than Chinese arithmetic. I watched as Michelle licked up and down Tom's massive shaft and washed his balls with her tongue. She worked her tongue back up to the head and sucked it inside her mouth. As she sucked, she moved her lips up and down very slowly.

Damn, she looked sexy, wearing nothing but that tight shirt, her long hair loose and tangled, her hands clutching the boy's thighs, her lips puckered up—kissing, sucking and licking that dick with a lustful look on her face!

She cupped one hand under his balls and started running the tips of her fingers across his sac. Meanwhile, she was still sucking his big dick, pulling on the head with her lips on every stroke. Her slim fingers caressing his balls and her hot, pink lips pulling on his peter were starting to get to him. I noticed his scrotum starting to draw up. It was for resolution this good that I shelled out over two grand for these binoculars.

Anyway, Michelle quit sucking and started licking again. She stiffened her tongue, pressing it against the side of his hard, swollen dick. Her tongue was so stiff and his dick was so hard that when her tongue touched it, it bobbed around, slipping away from her tongue and rubbing against her face. Tom's face was blood red and he started coming in jets, straight into the air! Michelle licked and fondled his cock-head as he came, catching a good deal of his come with her tongue and mouth. The rest splattered onto the patio.

Michelle licked her lips clean and sucked the last of the come off the end of Tom's cock. It was still hard as a rock. She stood and peeled off her skirt and climbed onto his lap, sliding her hot little pussy down over his dick. Michelle has the tightest pussy

I've ever touched. Even though she and Tom were both wet and well-lubed, she still had to squirm to get his big dick all the way inside her.

Tom put his large, calloused hands on my wife's beautiful creamy ass and started squeezing and rubbing her sexy cheeks. She swayed slowly back and forth, impaling herself ever deeper on his hard dick. Michelle's creamy skin contrasted beautifully with Tom's dark skin. I watched her ass moving back and forth on his thighs, her tits with those hard pink nipples pressing into his huge hairy chest, her serious face kissing his neck and, most impressively, Tom's massive dick pumping in and out of her tight pink tunnel.

I thought it was all I could stand, but as I watched, things just kept getting better. Tom was thrusting and pumping while Michelle went into a fucking frenzy. The look on her face was something between pleasure and awe. Her hands and forearms flailed helplessly in the air as she was overtaken by the orgasm of her life. She was coming so feverishly that she tried to say something but couldn't. I thought they were going to stop, but they just slowed down a little and kept fucking.

When Michelle regained control, they established a slow, steady rhythm to their fucking. Michelle swiveled her hips around and around, bringing her gorgeous ass up high every time she rotated to the top. Tom's dick would almost pop out with every swivel. The head would slowly appear and poke at her tight opening before slipping back in.

One time, when his dick slipped out of her, she reached back and guided it back in with her sexy little hand. When it went in this time, it went all the way to the hilt, and Michelle gasped loudly. They both started thrusting and pumping at a faster pace, moaning and breathing heavily. He was pushing and pulling that whole nine inches of thick, hard dick in and out of my wife as she moaned loudly with pleasure. I couldn't believe I was standing in the bushes watching my horny little honey humping her heart out—fucking another man silly.

Suddenly Michelle leaned her head back, arched her back, stiffened her midsection and started jerking her pussy back and forth over Tom's dick. She started screaming as she came, her face turning red and tears of passion rolling down her flushed cheeks. Tom started coming inside my wife, moaning and gasping for breath as his scrotum tightened like wet leather in hot sunshine. They climaxed together and they weren't alone. I came in my pants and nothing had even touched my dick.

Later that night, while Tom and Michelle bathed and ate, I crept up to the house and set up my post outside the guest bedroom window. After dinner and drinks. Michelle led Tom to the guest room and dimmed the lights. He lay down on the bed on his back. She left and returned a few minutes later wearing a new negligee made of some see-through white fabric.

As I watched from the window, I found Michelle's bright red pubic hair and erect nipples startling under the translucent material. I couldn't take it anymore. I sneaked into the house for a better vantage point. I hid in the dim light behind my bedroom door, which was just across from the guest room.

Now I could hear them as well as see them. As Michelle climbed on top of Tom, I noticed she wasn't wearing panties. She sat on his stomach, and Tom reached up and started rubbing her beautiful tits. Michelle started grinding her pussy into his hairy chest. She carefully placed her wet pussy right on top of one of his stiff little nipples and pressed and rubbed against it. Watching her beautiful white flesh mash against Tom's tan muscles was arousing as hell!

She touched his large, hard dick and brushed her hand provocatively all over his balls and dick. Then she leaned over and started massaging his neck and caressing his chest. Tom reached up, tore the flimsy gown from her body and pulled her to him. She sucked his nipples awhile, then moved backwards, raking her tits across his chest and stomach before stopping at his dick. She rubbed both tits over his dick and balls. Then she took one tit and mashed it nipple-first into the top of his dick, causing pre-come to soak her nipple. Finally she put his dick between her tits and played with it. After a few minutes, she sat back on his chest and started humping with her ass again. I could hear her moan as she ground her cunt into his chest.

Tom grabbed her by her butt and pulled her hot pussy up to his face. He licked and kissed for a while, then started tongue-fucking her. It only took about a minute before she started coming. He rubbed his face back and forth against her pussy, really turning her on. He kissed her stomach and waist then concentrated once again on her hot cunt. This time he sucked. He was trying to suck her clit up into his mouth when Michelle started coming again. She bucked wildly while he fucked her with his tongue.

Tired of foreplay, Tom mounted Michelle, putting his monster cock inside her and pounding her pussy with everything he had. Michelle was whining with ecstasy. His balls bounced off her pussy every time he entered her. Tom was fucking so hard, the bed started shaking back and forth. All of a sudden Tom's muscles flexed. He withdrew his excited, reddish-purple cock and aimed it right at Michelle's tits. His come was under so much pressure it sprayed warm jets of semen all over her belly up to her chin.

That was the last round I witnessed. I tended to my business and gave them the next two days alone.

I still get a hard-on every time I think of Michelle putting Tom's big, tan dick in her mouth or in her tight pussy. I almost come thinking about how their bodies looked together—his hard, dark muscles mashing and pressing against her sweet, pink, tits and white body.

Despite all the lovemaking, Tom got through with the yard work. Now, every time I see him he asks me if I need help. I tell him not to worry. I'm saving all the chores for him since I know he can get the job done. Michelle seems happier than ever; but I know she's going to want some more of Tom before the leaves need raking.—N.A., *Chesapeake, Virginia*

Girl Meets Girl

A MASSAGE IS JUST THE THING TO GET THOSE
SAPPHIC FIRES FLAMING

*B*eing a senior executive in an international accounting firm, I have little time for a social life, let alone sex. As a matter of fact, the most exercise I get is a steady workout in hotel exercise rooms. It was stressful, to say the least, and I guess it must have shown, because one day a friend of mine suggested that I get a total body massage to relieve my stress.

I put it off and put it off until I was finally able to work it into my busy schedule. When the day rolled around, I arrived home just minutes before the masseuse showed up. When the doorbell rang, I opened the door to find an attractive young woman of medium height and build with soft, brown hair shimmering in the afternoon sunlight. Her eyes were warm and riveting. Strangely, I was immediately attracted to her. I reacted to her as I'd reacted only to men in the past, yet toward this woman my attraction felt very right.

When she came in, she noted the fact that I was still dressed and that our time, though not rushed, was limited. I watched as she immediately started setting up her equipment and preparing the oils and scents. I should have been getting ready, but all I could do was watch, mesmerized by the beauty of this woman's lithe body covered by a light cotton shift. I finally broke the silence by asking if she would like a glass of wine, and in the same anxious breath I asked her name. We laughed together at the awkwardness. Then she said, "Yes, and it's Alice."

Alice threw a jazz tape into my stereo system, and when she went to draw a warm bath, I turned on the speakers in the bathroom. Soon I was being led into the bathroom. Motioning in a questioning manner, she began to remove my clothes. She slowly pushed my jacket over my shoulders and placed it on a chair. Gently she turned me to face the full-length mirror and, standing behind me, she reached around and began to slowly rub my breasts through my blouse, searching out each button and carefully and deliberately unbuttoning me top to tail. My heart began to race and my breathing became deeper and shorter as a warm glow began to sweep over my entire body. Soon I began to tingle all over, and then I felt the juices flowing in my pussy.

Alice further heightened my excitement by rubbing my thighs and fondling my buttocks as she unzipped and removed my skirt. Not letting it fall to the floor, she gently pushed it down to my ankles and guided my shoe-encased feet out of the gathered material.

Alice stepped back from me and removed her cotton shift. I watched, a voyeur from my position in front of the mirror, and I gasped at the beauty being revealed before me. Alice was wearing a pair of white silk exercise shorts and a thin, white cotton tank top which left little to the imagination. Her breasts were firm and round, with the darkest areolae I have ever seen, easily visible through the material. Her nipples jutted out at least three quarters of an inch.

Obviously noticing my interest in her body, Alice whispered that my strong nipples were pushing out of my bra and that maybe they would like to be released. Before I could answer, she unfastened my bra and slipped her smooth fingers over my shoulders, pushing the straps forward, letting the material fall free of my aching orbs. Alice reached under my arms and gathered my breasts into her strong hands. She fondled them with the gentlest of touches, paying particular attention to my sensitive nipples. As she continued her ministrations, I began to moan and feel the waves of pleasure surround me even more—I felt an intense orgasm building deep within my body.

Not wishing me to reach that ultimate point of pleasure so quickly, Alice moved her hands slowly down my stomach and penetrated the waistband of my panty hose with two of her fingers. Then, ever so slowly and gently, her hands moved down my legs, pushing my panty hose down to my ankles. Removing my shoes, Alice pushed the bunched up nylon off my feet. With her soft, pert lips she began to kiss my toes, then she slowly worked her way up my legs to the lacy softness of my panties to begin the process all over again.

Alice's applied magic, through the sensitivity of her mouth, sent my senses into orbit. As she neared my rounded butt-cheeks, I fought the urge to reach around and guide her head into my crack. My mind was filled with images of past experiences of rear entry, but the desire was heightened by a wanton desire to be taken by another woman. Alice continued to massage my ass with her lips and tongue as she slowly moved her soft hands gently around my hips to my love-mound.

As she touched my pussy, I exploded into an intense orgasm. Weak-kneed and wobbly, I almost fell over but for Alice's steadying arms. She said softly to relax and allow myself to be swept away. As my breathing subsided, I realized that I had my eyes clamped shut and that I was clutching Alice's hand to my pussy. Alice hugged me and gently reassured me that I was in good hands.

Easing me into the tub, Alice began the most sensuous massage I have ever felt—from a man or a woman. Using the loofah sponge to heighten my sensitivity, she tweaked my nipples to near orgasmic levels and rubbed my pussy with wanton abandon. Paying particular attention to my clit, she repeatedly brought me to the edge of orgasmic release, just to let me slide back again. The feeling she gave me was filled with waves of pleasure that took over my body and were so intense that I nearly passed out. In fact, all I really remember is Alice's sweet, soft voice whispering the question of whether I wanted more in the tub or did I need something else? I couldn't imagine what else there could be, but I was so totally captivated and relaxed that I said I was game for anything she had in mind.

Helping me out of the tub, Alice led me to the massage table. Pouring warm oil all over my back, butt and legs, Alice systematically massaged and rubbed each inch of my skin, releasing the last vestiges of tension in each muscle. Working up my legs, my anticipation grew as she neared my butt, only to be disappointed by her avoidance. She did the same starting from my neck down. This time I found myself unconsciously humping the table. Alice sarcastically asked if I had a problem.

To this I responded, "I want more, I want to feel you. I need you to touch me!" I surprised myself. I'm usually a demure person when it comes to sex.

Alice asked me to be specific: "What do you need? What do you want to feel? Where do you want me to touch you?"

I could only respond with, "My butt."

Alice poured more oil down the crack of my ass and ever so slowly began kneading my ass-cheeks. I responded by humping in time with the rhythm of her motions.

It was then that I realized that if I wanted something, I would either have to ask for it specifically or take more control of the situation. But I was hopelessly lost under the control of Alice's magical fingers. All I could do was roll over as Alice moved to the head of the table. A bit surprised, Alice asked, "What's this? Do you want something else?"

I said yes, in a deep, throaty voice, and added, "Concentrate on my tits and pussy!" Alice responded immediately by placing her fingers on my pussy mound and working them aggressively into my soaked love-hole, saying, "Now, there is the real woman I've been searching for."

Becoming more bold, I reached behind my head and began to slowly rub up and down the backs of Alice's legs and ass. Responding to her moans, I began to slowly remove her silky shorts. Alice was totally nude in seconds and inches from my head. I asked that she spend time on my tits and nipples, and Alice serviced them as only a woman can. Alice asked if I wanted them kissed and sucked, and I surprised myself by saying, "Yes. Oh, please, yes!" As she was sucking and rubbing, I became more involved: "Rub my pussy, finger-fuck me until I come. Alice, don't stop this time. Fuck me, make me come." Fingering me hard, harder than I have ever done for myself, but gently and knowingly as only a woman can, Alice brought me to an intense orgasm that had me shaking for what seemed like hours. As my spasms subsided, Alice gently rubbed my pussy and kissed my mouth.

I'd never kissed a woman before, and I'd always thought it would be strange, but at that moment I wanted and got the deepest, wettest, longest and most sensual kiss of my life. Alice captured my mind with it. I still can't imagine how long it was before Alice, panting sensuously, said that it was time to wrap things up. She had enjoyed herself so much, however, that she offered me a special treat, if I had the time.

Nodding approvingly, I let her take control again as she moved to the other end of the table. Again, she began a slow, deliberate lip and tongue massage of my feet, legs and pussy. When her hot tongue reached the inside folds of my pussy, Alice lit my fire and quickly brought me to the boiling point of orgasm. I was out of control, screaming, "Yes, suck my pussy, you're making me come, fuck me with your tongue, yes, I'm coming, coming . . ."

Bidding Alice good-bye at the door was much like seeing your best friend leaving you. Tenderly I kissed her lips, tasting my pussy juices for the first time in my life.—*T.L.*, *Fairfax*, *Virginia*

STRANGE INTERLUDE LEADS TO
A ROOM OF THEIR OWN

*F*or my birthday a few months ago, a friend of mine gave me two tickets to see a Broadway show. Naturally, my husband and I were excited to be going the minute we received the tickets. The night before the show, however, my husband came home from work and said he had a very important business meeting the next day and wouldn't be able to go. I was upset at first, but then I decided to call my friend Darlene (who had given me the tickets) to see if she would be able to go with me. She said she didn't have any plans and would be happy to come along.

The following morning I picked Darlene up at her house and we drove to the train station. The conversation on the way into the city was about our husbands. Darlene explained to me that she doesn't enjoy having sex with her husband anymore.

"I'm tired of him humping me and then falling asleep. It seems like it's usually over in five minutes or less," Darlene said. "Is your husband good in bed?"

"He's okay, but I would prefer more foreplay," I said.

As the conversation continued, Darlene looked at me all of a sudden and said, "I've always wanted to see what it would be like to make love to a woman." When she said this, she gently slid her hand up my thigh and squeezed my hand. My heart beat a little faster as she looked into my eyes. I have always had feelings for Darlene, but because we were both married, I never pursued anything.

She held me for a little while and then eventually let go. We didn't say anything more until we arrived at Grand Central. When we stood up to get off the train, we faced each other and she moved her body close to me. So close, in fact, that I could feel her hard nipples press against mine through our clothes. I had to resist the urge to kiss her since people were all around us.

We finally made it out of the station and started walking toward Broadway. After we walked for ten minutes, Darlene announced that she had to go to the bathroom. Since I've been to the city many times before, I suggested we stop at a hotel. They never know if you're a guest or not. When we reached the bathroom, Darlene grabbed my hand and we both went into the handicapped stall.

"What are you doing?" I asked. "Someone will catch us, crazy!" As I said this, I just kept smiling because the only thing I wanted to do was kiss her.

"I'm not doing anything," Darlene said as she pushed her body up against me.

Darlene moved her face right up to mine and said, "Now I got you right where I want you." She licked my lips gently before she softly kissed them. Next thing I knew, she was unbuttoning my shirt as we kept on kissing. I could feel my pussy getting wet just from her kissing me, so I couldn't imagine how wet it would be if we started doing anything else.

When my shirt was all the way undone, and my bra as well, Darlene pulled away from our kiss and looked into my eyes. She brought her index finger up to her mouth and licked it with the tip of her tongue. Then she moved her hand down to one of my hard nipples and started to circle the areola with her wet finger. Darlene did the same thing with her other hand to my other nipple. My knees were about to buckle.

Darlene kissed me gently on the lips one more time and moved her head down toward where her hands were. I looked down to see Darlene push my breasts together with her hands as her head moved back and forth, the tip of her tongue gently flicking one nipple and then the other. I didn't think my nipples could get any harder, but I was wrong. Each time her tongue touched one, it seemed to get a tiny bit harder.

I could feel my pussy throbbing, and I knew I was going to explode soon. I was moaning so loud, I thought for sure we would be arrested. As Darlene's tongue massaged my nipples, her hands were massaging the under parts of my breasts, squeezing them lightly and lifting them up at the same time. It felt so wonderful that I didn't want her to stop. I grabbed her head and pulled her closer to my chest. She was making me crazy.

As I grabbed Darlene's head, she reached under my skirt and

moved my panties to the side. Her middle finger moved into my slit.

"You are so wet," Darlene said. "You must like what I've been doing so far."

All I could do was moan louder. Darlene pushed her finger gently into my soaking wet hole and then slid it almost all the way out.

"Do you want me to put it back in?" Darlene asked.

"Oh, yes! Please don't stop. You're going to make me explode," I said.

"Then tell me what you want," Darlene said.

"I want you to put your finger in my pussy and make me come," I said.

Darlene slid her finger into my hole again and just twisted it around really slow. That was when I lost it and started coming all over her hand. I could feel my pussy contracting around her finger, and I didn't ever want her to remove it.

As my breathing returned to normal, we heard someone enter the stall next to us. That's when I suggested to Darlene that we get a room.

"What about the play?" Darlene asked.

"Who cares," I said. "I want to make love to you for the rest of the day."

When we checked in and got up to the room, we ordered a bottle of champagne. It didn't take us long to pick up where we'd left off.

After the champagne was delivered, I popped the cork and poured two glasses. I turned to Darlene, who was standing by the bed watching me. We didn't say a word, we just gazed into each other's eyes. I could feel my body tingle as we stepped toward each other and kissed. We started taking off each other's clothes as we kissed. I laid Darlene down on the bed and positioned myself on top of her.

"Now I have you right where I want you," I said to her.

"Prove it," Darlene said, kissing me again. I moved my face away and reached for a glass of champagne. I took a sip of it and put the tip of my finger into the glass. With my wet finger, I traced around her nipples with the cold champagne. I could feel her nipples getting hard from my touch.

"I love that. I love when you touch my nipples," Darlene moaned. When both her nipples were rock-hard, I lifted myself up so my breasts were above hers. I lowered myself slowly so that the tip of her nipples touched mine. I moved my body up and down so that just our nipples rubbed against each other. As Darlene moaned louder, I moved a little faster. Then I repositioned my body so that my nipples rubbed against Darlene's stomach. My tongue started going to work on her nipples, licking and flicking the tips of them.

"Oh, yeah, suck my nipples! Suck on them. I love it!" Darlene moaned.

So I started sucking on her nipples. They were rock-hard in my mouth. As I sucked each one, I continued to flick the tip with my tongue.

Darlene was going wild. Her hips were moving against my body, so I reached down and felt her pussy lips with my finger. She was soaked! I pushed my finger gently into her hole and pulled it out. I stopped sucking on her nipples for a minute so I could circle her nipples again with my finger. I spread her pussy juice all around each nipple and then looked into her eyes. I put my finger into my mouth and sucked the rest of the juice off. After I pulled my finger out of my mouth, I started sucking her sweet nectar from her nipples.

"Oh, my God, you're making me crazy," Darlene said. She was moaning so loud that I thought I would have an orgasm just listening to her.

While I was still sucking on Darlene's nipples, I moved my hand back down toward her pussy. My body was on top of hers, so it was easy to slip my finger back into her juicy hole. As I did this, I stopped sucking her nipples and moved up to kiss Darlene on the lips. Darlene reached down with her right hand and I felt her finger slide into my pussy.

"Oh, my God, you're so wet!" Darlene said.

This seemed to arouse her even more. We both moved our fingers in and out of each other's pussy with the same rhythm.

"Oh, yeah," I said. "You're going to make me come!"

We moved our bodies against each other as our fingers moved slowly in and out of our slippery pussies.

When I felt Darlene's pussy start to contract around my finger, I slowly pushed it in as far as I could. She went crazy. You should have heard her scream. Right about the same time, I exploded, and I could feel my own contractions pulling Darlene's finger in and out of me!

Our orgasms were so similar, it was hard to tell who was who. Needless to say, we never made it to the show. But we do go to New York City a whole lot more often.—*L.S.*, *Mamaroneck, New York*

ROOMMATES FIND SOMETHING ELSE
THEY HAVE IN COMMON

I have a story to tell you, and I'm actually kind of excited that I really have the nerve to write it down.

I have been reading *Penthouse Letters* since I first found a copy in a friend of mine's dad's room one night during a sleepover. I'm twenty-two now, and I read it every time I get drunk enough to go buy one. I may be an anomaly among women, but I must admit that after reading the letters and looking at the pictorials (especially the multigirl ones) I masturbate fiercely. When I see three girls going at it, it really puts me over the edge. Keep 'em coming! (No pun intended.)

I am at work right now, but in my office things are slow so I decided to relate this story.

I live in a small-town suburb of Philadelphia where you don't expect much to happen, and not much does. My name is Jenny

and I have shoulder-length brown hair, a rather skinny body—
but decent enough to look at, I guess—and since high school I
have generally been regarded as preppy.

I rent a part of a house with my best friend Samantha. She is
really pretty, half-Spanish with long, curly, jet black hair. Her
face, with its dark eyes, looks like a model's. She comes from a
wealthy family, and her stepdad owns the house we live in.

Samantha always had it all, and every girl in school envied
her, even her friends, even me. I come from a small and not so
well-to-do family. I couldn't go to college, and since Samantha
didn't even want to go to college, we ended up moving in together.

Sexually, Samantha is pretty much a whore. I don't mean anything bad by this, it's just that she has to have sex all the time. I,
on the other hand, have only recently found out what an actual
hard cock looks like. I've always been shy, and I guess I still am,
and yet I've always had a secret sex life in my mind that would
rival anyone's.

I was always fascinated with Samantha and her attitude, and
she has helped me enjoy sex. It started out as a game. Samantha
has always had a maid, and when we moved in together I found
out that without domestic help, she's a slob. The good thing is
that I don't mind doing housework, and it's a pretty good trade-
off, when you get down to it. I mean, I pay next to nothing in
rent, we don't have to pay the utilities, and we've got all the best
appliances, a killer sound system—home entertainment center,
as Samantha calls it—and a computer apiece, with all the latest
software and access to the Internet.

Anyway, one day, when I was doing the dishes, Samantha
came up behind me just out of the shower and hugged me. I could
feel her boobs rubbing against my back as she kissed me on the
cheek good morning. This wasn't too unusual—we always walk
around topless. I giggled and turned around, only to find that
Samantha was buck naked. I ran my eyes over her perfect body—
it was the first time I'd really seen her completely naked.

I couldn't help but stare at her shaved pussy. I blushed and she laughed. "I think that somewhere, deep down inside, you're thinking about what it would be like to be a man right now," she said to me.

She laughed, but I felt a little self-conscious. And do you know why? Because it was true! I wasn't just admiring her body objectively; I was admiring her sexually.

I asked her what she wanted me to do. She suggested I massage her entire body, and then she just walked back into the bedroom. I didn't know if she was serious, and I finished the dishes and walked into her room expecting to see her dressed and giggling like usual—she's such a kidder. But she wasn't kidding, and she was lying on her back on the bed.

I didn't say anything. I didn't know what to say or do, really.

"Go get your lotion. It smells so good," she said. I felt a shiver of apprehension and sexual excitement at the prospect of feeling her naked body. I was still a virgin, and she looked so calm and reassuring. I went to my room and found my lotion, my hands shaking and mouth dry as I returned. She was sitting up.

She somehow knew I needed to be prodded a little to open up, and I was playing like a lost puppy into her hands. She was so beautiful that at that moment I would have done anything for her; I did actually, and I still do. I love her so much.

But anyway, she smiled and said, "You don't have to, Jenny, if you don't want to. I'll understand if you're not into it. We can forget it all."

"Not into what?" I asked, even though I knew damn well.

"You know, get sexual."

I told her I wanted to and that she was just the person I wanted to do it with my first time. She asked me what I was willing to do with her, and I felt an electric shock enter my slit when I said, "Anything."

I went to shut the door, I guess as a habit, and when I turned back around Samantha was rubbing her pussy. I just stared in fascination. She knew she had me. I silently and slowly undressed, embarrassed because my pussy wasn't shaved. But I'm not a hairy person, so I tried to calm my nerves by thinking that it wasn't too bad—like that really mattered.

Samantha smiled at me and looked at my pussy. Then she took my breath away when she reached out and fingered my pussy lips. I was so wet I thought I would faint. She picked up the lotion that had fallen to the floor, then tossed it aside.

"Together we have enough of our own lotion, Jenny," she said. She then stood up and, with the swiftest, smoothest steps, walked up to me and put her tongue in my mouth. I felt the first stirrings of orgasm as she kept rubbing my pussy. I could feel her saliva dripping into my open mouth, and I sucked it in and drank it like a hungry wolf.

Samantha pushed my head to her boobs and I suckled and kissed each one. She started screaming like mad, and finally she yelled out, "I can't take it any longer!"

She bent her head down to my nipples and started feverishly licking and nibbling them. My knees started to go weak, and she must have sensed this, for she immediately told me to lie back on the bed. I did, and she then got on top of me and pressed her body against mine. After kissing my mouth and my neck, she went back to work on my modest boobs as her fingers slipped into my now soaking pussy. Eventually she licked and kissed down my stomach, and I can't describe the anticipation that I felt when she began to lick all around my pussy.

Finally, she spread my pussy and then looked up at me. "What would you like me to do? Would you like me to take my time, or do you want me to give you the most incredible orgasm you have or ever will experience?"

I must have zoned for a moment, because I didn't really hear her question.

"Jenny?" she asked.

"What?" I answered.

"What would you like?" and then she repeated her question.

I giggled, and then we both broke up laughing.

"Do me," I said, and for the next ten minutes I really zoned out. I've never done drugs, but I felt the way you must feel when you're high. She knew exactly where everything was (which I guess is pretty obvious). She licked my inner thighs all over, and then she started fucking me with her tongue, darting over and around my clitoris. And when I started heaving, she stayed right with me until the very end.

I was looking at her while she continued to lick me, and all I wanted to do was lick her pussy. It was, like, the most important thing in the world to me then. Samantha's face was so wet with my come that when she kissed me I could taste myself. I had tasted myself before, because I like licking my fingers clean after a masturbation session. But this time it was so awesome, tasting me in her mouth.

Samantha got up and went over to her little couch next to her bed and sat down. I waited until everything calmed down a little and then looked over. She had a dildo in her pussy really deep, and I watched amazed and subdued. Then she reached to her side, grabbed a smaller dildo and stuck it up her ass. Good God, I would never have dreamed that this kind of stuff could be arousing. It was a very educational day for me.

All I could do was watch, so horny I didn't know what to think or do. She suddenly pulled out the front dildo and tossed it to me on the bed.

"Lick it and tell me if you like it."

Oh, I liked it very much, and I told her so.

"Why don't you come over and lap my pussy like I did yours."

I smiled and looked at her pretty face. She spread her wet pussy lips really wide. I still couldn't think of anything to say. I looked at the dildo in my hand. It was glistening and slimy. I did love how she seduced me, and I loved being sexual with her.

She was opening me up and making me feel like a vixen. I wanted to be hers, even though I really didn't think of myself as a homosexual. I don't think of it that way, really—it's just sex. Once I tasted the goo on the dildo, I knew I was hooked.

Samantha leaned back on the couch and spread her legs. I could see the wetness in her pussy and knew I would eat it. I sexily crawled off the bed and across the floor to her waiting hole. She caressed my hair and then arched her back, pushing her pussy out to me. I didn't even touch it; I stayed on all fours and began to lick all around it. I wasn't apprehensive, anymore. I was just into it, and I wanted to work her up like she did me.

I began licking her smooth pussy and then, as I got more into the groove—literally—her taste and smell subdued me and I lapped away like a kitten, pushing my tongue as far into her warm and salty hole as I could. As soon as Samantha began to moan a little, I sucked her whole pink pussy into my mouth.

Soon I felt Samantha's hands on my head as she gently pushed me back onto the floor, sitting on my face.

I could taste her and feel the wetness on my face. She squealed and continued to grind her pussy on my chin. That's when she really came, and I was almost smothered with her pussy. I swallowed eagerly every drop of cream as if my life depended on it.

I'd never thought about sex with a girl before that morning, but I suggest trying it because it is like nothing you'll ever experience. I am happily sexually active with Allen (my man), but he doesn't know that his fun with me is due to Samantha's fun with me.—J.A., *King of Prussia, Pennsylvania*

THE ONLY THING BETTER THAN A
TONGUE IN YOUR PUSSY? THREE TONGUES

I recently went on an all-girl vacation to an island, with three buddies. Tracey is my closest friend, and we were joined by two girls, Giselle and Dierdre, that Tracey works with. Dierdre and I are married, and Giselle and Tracey are single. We are all in our late twenties and attractive.

Of course, on the flight down Giselle and Tracey were talking about meeting some guys at the resort. Dierdre and I, being married, kept quiet, but I was thinking that a little sexual encounter would be fun. I've had a few affairs that my husband has no idea about.

The four of us spent the first day on the beach, just relaxing. All of us except Dierdre were wearing thong bikinis that left little to the imagination. Dierdre wore a one-piece. We were approached by a lot of guys, but nothing really interested us.

After dinner, with nothing promising, we decided to go back to our villa and just hang out with each other. Tracey ordered a few bottles of champagne. We all had a few drinks, and I was getting to know the other girls better, when Tracey suggested we each tell a secret about our sex life. Tracey volunteered me to go first. Dierdre didn't think our game was a good idea, but I started anyway.

I told them that my boss Eliot is very good-looking. When he was away on a recent sales trip, I got a frantic call that he had left some important files in his office. He wanted me to get the next flight out and bring him his work. He said he'd need my help all week, and that I should plan on staying.

I'd never gone on a sales trip before, and getting away sounded interesting. I called my husband, told him about the emergency, and got the next flight. I got there in the late afternoon, and was met by Eliot at the hotel. He decided that his customers Tom and Earl would meet us there to finish the contract. I checked into my room, then went to Eliot's suite. Tom and Earl were already there.

We finished our work around eight P.M., and I got up to leave. Earl, who was really hung, suggested that I stay for a drink and some coffee. Tom, also very handsome, sat next to me on the couch and, after a drink, placed his hand on my thigh while we talked. Eliot was soon on my other side. As Tom went to kiss me,

I could feel Eliot's hand on my other thigh. I was incredibly horny, and offered no resistance to his kiss.

Before I knew it, my dress was up around my waist and both men were rubbing my pussy through my panties. Earl came around the back of the couch, pushed my dress down off my shoulders and took my bra off. Tom now had his hand in my panties and began to remove them. They then removed my dress, so all I had on was stockings and pearls. I was sitting, totally nude, with my legs spread wide open for three studs.

Eliot told me he'd always wanted to fuck me, and that I was about to be completely and thoroughly fucked. They brought me close to orgasm several times, playing with my pussy and tits for an hour while they remained clothed. When Earl asked me if I was ready for three cocks, all I could mutter was, "My pussy is ready."

Eliot began to remove his clothes first. When he took his underwear off, he had the biggest, fattest cock I'd ever seen. Eliot began to eat my pussy out, as Tom and Earl also stripped. Eliot got up, and Tom put the head of his cock just inside my pussy. Eliot put his cock in my mouth. I held Earl's organ in my hand. Earl and Tom each took turns fucking me as I sucked on Eliot's enormous cock. I had several orgasms.

Eliot finally withdrew from my mouth and began to penetrate my already well-fucked cunt hole. I could feel every inch sliding in. When he got all the way in, he withdrew, then slammed back into my pussy, and set me off on the most intense orgasms I'd ever had. I was writhing and bucking in a frenzy. Eliot completely filled my pussy with each thrust. I was in heaven when he finally filled my hole with cream.

I fucked and sucked the three guys all night, in every position we could think of. My favorite was when I was on top of Eliot, with my back turned to him. I humped his huge cock while Earl and Tom took turns filling my mouth. On Tuesday morning we quickly finished up our work and had an orgy that lasted until Friday morning, when I went home. Eliot was right when he said I would be thoroughly fucked.

When I finished my story, Giselle asked me if I still fuck Eliot. I told them he knows my pussy is his anytime he wants it. I turned to Tracey and said, "Now it's your turn."

To be brief, Tracey told us she loves to be facedown on the bed while her boyfriends fuck her ass. I could feel my panties soak when she told us she has huge orgasms when her lover comes in her ass. I could see Dierdre, who was really shy, blushing from all our sex talk.

Tracey told Giselle it was her turn. Giselle began by telling us she'd been to bed with other women. She had been sleeping regularly with a girl from work, and her boyfriend didn't know it. She went on to tell us that only another woman knows how to eat pussy, and the best is the feeling of your tongue in another girl's pussy when she is coming. The first time she had sex with a woman, an older woman seduced her. In their many love sessions, the woman had taught her how to make love to another woman's pussy. While she said she loves her boyfriend's cock in her cunt, her orgasms are much longer and more intense with women.

I was getting hot as she gave us all the details of how her older woman had used vibrators and dildos on her. I had often fantasized about having sex with women.

Tracey told Dierdre it was her turn. Dierdre very nervously told us she'd only had two lovers, and that she was true to her husband. We asked her if she'd ever had an orgasm, and she said, "I think so." She told us she had a "regular" sex life, that she sometimes gave her husband blowjobs but he never came in her mouth. She also said they have sex about once a week.

I asked her if she ever fantasized. She admitted that she had found other women attractive, and wondered what it would be like to be with another woman. I was sitting closest to Dierdre who, while shy, was the prettiest and had the best figure of the four of us.

I leaned over to kiss her, and found no resistance. This was the first time either of us had ever kissed a woman passionately. In no time, Dierdre and I were embracing and I was removing her panties. With her panties off, I spread her legs wide open and had my first taste of pussy. Giselle and Tracey were now alongside Dierdre, rubbing her tits and kissing her all over. Giselle was telling her how sexy she was. I had my tongue deep in her pussy. We were all working on a different part of Dierdre when I sensed she was about to explode in orgasm. She started bucking and moaning uncontrollably. I kept my mouth firmly planted on her soaked little slit as she came.

When things calmed down a bit, Dierdre realized that that had been her first real orgasm. We all decided that we should forget about men for the week, and have our own private orgy, with Dierdre being our little slut. While we all had sex with each other, we paid special attention to Dierdre's pussy, making sure she had as many orgasms as she could stand. We sucked each other's pussies out constantly. Several times Giselle, Tracey and I ate Dierdre's pussy out at the same time. I got really turned on when Dierdre was thrashing around in orgasm, with my tongue stuffed up her pussy.

By the end of the week, Dierdre was also an expert at eating our pussies to orgasm. When we got home, we never repeated our experience together, but at least we all have another story to tell if the situation arises.—*N.D.*, *La Crosse, Wisconsin*

Serendipity

CRAWLING: UNDER CARS, OVER COCKS

I was driving through southern Pennsylvania on my way home from Baltimore when the inevitable happened. It was late January and the roads were really bad. I was trying to make it to a motel when my car gave a tortured gasp and quit. I suppose it could have been worse, but I nearly froze my ass off getting to a phone to call a garage.

When the tow truck arrived I warmed up immediately. The tow-truck driver was a female, a tall, well-built woman of about twenty-five, with long blonde curls dangling out from under her woolen cap. Her smile was enough to melt the ice on my coat. Even through her parka I could tell she had a great body. She was big boned, but well proportioned.

Kelly was every bit the professional. Ignoring the snow and slush, she crawled under my deceased vehicle and hooked it up to the truck. In a matter of minutes we were bouncing down the road in her rig. If you've ever ridden in a tow truck, you know they're real bumpy. I glanced over at Kelly. With the warmth inside the cab she unzipped her coat to expose a cold-hardened set of nipples poking through her work shirt. Her magnificent chest came close to bursting free of her clothing with each bounce. Somehow I managed to keep my cool, but I was warming up fast.

As we crawled through the traffic we struck up a conversation and got along really well. Pulling into the service station, I asked Kelly where I could find a place to spend the night. She offered to take me to a motel and, to my surprise, led me to a beautifully restored MGB roadster for the trip. "You don't think I drive that hulk when I want to have fun, do you?" Kelly asked.

Once I was checked in at the motel, I screwed up my courage and invited her to dinner. To my surprise and delight, she accepted. We made an interesting pair in the motel dining room—me in my traveling suit and Kelly in her stained work clothes. We flirted through a mediocre dinner. By the time dessert rolled around the conversation had gotten uninhibited. I invited her back to my room, then paid the check before we made a mad dash to my room through the snow.

I have undressed many women in my time, and I flatter myself that no combination of hooks, buttons, clasps or other obscure fastenings can defeat me. But as I nuzzled the back of her neck and reached around to remove her uniform, I found that her large frame and bountiful boobs made it difficult to unbutton her shirt. With a laugh she turned in my arms and began to work the buttons herself, stopping when just a hint of black bra showed. "Come on, big boy," she teased, "let's see if you can take it from here."

I gladly reached over, undid the front of her shirt and dropped it to the floor. No frilly bra for this large and bountiful woman! She needed functional, heavy-duty support for her 46DD boobs. I eased one bra strap over her shoulder and lovingly slid the cup down over her lusciously chubby breast until her taut, dark-brown nipple was exposed. I bent over and gently ran my tongue around it in circles. She began to purr as I tasted her mushy tits. When I finally took her nipple in my mouth and gently began to suck it, she stiffened and groaned with pleasure.

As I continued feasting on her succulent flesh, I reached down and undid her belt, easing her khaki trousers to the floor. I was about to go for her panties when I discovered something I hadn't expected: boxer shorts! She was wearing men's cotton boxer shorts! I couldn't help it, I started to laugh right into her fleshy boobs.

"Hey, come on! What did you expect to find on a working

woman?" she said. "You can't wear sexy lingerie when you crawl under cars for a living."

I slid her boxers down to the floor and led her to the bed. Since my tool was still in my pants. I elected to use my tongue to its best advantage. I slid my way down her magnificent body and parted her legs, exposing her blonde-bushed pussy. There were little beads of cunt juice on the delicate hairs between her legs, just begging to be lapped up. I parted her bush with my fingers, stroking back the wisps of curly hair to reveal her soft, pink cunt lips. I stroked upward with a finger to part the covering of her clit, and then gently began to brush my hot, wet tongue over it.

She had a strong, musky taste that I found very exciting. I began to eat her out in earnest, like I could swim in her gushing cunt forever. Soon her hips were moving about, and she was raising her big ass to meet my mouth while moaning with rapture. Each time she rose off the bed I gave her clit a suck. She was a lusty woman with a healthy appetite for life's pleasures; the work hard, play hard type. I licked a finger and plunged it deep into her love-tunnel while I continued to lick Kelly's budding clitoris. Each time I plunged into her she cried out, "Yes, yes!" over and over again.

Her moans increased as I continued to finger-fuck her, and I started having a hard time keeping my lips on her snatch as she writhed about. Suddenly she exploded in orgasm, writhing wildly as I desperately tried to keep my mouth over her love-knob. Eventually she calmed down. She lay there breathing hard while I rested my head on her crotch, occasionally giving her a playful lick to remind her I was there.

As soon as she had recovered she maneuvered her way down to my cock. Her hot breath sent chills through me as she began to nibble the tip of my cock through my underwear. Kelly's fingernails delicately traced the outline of my cock and balls. Then she gently pried my boner out of its covering.

She sucked eagerly, expressively, artfully. She alternated between darting her tongue around the tip and engulfing my entire member in her steaming, wet lips. Kelly delicately stroked my testicles throughout the blowjob. I was in heaven! With each stroke she did something new and exciting, using her tongue in ways I had never imagined. Kelly's fingers danced over my balls and slowly worked their way between my legs. Soon I felt her fingers stroking my asshole. I began to purr. Taking my reaction for a sign of approval, she delicately worked one digit up my asshole. Her finger probed my back door, sending waves of heady pleasure through my body as her talented mouth rode up and down on my prick.

All too soon, I felt my balls begin to shrink and my sperm begin to rise. I lay back helpless as I pumped load after load of hot spunk into her waiting mouth. She sucked each drop from me, draining my load until I began to think she would suck the life out of me. It was my turn to collapse in a panting, satisfied heap. I felt her crawl up beside me and I turned to hold her.

I don't know how long we cuddled, but eventually my lust began to rekindle and I began to play with her massive mammaries. She rolled over on her back and I began to lick and suck her silver dollar-size nipples. As I teased her tits, I reached down and began to trace the outline of her pussy lips through her thick bush, slowly working my way to the moist, pink flesh below. Her pussy was dripping wet, aching for a finger or a cock to slide right in.

I slipped my index finger into her gaping hole and pulled it out again. Then I ran my finger over her clit while I continued sucking on her juicy tits. Kelly spread her legs wide and began to roll her hips in response to my attentions. She began making little sounds of animal pleasure deep in her throat. I began to finger-fuck her and her hips moved faster. I shifted my attentions to her clit, and began to tweak her where it felt best. In no time she was thrashing wildly on the sheets as I rubbed her clit and sucked her nipples.

She reached down, grabbed my hand, placed it over her crotch and began to rub herself with it hard. I got the message: No more delicate teasing; it was time to come now. Kelly rubbed herself with my hand and began to cry out. I felt her grow rigid as an orgasm overtook her. I took over as she lost control, furiously rubbing her crotch and desperately trying to keep my mouth over her nipple as she shook and bucked. As her orgasm reached its peak she cried, "Fuck me, fuck me!"

Eager to comply, I pulled her up onto her hands and knees and plunged my rigid cock into her from behind. I pounded away like a madman, feeling my balls slap against her fat ass with each thrust. She was hot, wet and tight, too tight for such a big woman, I thought, and with each thrust I penetrated her delicate nookie as deep as it would go, driving her body forward with the force of my ramming.

"Your pussy is so tight," I said. "You like this cock in your tight pussy don't you?"

"Oh yes, fuck me, oh yes," she cried. Soon I heard her begin to cry out again with each jab of my prick, but this time it was an oncoming discharge. This big woman was multi-orgasmic. She was coming again. As she twisted in delirious delight I grabbed her hips and redoubled my speed, driving home my rigid rod faster and faster. Her ass rose higher to meet my furious thrusts. I continued to pound away before my prick pulsed and shot its load. I came close to blacking out with the force of it all.

We collapsed onto the bed and spent the rest of the night comfortably snuggled together, waking in the morning to once again take pleasure in each other's bodies before returning to the garage to get my car fixed. I'll never complain about car trouble again.—*R.J., Trenton, New Jersey*

REKINDLING DISTANT SPARKS WITH A TONGUE UP HER ASS

*D*o you know who this is?" a sultry female voice asked over the phone.

"I think so," I cautiously answered, looking about my office suite. My secretary continued to type away, oblivious. Traffic forty floors below was as still and blurry as an old photograph. "I hear you're married," I commented awkwardly.

"Miserably so."

I wasn't prepared for this conversation. I hadn't expected to ever hear from Alicia again. I shut the door to my office and asked her what had happened since we'd last seen one another. She related that she had married a wealthy stockbroker and promptly settled into a boring life filled with charity galas, lady friends who did lunch, gallery openings, and no sex.

"That's the part I can't handle," she confided. "You told me I'd never forget you, and I guess I wanted to let you know you were right."

Alicia and I had met years before, when she was a nineteen-year-old sorority queen. The summer we shared was filled with travel, great food and wine and unbelievably good sex. I had been only her second lover, but what she'd lacked in experience, she'd more than made up in enthusiasm and curiosity to try new things. I had been her "summer fling" that year—an older lawyer with a Jaguar, which she loved to drive to her friends' homes. She'd been eager and adventurous. In the seven years since I'd last seen her, I had often thought of her lithe body wrapped around mine in the middle of the night. As we spoke on the phone, I felt a long for-gotten—yet suddenly familiar—aching. I knew we would have to meet.

In the nights that followed I could scarcely keep my hands off my turgid cock for thinking about her incredible ass and tasty pussy. This young enchantress had once again cast a spell on me. After raising blisters on my palms for several days, I was delighted when my secretary told me I had a deposition scheduled in Alicia's city at the end of the week. I instructed her to call and reserve a suite at my favorite hotel. Alicia had a reception to attend that Friday; however, she agreed to meet me in the lobby at ten o'clock. When I called to finalize our plans, she coyly informed me that her husband would be out of town until Sunday.

At the end of the appointed day, I had drinks with friends and sped to the hotel. Standing at the reception desk was a vision of loveliness that took my breath away. Alicia's girlish charms had given way to the ripe sensuality of womanhood. Her five-foot-eleven-inch frame was wrapped in a gold and black sequin gown that accentuated her every curve. Her blonde hair fell over her bare shoulders, draping her pert, pointed breasts. A daring slit showed her tanned legs off. Every man in the room watched with envy as she greeted me with a kiss on the cheek. I returned her kiss and gave her a hug. Her hard nipples burned holes in my chest. I felt my organ stir.

"I have to use the rest room," she said. "Can we go to your room for a moment?" I waved her towards the elevator, watching her shapely ass strain against the confines of her dress with each step. The elevator attendant gave me a knowing smile. Something told me our dinner reservation was going to be wasted.

We took turns in the bathroom. I emerged and found her standing next to the bed. A single lamp lit the room. The sequin dress highlighted her shapely breasts, which now looked flushed and heavy in the soft light. "Care for a mint?" I jokingly asked. She wrapped her arms around me and our mouths melted in a kiss. Her soft, pink tongue probed deeply into my mouth, demonstrating the intensity of her passion.

I unzipped her dress from behind and watched her erect nipples and the smooth curve of her belly come into view. The haute couture dress fell to the floor, leaving her wearing only a small thong and high heels. My fingers slipped into her panties, grazing her wet lips and bush. I pushed between her hungry sex, mashing her pearllike clit with my finger, the way I remembered she loved to be stroked.

"God I've missed you," she gasped. My touch became more insistent, and I felt her legs give as she shuddered with her first orgasm.

"Lay over the bed," I said. Alicia spread herself facedown over the quilted duvet, arching her back to display her firm and well-defined ass-cheeks. I quickly removed my clothes and lay on top of her. My hard, seven-inch cock probed the soft crack of her ass, its sticky pre-come mixing with her perspiration. She moaned as I kissed her earlobes and shoulders. I reached beneath her quivering stomach and stroked her pink nub in time with the insistent probing of my swollen glans. Her pussy lips swelled, soaking my fingers with their wetness. "Come for me baby. Come all over my finger," I whispered huskily.

"God! Yes!" she cried. Groaning, her knees spread further and she collapsed on the bed. "Put your tongue in my pussy. I need it. Please, eat me," she implored. I kissed lazy trails down her smooth, tan back and slid her thong panties down her muscular thighs.

"Do you remember the position?" I asked. Alicia responded by grabbing her ass-cheeks and holding them wide apart.

"Yes," she whimpered. "Eat my ass."

I pushed my tongue deep into her puckered bunghole. Her hips thrust backward involuntarily as I turned my attention to her now sopping slit. Her curly, brownish-blonde cunt hairs were matted with her wetness. Two fingers filled her tight snatch, as my thumb busily worked her swollen clit. I sucked her wrinkled pussy lips into my mouth one at a time, savoring their salty tang.

"Oh baby, I'm coming again!" she cried. I licked her crack from top to bottom, sliding my fingers in and out of her pink hole as her pungent juices soaked my face and fingers.

"I want my fat cock in your mouth, girl," I groaned. Alicia whimpered and began to slather my huge, purple head with her long tongue the way I had taught her years before.

"I want you to shoot in my mouth, honey. Empty your nuts so I can taste it," she panted. I responded by pushing my meat past her pouting lips, filling her mouth with bulbous head and thick, veiny shaft. She renewed her insistent slurping, squeezing the swollen nuts that hung heavy between my legs. I watched her blonde mane bounce over my cock as my orgasm grew from within. My hips began to thrust forward involuntarily. Turning her blue eyes to mine, she paused and implored, "Shoot it." I responded by pumping out thick, salty ropes of white lava that she sucked from my jerking prick as if she were starving. Alicia covered my face with kisses as she stretched her long frame over my body.

"I've missed you so much," she sighed. I stroked her hair away from her face and kissed her. I cupped her ass in my hands and pressed my cock against her until it slowly swelled to fill the tight space between her thighs.

"Do you want that in your pussy?" I asked. She nodded. "Then put it in, baby," I told her.

Placing her feet on either side of my hips, Alicia lowered her swollen sex onto the hard, hot length of my rigid phallus. I raised myself on my elbows, as she wrapped her graceful arms around my neck. Fully supported, she stabbed my penis deep inside her, sucking in her breath as my cock crashed into her again and again. Her breasts bounced in time with her insistent bucking; her sex clenched my cock in a velvet vise. "I can't stand it!" she screamed. "Fuck me harder!"

I watched my throbbing penis pound into her young pussy without mercy. "That's it baby," I yelled. "Fuck my cock! Come for me!"

I shoved two fingers into her hot ass as she went over the edge in yet another mind-shattering orgasm, collapsing on my chest and biting my nipples. I threw Alicia on her back and worked my fat pole into her tiny sex hole one last time. Her legs entwined with mine and her breasts mashed against my hairy chest. Her mouth melded to mine as I pumped the thick shaft of my cock in and out of her hole. We fucked forever, it seemed.

"Faster," she panted, "I think I'm going to come again!" Her nails ran across my back as her sticky hole clutched my cock. Rising on my arms, I looked down and watched my greedy prick take its pleasure. Alicia's manicured nails tweaked my nipples, sending spasms down my spine. I could feel my shaft grow harder and longer as Alicia's cries of pleasure increased in volume and intensity.

"I'm coming, love," I shouted.

"Yes! Shoot your come in my pussy," she cried. With a loud groan, I blasted my white-hot load into her tightness. Alicia came at the same time and we collapsed in each other's arms.

When we recovered, Alicia poured a bubble bath while I called room service for champagne and hors d'oeuvres. What followed will have to wait for another letter!—R.L., New York, New York

A TEENY BIKINI AND A DIP IN THE POOL THAT ENDS UP OBSCENELY

*L*ast summer, my wife Dorothy and I were driving home from my niece's wedding in the next state. We decided to make an overnight stop, as once we got home there would be three teenagers in the house to kill any romantic ideas on our part.

The day was hot, and Dorothy said she wanted to try out her new bathing suit and see how I liked it. We pulled into a small motel just off the highway. I put on my suit and said I would meet her at the pool. Two young couples shared a table on one side of the pool, and a man in his sixties sat by himself on the other. When they all started to look behind me, I turned and saw my wife walking toward me in the smallest string bikini I have ever seen. Dorothy is a long-legged, forty-year-old blonde, with blue eyes and lovely measurements. Her suit covered her nipples and about twenty percent of the rest of her tits. The bottom covered so little that I didn't understand why I couldn't see her pussy.

Dorothy told me she was sorry she had taken so long, but she had ended up shaving her pussy bald so she could wear the suit at all. Then she asked me how I liked it, and I told her I liked it fine.

All the others were staring at us with envy and lust. She asked me if she still turned me on, and I told her to look at the bulge in my suit if she wanted an answer. She smiled and said she was so wet already she was ready to come without the fucking she expected me to give her in about five minutes.

"Why wait five minutes?" I asked.

Dorothy replied, "You'll see." She stood up and walked around to the end of the pool. When she got there she took a while carefully adjusting her bikini. She walked to the end of the diving board, adjusted the suit once more and dived in.

When she came up, she was shrieking at the top of her lungs. She swam to a ladder that was only a few feet from the older man and climbed out of the pool. She had lost her suit and was completely naked. She stood at the top of the ladder directly in front of the man for the length of a breath. With one arm covering her tits and the other between her legs, she ran off to our room. I noticed as she ran by that two of her fingers had disappeared into her cunt.

Everyone was frozen for about thirty seconds. Then a babble of conversation began as I stood up and hurried to our room.

I opened the door to find Dorothy lying on the bed, her fingers sliding in and out of her pussy at a furious rate. I closed the door behind me, and she was instantly on her knees in front of me, pawing at my bathing suit. As the suit dropped to my knees, she pushed me back onto the bed and began to slip her lips over the swollen head of my cock. Her mouth slid all the way down my shaft until her nose was buried in the hairs on my stomach. Then she began to bob her head up and down on my prick as fast as she could. She didn't slowly lick or nibble the way she usually does. She was just so hungry for my cock and the juice that it contained that she wanted it right away. She got it in less than two minutes. When she'd gotten as much of my come as she could from my prick, she threw herself on her back on the bed and pulled my face down to her newly shaved pussy.

"Eat my pussy now. Lick my cunt. Make me come with your

mouth." My wife had never been like this before. She was ramming her pussy against my mouth as hard as she could, and I had just begun to obey her, when she started spasming and let out a scream that I was sure would bring the police. She was gushing so much pussy juice onto my face and tongue that it was like a man coming. I was getting pretty wild myself, and refused to stop my box lunch just because she had one orgasm. I continued on until she had gone over the top twice more in quick succession.

She was still trembling from her third orgasm when she whispered that she wanted me to fuck her doggie-style. Dorothy rolled over onto her hands and knees on the bed. I stepped up behind her and my rod was buried in her gash before she finished asking. She was coming again in less than half a dozen long, deep strokes. I continued slamming my hips against her ass, filling her cunt with my seven inches as fast and as hard as I could. I had never felt as turned on in my life, and it seemed to me that my dick was bigger than it had ever been. She was coming every couple of minutes now. In contrast, I seemed to be able to go on forever. I must have plowed her cunt for about forty minutes before I felt what seemed like an explosion in my balls and pumped jet after jet of creamy white come into her love-tunnel, driving her to one last shuddering orgasm.

We sank down on the floor and fell asleep, my dick still buried inside her. We awoke about an hour before dawn and made love again, but more slowly and gently. We had showered and were ready to leave by six.

As we left our room, the door to the next room opened. The older man from the pool stepped out and called to us. He handed Dorothy her bathing suit, and thanked her for the chance to see "the prettiest sight I've seen in a long time." By way of thanking him, Dorothy pulled her skirt up to her waist, took off her bikini panties and handed them to him. Then she placed his hand on her pussy and leaned forward to kiss him full on the mouth. After that we left.—K.T., Tuscaloosa, Alabama

A FRIEND IN NEED BECOMES A FRIEND FOR LIFE

My name is Ray. I'm fifty-two and a widower. About five months back I was shopping at the local supermarket, getting some beer and smokes. At the checkout a young girl of nineteen was in front of me. She had a baby with her. Her bill came to forty-six dollars and change. She only had forty-one bucks, and was almost in tears. I said, "Let me help you," and gave her what she needed.

She waited till I checked out and I walked her to her car. She said, "How can I repay you?"

I responded, "How about having a beer with me?" She said okay, so I followed her home.

She had a small two-bedroom apartment, very clean, very nice. She said, "Let me put the baby down. It's time for his nap." I popped open two cans of beer and we sat on the couch. During our conversation I found out that her name was Nancy. She told me that the baby's father was a real bum. He didn't work, so she kicked him out. We finished off two beers and she finally said, "I don't have any money to give you, but I'll give you a blowjob, if that's okay."

I said, "No, I don't want anything for my money. But if you'll let me eat your little pussy I'd be delighted to have you blow me."

Nancy's eyes lit up. She stood up and said, "Let's go to the bedroom." We took off our clothes. I swallowed hard as I took in the curves of her body. Her tits were the size of oranges, with big, full nipples. I could see the pink of her cunt lips through the golden hair of her beaver.

Smiling shyly, Nancy asked, "How do you want to do this? My boyfriend was never one to go down on me." We lay on the bed and I started French-kissing her. I put my hand on her pussy, rubbing my finger in her little slit. Her button soon got hard and she started to moan softly. I moved my mouth down to her little tits and started sucking on her nipples, which were now puffed out and hard as pebbles. She started moaning much louder and put her hand on my cock, jerking it up and down.

After a few minutes of tit sucking I said, "I'm ready for some pussy licking." I told her to straddle my head, with her head facing toward my cock. Her cunt lips were swollen and wet with her excitement. Her clit was quite the size, and the head was out from under the hood. Her cunt was so small I could put my mouth around the whole thing, which I did. I shoved my tongue up her hole and fucked it like it was a small cock. Nancy shuddered and mashed her cunt to my mouth, then started sucking on my cock. It wasn't long before her thighs squeezed my head. She said, "Oh God, you're making me come!" and creamy juice started oozing from her hole.

I licked up all her cunt cream, then put my lips around her love button, sucking it in and out of my mouth. Nancy said, "Oh my God, I'm coming again already. Don't stop! Please don't stop!" Her cunt flooded my mouth for a second time. When her orgasm subsided she lifted her cunt off my mouth, saying, "I can't take any more. My cunt is too sensitive."

She sat on my belly and kissed me, saying "That was wonderful. I never came so hard in my life. But you never got off. Would you like to fuck me?"

I said, "I sure would." She lifted her ass up and straddled my hips. I felt her hand on my cock as she lovingly put it at the mouth of her cunt. I soon felt my cock sliding into the tightest cunt I've fucked in a long time. She was moaning, as inch after inch of my cock pushed into her tight, wet hole.

When she finally got it all, she said, "God, you're big." I could feel her cunt muscles pulsing around my cock as her cunt adjusted to the girth.

She started fucking up and down on my shaft, leaning over me so I could suck and chew on her big nipples. Her clit must have been riding up and down on my cock because she giggled and said, "Oh God, fuck me hard. I'm coming again! I can't believe it! I can't fucking believe . . . Oh, sweet Jesus!" I'd been holding back, but when she said that I started pumping hot come into her cunt. She kept moaning, "Oh God, oh God, I can feel your hot come. Don't stop. It feels good." I wish it could have lasted for hours, but I was soon drained.

When I got ready to go I told Nancy I had a lot of connections, and maybe I could get her a job. Within a week I had her a job as a receptionist.

That weekend she called and asked me to come over. When I got there she was dressed in a sheer robe. She handed me a beer and sat me down on the couch. Within minutes she had my cock out, giving it a tongue bath. I took my clothes off and Nancy dropped her robe. Her body looked even better than the first time. I told her I wanted to eat her pretty pussy. I had her sit in an easy chair and put her legs up over the arms, then knelt between her legs and started licking her slit. I soon had her cunt juice oozing out of her hole. She kept moaning, "Oh God, Ray, oh God. I can't stop coming with you. You make me come all the time!"

I told her to kneel so I could fuck her from the rear. Beads of cunt juice clung to her pubes. I wet the head of my cock with her juice and eased it into her hole. She moaned and pushed back, and I soon had it in to the hilt. I was looking at the little rosebud of her asshole, and I knew I wanted to fuck it. I wet my finger and eased it into her ass. She moaned, "Oh God, what are you doing?" I told her I was getting her asshole ready for my cock.

She screamed, "Oh God. Do it!" My cock was coated with cunt juice when I pulled out. I put the head at her rosebud and pushed. She moaned loudly as I pushed in. I told her to relax, that the hardest part was over. I soon had all of my cock in her ass and she started moaning, "Oh yes. Fuck it, fuck it." I put my hand on her cunt and rubbed her clit. She started fucking back and screamed, "Here I come, here I come. I'm coming!" Hearing that, I flooded her ass with hot come.

We fucked all weekend. I must have come seven or eight times. That was a few months ago. We still see each other on weekends, and her cunt is still as tight as the first time we fucked.—R.C., *Abilene, Texas*

DON'T PLAY WITH YOUR FOOD, FUCK AROUND WITH IT

*H*aving been twice married and twice divorced before the age of twenty-seven, I believed I had experienced everything a man and woman could do together sexually.

That held true until I met Veronica. She was in her midtwenties, had long naturally blonde hair, a perfect hourglass figure and beautiful legs. I entered my local bar, which was almost empty, and boldly sat down next to this blonde beauty. After a drink I struck up a conversation. She was charming, intelligent and nursing a broken heart. While we were talking I tried to look up her leather miniskirt, but every time I did she'd move just enough so I couldn't see anything. After some more conversation and drinks, I learned that her last boyfriend had left her horny and wet instead of high and dry. As she phrased it, she was kinkier than a knot in a rope while he was straighter than a monk.

As we continued to talk, I was finally rewarded for my efforts by catching a glimpse of a beautiful shaved pussy nestled between those long legs. The sight of that smooth pussy made my cock throb instantly. The bar was getting crowded, and Veronica asked if I'd like to go over to her apartment for a drink or two. I said yes. Actually, I think I yelled it.

I followed her in my car. She stopped at a grocery store, popped inside and quickly returned carrying a small bag. We finally got to her apartment and she offered me a drink as I sat down on a leather couch. After putting some soft jazz on the stereo she went to the kitchen, soon returning with two orange Popsicles in a glass. I leaned over and gave her a kiss, which turned out to be a tongue-probing adventure, and she ran her fingers around my steel-hard cock.

She then took a Popsicle and ran her tongue over it like it was a hard cock. All at once Veronica lay back on the couch and hiked her legs up on the coffee table, exposing her beautiful hairless pussy. I thought that was my cue to go to work but, as I watched in amazement, she eased the frozen Popsicle into her wide-open pussy. She was getting hotter by the minute as she forced the Popsicle in deep, then slowly removed it, rubbing her clit. Her ass began to lift up off the couch to the rhythm of the Popsicle dildo, until she reached a very intense climax.

Veronica looked over at me and asked, "Did you like it?" I nodded excitedly, as I undid my jeans and underwear to release my throbbing cock. She leaned over and flicked the pre-come off my cock with her soft tongue, then wrapped those wonderful lips around my cock like a velvet vise. Her blowjob skills were perfect. She quickly brought me near the limit, but as I got very close she quit and said she'd be right back. Veronica came back with two more orange Popsicles. Dropping to her knees, she started where she had left off. I felt a strange excitement as I felt the coldness of a frozen Popsicle and the warmth of her mouth going up and down my meat. I took hold of her head and fucked her mouth like it was an overheated pussy, finally filling her mouth full of come. She gladly swallowed it down, her lips milking my cock to the last drop.

Feeling very relieved, I told her it was my turn, and went and got a couple of Popsicles of my favorite flavor, which happens to be cherry. I eased one into her sticky gash while licking her clit. Soon she was moaning for me to fuck her with it, so I buried it in her hole up to the stick and lapped up the overflowing juices like a dog on a summer day. The Popsicle had melted to nothing, and I was about ready to give her a royal fucking, when she told me to go get the whole box of Popsicles.

I returned to find her with one leg over the back of the couch and her fingers buried deep inside her pussy. I set the box of Popsicles on the coffee table and eased my cock into her soft, wet pussy. I could feel her little pussy contracting when she said, "Sit up and fuck me."

We changed positions so we were sitting up facing each other. I was in heaven as I pounded her pussy and nibbled on her nipples. Veronica leaned back, picked up a Popsicle and handed it to me, saying, "Use it!" I told her my cock was a lot better. She said, "I've got more than one hole that needs to be filled," and she guided the hand with the Popsicle to her ass. I eased the Popsicle into her tight asshole. It broke, so I eased one of my fingers into her back door, since I've always liked to play with asses.

She moaned, "Oh, yes. Fuck me. Please, fuck me hard." I slowed down and bent her over the couch to give me a perfect shot at her sweet ass. I eased my cock into her tight ass until I felt the broken Popsicle. "Mmmm, yes" was all she said as I gave her ass one ball-busting fuck. Very soon I reached the point of no return. Grabbing hold of her shoulder and forcing my cock deeply into her ass, I filled it with come. We were both totally drained of energy, so we took a long, playful shower to rid ourselves of the stickiness.

I stayed that night with Veronica, and many since. We always search for more fucking food while at the grocery store.—A.F., *Topeka, Kansas*

RELOCATION RECONFIGURES WORKING RELATIONSHIPS

*T*his letter is to prove to everyone that fantasies can come true. Sometimes they just need a little push! Recently the object of my desires gave me the most incredible night of sexual pleasure I have ever experienced. Even now as I'm writing this, I can feel the wetness between my legs just thinking about him. Since then

I've been trying to think of a way to thank him. Seeing this letter in print in your magazine is the best way I can think of.

My fantasies about this guy began years ago when I first started working with him. I dreamed of ways to seduce him every time we traveled together, but my fear of rejection always won out (not to mention the fact that we were both married to other people). Then, unfortunately, he moved far away, leaving the telephone our only means of communication.

After not seeing each other for two years, we discovered we would both be attending the same convention. I made sure my company made my reservations at the same hotel he would be staying in.

After checking in and waiting for him for hours, he finally knocked on my door. While we were catching up on each other's life, my eyes kept wandering to his crotch, mentally undressing him. It didn't take long for us to realize our attraction was definitely mutual. He leaned over and gave me the most sensual kiss, which slowly became a powerful, hungry kiss. I couldn't believe this man's body was pressed against mine. We undressed each other, savoring each other's body with our eyes. As I finally got to unzip him, I ran my tongue down his smooth, sexy chest to the bulge in his pants. As his dick escaped from its constraints, I took him into my mouth.

Pushing me down on the bed, he kissed his way down my neck and shoulders, stopping at my breasts to squeeze my nipples with his fingers and then suck each one. I had to keep telling myself this wasn't a dream.

He worked his way down to my aching cunt. His tongue did things to my pussy that I had never experienced before. He explored every crevice. I had a tight grip on his head and pulled him closer, then pushed him away, begging him to put his cock in me. I had to feel him inside me!

With his body on top of mine, he slipped inside me easily and naturally. He told me to stop moving because he didn't want to come yet. That was all I needed to hear. I started bucking my hips to meet his. It was so intense that we exploded together almost immediately.

We both knew that this was only the beginning of our night together. We had a lot of years to make up for! After some time I decided it was my turn to let my tongue do the work. I slowly ran my tongue down his gorgeous body until I reached his inner thighs. I teased him by lightly licking his cock up and down. As I felt him get hard in my mouth, it made me wet and willing to do anything to please him. I began sucking his entire shaft while circling the head with my tongue. He grabbed my legs and had me straddle his face in a 69 position. His fingers spread open my pink lips and he slowly flicked his tongue over my clit.

We were fucking each other's face, giving each other the highest form of pleasure. He then asked me to sit on his cock. I turned around and placed his prick in my hole. I slowly slid up and down on his cock, then leaned over to kiss him. Tasting my own juices on his lips made me ride him faster and faster. Both of our hands fondled my tits. He put his hands on my hips and started fucking me harder. We finally collapsed in each other's arms after another phenomenal simultaneous climax.

I told him I couldn't get enough of him. We simply couldn't keep our hands and mouths off each other. Little did I know the best was yet to come.

He rolled me on my back and kissed me with the same sensuality as our first kiss. Before I knew it, he entered me again, slowly yet passionately. I took his hand and started licking and sucking each finger with the same ferocity I felt when I had licked and sucked his cock. With each lick of my tongue he pounded me harder and faster.

I told him I wanted him to fuck me from behind. I needed to feel his hard tool deep inside my wet pussy. As he entered me, he told me to touch myself. I didn't hesitate for a second. My thumb rubbed my clit as my fingers felt his cock going in and out. His shaft was dripping with my juices. He started running his tongue up and down my spine, causing the most erotic sensations I have

ever felt. His hand joined mine, bringing me to the most powerful orgasm I've ever had. Every nerve in my entire body tingled
with pleasure. He then came inside of me with the same intensity
as the first two times. The evening ended as perfectly as it had
begun, with the two of us passionately holding and kissing one
another.

I don't know when I'll see him again, but every night I think
about the next time we'll be together, fulfilling more fantasies
and creating more memories.

Thank you, my love, until we meet again.—*Name and address
withheld*

SHE KNOWS WHAT SHE WANTS—
NO IFS OR ANDS, JUST BUTTS

*L*ast fall I traveled to the East Coast for a two-day business trip.
Being single and horny, I decided to look up a girl whom I had
dated six years earlier, when I was in college. A mutual friend told
me that Joan was running a sales agency and was apparently
doing quite well.

After checking in at my hotel I looked up Joan's agency and
telephoned. She remembered me and seemed pleased that I'd
called her. Before I could issue an invitation, she suggested that
we meet for a drink at five and then go to dinner. She gave me
the name of a nearby lounge. After spending the afternoon going
over the next day's presentation, I decided to take a quick shower
before my date.

As I showered I tried to remember Joan, but in my memory she
blended in with a number of other girls I'd dated. I did remember
that she was quite studious and dressed rather plainly. Still, she
had a fine figure with a great set of tits. We never got much beyond a few kisses and a furtive grope now and then. My expecta-

tions were not very high but at least I would have some company for dinner.

We met at the designated spot, and I must say that Joan had chosen a very nice watering hole. Although she readily recognized me, I wasn't sure at first if the woman who said "Hello" was really Joan. For one thing, she had gone blonde and wore her hair in a short, businesslike style. Her basic blue business suit did a good job of hiding any curves, and she now wore glasses, making her look even more the successful businesswoman.

We sat in a booth and I went through two Jack Daniel's while Joan sipped white wine. We caught up on each other's career and talked about people we knew until Joan checked her watch and suggested we leave for dinner. On the way, I marveled at the self-assurance she had developed. It even showed in her driving—aggressive but safe. It was obvious she liked to be in control.

Dinner was excellent. Joan drank martinis while we ate, and by the time coffee arrived she had become a little more relaxed and much friendlier. Halfway through our first cup, Joan leaned over to me and, in a husky voice, asked if I would do her a favor. "Gladly," I responded.

She told me that she had been working very hard for months and, as a result, her social life was practically nil. "What I really need," she said, without batting an eyelash, "is a good fucking. You do like to fuck, don't you, Ron?"

Needless to say I was taken aback, but I managed to answer calmly, "Joan, not only do I like to fuck, I suspect I like to do just about anything else you'd want to."

Joan looked at me and said, "Good, let's go to my place for a brandy, and then some fun and games."

We drove to her place in silence—I guess both of us were wondering what was to come. Her apartment was expensive and nicely decorated, with a great view of the city from a small balcony. She poured a couple of snifters of very good brandy and we headed for her bedroom.

Joan's hands were all over me as we kissed. Her breath was hot and sweet, her tongue like a flaming sword. She began to undress me expertly as her hands and tongue worked me over. In a short time she had me naked. "Lie back and sip your brandy while I get ready for you," she whispered.

I did as I was told as Joan disappeared into the bathroom. While I waited, I couldn't help but be impressed by the size and hardness of my cock. I found myself sliding into a state of total sexual arousal, both physically and mentally. As I considered my good fortune, I heard Joan and looked up to see her standing in the doorway. "I'm ready now," she said.

My eyes took in her naked, slender figure, topped off by a magnificent pair of tits. My breath caught as I realized what she was wearing around her waist. She had donned a black leather harness, and projecting from the front was a very lifelike dildo.

The look in Joan's eyes had changed from wide-open and friendly to narrow and hard. She had applied dark mascara, which gave her a totally different look. "I suppose you're like most men. Get to a girl's apartment, have a quick fuck, leave her up in the air and go on your merry way. Well, if you want to fuck me, it's not going to be like that. I'm going to fuck you first—at my leisure and until you make me come."

I couldn't believe this was happening. She continued. "If you want me, you're going to have to serve up that cute ass of yours. The choice is entirely up to you. If it's a deal, we'll continue. If you don't want to, we'll have a nightcap, shake hands and you can leave—no hard feelings."

My mind was in a whirl. I had never been so aroused, but I'd never taken it up the ass either. In the end, excitement overcame trepidation and I said, "It's a deal, but please be gentle."

Joan promised me she'd go easy. She came over to the bed and positioned me so that I was facedown, on my knees and elbows, my ass stuck straight up. "I think I'm dealing with a virgin," she said. "I guess I'll have to do some breaking in first." I heard her fumbling in the nightstand and then felt my ass-cheeks being parted. The next thing I knew, she had coated the length of my crease with some sort of lubricant. Then I felt her finger gently probing my opening.

To be quite honest it was extremely arousing and I relished feeling more. She worked her finger in and out until I no longer resisted. "That was step one, sweetie," she said. "I think you'll need a little more work before we really get down to business."

I heard her reach into the nightstand again. Then I felt something pressing against my opening, some sort of butt plug. Joan proceeded to work it into my asshole, all the time talking dirty, telling me how much she wanted to fuck my virgin ass.

The next thing I knew Joan had me roll onto my back. Then she straddled me, putting her knees on either side of my chest. She thrust her "cock" between my lips and told me to suck her off until she came. I tried to remember how my girlfriends did it, and how it was done in the movies I watch.

I began sucking and stroking the dildo. It must have been rubbing against Joan's clit, because she started bucking wildly, exhorting me to suck her harder and harder. Finally she came with a great shudder and lifted herself off my face. "I think it's time we take that cherry of yours," she cooed.

Again Joan positioned me facedown. She removed the plug from my ass and I felt the dildo against my anus. I prepared myself for Joan's onslaught. Fortunately she was gentle and took great care in easing the dildo into me. She moved in and out at a steady pace and, with a free hand, reached under me to stroke my cock. It didn't take long before I came into her hand with a mighty spurt.

My orgasm sent Joan over the top again and we came almost simultaneously. When Joan pulled out I thought I was done for the night, but she had other ideas. "I'm ready to get fucked now," she purred. "Just lie back and relax until I get you ready." I looked at my limp stalk and doubted that it could rise again. Joan went out into the kitchen and returned with two large margaritas filled with crushed ice. "Sip this," she said, "You'll find it revitalizing."

As I did, she raised her glass to her lips and then engulfed my cock in her ice-filled mouth. The effect was instantaneous and my cock once again became hard as a rock. Joan looked deep into my eyes and said, "Now I want you to fuck my brains out, any position, any way you want."

I don't know how long it lasted. We fucked in every conceivable way. We started out with her on her back, then we fucked doggie-style and we finished with her on top. She became a wild woman, moaning and groaning, shouting and talking as dirty as any porno star I'd ever heard. Her cunt was insatiable and her clit was a hair trigger for her orgasms. Since I'd already had one massive shot, I was able to stay in control and put Joan through her paces. Never had I experienced anything so wanton, so unabashedly sexual, as this encounter with a woman who had been so shy and demure back in college.

Finally, when I felt an orgasm stirring in my loins, Joan sensed it also. "When you get ready to come," she said, "I want you to stick your cock up my ass and load me with your jism." That's all it took. I pulled out of her steamy cunt and easily slid into her asshole. Neither one of us lasted very long. As Joan diddled her clit, I let go another load. When we finally relaxed I disengaged and rolled onto my side. Joan looked at me, laughed and said, "I hope you don't think I'm forward or anything."

After cooling off and having a nightcap, Joan called me a cab. As I left she shook my hand vigorously, and said, "Nice job! I hope we can get together again." Somehow I felt like I had just received a promotion.—R.D., *Baton Rouge, Louisiana*

Gang Bangs

SERVICING THE TROOPS TO KEEP UP MORALE

*T*he experience I'm about to relate happened to my wife and me several years ago. I was a lieutenant in the army, and we had just gotten married. Alanna, my bride, was a petite, twenty-year-old honey with blonde hair and a body that wouldn't quit—and still won't!

It was Saturday night and we had gone out to dinner at a nice restaurant in the country. Alanna looked particularly sexy that evening in a clingy knit dress that hugged every curve of her luscious body. Beneath it she wore matching beige undergarments, complete with garter belt and stockings.

One the way back to post, I decided to fuck my sexy little wife under the stars. I pulled my car off the road and drove to a secluded area overlooking a large lake. As we kissed, my hands roamed over her body. I caressed her tits with one hand while the other was up under her dress exploring her dripping pussy.

The car was small, and the gearshift kept getting in the way, so I got out and went around to the passenger side. Opening the door, I took Alanna by the hand and helped her out. We stood and kissed for a moment, then I told her to turn around and hold on to the door. She bent over and grabbed the door, placing her head partly through the open window. I raised her dress, pulled the crotch of her panties to one side and shoved my rock-hard dick into her slippery cunt.

Alanna let out a groan as my dick slid firmly up the heavenly space between her smooth thighs. I began rocking in and out of her, and she bit the back of her hand and pushed back at me, urging me to fuck her harder. I started pumping into her with long, firm strokes, and she was really moaning. I pushed her dress up higher and higher until it was up around her neck. She pulled it over her head and tossed it into the car. Next, I unhooked her bra. Her 34C tits bounced free and began swaying to the rhythm of the fucking she was getting.

Not wanting to come too soon, I pulled out, turned my lovely wife around and gently pushed her to her knees. She knew what to do and hungrily took my cock into her mouth, sucking for all she was worth. I held her head and pumped my cock into her warm mouth. After a few minutes, I pulled her back up and removed her panties. Now she was standing under the starry sky clad only in her garter belt, stockings and high heels.

I took her around to the front of the car and lifted her onto the hood. Holding her legs up over my shoulders, I pushed into her cunt again and began fucking her as hard as I could. Holding on to her luscious ass-cheeks, I pulled her cunt up to meet each powerful thrust of my cock. With each stroke, her cunt made a loud sucking noise. Soon, Alanna began moaning as an intense orgasm swept over her. Unable to hold back any longer, I increased my pace and shot a huge load in her pussy.

I still had my dick buried deep in Alanna's cunt when, suddenly, a bright light hit us. Alanna jumped down and got behind me, trying to hide her nudity. It was an MP sedan. Alanna was frightened that we would be arrested and that all our friends would find out. I told her we were in big trouble, and maybe we could talk our way out of it.

The sedan pulled closer and two burly, young MPs got out. They were trying to act official, but they were clearly having a hard time keeping their eyes off of my sexy wife. From the bulges in their trousers, I knew they liked what they saw. They told my wife to step out from behind me and, after some hesitation, she did. Then they asked me to come over to them.

When I got to them and the light was out of my eyes, I realized that I knew them!

"Shit, lieutenant, we didn't realize it was you. What you doin'?"

I guess he was joking, because I think it was fairly obvious what I was doing. Still, I played along.

"I'm doing some top secret investigations. Can I enlist you men for some help?"

My wife and I had often talked about a gang bang, and here it was happening without any planning at all.

We went over to the car and one MP stayed outside while the other got in the backseat with Alanna. I couldn't hear what he was saying, but the next thing I knew Alanna had her legs up on the front seat and the MP was between them, banging away at her. He was really fucking her good, because Alanna was moaning loudly and her stocking-clad toes were curling up, a sure sign that she was enjoying herself.

After the first MP fucked her, he got out of the car and brought Alanna with him. He gave my young wife to the second MP, who reached between her legs with both hands and lifted Alanna up in the air. She grabbed him around his neck and looked straight into his eyes as he lowered her onto his huge, meaty cock. With my wife holding on for dear life, the second guy fucked her with such intensity I thought she was going to pass out. Alanna was screaming for more and, when the guy came, his load immediately began dribbling out of Alanna's gaping love-hole.

After the second MP had finished, they "let us go." We departed so fast that I left Alanna's panties on the ground and she didn't even bother putting her dress back on. When we got home, gobs of thick come were still dripping from her freshly fucked pussy. As soon as we got inside, Alanna was all over me and we fucked till dawn!

About a week later, Alanna called me at work. She told me that her two MP friends had just paid her a visit, to return her panties. She said they stripped her naked and fucked her doggie-style for over two hours. She said she came several times and her pussy was sore. She added, "Hurry home, 'cause I'm one horny bitch!"

We were reassigned about a month later and left that post forever. But in those last few weeks, Alanna became a good friend of the MPs. They visited her almost daily. On our last weekend on post, they took Alanna to their barracks for a farewell party where she took on all comers, sucking and fucking from Saturday night till early Monday morning. When I got her back, she smelled of booze, sweat and sex, and her pussy and asshole were flaccid and oozing come.

We've had a couple of threesomes since those days, and we've gone to a few swingers' parties, but nothing beats the memory of that night and the time Alanna "serviced the troops."—*Name and address withheld*

SERVICING THE TEAM TO KEEP THOSE BATTERS UP

*M*y wife Maureen and I are regular readers of *Penthouse Letters*, and we both enjoy the Gang Bangs the best. We have had a few group gropes over the years and, to my surprise, I most enjoy seeing my wife pleased by two cocks—as does she.

Maureen is in her mid-twenties, has long blonde hair, a wonderfully small, tight figure, great tits—and she's an avid semen connoisseur. In all the orgies we've had, Maureen always comes two or three times before insisting that she take care of the rest of us. The first time, I was a little hesitant about my wife swallowing another man's come, but in the heat of the moment I'll let anything happen as long as I get off.

During a recent threesome with Brad, a friend of ours from the local college, Maureen suddenly mentioned that she was very satisfied, but something was missing. I asked her what she meant, and she looked at Brad and me with a smile on her come-coated face and replied, "More guys!"

We didn't do anything about it that night, but a few days later, Brad and I decided to throw a little party for his school's baseball team. I told Maureen that I had a surprise for her the night of the get-together, but she had no idea what was in store for her. All that I said was that she would have to do a little entertaining that night. "I would love to," she replied.

At about six o'clock, the guys started showing up at our house. Each one had been told to bring some booze and an open mind. Maureen answered the door and introduced herself to the guys, giving each a kiss on the lips.

After all seventeen players had arrived, Maureen served appetizers in her skimpy French maid outfit that barely covers her tits and ass. She accentuated her long legs in fishnet stockings. The booze flowed freely and it wasn't long before everyone was feeling good, including my wife. It was at this point that Brad and I decided to get things started.

We made up a little drinking game in which there was a bucket full of pieces of paper with the letters B, P, A and O printed on them. Before each could draw from the bucket, he had to first down a glass of beer, wine or a shot of the hard stuff. The bucket moved around the living room, and each time it came to Maureen, she would drink but would receive no ticket. She was becoming suspicious of this game but played along willingly.

After the first round, I told the guys to save their valuable coupons, which they could redeem later. After four rounds, I told the crowd that each ticket had significance and, with Maureen's permission, each would be fulfilled. I asked my wife to come to the center of the room and then proceeded to say that anyone with a P ticket could fuck Maureen's pussy, an A ticket could fuck her ass, a B ticket could receive a blowjob and an O could not touch her but only jack off. Anyone having a combination of letters could do what each letter entitled them to do. The only catch was that nobody could come until I said so.

I'd loaded the bucket mostly with Os, and it turned out that six guys couldn't touch her at all.

We all took off our clothes, and soon my wife was surrounded by seventeen hard cocks, each guy taking his turn as his ticket dictated. Maureen looked so happy.

I got the video camera to catch some of this once-in-a-lifetime experience on film, and when I returned, I was surprised to find my wife in a most overwhelming position. As I looked through the camera she was straddling one guy and riding him hard while alternating between sucking two well-hung studs in front of her and jacking off two others, one on each side of her. She was soon anally penetrated by one of the largest shanks I have ever seen. It must have been ten inches long and as big around as a large cucumber.

So there I was, taping my wife simultaneously servicing six studs from the local college baseball team as the rest were yanking their puds as they waited for their turn at my petite wife. She, meanwhile, seemed to have turned into a dick-hungry slut who couldn't get enough cock in her. I got a good close-up of what still seems physically impossible.

None of the guys came, however, and after an hour and a half of group fucking, the entire team was lined up against the wall pulling their hard dicks. My wife was going up and down the line giving each dick a few minutes of attention before moving to the next. When she got to the end of the line, I gave her a glass and told her that she could now suck the men to the point just short of coming, at which time they could jack off in the glass.

With a smile on her face, she started to suck the first dick, and because he had been so close before, he quickly unleashed a giant load of cream right into her mouth and on her chin.

She licked the last of the come from the guy's rod and then went happily to the next dick. As this guy started to arch his back and moan, she stopped sucking and placed the glass over the tip of his cock, milking his cock for every last drop of spunk. She licked the second man's dick clean of come and moved to the next.

My wife continued down the line working the well-hung studs with her mouth as she stroked the next guy in line. She continued to suck off each guy with slutlike enthusiasm, having them pull out and either shoot their loads on her face or in the glass. She was being my dream whore, and I was capturing it all on film.

After the seventh or eighth guy, she would move to the next guy in line and within seconds he would come on her waiting face. It was a come depository assembly line, and the guys were enjoying it almost as much as my wife.

The last guy in line was a well-hung man with a horselike dick. When she got to him, she put his meat well down her tiny throat and stroked the exposed six inches that she couldn't swallow with two-handed enthusiasm.

When he was close to coming, he told her to sit back and open wide. His first two shots went well over her head, but they were followed by eight to ten more streams of thick semen that completely covered her already sticky face.

Seeing the woman of my dreams drain the semen from seventeen hard dicks was more than I could handle. I handed the camera to the big-dicked man and told him not to miss a thing. I laid Maureen down and began to fuck her yearning vagina. Before I came, I pulled out and asked her where she wanted my load.

"On my face," she replied, as I sent what seemed to be a gallon of come showering over her pretty face. As she lay there in exhaustion, sucking my limp cock, I picked up the twelve ounces of collected come and slowly poured it in her mouth, which she swallowed one gulp at a time.

The day after the party we watched the tape several times, fucking all the while.—L.M., Fayetteville, Arkansas

SWINGING BOATERS HEAT THINGS UP, BUT IT'S NOT CABIN FEVER

*M*ia and I have been married for five years. We enjoy your magazine, especially the letters about threesomes and crowds.

We were reading a letter about a threesome one night when

we were both naked in bed. My cock was up and hard, and Mia's nipples were like two hard pebbles.

"How would you like to add another guy or girl to our love-making and have a threesome?" I asked.

Mia said, "I'd rather add a couple. That way we'd both get to fuck a new person."

A week later I stopped in an adult-book store and picked up a local swingers magazine. That night, while lying in bed, I handed it to Mia and said, "See if you can find a couple we might like to get together with."

Mia said, "You're really serious about this, aren't you." Mia went through the magazine a few times and finally said, "How about this couple."

The ad showed a man and a woman in swimsuits and read "Late twenties new to swinging would like to meet same. Must be discreet."

We sent a letter off the following day and waited for an answer. A few weeks later we received a reply saying they would like to meet us. They named a hotel lounge where we could meet and gave a phone number.

Friday night arrived and off we went. Mia was dressed to kill in her favorite minidress.

When we got to the lounge, we sat at the bar and ordered drinks. After a few minutes a man walked up and asked, "Are you Bob and Mia?"

I said, "Yes, are you Broderick?"

He said, "Yes, we're sitting over at a table. Bring your drinks and join us."

Broderick introduced us to Heather, an exceptionally nice-looking brunette. We hit it off real good. After about an hour, Broderick said, "Why don't you two talk it over while me and Heather hit the johns."

I asked Mia, "What do you think?" She said, "Okay with me, if you want to."

When Broderick and Heather came back we said, "Let's do it."

Broderick gave us the name of a marina and said he would see us there around ten the next morning.

He had an awesome boat with plenty of sleeping room, if you know what I mean. We went about six miles offshore and dropped anchor. The ocean was flat. The girls had on bikinis and were enjoying the sun.

Broderick said, "Let's go down in the cabin and have a few drinks."

I sat with Mia on one bed and Broderick sat on the other with Heather. We were new at this, so I took Broderick's lead when he took off Heather's top and started playing with her tits. I did the same with Mia. After a few minutes Heather came over and sat next to me, telling Mia to go over with Broderick.

Heather's hand went to my cock as I sucked on her tits. She said, "Let's get these off," and knelt on the floor pulling off my trunks. I glanced over at Mia right as she was doing the same for Broderick. His cock sprang free. Christ, it was big. It had to be all of eight inches and big around as a Coke bottle.

My attention was soon on my own cock as Heather took it in her hot mouth. I heard Broderick say, "Oh, yeah, suck it, suck it."

I felt that tingling sensation in my balls and knew I would be coming soon. I wanted my cock in Heather's cunt when I came, so I sat her on the bed and started eating her pussy. She was very verbal, just like her husband, and started screaming, "Oh, fuck, baby, eat me, eat me, make me come." Man, she tasted sweet.

When I heard Mia moaning, I looked over to see that Broderick was eating her cunt. It was like making out in front of a mirror. Meanwhile, Heather's ass came off the bed and her hands held my head on her cunt. She screamed, "Oh, fuck, I'm coming."

Her juices started flowing from her cunt. I tongue-fucked her till she relaxed. "God, that was good," she said. "This is so fucking awesome."

My cock was throbbing as I knelt between Heather's legs. She put the head in her hole and put her legs around my ass as I slammed all six inches into her cunt. She screamed, "Oh, yes, baby, fuck me good."

Her cunt muscles tightened around my cock as I fucked in and out of her wet hole. I heard Mia whimper, "Easy, easy," and so I glanced over at her and Broderick. He had her legs bent back with her knees smashing into her tits. Her cunt lips were spread wide and his monster dick reamed in and out of her like a pile driver.

She moaned as inch after inch disappeared in her cunt. Her cunt was soon mashed up to his balls. She wrapped her legs around his ass and said, "Don't move. Let me get used to your big cock." Her legs soon pulled on his ass and he started fucking her nice and slow.

I glanced over at Mia so many times because this was a first for us, and I was as excited to see that big cock fucking her cunt as I was to have my own cock in some strange pussy.

Heather's cunt muscles were milking my cock, and I was soon shooting hot come in her cunt. We lay back and watched as Mia and Broderick continued to go at it. He lasted much longer than I did. Mia finally moaned, "Fuck me hard with that big cock. I'm coming." Her legs tightened around his ass and his cock was soon coated with her cunt cream. He screamed, "Oh, fuck, here it comes."

His ass muscles tightened as he shot his hot sperm in her cunt. A river of come was soon funneling down the crack of her ass.

Both girls went to the head to clean up while Broderick made us more drinks. We sat around the cabin naked, Mia and Broderick on one bed, Heather and me on the other. Presently, Broderick started kissing Mia. His hands went from her tits to her pussy. His cock was rock-hard as Mia jerked up and down on it. I followed his lead and started finger-fucking Heather. Broderick laid Mia back and straddled her chest, fucking her tits. Her legs were spread as his hand rubbed her cunt.

Heather then slipped off the bed and knelt between Mia's legs.

She pushed Broderick's hand away and started eating my wife's pussy.

Mia moaned. "Oh, yes, honey, eat me." She thought it was me eating her cunt.

Heather was waving her ass at me, so I knelt behind her and slid my cock up her cunt. Mia soon started moaning, humping her cunt at Heather's mouth. Heather feasted on her cunt juice.

Broderick said, "Oh, fuck, here it comes. Suck it, suck it."

Hearing this, my cock started unloading hot come in Heather's cunt. Broderick rolled off Mia and lay back on the bed. My cock was still spewing wildly in Heather's cunt, and when I was spent, I pulled out and sat back on the bed.

Mia's eyes were closed, and Heather was still feasting on her cunt. Mia's hands went down to Heather's head, and when she felt the long hair her eyes sprung open. This was the first time a woman had ever gone down on her. She just moaned, "Oh, yes, yes, eat me, girlfriend." Her ass came off the bed as she fucked her cunt at Heather's mouth.

Her orgasms came crashing down and she came for nearly five minutes. My wife unleashes a torrent of juices, and Heather was good to lap it all up.

When the girls were done, Broderick suggested we all go up on deck and get some sun. We grabbed our drinks and off we went. We were naked, but there were no boats in sight. Broderick said, "Why don't you put some oil on Heather and I'll do Mia." We spent a lot of time rubbing oil on the girls' tits, and their nipples were soon stone-hard. They were lying side by side. Mia's cunt lips were swollen and her clit poked out about a quarter of an inch.

After about an hour, Mia said, "I've had enough sun, I'm going down below." Broderick said, "Me too," and off they went.

The cabin windows were open, and I watched as Mia lay back on the bed. Broderick knelt between her legs and started eating her pussy. I heard her saying how good his tongue felt. I was sitting Indian style on the deck and Heather maneuvered around till her head was between my legs. She started sucking my cock.

My wife gives great head, but I have to say, Heather has some kind of technique that she ought to have patented. I don't know exactly what she was doing, but my dick practically mushroomed up into her mouth. I felt like the head of my dick was banging against the back of her skull. The more she sucked, the harder I got, but it wasn't like blue balls or anything. It was only like I had a huge cock all of a sudden.

I didn't want her to stop, and I was in luck. Judging from the sound of her moans, she was enjoying this every bit as much as I was.

From the sound of it, Broderick was doing a good job on Mia's pussy. She kept moaning, "Oh, oh, God, I'm there."

I looked back into the cabin to see Mia's legs wrapped around Broderick's back. She started to shake, and I knew she was about to come again. Her ass arched off the bed and she flooded his mouth with her cunt cream.

When Broderick sat up on the bed, his cock looked even bigger than it had before. He told Mia to sit on it. She straddled his hips and put the head in her swollen cunt. I watched as inch after inch disappeared in her cunt. She kept moaning, "Oh, God, you're big." She leaned over and he started sucking on her tits. His cock was slick with her cunt cream as it reamed in and out of her cunt. After a few minutes Mia moaned, "I'm there again. Fuck me hard with that big cock."

Broderick stood up and turned my wife over the bed. Slamming her from behind, he gave me a perfect view of his monster dick flying in and out of my wife's steaming gash. I felt like I was watching a porn flick. Hell, I felt like I was living a porn flick.

All of a sudden, Broderick moaned, "I'm coming." Frothy cream soon coated his cock as their combined juices ran out Mia's cunt. Seeing this, my cock swelled and I shot my own cock cream down Heather's throat.

Heather and I went down to the cabin and we all got dressed.

We had been anchored for about five hours. Broderick said, "Well, guys, it's time we went in. I think we had one great adventure. We'll have to get together again soon."

We all had one last drink to toast the afternoon and then headed back to port.

On the way home, Mia and I talked about our first swinging session. Mia said she enjoyed herself but that her cunt was a little tender from Broderick's big cock.

If you've never had a swinging session, you don't know what you're missing. Even if your sex life is the greatest you can imagine, fucking someone else's wife while he fucks yours is like moving into the stratosphere.—*B.V., West Palm Beach, Florida*

HEAVYWEIGHT CHAMP GIVES GROUPIE KNOCKOUT HUMP

I have always been a confident guy, full of arrogance and fury. From childhood I have known that I am destined to be the world boxing champion in my weight class. Accordingly, several months ago I joined a gym that is well known for producing champions.

I spent my first day at the gym sparring, shadowboxing and working out with the other fighters on various pieces of high- and low-tech equipment.

A week later the guys introduced me to a boxing groupie named Wanda. Wanda is a sexy blonde fox if ever there was a sexy blonde fox. She really has a big thing for boxers, I was told, and just about any fighter who wants to fuck her is welcomed with open arms—and legs.

As a matter of course I tried to seduce Wanda but to my dismay she rejected every one of my advances. She wouldn't give herself a chance to find out that, while I may not be as handsome a hunk as some of the other guys, I do have one asset that few men can match: a ten-inch cock. Wanda would have all the prick her hands, mouth and cunt could handle if only she tried me out. But as week after uneventful week rolled by I began to think I would never get my chance with Wanda.

One month after I joined, the gym held a Golden Gloves tournament. I fought hard in my match and quickly knocked out my opponent. After the match I rushed into the locker room to shower and change before heading out to celebrate.

To my astonishment, Wanda suddenly strolled into the locker room. She matter-of-factly checked out the naked boxers with unmistakable lust in her eyes. I didn't know what to make of it. I was shocked and visibly aroused by her boldness.

When Wanda caught sight of my jumbo tube steak, her mouth dropped open and her eyes widened. Now was my moment, it appeared. With a visible effort, Wanda finally managed to tear her eyes away from my cock and balls and address the roomful of fighters.

"Hey! It's time for my workout, boys!" she announced loudly as she started taking off her clothes. "I need a big prick and I need it now." While the guys gathered all around her, Wanda hopped onto the massage table and peeled off her few remaining garments. Now she was altogether naked—stripped for action.

"Who do you want, Wanda?" one of the boxers called out in the crowd.

"Whoever has the biggest dick!" she shouted with no hesitation, and pointed a steady finger directly at me. A bunch of fellows pushed me in her direction. She anticipated the move and lay back with her legs spread wide to receive my tallywhacker.

Wanda screamed with joy as I plunged my hambone into her steamy cunt. To my surprise, she was able to take it almost all the way in on the first stroke—something no other woman had ever done before! I marveled at her sexual talents and abilities, and I blew my wad in a very short time.

Wanda, bless her heart, was insatiable. She fucked several more boxers and also delighted some do-it-yourselfers who stood around and jerked off as they watched the sex show. She was a happy camper, ravishing, energized and eager for more.

Sitting up on the massage table, she spoke to me in a sexy, sultry voice. "I still haven't come yet," she cooed. "Would you be a dear and eat me out?" Her sopping cunt was dripping with sperm; but the guys urged me on and, next thing I knew, I was down on my knees facing her wet, sloppy cunt.

I tenderly tongued her swollen clit before I started work on her pussy. Soon I was sucking on her labia and slurping up the orgasmic mixture overflowing from her well-fucked cunt. She shrieked and writhed as she came, drenching my face with a mixture of sex juices.

Then I realized all at once that all my fellow boxers had been standing close by, taking in this cunt-lapping show and enjoying the spectacle!

I had eaten their come right out of this gorgeous babe and they were pleased as Punch about it. "How did I taste?" one of them shouted.

"I hope you didn't spoil your appetite for dinner," another called. Others laughed and chimed in with clever comments of their own. I was humiliated and I was feeling betrayed and uneasy.

Fortunately the guys were too good-natured to let me suffer long. While chuckling and patting me on the back, they explained that the entire orgy had been a setup. It was their way of initiating new boxers into their exclusive circle.

I am now officially on the team and I'm looking forward to setting up the next cocky kid who wants to join. Meanwhile, Wanda and I have become lovers. She is truly the undisputed mistress of boxing.—*W.S.*, *Brooklyn, New York*

Boy Meets Boy

A ROUTINE WORKOUT LEADS TO A RADICAL
CHANGE OF ROUTINE

A few months ago I had my one and only sexual encounter with another man, and I'm beginning to realize that it has changed my life forever. I find myself thinking about this guy almost all the time.

I'm pretty much an average guy, forty-nine years old, been married twice. I have been a school teacher for twenty-five years. There are two things about me that people tend to notice and remember. First, I'm a bodybuilder, and I get a lot of comments about my body. Second, I have a large dick. My cock seems to draw as much attention from the guys in the shower room as it has from my two wives and the one woman that I've had an affair with. My dick is fairly long, but I think it's the thickness that makes it so exceptional. My second wife and the lady I had the affair with called my cock "Mighty Dog." A couple of guys that I work out with at the gym nicknamed me "Wonder Boy," so you get the picture: I have a larger than average penis. Angela (she was the school teacher that I had the affair with) kept K-Y jelly in her night stand the whole time we were seeing each other.

Anyway, I was at the gym very late one night about five months ago when this big hunk of a guy walked in and started working out. We were the only two people there, so we spoke and made small talk while we were working out. After a while I started to get this embarrassed feeling, and soon I realized it was because I was staring at this guy's body. He must have been about six foot seven or six foot eight, and he must have weighed at least two hundred and seventy-five pounds. To put it plainly, he was beautiful. I know that I have never seen such a perfect man in my life, and I'm around a lot of very well-built guys all the time.

I finished my workout and hit the showers. I had just lathered up my whole body when in walks this guy. I must have gasped as I first saw this giant's cock, because he looked right at me and smiled as he walked by me. He stopped at a shower just across from me and turned the water on very hot. He turned and asked me if he could borrow my soap, and when I nodded yes, he walked by me very close and took the soap out of the soap dish on the wall behind me. As he turned to go back to his shower, he let his meat loaf brush against my ass and upper thigh. My normal reaction would be to punch him right then, but to tell the truth, I guess I realized that I was aroused by it.

He was facing me as he started soaping his very large and hairy chest. Then he went on to his cock and balls. He was making small talk as he did this, and I can't even remember what he said or if I answered him. All I can remember is staring at what must have been the world's biggest prick, and I am not excepting my own.

He continued to make small talk as he slowly soaped his cock. He said that he was from another part of the state and that he stopped here to work out a couple of times a year. He started talking about how horny he was. He had been on the road all week and hadn't seen his girlfriend in ten days. I was just listening and watching him wash his huge cock when I realized he was starting to get hard. I was getting really turned on by the thought of seeing him hard.

He asked if I would mind washing his back, and he held out the bar of soap to me. I moved forward and took the soap with no hesitation. Mr. Wonderful turned toward the shower wall and placed his hands high and wide against the tiles. I started washing his back slowly, and I kept thinking that I should stop because

I'm not gay and I had never touched another man in this way before.

He turned suddenly and faced me. My knees almost buckled when I saw that his cock was rock-hard and standing straight up. Once again, he smiled at me and asked if I would like to wash his chest. I felt weak and didn't say a word as I started washing his chest, and for the first time I believe I knew what was going to happen. I stopped trying not to look at his cock and just stared at it as I washed his chest. He then took hold of my wrist with his huge hands and, looking right into my eyes, pushed my hands down onto his cock.

I didn't resist. I started soaping a cock that felt as big as my arm, and for the first time started wondering what it would be like to have a man's cock in my mouth. I didn't have to wonder long, because things happened very fast after that. He put his long arms around me and pulled me hard up against him. His cock was pressing against my stomach, and I can't began to tell you how large and hot it felt between us.

After a minute, we backed away slightly and I stared at his cock as I fondled it. I thought that I would explode with excitement because I knew for sure that I was going to suck him right then. I held on to his cock with both hands as he pushed me down to my knees. I was scared and not sure what to do first. I held my face against the side of his cock and again thought how hard and hot it felt. I started sucking him slowly and he then put his hand behind my head as he started to fuck my mouth. This lasted only a few more seconds, when he started to come into my mouth. I started swallowing as fast as I could, but it's very hard to do with your mouth open that wide. I started choking and he pulled his cock out of my mouth and shot huge globs of come on my face and chest.

I was still on my knees and swallowing come when I reached down and started pounding my own cock. I came in about five seconds. I shot my load onto the shower floor between his legs. It felt so good.

I felt slightly embarrassed as he helped me up and I walked back to my shower. I started washing the come off my face. I was facing the showerhead, so I was startled when he put his arms around me from behind and hugged me firmly. I could feel his cock lying between the cheeks of my ass as he held me very tight and whispered in my ear, "Thanks, that was great, and I wish that I had time to fuck your ass." He slapped me on the ass as he walked away from me and said over his shoulder, "I hope I see you on my next trip."

I waited for a while before I left the shower. I wasn't sure that I wanted to face him. By the time I went into the locker room, he was gone.

For the first couple of months after this happened, I was pretty much in a state of denial. I tried not to think about it, and I screwed my wife harder than I had screwed her in years. I guess I wanted to reassert my manhood. Well, I have finally given up trying not to think about Mr. Wonderful. Even if I never see him again, I don't ever want to forget what we had. And I've even started dreaming up scenarios in which we see each other again. This is one of my dreams: I'm going to invite him to spend a weekend at my house. My place is great for lovemaking. I have a huge shower with a large seat in it and, of course, there's also a hot tub. I have several large mirrors in the bedroom that always make for great viewing. When I get Mr. Wonderful in my house, I'm going to do a lot of the things that my lover used to do to me. I'll wash him slowly in the shower and then I'll dry him as I admire his body. I'll ask him to lie on the bed while I massage him and make loving comments about his muscles. And I definitely want to rub his cock with oil while I kiss it gently.

I'm sure by now both of our cocks will be rock-hard, and when I lie down beside him, our cocks will rub against each other while he puts his arms around me and holds me very close. I then want to feel his huge cock resting against my stomach. I want to feel it gently throbbing as he holds me.

My dream then calls for him to kiss me over and over and to

push his tongue deep into my throat as he starts to grind his cock against me. I'll then start kissing and licking his body as I slip down under the sheets to position my mouth in front of his cock. I start licking and sucking him, and I know that he'll hold the back of my head as he starts fucking my mouth like he did in the shower. This time I'll be ready for him, because I have been practicing with a huge dildo that I bought. I can put most of it in my mouth, and I'm able to put the whole thing up my ass. When he comes this time, I'm not going to miss a drop, and I hope he pushes his dick into my mouth so far that it slides down my throat. I can't wait.

Most of all, I want Mr. Wonderful to fuck my ass from the missionary position. I want to feel his body all over me as he drills my ass. My lover used to kiss my neck and lick my ears as she would keep repeating, "Fuck me, fuck me harder. Please, fuck me." I want to do the same thing to Mr. Wonderful, and I hope his nipples are as sensitive as mine, because I want to pinch them and lick them as he fucks my ass very hard. I want it all, I want all of his cock in me.

After I have cleaned him and rubbed him a while longer, I can fall asleep in his arms with his cock lying between my legs. I want so much for him to kiss my neck and ears as we fall off to sleep.

I plan to wake up first so I can slip under the covers and wake him by slowly licking and sucking his beautiful cock until he gives me one more load of his hot come. When he is finished throbbing, I will slip up beside him and he will kiss me so that he can share the taste of his gorgeous cock as we hold each other for a while before he leaves.

I have given up trying to convince myself that I'm not gay, and now all I can think about is Mr. Wonderful coming back to town.

If he reads this, I hope he gets superhorny and plans a trip my way.—*Name and address withheld*

FRIENDS DON'T LET FRIENDS WASTE SPUNK

Since this isn't the kind of story you can share at work, I thought it might be fun to share it with your readers.

Last spring, three of my buddies and I took a weekend fishing vacation. On Friday, we said good-bye to our wives and headed up north to Glenn's cottage to catch a few bass. After a six-hour car trip, we were all pretty tired and hungry. So Martin and I carried in the bags and gear, while Owen fired up the grill and Glenn checked out his boat.

After grilling a few steaks and drinking some beer, we all went out on the lake and spent a few hours hoping for fish. While we waited for a bite, Martin told us some wild stories about fucking his wife with, as he described it, his "incredibly huge" cock. He said his orgasms were so enormous, they'd always have to change the sheets, and the mattress would be soaked. This brought out bursts of laughter from Owen, Glenn and myself. After a time, Owen caught an eighteen-inch bass. Martin caught a fourteen-incher and I caught a snapping turtle, earning the biggest applause.

Around midnight, we got back to the cottage and sat around the living room talking. That's when Glenn sprang two surprises on us: He pulled out a box of fine cigars and produced a selection of porno tapes. We sat through the first tape laughing, smoking and drinking, just like a small bachelor party.

As Glenn put in the second tape, Owen started complaining, saying that he didn't like getting so turned on with his wife nowhere around.

"Looks like you'll be stroking the pickle tonight," Martin said, slapping Owen on the shoulder.

"Yeah, unless you can get one of us to stroke it for you," I added.

"Oh, man," Glenn said, "that'd be hilarious. We should all play a round of poker and the loser has to stroke off Owen."

Martin jumped in, "Why stop there? Why should the other

two be left out?" Now, normally this idea might have been quickly dismissed, but with four close friends and a lot of beer and a porno tape . . .

So Glenn dealt out the cards and said we would play one hand and the loser would have to jerk off the winners.

"Well, if we're going this far," Martin said, "let's double the stakes so I can get a blowjob out of the deal."

"You may be giving the blowjob," I said. This was followed by a round of laughter, and the bet was on. I have to say that my cock was pretty damn hard from all this talk, and I was excited about the prospect of getting a blowjob from one of my good buddies. With my five cards in hand, I put on my best poker face. In a matter of minutes, the hand was done . . . and I'd lost!

The next thing I knew, my three good buddies were sitting bare-ass naked on the couch. There was a lot of chuckling going on as they cued up a new tape. As the movie started, they all looked at me to see if I was going to weasel out of the bet. Being a man of my word, I knelt down on the floor in front of Glenn and took a long look at his cock. It was about five inches long and covered in a bush of pubic hair. To say the least, I was nervous about blowing my friends. But as the tape got kicking, I could see three eager smiles and three hardening cocks. They weren't letting me out of this.

So as Glenn puffed on his fresh cigar, I leaned forward and began stroking his cock. As I grew comfortable with his rod in my hand, I leaned forward, opened my mouth and began smoking his bone. The uneasiness left me immediately. The feel of his rigid tool in my mouth was exhilarating! As my head bobbed forward, I took in deep breaths of the wonderful aroma coming from his crotch. It made my own cock hard with enjoyment.

Each bob of my head made me happier that I'd lost the game. Glenn soon stopped watching the film, closing his eyes and enjoying my work. His moans and body rhythm told me I was handling this like a pro. As his hips moved with my bobbing head, I reached up and ran my fingers through that wonderful pubic hair.

Glenn put down his cigar and placed his hands on the back of my head, urging me on. Holding his balls tight in my hands, I gave a nice tug and Glenn blew a hot load into my waiting mouth.

I felt quite good after my first blowjob, and I was eager to try again. Martin and Owen were quite pleased to see this, as I saw each of them holding their cocks, ready to be the next recipient. I decided to go with Owen's smaller cock, since Martin wields a long, nine-inch pecker with an enormous set of balls. I started to believe all of his stories were true. He was going to be a challenge.

As the movie continued, I opened my greedy mouth and took in Owen's scrawny rod. His cock fit so nicely that I began running my tongue around it as if it were a Popsicle. It wasn't long before Owen followed Glenn's example and forgot all about the movie. I was having so much fun sucking his cock. It felt incredible to please my friends like this. Now I realize why my wife loves sucking my cock so much!

Owen swung his legs up over my shoulders and wrapped them around my head. Beads of sweat were dripping from Owen's bald head, and I could tell by his increased moans that the end was near. After a few seconds, Owen let loose a tremendous orgasm, dropping his beer in the process! It was hard to believe that his small dick carried so much jam. Half of his load flew out of the sides of my mouth and dripped onto his thighs. Gulping down as much of his juice as I could, I found myself sliding his spent cock across my face until I was covered with his load. With a happy sigh of relief, Owen thanked me and got up to clean off.

Even with two satisfied customers, I knew my real work was still ahead of me. Drinking down the remainder of Owen's beer, I took a long look at Martin's enormous cock. It must have been seven inches hanging limp! And as I moved toward it, it began to stiffen. I grabbed that incredible rock-hard bone and readied myself. Martin sucked on his cigar and, with a smile, said, "Now, suck me like a good bitch, Howard."

He need not have worried. I was just hitting my stride. I started slowly tonguing his balls, making him anticipate my warm mouth around his huge organ. Lifting his balls, I licked my tongue around the perimeter of his cock. Finally, my warm lips locked around the luscious bone. Martin's cock was so big, it took me a long time before my throat accepted the whole shaft. I must have slurped on that cock for half an hour! Owen and Glenn had completely forgotten about the video. They just stared at me in amazement, jerking their recharged rods.

Martin was just a cool customer, smiling as he smoked his cigar and talked with them. He didn't moan, and I couldn't figure out why he wasn't enjoying himself—I sure was! Finally, as Martin finished his smoke, his balls gave a shudder and his cock blasted me with a gallon of burning juice. There was no way possible I could have been prepared for that load!

I swallowed as much of his wad as I could, but I looked down and Martin's legs were drenched with come. I knew what was coming next.

"Well, Howard, looks like you'll have to try again," Martin said with a chuckle. Owen and Glenn each cracked up, and I started laughing through my sloppy wet mouth as I licked his legs clean. Now I realized why Martin hadn't enjoyed my blowjob—he expected a second one. I didn't complain. In fact, this turned me on. The thought of engaging his bone again made my cock squirt out its own ample load. Knowing this situation might never happen again, I was fully prepared to let his second load slip so I could go for a three-peat.

Owen and Glenn said good night as Martin stretched back on the vacant couch and led my face back to his ready member. As I resumed my cocksucking, Martin helped himself to another cigar and a couple of brews. I could tell by the look in his eye that he was planning on being up for a while. I must have spent half the night working that cock, and I loved every minute of it. Martin never failed to fill my mouth with his scorching loads. By the end of the night, I was drunk with his come.

On Sunday, our trip ended and we headed back home. Everyone agreed we'd have to come back again. And I'm sure we'll find our way back to the poker table. I think I'll ask my wife for a few pointers on cocksucking, because next time I plan on losing on purpose.—*H.L.*, *Sterling Heights, Michigan*

NUPTIALS PROMISE BRAND-NEW BOND FOR THESE MEMBERS OF THE WEDDING

I had driven most of Friday afternoon to attend the wedding of my closest college friend, Mark. He and Margaret were to be married the next afternoon. Mark had made reservations for me to share a room with Brian, a cousin of Margaret's, who had just returned from a two-year stay in Europe.

I checked into the motel and went to the room. Clothes were strewn over the two double beds. I unpacked and showered.

As I was drying off, I heard the door open. I wrapped a towel around my waist and walked out to meet my roommate.

"Vernon, I'm Brian. Mark told me all about you. Glad to meet you." We shook hands.

Brian was very handsome. Only his slightly hawkish nose kept him from looking pretty. He wore only a brief bikini that hardly covered his cock and balls. I couldn't help but admire his well-proportioned body. He was tall, about six foot two, lean and muscular, though not overly.

"We'd better hurry if we're going to make it to the party on time. I stayed too long in the pool," he said. I couldn't help but notice that he was staring at me as I dressed.

We drove to the party in separate cars. Much later that evening, Brian told me that he was leaving and asked that I give him an hour head start. I saw him go out with one of the bridesmaids. With his looks and obvious sex appeal, he probably could have gotten any girl there.

My date was more cute than good-looking. We danced for another hour before I drove her home.

There wasn't any action in the motel lounge, so I went on up to the room. The drapes were drawn and the room was dark.

Immediately, I saw that Brian was fucking the girl he had left with. They were illuminated only by the light from the bathroom. Her legs were wrapped round his waist as he pounded her. Brian glanced at me and kept on screwing. I waited outside until I saw them leave. Then I went in, undressed and crawled naked into bed. I did not awake when Brian returned.

I woke up late in the morning with my usual erection in hand. I lay quietly for a while, then opened my eyes. Brian was propped up in his bed watching me slowly stroke myself.

"Good morning, Vernon," he chuckled. "What are you going to do with that big hard-on? It would be a pity to waste it."

"Just try to piss it away, I suppose. I don't have any use for it. Sorry I walked in on you last night."

"That's okay. I thought it was funny." His eyes were glued to my extended prick as I walked across the room.

It was about noon and we were due at a brunch. The affair, which was over by two that afternoon, was uneventful, and when the girls all left to prepare for the wedding, Brian and I decided to spend the rest of the afternoon by the motel pool.

Brian laughed at me when I put on my baggy swim shorts. "American men are so modest. In Europe, they wear as little as possible, and often swim nude. The women also. Men here are even afraid to be caught looking at another guy. I like to look at sexy bodies like yours." I blushed. "Do I embarrass you? You should learn to be more open about sex."

"You sound like you're hung up on sex," I said.

"Sure, I go for whatever sex I can get," he replied.

The pool was almost deserted. We swam some laps and lay in the sun for an hour or so. All the while, I couldn't help but think about what Brian had said. It began to dawn on me that if you're on this planet for a finite period of time, there doesn't seem to be much reason not to experience all it has to offer, even if this means only checking out another guy's package every once in a while.

I rode with Brian to the wedding. It was all very nice, but I had a little too much champagne at the party afterwards. Brian suggested that he take me home before I made a fool of myself. I resisted, but he insisted. Somehow, he got me into the room still on my feet.

"Here, take these aspirin and then take a hot shower, or you'll have one hell of a hangover." Brian helped me undress and then turned on the water in the bathroom.

I must have stayed in the shower a long time, because I was actually starting to sober up. When Brian came in and got me, he was buck naked.

"Feel better, don't you? Stand still and I'll dry you off." He started with my head and worked his way down my back to my ass and legs.

"Now for the front. Turn around," he said. He carefully dried my crotch, and it felt good. I have to report that my cock started to swell.

"Look at yourself in the mirror. You're beautiful. See what's happening. You're not such a prude, after all. Let's see if it will get hard."

Brian held the base of my dick in one hand and tickled the tip with the other. I just stood there and watched my cock rise. It felt strange letting a guy fondle me like that.

"It's beautiful. Thick and growing. Come on, I'm going to put you to bed. Maybe you won't waste this one."

I sat on the side of my bed. My shaft stood straight up. Brian yanked on his own prick as he stood looking at me.

"Do you want me to bring you off?" he asked. I fell back sprawled on the bed and didn't answer.

His hands began to run lightly over my body. He pinched and sucked my nipples. My heart was pounding. I didn't know a guy could make me feel this way. He held my balls and licked my navel. It tingled all over. His lips followed his exploring fingers, and my cock leapt at his touch. It was growing bigger and bigger, feeling like it was going to burst. Brian's tongue swirled around the sensitive knob. I lifted my head and watched as his head moved up and down. Twice he took me to the brink of explosion and held me there, only to stop and start again. He was driving me crazy. I don't think I had ever been so sexually aroused.

Then Brian crawled up over me and sat lightly on my stomach, holding his long cock in front of my face.

"Go ahead, touch it. It's not going to bite you."

I'd never held another guy's dick. I jacked it with both hands. It felt different from my own, the same way his hands felt different on me. He leaned forward and brushed the head against my cheek.

"Okay, that's enough. I might cream all over your face. Unless you're ready to suck some cock."

I didn't care. I grabbed his ass-cheeks and pulled him into my mouth. I was impressed by the way his cock completely filled my mouth. I swirled my tongue on the head for a while, just as I'd experienced it with my girlfriends, and sure enough his penis started to throb.

Pulling out, he gasped, "No, I want to do you first."

I thought I was going to come right when he engulfed my cock. I started humping my hips, and he slurped with wild abandon. When I felt like I was starting to come, I yelled out, "I'm coming," just in case he didn't want to swallow. But he just kept right on sucking.

Spurt after spurt of creamy jism flooded his throat, and he sucked and slurped for more.

When I calmed down, I asked Brian if I could return the favor. When I opened my eyes, I realized I was too late. Brian was on his knees beside me, jacking off, and soon I felt warm jets of come start to tickle my tummy.—*V.J.*, *North Myrtle Beach, South Carolina*

THE ROAD TRIP, THE MOVIE, AND
THE ROMAN-NOSED MAN

I had a hell of a row with my girlfriend the night before I left on this sales trip. There was a lot to it, but the catalyst that kicked it off was her remark that she sometimes misses her ex-husband. She said that after all, he was an interesting guy when he wasn't being nice to her. That cheesed me off real good, and I remarked that maybe that was when he was most interesting. That cheesed her off. No legs around me that night!

It was a pretty dreary plane ride the next morning, some pretty dreary driving around in a rented car with a kind of reluctant transmission and some pretty dreary stories from customers who like to make me strain harder for a reorder than I've ever strained for sexual favors. Adding to the dreariness were the hotel room where I was staying and the restaurant I chose the first night. A couple of double bourbons washed away the taste of the restaurant fare, but as I left that miserable grease trap I wondered which was worse off, my mind or my stomach.

I sometimes get mildly perverse desires when on the road; among them, all-male movies. I went to an X-rated movie theater in that city that features such movies, and when I go to see something there I always make it plain I'm interested only in what's onscreen and not in any of the live performances going on in or under the folding seats. So it seemed I'd be spending that evening just watching a movie called *Rising Star*, starring Billy Hungwell, who's a favorite with all-male audiences everywhere.

I sat in one of the back rows, on the aisle, the way I usually do. That way, I know that anyone coming along to sit beside me is probably up to something I'm not interested in and I'll tell him so. And sure enough, along came a dark figure, just when I was becoming amused at Billy's antics. Not long after this guy sat down, he put a hand against my leg, but not on my knee. I pulled the leg away. He tried again, and normally I'd be ready to murmur, "Fuck off, queer!" But I didn't, not that night. I let him keep going this time. His hand was soon on my knee, then up my thigh. By the time his hand pressed lightly against what he was looking for, I was surprised to find it was hard.

Fondling followed. I pushed the hand away but welcomed it back a couple of minutes later. I concentrated on Billy until the fondler became more interesting. I looked sideways and saw, by the light the screen reflected, a Roman-nosed face. How young, how old? I couldn't tell. The bourbon buzz and that gentle male hand, moving now to caress my tight scrotum, gave me a good feeling, but one I nevertheless felt uneasy about.

"Unzip your fly."

It was a low but clearly audible tone, with a Continental tinge. In response, I made a grunt that was negative and unfriendly. Suddenly, Billy was no longer amusing and Roman-nose was disgusting. I lurched upward and to the left, springing into the aisle. I hurried up the aisle toward the exit, hearing somebody's high voice in the dark saying, "Another satisfied customer!"

On the street, I started roaming around, not wanting to go back to the hotel. I sat on a park bench for a few minutes, then walked around again, looking in store windows. I wasn't paying attention to what I was looking at, so I don't know whether it was a bookstore or a men's clothing store I was standing in front of when I heard that Continental voice again, this time saying, "I'm truly sorry if I've upset you." I turned to look at Roman-nose. I couldn't think of any sensible thing to say, so I hoped the guy, who was a little taller than I was and very well dressed, would keep talking.

"I saw you in the lobby of the Broadwood Hotel. I'm staying there too," he said. "I wouldn't have bothered you if I hadn't seen you later, in the theater."

"You can see real good in the dark, is that it?" I replied.

"Sometimes." He smiled, looked down, and brought his hands together in a nervous-looking gesture, in front of the place where his fine houndstooth jacket was buttoned. They were slim hands, with long fingers.

"Look, can I buy you a drink?" he asked. He looked at me sincerely and I found myself wondering just what guys like him go through. I mean, he must have had that Roman nose bent sideways a few times by those who didn't take to all his sincerity and concern.

"No," I answered. "Tell you what, if you like bourbon, knock on the door of room four-twenty in about a half hour. I'll be there." I turned and walked away quickly, making it plain we were to find our way back to the hotel separately.

I'd carried a bottle of Old Grand-Dad in my briefcase and had knocked back one shot already by the time I heard my phone ring. He was calling first, just to make sure. Why didn't he just come ahead and knock? But I told him the invitation was still open and he was soon in my room.

I offered him a hanger for that fine jacket and then a tumbler with bourbon in it. He stood in the middle of the room, looking nervous again and not interested in the glass or its contents.

"May I be frank?" he asked. "I don't think we need hesitate any longer. I'm here in the hope of giving you a blowjob."

"I don't know if I'm in the mood for one," I answered.

"It's more like you aren't quite ready for one," he countered, "not as ready as you were in the movie theater. But I can attend to that. Please, sir. You'll enjoy it."

His nervousness was replaced by a sense of authority. He put the glass on the counter by the television set, then went to the windows and pulled the shades. He came back to me and lightly put his hands on either side of my waist. What the hell, I thought, sucked off by a Continental queer. Could be worse.

After making me pry off my shoes with my feet, he dropped my trousers to the floor, then picked them up and placed them over the chair by the writing table. As he came back to me, he was loosening his tie. With that light touch again, he took my drawers and pulled them down my legs.

"You might wish to sit on the edge of the bed?" he said, as if asking me. I knew it was a strong recommendation. I sat down. "There," he said, "now you can relax."

He parted my knees, slid his hands up my thighs, and took my half-staff penis in his right hand, while his left slid beneath my balls. His thumb worked skillfully, just under the head, and built me up, giving me a good feeling. I did relax, leaning back on the bed, on my elbows. I thought of my girlfriend as his mouth enclosed the head. Then he slid up the shaft until my entire dick was in his mouth and his large, stately nose was buried in my hairy bush.

He sucked me with his eyes closed, grunting small exclamations of approval, looking like a gourmet of fellatio. Thoughts of my girlfriend faded. She wasn't doing me any good. I looked at the man's neatly combed, graying hair as it started to fall forward. Here was my girlfriend now, for tonight anyway.

I pushed my hips upward, thrusting my dick deep into his mouth. My gesture broke his rhythm, and I was amused by his annoyance. I wanted to assert a little more authority. He quickly adjusted, slipping his hands around my hips and taking the rhythm back. He had a smooth touch on my bare flanks and buttocks.

I brought one of my hands around to touch his face. His forehead was moist with small beads of sweat. I got the feeling this was a critical moment, when I'd decide whether I wanted this blowjob to be merely an experience or an outright pleasure.

I could feel myself choosing pleasure. I was struck by the odd beauty of this sight, this dignified-looking stranger bent to what seemed to be the indignity of giving head to a total stranger. If anyone could make it look good, he could, by enjoying it thoroughly.

Then he surprised me. As if aware of my appreciation, he opened his eyes and looked upward till they met with mine. It was all I needed. I could feel the final surge coming on. He pulled on me with his mouth, sensing how close to the end I was. He pushed downward, taking in all my dick, then brought himself back. As he was ready to push forward again, I came. It was intensely good.

He moaned deeply and swallowed my rod so he could hold it deep in his mouth as long as it was hard. My come shot, then oozed out of me. He eagerly drank the drink he'd really wanted when he'd come to my room. As I became limp he gave me last licks, then arose, pulling a handkerchief from his pocket and pressing it to his mouth.

I lay on the bed, my legs spread and my wet, droopy genitals exposed. He might be dressed again, houndstooth jacket and all, before I got my underwear back on.

But he turned and went to the bathroom, where he turned on the light and stood before the mirror. I looked at him only briefly, then scrambled to get dressed again. I was grabbing for my pants on the chair when I heard him say, "Would you—"

"Would I what?" I asked, looking around for a shoe instead of putting my pants back on. I looked into the bathroom to see that he faced the mirror as he spoke.

"There are some who might find fault in what I've just done, or the way I did it," he said. "They might wish to show their disapproval or displeasure by—" He turned to look at me and I noticed his tie was back in place. He swept both his hands over the crown of his head, leaving his hair once again neat.

He came out of the bathroom and I went in. I hung my pants on a hook on the door and stood over the toilet bowl. I could hear him behind me, putting his jacket on and opening the door. He shut it quietly, before I was finished.

I'm in another town now. I closed a new sale today, one that should get me the best commission I've had all year. I phoned my girlfriend, and after a half hour, I felt better off than when I'd last seen her. Things are back to normal, or even better. But as I lie here on my hotel room bed, drinking the last of the bourbon I brought with me, I don't think so much about her as about him.

Never mind what might have been, I must remember what was. He went down on me. He would have done it in the dark of that smelly movie theater, just the way he actually did it in my room. His mouth offered me a better climax than I'd lately gotten from my girlfriend. Certainly better than the one I'm trying to raise with my right hand is likely to be. As I massage myself under the head with my index finger, I think about her and try to feel the stimulus. Then I think about him and the effect is improved. Just a little rub while I remember ... how nice it was ... nothing to feel ashamed of ... just a little more ... feeling better ... better ... better ... just about ... there ... there ... there.—A.M., *Dayton, Ohio*

Pursuit & Capture

BIG DICKS: WHOSE FANTASY IS IT ANYWAY?

My girlfriend and I have just recently gotten back together after one of our many breakups. That first sex after getting together again is always the best, which is perhaps why we don't stay together for too long. This time was no exception. Afterward, I couldn't help but ask if she had been with anyone, which she never had previously.

"Don't start that shit again," Tammy retorted. Instantly I knew she had. I was amazed. She'd only slept with one other guy, one time, before me.

"Honey, you've got to tell me about it," I said, but Tammy refused. I was pissed, but it also seemed to me that if she'd broadened her horizons a little it might be good for us. I persisted. "C'mon, you have to tell me about it." She told me that she'd been drunk, and that it was no big deal. I tried to explain that I wasn't mad, just interested.

She finally conceded. It seems she was at a party at a friend's place. A guy she works with named Ronnie, who lived in the same building as her friend, asked if she wanted to get high at his place. They went to his apartment and started making out on the couch. "I was so horny, but I asked him to stop and he did," she told me. "Ronnie went to another room to get his weed, and the next thing I knew he came out completely nude." She paused.

"Well?" I asked.

"Honey, his dick was so big."

"How big?" I asked her.

"Well, you remember that video you showed me? It was that big."

I said, "Oh my God."

"And he just smiled and walked over to me. I couldn't stop staring at his dick."

"Honey, say cock," I broke in. "It's more erotic."

"Okay, cock," Tammy said sensually. "God, it hung about halfway down his leg, and it wasn't even hard! He didn't say anything, just put both my hands on his cock. I was hypnotized. I couldn't close my hands around it." She started pumping it with both hands. I was so turned on as the words fell from her lips. She has the loveliest lips and the softest skin I've ever touched. "He ran his hands through my hair, and urged my head toward his cock. I started licking it all the way up and down and massaging his balls. Then I brought the tip to my lips and took it in as far as I could. It was really hot. I could feel it pulsing in my mouth."

As Tammy told the story she started slowly jerking me off. I could see the primal lust in her eyes as she went on. "I was so wet. It was like I lost control. I just started pumping with both hands as I sucked the head. I just wanted to feel every inch of that cock inside of me."

She quickly undressed, and he positioned her on the couch with her ass hanging over the edge. He took her right leg and held it high in the air as he brought his cock to her sopping lips. He started rubbing her clit with the massive head. She began writhing in pleasure and cried out. "Put it in, please put it in!" He pressed the tip inside, then reached down and grabbed her other leg, holding them both in the air far apart. He began easing it in little by little. "Oh shit, it's so fucking big!" she cried. "I want all of it."

He sank his cock all the way inside of her until his balls were pressed against her ass. "I just started screaming," Tammy continued, her face glowing with the memory. "I didn't care if anyone heard me. It felt so deep and good. He would pull back all the way and then stuff it back in." She said that her pussy lips were wrapped so tight around his pole that with every move her clit rubbed against his shaft.

"I came so hard, and it lasted forever. It drained the life out of me. Then he turned me over and kept slamming it into me." She said that she was so weak from her orgasm that she just lay there whimpering with lust, unable to move. With both hands he massaged her ass.

He was squeezing her ass-cheeks and saying, "You like that big cock, don't you?"

She groaned back, "Yes, yes! I love it so much!" When he pulled out she collapsed against the couch, and he blew a copious load all over the sofa.

When Tammy got to that point in the story I tensed up and came like a champion.

Well, since then things have been going pretty good, especially in bed. I think Tammy's experience renewed an enthusiasm in her that I hadn't seen for a while. I still wish I'd been there to see it.—K.V., Austin, Texas

STUDENT OF TONGUES TAKES HER TO PLACES SHE'S NEVER BEEN

I'm the branch manager of a financial institution near where I live. In our building are offices which we lease to other businesses. The ladies' rest room is located down a corridor. I noticed that a certain tenant invariably came into the corridor and started making small talk every time I finished using the rest room. His office door was always open, so he knew when I was in there. When we had our little chats, his eyes constantly strayed to my breasts, and sometimes he would also glance at my crotch and shapely legs.

As time went on I actually found myself dressing for him and looking forward to our chats. I also found that his eyes were getting bolder. Also, when I returned to my desk and slipped a hand into my panties, they were usually damp.

One day I sat behind my desk, unable to do any work. I kept thinking about Gary, and decided that the very next day I was going to make a move.

On my way to work the next morning I went over the details of my plan. When I was satisfied that the business of the day had been taken care of, and the customers all served, I called my capable assistant to my office. I explained that I was going to be away from my desk for a while, that I was required to review the terms of a tenant's lease and that I didn't want to be disturbed. I knew that Rhea would take care of anything that might come up.

As I started toward Gary's office I was very nervous, and so unsteady I almost backed out. His door was closed, and I felt relieved, thinking he was out. I knocked softly, hoping he wouldn't answer, but instead I heard him say, "Come on in. I'll be with you in a moment."

When I entered he was on the phone, discussing an insurance policy with a client. I stood there, my back against the door, and carefully and silently locked it. All the while he talked on the phone his eyes were glued to my crotch and boobs. Finally he finished his conversation. I walked over to his desk and lifted my skirt, revealing stockings but no panties. I could feel my juices already starting to flow down the inside of my thighs. I lifted my leg and placed a foot on the corner of his desk. Looking him straight in the eye I confidently said, "Go ahead. Eat it! I know you want to, so go ahead, feast yourself." I almost passed out with the boldness of what I was doing. I suddenly felt a rush of pleasure just at having said the words.

I've never seen a person move so quickly, as he immediately dropped to his knees and began lapping away. His tongue traveled in long slurps from the back of my pussy to the front, then circled my clit. I groaned and put my hands on the back of his head, urging him on.

This went on for several minutes, and he must have sensed that I was about to orgasm as he stopped and asked me to lean forward across his desk. He spent the next ten minutes on his knees lavishing kisses all over my derriere. He would start at the bottom of my buttocks and gently lick and kiss the entire length of my crack, stopping to tongue my nether hole. His tongue felt as if it was on fire as he plunged it in and out, then continued his journey all over my ass with hot, wet kisses and licks. All the while he was working his fingers into my slit, occasionally flicking my clit. I felt that at any moment I would come, but he skillfully stopped for a few seconds each time I was on the edge, then continued, always keeping me on the brink, not allowing me to come.

Gary stopped what he was doing and had me sit in the chair behind his desk. The chair was one of those expensive, leather-upholstered executive chairs that tilt way back. He sat me on the very edge and told me to lean back. He dropped to his knees again and placed my heels on the desk. It was the perfect position, as my cookie was pointed toward the ceiling, which provided him just the right position. He greedily returned to tonguing me. First he would lap my entire slit, then suck on the labia, then suck on my clit, and was forever dashing his tongue in and out of my honey-pot. My husband gives good face, but I have to tell you, this guy is a world-class cunnilinguist.

Finally he focused his attention on my clit, sucking it hard. He held it gently between his teeth and used his tongue to flick it back and forth. I could barely keep from crying out. His fingers ran in, out, in, around my pussy walls and out. I found myself begging him to allow me to come, something I've never done before. Finally Gary glued his mouth to my cunny and I knew this was going to be it. For the next few seconds he worked magic on my clit, then replaced his fingers with his tongue and plunged, deeper and deeper into my crevice, faster and faster, harder and harder, his nose hitting my clit. It happened. I felt myself climbing higher, reaching for the stars. I forced my bottom out to meet his tongue thrusts, and for the first time in my life I saw fireworks—rockets, Roman candles and bright rainbows—as I came and came.

He brought me down slowly and gently, lovingly and tenderly continuing to lick and suck, until my trembling stopped and I was finally back down to mother earth.

Suddenly there was a knock at the door. My assistant informed me through the locked door that my boss was on the phone. I stood on wobbly legs, straightened my skirt and told Gary that I had to go. He understood, and gave me a playful pat on the butt and a kiss on the lips. I could taste my own juices and enjoyed the smell of my sex. I left his office, went to the ladies' rest room, replaced my panties, did all the usual things a lady has to do to be presentable in public and returned to work.

I didn't see him for the next two days. On the third day I was having lunch and he approached the table, asking if he might join me. I invited him to sit and we had a long chat about what happened. I apologized for not having returned the favor, but he brushed it aside. He's a happily married man and not interested in making love with another woman. He told me, though, that he can't get enough of eating pussy and that he'd wanted to go down on me from the moment we met. He also told me that when I reached orgasm I had let out a scream, and all the while I had been moaning loudly, none of which I can recall.

Since that first day we have had many such encounters. I find myself looking for reasons to work late so we can be more comfortable on my office furniture. It has never progressed to more than him pleasing me. He's never made any demands on me to do anything at all for him. I've never even so much as touched his cock, although I have seen the imprint of it and feel that his wife is one lucky woman.

For two years now Gary has been servicing me at least twice a week, and I have been delighted to allow him. All he wants to do is eat pussy, and I'm determined to keep my tenants happy.—A.A., *Tampa, Florida*

CHEMISTRY MAJOR GETS A LESSON IN ELEMENTARY BIOLOGY

I'm a sophomore chemistry major at a big university in the Midwest, and this is the story of the most intense sexual encounter I've ever had. I spend long hours in the lab with professors and graduate students, performing experiments and analyzing data. It was in these intimate circumstances that I met the most sensual, sexual woman I know.

Ratchanee was a visiting professor from India, brilliant and beautiful. I loved coming to work every day because I knew she would be there waiting for me. Her body was absolutely astounding. It is hard for me to decide what aspect of her magnificent form captivated me the most. When we first met, she was wearing a snug blouse that accented her full breasts. Her skirt stopped eight inches above her knees, and for a moment I couldn't take my eyes off her legs. I think she must have noticed my attention, but she didn't let me know.

We worked side by side in the lab for weeks. One day we went out to lunch together. Nothing special, just one of the restaurants around campus. When Ratchi discovered I spoke Bengali she was surprised and impressed.

One Friday night I decided to come into the lab and do some work. I'm a pretty social guy, but the lab group was behind on an experiment that Ratchi had to write an article for by the end of the quarter. I had no plans that night, so I decided to help her out. After all, we were good friends by then. About half an hour after I arrived I heard keys jingling in the lab door and Ratchi came in.

"What are you doing here?" she asked. When I told her, her full lips parted in a smile. We worked together for an hour. Ratchi suggested we take a break. Her shoulders were tired and sore, so she asked me to rub them for her.

We went to her office and sat down on the couch. She let out a slow, low moan as I rubbed her back. I found the circumstances extremely arousing and became erect immediately. When I was finished massaging her she turned around and noticed my penis pointing right at her.

I was about to apologize when she suddenly kissed me on the lips. I was stunned. She kissed me a second time, this time sliding her moist tongue into my mouth. All I could say was "Yes." She told me to take off my clothes, which I did willingly. Ratchi stood up and began undressing in front of me. I slowly began to jerk off to her naked body. She teased me, slowly unbuttoning her blouse and then unzipping her skirt. My self-service action intensified as she removed her underwear and hovered over me, completely naked except for her lab coat.

What happened next was totally embarrassing. I was so intent on her figure that I didn't notice how close I was to orgasm. As she walked toward me I came all over myself, all at once. Ratchi looked at me sitting on our lab couch, covered with my own come. I was about to get up and clean myself off when she said, "Oh no! Don't you even think of moving!"

Ratchi walked over to her desk and bent over it. Then she began to stimulate her pussy with her long fingers. I could see the cream forming in her vagina as she repeatedly dipped her finger in and out, playing with her clit. She did this for several minutes, getting off on her own hand. Ratchi took an empty test tube in her mouth and began sucking on it, as if performing fellatio on it. The scene was amazing. Finally Ratchi came, with a slight shudder.

The sight of this beautiful woman masturbating had made me hard again. She walked over to me and began sucking me off. Ratchi lapped up the come I'd sprayed earlier, tracing her tongue over my torso and chest. She proceeded to run her lips over the length of my rod, pausing intermittently to suck hard on the head. I wanted to taste her, but she wouldn't give up my cock. She was kneeling between my legs on the floor as I sat on the couch so I grabbed her by the waist and lifted her, turning her in midair, so her pussy was in my face and my cock was in her mouth.

We remained in this vertical 69 for at least five minutes. I held her waist so she wouldn't fall forward and she braced herself with one of her hands. Her legs were draped over my shoulders. She came over and over again as I dove into her dark, warm pussy. It was difficult to keep her frame from toppling over at times, because when she came her body jerked wildly.

After her third orgasm I knew I was not going to be able to hold it for very much longer. I told her I was coming, and she intensified her blowjob even further, stroking me with her hand and running her lips over the head of my penis, penetrating the hole with her tongue. I came in her mouth, and she swallowed every drop like it was liquid gold.

Ratchi gradually eased off, and I sighed in satisfaction.

"You sound like you think we're done here," she said. Ratchi went over to the lab table and brought back a graduated cylinder, a slim, twelve-inch container used for measuring liquids. She positioned it on the floor and knelt over it, then gradually lowered her ass over it. The smooth glass penetrated her wet pussy, and she deeply inhaled the thick scent of sex in the air.

Watching Ratchi hump the glass phallus, I became erect again. I beckoned to her, but she was intent on coming with her makeshift dildo. Her breathing increased, and as she came she screamed "Oh my God!" in Bengali.

I stood up, gingerly lifted her and placed her on the couch. She lay flat on her back and spread her legs for me. I began moving my penis over her pussy lips. The juices flowed almost instantly, and I slid myself into her.

I had waited for this for a long time, so I didn't rush the process. I steadily worked her pussy in a regular, undeviating rhythm. As we fucked, I eased my hands under her ass and used my thumbs to help work her open a little further. She was unbelievably tight for a woman of her age, and I enjoyed every inch of her. She came twice while I was on top of her and she left four huge wet spots on the couch.

I was approaching ecstasy for the third time, but I didn't want to come without her, so I pulled out and told her to get on her knees. Ratchi complied, giving me an excellent view of her slim, round, brown ass. She arched her back and dipped her head down so that her ass lifted high in the air, making her glistening womanhood gape at me. I carefully inched my way into her and we began doing it doggie-style. As we fucked, I noticed that she was pushing back against me as I penetrated her from behind. We were both sweating from our exertion, and I knew that this would be my last performance of the night. Ratchi's long black hair flew in the air as our fucking continued. I gathered it all in my hands and rubbed it against my chest.

I slowed down, pulled out and sat on the couch, my cock standing straight up in the air. Ratchi pounced on me like a cat in heat. She sat on my cock and began rapidly moving up and down my length. This position excites me, because it puts my lover in complete control of our tempo. Ratchi's full, round breasts heaved in the air as she brought me closer and closer to orgasm. I reached out and grabbed them, cupping them with my hands and bringing the stiff nipples to my lips. My professor/lover called out my name and begged for more. Having her tits as a distraction was enough to let her catch up with me. I knew we were going to come together. Her cream was running all over my legs, so I took one of my hands and began fingering her pussy. Ratchi stiffened and jerked, then one of her hands disappeared under us and she began rubbing my balls. We were both prolonging the pleasure for as long as we could because we didn't want it to end. Ratchi began making more noise than she had made all night. My cock and right hand stimulating her pussy, coupled with my tongue licking her nipples, was making her wail in ecstasy. In one final sensual explosion, we came in a resounding clap of orgasmic thunder.

Ratchi fell off me and onto the couch. I fell asleep almost immediately. I woke up early Saturday morning to discover Ratchi had already left. I noticed the graduated cylinder she had used as a dildo lying on the floor. I sat for a while reliving the night, then, smiling and whistling, I locked up the lab and left.—S.S., *Evanston, Illinois*

WILL SHE PASS UP HER FIRST CHANCE TO SWING? DON'T BET ON IT

*I*t happened shortly after Kevin moved in next door. He struck me as a nice enough guy in most ways, but a blowhard, always bragging about his sexual exploits. Then one day he went too far when he said, "I can fuck any woman. There isn't a female alive who can resist me."

To make a long story short, I just couldn't pass up a challenge like that. After getting him to commit to a two-week time limit, I bet him he couldn't bed Maria.

He was eager for a shot at my beautiful 36C-24-35, five-foot-five-inch, twenty-six-year-old wife, but I cooled him out by saying, "Now wait a minute. If you win you get to screw my wife. What do I get if you win?"

He was so sure of himself he said, "Anything. You name it."

I replied, "Your '65 Mustang."

He thought about it for quite a while, then came back with, "Sure man, but be fair. That car's worth tons of money. When I win you have to let me have a whole week alone with the lovely Maria."

"Well, that's up to her, isn't it?" I replied with a smile. Now, my wife was raised by very traditional southern parents. She had been sent to nothing but church schools, wasn't allowed to date at all until she was sixteen, and only then at chaperoned church activities. Even though she's loosened up a lot in the six years we've been married, she's still very religious, and sexually conservative. When I put that together with Kevin's cockiness, I was confident I'd be driving his classic Mustang within the month.

Before that afternoon was over we had set the ground rules. Neither of us would ever tell Maria about the bet, no matter who won. Kevin had to get a blood test and promise not to have sex with anyone else during the challenge. He had to seduce her using only his looks, charm and sexual prowess. No drugs or alcohol could be used to lower her resistance. Near misses wouldn't count. He had to have actual intercourse with Maria, ejaculating inside her vagina. I wasn't allowed to interfere in any way. To prove he had succeeded, I had to witness the act. However, if Kevin won, I would fake a business trip and arrange for him to have seven full days and nights alone with her. But most important, regardless of our agreement, at no time during or after the bet did Maria have to do anything she didn't want to.

The two weeks started on a warm Friday evening with Maria and me going to Kevin's for dinner. I was sure he'd act like an arrogant ass, putting on some macho routine that would turn Maria off, ending the contest before it began. Boy, was I wrong. To my surprise Kevin had a date, and what a date she was. Her name was Cynthia and she was a stunningly beautiful, sweet individual.

She and Maria immediately hit it off, quickly giggling and gossiping like old friends. This included a conversation in the kitchen, where I overheard Cynthia going on and on about what a great lover Kevin was.

Even though Kevin was the perfect gentleman, not making one false move or statement, his plan for the evening worked, because when the girls rejoined us, Maria kept sneaking peeks at the front of his pants. Kevin noticed it too, so the next day he made sure she could check out his bulge to her heart's content.

He came over wearing a tiny men's bikini bathing suit and stood over her while she was lying out getting some sun. As he stood right next to her, his crotch about a foot from her face, I could understand how any woman would be attracted to him. He's tall, good-looking, with a muscular build, a trim flat stomach and the kind of tight butt that girls love. His bright yellow suit contrasted with his dark skin, drawing attention to what was obviously a very big cock hidden underneath.

As per the agreement, I stayed inside the house, even when Maria became comfortable enough with him to roll over and allow him to unhook her bathing suit top to rub suntan lotion on her back. Next he got a lawn chair, and positioned it at the head of her lounge chair. He then sat with his legs spread, once again putting his crotch right in front of Maria's face.

If nothing else, my wife was flustered by Kevin's display. I know because when some squirrels made a commotion behind her, she twisted around without thinking, exposing her breasts.

Kevin whispered something that made Maria turn bright red with embarrassment, and she playfully hit his knee. It worried me to think that less than twenty-four hours of the bet had passed, and Kevin had already seen Maria's titties. Plus she was relaxed enough around him to be joking about it.

That was nothing compared to the shock I got on Sunday night. We invited Cynthia and Kevin over to watch a movie. It was late when it ended, so I excused myself, saying I had to get up early for work. The three of them went out by our pool, where the conversation drifted around to skinny-dipping. They kidded about it for a while, then Cynthia told Maria, "I will if you will."

My heart sank when Maria gave Kevin another playful smack, smiled and said, "So, it's payback time. Now I'll get to see what you've got."

I was amazed at how casually my wife undressed along with the others, then walked hand in hand down the steps with them into the shallow end of the pool. As they splashed around in the waist-deep water, the girls teased Kevin about the way the cold water was making his cock shrivel up, and he came back with a comment about how swollen and hard their nipples were for the same reason. This led to the three of them taking turns standing on the steps wiggling and acting silly while the other two laughed. I don't think Maria would have done any of this if Cynthia hadn't been there, but I could tell my wife was aroused by the group nudity.

Kevin spent time with Maria every day that week. They had a lot of fun, but nothing happened until the following Saturday, when he made his first real attempt to get into her panties. Per his instructions, I told Maria I was going out with the guys, then sneaked back to Kevin's place. Once I was there and safely hidden away, he called Maria and asked her to come over.

When she arrived, Kevin put on a performance that was worthy of an Academy Award. With tears in his eyes, he told her Cynthia had broken up with him. He milked it for everything it was worth. Playing on her sympathy, he got Maria to hold his hand, give him hugs and squeeze him close. Then, supposedly to get his mind off Cynthia, he and Maria went around the house collecting all the little personal things that reminded him of her.

In the bedroom they found some of Cynthia's lingerie, including a teddy Kevin had given her. After reminiscing about the significance of the garment, he asked Maria to put it on. At first she balked, but he kept the pitiful routine going until she consented and went into the bathroom to change.

When Maria came out, wearing only the teddy, she looked better than naked. It was very feminine, very brief and very sheer, emphasizing her breasts and pussy rather than concealing them. It was obvious by the way she was carrying herself that the garment didn't just make Maria look sexy, it made her feel sexy too. She went over to where Kevin was sitting and did a slow pirouette in front of him, then asked, "So, what do you think?"

Unable to take his eyes off her, he replied, "God, Maria. You're beautiful." She smiled and bit her lower lip, then stepped forward into his arms. Maria's eyes drifted shut, and her breathing became strained as our new neighbor's hands roamed over her body. He started with her arms, waist and hips, but moved around back to lightly massage her tush. When she didn't resist he worked his way up to firmly squeeze her titties and pinch her nipples. A whimper escaped from Maria's throat when Kevin's lips replaced his fingers on her right breast.

Up till then I was holding out hope that Maria would put an end to this and I would still win the bet, but I got a really hollow feeling when she only pushed him away long enough to let the teddy slip down around her waist, then pulled him forward again, burying his face between her breasts. Maria held the back of Kevin's head, guiding his mouth back and forth between her aroused nipples. His hands were busy pushing the teddy off her hips and down to the floor, where she raised one foot then the other, stepping out of the lacy garment. I watched my wife open her stance, giving Kevin access to her pussy. His hands slid back up and between her legs, one from the front and the other from the rear. A few seconds later Maria gasped and bent her knees, squatting down slightly to meet his fingers as they wormed their way into her vagina and her tight little rectum.

Watching my sexy wife humping her pelvis in response to Kevin's fingers pumping in and out of her two openings, while she held his face to her soft mounds, was giving me a raging hard-on. Don't misunderstand, I was still jealous, but the graphic sex scene in front of me was still turning me on. It dawned on me that this was the first time I'd ever actually seen Maria having sex, and it made me realize how lucky I am. When she erupted into a tremendous orgasm I was glad she was having so much pleasure.

Suddenly she pulled away from Kevin and started getting dressed. He protested, pointing out the tent in his pants, and saying, "Maria, please, you can't leave me like this."

She gave him a wicked little smile and said, "Sorry, Kevin, but I've got to get home before my husband gets back. At least I helped you forget about Cynthia for a little while."

That evening Kevin came over for dinner. During the meal

he and Maria kept exchanging knowing glances. After we ate I excused myself, saying I was exhausted and needed to get to bed.

While I pretended to be sleeping, the two of them did the dishes. Of course, the only thing Kevin wanted to discuss was what had happened earlier, and how hot and sexy Maria was. As they talked it came out that Kevin was the first one to ever finger-fuck her bottom. When he asked how she liked it she gave him a little peck on the cheek and said, "I never imagined that having both my holes penetrated could feel so good. Thank you, it was wonderful."

She smiled and turned slightly, responding to his advances. Without saying another word Kevin unzipped her jeans, and slipped both hands inside, one in front, the other in back. She halfheartedly resisted saying, "We shouldn't be doing this," but when he asked if she wanted him to stop, she replied, "Truthfully? No."

With Maria breathing hard, and once again rocking back and forth to the tempo Kevin was setting between her legs, he asked if there was anything else she'd never done. She was having a great deal of difficulty talking, but finally blurted out, "I've never sucked anyone off."

Kevin waited until she was nearing a climax, then said, "Come on Maria, make me the first."

Since Maria had always refused to perform any oral sex, saying she'd never put the thing a man pees from into her mouth, you can imagine how I felt when she dropped to her knees, pulled his semierect manhood out and took it between her lips.

This was the first time I'd gotten a good look at Kevin's cock. It quickly inflated to its full size as Maria lovingly licked, nibbled and sucked it. Once she got him hard she looked up, smiled, then cut me to the quick by telling him, "Your cock is beautiful. It's much bigger than my husband's."

More aggressive than she'd ever been with me, Maria wrapped both arms around him, then squeezed and kneaded his butt, while taking as much of his cock down her throat as she could. For a woman who had never done this before, she sure looked like she had an idea of what she was doing. Kevin didn't have to give her any hints about what he liked. She could tell from the loud groans every time she got it right. When she wrapped her hand around the base of his cock and jerked it up and down while circling his dickhead with the tip of her tongue he grabbed her shoulders and said, "Oh, babe, that's so perfect!"

He held out for about ten minutes, but when Maria spread his buns and pushed one of her fingers into his ass, even Kevin couldn't hold back any longer. He shot a huge load of sperm into her mouth. As far away from them as I was, I could still hear the gulping sounds she made as she tried to keep up with his pumping cock.

Maria continued sucking until he went soft, then carefully stuffed his equipment back inside his pants and zipped him up. After handing him a clean towel, she leaned against the counter with her hands behind her back and told him, "We have a rule here. Whoever makes a mess has to clean it up."

He gave her a big grin and went right to work on the front of her blouse, where some drops of come had fallen.

For a few seconds Kevin actually wiped the come stains, before Maria pulled her shirt and bra up around her neck. Taking the hint, he lavished attention on her titties, squeezing, kissing and nibbling the sensitive orbs. When she began moaning and sighing in response to his caresses, he said, "Maria. I want you. Let me give your whole body the pleasure you're craving. Let me do you doggie-style. That way I can fill your pussy with my cock and finger your ass at the same time. Just imagine how that will feel."

Maria sighed, mesmerized, "Mmm, yes, that sounds nice."

I thought he had her, but a few seconds later she continued, "Kevin, wait. This is happening too fast. I sucked you off because I wondered what it was like, and to repay you for earlier. I need to think, okay? We can get together again tomorrow."

* * *

On Sunday Maria was very quiet during church, and later when we worked in the yard. Kevin came over while we were outside, but she avoided both of us. We puttered around for a while, then Maria went inside. I gave Kevin my keys, and yelled out, "Honey, I'm going jogging."

After giving him a few minutes lead time, I crept through the house to our bedroom, where I found them standing at the foot of our bed. Maria was rubbing and squeezing Kevin's cock through his pants and saying, "I don't know. What if he comes home and catches us?"

Kevin, who was lightly tracing circles across her blouse, kind of chuckled and responded, "We don't have a thing to worry about. He can't get in. I lifted his keys and locked the door."

That's when Maria's expression changed, and I knew she had made up her mind. She threw her arms around his neck and gave Kevin a long, passionate kiss. When their embrace broke they urgently pulled off each other's clothes.

In all the years I've known Maria I can't remember ever hearing her say fuck, so it was quite a shock when she told Kevin, "God, I'm so horny I feel like I'm on fire. I've been soaking my panties just thinking about your fucking me doggie-style while fingering my ass. Both my holes have been tingling ever since you mentioned it. Do me like that. Fuck my pussy with your cock, and my ass with your finger. Hurry. I want you inside me."

Once they were naked, Kevin made sure Maria was positioned so I could see everything from my hiding place in the hallway. Moving in behind her, he rubbed his dick up and down her wet, swollen slit, then gently eased the head in and out of her opening a few times. Then, with one slow steady push, it was done.

A loud moan escaped from my wife's throat as her love-hole was stretched and filled for the first time by a cock other than mine. When he was all the way in, she gasped, "Oh God, Kevin, I've never felt so full in my life. Oh yes, you're driving me wild." He pumped into her juicy pussy a few times, then eased a finger into her ass. With a look of pure ecstasy on her face, Maria moaned loudly and exclaimed, "Oh God, yes! Oh yes. Oh, Kevin that feels wonderful. Yeah, yeah. Oh, I can feel your big, beautiful cock way up inside me. I love it. Yeah, like that. Oh God, Kevin, I'm going to come! Fuck me harder. Oh yea-h-h, fuck me, fuck me, fuck m-e-e!"

Grinning in my direction, Kevin was only too happy to oblige Maria's wishes, furiously pounding into her two holes until she gave out a long, hissing, sighing sound. Her body went rigid and shook for several seconds, as she was rocked by a titanic orgasm. When he couldn't hold back any longer, the tempo of his thrust increased to a fever pitch, ending with him blasting a massive load of hot, sticky sperm deep inside her.

Maria was wild with ecstasy, and didn't want him to stop, yelling, "I can feel you squirting inside me. Oh Kevin, fill me with your wonderful seed. Pump my pussy full of your hot spunk!" She held him tight, and continued to hump against him until his spent cock went soft and popped out of her overflowing pussy. When she finally allowed him to roll off, she had an unbelievably satisfied look on her face.

I'm not one to renege on a bet, so after work the next day I told Maria I had to go on a business trip. It was one of the hardest things I've ever done, but I stayed away for the entire week. When I returned, other than my wife's pubic hair being shaved off, everything appeared normal. I was dying to know what happened, but I guess I never will, since the only thing Kevin will say is, "Man, it was fantastic. We did it all. If you can imagine it, we did it. That wife of yours is one hot lover."

I actually asked Maria if she had seen Kevin at all during the week I'd been away, mentioning that it seemed like he'd been hanging around a lot lately. "Yeah, he came over a few times," she said.

When she didn't add anything more I asked, "Well what did you do?"

"Oh," she replied, "We just played a lot of games." I guess that's all I'll ever know.—*C.H.*, *Santa Monica, California*

WHEN IT COMES TO PAINTING, THERE'S NOTHING LIKE THE MASTER'S PIECE

*L*ike most of the letters I have read in your magazine, this one starts the same. I never thought it would happen to me. But it did.

It was a couple of years ago when I took early retirement. I started doing a few minor repair jobs and a little painting to pick up a few bucks and to keep busy.

One friend of a friend asked if I would paint a room for them. The wife wanted it done and he was too busy at work to take a couple of days off, and he did not like to paint. I went over and took a look at the room and agreed to paint it on the next Tuesday and Wednesday. Since he and his wife both worked I would be in the house alone so it seemed like a pretty good job.

I arrived about eight Tuesday morning and met the husband as he was leaving to go to work. He informed me his wife was not feeling well so she was staying home, but that I could go ahead and paint. She would sleep late and if she felt better later she would go in to work for the afternoon, he said.

I went on in and moved the furniture around and got all set up. Then I started to paint. I had just about finished the ceiling when the wife came to the door and asked me if I wanted a cup of coffee. It sounded nice and I was at a stopping point so I told her a cup of coffee would be great. In a few minutes I finished the ceiling and went into the kitchen.

She didn't look like she felt bad; in fact, she looked great. It looked like she had showered and fixed her hair. I also smelled perfume. Man, she looked and smelled great. When she asked if

I wanted cream in my coffee I said yes. As she reached up to the top shelf of the cabinet for the powdered cream, her short robe rose to reveal about a third of the cheeks of her well-rounded ass. She had the smallest bikini I had ever seen on a woman. I began to feel something stirring between my legs, and you all know what that was.

As she put the cream on the table and sat down, she let the robe slide off her shoulders, remarking how warm it was in the house. The sheer, blue dressing gown clearly revealed her hard nipples. I knew she had big breasts. I had seen her on a couple of social occasions, but she had never before worn anything so revealing or tight, so the sight of those knockers really made my eyes bug out.

She talked as though nothing strange was happening, so I tried to talk and act as if nothing was out of the ordinary, like the monstrous sausage throbbing away in my underpants. She asked if I wanted another cup of coffee and, of course, I said sure. She picked up the pot and instead of walking around the table leaned over directly in front of me. The gown gaped open and I could see her big beautiful breasts. She finished pouring the coffee and looked me right in the eyes and asked if there was anything else I wanted.

I figured now was the time. I said I see a lot that really looks good to me. When she smiled I reached up and felt her breasts, which were as soft as a jumbo-size bowl of Jell-O. She smiled and said she thought she had made the right decision—that this would be a good morning to stay home and spend some time in bed.

With that she put the coffeepot down and took me by the hand and led me to the bedroom. She undressed me while I felt her breasts and her pussy, which was really wet. Then I removed her gown and bikini panties. She had satin sheets on the bed. She pushed me back and then she slid in on top of me. Before I knew anything she had her pussy wrapped around my dick like a hot dog on a bun. I came so quick that it surprised me, but she was just starting to get warmed up. She drained me dry but her pussy kept a tight grip on my cock.

As she rolled off me and lay down, I began to kiss and suck on one breast and then the other. Her nipples were like hard candy of the sweetest kind. As I rolled on top of her, her legs automatically spread, and when my dick slipped into her pussy I felt a contraction like a steel ring. She had the strongest pussy muscles of any woman I have ever been with.

Even with those taut cunt muscles, trying to stay inside her was tough as she could move her ass in several directions at the same time. Since I am an older man, and had already come once, I really had to work at it to reach a second climax. This suited her just fine.

As I felt that great sensation rising in my groin I felt her begin to stiffen and her head arched back. She growled and then began to writhe and twist. Her breath came so hard I wondered if the neighbors would hear her. To say that we both reached a thunderous climax would be an understatement. What we reached was the climax of climaxes for me. She lay there in a pool of sweat breathing hard and sighing.

She said this was the nicest paint job she had ever seen done, and she was sure that she would find another room that needed painting before too long. She also wanted to know how my morning break had been. I was so busy sucking on those beautiful breasts that I mumbled that the break was fine, but what about lunch. She said she had thought about going in to work for the afternoon, but maybe she did feel a lingering headache.

I got up and dressed and went back to my painting. I figured I better paint some so the husband would not wonder what I had done all day. I heard her rattling around for the next couple of hours. I painted as fast as I could because I was really looking forward to our lunch break. About noon she came into the room while I was on the ladder.

It was clear that she only had on that short robe as she walked over to me and unzipped my pants. She took my dick out of my pants. Since I was standing on the third step of the ladder it was just at the right level, and she put it into her mouth. She then said she knew what her lunch was going to be but I would have to find something I liked for myself. She then unbuckled my pants and as they dropped I stepped down off the ladder. In the bedroom she wanted to finish what she had started, so I moved around and found a warm wet pussy just ready for slurping. As I put my tongue up her pussy I felt it tighten and heard a groan from her, but she never stopped sucking on my dick. She sucked like it was the best thing she had ever had in her mouth, and I was having trouble concentrating on what I was doing. I stopped and just looked down at her face. She had her eyes closed and was letting out a low groan.

As I started to come she just sucked harder and I almost cried out it felt so good. As I watched my half-soft dick slip out of her smiling mouth, she had a glow like nothing I had ever seen. After a few moments I returned to my pussy sucking for she surely deserved the best I had to offer. I nibbled, I sucked and I tongue-fucked for all I was worth. "Yes, yes, yes," she moaned, over and over, louder and louder.

Finally I felt her begin to come. She squeezed my head so tight I could hardly get to her pussy but I gave it all I had. She went limp. Her legs fell apart, leaving her pussy wide open. I softly kissed it several times as she reached down and patted me on the shoulder.

After a moment I turned around and she held out one of her breasts, asking me to suck it while we rested for a moment. As I slowly and softly sucked her big nipple I slowly fondled her body. She began to purr like a kitten and snuggled closer to me. My dick was done for the day, or so I thought. After all, I am sixty while she was probably in her thirties.

We lay there quite a while and then she began to play with my little nipples, nibbling on them. She then bent over me, dragging first one nipple and then the other over my lips. Then she got on top of me and ground her rough pussy hair into my skin. She took my limp dick and began to rub the head with her nipples. Boy, what a feeling as those two little bullets slickened.

As my dick got hard she licked my balls and sucked them. She then rolled me over on top of her and said, "Hang on, baby." She rolled onto her back with her legs still wrapped around me. She moved her pussy every which way and it felt like my dick was stuck inside a vacuum cleaner hose. Her legs got tighter and her pussy moved faster until I saw her stiffen again and get red in the face. She let out a groan that I know could be heard next door, but by then I didn't care because I was coming.

I latched onto her nipple and sucked. When she had finished her climax her legs spread open wide, but my limp dick was still in her. I just lay on top of her with my head on her ample breast as my soft dick slowly slid out of her wet pussy.

When I awoke I was still on top of her and she was asleep. I kissed her nipples and slowly got up. I dressed and went back to the room I was painting but there was no way I could paint anymore that day. The thought of climbing a ladder was too much.

After I cleaned up to leave I went back to the bedroom and as I kissed her she began to move. When I touched her nipples they became hard immediately. She was lying there naked, spread-eagle on the bed. She opened her eyes and I thanked her for the coffee and, as I patted her pussy, the snacks that I had that day. I told her I had done all I could do for that day, painting and otherwise. I gave her another soft kiss and left.

When I arrived the next morning the husband said the room was looking really nice. I asked about his wife and he said she was fine. He said she told him she had spent most of the day in bed and it had really made her feel better. In fact, she had gone in early to catch up on her work from yesterday.

I never saw her again on that paint job but the husband was happy and paid me very well for my labor. The next time my wife and I were in their company, she mentioned she and her husband were thinking about getting another room painted. She wanted to know if I was interested. She said she would be trying to think up some new snacks to go along with the coffee. I told her the snacks last time had been great; in fact, memorable and about all a man my age could take. —D.M., *Corpus Christi, Texas*

UMM, WHAT'LL I DO TODAY?
THINK I'LL LOSE MY VIRGINITY

My parents moved to California when I was a little girl. It's still too bad they treat me like I was one. They would flip if they ever found out that I've sucked and fucked every boy's cock in our apartment complex. But what's a poor girl to do stuck inside of San Francisco with the Manhattan blues? And how else is a girl supposed to have a good time?

I've tried my hand at chess and didn't like it. As for swimming, I didn't care for it. Aerobics is too sweaty. So for me, the answer came to me one day while I was out walking around. It sort of flashed in my brain—Sex! Yeah, good ol' sex. That was the solution to my boredom. I had the equipment—incredibly large tits and a tight, sweet snatch. I didn't need much training to use them. So right away, without really considering any consequences, I dove in and quickly began to have sex.

Now, don't get me wrong. I'm no slut. Sure, I enjoy having big cocks between my tits, but I'm somewhat picky. I just don't let any man fuck me or come on my huge tits. No way. That's why I fuck the boys in my apartment complex because I know them and they know me. Boy, do they know me.

I can still remember the first time.

I woke up wet. My pussy was pulsing for a real dick. The only thing I had was a ten-inch dildo that I had ordered from one of my father's girlie magazines. It satisfied me for a good month, but then the need to have the real thing became a throbbing, frustrating itch. I tried to ease the sexual awakening within me by sliding that big dildo in and out of my cunt, feeling the artificial veins touching, stroking, caressing my nerves. Then I'd slide it between my sweaty breasts, which I would sometimes massage with baby oil. It just made me crazier for the real thing. I couldn't hold back my desires any longer. I had to have it.

I made sure my parents had left for work before I got dressed. I put on a tiny pink and white miniskirt, a tight top, a spangle in my hair and no underwear hindering my sweet ass and cunt. The alarm clock on my dresser read ten-forty. I was seriously late for my class at City College, but I didn't really care.

Today was the day I was going to lose my cherry. Not that my dildo wasn't a good plaything, but I had to feel some hard flesh moving inside of me—not rubber—or else I was going to lose my mind. I felt my nipples become hard under my cotton top as I thought about fucking my way to an orgasm. I smiled and left the kitchen for the hall.

I rushed for the elevator. The door was about to close. I called out. "Hold it, please!" And a hand did. A green stone glittered on the third finger. A school ring. It was my neighbor's son. He was late too. He was covered in flannel with a big, black backpack over his right shoulder. He let the door go as I got into the elevator. He smiled, his brown eyes gleaming. I smiled back and my flesh tingled. My nipples became harder if that were possible. I knew he could see them standing out, and I got embarrassed. I crossed my arms over my chest, trying to cover up my excitement—then I thought to myself—Why are you embarrassed? Aren't you looking for a real cock?

I glanced over at my neighbor. He was no wimp. His chest heaved in and out as he watched the floor numbers light on, then off, on, then off. He looked at his watch. I eyed his crotch and saw a nice bulge. My pussy pulsed like a second heart. He is what you want, I thought to myself as we hit the ninth floor.

Shit, in a few seconds he was going to be gone. If you're going to act you better act now. So I did. I reached out and pushed the stop button. The elevator stopped with a jerk. The alarm sounded out softly. I knew I only had a few minutes before building security would get the elevator working again, but a few minutes were all that were necessary. I smiled at him.

He looked at me with one of those "what the fuck are you doing?" expressions. I rolled down my top and flashed him my perfect tits, which are full and tan all over with sharp, sugary brown nipples. I noticed his bulge twitch—then grow against the zipper. It was an amazing sight. By now my twat was dancing with the dewdrops of sex. I couldn't wait to feel that glorious thing of his inside me. I squeezed and licked my sweet breasts as I watched him take out his erection.

My mouth dropped open. It was deliciously large with veins flowing like tree branches just under the skin. He stroked it, and it grew even larger. My dildo at home did not compare at all to the natural beauty of this guy's prime-of-life erection. A warm drop of my juice dripped free of my cunt and hit the floor as the emergency phone began to ring.

I grabbed hold of that cock and jerked it. The flesh was loose, velvety smooth. I moved back and forth with ease. I imagined feeling it inside me pistoning fast, then slow, and faster again as he licked my nipples slowly into his mouth. He bit the nips, then swirled his tongue around them. I knew I wouldn't have to imagine feeling it inside me any longer.

We slid to the floor and he pushed my skirt up. He buried his head between my shapely legs, licking and sucking. He kissed my cunt with such heated passion that I thought I was going to come right then and there. Somehow I managed to hold it back. I grabbed and ripped at my tits as he burnt tracks across my clit. My legs embraced his head. I couldn't believe how good his lips felt.

I closed my eyes and rocked my hips, wanting to fuck his mouth with my cunt. I heard him moaning through my drenched pink sex. The phone was buzzing next to my head. I licked my lips. Stop ringing, damn it, my mind screamed through a thick haze. Stop fucking ringing! But it wouldn't.

Quickly I felt something new. Oh, shit! My mouth opened as

I felt it. It pushed inside of me, slowly. The walls of my cunt stretched. God, did they stretch. I could feel a stiff mass filling me as I had never been filled before. He was on top of me. My legs were on his shoulders. I could see his mouth moving but no words were coming out. His hips fell on mine. Then he lifted. The feeling inside me moved out, then thrust back. It was incredible!

I could feel my orgasm growing fast. He bent forward and took my right tit into his mouth. The muscles of my pussy opened and closed around him. Rivulets of sex juice oozed from my crack. It wasn't going to be long now. My legs started to tremble.

I grunted with each forward thrust of his massive cock. Then I came—I came so hard that I thought I was going to die or pass out. My tits bounced and swayed with the power of my orgasm. I never thought I could come so hard and for so long. Then something I had not expected happened—he came. That scared me because my dildo never came.

He pulled out of my twat and shot white lotion all over my tits. Hot, delicious lotion, something I imagined bathing in if I could get the opportunity. It splattered all over me. I rubbed the come all over my tits and worked the stuff in slowly, talking about how sweet it looked and how much I wanted to do it again.

I still sometimes play with my dildo. I think toys for women are the greatest. However, now that I have all these new friends, I get the real thing all the time. The real thing is a hell of a lot sweeter than rubber. —*P.N., San Francisco, California*

A WARM FIRE, HOT FOOD AND
A GOOD FUCK FOR THE SNOWBOUND

My wife and I are both trained Emergency Medical Technicians, often working different schedules with long hours and for long stretches of days. When we finally had three consecutive days off, we rented a secluded cabin near a ski resort about an hour from our home.

We arrived at the cabin and unloaded the car. As soon as we had the last suitcase in, we literally ripped each other's clothes off and dove right into some long-delayed pleasure. We, in fact, didn't wait till we made it to the bedroom; we fucked right on the kitchen floor. I have to say that even though we both have had different work schedules, our sex has always been electric.

No sooner had we gotten dressed when there was a knock on the door. We looked at each other rather surprised. Who could it be? No one knew we were here. I went to the door and carefully peeked out. A young man in his twenties, looking extremely cold and disoriented, was standing outside. As I opened the door further, he said, "Help me please!"

I yelled to my wife that the man was suffering from either hypothermia or possibly frostbite. We reacted quickly and methodically to the situation, bringing the young man inside and checking his hands and feet for signs of frostbite after removing his boots and socks. Neither of us found any signs of frostbite, so we moved on looking for other signs.

The next thing we did was remove his wet clothing. As my wife began to remove his jeans I began to get the fireplace ready for a fire. I wanted to get the room warmer. I had just gotten the kindling wood ablaze when I heard Jenny yell, "Whoa!" I turned and looked.

As she was pulling off his jeans his long underwear came off, too. Now you guys know what happens to a penis when it gets into something cold. It's a common enough bodily response. I have always termed it "turtle dick." The penis shrinks into the warm part of the body. Well, needless to say, our patient had this condition; however, there was still quite a massive dong hanging there between his legs. Jenny quickly pulled the guy's drawers up, and I think she was relieved that the young man was still disoriented enough not to know what had just happened.

I went to the bedroom and grabbed a blanket to help keep him warm. When I returned he was a little more conscious of what was going on. He was telling my wife that he had been hiking and had gotten lost. I covered him with the blanket and told him to rest quietly while I got the fire started.

As I was leaving I heard my wife apologize for looking at his cock and making such a show of how large it was. It was quite out of character for her, especially considering the amount of training she has had. I thought it was probably because she was still horny from our earlier romp on the kitchen floor.

Outside it had started to snow quite hard. I waded my way through the snow to the woodbox located at the back of the cabin, and dug out several good-sized logs as well as some smaller ones to help the kindling along. The whole process took me about eight minutes. I added a few more taking in the quiet beauty of the snow falling in the woods and all along the surrounding hills.

I returned to the cabin, opened the door and saw our patient sitting forward on the couch with the blanket tossed aside. As I walked toward him in the direction of the fireplace, I looked again. Jenny had her lips tightly wrapped around his big cock; she had her eyes closed and was quite oblivious to my presence in the room. Our patient just looked at me and smiled.

"Jenny!" I yelled. She stopped and looked up at me, rather bewildered.

"You saw it, the poor thing needed resuscitating," she said.

I looked at his penis. It must have been at least ten inches long. It was also hard as a railroad spike. I dropped the wood on the floor in front of the fireplace, my mind swirling with all kinds of conflicting emotions. When I turned around I saw our patient place his hand on Jenny's head, pulling her back to his prick, which she obligingly did.

Totally confused, I turned and started the fire, listening to the familiar sounds of slurping, Jenny's moans and his rather guttural groans. My wife loves to suck cock and knowing what this guy was experiencing got me excited. I could feel myself getting hard as I listened to this oral escapade.

After the fire was roaring I turned to see Jenny really bobbing on the young man's cock. Encouraged by his guttural coaxing, she was desperately trying to take the whole slab into her mouth, while she used one hand to manipulate and fondle his large balls. The whole thing was beginning to make me extremely horny. I didn't think I could take it anymore.

"Jenny, would you stop that," I pleaded, but she didn't even slow her pace.

"Give it up, man. She's into sucking my cock, and she doesn't want to stop," the unexpected visitor announced at this point.

I had to admit he was right. She was enjoying every stroke she made on that glistening rod. The bulge in my own pants was no-ticeable, and I did the only thing that I could think of—I joined them. I removed my jeans and got on my knees behind Jenny, who had pulled her stretch pants down to her knees in order to finger herself while she fellated our new friend.

I grabbed her hand and moved it out of the way, then eased my cock into her wet pussy. She let out a big moan but never took that cock from her mouth.

Jenny was coming all over in a matter of moments. During her orgasm she stopped sucking, seemingly frustrated that this cock she had been working on hadn't spilled a wad yet. She began stroking the shaft with both hands as she continued to suck on it. That must have been what he needed. At that mo-ment his whole body began twitching. Jenny removed her mouth and watched as his huge cock shot its load high into the air, then down his cock and balls. He reached down and pulled her T-shirt off over her head, rubbing sticky come all over her 36C tits.

Now it was my turn. I thought that my come was going to shoot out of Jenny's mouth, I blasted so hard. She came again with another swooping orgasm before sitting up to continue rub-bing our new friend's jizz all over her boobs.

The three of us sat there, all of us in some form of undress, not really knowing what to do or say. An awkward moment, especially for Jenny who had her pants around her ankles and sperm splashed all over her breasts. She didn't act unusual about it at all. I finally broke the ice and asked our friend what his name was, and if he had been with someone else that might be looking for him.

"My name is Phil," he said. "And I should call, or get going back to my hotel if you folks know the way."

I showed him to the phone and I watched Jenny's eyes follow his half-naked frame walk to the phone. The snow was coming down harder, and the wind had kicked up, too. Jenny joined me at the window. The thought instantly came to me that we probably shouldn't let him venture out into the storm. He could get lost again.

Phil hung up the phone and said that his friends hadn't even noticed that he was gone. Jenny found this to be curious. "What about your significant other?" she asked.

Phil smiled, "I don't have anyone in my life right now."

Jenny, who was still naked, began acting sexy. She was leaning back on the couch, massaging her thighs and arching her toes. The two of us were watching her, growing harder. Phil walked towards the couch and began gathering up his clothes. "Thank you both for helping me but I'd better get going."

Before I could say anything Jenny said, "You can't leave, it's snowing way too hard out there, the wind is up, and we don't want you to get lost again." She walked towards him, reached out and pushed his hard-on downward, letting it slap back against his belly. "Besides I think you're ready to go again." She then removed his coat, sweatshirt and knit cap and pushed him back onto the couch. She straddled his large organ and began lowering herself onto it.

Again I was shocked by her actions and decided that I would join rather than protest. I removed my shirt so that we were all naked. Jenny was having some difficulty taking his whole cock

into her pussy, but she found a happy medium pumping half to
three-quarters of the full length into her vagina. Occasionally she
would go too far down, yelping slightly but never being too uncomfortable to stop.

Phil noticed my bewilderment with the situation. I was watching it all, slowly stroking my dick to an aroused state. He smiled
at me, then grabbed Jenny and lifted her off of his engorged prick
just as she was about to come. He had her kneel on the couch
with her elbows resting on the back of it. He then motioned me
around to the backside of the couch, where Jenny immediately
shoved my cock into her mouth. Phil, of course, loaded his manhood into her exposed pussy from behind. It was not long before
all three of us came, not without loud moans and groans from all
parties involved.

After we all gathered ourselves together, and Jenny excused
herself for a bathroom trip, Phil and I began to dress.

"If you don't mind my saying so, your wife is one hot lady and
you are very lucky," he said.

"I would agree with you. We don't get an opportunity to be
alone like this very often, and I think this had made her unusu-
ally horny."

Phil took a big joint from his pocket, asking if I'd join him in
a smoke. I declined, but told him it was okay if he did. We talked
sparingly while he sucked on the joint. When his eyes glowed
with the ubiquitous look of being stoned, he introduced a completely off-the-wall idea.

"How do you feel about making your wife a sex slave from now
until I am able to leave?" Phil went on to explain how he and his
best friend often do it with his friend's girlfriend, and all of them
really get off enjoying the fantasy as well as the great sex.

I told him that I didn't think so. I was sure that Jenny would
never go for it. Quite honestly, I had no interest in sharing my
wife any further. Just then Jenny walked in. "I probably won't go
for what?" she asked.

"I was talking about you being our sex slave, just until I can leave, but your husband said you wouldn't be interested," Phil said.

"What would I have to do?" she asked curiously.

"Anything we wanted you to."

Jenny smiled. "Okay," she said, "as long as it's nothing too outrageous or painful. I love the idea." I was again shocked. I was so sure that she would want no part of this scene.

She eagerly asked when we could get started. Phil said right away. We were hungry, he said, and wanted some food. Jenny scampered off to the kitchen to fix us something to eat. I went out to get some more wood for the fire. The snow was still coming down and I really tried to load up on wood so I wouldn't have to come back out later. On my way in I looked into the kitchen window to check on Jenny. Her tits were bare and hanging over the sink, slinging back and forth and up and down. Phil was fucking her from behind, causing her tits to shake with each pounding thrust.

I threw another couple of logs on the fire, then both Jenny and Phil brought dinner out and set it on the table. We ate but I didn't say a word. I was convinced that Phil was in this slave thing for his own pleasure. After dinner Phil got up to clear the table as Jenny walked over to me and said that she wanted dessert. I looked at her and said, "Yeah, so what?"

"So get up on the table, but take those jeans off first."

I removed my jeans and sat on the table. Jenny took my limp cock in her mouth and began sucking me. Meanwhile, Phil continued to clear the table off. Soon I was filling my wife's hot mouth with my come.

We sucked and fucked the night away. In the early morning hours, when I was sure that Jenny could not take any more, Phil suggested that we try some variety. Jenny didn't fight it, but she had hardly any strength left. She asked us not to fuck her, and I think Phil actually hesitated, but I was now the aggressor. Soon Phil was shoving his big prong into Jenny's Vaseline-lined cunt. It wasn't long before she was bucking and squirming. I rolled her over onto her stomach and Phil, underneath her, continued to fuck her pussy. It was the opportunity I had always looked forward to. I could see her anus exposed and ripe for fucking. She had never let me fuck her there. I drove my cock slowly into her goo-slickened asshole. Jenny went nuts, as Phil lay underneath, cheering me on. I filled her butt with my hot juice and allowed the last bit of my come to shoot over her hot little ass. Phil came, too, shortly thereafter.

We left Jenny lying on the bed and grabbed a couple of beers by the fire. We talked, and at sunrise I pointed him in the direction of the lodge. Jenny and I have since brought other friends to our bed. All it took was adding a third party to open us up to the full experience of sharing. Now we want to go a step further, exploring other varieties of swinging and swapping. Multiple partners interests us a lot, and it's all because of this one unannounced visitor at our door. Life is strange that way. —Z.R., Laramie, Wyoming

SEXUAL LIBERATION WITH A POOLSIDE EPIPHANY

There are many things in this crazy world that happen without explanation or without reason. Perhaps this is one of them.

My wife is a beautiful blonde with short hair, a buxom figure, and a sexual appetite that meets mine. Cindy and I have found other partners that share our thoughts, actions, and desires. It was she that brought about this happening, although I know she didn't plan it.

One of the best friends I had was Mike. Mike is a few years older and, like me, he is going bald. He is jovial and very outgoing, which is proper for someone in the public relations business. His wife Kathy has always struck me as a very educated snob who put up with me because of Mike. I got the impression she didn't think much of either Cindy or me. Kathy is a petite brunette with magnetic blue eyes.

Cindy decided to have a surprise birthday party for me and invited several friends, including Mike and Kathy. When I got home I found our swimming pool surrounded by swimsuit-clad bodies, all singing happy birthday to me. Cindy kissed me, held out my trunks and said, "Get with it, birthday boy." We had a great time, splashing and drinking it up in one wild celebration.

Around ten everyone had left, except Mike and Kathy. Mike had been putting away the Jack Daniel's and Kathy had emptied at least one wine bottle. They weren't drunk, but they were feeling no pain.

"Let's go skinny-dipping," Mike yelled as he pulled his trunks off and stood at the edge of the pool. Kathy moved to stop him, but he untied her bikini top.

"Michael!" she scolded. "What the hell do you think you are doing?"

"I'm going skinny-dipping, and so are you. So is Don. So is Cindy. The last one with clothes on is a wimp." He began untying the bows holding her bikini bottoms in place. She protested, but not enough to keep him from completing the task. Before her bikini bottoms hit the poolside I was stepping from my trunks. Cindy wasn't shy; she was halfway out of her suit. Four naked bodies splashed into the pool amid roars of laughter.

Needless to say, there was some underwater groping, and it wasn't all directed toward our respective spouses. For a while I had Kathy's breasts in both hands, and later I managed to get one finger in her cunt. From Cindy's giggling I guessed Mike was getting some feels for himself. I wasn't sure how far this was going to go.

It was surprising to see Kathy let her guard down. I thought it was probably the wine. Cindy pressed me against the side of the pool, one hand on my cock, her lips against mine.

"You, sweet lover, or your friend Mike over there, are going to have to fuck me tonight," she whispered. "I'm so damned hot I could screw the water hose."

"What about Kathy?"

"What?"

"Yeah," I replied. "Why not get Kathy to fuck you. Maybe a good woman-to-woman encounter would make a good birthday present for me."

"You bastard!" She started to move away but then turned back. "Okay, I'll do it. I'll try to get Kathy, but if I do, you're doing it with Mike."

"Come again?" I said. I thought I was hearing things.

"You heard me. If you want to watch me fuck Kathy, then I want to watch you and Mike. What's the matter? It's okay for two women but not two guys? Double standard?"

Cindy knew she had me. We had discussed this before: the heterosexual prejudice against male-to-male sex, and how woman-to-woman was somehow considered sexier and more titillating. "Alright, alright. I don't know how Mike is going to go for this, but alright."

Cindy moved across to Kathy, and the two of them left the pool. Later she told me how she convinced Kathy, or coerced her, but that isn't important. I motioned to Mike to join me at poolside for a drink.

"Don't worry about your trunks, we'll just pretend we're nudists." He laughed and sat naked in the lounge chair.

"Where did the girls go?"

"I think they're going to do something special for my birthday."

He nodded and sipped another Jack and water. It was only seconds before Cindy and Kathy emerged next to the pool, arm in arm. Kathy lay on the large beach towel with Cindy propped above her. Cindy leaned forward and kissed Kathy and I watched Mike. He leaned forward in his chair but said nothing.

In moments Cindy was between Kathy's splayed legs, eating her cunt. Kathy's head was rolling from side to side and deep moans were emerging from her throat. "Shit!" was all she exclaimed as her body arched in orgasm. Cindy licked her way from Kathy's mound to her lips and kissed her again, deeply.

Cindy rolled to her back and beckoned Kathy to come to her. Kathy began by sucking Cindy's generous breasts, then moved down her stomach until she could position herself at the tunnel opening. I could tell when Kathy's tongue met Cindy's clitoris. The look on her face and the arch of her back were signal enough. Kathy took her role seriously and kept lapping at Cindy's tunnel until she brought my beloved to her climax.

Cindy turned to look at me, smiling. Kathy moved to remain beside her, touching, still enjoying their sex. I knew what the look was. "Mike," I said, putting down my drink, "I made Cindy a promise, or rather a deal, and it's my turn."

"Jesus," Mike breathed, still looking at Cindy and Kathy. "Don, I've wanted to watch Kathy with another woman for years. Do you know how magnificent that was? She's talked about it before but only in wondering. I didn't think it would ever happen."

He looked at me, remembering that I had said something. "What kind of deal?"

"If Cindy would make it with Kathy, I would put on a show for her." I reached down and placed my hand on his cock, closing my fingers around it. "I've never considered myself even remotely gay, but if I was ever going to make it with a man, I'd want it to be with you."

Mike just looked at me. I'm not sure what was happening in his mind at that very moment, but I felt his cock quiver in my hand. I began to stroke it very slowly and it began to harden. I moved my mouth toward his, unsure of how this was going to be. He moved to me and we kissed. I closed my eyes and his lips felt no different from a woman's, aside from the rough skin and whiskers. I moved down his chest until I could suck the nipples of his breasts. It affected him. His cock reached its full length, very hard. I edged down until I was kneeling between his legs, staring at his seven-inch penis, the veins of which were rising visibly on each side. The head was purple and thick. It seemed right to open my mouth and take him in.

I moved my lips and tongue up and down the shaft of his hardness, feeling the rubbery skin, the blood-filled veins and the small bumps beneath the penis head. I let my tongue drag purposely into the crevice at the base of the head and licked voraciously at that point. It affected him as it does me, and he was reacting. I reached down with one hand and gently held his balls, not squeezing, but softly rubbing the sack.

I began rapid movements of my mouth over the head and his groans aroused me. I could tell he was about to come. With my other hand I began to stroke his cock as I sucked. In a matter of moments I had milked the man; he was spurting into my mouth. I kept sucking until he stopped coming. My mouth was full of his warm sticky semen. I swallowed and I licked his red cock as it began to recede. When I looked up, Mike was looking at me. His expression was a mix of pleasure, surprise and wonderment. I knew he was wondering if I wanted him to suck me, or wondering if he could.

I kept my hand on his cock as I moved to sit beside him. I kept stroking it and massaging it as it deflated. I looked over at Cindy and Kathy. I saw an acceptance on their faces, one of knowing reality.

"I'm not sure I can." It was Mike, looking at me, then down at my cock. I took his hand and placed it on my growing member.

"You don't have to do anything if you don't want."

He looked over toward Kathy and Cindy. Neither woman said anything. He began to stroke my cock, slowly. As I began to get hard he was still looking at Kathy, stroking me. I was enjoying the feeling of his hand on me and reclined to accept his handjob. I closed my eyes to relax with the feeling. Then I felt his head rest on my stomach. He was watching my cock, watching his hand masturbate me. He was good.

"I can't," he said as he kept stroking my cock. "I can't suck it."

"It's okay," I consoled. "It's alright."

He kept stroking me, doing what he could for me. I relaxed

and was about to come when I felt lips on my cock. I looked up to see his mouth over my cockhead. Just then I came in a gush of hot spunk.

The women joined us. Kathy kissed Mike and Cindy kissed me. Kathy looked at Mike and stroked his head. She moved toward me and took my cock in her mouth. She sucked my soft cock for a few moments while Cindy sucked on Mike. Mike watched his wife, got hard and then erupted in Cindy's mouth. Kathy also got me hard and then brought me off. Mike understood. I understood. It was alright. This is the way sex should be.
—N.H., *Miami, Florida*

WHERE LOVE AND AGGRESSION COME TOGETHER

I can't wait to tell you about the most exciting evening of my life.

My fiancée and I have been together for four-and-a-half years. I had always fantasized about a threesome with my wife-to-be and another man, but knowing her as I do I didn't think she would ever agree to it.

Last night I came home from work expecting a quiet evening with a small celebration for my birthday. When I opened the front door, I found a small box with a note from my wife explaining that I should go upstairs and follow the instructions in the box. I rushed upstairs and ripped open the box. Inside I found a pair of black silk underwear and a black bow tie. The instructions said I was to put on the underwear and get dressed in my silk Pierre Cardin tuxedo.

I was very excited, and I did exactly what the note said. Inside my jacket was another note. This was even more of a surprise. It said to come downstairs to the living room when I was done. It also said not to turn on any lights.

*   *   *

When I got downstairs and edged my way carefully into the living room, the lights went on and my wife-to-be yelled "Surprise!" I was more than surprised; I was stunned. She was surrounded by at least a dozen handsome young men in black tie. My wife was dressed in a beautiful black evening gown, diamond earrings, the whole elegant bit. She looked stunning.

She explained that she was going to fulfill my fantasy, but she was going to do it her way, enjoying it by calling the shots and setting the right tone and atmosphere to the occasion. Hence, the black tie.

She told me all the men were professionals. They would do anything she asked them to do. She added that they were being paid by the hour, and most of them were out-of-work actors, while several of them moonlighted at the local amusement park as furry animals.

She then told the nearest man to lift up her dress, and to start licking her bottom. She lay down on the couch as the man pulled her dress up and found her bare pussy, which he delightedly began to lick immediately. She asked me to choose the most handsome man in the room and to unzip his pants, and put his penis in my mouth. She told me to get him ready to fuck her.

I did as she said. I reached for a blond surfer-type and opened his pants. I started fucking him with my mouth and my hand. I had never done this before but I knew what I liked, and what felt good. Before long I heard my wife moaning with pleasure from her tongue-lashing, but her dark eyes were riveted on me. I saw her smile when this hunk exploded in my mouth. I drew away as the spurting dollops of cream landed on my face, but then I went back to him and finished every drop.

My wife-to-be thought that I had somehow spoiled her fuck, but she was just toying with me. She told me to bring her another one. This time she positioned me on my back while she kneeled over my face. She guided this next man's hard penis into her steaming cunt. When he started to pump her, his hairy balls slapped against my face. I licked both of them as they fucked.

When he groaned and fell away from her, she was quick to place her cunt on my mouth so I could lick it clean of his come.

Now it was my turn. "Look," she said. She spread her legs and gave me a peep of her pussy. There was juice between her thighs; she had a small river under her ass. She lay back in my arms while I felt her up. I know her this way—if she could've reached flesh her teeth would've pricked me like hot needles, but as it was she was content to grind them dreamily, hungrily while I diddled her squishy hot peach.

I gave her what she wanted. She grabbed my balls and rubbed the knobs of her tits against my chest, then her fingers caught my prick by the throat. She yanked my cock and tickled its chin, making soft pleased sounds like a cat when she discovered how fucking hard I was.

She squeezed my thighs between her legs, rubbed her bush and cunt against me. She was playing with herself against my leg, enjoying the hunk punk audience, and that hairy belly was tickling my hip and driving me wild. She knew what I wanted. My cock quivered in front of her. She placed her hands against my knees and bent, taking my prick into her mouth and sucking, waiting for me to push her back and give her the fuck of a lifetime.

She began to laugh, teasing me like it was all a game. At this point she told everyone in the room to take off their clothes and join us on the floor in front of the fire.

"Hold on a second," I said. "This woman is going to be my wife, and I am going to take her now. You guys can watch or go make a drink, but for now, this is between me and her." She started laughing, not accustomed to my being so powerfully sure of myself.

Laughing at me that way, I was able to understand where she was coming from. But I wasn't thrilled to be spending my birthday with a bunch of naked pro hunks. I used the anger to my best advantage—sex is, after all, a place where love and aggression come together.

"Laugh now, honey! Try to laugh with a cock in your mouth. Try to spill your laugh around the edges, into my bush—it will catch in the bristles. The laughter you have will come from your throat. But you'll feel it in your belly too. I'll make you laugh and slobber with my cock. And after I've come, your laugh will sound as if you are gargling with semen. When you giggle, little squirts of jism will drip out of your ears, and for hearty laughter you'll have special tears of jism, to drip from your nose."

"Wow," she said. "That almost sounds poetic." Whatever it was that I said made her overcome with lusty delight. She was sucking my cock like she'd never done in all the years I'd known her. She had her fantasy, her whims had been acknowledged.

The studs gradually filed out, dressing and leaving the house. Now she was mine—she belonged to only one thing: my burning cock. She let me fuck her in the most exciting and powerful way imaginable. It was utter ecstasy, and our sex life has never been better. I can't wait to help her celebrate her birthday. —*Name and address withheld*

HOOVERING DARK JAM FROM A HONEY POT

*Y*ou've heard about women fantasizing over mythical, big fat black cock. You've had a few stories about guys getting their kicks having their wives fucked by gargantuan black dick. What actually happened to me and my wife is as follows.

It is true that Mary and I had fantasized during foreplay and sex about sharing our bed with—and her getting fucked by—a big black stud. I don't know if it's every white woman's dream, but I do know it's always fascinated Mary.

It's true that I'd purchased a large black dildo which we'd sometimes use, pretending it was attached to a well-built stud while I throttled her teeming cunt with it. I enjoyed watching that black monster fuck in and out of her cunt while my gorgeous wife sucked me off. The contrast of her puffy pink pussy lips and the thickly-veined black tool was erotic to watch.

We went one Saturday night to an office party, where one of my co-workers was a really well-built, handsome black dude who came across real sharp and sophisticated. I'd told my wife about Troy, but this was the first time she'd met him. She was very impressed with him, and I could tell he, likewise, had similar impressions of her.

The place was crowded, but a lot of people still tried to dance. Troy and Mary made a great pair on the dance floor. I have always had two left feet, so I was content to watch Troy dance with Mary quite a bit.

When the music slowed to an easy, romantic tune, many more people jammed together onto the dance floor. I could see that neither Mary nor Troy minded being crushed together in the swirl of bodies. It got rather warm out there, so they came back to the table where I was sitting. I noticed Troy was sporting a hard-on, which with his pleated, tailored trousers, could not be concealed no matter how he adjusted his pants. I was amazed at the length of the protrusion. He definitely fit the stereotype of the big, hung black buck physically, but speaking with him was like talking to an urbane gent with a master's degree in elocution.

At this point, Troy up and announced he was leaving. Mary protested, saying he was such a good dancer she didn't want him to leave. She said she was having a great time.

Troy said his roommate Chet was throwing a party back at their apartment. He invited us to come along if we wanted, saying that Jack and Susan were actually coming so that we wouldn't be the only non-black couple—if that was a concern.

Mary jumped up and said, "Of course not!" Then she kissed Troy on the lips briefly, saying to me, "Let's go, love." So off we went.

The apartment was packed. We squeezed through the living room and went into the kitchen, where Troy introduced us to Chet and Chet's brother, Dwight. There was an obvious odor of marijuana, a load of half-gallon jugs of liquor, lots of cigarette smoke and loud, loud music. Everyone was having a great time. A lot of attractive young couples were making out pretty well, kissing and petting uninhibitedly. But there was no out-and-out sex. Some of the dancers—curvaceous black women with big round butts—got really erotic.

The brothers quickly provided some weed for me and my wife. We were seated at the table with Chet, Dwight, Troy and several others. A lot of sexy, raunchy jokes were being told. Troy was standing behind Mary, who was seated at the table. He began massaging her neck and shoulders. I saw his hands out of my peripheral vision slip down to grab her breasts as he lowered his head to whisper something in her ear.

She stood up and they headed to the living room to dance. I could see them occasionally as they danced. I'd never seen her dance so suggestively, even crouching down closely in front of Troy's crotch in a manner which seemed to simulate fellatio. They were all cheering this white chick on; she was floating mesmerized on the pot and the longing in her soul to be finally fucked by a man of color.

I started to get up and go watch in the living room, but Dwight said not to get upset, to sit down, because he had another joke for me. I was smoking and drinking heavily, a lot more than I ever had. Time became lost in the haze of booze and smoke, and I soon found myself enchanted by a pretty, overweight black woman, who kept rubbing her meaty tits against my neck and shoulders every time she passed by.

Eventually, I somehow realized that Dwight, Chet and Troy were no longer there—nor was my wife. The crowd had thinned out. The living room was full of black couples, all involved with each other in some wild heavy petting, which included a lot of exposed tits and men with their hands submerged under the skirts and panties of the moaning women. One guy, sitting on the floor in the corner, was getting head from his girlfriend, who looked so eager and pleased to see me watching as she engulfed the slick, black penis.

I passed out on the chair in the living room, while everyone else was getting it on.

I kind of remembered Jack and Susan leaving earlier in the evening, asking me if we wanted a ride home. I can't remember what I told them, but I realized at this point that we'd left our car at the office party and rode with Troy back to his apartment.

I came awake, not knowing how long I'd been out of it. I got up and staggered around a bit, looking for Mary, hoping she'd not abandoned me and wondering if, in fact, she'd gotten a lift from Jack and Susan. If she had left, I wondered why. Had I done something to offend her? Was I out of control? I don't think I would have said anything to offend our guests, but then again, I'd never gotten this blasted before. Anything was possible.

I opened a door and, as I stared in the dimly lit room, someone ordered me to "Shut the door, motherfucker!"

So I did.

I slumped into a chair, and someone handed me a drink. I think it was Troy but I'm not sure. I became aware that I was in a bedroom and several other people were there too. I was looking around for that pretty black girl, but she wasn't around. My eyes began to focus a bit more as I adjusted to the soft light. What I saw really didn't surprise me as much as I thought it would.

Everyone was naked. There were three black men and a white woman. The woman was taking a toke on a weed, and then I knew it was my wife. "Oh," I said. "There you are Mary, are you okay?" Someone lit up a weed for me and put it in my mouth.

"Don't worry, Tom," someone said. "She's having the time of her life."

"That's good, so am I," was all I said. Dwight had just rolled off my wife, his long, black dick gleaming in the soft light with my wife's cunt juices. I remember thinking that his cock was not rigid-hard, but still long and quite thick.

Chet seemed to pull my wife over; he sat up on the edge of the bed, got Mary in an upright position, and told her he was ready to fuck her again, this time with a rapt audience. He wanted her to sit on his huge black dick and fuck herself, while he played with her "pretty pink clit and tits."

She went into ecstasy as her cunt was again stuffed after just losing Dwight's bona fide black boner.

Troy walked up to my wife stroking a fat, black horse-cock. He rubbed it over her face and lips. She opened her mouth to take it as best as she could.

"She's an absolute bon vivant when it comes to dark, blood-engorged cock meat," Troy quipped, looking my way.

I asked Mary what she was doing, and Troy said, "She's enjoying herself, dude."

I asked Troy what he was doing. He said, "I'm fucking your wife's face, man, just the way she likes it. Just helping you out, you understand."

Chet was getting ready to shoot another load of come up her twat. He was shouting, "Go mama, take that black cock up your lily-white poozlet. Yeah, uh-uh, take it, fuck me honey, take it, yeaahhh!"

Sometime later Troy grabbed my wife's head in his large hands and pumped a good hot load into her mouth.

I said, "Troy, she doesn't like to swallow come."

"She does if it's from a dark and chocolate cock that's as big as mine," he said.

"Really?" I was still pretty addled, not sure if this was really happening or if I was dreaming it.

"Come here, dude. Your wife wants you," Dwight said. I was led over to the bed and stripped. Mary was lying there on the bed, her legs spread and seemingly worn out, like she'd been exercising hard. When I moved to touch her, she was very limp, totally relaxed.

The guys said I needed to soothe my wife's pussy because she'd been fucked so much; she needed me to lick the puffy pink lips of her well-fucked sex organ to get her back into shape.

Someone pushed the back of my head down towards her come-soaked pubic hair and come-filled cunt.

"That's it, lick her clean, be gentle."

"Suck her out, man. Hoover that honey-pot. She's loaded, take it. Clean her out."

They were all laughing.

"Hey, dude, you're doing great. Get your tongue up in there and swab that black man's seed." There was more laughing.

Dwight said, "Aren't you going to fuck your wife, man? She needs more cock. Show us how you do a honky fuck."

"Right," I said, and slid right on it. She was so juicy. I'd never felt pussy so wet and slippery before.

"Like boppin' a melon, ain't it? A tight juicy watermelon."

While my cock found a tight, wet paradise, I hugged and kissed Mary until we both fell out—well-fucked and exhausted.

When we awoke, Troy was in bed with us. Dwight was slouched in the chair fast asleep, and Chet was stretched out on the floor. The room smelled of sex. Mary woke with a hangover and a cunt sore from overexertion.

Mary went to shower, where Troy joined her, doing God knows what with the bar of soap. When I came out of the shower, Troy was giving my wife a slow gentle fuck. We finally left sometime before noon.

To be frank, we really get off on the memories of that evening, time and time again. I can instantly attain an erection just remembering what Mary looked like with those three black hunks hovering over her with their long dicks.

We get together with Troy occasionally. When we do, it is uninhibited sex! We haven't seen Dwight again, as he was visiting from Chicago. As for Chet, we accidentally met one day when I was pulled over by a motorcycle cop. Under the helmet and black leather, it was Chet.

"I almost didn't recognize you with your clothes on, man," I told him. He asked me if the wife and I ever needed some special police attention some nights. I said we would, and he took our phone number and address. Later, he phoned and came by in uniform.

Let me tell you folks, I got a serious charge out of watching my wife suck off a uniformed cop, a black one at that. We only got together with Chet twice because he recently got married.

In closing this correspondence on behalf of my wife, I would like to stress that Mary and I are very happy and content with our marriage arrangement. It took a deep plunge, and left us drenched, good and drenched. —*R.P., Baltimore, Maryland*

THIS LITTLE PIGGY LIKES DARK MEAT, SO HUBBY HAS HIS PALS OVER

*M*y wife Jean is a twenty-three-year-old dirty-blonde beauty who is always ready to fuck, anytime, anywhere. She is a real flirt and cock-tease, and has no trouble attracting men. We'd often discussed the possibility of Jean sampling some meaty black cock, as she'd never been with a black man but often fantasized about it. When it was time to turn her fantasy into the real thing, I invited Jimmy and Horace, two of my coworkers, who happened to be black, to our house for a few drinks.

About the time the beers were kicking in, Jean said she was going to change into something more comfortable. The men suggested she put on something real sexy, but I don't think they actually expected her to do so. Imagine their surprise when she reappeared a few minutes later in a gauzy white negligee, underneath which was a black G-string so narrow it disappeared within the fleshy folds of her cunt.

Her tuft of wispy blonde pussy hair was plainly visible as she sat on the couch between Jimmy and Horace. Jimmy was just coming off a recent divorce and was horny as a virgin. Jean put a hand on his lap, rubbed his bulge slowly and sensually, then leaned over and kissed him. Jimmy responded with equal passion, and soon they were locked in a heated embrace, their tongues dueling.

Horace got up to give them plenty of room on the couch. Jimmy lifted Jean's negligee and played with her round titties. She moaned as he tweaked the stiff, long nipples. He soon slipped off her negligee, then stripped himself naked. Jimmy's mouth moved to her tits, massaging each nipple with his bright pink tongue. His hard black cock looked huge, and Jean's eyes opened wide, gleeful at the size of it. The only thing that stood between her hot pussy and his extremely huge dick was that tiny strip of G-string. Jimmy worked it over her erect clit, getting the fabric soaked and making her cry out in orgasm. Then his hand dropped to her pussy. With a quick, hard pull, he yanked down her G-string and slipped it over her bare feet, then tongued my wife's clit until she was shaking with another climax.

Breathless and grunting hungrily, Jean got on her hands and knees. Jimmy positioned the head of his dick at the opening of her cunt. With a single hard thrust he penetrated her, burying his cock deeper inside her than she had ever been penetrated before. Jimmy's giant pole plunged in and out of her cunt with alarming speed. My wife responded by wiggling her ass back against his crotch, milking every ounce of sensation out of this master fuck. Soon she began moaning loudly, and I knew she was coming again. Jimmy was also gasping and growling. His back stiffened as he slammed into her cunt one last time. He cried out as his seed splashed the walls of her slick cunt.

Jimmy's hose slipped out of her, and Jean lay back on the couch. I stroked my cock through my pants as the black man's thick jam dripped from the slit between my wife's legs.

Needless to say, Horace put up no resistance when Jean knelt before him, ready to give him a shot at her eager mouth. Horace offered her his big black cock, a seven-incher that shone like a piece of polished oak. Taking it in both hands, Jean caressed its length and admired its beauty. It twitched in her hands, and a drop of pre-come oozed from the slit in its dark brown head. She licked the drops and teased the small opening. Horace ran his fingers through her thick auburn hair, told her to get ready and then rammed his cock down her throat. Jean never has a gag reflex—her throat muscles instinctively relax when a cock is coming their way. This allowed Horace's full length to plunge down her throat over and over again. She bathed his prick with a thick coating of saliva, running her tongue up and down the veiny shaft.

With increasing urgency, Horace fucked her red-lipped mouth. By this time I had my own stiff cock in my hands. I jacked it back and forth as I watched Horace and Jean get it on. I could feel my balls boiling, and fought hard to keep from coming too quickly. As Horace fed her his frank, his huge black balls slapped her chin. Jean took them both into her mouth and sucked them like candy.

Horace told her to lie on her back. He knelt between her legs, bending her knees back until they rested against her tits. Her freshly fucked clit stood out prominently through the damp curls of her pussy hair. "Fuck me!" she cried out as he eased his prong into her hole. As he nailed her, she locked her legs around his neck and cried out for him to do it harder. "Ooooh, give me that black cock! I love it!" she wailed.

In a few moments Horace announced that he had to come. Jean squealed that she was coming too. As he pumped his load into her, my balls erupted furiously. A ton of hot, sticky sperm shot out of my cock and squirted between my fingers. It was probably the most intense climax of my life.

I jacked off three more times that night while watching my friends repeatedly fuck my beautiful wife. Jean says that the next time they come over, she wants me to videotape it. I can't wait.

Then I'll be able to watch her fuck anytime I like. —B.T., Hartford, Connecticut

GROUP GROOMING TURNS TO
GROPING ON THE HAIRDRESSER'S DAY OFF

I'm thirty-four, with short blonde hair and a well-built figure.
My greatest asset is my 36D breasts.

I am the owner of a beauty salon, and since it was a Monday
the salon was closed. My husband was away for the day, so I decided to do some sunbathing and just relax.

I had put on my skimpiest bikini, and was lying in the backyard catching some rays, when I heard a car pull into our driveway. I wasn't really too excited about having company, as I'd just
gotten relaxed. When I got out front, though, it was my friend
Theresa with her husband Slade and his best buddy Dave.
Theresa wanted to know whether Slade could get a haircut. I told
them I had my clippers inside and would be glad to give him what
he wanted.

I had Slade sit down in the kitchen. While I trimmed his hair,
his eyes were fixed on my big boobs. I could feel Dave staring as
well, as I was still wearing the bikini.

After I was finished with Slade's hair, Theresa asked if I was
going to give Slade a sucker like his barber did when he was a kid.
Well, I'd never thought of fucking around on my husband, but I
couldn't pass up an opening like that. I pulled off my top and told
Slade, "Suck on these tits, big boy. I'll bet your barber never gave
you an offer like that."

Slade was on my tits in a flash. Dave pulled down the bottom
of my suit, and they had me lie down on the table. As the three
of them undressed, Dave took his hard cock, slipped it into my
pussy and began to fuck me like a stallion. Slade asked me to

suck his big pecker, and he didn't have to ask me twice. Theresa sucked my swollen tits as her men pounded their dicks into me.

I was already coming like crazy when Dave flooded my cunt with his foamy seed. Feeling Dave's sperm shooting inside me caused me to suck harder on Slade. Theresa told Slade, "Give her a good dose of vitamins and protein," and Slade responded by filling my mouth with his warm, sweet health shake.

Theresa said, "It looks from where I stand like you're a really good cocksucker. I'd love to see if you can eat pussy as well as you do dickmeat." When I nodded my head and lay back down, she sat on my face and slowly lowered her musky cunt over my mouth. I lapped at her tasty snatch as if I'd been doing it all my life.

"Oh God, suck my clit harder, you sexy bitch!" Theresa screamed, as she began to fill my mouth with sweet, syrupy honey. I made sure to lick every bit of her nectar out of her hot crack.

We rested awhile, then went into the bedroom. Slade lay down on his back, looked at me and said, in a raspy voice, "Fuck me." As I lowered myself onto his spear, I told Dave I wanted to eat him. Theresa said I had such a nice ass it would be a shame to let it go to waste.

She left the room, returning shortly with a frozen hot dog and a jar of Miracle Whip. She spread my sweet ass cheeks apart with one hand while pushing her new toy up my asshole. The combination of the coldness and the strange sensation of having that hard little meat-stick shoved up my butthole made me cream like crazy.

The three of them ravaged me. I loved having all my fuck-holes filled. My cunt muscles began to put the big squeeze on Slade's dick, causing him to come deep inside me. Dave saw his friend pumping and heard him groaning, and he filled my throat with love-cream.

Excited beyond belief by all this, Theresa rolled me off her husband and continued to fuck my butt as she sucked Slade's come from my pussy.

Before they left I took both Slade and Dave one at a time in my pretty ass, and even drilled my darling Theresa's cunt with a strap-on dildo.

I was pretty well fucked out when my husband got home, but I managed to give him a fine blowjob after telling him the whole story. I'm so glad I've learned so many extra services I can perform to keep my clients coming—back. —B.G., *Ocalala, Florida*

A HAND OF SOLITAIRE GETS DOWN AND DIRTY IN A FROLICSOME FOURSOME

*M*y wife and I have been subscribers to your magazine for years, and I feel we owe it to other *Penthouse Letters* letter writers to relate an experience we had six months ago.

We're quite a liberated couple. We've always openly talked about sex and masturbation with our friends, and have often gone to nude beaches with them. Although Elizabeth and I had often fantasized about group sex, we had never gotten up the courage to actually do it. Elizabeth has a great body and has caused more than a few guys at nude beaches to get obvious and embarrassing erections.

Our story began when Elizabeth went away on business, leaving me alone for an entire week. It was Thursday night, and I was alone on the couch in the den, reading your magazine and massaging my hard cock. Just as I was approaching orgasm the front door opened. In walked Elizabeth's best friend Trudy. She giggled when she saw my situation, and said that I must be eager for Elizabeth's return. Then, to my surprise, she sat on the chair across from me and asked if I'd mind if she watched. The idea turned me on, as Trudy is a knockout blonde, so I agreed. I resumed stroking my stiff cock, feeling a little tentative at first, but soon getting into the exhibitionistic thrill of the whole thing. Trudy asked me to read some letters to her, so I read her a few from the Crowd Scenes section.

At the end of a few letters I was throbbing and tingling so much I couldn't hold back. I shot a huge load of come, throwing back my head and letting out a good groan at the same time.

I looked over to see Trudy with her skirt up over her waist and her legs spread, fingering herself to a very intense orgasm. I could see the juices glistening on her fingers as she shoved them in and out of her lovely pussy. I loved the long, moaning sigh that she let out as she reached a crescendo.

After we'd both calmed down, we talked about how much those letters had turned us on. We decided to get my wife and Trudy's boyfriend to help us live out the fantasy we were plotting out together.

I invited Trudy and her boyfriend Gary to join us for dinner. Trudy and I then related the story of her catching me "red handed," and everyone had a big laugh over it. The conversation then began to focus on group sex. Trudy and Gary said they had never tried it but had fantasized about it often. When I told them we felt the same way there was a long, awkward silence. It felt as though none of us breathed. "Well," Elizabeth finally said, "It sure looks like now would be the perfect opportunity."

Elizabeth then motioned for Trudy to follow her to the bedroom, telling me to put on some music and sit on the couch with Gary. We quickly obliged, talking and laughing like kids, wondering exactly what they had in mind.

The girls came out of the bedroom five minutes later wearing Elizabeth's lingerie. Trudy was in a red G-string with a matching push-up bra, and Elizabeth had on a see-through teddy that showed off her perky tits and neatly trimmed bush.

Gary and I whistled appreciatively, and Elizabeth started doing a lap dance on Gary. She was grinding her body against his, but not letting him touch her in any very intimate way. Trudy followed suit with me, and I quickly developed a raging hard-on. I looked over to see Gary take off my wife's teddy and begin sucking her tits. Beginning to breathe hard, Elizabeth released his cock from his pants, and started to stroke it. Gary's cock was the largest I'd ever seen, and Elizabeth wasted no time in lowering herself onto it.

Just as they started fucking, Trudy began sucking my cock. I hadn't noticed that she had even unfastened my zipper. I played with Trudy's tits. Watching my wife fuck another man was turning me on enormously, and as they orgasmed I shot my load into Trudy's mouth.

After a moment's rest I had Trudy lie on her back, and began licking her beautiful blonde pussy. I shoved my finger in and out of her steaming hole and licked her clit. She soon started bucking and came, soaking my face with her musky juices.

I looked up to see Elizabeth sucking Gary's dick back to life. Watching her practice her private arts on another man quickly made me hard again. I mounted Trudy doggie-style, and rubbed her tits while watching my wife suck Gary to orgasm. Trudy and I quickly followed, clutching each other, sweating and shouting, as we exploded in massive orgasm. Then we all collapsed in a pile on the floor.

It was two A.M. by the time any of us stopped fiddling around. Without saying a lot, Gary and Trudy gathered their clothes and went back to their own house.

We've all talked about it since. Everyone seems to be happy that it happened, and we're planning to take a vacation together soon so we can relive the experience and explore some further fantasies. —A.R., *Medford, Massachusetts*

Different Strokes

WHAT'S GOOD FOR THE GOOSE
IS GOOSING THE GANDER

*I*t all started last Halloween. Lori, my girlfriend, decided that I was unsympathetic to women, and all the work she puts into being a woman. She said that for Halloween we should switch roles for a day. I agreed.

On Halloween morning I woke up to see Lori dressed in my sweats. I asked her what was going on. She replied, "Did you forget we switch roles today? I prepared a bubble bath for you. Don't worry. It will be fun."

As I got into the tub, Lori came over to me with a razor and some shaving cream. "To be a proper lady, you're going to have to shave," she said. "Don't forget to do your chest, your legs and under your arms." I did as instructed. When I was done, Lori came back and said my pubic hair would have to be trimmed also. She offered to help me, and I asked for her assistance. She proceeded to trim and shave my pubic region into a heart.

When I got out of the bath Lori dusted me with some of her powder and led me into the bedroom. She saw me becoming aroused and said, pointing to my erection, "You're going to have to get rid of that. Go into the bathroom, jerk off into this cup and bring it back to me." When I returned with the cup full of my come, Lori took it, called me a good girl and told me to get dressed and make lunch while she ran some errands. She left, so I put on some clothes and proceeded to make lunch.

After an hour, she came back carrying several bags and

brought them into the apartment. "Did you make lunch?" she asked. She then told me I was improperly dressed and that she would correct that after we ate.

After lunch Lori led me back to the bedroom to show me what she had bought. She opened the bags and showed me all the makeup she had bought for me. Lori led me into the bathroom, sat me down and started my transformation. First, she plucked my eyebrows slightly to give them more of a feminine look. Then came foundation, eyeliner, four shades of eye shadow, mascara, blush and lipstick. She also applied fake fingernails. Knowing that I find redheads very attractive, Lori had bought me a wig of long, red hair. She put that on me last. Seeing myself in the mirror for the first time, I became highly aroused at what I saw—a beautiful girl looking back at me. Lori reminded me that a lady does not get erections and gave me the cup again. After I went into the bathroom and filled the cup, I returned to the bedroom.

Lori then showed me the clothes she had bought me and proceeded to help me get dressed. We started with the light-blue panties and matching bra. She filled out the bra with falsies and helped me with the blue garter belt and blue stockings. The feeling of the silk on my shaven legs gave me another erection and Lori handed me the cup again. With a laugh, she reminded me that I was a lady.

When I came back, Lori helped me into a lacy white dress and gave me a pair of shoes to put on. She then dressed herself in my clothes and asked if I was ready for the Halloween party. I wasn't too thrilled, but we went.

After we got back, I told Lori that I had a new appreciation of women and the troubles they go through. Smiling, she said, "The night is not over. Take off your dress and panties but leave on the rest of your clothes. Lie down on the bed and I'll be right back, baby." I lay down and nervously waited for her. She came back wearing a robe and said, "Since you're playing the role of the girl, I'll play the role of the man, and make a woman out of you." She opened the robe, showing me that she was wearing a strap-on dildo, and asked me if I was ready.

Too late to turn back now, I thought. I told her, "I'm yours, but be gentle, I'm a virgin." Lori laughed and told me to kneel down.

"Suck my cock," she said, and put the rubber dildo in front of me. Licking the head and shaft of her cock, I made my first attempt at deep-throating her but gagged halfway down. Pulling it back, she grinned and said, "Not as easy as you thought, is it? Now lean over so I can lick your pussy." I bent over and Lori started to lick my ass. While tonguing and fingering my ass, she reached around and slowly jerked me to a climax. "Now it's time for you to lose your virginity," she told me. She slowly eased the head of the dildo into my ass. At first it was painful, but then pleasure set in. Lori then shoved her cock in up to the hilt and slowly started to fuck me. In time she started to increase the rhythm. She was moaning and grunting as if the dildo was a part of her. She continued to fuck me for what seemed like hours. When she finally pulled out of my ass she told me to kneel so she could feed me her orgasm.

After she took off the condom and cleaned the dildo I started to lick it, beginning at the head. As I was licking it, I noticed there was a small hole in the head. Lori yelled. "Suck it, don't lick it! How do you expect me to get off? Now suck me baby!"

I did as Lori said. I wrapped my mouth around her cock and started to bob up and down on her shaft. "Try to deep-throat me again," Lori said, "but go down on your exhale." Doing as she told me, I managed to deep-throat her on the third try. She giggled with delight when I succeeded.

"Faster baby, faster," she screamed. "You're one hell of a cock-sucker. Are you ready for my come, baby?" Not really sure what she meant by her come, I moaned and nodded yes. "Open your mouth so I can watch you swallow," she said. "I expect you to eat every bit of it." She said that the dildo was equipped with a special feature. The balls could be filled with a fluid and squeezed to simulate a male orgasm. Kneeling and looking up at Lori with my mouth open, she laid her cock on my tongue. "I filled it with all the come you gave me today. Eat up, baby," she said, and squeezed the dildo, coming in my mouth and on my lips and face. "Lick your lips and swallow it, baby," Lori giggled. "It's an acquired taste."

I swallowed as much as I could, licking my lips and not feeling too bad, since it was my own come. Lori bent over and pinched my nipples and kissed me, saying how much she loved me. She also told me that if I ever forget how hard it is to be a woman, this night could be repeated. I hope so. —D.L., *Baltimore, Maryland*

WHEN THE TIMING'S JUST RIGHT, FANTASIES TURN REAL

*M*y boyfriend has been gone for nearly two weeks now, on a business trip to Los Angeles. He should be home any day, but that doesn't help me now. I miss our frequent lovemaking sessions.

We both love sex and aren't afraid to show it. Even though our phone sex is great, I miss the real thing, and sometimes you just have to improvise.

I have this wonderful vibrating dildo he bought me when we went to a convention in New York City. It looks just like a real penis. It has veins and is at least eight inches long and three inches around.

I sit watching a really good fuck flick. They are getting it on so good! I put the dildo on the coffee table so that it stands straight up. I rub my hard nipples and take one in my mouth. I lick it, suck on it and then move on to the next one. I can just imagine Billy doing it instead of me.

I put a finger deep inside my cunt. Oh God, I'm so wet. Just a rub on my clit, then maybe a few more strokes, then I mount the dildo with it set on low speed. I ride it just like I would ride Billy, if only he was here. Then the door opens and he's home. I start to dismount and he says, "No. Don't. I love watching you fuck yourself on that big thing." He undresses and strokes his cock, then kisses me deeply, then kisses my neck and breasts. His hands move to my cunt and as I ride my toy, he rubs my clit and fingers deeply into my ass, spreading my juices all around, making me so wet.

He removes his finger and takes the lotion off the table and rubs it all over his cock and on my ass. I lean forward, being sure to keep my toy deep inside. He slides his hard hot cock deep in my ass. Grabbing my hips, he fucks me deep and hard until I come. He says, "It feels so good, your hot, tight ass and the vibrations from the dildo." He pinches my tits as he presses deeply and erupts into my waiting ass. It is so good to have him home. We move to the shower and on to the bedroom. The fun is just beginning. Billy lies flat on his back. I kiss him deeply, using lots of tongue, then I lick his neck. I move to each nipple, licking and nibbling. He moans, which excites me further. I feel his cock—it is hard as rock.

I make him turn on his side and I lick his butt. I move my mouth and tongue to his asshole. I love licking all around, he always moans so good. I grab his cock and give it a few strokes, all the while tonguing his hole. I put my finger in my mouth and get it slippery, then slide it into his asshole, moving it around and fucking him. I have him turn on his back while my finger is fucking him, then take his long, hard cock in my mouth, licking and sucking up and down his shaft. I let it slip out, and I lick the underside. He says, "Oh God, that feels so good, but stop, stop." I stop because I know he is about to shoot down my throat. I take my finger out of his ass. "What do you think I'm going to do to you now? I'm going to mount you and ride you till I come." I move up to him and feed him each breast in turn as I slide onto his wonderful hot cock. I ride him hard and fast. Oh God, I love the look on his face as I ride that wonderful prick! Then I lean back and rub my clit. I explode. I tell him how much I love him. I quickly move between his legs and take him in my mouth. I have a special, small dildo, which I like to lubricate and slide into his ass.

He moans and his cock expands. He can only take this for a short time and then I taste his beautiful come. I love having him shoot in my mouth. I always feel as if he's giving me a piece of himself.

We shower, then return to bed to hold each other tight. I never thought I'd find someone so sexually compatible. Lucky me. —C.F., Des Moines, Iowa

THEIR BATTERIES GET CHARGED WHEN SOMEONE ELSE PLUGS IN

*M*y wife and I are occasional readers of your magazine. Since we were inspired by the letters we've read, we decided to write and share our experience. Though we love each other dearly, the tedium of nine years of marriage has taken some of the sizzle out of our romance. Our sex life, though good, had become somewhat humdrum. So, after reading about the experiences of other couples, we decided to add spice to our own lives.

Jennifer is twenty-nine, very beautiful and, after two kids, has kept her dynamite 38-23-36 figure. She still turns men's heads in lust. For my part, I've never been interested in another woman sexually since we've been married and I had no desire to try sex with anyone else. Jennifer, however, admitted to occasional feelings of lust when men hit on her and, quite frankly, I would get quite turned on thinking of her in bed with another man.

After discussing it, we decided our marriage was sound enough to try a little experimenting. We agreed Jennifer would go on a date or two, engage in extramarital sex and fill me in on the details when she came home.

I still remember that first evening. I looked at my wife in her short, tight, split-up-the-thigh, low-cut, revealing dress, her hair and makeup impeccable as usual, and her sexy spiked heels. I inhaled the fragrance of the enticing, alluring perfume she was wearing and had to restrain myself from attacking her. But I managed to control myself until Andrew—one of her coworkers, who had been quite amazed by Jennifer's sudden change of attitude toward his suggestive remarks—came to pick her up. I kept the kids in the family room, peering through the partially opened door at Andrew, staggered by the sultry seductress who greeted him when he rang the doorbell. He couldn't take his eyes off her as she got her purse. I saw Jennifer smile at him when his hand touched her sexy, shapely bottom as he escorted her out the door.

I fed the kids, put them to bed at nine and tried vainly to watch TV and read. I could not keep my mind off Jennifer and Andrew, wondering what they were doing all evening. I turned in at eleven but got no sleep. I lay there with a raging hard-on, imagining my wife naked in bed with Andrew screwing her as the hour turned to midnight, then one, then two in the morning.

By that time, I had little doubt Jennifer's evening had gone well and that Andrew was getting the best piece of ass he'd ever had in his life. I was so horny I dared not touch my throbbing cock lest I lose my ardent fervor for the erotic encounter I was anticipating when Jennifer came home and told me about her evening.

A little past two-thirty I heard the car drive up. I slipped to the darkened hallway at the end of the stairs, where a window overlooked the driveway and the front door below. A streetlight illuminated Andrew and Jennifer kissing passionately in the car.

He escorted her to the door and they kissed again, Andrew's hands raising her skirt to her hips, cupping her ass as their bodies ground together.

I went back to the bedroom, turned on the lamp and watched Jennifer's entrance. She came into our bedroom and smiled at me with a dreamy sigh as I looked her over. Her mussed hair, smeared lipstick, and rumpled dress, along with the freshly fucked look on her face left little doubt as to what had transpired, but I had to ask. "Did something happen you want to tell me about?"

Jennifer grinned. "I do if you want to hear about it." My wife then relived her evening for me, starting with dinner and drinks, their passionate kissing in the car and the ride to Andrew's apartment. All the way there, she stroked his bulging trousers while his hand rested on her inner thigh, a finger in her hot, sopping-wet hole through her crotchless panties.

Once at his place, their passion and lust was completely out of control. They frantically undressed and pawed each other. Once stripped, she told how Andrew expertly ate her out on the couch, bringing her off twice with the expert ministrations of his tongue before he carried her into his bedroom.

Incredibly turned on, I listened as Jennifer described how Andrew had mounted her, sinking what turned out to be a very large cock deep in her pussy. She came twice more before Andrew shot a gusher of his semen in her, filling her cunt with come. He then fucked her twice more—once with her on top, then doggie-style, blasting two more creamy loads of sperm into her snatch. I gazed at her, rapt. "Did all that really happen?" She grinned naughtily and took off her dress. "Exactly as I said," she told me.

Jennifer's black, lacy, crotchless panties were stained white and soaked with jism. Her dark pubic hair was wet, matted with come.

White globs of semen clung to her pussy and an oozing white river of sperm seeped down her thighs.

I could stand no more. Pulling her down on top of me, still clad in panties and heels, I impaled her sloppy pussy on my rigid cock, sinking my dick deep into my wife's come-filled hole. I ejaculated almost immediately. Jennifer's pussy overflowed, gushing her juices, mixed with Andrew's sperm and mine, all over my cock and balls. We lay there together, in love and in lust, knowing we'd added a new dimension to our relationship.

Over the next three months, we repeated this erotic experience sixteen times, with Andrew and two of her other coworkers.

We've pretty much stopped for now, but if things ever get dull again, we'll know exactly what to do. —*T.A.*, *Bethesda, Maryland*

WAITING TO INHALE THE STAFF OF LIFE AND LOVE

*H*ere I am, just lying on the bed naked. My legs are slightly parted and I'm sort of dozing and thinking dreamily of you. I wish you were here, so you could place that hot hard dick in my mouth.

Suddenly you appear! Immediately I notice that you have a huge hard-on already. Ahh . . . so you've been thinking about me too, huh, lover? Well come over here and sit down on the bed. I want to talk to you.

The instant you sit down I slide my leg over your lap and start to rub against you. Ahh, the feeling of my soft skin touching your hot cock is wonderful. I reach out my hand and grab your cock. I feel the quiver your cock makes as I touch your flesh. I slowly start to stroke you. Yes lover, I have been waiting too long for you. I've been wet, and my poor pussy has been waiting for you all morning.

I climb over and sit down in your lap, facing you. You gently slide back until you are lying down on the bed. I move forward, pressing my tits against your chest as I lie on top of you. I reach for your mouth with my soft lips. Oh, my tongue finds yours and we share an electrifying kiss. My tongue meets yours as ripples of pleasure pour through my body.

I start to grind just a bit against you. My pussy is in control, not me. As my tongue continues to search your mouth I start to slowly move up and down against the shaft of your dick, making sure it is nice and hard before I take it into my mouth. Yes, you do want me to take it into my mouth, don't you? I move my head down from your face, kissing you every step of the way. As I get closer to your cock, I can feel my own excitement rising. I want to suck your cock, babe! I want you to fill my mouth with your hot, hard piece of flesh. My lips lightly touch the head of your cock softly, and then more firmly, as I take you into my mouth. Ahh, I just slide my wet mouth up and down on your cock for now, sucking lightly at first. I'm giving my mouth all of you, and then teasing myself and just letting the head of your cock in my mouth. My tongue runs circles around your head, with my lips wrapping tightly around it at times. Oh, your cock is just glistening with moisture, so slippery, so easily sliding in and out of my mouth.

I climb on top of you and put my pussy in front of your mouth. I need you to kiss it for me. I need you to lap up my juices! I need to feel your hot tongue on my clit while I suck and lick your hard cock. Yes, that's it lover, slip your tongue up inside me. Mmmmm, it feels so good I almost forget what I'm doing to you. Almost!

I take my hand and slowly, teasingly, stroke your dick as I suck on the head of your cock. I want to just slide my head all the way down. I want to take you all the way into my mouth and lick your balls when my mouth gets to the base of your dick. As I slide back up I keep my tongue nice and flat as it presses against the side of your cock. You have my cunt lips completely parted and are sliding your tongue up and down my slit. I am wriggling against your tongue. Lover, you feel so good! I move down to sit on top of you. I just have to feel your cock inside my soaking wet pussy. I move up and down so just the head enters me and then all of a sudden I just sit down on your cock.

My God! The intensity is too much. I begin to fuck you uncontrollably. I can't stop! My pussy is aching to come. I have to fuck you and fuck you hard, grinding my ass into your balls on each downstroke. I am bouncing wildly now, in a frenzy, and I'm about to come. Yesss!

You grab the base of your dick and hold it tightly. You don't want to come yet, and try to make it through the tight spasms you feel from my orgasm. You know that I'm not done with you yet!

I jump off you and place your cock back in my mouth, licking all my come juices off your dick. You are slowly pumping into my mouth, using your hand to slowly jerk off into my mouth.

I replace your hand with mine. I want to control your orgasm and you seem way too close. I suck on your dick for a few minutes more and then go back to fucking you, only letting the head of your dick into my pussy. Every now and then I just slide the whole length of you in, but not too often, because I am scared that you will come. I fuck you, ever so slowly, then move back so I can suck your dick with my wet lips and tongue and mouth. I let you pump your cock into my mouth a few times furiously, then I slow down the pace, only giving you a little. You are on the edge of coming, but not yet, not yet, lover. You have one more thing you have to do before I can let you come.

As I am sucking on your cock, you take a finger and slip it into my dripping pussy. You get it well lubricated and then insert it into my ass. This drives me wild! I start to buck against your hand, wanting more up my ass. I need you, lover! I need you to put that hot cock of yours right up my ass. I want to feel your balls slapping against my pussy as your cock is hammering in and out my tight asshole. I move around onto all fours and you press your cock up against the entrance of my ass. You know how wild I'm going to get when you drive your rod into my tight little opening. Your excitement heightens as you think about how good and hot and tight my ass is going to feel. You are ready to fuck me and start to move into my asshole. I am crazy for it. I take one hand and start to play with my clit as I back onto you, meeting your increasing thrusts. You are fucking my ass, and I am slamming into you, meeting your raging passion. Yessss! I am going to come again, a most intense orgasm. You feel this and scream out! We both come together in wild abandonment. —S.P., Missoula, Montana

THESE BIRDS OF PLAY FLY SOUTH
TO GET THEIR KICKS

*A*fter reading your magazine for the last few months in total enjoyment, we decided to write and tell you the fun that we had on our last holiday.

First, a little bit about who we are. I'm Natalie: 36C-25-36, blonde hair, blue eyes and always ready for a lot of fun. I'm pretty successful, too, given my hot little body. Can you picture those tits on a five-four, one-hundred-and-ten pound frame?

Michael, my husband of twelve years, is slim, firm and tan at a hundred and fifty pounds. We started reading *Penthouse Letters* about four months ago and have relished every issue.

Michael has a lust for eating pussy that every woman who loves to be eaten out longs for in a partner. I'm sure you know there is nothing like being manipulated by a warm and skillful tongue. But on to our fun!

When we started planning a spring vacation on the Gulf coast, one of the main things we wanted to do was try some of the thrilling things we'd read about in your letters. We were looking forward to a lot of fun, sun and what I'll call risky sex.

The flight was a short one, but we were determined to have the fun begin the minute the vacation began—that is, the minute our everyday routine ended. I chose my traveling clothes very carefully. I decided upon a strapless dress with full skirt, for easy access. Even before everyone had boarded, Michael had one finger already working on my hot pussy. I raised my skirt to avoid any telltale wet spots. Soon (but not soon enough) the plane took off and the lights were dimmed. With two fingers in my twat and my own fingers rubbing and teasing my clit, it was almost impossible for me to remain quiet and still.

With no one the wiser to our antics, Michael pulled down the front of my dress and starting licking and sucking on my firm and full breasts. The guy in the next seat didn't seem to notice what was happening right next to him. Michael took his fingers out of my pussy and licked and sucked off all my juices, telling me how much he wanted to eat my pussy. So right there he put his head in my lap and started finger-fucking me while licking and sucking on my clit. I never thought it was possible to enjoy oneself so quietly—right there, with all our company unaware of what was happening, right under their noses, so to speak. But as I said, it was a short flight.

After finding our rental car, we went right back to making our trip a memorable one. The drive to the motel was ecstasy. After a few good licks, we were on our way again. Michael stuck his amazing finger in his mouth and then slipped it up between my legs again. Michael brought me to another wet and tasty orgasm while driving down the ocean highway. As you might have guessed, Michael's seven inches were rock-hard and ready for action. With my hand in Michael's pants and my dress around my waist, we raced to the motel.

It felt like forever getting the keys, and the minute we were in the room, I was on my knees and freeing Michael's anxious member. I sucked that thing down my throat so fast I almost choked. Poor fella, he must have been wanting to come ever since the plane took off. I hadn't swirled my tongue once around his cockhead before he was shooting his warm, tasty come down my throat. It sure got the taste of the airplane snacks out of my mouth.

Well, it was great to taste his come, but we wanted to do more exhibitionism like on the plane. So, after some good clean fun in our room, the next stop was the Jacuzzi, in hopes of finding our next audience. Our luck was good. Three guys were cooling off down by the pool. So with a quick walk around the pool just for show, I took off my robe and got in the Jacuzzi with Michael, all the while sure that my every move was watched.

After only a few minutes in the hot water, I decided to go down again on my favorite shaft, knowing there were probably three more just as hard less than fifteen feet away. But, alas, two kids came out for a late swim and we had to move our fun back up to the room. We watched the pool for a long time after that, but those kids just stayed and stayed. We went out on the landing several times, Michael in his birthday suit and me in only my little teddy. I thought at least the three grown guys who were also still out there would get a glimpse of what they were missing.

When the kids finally went in, those three guys were still waiting down at the pool for our return.

So we threw our suits back on and headed out to the pool. It was after dusk now, and the only light was the light coming from the pool and the Jacuzzi. Michael jumped in and immediately took off his shorts. I sat beside him and started to stroke his fine prick. He is so big that the head poked out of the bubbling water. I leaned over and took the head in my mouth. I licked it for a while and then Michael untied the back of my bikini top. I held my breath and went all the way down on his pole.

When I came back up, he grabbed me by the waist and sat me on his lap. I could feel his throbbing shaft against my mound through my bottoms, and I knew I had to take him. I pulled his head (his real head) down to my breasts and urged him to take my huge nipples into his mouth. While he was sucking my tits, I looked around to see the three guys watching us, each of them stroking their rods through their suits. That's when I decided to really give them a show.

Reaching under the water, I slid my bikini off and started rubbing Michael's cock against my lower lips. That was all I had to do. Michael's cock shot up into my snatch without the least bit of effort on either of our parts. I started humping high and hard on my baby's tool, and immediately the three guys let up a resounding cheer.

I was coming almost immediately, and when I felt Michael's dick start to throb, in orgasm, I threw caution to the wind and started whooping and hollering.

My tits were bouncing all over the place, Michael's head was thrown back and I noticed that the three guys were suddenly quiet. After Michael loosed his load in me, I turned around to see what was up with the other guys.

Needless to say, I was very pleasantly surprised to find that all three of them had dropped their shorts and were whipping their puds. When I showed Michael what was happening, he said, "Well, let's give them something more to jack off to." With that, he lifted me up out of the water, sat me on the edge of the Jacuzzi and buried his face between my legs. As Michael sucked me to a shuddering orgasm, I watched amazed as each of those guys, their eyes glued on me, shot their wads high in the air, one after the other.

Now we're having a Jacuzzi installed by our own pool here at home. It's a strange thing some people will do to live their fantasies, but we now like to fuck in the backyard and imagine that all the world is watching. Call us crazy! —N.M., *Memphis, Tennessee*

A SCHOOLGIRL'S PRIMER ON HOW TO DO IT RIGHT

I'm sitting here in this hotel room reading your magazine. I use it to give me ideas of things to do to the guys when I'm back at school. I've done this for quite some time: Read your magazine, try stuff out on my conquests. It is one of the best ways I know to get into the male mind and see what turns them on.

Well, since I've nothing going on right now, I thought I'd relate a couple of adventures I had during the last school year. They were definitely inspired by *Penthouse Letters*.

First, let me describe me and my roommate, Alicia. I'm tall and thin with large, firm tits. They're my most distinctive characteristic. They have dark, sensitive nipples that really contrast with the rest of my body. My bush is dark and I have full, pouting pussy lips that just love a stiff cock passing through them. Alicia is blonde, has a great set of tits that the guys love to ogle and shoot off onto, and a tight pussy that is covered with curly brown hair. Neither of us has trouble attracting guys.

Well, Alicia and I have a little friendly competition between us concerning our sexual abilities. The root of the competition is our love of dick. We are both extremely lustful. She and I have a couple of steady fellas, but they both understand (her boyfriend and mine) that we are free to do as we please, sexually. My boyfriend, Dylan, likes to watch me take on other guys, anyway, so it really isn't an issue. The four of us (including Woody, Alicia's boyfriend) have had sex together, but not an orgy. I mean, I've never had sex with Woody, and Alicia has never had sex with Dylan, we've just fucked in each other's presence.

One time, the four of us were in our apartment and Alicia and I were in a playful mood. After a little "arguing" about who could get their guy off the fastest by sucking his cock, we decided to have a contest.

When Dylan and Woody stripped, they were already sporting nice erections. Both cocks are about the same size, but when Dylan gets hard, his cock arcs upward, whereas Woody's stiffens straight out. Dylan's balls tend to be higher in his sac than Woody's too. (This actually was another of our contests, comparing our boyfriends' erect cocks. Guys love that kind of shit—they're so competitive.)

Anyway, we had them sit down in front of a TV showing erotic videos. We wanted to get the guys really hot for the contest. We watched a couple of hot scenes where the actor's cock sprays a nice load of jizz. (Guys love that too. Watching another guy lose his load on some pretty girl's face or tits is a real turn-on for a guy. Males are so visual, and I like to use it to the max.)

After a while, we knelt in front of the guys and had them stand up so that their cocks were bobbing before our eyes. The whole time there was a lot of sexual banter going on. It was a lot of fun. We each reached up and grabbed our guy's cock at the base, saying, "One, two, three, go!" We started sucking their cocks for all we were worth. I was watching Woody's prong disappear into Alicia's mouth and she watched Dylan's cock slipping in and out of mine. The deal was that we had to make our guy come first. In order to make it fair, when the guy started squirting you had to remove your mouth so you could see the jizz. Another reason for letting the come fly and not cover it up was we knew Dylan wanted to see Woody's load and Woody wanted to see Dylan's.

And sure enough, the guys were watching how the other guy's cock was doing.

I could see by Woody's balls rising up in his pouch that he was getting there pretty quick. And the thing of the deal was, the better I went at Dylan's cock, the better it looked to Woody and the faster he was going to drop a nut. So I had to change tactics. I put Dylan's cockhead in my mouth and sucked and rolled all the sensitive parts with my tongue. Alicia continued to work all along Woody's cock, letting it bob and flop along her face and mouth as she tried to coax his load. Well, she looked like she was giving really good head, which is what I wanted Dylan to think as I tickled his plum. I felt Dylan start shivering and felt his balls contract. I removed my mouth and said, "Ta-da!" as Dylan shot his load in the air. When Woody saw the first stream of white goo, his cock spasmed and started squirting. Just like I knew it would. Alicia and I were both fucked good that night.

Another time, Alicia and I came up with the idea of trying to get two cocks to shoot off on each other. We thought we could do it, so one night we tried. We had a couple of our other guy friends over and Dylan. Dylan is friends with both of the guys, so he was excited, also. We started with some videos (videos: never leave home without them) and eventually we were all naked. Dylan was in the easy chair watching the action, which consisted of the guy I was with doing a good job eating my pussy and Alicia getting her tits rubbed and sucked. When the action was getting pretty hot, Alicia and I asked the guys to stand up.

We both got to our knees in front of their erections and started to give them head. Now, both these guys had long cocks, longer than either Dylan's or Woody's, which is one of the reasons we (Alicia and I) picked them. As we were sucking these big cocks, Dylan was pulling his in the easy chair.

After a short while, Alicia and I maneuvered the guys together where we could each suck the other guy's cock. Alicia would offer me her guy's cock and I'd do the same with my guy's dong. We swapped off like that for a while, the guys getting pretty close to losing it. Soon, we had their cocks inches apart, Alicia on one side and me on the other. Both guys had their pelvises thrust forward. Alicia and I started jerking on each guy's cock, trying to get the heads to touch. Eventually, we did get their cocks touching, and they formed a triangle with their cockheads forming the apex. Suddenly, Alicia's guy started to squirt, followed by my guy. That was a wonderful sight. Each guy's jizz coated the other's cock. We kept coaxing their loads and aiming them at the other's plum. When they were finished, they looked a little awkward, but extremely satisfied. I looked at Dylan and he had come running down his dick and hand. He'd obviously enjoyed it too. And I enjoyed the fucking he gave me later.

I have one more time that was outstanding in my mind. Dylan's fraternity was initiating some freshmen, and they wanted to do a little good-natured hazing. Alicia and I said count us in.

To cut to the chase, Alicia and I decided to have the pledges sit through a cocksucking lesson—nude. We picked our favorite upperclassmen with long cocks and got them in on it.

The night of the event came. Dylan had the pledges (there were four of them) in a room naked, sitting on some folding chairs, all in a line. Dylan had a chair in the corner, out of the way. You should have seen the looks on those pledges' faces when Alicia and I walked in—nude! Their eyes were darting from pussy to titties back to pussy. They were all attempting to hide their cocks, but Alicia and I soon made that impossible.

Alicia said, "Since you are soon to become members of this fraternity, we wanted to show you how your sisters will take care of your needs." I didn't have a clue what she was talking about, but it sounded good. We had one of the guys come in.

Anyway, Alicia said, "This is how we service a nice cock." I interrupted, "All you pledges, stand up." They did, but you could tell they were embarrassed. Their hard-ons were revealed to everyone in the room. Nice, young, hard cocks. Full of come. Four of them standing straight up at attention. What a sight! I told them to move their chairs a little further apart and sit down with their legs open. I wanted to judge the effect we were going to have.

Alicia moved her guy right up in front of the pledges. She squatted down in front of them, spreading her legs so the pledges could see her pussy. She was damp (as was I). She said, "These are balls." She cupped them in her hand. "I'm going to show you the proper way to suck the jism out of them." All the pledges' cocks twitched and they shifted in their seats. Alicia said, "First, you need to prime the pump." She started to slowly jerk her guy's long cock. Her hand looked good sliding over his hard shaft. She said, "By the way, isn't this a nice specimen of a cock?" She shook it gently. "Here is the most sensitive part, the cockhead. And here is where you will soon see this guy's load shooting out." She licked his hole. She then positioned him sideways to the pledges and started to really give him head. She licked up and down his shaft and twirled her tongue around his knob. I watched the pledges and they were mesmerized.

Soon, Alicia had her guy's cock squirting long strings of sperm across the room. She stood up and kissed him and said, "Now, that was a load."

I then had my long-dicked guy come in, and I sucked him off for them, except I had him facing the pledges, so they could watch the changing expressions on his face. It made me hot thinking about the view of my bobbing head from behind. When I felt my guy's dick start to throb, I pulled away and continued to jerk his shaft. Presently, he was shooting wildly all over the place, and a little landed on the legs of a couple of the pledges.

I said, "Okay, time to become brothers!"

We told them if they failed this test, they would not be allowed to enter the group as a frat brother. We had the pledges face off. Alicia had two and I had two. We grabbed a cock in each hand and started to slowly jerk them. All the pledges were hair-trigger, so we had to be careful.

Alicia said, "In order for you to become brothers, you must

perform this ritual. You and the pledge in front of you will press your cocks together. Then, my partner and I are going to jerk the both of your cocks, together, until you come. If you cannot come, or will not come, you will not be admitted." Sounded good to me.

I had my two guys and I could watch Alicia and her two guys. We were facing each other across four cocks and eight nuts. When we had them like we wanted them, we began to jerk all of their cocks at the same time. I put saliva on my hands to make the sensation slicker. It wasn't long before my pledges were both shooting off. They each had a tremendous load of come. Each guy's load landed on the other's tummy and ran down his cock and balls. I looked over at Alicia just as her guys started emptying. She cheated—she let a couple of squirts go, then she started sucking on both their knobs. She later told me she couldn't resist.

Then Alicia said, "You are now brothers." We then left and Dylan and I fucked until morning. Alicia probably did too. With Woody. —R.B., *Statesboro, Georgia*

I HAD A DREAM, CRAZY DREAM. AW, COME ON, NOW

I'm not going to tell you their names, but they have to be two of the sexiest gals I've seen in the market since I moved here, which was five years ago. When I first saw them, they were both dressed in miniskirts which did not leave much to the imagination.

They both were sporting at least 36-24-36 bodies, with long, voluptuous, tanned legs clear up to their asses. Their tits just seemed to be trying to pop right out of their tops. It was a hard-on just waiting to happen. Standing in front of the meat counter, checking out my grocery list, I tried not to look too obvious, even though it was almost impossible not to stare at both these gorgeous gals.

I guess we all had the same thoughts, because there they were, checking out the meat too. To my welcome surprise, they had turned their attentions toward me. Well, needless to say, it had been quite some time since the last time, so I had to ask, "What looks good?" and they both gave me the biggest, sexiest smile. One of them looked me over from head to toe and stopped at the middle, saying, "You're not looking bad. What are you doing for dinner?"

Little did they know about my somewhat lonely situation as of late. So the natural reply was, "Nothing I wouldn't mind sharing with the both of you."

It was confirmed. I was to bring my meat and myself to their apartment at eight. I had a feeling, a wonderful, delightful feeling.

Of course, I arrived exactly at eight. Okay, so I arrived a little early and waited outside their apartment till eight. I rang the doorbell, and before I knew it, I heard those sweet voices, "Hi, sweety, we're so glad you made it." They were definitely an eyeful, one dressed in a short, red teddy and the other dressed in a short, hot pink chemise. I was almost hard already, just following them inside. It was quite obvious that they had nothing on underneath. As they walked, the delicate fabrics clung to every curve, and my cock responded to all of them.

I could smell the bouquet of a delightful dinner cooking, and we all decided to have a cocktail before dinner. They took me into the living room, these two gorgeous, sexy females, handed me a drink—Crown Royal, of course—and got me comfortable on the couch, one on either side of me.

It was almost alarmingly uncomfortable to know that these two beauties definitely had no other clothing on whatsoever. When they crossed their legs, there was definitely nothing left to the imagination. My cock was bulging right through my jeans. I gathered they both noticed the strain on my swollen member, because they proceeded to remove every stitch of my clothing. As they did, it was not very hard to notice that both of them were shaved completely.

One said to the other, "I think he could use a shave too, don't you?" The other didn't hesitate to get a basin of hot water, shaving cream and razor.

"You lather, I'll shave."

At this point, we were all naked, and they were even more gorgeous than I could have dreamed. One started slowly applying lather all over my cock and balls. Between the warmth of the water and the application of the lather, I thought I was going to blow a load right then and there. Especially with both of these naked beauties touching me with their tits and rubbing their pussies on me. It seemed that with every stroke of the razor, the other girl would apply more lather, making my cock as hard as a rock. I was determined to hold out at least till they were done shaving me.

To watch these two beauties shaving me while staring at their baldness was simply exquisite. I wanted to lick their shaved pussies so bad I could literally taste it. After they had completely shaved my pubes, one said, "Roll over, we're not finished yet."

I couldn't believe what happened next. They spread my cheeks, lathered my ass and then shaved my asshole and ass completely clean. I mentioned, "Then I guess I'm done."

They both replied, "Not yet. The fun has just begun."

After a light dinner, we retired to the bedroom. Since we were already naked, we started right in kissing and fondling one another. Then both girls laid me back and told me to enjoy. One started at the top with her light fingers and tongue, and the other started on my inner thighs. Just watching these hairless pussies teasing me all over made my cock hard as steel, to say nothing of the exquisite feelings tingling in my balls. Then it was my turn to return the delightful fantasy. I proceeded to lick every inch of both their glistening bodies, softly running my fingers over the curves of their breasts, teasing all around their nipples while working my way down to lick and tease each pussy till it bloomed open like a rose petal. Not to let the one cool down while I was eating the other, I had my fingers inside her, tantalizing her pussy lips while I ate her friend out.

After a few minutes of this, the one I wasn't eating came

around and gobbled my dick down. I knew I was going to blow a load and a half. God almighty, could this gal suck a cock. Her friend started telling me, "Come, baby, come for us."

That was all I could take. I thought my dick was exploding, and that beautiful creature licked every bit of juice from my cock while I teased her friend's clit till the cows came home. —*Name and address withheld*

RITES OF PASSION, RITES OF SPRING, RIGHTS OF INITIATION

*G*rowing up together, my best friend Jamey and I shared many experiences. When we turned eighteen, these included masturbation. This slowly came to a head as the summer before college wore on. Sometimes, when I was over at Jamey's house, we would read his *Penthouse* magazine and beat off.

Since I was one of a very few guys in our group of friends who was not circumcised, I could tell that Jamey was intrigued by the appearance of my cock. Fortunately, I started developing fairly early and have nothing to be ashamed of in the size department.

Even though I looked mature, though, I was still a frustrated virgin, and I was pretty sure Jamey was too. Jamey went on to attend a university about two hundred miles away, while I went to the local community college. We saw each other several times that first year, when he came home for a weekend or when I went to visit him.

The first quarter of school was uneventful. Jamey's roommate was a senior finishing his last quarter, so they didn't have much in common and pretty much kept to themselves. The next quarter was entirely different. His new roommate was a sophomore transfer, so their ages were closer and they had more interests in common. The first time I met Perry, Jamey's new roommate, was quite memorable.

As usual when I visited, I arrived fairly late in the evening. Jamey was working at his computer and asked if I had eaten yet, to which I replied no, I hadn't. Jamey said that he had to go downstairs to get his laundry. When he got back, we could go to the pizza place down the street. After my long drive, I needed to take a major piss, so I went down the hall to the bathroom. When I got back, I sat at Jamey's computer and saw that he was working on some boring report for school. I put that aside and looked around his files until I found a "*Penthouse*" folder. Now that's more like it!

There were literally hundreds of letters that had been scanned in and saved by subject. Then I found a "Sex" folder with lots of large files in it. Probably porn pictures downloaded from the Internet, I thought. There were some of those, but mostly they were nude pictures of Jamey and some other guy I assumed to be his new roommate. In some pictures they were together, some alone, and in various states of arousal. There were a few in which they were ejaculating.

I called up a picture of Jamey coming and left it on the screen while I paged through some of the magazines on his bed. When Jamey got back to the room I told him, "I always did like to watch you shoot your wad."

"I thought you might find those," he said as he put his laundry down and called up a picture of a guy stroking his hard-on. "That's Perry, after I told him about your foreskin. He's been eager to meet you ever since. Are you still up for pizza?"

We walked down the street to the pizza place. Along the way he told me about Perry. "I think he was testing me from the day he arrived. First he offered me use of his extensive *Penthouse* collection. After a couple of weeks, probably when he figured I didn't have a steady girlfriend, he started reading them in bed, and after we shut out the lights he would jack off. You can't be in the same room and not get turned on, so I would quietly slip my shorts down and beat off along with him.

"After a couple of nights of that, he said, 'Here's one that'll make you hard,' and he read one out loud. Then, Saturday morning, Perry finished his shower a few minutes before I did. When I got back to the room, he was sitting naked on his bed reading a *Penthouse* and playing with his cock. He said, 'This one turns me on every time,' and read a letter. I picked a magazine from his collection and sat on my bed. We took turns reading letters until we were both really hard. Perry said he couldn't let a good hard-on go to waste and started stroking away. I followed along and we both came quickly. A few days later, I was jacking off when he got home, so he stripped, sat next to me and we jerked each other off.

"Once, when we were looking at some of his magazines and jacking off, we found a couple of pictures of uncircumcised guys, and Perry said he wondered what it was like to have foreskin. He asked if I had ever played with one, and that's when I told him about you."

When we got back to the dorm, Perry was in his swimsuit and said he was going out to soak in the Jacuzzi to unwind before going to bed and asked if we wanted to join him. We agreed, though I said that I hadn't brought a swimsuit, so I'd just go in my underwear. I stripped down to my briefs, giving Perry a good view of my bulge, but no more.

We had a nice soak, and the warm water was indeed relaxing. When we got back to the room, I said I was going to take a shower to wash off the chlorine. Perry readily agreed that this was a good idea, and Jamey followed along to watch.

I peeled off my wet shorts and stood under the running water. As I soaped up my hair, I casually turned toward Perry to give him a tantalizing view of my gently swaying balls. I rinsed off my hair and continued washing, casually pulling back my foreskin to clean the head of my penis. Perry's cock stiffened a little and he turned his eyes away. A virgin, I thought.

We dried off, went back to the room and hung up the towels. As Jamey and Perry pulled back their bedcovers, I knelt down to pull my sleeping bag out of my duffel. With my back to Perry, I was giving him a nice view of my testicles which, due to the hot shower, were dangling very low between my legs. I could see in the mirror on the wall that Perry was staring at them. When I turned to spread out the bag, he quickly looked away, but I could see that he was starting to get hard. Jamey was getting hard by watching Perry trying to hide being turned on. I pointed at Jamey and asked Perry, "Did Jamey ever tell you that we use to jack off together? He always liked to play with my foreskin. It looks like you would too." I sat up on Jamey's desk. "Come on, it's what you want, isn't it?"

He sat on the chair before me, lifted my cock and carefully examined it, gently tugging at my foreskin to expose the head, which he licked. Then he put all of it in his mouth and sucked it to its full hardness. Then he pulled it out and stroked it, playing with the foreskin some more, followed by some licking and sucking of my balls. It wasn't long before he was back to chowing on my meat. He certainly had the best lips that had ever been around my cock. He soon had me shooting my load down his throat. He swallowed most of it, with a little semen dribbling down his chin.

After that I introduced myself to my new seven-inch friend between Perry's legs and got to watch sperm shoot from Jamey's familiar penis while I squeezed his balls.

The next day we hiked up to some hot springs in the hills behind the school where we could skinny-dip and generally be naked and play with each other. Perry showed me how he got all those great pictures that I'd seen on Jamey's computer. He had both a video camera and a digital camera which we used to take pictures of us doing everything to each other.

When we got back to their room, they transferred the pictures into the computer so we could see what we'd done that day. That set us off for another night of sex.

The next morning, after we had all been drained, we went to the local nude beach to check out the scenery. After swimming around to a more secluded cove, we had another round of sex on the sand before I had to pack up and go home.

I went home with a tape full of pictures of the three of us that I can enjoy on my computer at my leisure. I visited Jamey and Perry several more times that year. And when I'm not with them in person, I always have them on my computer. I must say, I look at them more often than I care to admit. —*Name and address withheld*

AMOROUS PAIR PERFORM FOR IMPROMPTU GATHERING

It was Valentine's Day, and I was with my girlfriend Minnie. We were on a Caribbean cruise, and one day we were offered the opportunity to go to a nude beach.

When we got there, there were only a few other people on the beach, but as the day went on, more people arrived, including some good-looking younger couples. I was completely naked, and my girlfriend was topless. I don't mean to sound egotistical, but we are both good-looking and were receiving quite a few appreciative glances.

We played around a little in the water and mostly just relaxed in the beautiful Caribbean sun. We started talking about sexual fantasies, and Minnie asked me what was one of mine. I told her I always wanted to make love in an exotic locale.

"Oh, you have, have you? What ever gave you that idea?"

I looked at her sheepishly and swore to her that this was not the first time I'd thought of it. We started kissing and gradually (and then suddenly) my dick started to get hard. Minnie reached down and started stroking my cock while I placed a finger or two inside her wet snatch. I looked around and saw a handful of people casually watching. What a turn-on.

All of a sudden, someone yelled, "Look at the size of that lizard!"

Well, I have a larger than average penis, but I have to admit that they were not referring to me or any part of my anatomy. There was a large iguana coming out of the hills. We laughed and decided we needed to cool off.

Standing up to walk into the water, there was no hiding my hard-on, but I didn't care. Once we were in the water, we kissed some more and decided to swim around the corner and look for a secluded cove or something.

We found a little cove, but there was a house and we were sure there were people in it. This started to turn me on more, and we started to make out in a little tidal basin. I lay down on my back and stuck my dick up in the air. The warm water felt good, and my girlfriend's mouth around my dick felt even better.

Presently a small motorboat rounded the point and immediately we heard a group of men yelling us on. Minnie pulled away from my dick and said, "Let's wait till they pass," but just then their engine stalled—yeah, right!

After a few minutes of a great blowjob, Minnie turned around into a 69 (to more cheers) and I ate the most beautiful pussy in the world while fucking her lovely face. When I couldn't take it any longer, I pushed Minnie away, put her on her knees and entered her from behind. Now I was fucking like a madman and watching our audience watching us. Now the guys in the boat had very somber looks on their faces, and I couldn't blame them. I, too, believe that sex is sacred and not to be entered into lightly.

We were both very excited about being watched and wanted our audience in the boat and in the house to enjoy the show. Minnie was howling and, soon, I was too as I unloaded a pint into her hole. Minnie was coming when I was, and when we were done, we splashed down into the shallow water and started kissing each other feverishly.

Miraculously, the guys got their boat restarted just then and roared away.

Now that we were finally alone (at least, if no one was in the house) we decided to finish things up in style. My girlfriend likes to have her asshole licked, and guess what? I like to lick her asshole. So she lay facedown in the shallow water with her head on the sand (kind of like a pillow) and I buried my head between her cheeks. Minnie started screaming and I knew I was giving her what she wanted. I love nature! —M.M., *Orlando, Florida*

SINGLE-HANDED AND BAREFOOTED, SHE TAKES ON THE CROWD

I have always been an avid reader of your magazine and have found both the pictures and the letters from your readers very stimulating. Recently I read two letters from fellow foot fetishists that made my prick hard to control.

My girlfriend Val likes to walk around the house barefoot when she comes to see me. She doesn't know it, but it drives me mad to see her sexy feet with her dainty painted toes. I've even seen her add a spritz of perfume to them as a finishing touch.

Last Sunday we dined out for the first time in months. Val decided to wear a semitransparent green chiffon dress, white panties, sheer pantyhose and a pair of gold high heels that I had never seen before. Her dress was fucking sexy. It had a bodice that lifted up her tits, which were somewhat visible through her extremely sheer bra.

We got into my car. Val looked stunning. Her blonde hair fell over her shoulders, and she crossed her ankles while we were traveling. "These shoes are a little tight, love," she reported. I hoped that meant she wouldn't have them on for too long.

When we arrived at the restaurant, we were seated at a quiet table in the corner. We sat gazing at each other over a glowing candle. It was all very romantic. I noticed a middle-aged chap at the bar casting a longing look in Val's direction.

"I love you," I whispered to Val.

"So do I, love," she smiled.

The chap I had noticed at the bar came over to our table and asked if he could join us. Men are always attracted to Val, and I know she loves the extra attention. I'm secure enough in our relationship that I don't mind sharing her sometimes. When I said he could join us, he sat down and introduced himself as Bill. He was well-dressed in a nice suit, and had his white hair combed back. His rugged face showed signs of his battle with the bottle.

Bill stared at Val, and I could tell he was thinking about fucking her. She seemed relaxed as she quietly sipped her bubbly. I excused myself and headed for the men's room. I saw that Val's feet were shyly tucked under her chair, her right foot bare, her shoe next to Bill's chair. I saw him reach down, pick up the shoe in his big hand and hold it in front of him.

When I returned to the dining room, the live band started playing. I noticed both Val's feet were now bare.

"I bet you won't, my sweet," Bill was saying to Val.

"Bet what?" I quizzed.

"I just bet Val that she wouldn't get up and dance barefoot on the bar," he replied.

I sat down and gazed at her shoes, which were now sitting on the table. When I picked them up I could smell the lingering perfume of her scented feet. Val blushed and looked at Bill.

"If I do, it'll cost you fifty bucks, Billy," she said.

"Okay, love, you're on!" was his retort.

A short while later, I went over to the bandleader and made a request. Val slipped her shoes back on to go to the ladies' room. She returned to the table just as the song I'd requested began. It was one of Val's favorite songs, and she asked Bill to join her on the dance floor.

She soon left him on the floor and headed toward the overcrowded bar. I was wanking myself, discreetly at the table. Billy slid back into his chair.

Val climbed awkwardly onto the bar, shoes and all, amid the deafening rock 'n' roll. The crowd cheered her. Her body was incredibly sexy. She gyrated her hips and played with her cunt through the sheer material of her dress.

My eyes were hazy with booze as I watched eager hands paw at her legs and feet. She lifted her feet to willing hands, and the straps of her shoes were quickly unbuckled. Then her shoes were gone! My dick was hard and red as Val dipped her right foot into a mug of beer. She lifted it out, dripping, and someone sucked on it.

She turned, squatted on the bar and pulled down the zipper in the back of her dress. She stood and slowly, very slowly, let her dress slide down her body until it puddled on the bar. Christ! Now her boobs were revealed, her big, brown nipples visible through her sheer bra.

Val's eyes were closed, her face was gleaming with perspiration and her hands were working on the waistband of her hose. "Take 'em off!" someone in the corner shouted. Val complied.

I couldn't believe it. My Val was standing on a bar clad in only a bra and panties. I staggered toward the bar, my prick still in my hand, trying to get to her through the crowd. I wanted to fuck her right there on the bar. Her shoes were drenched in a puddle of beer. Her nylons were on the floor in shreds. I picked them up and sniffed the crotch. I could detect the aroma of her cunt. The toes smelled sweaty and were sticky from beer.

The atmosphere was heavy with smoke, booze and the scent of sex. I looked up at her just in time to see her bra disappear into the crowd. Her beautiful boobs were bouncing around and her nipples were erect.

A guy next to me at the bar had poured sherry over her left foot and was licking it off her toes. Val reacted by putting her toes in his mouth. "Suck my toes, love. Come on!" she urged.

She seemed to be in a trance as her legs were caressed by many hands. Her white panties were still on when Val did the unexpected. She sat on the edge of the bar with her legs stretched out in front of her, her feet touching one guy on the nose and another on his hairy chest.

"You all want to fuck me, don't you?" she teased.

A resounding "Yes!" was the answer.

"Before I show you what I've got, you've got to make love to my legs and feet. Drive me wild," she instructed, "while the music lasts."

The crowd went mad. Val sat on the bar, visible from the waist up, leaning back on her arms, her legs stretching out into the crowd.

Her feet and toes were kissed and sucked, pricks were rubbed between her toes and come flew through the air. Her feet pressed against chests, pricks and faces.

When the music stopped, the action slowed. Val beckoned a young blond guy to her. "Drop 'em," she instructed, pointing to his pants with her foot. Hesitantly he did as she wanted. His tool was pink and large. She held it between her feet and started to masturbate him. The crowd hushed as the young guy squirmed and moaned. Val stopped and instructed. "Now take mine down." The crowd cheered as he obliged.

She took her panties and threw them at Bill, who put them in his pocket as a souvenir. "Come here," she said, pointing at him. "Get up here and fuck me!"

Bill's cock was bigger than I expected. When he sat on the bar, Val took his massive tool in her hands and began rubbing it enthusiastically. Then she lay down, her legs wide open, her cunt dripping wet.

Bill climbed atop her and entered her. He came within seconds.

I walked closer and stroked the soles of her feet. Bill was still inside her. He bent his head and began sucking her nipples. She wrapped her legs around him and crossed her ankles behind Bill's ass.

"Fuck me! Suck me! Harder, harder!" she urged. Her hands clutched at his back and her toes curled in intense passion as their bodies moved together.

When it was over, Val yelled and screamed with her climax.

Bill sat up, his softening prick dripping with her juices. I helped her from the bar and we collected her clothes from the floor, except for her panties and her nylons, which were never found. For the rest of the night Val danced with me barefoot, which kept me horny all night long. And when we got home that night, we had a lovemaking session that lasted until the wee hours of the morning. I think we'll be going out for dinner more often now.
—T.K., London, England

THE ONLY THING BETTER THAN A NURSE IN UNIFORM IS WEARING IT YOURSELF

I've always had a thing for uniforms. Maybe that's why I married a nurse. Tracy's starched white uniform really turns me on, and her long legs in white stockings always get me hot and bothered. The only problem is that she works nights, and our schedules make it hard to find time together in bed.

The night shift does have its advantages though. There have been many mornings when I've been awakened by an angel in white standing alongside the bed.

One of the games we have developed over the years happens on mornings like these. She pretends I'm a patient, telling me it's time for my rubdown. Tracy reaches out, unbuttons my pajamas and starts to rub my body, slowly and sensually.

Just as if I were one of her patients, she explains just what she is about to do. "Good morning, Mr. Smith, it's time for you to get up," or, "Mr. Smith, it's time for your sponge bath." I'm always Mr. Smith on these occasions, and she is always Nurse Jones.

I look up at her beautiful tits encased in the virginal white of her uniform and watch them jiggle as she presses her hand into my body. She works her way down my body and snaps open my fly, revealing my semierect cock. With a smile she begins a massage of my member, and I am soon aroused and pointing skyward. Fumbling off her pantyhose, she leaves her uniform on as she climbs on the bed and impales herself on my rigid cock. Her long, lean legs flex, raising her delectable body up and down, and I watch her tits bounce each time she slides down my pole. I reach out and unbutton the front of her uniform but I'm frustrated by the heavy fabric of her bra, built for support and not for sex.

"Nurse Jones, there seems to be something covering your lovely tits this morning," I say.

"Of course, Mr. Smith. A professional must wear the proper clothing at all times," is her usual response.

Still, I locate her nipples and gently tweak them each time they come within reach. I can feel her juices dripping down on my balls as she continues to ride my peter, smiling down at me and asking if I approve of my therapy. I very much approve and tell her so, praising her medical abilities. I can feel the coolness of the air as she slides up off my cock and the incredible warmth each time her slippery slit engulfs me. Soon that familiar feeling starts to build, and I spray my white seed deep into her white-sheathed body, grunting and clenching my fists as I pound on the bed in orgasm. When I have finished, she sits still for a moment and then, rising gracefully, sits on my face for her reward. I greedily reach out with my tongue and lick her cunt, tasting her womanhood and my come mixed together. I explore the many folds of her vagina, sliding my tongue into the myriad nooks and crannies of her cunt lips. Each time I probe into her slit I can feel her shudder in pleasure, and I am rewarded with a little spurt of my own sperm. Clutching her magnificent ass, I press her clit to my hungry mouth and suck her until she comes, trying desperately to keep my lips fastened to her as she writhes in orgasm. As she calms down, I release her from my embrace and tell her how much I love her.

But while the mornings can be a pleasure, she needs her sleep and I have to get ready for work. The nights without her are long and lonely. I don't remember when it first happened, but one day, while thinking about her, I tried on my wife's silky white pantyhose. They're too small for me, of course, but seeing them on me when I looked in the mirror was a real kick, and somehow I felt closer to my missing wife. I suppose it was inevitable, but one night I fell asleep before I had taken them off. I awoke to feel her unbuttoning my pajamas and blearily realized I was still wearing her pantyhose. There was nothing I could do about it.

I could tell she was surprised. Her hands stopped as she went to free my cock for its therapy. Deeply embarrassed, I tried to sink into the bedclothes.

"Mr. Smith, there seems to be something covering your lovely cock this morning." Pulling down my pajama bottoms, she uncovered her white nurse's panty hose encasing my crotch. "Mr. Smith, I had no idea you wanted to be a nurse," she said. "You haven't told your wife about this, have you?"

I was dumbfounded. I didn't know what to say but stammered out something about taking them off right away.

To my complete surprise she replied, "Oh no, Mr. Smith. I think perhaps you need a new kind of therapy." With that, Tracy slid the elastic waistband of the pantyhose down past my cock and quickly sucked my flaccid member into her mouth. It didn't take long for her ministrations to overcome my embarrassment, and I felt myself growing in her mouth as she sucked on my cock with gusto. Soon she was sliding her lips up and down my prick while stroking my balls through the white nylon. I forgot everything except the circle of fire rising and falling on my rigid prick, and blasted a load of come into her as she sucked me dry. Removing her lips from my spent member, she lifted her skirt and tore out the crotch of her panty hose. "Seeing as you like them so much, I won't take mine off either," she said. "It's my turn now, Mr. Smith!"

Pulling side the skimpy panties she wore underneath her hose, I began to finger her cunt, playing with the hair that protruded through the jagged opening in her lovely white stockings. I slid my finger over her outer lips, outlining them and brushing lightly into the crack between them. I was really turned on by her impulsive actions and began to rub her clit through her panty hose. Soon she was grinding her crotch against my hand as I rubbed her, pumping her hips and crying out, "Harder, Mr. Smith, harder!" I obliged, and she came with a roar. With a guilty look at the clock, I left her smiling in bed as I quickly removed her pantyhose, dressed and headed to work.

I was very nervous coming home that evening, but Tracy was not at all put off by my behavior that morning. I explained how much her nurse's uniform turned me on, which made her laugh. To her it was just what she had to wear for her job. A funny look crossed her face as she told me not to worry. She said if her uniform turned me on it was all right. Perhaps she could come up with a new therapy for me.

I was relieved, to say the least. The evening passed much as usual, and she left for work early that night. The following day was Saturday, so I puttered around the house as quietly as I could to keep from waking her. She arose about noon, which was unusual, and said she couldn't sleep anymore. To my surprise she had put on her uniform. She asked me to go out to her car and bring in the box in the trunk.

As I returned with the box, she greeted me with, "Good afternoon, Mr. Smith. I'm glad you arrived on time for your therapy session." So that was to be the game. "Please follow me, Mr. Smith."

She led me to the bathroom and said, "Please put the box on the sink and remove your clothes, Mr. Smith." I complied as she began to fill the tub. Following her instructions, delivered in a cool, professional voice, I climbed in the tub and was scrubbed quickly, impersonally and professionally. Tracy then shaved my face and drained the tub, but instead of telling me to get out she lathered my legs and started to shave them. By this time I had some idea of what she had in mind and enthusiastically cooperated with her. She rinsed me off, toweled me dry and opened the box.

Breaking her character as the cool, professional nurse, she said, "I borrowed a few things from my coworkers for your therapy. I hope you like them." She handed me a pair of plain white panties and told me to put them on. I did so. Next came a garter belt and white support stockings. "I thought these might be better than pantyhose, considering that you're built different than the average nurse. Do you know how hard it is to find stockings and garters these days? I hope you appreciate this," she said. I did, and told her so. I was taken aback as she handed me a utilitarian white bra. I hadn't figured on things going this far. With a look of exasperation she said, "Come on, Nurse Smith, you have to go on duty and you have no time to dilly-dally." Nurse Smith?

I held out my arms and she slipped on the bra, expertly fastening it around my chest. Out came two pliable bags of saline solution, which she inserted into the cups of my bra. Then she produced a slip and a nurse's uniform, one of her wigs and even a white nurse's cap. My own white sneakers completed the outfit. There in the bathroom mirror were two nurses, one taller and definitely scruffier than the other, but two nurses nonetheless.

I couldn't believe what was happening—my own wife had dressed me as a nurse. I had fantasized about this, but hadn't mentioned a word of it to her. I guess I should have had more faith in Tracy. She is always willing to try something new, and her years as a nurse have inured her to shock. She stepped back and scanned me from head to toe. "You'll do. Nurse Smith. At least for now. If you find it comfortable here at nursing school, I'll help you perfect your image in the future."

The day passed all too quickly. In my white uniform I helped with the housework, made the bed (with hospital corners, of course), played a game of cards and helped cook dinner. Tracy decided we should eat on the deck and, although I was nervous about leaving the sheltering walls of the house, I agreed. We live in the country with no close neighbors, but I was still a little apprehensive. After supper Tracy stood up and said, "It's time for my dessert."

To my astonishment she came over, knelt at my feet and lifted up my skirt. Drawing aside the white panties, she began to suck my cock. I was floored. What if someone came and saw us? What if . . . I soon forgot the "what ifs" as my prick grew under her attentions. There I was, a man in a nurse's uniform sitting out on my deck while being sucked off by another nurse. It was great. I loved every minute of it. I couldn't see my prick because of the jutting boobs on my chest, so I had to follow the action by touch. Not hard to do, as every little sensation was driving me wild. As my member stood straight out she began to tease it, just running her tongue lightly over my balls and cock, keeping me hard but not getting me off. She would concentrate on my balls, nibbling, licking and sucking, first one, then the other.

My pecker flagged with this attention to my balls, but before it could sag too much she latched onto the tip of my cock and slid her lips slowly and sensually down my pole, her tongue flicking at my manhood. As she slid her mouth back toward the tip, I felt the suction drawing my come from deep inside my body. With each breath I felt the tightness of the bra around my chest, and my eyes saw only the pure white of our uniforms. With exquisite slowness, she moved her mouth over my aching cock, sucking expertly, sending ripples of delight through my body. I felt the tightness in my balls that signals imminent release, but she must have felt it too: suddenly my pole was hanging all alone in the cool evening air.

Without a word she rose and seated herself on the edge of the deck and spread her legs. I know a hint when I see one, and I quickly descended the porch stairs. When she pulled back her skirt to reveal her bare cunt, I raised my own skirt and plunged my pecker deep into her. I held my position, crotch against crotch, and leaned over to kiss her. I withdrew my penis and, after a second of suspense, plunged back in and began to fuck her for all I was worth.

It was a strange and exciting feeling to be wearing a nurse's uniform, to feel the weight of the ersatz boobs on my chest as I rammed my manhood deep into her slit. I savored the subtle pull of the garters and stockings as I flexed my butt and drove my pecker home. Her warmth surrounded my cock over and over. I could hear the slight sucking sound as I pulled out, and her moans of lust as I pushed in again. Orgasm took her suddenly, her eyes wide open, staring at my white-clad body. "Fuck me! I want you to keep fucking me forever!" she yelled. "Don't stop! Oh God!"

After that nothing was intelligible, but I kept on fucking her. I felt as if I could keep this up for hours, driving my aching prick deeper and deeper into her cunt, savoring the rush of sensation as I penetrated her and the moment of coolness as I withdrew. Her moans rose in pitch and she again climaxed around my probing prick, clenching her muscles as the orgasm overcame her. With that I felt my balls tighten to propel my juices into her wet hole and I blew my own load, pumping spurt after spurt of sperm into her. As my sperm filled her, I kept pumping my pole until I was no longer able to keep it up.

I stood there, outdoors in the twilight, dressed in white, with my pecker inside my wife, holding her as much for support as for affection. She smiled up from the cedar planks of the deck and said, "Nurse Smith, you are one hell of a lover, but you look funny without your hair and cap!" I'd totally failed to notice that I'd lost my wig in my exertions, and it lay there at my feet.

"Nurse Jones," I replied, "I don't give a damn!" —*Name and address withheld*

ALSO AVAILABLE FROM WARNER BOOKS

PENTHOUSE UNCENSORED

Two classic collections of *Letters to Penthouse* come together in this extraordinary volume. *Penthouse* magazine dared to bring the voices of the sexual revolution to a world eager to listen. And its readers dared to bare it all—the good, the bad, and the very, very naughty—revealing, in their own inimitable words, just how free, just how fabulous, and just how sexy their lives (and yours!) can be. Now, in *Penthouse Uncensored*, share the thrill all over again, page after scorching page.

PENTHOUSE UNCENSORED II

Here together are two timeless collections of *Letters to Penthouse* combined in one electric and erotic volume. These all-true tales of real people making love in all its delicious varieties are guaranteed to scintillate and to sizzle. See how America's most enthusiastic, most uninhibited couples keep the primal way to pleasure always fresh—and forever exciting.

9 780446 679749